THE
BRIDES
of
LANCASTER
COUNTY

THE
ℬRIDES
of
LANCASTER
COUNTY

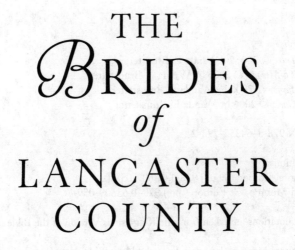

WANDA &
BRUNSTETTER

BARBOUR

PUBLISHING

A Merry Heart © 2006 by Wanda E. Brunstetter
Looking for a Miracle © 2006 by Wanda E. Brunstetter
Plain and Fancy © 2006 by Wanda E. Brunstetter
The Hope Chest © 2006 by Wanda E. Brunstetter

Print ISBN 978-1-64352-793-2

eBook Editions:
Adobe Digital Edition (.epub) 978-1-63609-058-0
Kindle and MobiPocket Edition (.prc) 978-1-63609-059-7

Scripture quotations are taken from the King James Version of the Bible.

Scripture quotations are also taken from the Holy Bible, New International Version®. NIV®. Copyright © 1973, 1978, 1984 by Biblica Inc. Used by permission. All rights reserved.

All German-Dutch words are taken from the Revised Pennsylvania German Dictionary found in Lancaster County, Pennsylvania.

This book is a work of fiction. Names, characters, places, and incidents are either products of the author's imagination or used fictitiously. Any similarity to actual people, organizations, and/or events is purely coincidental.

For more information about Wanda E. Brunstetter, please visit the author's website: www.wandabrunstetter.com

Published by Barbour Publishing, Inc., 1810 Barbour Drive, Uhrichsville, Ohio 44683, www.barbourbooks.com

Our mission is to inspire the world with the life-changing message of the Bible.

ecpa Member of the
Evangelical Christian
Publishers Association

Printed in the United States of America.

A MERRY HEART

Brides of Lancaster County

1

*In loving memory of my sister-in-law, Miriam (Mim) Brunstetter,
who always had a merry heart.*

*A merry heart doeth good like a medicine;
but a broken spirit drieth the bones.*
PROVERBS 17:22

CHAPTER 1

"I wish our teacher wasn't so cross all the time."

"*Jah*, my brother Sam says she's just *en alt maedel* who never smiles. I think she must have a heart of stone."

Miriam Stoltzfus halted as she stepped out of the one-room schoolhouse. She recognized the voices of Sarah Jane Beachy and Andrew Sepler and noticed that they were playing on the swings nearby.

Perhaps some of the children's words were true. At the age of twenty-six, Miriam was still unmarried, and as far as she was concerned, that made her an old maid among the Old Order Amish group to which she belonged.

Miriam pursed her lips. "I'm not cross all the time, and I don't have a heart of stone." But even as she spoke the words, she wondered if they were true. She did tend to be a little snappish, but that was only when the children in her class didn't behave or whenever she suffered with one of her sick headaches.

Miriam glanced at the swings again and was glad to see that Sarah Jane and Andrew had left the school yard. She didn't want them to know she had heard their conversation, and she wasn't in the mood to hear any more talk against herself. She would be glad to leave the school day behind and get home to whatever chores awaited.

She hurried around back to the small corral where her horse was kept during school hours and soon had the mare hitched to the box-shaped buggy she had parked under a tree that morning. She wearily climbed inside, reached for the reins, and, for the first time all day, experienced a moment of solace. Speaking a few words of Pennsylvania Dutch to the mare, she guided it out of the school yard and onto the road.

A short time later, Miriam directed her horse and buggy up the long driveway leading to the plain, white farmhouse where she lived with her parents and Lewis, her only un-married brother. She spotted her mother right away, sitting in a wicker chair on the front porch with a large bowl wedged between her knees. "Look, daughter, the first spring picking of peas from our garden," Mom called as Miriam stepped down from the buggy.

Miriam waved in response, then began the ritual of un-hitching the horse. When she was finished, she led the willing mare to the barn and rubbed her down before putting her into one of the empty stalls.

"How was your day?" Mom asked when Miriam stepped onto the porch some time later.

Miriam took a seat in the chair next to her mother, her fingers kneading the folds in her dark green cotton dress. "It went well enough, I suppose, but it's good to be home."

Mom set the bowl of peas on the small table nearby and pushed a wisp of graying hair away from her face where it had fallen loose from the tight bun she wore under her stiff, white head-covering. "Problems at school?"

Miriam released a quiet moan. Her mother always seemed to know when she'd had a rough day or wasn't feeling well, and she knew if she didn't offer some word of explanation, Mom would keep prying. "It's probably not worth mentioning," she said with a sigh, "but after school let out, I overheard two of my students talking about me. They seem to think I'm cross and have a heart of stone." She clasped her hands tightly around her knees and grimaced. "Oh, Mom, do you think it's true? Am I cross all the time? Do I have a heart of stone?"

Mom's forehead wrinkled as she shook her head. "I don't believe any Christian's heart is made of stone. However, I have noticed how unhappy you are, and your tone of voice is a bit harsh sometimes. Does it have anything to do with William Graber? Are you still pining for him?"

Miriam's face heated up. "Of course not. What happened between William and me is in the past. It's been almost two years, and I'm certainly over him now."

"I hope you are, because it would do no good for you to keep fretting or dwelling on what can't be changed."

An uncomfortable yet all-too-familiar lump formed in Miriam's throat, and she found that she couldn't bring herself to look directly into her mother's brown eyes. She was afraid the hidden pain in her own eyes would betray her words.

"If your troubled spirit isn't because of your old beau, then what is the problem?" Mom asked.

Miriam shrugged. "I suppose everyone feels sad and out of sorts from time to time."

"Remember what the Bible tells us in Proverbs: 'A merry heart doeth good like a medicine: but a broken spirit drieth the bones.' Happiness and laughter are good medicine for a troubled spirit, Miriam."

"I know that, Mom. You've quoted Proverbs 17:22 to me many times. But it's not always easy to have a merry heart, especially when things aren't going so well." Miriam stood. "I'd best go to my room and change. Then I'll help you get supper started."

"Jah, okay."

Miriam hurried inside, anxious to be alone.

⁂

When the door clicked shut behind Miriam, Anna bowed her head. *Heavenly Father, I know my daughter says she is over William, but her actions say otherwise. I believe she's still pining for him and hasn't found forgiveness in her heart for what he did. Please take away Miriam's pain, and help her to find joy in life again. Show me if there's anything I can do to help her be at peace with You. And if it's within Your will, please send Miriam someone who will love her in a way that will make her forget she ever knew a man named William Graber.*

Anna felt something soft and furry rub against her leg, and she opened her eyes. One of the calico barn cats sat at her feet, staring up at her with eyes half closed, peacefully purring. She leaned over and stroked the animal behind its ears. "I think Miriam could learn a lesson from you, Callie. She needs to take the time to relax more, enjoy each precious moment, and carefully search for the right man to love."

The cat meowed as if in agreement and promptly fell asleep. Anna reached for the bowl beside her and resumed shelling peas.

Miriam's upstairs bedroom looked even more inviting than usual. The freshly aired quilt on the bed was neat and crisp, giving the room a pleasantly clean, outdoor smell. The bare wooden floor was shiny and smooth as glass. Even the blue washing bowl sitting on the dresser across the room reassured her of the cleanliness and orderliness of her plain yet cozy room. On days like today, she wished she could hide away inside the four walls of this familiar room and shut out the world with all of its ugliness and pain.

Miriam took a seat on the comfortable bed and pulled her shoes off with a yawn. *How odd that some of the young people among my faith desire to leave this secure and peaceful life for the troublesome, hectic, modern world. I don't believe I could ever betray the Amish faith in such a way. Modern things may have their appeal, but simplicity and humility, though they separate us from the rest of the world, are a part of our culture that I treasure.*

She fluffed up her pillow and stretched out for a few moments of rest before changing her clothes. Staring at the cracks in the plaster ceiling, she reflected on the voices of the two children she had heard talking about her earlier. "How little they really know about their teacher," she whispered. "They don't understand my pain. They truly believe I have a heart of stone."

Her vision blurred as tears burned her eyes. "My heart's

not stone—it's broken and shattered, and I'm afraid it always will be so."

A tear slid down Miriam's face and landed on the pillow beneath her head. She squeezed her eyes shut, refusing to allow more tears to follow, for she knew if she let her emotions take over, she might lose control and never be able to stop crying. Miriam longed to be loved and feel cherished, and she knew in her heart that she was capable—or at least had been capable—of returning that same kind of love to a man who was willing to give his whole heart to her. She thought she had found such a man in William, but after his betrayal, she was certain that no man could ever be trusted. So she would guard her heart and her emotions and never let anyone cause her that kind of pain again.

Unwillingly, Miriam allowed her mind to wander back to when she was a twelve-year-old girl attending the one-room schoolhouse where she was now the teacher. . . .

Miriam sat upright at her desk, listening attentively to the lesson being taught until a slight tug on the back of her small, white head-covering caused her to turn around.

William Graber grinned, and the look in his deep, green eyes seemed to bore into her soul as his gaze held her captive. Even at her young age, Miriam knew she wanted to marry him someday.

William handed her a crumpled note he'd taken from his shirt pocket.

Miriam took the piece of paper, turned back around, and opened it slowly, not wanting the teacher to hear any rumpling. She smiled as she silently read William's words:

> *Dear Miriam:*
> *I want to walk you home after school lets out. Meet*
> *me by the apple tree out behind the schoolhouse.*
> > *Your friend,*
> > *William Graber*

Miriam turned and gave William a quick nod; then she folded the note and placed it inside her desk. Impatiently, she waited for the minutes on the battery-operated wall clock to tick away. . . .

Miriam's thoughts returned to the present. Releasing a sigh, she crawled off the bed and shuffled across the room to stand in front of the open window, where she reflected on the first day she had walked home from school with William. It was the beginning of many walks home together, and over the next few years, their friendship had grown as he continued to gain her favor.

Miriam and William's eighth year in school was their final one, and they both spent the next year in vocational training at home. William was instructed in the best of Amish farming methods, and Miriam learned the more arduous homemaking skills. She was sure they would eventually marry and settle down on a farm of their own, and she wanted to be sure she could run an efficient, well-organized home.

William was given a horse and courting buggy at the age of sixteen, and a few days later, he asked if he could give

Miriam a ride home after a young people's singing. That had been the beginning of their courting days and the night Miriam had known she had fallen in love.

The months melted into years, and by the time the young couple had turned twenty, they still hadn't made definite wedding plans. Though they often talked of it secretly, William said he didn't feel quite ready for the responsibilities of running a farm of his own. After working full-time for his father since the age of fifteen, he wasn't even certain that he wanted to farm. He knew it was expected of him, but he thought he might be more suited to another trade.

The opportunity William had been waiting for arrived a short time later when he was invited to learn the painting trade from his uncle Abe, who lived in Ohio.

Miriam cried for days after William left, but he promised to write often and visit on holidays and extended weekends. It wasn't much consolation, as she had hoped that by now the two of them would be married, perhaps even starting a family.

Impatiently, she waited for the mail each day, moping around in a melancholy mood when there was no letter, and lighthearted and happy whenever she heard from William. His letters were full of enthusiastic descriptions of his new job, as he explained how he had learned the correct way to hold a paintbrush and apply paint quickly yet neatly to any surface. He told her about some of the modern buildings in town they had been contracted to paint, and he promised he would be home soon for a visit.

William's visits were frequent at first, but after he'd been gone a year, his visits came less often, as did his letters. On

Miriam's twenty-fourth birthday, a letter arrived with the familiar Ohio postmark. Her heart pounded with excitement, and her hands trembled as she tore open the envelope. It was the first letter she'd had from him in several months, but William's words had shaken her to the core.

Miriam groaned at the memory as she pressed her forehead against the cold window. When the pain became unbearable, she moved away from the window. Slowly, as though she were in a daze, she made her way across the room to her dresser. She knelt on the floor and pulled open the bottom drawer with such force that it nearly fell out. As she removed the stack of letters she had received from William during his time in Ohio, a sob caught in her throat. Her hands shook as she fumbled through the envelopes until she found his final letter. In a shaky voice, she read it out loud:

Dear Miriam,

I've always thought of you as a special friend, so I wanted you to be the first to hear my good news. I've fallen in love with a wonderful Amish woman—Lydia Stutzman. I love her so much, and we plan to be married in a few months. We'll live here in Ohio, and I'll keep painting for my uncle, as I'm sure you know that I could never be happy working as a farmer.

I hope you will fall in love with someone, too—someone who will make you as happy as Lydia has made me. I'll always remember the friendship we had as children, and I wish you the best.

Your friend,
William

Even though William's final letter had come nearly two years ago, to Miriam it felt like only yesterday. Her heart ached whenever she thought of him or read one of his letters. Did he really believe she would fall in love with someone else the way he had done? She had been crushed when he'd referred to their relationship as only a friendship. Had their years together meant nothing at all?

Miriam shuddered and leaned heavily against her dresser. The bitterness she still carried created a feeling of fatigue that never allowed her to feel fully rested. Suddenly, the room felt stifling, and she wanted to race out the door and never look back. But that wouldn't solve a thing.

With a determined grunt, Miriam grabbed the stack of envelopes, marched across the room, and flopped onto her bed. As tears streamed down her cheeks, she ripped each one of William's letters to shreds and dropped the pieces into the wastepaper basket near her bed. William had left her with a heart so broken she was certain it would never mend. But at least his letters could no longer remind her of that horrible pain.

CHAPTER 2

In the kitchen, Miriam found her mother standing at the counter, rolling out the dough for chicken potpie.

"Are you feeling better now?" Mom asked with a cheery smile.

Miriam reached for a clean apron hanging on a nearby wall peg. "I'm fine."

"That's good to hear, because we have guests coming for supper, and it wouldn't be good if you were gloomy all evening."

"Guests? Who's coming over?"

Mom poured the chicken broth into the kettle before answering. "Amos Hilty and his daughter, Mary Ellen."

Miriam lifted her gaze toward the ceiling. "Oh, Mom, you know I'm not interested in Amos. Why must you go and scheme behind my back?"

"Scheme? Did I hear that someone in my house is scheming?" Papa asked as he entered the kitchen.

Miriam slipped her hand through the crook of her father's arm. "Mom's trying to match me up with Amos Hilty. She's invited him and Mary Ellen to supper again, and they were just here a few weeks ago."

Papa leaned his head back and chuckled. His heavy beard, peppered generously with gray, twitched rhythmically with each new wave of laughter. "Daughter, don't you think it's high time you married and settled down with a good man? Amos would make you a fine husband, so please don't close your mind to the idea."

"I think it's her heart that is closed." Mom glanced over at Miriam and slowly shook her head. "A heart blocked off from love soon grows cold."

Miriam turned away and began setting the table.

At that moment, Miriam's youngest brother, Lewis, came in from outside, sniffing the air as he hung his straw hat on one of the wall pegs near the back door. "Somethin' smells mighty good in here, and it's makin' me awful hungry."

"We're having company for supper, so hurry and wash up," Mom said, nodding toward the sink.

"Who's coming?"

"Amos Hilty and his daughter," Miriam answered before Mom had a chance to reply.

"Aha! I think Amos is a bit sweet on you, sister."

"Just because he's a widower and his little girl needs a mother doesn't mean I'm available. Why can't you all see that I'm content with my life as it is?" Miriam compressed her lips. "I don't need a man."

Lewis gave Mom a knowing look, and she smiled, but neither of them commented on Miriam's remark. Did they really believe she would be happier if she were married to Amos, regardless of whether she loved him or not?

Miriam clenched her teeth so hard that her jaw ached.

I won't give up my freedom to marry a man I don't love, and since I will never allow myself to fall in love again, my family will have to get used to the idea that I'm en alt maedel and will always be one.

Amos Hilty clucked to his horse and squinted against the setting sun shining through the front window of his buggy as he and his six-year-old daughter headed for Henry and Anna Stoltzfus's place. This was their second time eating supper at the Stoltzfus home in less than a month, and Amos wondered if Anna had extended the invitations because she knew he couldn't cook well or if she simply enjoyed entertaining. He was fairly sure that Anna had no idea he had agreed to come for supper again because he wanted to spend more time with Miriam and hopefully win her hand in marriage. More than likely, Miriam's mother thought he kept accepting her invitations because he was without a wife and needed a decent meal.

He glanced over at Mary Ellen, who sat on the seat beside him with her head turned toward the side window. A little over a year ago, the child's mother had been killed in a tragic buggy accident, and even though Mary Ellen seemed placid and well-adjusted on the outside, Amos wondered if she might be keeping her feelings bottled up. He figured what his daughter needed was the hand of a woman—someone who would not only care for her needs but also share in her joys, sorrows, and hopes for the future.

That sure isn't me, he thought with regret. Mary Ellen rarely spoke of her mother or expressed her feelings about anything of a personal nature. He had a hunch she might be hiding behind her forced smiles and the pleasant words that seem to slip so easily off her tongue. Someone like Miriam Stoltzfus, whom his daughter seemed to admire and respect, might have a better chance at getting through to Mary Ellen than he ever could. At least he hoped she would.

As the Stoltzfus place came into view, Amos drew in a deep breath for added courage. *God willing, I hope that someday I might be able to get through to Miriam, too.*

Shortly after six o'clock, a knock sounded on the back door. Since Miriam was alone in the kitchen at the moment, she went to answer it. Amos and Mary Ellen stood on the porch. He held his straw hat in one hand, and Mary Ellen, who stood beside him, held a small basket of radishes. The little girl smiled up at Miriam and handed her the basket. "These are from Pappy's garden, Teacher. I picked 'em right before we left home."

"*Danki*, Mary Ellen. I'll slice a few for supper." Miriam motioned them inside and then placed the basket on the counter.

When Miriam turned around, Amos nodded at her and smiled. "It's good to see you this evening. You're. . .uh. . . lookin' well."

Miriam didn't return the smile, nor did she make any response. Instead, she rushed over to their propane refrigerator, retrieved a bottle of goat's milk, and placed it on the table.

Amos shuffled his feet a few times and cleared his throat. "Mary Ellen tells me she's doin' pretty well in school these days. She says that's because you're such a good teacher."

"I do my best," Miriam mumbled, refusing to make eye contact with him.

Mom, Papa, and Lewis entered the kitchen from the living room just then, and Miriam sighed with relief. At least she wouldn't be expected to carry on a conversation with Amos anymore.

"*Gut-n-owed*, Amos," Mom said with a friendly smile.

"Good evenin' to you, as well. It was nice of you to have us to supper again."

"Our *mamm* knows how important good food can be for a man," Lewis said, giving Amos a wide grin.

"That's true enough." Amos cast a glance in Miriam's direction, but she chose to ignore it.

Papa pulled out his chair at the head of the table. "I think we should eat now, before the food gets cold."

Everyone took their seats, and all heads bowed. Miriam pressed her lips tightly together as she folded her hands. She was only going through the motions of praying tonight, and she felt too frustrated over Amos being here to even think about the food set before her.

When Papa signaled that the prayer was over by clearing his throat, he helped himself to the potpie and passed it to their guests. The main dish was followed by an array of other homemade foods that included coleslaw, sweet relish, sourdough rolls, and dilled green beans.

Miriam couldn't help but notice how Mary Ellen seemed to be studying everything on the table. It made her wonder if the last time the child had been served a decent meal was when she and her father had eaten supper here a few weeks ago. *I know Amos isn't much of a cook,* she thought, *for I've seen some of the pathetic lunches he's made for Mary Ellen.*

"You forgot to put the radishes on the table, Teacher," the child announced, pulling Miriam out of her musings.

"I'll see to them now." Miriam excused herself and moved across the room to cut up the radishes, wishing she could be anywhere but here.

"Teacher's real *schee*, don't ya think so, Pappy?" Mary Ellen asked her father.

"Jah, she's quite pretty."

Amos's words had the effect of fingernails raking across the blackboard, causing Miriam to grit her teeth as she returned to the table. This meal couldn't be over quick enough to suit her.

Amos helped himself to some of the potpie. "The women of this house make a good *nachtesse.*"

Lewis grabbed one of Mary Ellen's radishes from the bowl. "Jah, Mom and Miriam always put together a mighty fine supper."

"Please, have some bread," Mom offered, handing Amos the breadbasket. "Miriam made it, and it's real tasty."

"Danki." Amos grabbed two pieces of bread and slathered them with butter.

Papa chuckled. "You certainly have a hearty appetite."

"Guess that comes from eatin' too much of my own cooking." Amos smiled at Miriam, but she turned slightly sideways in her chair and focused on her plate of food, which she hadn't yet touched. She had no appetite and would have excused herself to go to her room but knew that would appear rude. Besides, she rather enjoyed Mary Ellen's company.

Miriam felt relief when supper was finally over and Papa announced that he and Amos were going to the living room to play a game of checkers. Lewis left the house a few minutes later, saying he needed some fresh air and thought he would go for a buggy ride. Miriam had a hunch he might have a date and didn't want to say so.

The women remained in the kitchen with Mary Ellen, who sat on the floor playing with Boots, one of their kittens, while Miriam and her mother did the dishes.

Miriam pulled a kettle into the sink of soapy water and began scrubbing it vigorously with a sponge, as she watched the child out of the corner of her eye. The young girl's brown hair, twisted on the sides and pulled to the back of her head in a bun, looked a bit limp, as though it might come undone at any minute. Miriam tried to visualize Amos, his large hands clumsily trying to do up his daughter's long hair and never quite getting it right. She realized how difficult it must be for him to raise the child alone, as there were so many things only a woman could do well. He did need to find another wife—but certainly not her.

Amos had a hard time keeping his mind on the game of checkers, when all he could think about was the woman in the next room who hadn't said more than a few words to him all during supper yet obviously cared for his daughter. Mary Ellen seemed to like her teacher, too, and Amos wondered if she saw something good in Miriam, the way he did—something that lay hidden deep within Miriam's heart.

After listening to Henry gloat because he had won nearly

every game, Amos finally decided it was time to go. He slid his chair away from the small table that had been set up in the living room and stood. "It's about time for Mary Ellen to be in bed, so guess I'd better head for home."

"Jah, okay," Henry said, as he cleared away the checkerboard. "I'm sure my wife will have you over for supper again soon; then we can play again."

"Maybe I'd better do some practicing before then, because you've sure skunked me good this evening."

Henry chuckled. "When you're as old as me, you'll likely win every game, too."

Amos smiled and bade Miriam's father a good night, then he headed for the kitchen. He found Mary Ellen kneeling on the floor with a kitten in her lap, and Miriam and her mother at the table, drinking tea. He nodded at Anna. "Danki for havin' us over. The meal was good, and it was much appreciated."

"Gem gschehne—you are welcome," she replied with a smile.

He glanced over at Miriam, but she never looked his way, so he directed his focus back to his daughter. "Kumme, Mary Ellen, come. We must get you home and into bed now."

"Oh, Pappy, do we have to go already? I'm not even tired yet."

"You might not think so at the moment, but half an hour from now, I'm guessin' your eyes will be droopin'."

Mary Ellen released a small sigh, placed the kitten on the floor, and stood. "See you in school on Mondaag, Teacher."

"Jah, Monday morning," Miriam said with a nod.

Amos grabbed his hat off the wall peg where he'd hung it earlier and steered Mary Ellen toward the door. Before his fingers touched the knob, he stopped and turned toward the table. "It was. . .uh. . .good to see you again, Miriam. Maybe I'll come by the schoolhouse soon."

"I'm sure Mary Ellen would like that," she mumbled.

Amos knew that many of the scholars' parents dropped by the school during the year—some without warning; some after letting the teacher know ahead of time. Since Miriam didn't seem too friendly toward him, he wasn't sure if he should let her know when he planned to come by or if it would be better if he just stopped at the schoolhouse unannounced. Knowing he could make that decision later on, he tipped his hat and said, "*Gut nacht,* Anna. Gut nacht, Miriam."

"Good night," they said in unison.

CHAPTER 3

On Monday morning, a few minutes after the school bell rang, Mary Ellen entered the classroom and presented Miriam with a small pot of newly opened heartsease. "These are from Pappy," the child explained. "He said he hoped some pretty flowers might make you smile." She stared up at Miriam, her hazel-colored eyes looking ever so serious. "You always look so sad, Teacher. God doesn't want us to be sad; Pappy said so." She placed the wild pansies on the teacher's desk and hurried to her seat before Miriam had a chance to respond.

Miriam studied the delicate flowers; they were a lovely shade of purple. It was kind of Amos to send them, but she was disturbed by the fact that he could look into her heart and see her sadness. *Perhaps I do seldom smile,* she thought, *but then there needs to be a reason to smile. If God wants me to be happy, then why did He allow William to crush my heart with his deception?*

She forced her gaze away from the pot of flowers and scanned the room to see if any of the children were absent. Satisfied that everyone was in their proper seats, she said, "*Guder mariye,* boys and girls."

"Good morning, Teacher," the class replied in unison.

Miriam opened her Bible and read from Proverbs 18. " 'A man that hath friends must shew himself friendly; and there is a friend that sticketh closer than a brother.' "

The passage of scripture made Miriam think about her friend Crystal, who had always been there for her. If not for Crystal's friendship, Miriam didn't know how she would have gotten through her breakup with William. Crystal never reminded her that William had married another woman or that Miriam was an old maid.

With a concentrated effort, Miriam pushed her thoughts aside, reminding herself that she had scholars to teach and knowing that it did no good to dwell on the past. "And now we shall repeat the Lord's Prayer," she said to the class.

❧

As Amos left his blacksmith shop and headed down the road toward Jacob Zook's place to shoe a couple of horses, he thought about Miriam and wondered if she liked the pot of heartsease he had sent to school with Mary Ellen. It was the second time he'd sent Miriam flowers using someone to deliver them in his place; only this batch of wild pansies had been delivered via his daughter and not his so-called friend.

Unwillingly, Amos allowed his mind to wander back in time. Back to when he was sixteen years old and had just received his courting buggy. . .

❧

"I'm a little *naerfich* about being here tonight," Amos told

William, as they simultaneously pulled their buggies up to the Rabers' barn, where the young people's singing was to be held.

"How come you're nervous?" William asked, stepping down from his open buggy. "I thought you were looking forward to coming."

"Jah, but that was before I learned you had given Miriam the bouquet of flowers I'd asked you to deliver and then you let her think they'd come from you." Amos clenched his fists until his fingers dug into the palms of his hands. "That was a sneaky thing to do, and it made me wonder if you're really my friend."

William snickered and thumped Amos on the back. "Miriam's had her eye on me ever since we were *kinner*, and when I gave her the flowers, she just assumed they were from me."

"You could have told her otherwise."

"I didn't want to disappoint the girl." William gave Amos a wily smile as they led their horses to the corral. "You may as well accept the fact that it's me she likes and find yourself someone else, because Miriam Stoltzfus is my girlfriend now."

❧

When a car whizzed past, the horse whinnied, snorted, and stamped his hooves, causing Amos's mind to snap back to the present. As far as he knew, Miriam had never learned that the flowers William had given her a few days before the singing had really come from Amos. As much as it had bothered him to do so, Amos had stood by and watched William lead Miriam along, allowing her to believe he planned to marry her and then leaving her in the lurch when someone he thought to be more appealing had come along.

Amos had been in love with Miriam ever since he was a boy, and William knew it. Yet that hadn't stopped him from making a play for her, and it hadn't stopped him from breaking her heart, either. When William started courting Miriam, Amos had looked the other way and made every effort to forget that he'd ever loved her. After a time, he'd met Ruth, whose parents had moved to Pennsylvania from Illinois. Soon after, they had started courting and eventually married. Even though Amos hadn't loved Ruth as intensely as he had Miriam, they'd had a good marriage, and their love had grown during their six years together. The product of that love had been a delightful baby daughter.

Amos flinched and gripped the reins a little tighter as the memory of his wedding day washed over him like a drenching rain. Ruth was a sweet woman, and he still missed her, but she was gone now, and Mary Ellen needed a mother as much as he needed a wife—maybe even more. Truth be told, Miriam needed a husband, too; she just didn't seem to know it.

"She's been gloomy ever since William jilted her," Amos muttered. He hoped maybe some colorful flowers would cheer her up and put a smile on her face. It might make her more inclined to accept his invitation when he stopped by the schoolhouse after he finished shoeing Jacob's horses, too.

Amos's buggy horse whinnied as if in response, and he chuckled. "You agree with me, Ed? Jah, well, for Mary Ellen's sake, I hope I'll be able to make Miriam see that we could all benefit if she and I were to marry. And maybe someday she will come to love me as much as I love her."

By the end of the day, a pounding headache had overtaken Miriam. Fighting waves of nausea, she leaned against the schoolhouse door, feeling a sense of relief as she watched the children file outside. She would be glad to get home again, where she could lie down and rest awhile before it was time to help Mom with supper.

Just as she was about to close the door, a horse and buggy pulled into the school yard. Amos Hilty stepped out, his large frame hovering above the little girl who ran to his side. With long strides, he made his way to the schoolhouse, meeting Miriam on the porch.

He removed his straw hat and nodded. "I came to pick up Mary Ellen, but I wanted to talk with you first."

"Is there a problem?" Miriam asked, stepping back into the schoolhouse.

When Amos and his daughter entered the room, he motioned to the flowers on Miriam's desk. "I see you got the heartsease. Do you like 'em?"

"They're very nice." Miriam, feeling a bit dizzy, sank into the chair behind the desk. "Is there a problem?" she repeated, knowing that her patience was waning fast and might not hold out much longer.

Amos shook his head. "No problem. I just came by to. . . uh. . .offer you an invitation."

"Invitation?" Miriam stiffened on the edge of her seat. She hoped he wasn't about to ask her to go somewhere with him.

"I was wondering—that is, Mary Ellen and I would like you to go on a picnic with us on Saturday afternoon. We're planning to go to the lake, and—"

"It will be a lot of fun, and we'll take sandwiches and cookies along," Mary Ellen interrupted. "Pappy said he might bring some of his homemade root beer. It's real tasty, and I know you'd like it. The cookies won't be homemade, but I'll pick out some good ones at the store. . . ." The child babbled on until Miriam thought her head would split wide open.

"I appreciate the offer, but I—I really can't go with you on Saturday," Miriam said, when she could finally get in a word edgewise. She pushed her chair aside and stood, then moved quickly toward the door, hoping Amos would take the hint and leave. "Now, if you'll excuse me, I must be going home."

At first Amos stood there with his mouth hanging slightly open, but after a few moments, he took hold of Mary Ellen's hand and went out the door.

As Miriam watched them go, she noticed the look of rejection on Mary Ellen's face. She knew she'd been rude to them and hadn't even bothered to thank Amos for the flowers, but her head hurt so much, she'd barely been able to think. Placing her hands over her forehead and leaning against the door, she prayed, *Dear Lord, please take away this headache—and if it's possible, remove the horrible pain in my heart that never seems to go away.*

Amos glanced over at Mary Ellen, who sat in the front seat of the buggy beside him, wearing a scowl on her face. The child was obviously not happy about her teacher's refusal to join them for a picnic on Saturday, and he felt bad about that. However, it was a relief to know that his daughter was still capable of frowning, since she normally smiled even when things didn't go her way.

Amos hoped Mary Ellen didn't take Miriam's unwillingness to join them in a personal way. He was sure it was him Miriam didn't care for, not his daughter.

I wonder what she would have said if I'd told her the truth about William. He shook his head. *No. I don't want to hurt her any more than she's already been hurt.*

They traveled nearly a mile before Mary Ellen spoke; then she turned to face Amos and said, "Pappy, do you think maybe Teacher don't like picnics?"

"Most people enjoy picnics, and I'm sure Miriam does, too."

"Then how come she didn't want to go with us on Saturday?"

"I can't rightly say. Maybe she's made other plans for the day."

Mary Ellen tipped her head, as her eyes squinted into tiny slits. "Then how come she didn't say so?"

"I–I don't know," Amos answered as honestly as he knew how. If he could figure Miriam out, he might have been able to get through to her by now.

"Some of the kinner at school think Teacher Mim is mean, but she's never been mean to me."

" 'Teacher Mim,' is it? When did you start calling her that?"

She shrugged her slim shoulders. "It just popped into my head this minute."

"Jah, well, you'd best not be callin' her that at school, because she might not like it."

"How come?"

Amos gritted his teeth, unable to offer his daughter a responsible explanation.

"Pappy?" the child persisted. "Why can't I call her 'Teacher Mim'?"

"She. . .uh. . .might not appreciate it, Mary Ellen."

"Would it be all right if I asked her?"

"Sure."

"And if she says it's okay, then can I call her 'Teacher Mim'?"

"It's fine by me if it's all right with her." He reached across the seat and took hold of Mary Ellen's hand. "Let's talk about something else, okay?"

She offered him one of her cheery smiles. "Can we talk about the food we'll take on the picnic?"

He grimaced, no longer in the mood for a picnic. "How about if we go to the farmers' market on Saturday instead? I could rent a table and try to sell some of my homemade root beer."

"Can I help?"

"Jah, sure."

"Okay then."

Amos wasn't sure if Mary Ellen really wanted to go to the farmers' market or if she was merely giving in to what she thought he wanted, but he decided to leave it alone.

❦

Anna was in the kitchen, peeling vegetables over the sink,

when Miriam arrived home from school, and she felt immediate concern when she saw her daughter's face. It looked
paler than goat's milk, and her eyes appeared dim. "Sit
down, Miriam. You don't look so well." Anna left her job
at the sink and pulled out a chair at the table. "Are you sick
or just tired?"

"A little of both." Miriam placed a pot of pansies on the
table and dropped into the chair with a groan. "I have another one of my sick headaches. They seem to be happening
more often these days."

Anna went to the stove and removed the teakettle filled
with boiling hot water. She poured some into a cup and
dropped a tea bag inside, then placed it in front of Miriam.
"Drink a little peppermint tea to settle your stomach, and
then go upstairs and lie down awhile."

Miriam nodded. "That sounds nice, but what about
supper preparations?"

"I think I can manage on my own. Anyhow, someday
after you're married, I'll have to do all the cooking without
your help."

Miriam released a sigh and took a sip of her herbal tea.
"I have no plans to marry, Mom. Not now. Not ever."

"My, what lovely pansies," Anna said cheerfully, feeling
the need to change the subject. "Did one of your students
give them to you?"

"Mary Ellen Hilty brought them. She said they were
a gift from her *daed*." Miriam grimaced as she made little
circular motions on her forehead with her fingertips. "It
was another one of his tricks to gain my approval, that's all."

"Miriam, please don't be so harsh. I'm sure Amos means

no harm. I believe he likes you, and he's no doubt been lonely since Ruth died."

"I'm sure he is lonely." Miriam slowly shook her head. "He came by after school today and invited me to go on a picnic with him and Mary Ellen this Saturday. I suppose he thought the flowers would pave the way."

"Did you accept his invitation?" Anna asked hesitantly yet hopefully.

"Of course not." Miriam pushed the chair aside and stood. "All he wants is a mother for his child and someone to do his cooking and cleaning."

Anna reached out and touched Miriam's arm. "I'm sure Amos wants more than that. He needs a friend and companion, just as you do."

"No, I don't!" Miriam's voice broke, and she dashed from the room before Anna could say anything more.

❦

Nick McCormick hurried across the parking lot of the Lancaster *Daily Express* and had almost reached his car when his cell phone rang. "McCormick here. Can I help you?" he asked after clicking it on.

"Nick, it's Pete. I was on the phone when you left your office, but I wanted to tell you about your next assignment."

"Already? I was just on my way to do a piece on the fireman who saved the kid who'd fallen in an old well, like you asked me to do."

"I still want you to cover that, but I'd like you to go to the farmers' market in Bird-in-Hand on Saturday."

"What for?"

"As I'm sure you know, tourism has started in Lancaster County, and I thought it would make a good human-interest story to have an article and a couple of pictures of the Amish and Mennonite people who shop at the market or sell things there."

"Can't you get someone else to do it?" Nick asked as he opened his car door. "I'm supposed to have Saturday off, and I'd planned to drive into Philadelphia for the day."

"Marv Freeman was going to do the piece," his boss said, "but he's come down with the flu, and it's not likely he'll feel up to working by Saturday."

Nick pulled his fingers through the back of his hair and grimaced. Walking around the farmers' market trying to take pictures of people who probably didn't want to be photographed was not his idea of fun, but he would do it in order to stay on the good side of his boss. Pete Cramer seemed pleased with his work these days, and if he played his cards right, in the future he might be given bigger and better stories to cover. "Yeah, sure, Pete," he said in an upbeat tone. "I'd be happy to go to the farmers' market on Saturday."

Miriam stood in front of her bedroom window, trembling from head to toe. *Why doesn't Mom understand the way I feel? Why does she keep coming to Amos's defense? Can't she see that he's not interested in me as a person? He only wants a mother for Mary Ellen.*

She leaned against the window casing as she thought about the eager look she had seen on Mary Ellen's face after

Amos mentioned going on a picnic. But the child's expression had quickly changed to one of disappointment when Miriam said she couldn't go.

Miriam moved away from the window and over to her bed. *I hope Mary Ellen didn't take it personally. It's not her I don't want to be with, it's her daed.* She sank to the edge of her mattress with a moan. Sooner or later, Amos was bound to realize there was no hope of them getting together. If she kept turning him away, eventually he was bound to look for someone else to be Mary Ellen's mother. At least she hoped he would.

Chapter 4

Early Saturday morning, Miriam and her family decided to go to the Bird-in-Hand Farmers' Market. While none of them would rent a table in order to sell their wares, they all agreed it would be fun to browse and visit with many of their neighboring Amish friends and relatives.

The sun gave promise of a warm day, and as Clarence Smoker, their Mennonite driver, drove his van into the market parking lot, Miriam wiped the perspiration from her forehead and groaned. She hoped this summer wouldn't be as hot and humid as last summer had been.

Papa climbed out of the van first, then helped Mom down. As the two of them started toward the market building, Miriam stepped down, followed by Lewis. "I'll be inside soon," he said, nudging her arm. "I want to speak with Clarence about givin' me a ride to my dental appointment in Lancaster next week."

"Jah, okay. I'll go on ahead." Miriam hurried toward the market and was halfway across the parking lot when she stumbled on a broken beer bottle someone had carelessly tossed on the ground. Her legs went out from under her, and she landed on the shattered glass. She winced and struggled to her feet, hoping no one had seen her calamity, and wondering what the nasty bottle had done to her dress and knees.

Suddenly, Miriam felt two strong arms pulling her to an upright position. She looked up and found herself staring at a tall English man. His sandy blond hair was neatly combed, and he wore a pair of sunglasses.

"Are you all right?" he asked, bending down to pick up the broken bottle.

Miriam's face heated with embarrassment. "I. . .uh. . . I'm fine, really—thank you."

He whipped off his sunglasses to reveal clear, wide-set blue eyes. "Your dress is torn, and I see blood showing through it. You'd better let me see your knees because they might be cut up pretty bad."

His resonate voice was as impressive as his looks, and Miriam had to tear her gaze away from him. "I—I appreciate your concern, but I'm fine," she stammered. There was no way she was going to lift the hem of her dress so the man could see her knees.

Miriam glanced down at her soiled skirt and rubbed her hand against it, as though in doing so it might take away the red stain and ugly tear. She took a few tentative steps and cringed but determinedly went on.

"At least let me offer you some assistance." The young man put one arm around Miriam's waist without even waiting for her reply. "I'll walk you to the building. I assume that's where you were heading before your little accident?"

"I was, but I can make it there on my own." Miriam

shook herself free from his grasp.

He smiled, revealing a set of gleaming white teeth and a boyish grin. "I didn't know you Amish ladies could be so liberated. I figured you might like to have a man look after you."

"I'm not liberated, but I don't need looking after." Ignoring the sharp pain in her knee, Miriam hurried on ahead.

The man continued to walk beside her. "I'm afraid we've gotten off to a bad start. I'm sorry if I've offended you." He extended his hand. "I'm Nick McCormick. Pretty catchy name, wouldn't you say?"

Miriam made no reply, nor did she make any move to shake his hand.

"I make it my duty to rescue fair ladies in distress." He reared his head back and laughed.

Despite her best efforts, Miriam found herself unable to keep from smiling. At least she thought it was a smile. She smiled so seldom anymore that she couldn't be sure.

After a few awkward moments, she finally took his hand and gave it a quick shake. "I'm Miriam Stoltzfus, and I'm sorry if I seemed rude. Now, if you'll excuse me, I need to catch up to my family."

"You're married, then?"

She shook her head. "I was speaking of my parents." Miriam wondered why she was answering this man's personal questions. It was none of his business who she was here with or what her marital status was.

"I see. Then perhaps you wouldn't mind giving me a guided tour of the place."

"A guided tour?"

"I'm a photographer for the *Daily Express* in Lancaster. I've come to take some pictures for a cover story about the Amish and Mennonite people who are here at the market."

Miriam eyed the camera bag hanging over his shoulder. She didn't know why she hadn't noticed it before. Her body stiffened, and the familiar frown was back on her face. "I have no intention of acting as a tour guide so you can photograph my people. And in case you aren't aware of this, we don't pose for pictures."

They had reached the market, and Nick dropped the broken bottle into a trash can and opened the door, letting Miriam step inside first. "I'm afraid it's my turn to apologize, Miriam. In spite of what you say, I am aware that a few Amish people do allow pictures to be taken, especially of their children. I can see that you have your guard up for some reason, and I've obviously offended you by asking for your assistance. Please accept my apologies."

"It's of no real consequence. I get my feelings hurt a lot these days," Miriam said with a shrug. "Good day, Mr. McCormick." She turned and limped off in the direction of the ladies' restroom.

❧

Nick watched until Miriam disappeared; then he turned in the opposite direction. He wished she would have been willing to show him around or at least talk to him long enough so he could get some information about her. Was she here to look around? Did she work at one of the places selling hot dogs, hoagies, or pretzels?

He thought about waiting until Miriam returned from the restroom but decided against it. She'd been anything but friendly during their encounter in the parking lot, so it wasn't likely that she would be willing to tell him what he wanted to know.

Not wishing to waste more time, he made his way down the aisle closest to him. English vendors selling craft items and souvenirs ran the first two booths, so he moved on until he came to a root beer stand run by an Amish man with dark brown hair cut in a Dutch-bob. A young girl sat on the stool beside him, reading a book. When Nick stopped in front of their table, she looked up and said, "Would ya like some root beer? My pappy makes it, and it's real tasty."

"Please excuse my daughter. She thinks it's solely her job to sell our root beer." The Amish man motioned to the jugs sitting on the table.

"It looks good, and I might come back for some on my way out," Nick said, "but right now I'm on a mission."

"What's a mission?" the child questioned.

"Mary Ellen, never mind. Go on back to your reading," her father admonished.

"That's okay; I don't mind her questions." Nick pulled a notebook and pen from his shirt pocket. "I'm a reporter for the *Daily Express*, and I, too, like to ask questions."

The Amish man's forehead wrinkled. "You're here to do a story?"

Nick nodded. "I'd like to ask you a few questions."

"About the farmers' market or about the Plain People who are here today?"

"Both," Nick said. No point aggravating the man if he

was opposed to him doing a story on the Amish.

"What do you want to know?"

"Well, to me and many other Englishers like myself, the Plain life is kind of a puzzle."

"In what way?"

"I've heard it said that you Amish want to live separately from the world, yet you integrate by selling your wares right along with the English here."

The Amish man nodded.

"I understand some of your men serve as volunteer firemen, working in conjunction with the English firefighters."

"Jah, that's true. We're willing to work with others outside our faith and have congenial relationships with them, but we still remain separate by the plain clothes we wear, our simple transportation and farming methods, and our restrictions on the use of media among our people."

Nick grimaced. *Ouch. That last comment was obviously directed at me.* He managed a smile. "We all have a job to do, and mine involves bringing people the news."

The man opened his mouth to say something, but an older Amish couple showed up, and he turned his attention to them. "It's good to see you both. How are you two doin'?"

"Real well," the woman replied.

The bearded Amish man who stood beside her nodded. "We were feeling kind of thirsty, so we decided to come on over and get some of your flavorsome, homemade root beer."

The little girl, who had returned to reading her book, looked up and grinned. "You think maybe Pappy and me

43

might get another invite to your house for supper soon?"

The Amish woman nodded and reached out to pat the child's head, which was covered with a small, white cap. "We'd like that." She smiled at the child's father then. "What do you think, Amos? Would you be able to come over again soon?"

He nodded with an eager expression and poured the man and woman each a glass of root beer. "If you think this is any good I'll bring a jug whenever we do join you for supper."

The older man took a quick drink and licked his lips. "Umm. . .it's *wunderbaar*."

"Wunderbaar. That means 'wonderful,' doesn't it?" Nick asked, butting in.

"That's right," the Amish man said. "Are you from a *Deitsch* background?"

"No, but I took a few years of German in high school, so I'm able to pick up on some of your Pennsylvania Dutch lingo."

"The man's a reporter for the *Daily Express*," Amos said. "He wants to do a story about the farmers' market and the Plain People who've come here today."

"We get too much of that already." The older man grunted. "Curious tourists askin' a bunch of questions is one thing, but I've got no time for nosy reporters."

"Okay, I know when to take a hint," Nick said, slipping his notepad and pen into his pocket. "Guess I'd better find someone else to interview."

He had already started to walk away, when the little girl called out, "Aren't ya gonna try some of Pappy's root beer?"

"Maybe some other time."

After inspecting her knees, Miriam found that only the right one was bleeding, but the cut didn't appear to be too serious. She wet a paper towel and blotted the knee to stop the bleeding; then she tried unsuccessfully to get the blood off her dress. She was afraid of scrubbing too hard for fear of tearing it more, so she decided to wait until she got home to tend to it properly.

Miriam was about to leave the restroom, when the door flew open and a little girl burst into the room. It was Mary Ellen Hilty. "Teacher!" she cried excitedly. "I seen your folks a bit ago, but I didn't know you was here today."

"Actually, I've only been here a short time," Miriam responded. She was tempted to correct the child's English but decided not to mention it since this wasn't a school day and she wasn't Mary Ellen's mother.

"Pappy will be glad to see you." The child's hazel-colored eyes shone like copper pennies, and her round cheeks took on a rosy glow. "He thinks you cook real good, Teacher. He said so after we had supper at your place last time."

Miriam tried to force a smile, but inwardly, she was seething. *Of course he likes my cooking. He would like any woman's cooking.*

"Your mamm said me and Pappy could come to supper at your place again soon." Mary Ellen twisted her body from side to side like a wiggly worm.

Oh, great. That's just what I need. Miriam tried to force a smile. "Are you happy it's almost time for school to be out for the summer?" she asked, hoping the change in subject might get Mary Ellen's mind on something other than their next supper invitation.

The child offered her a wide grin. "I'll enjoy spending more time with Pappy when he lets me come in his shop, but I'll miss school—and you, Teacher Mim. Is it all right if I call you that?"

"Jah, sure," Miriam mumbled.

"Some of the kinner don't like you so much, but I think you're real smart—and pretty, too."

"Danki." Miriam moved toward the door. "I must be going now, Mary Ellen. I need to find my folks."

"They're still talkin' to Pappy over by his root beer stand. Why don't you go on over and try some? Pappy gave your folks a glass for free, and I'm sure he'd give you one, too."

Miriam only nodded in reply, but when she left the restroom she turned in the opposite direction, away from the side of the market where the refreshments were sold. The last thing she needed was another meeting with Mary Ellen's father.

She didn't have to go far before she saw a familiar face. Her sister-in-law Crystal was heading toward her, holding hands with her two-year-old twin boys, Jacob and John.

"Aunt Mimmy, *dummle*—hurry," Jacob squealed.

"Aunt Mimmy, dummle," John echoed.

Miriam knelt next to her nephews to give them a hug, but the pain in her knee caused her to wince, so she carefully stood up again.

"Miriam, what's wrong? Are you hurt?" Crystal asked with a look of concern.

"It's not serious. I fell outside in the parking lot and cut my knee a little. I embarrassed myself some, too." Miriam made no mention of the brazen young English man who had offered his assistance. Why bring more questions from Crystal?

Crystal pointed to Miriam's dress. "You've torn your skirt. Let's go find your mamm. Maybe she has something we can mend it with. Your folks are here with you, aren't they?"

"Jah. I was told they're over at Amos Hilty's root beer stand."

"Let's go find them," Crystal suggested. "Maybe after Mom fixes your dress, she'll watch the twins for me. Then we can go off by ourselves and do some shopping. It will be like old times for us."

The idea of some time alone with Crystal did sound kind of nice, but Miriam wasn't eager to see Amos. She hesitated before answering. "Why don't you go on? I'll meet you over by the quilts. I'd like to look at some Karen Freisen has for sale."

"That's fine, but what about your dress?"

"It can wait until I go home."

"Come with us anyway, and I'll treat you to a nice cold root beer," Crystal prompted.

John tugged on Miriam's dress. "Dummle, Aunt Mimmy."

"Dummle, Aunt Mimmy," echoed Jacob.

Miriam shrugged. "Oh, all right. I can see that I'm out-numbered. Let's get ourselves some root beer."

❦

Amos was busy pouring a glass of frothy root beer for a

young English boy when Miriam showed up with Crystal and her twins. He handed the glass to the boy and offered Miriam what he hoped was a friendly smile. "It's good to see you again. Your folks were here a few minutes ago. You just missed them."

"Oh, wouldn't you know it? I wanted Anna to watch these two for me," Crystal said, nodding at her boys.

"Maybe we should try to find them," Miriam suggested.

Jacob pulled on his mother's skirt, and John pointed toward a jug of root beer.

"Jah, boys, we'll have some root beer first," promised their mother.

Amos lifted the jug that was already open and poured some root beer into four paper cups. He handed the two larger ones to the women and gave the twins smaller servings.

Frothy foam covered John's and Jacob's noses when they simultaneously took a drink. The grown-ups laughed—even Miriam. It was the first time Amos had seen her laugh in a good long while, and it sounded real nice to his ears.

After the drinks were finished and they'd engaged in some polite conversation, Miriam said they should be on their way. Amos nodded, feeling a sense of regret, and said he hoped to see her again soon and was sorry she had missed Mary Ellen, who had gone to the restroom.

"I saw her in there," Miriam said. "I'm sure she'll be back soon."

Amos shrugged. "If she doesn't run into someone she knows and gets to gabbing."

"That's the way I was when I was Mary Ellen's age,"

Crystal put in. "My daed said I was the most talkative child in our family."

Miriam glanced around with an anxious expression. "Well, as I said before, I really should be on my way."

"That's right," Crystal agreed. "We need to find your mamm so we can see if she's willing to watch the twins while we do some shopping."

The women headed off, and Amos, determined to get Miriam off his mind, busied himself by setting several more jugs of root beer on the table.

"Amos is definitely interested in you," Crystal whispered to Miriam as they walked away.

"Well, I'm not interested in him," Miriam replied with a firm nod. "Furthermore, it troubles me the way everyone keeps trying to match us up. Even his daughter is in on the plot."

Crystal touched Miriam's arm. "Mary Ellen's a sweet child. I'm sure no such ideas have entered her mind."

"Maybe not, but some adults, whom I won't bother to mention, are in on the scheme to marry me off to Amos." Miriam wrinkled her nose. "I'm afraid some of them might be using that poor child as an instrument of their devious ways."

Crystal laughed. "How you do exaggerate. No one's being devious or plotting against you. We just want your happiness; surely you can see that."

Miriam just kept on walking.

"Ever since we were little girls, all we talked about was

how we would marry someday and have a family. We both knew how happy we'd be if God gave us good husbands and a bunch of fine kinner to raise."

"That's easy enough for you to say, because you're happily married to my brother Jonas. And you have these *lieblich* boys to fill your life," Miriam added, pointing to her adorable nephews. She touched her chest. "I, on the other hand, am an old-maid schoolteacher, and I'll always be one."

CHAPTER 5

"That was a great story you did on the farmers' market," Pete said when Nick entered his office the next weekend.

Nick pulled out a chair and took a seat in front of his boss's desk. "Thanks. Glad you liked it."

"You must have some kind of a connection with the Amish, because the quotes you got were awesome, not to mention the pictures you included."

Nick nodded. "I took a few years of German, so I understand some of what they say when they speak Pennsylvania Dutch to each other, which is how I got some of the information included in my article."

"And the pictures? Did they willingly pose for those?"

"Only a few of the Amish kids did. The older ones don't like to have their pictures taken, so I had to get those on the sly."

Pete nodded, and a slow smile spread across his face. "You're not only good with words and pictures, but you're crafty, as well. I like that in my reporters. That's how great stories are born, you know."

Nick lifted his shoulders in an exaggerated shrug. "I do my best."

Pete's balding head bobbed up and down. "And I'm sure you'll do your best on the next piece I give you."

"What might that be?" Nick asked with interest.

"Covered bridges."

"Covered bridges?"

"Yep. There are a lot of them in the area, and some of the older ones are in the process of being restored. I think it would be good to do an article about the bridges so our readers will know where they are and how to find them."

"Do you know where they all are, Pete?"

"Nope, but that's your job to find out."

Nick felt a trickle of sweat roll down his forehead. Driving all over the countryside searching for covered bridges did not sound like an interesting assignment, and he told his boss so.

"You don't have to drive around aimlessly. I'm sure the Amish in the area know where the bridges are, so I would suggest that you stop by some of their farms and ask for directions." With that, Pete stood and motioned to the door. "Your assignment begins right now, Nick."

The morning sun beating against the windows had already warmed the kitchen when Miriam came downstairs. She squinted against the harsh light and turned away from the window. Her head felt fuzzy; another pounding migraine had sent her to bed early the night before, and the unpleasant remnants of it still remained. What she really needed was something to clear her head of the dusty cobwebs lingering from her disturbed sleep. Since today was Saturday and there was no school to teach, perhaps she would have a cup of herbal tea, wash her hair, and then go sit by the stream to dry it. Some time alone might do her some good. Papa and Lewis were already out in the fields, and Mom had gone over to her eldest son, Andrew's, place to help his wife, Sarah, with some baking, so no one would need Miriam for anything.

While she waited for the water in the kettle to heat, she cut herself a wedge of shoofly pie and took a seat at the table. She liked solitude, and the quietness of the house seemed to soothe her aching head a bit. By the time she had finished eating, the water was hot, so she poured some into a cup and added a peppermint tea bag. After drinking the tea, she went to the sink to wash her hair, using a bar of Mom's homemade lilac soap. A hint of the perfumed flower tickled Miriam's nose, and she sniffed appreciatively. She rinsed with warm water, reached for the towel she had placed on the counter, and blotted her hair, being careful not to rub too aggressively, which she knew would only aggravate her headache.

When she was satisfied that the majority of water had been absorbed from her hair into the towel, she wrapped another towel loosely around her head, picked up her hairbrush from the wall shelf nearby, and went out the back door.

Miriam found the stream behind their house to be clear and blue, so inviting. She sank to the ground, slipped off her shoes, and wiggled her toes in the sun-drenched grass. At moments like this, she wished she were still a child. Life seemed easier back then, and it wasn't nearly so painful.

She reached up and pulled the towel from her head, caus-ing her damp hair to fall loosely about her shoulders. She shook her head several times, letting the sun warm her tresses as she closed her eyes and lifted her face toward the sky.

Oh Lord, she prayed, *why must my heart continue to hurt so? I want to be pleasing in Your sight, yet I know that most of the time I fall terribly short. How can I have a merry heart, as Mom says I should, when I'm so full of pain and regrets?* Tears squeezed from her closed eyelids, and Miriam reached up to wipe them away.

The crackling of a twig startled her, and when she turned, she spotted the lens of a camera peeking through the branches of a willow tree. When she realized it was pointed at her, she gasped and jumped to her feet.

Nick McCormick stepped out from behind the tree and smiled. "Sorry if I surprised you."

"I—I never expected to see you again."

He smiled sheepishly. "I can't believe my luck—it's the liberated Amish woman I had the privilege of helping to her feet last Saturday. And what beautiful feet they are," he said, pointing to Miriam's bare feet. "I had no idea I'd be seeing you again today, either. Especially not like this."

Miriam pulled the hairbrush from her apron pocket and began brushing her tangled hair, knowing she must look a sight. "I don't appreciate you sneaking up on me. And I don't like the fact that you were taking my picture. I told you last week—"

"Yes, yes, I already know. The Amish don't like to be photographed." His smile widened, and he moved closer to her.

Miriam's teeth snapped together with an audible *click*, and she twisted the handle of the hairbrush in her hands. Why did she feel so nervous in this man's company? "The Bible tells us in Exodus 20, verse 4, 'Thou shalt not make unto thee any graven image,' " she explained. "We believe that includes posing for photographs or displaying them for impractical reasons. We also don't want to appear prideful."

"I can see that you're well versed in the scriptures," Nick said as he took a seat on the grass. Before she could comment, he quickly added, "And for your information, I photographed several Amish children at the farmers' market the other day, and none of them put up such a fuss. Is their religion any different than yours?"

Miriam lowered herself to the grass again, making sure she was a comfortable distance from the insolent intruder. "Children haven't joined the church yet, and they don't know any better. Besides, some English folks bribe them with money or candy. They're not strong enough to say no."

Nick laughed, causing the skin around his blue eyes to crinkle. "How about you, Miss Stoltzfus? Would you allow me to photograph you for a piece of candy?"

"I wouldn't pose for a picture at any price." Miriam looked the man squarely in the eyes. "Anyway, you've already taken my picture without my knowledge or my consent. I'm sure you probably have some prize-winning shots of the silly Amish woman sitting by the stream without her head-covering in place."

Nick's face sobered. "I've offended you again, haven't I?"

"To be perfectly honest, you have."

Nick held his camera in front of her face, and as he pulled

each of the pictures he'd taken of her onto the screen, he hit the DELETE button. "There. Is that better?"

Before she could open her mouth to reply, he added, "Please accept my heartfelt apology for intruding on your privacy."

Miriam's defenses dropped just a little. "Thank you, Mr. McCormick."

"Nick. Please, call me Nick." He grinned at her in a most disconcerting way. "You know what, Miriam?"

"What?"

"You're beautiful when you smile."

Miriam felt the heat of a blush stain her cheeks. She hadn't even realized that she'd given him a smile. She looked down at her hands, clasped tightly around her hairbrush, and noticed that she was trembling. "I—I don't know what to say." Her voice was strained as his gaze probed hers. How could this man's presence affect her so, and why?

"Now I've embarrassed you," he said. "I apologize for that, too."

Glancing out the corner of her eye, she admired the perfect line of his profile. He was the most handsome man she had met since William. Instantly, she halted her thoughts. How bold of her to scrutinize the Englisher like that. As much as she would have liked to get to know Nick better, she was eager for him to leave.

"What's wrong? Aren't you willing to forgive me?" he asked, his lips twitching with a flirty smile.

"Of course I am. It's just that. . .well, no one has ever called me beautiful before."

"Then they must have been wearing blinders." Nick rose

to his feet. "I'd better get going. I'm on a quest to find covered bridges, and so far I've only found two." He grunted. "I thought I could get some information from people living in the area, but you're the first person I've run into, and you probably wouldn't be willing to help."

"What makes you say that?"

"You didn't want to show me around the farmers' market last week, and I've offended you twice already today, so I just assumed—"

"You assumed wrong, Mr. McCormick."

"It's Nick, remember?" He looked at Miriam in such a strange way, it made her mouth feel dry and her palms turn sweaty. Maybe she just needed something to drink. "So do you know where some covered bridges might be?" he asked.

She nodded. "There are a few not far from here, and several more throughout the county."

"Can you give me some specifics?"

"Let's see. . . . There's one near Soudersburg, just off Ronks Road. Another is close to Strasburg, off Lime Valley Road." She paused and thought a minute. "There are two south of Manheim, one north of Churchtown Road, one east of Rothsville, and another one northeast of there. Then somewhere between Reamstown and Martindale you'll find one, and I believe there's one north of Ephrata, too."

He whistled. "That's pretty impressive. You must get around quite a bit."

"Not anymore. I spend most of my time teaching school. I used to travel the area a lot when I was a teenager."

"You're a schoolteacher?"

She nodded. "I teach at the one-room schoolhouse about a mile from here."

"So the liberated Amish woman is not only beautiful, but she's smart, too."

Miriam's defenses rose once again, and she clenched the hairbrush tighter. "I am not liberated, and I wish you would quit saying that."

"Sorry."

There was an awkward pause as they stood there staring at one another. Finally Nick smiled and said, "I've heard that the Amish only go through the eighth grade. Is that correct?"

Her only reply was a quick nod.

"Then how much training does a teacher for one of your schools need?"

"Same as the other scholars—we graduate eighth grade."

"That's it? No college or other formal training?"

She shook her head. "Amish teachers are selected on the basis of their natural interest in teaching, academic ability, and Amish values."

"What kind of values?"

"Faith, sincerity, and willingness to learn from the pupils."

"Ah, I see. Very interesting facts you've given me." Nick smiled. "One of the things I enjoy most about being a newspaper reporter is learning new things when I interview people."

"My mother's a reporter, too." Miriam hadn't planned on blurting that out, but she thought maybe Nick might be interested since he also wrote for a newspaper.

"What newspaper does she write for?"

"*The Budget*. Mostly Amish and Mennonite people read it, although I understand that some Englishers subscribe to the paper, too. Have you heard of it?"

"As a matter of fact, I have. I believe it's published in Sugarcreek, Ohio. Am I right?"

She nodded. "There are Amish and Mennonite people all over the country who write columns that go into the newspaper, and my mother is one of the scribes."

"That's interesting. What kind of news does she report?"

"Oh, just the happenings in our local community—things like weddings, funerals, those who have had recent out-of-town visitors, accidents that have occurred in the area—that type of thing."

"What's your mother's name? I might decide to pick up a copy of *The Budget* and check out her column."

"Anna Stoltzfus."

"I'd like to meet your mother sometime. Maybe we could swap stories."

Miriam wasn't sure if Nick was only kidding or if he really wanted to meet her mother, but she was pretty sure Mom wouldn't take to the idea of some fancy English reporter who toted a camera asking her a bunch of questions. So rather than comment on his last statement, she merely shrugged and said, "It's been nice talking to you, Nick, but I need to get back home now."

"Do you live near here?"

She pointed to the field behind her. "Our house is on the other side of that pasture."

"Just a stone's throw then, huh?"

"Jah, if you've got a long arm."

He chuckled and held out his hand. "It's been nice talking to you again, Miriam. I appreciate your help on the covered bridges, and I hope this won't be the last time we meet."

Miriam didn't respond to that comment, either, nor did she shake Nick's hand. The man had a way of getting under her skin, but something about him fascinated her, too, and that bothered her more than she cared to admit. "Good-bye, Nick," she murmured.

"Bye, fair lady."

As Nick walked away, Miriam pressed a hand to a heart that was beating much too fast and wondered why the thought of seeing Nick again held so much appeal.

$$\approx$$

"Oh, Sarah," Anna said, as she and her daughter-in-law sat at the kitchen table drinking a cup of tea, "I'm worried about Miriam."

"What's the problem? Is she feeling sick or something?" Sarah asked.

Anna shook her head. "My daughter's body isn't sick, but her heart seems to have been shattered, and I fear it might never be mended."

"She's not still pining over William Graber, is she?"

"I'm afraid so. She's rejected all suitors ever since William jilted her, and now Amos Hilty has shown an interest, and she's giving him the cold shoulder, too."

"Many young people have breakups with their boyfriends, but most recover after a reasonable time." Sarah clicked her tongue. "If there was only something we could do to make Miriam realize that life goes on when bad things happen. God is always there to help us through our trials; we just need to trust Him and look for the good."

"I wish she could see that." Anna released a sigh. "I really think Amos would be good for her, and from what I can tell, his daughter seems to like Miriam a lot."

"She's a good teacher; Rebekah has told me that often."

"If she can teach the scholars and make them like her, then she has what it takes to be a good mother."

Sarah's forehead wrinkled as she stared at the table. "Sorry to say this, Anna, but not all of Miriam's students like her. Some say she's an old-maid schoolteacher with a heart of stone. Rebekah told me that, too."

Anna nodded. "Miriam overheard some of the kinner saying that not long ago, and it nearly broke my heart to see how sad she looked when she told me about it."

"Maybe we need to look for some fun things we can do that will involve Miriam."

"Jah, maybe so. Although she doesn't seem open to the idea of doing many fun things anymore. I'm going to keep praying for my daughter—that the Lord will give her a merry heart and that, if it's His will, Miriam will fall in love and get married."

CHAPTER

6

By the time school had let out for the summer, the weather had become hot, and Miriam found it difficult not to complain about the stuffy, humid air. Some days, not even a tender breeze graced Lancaster County.

One evening, a summer storm finally brought wind and rain, but it only caused more humidity. That evening, Miriam sat on the front porch steps watching streaks of lightning brighten the shadowy sky.

"God's handiwork is a pretty picture, isn't it?" said a deep voice from behind her.

She turned and discovered her father standing on the porch, stroking his long, full beard. "You startled me, Papa. I didn't hear you come out."

"Sorry about that." He pointed to the sky. "God's quite the artist, wouldn't ya say?"

Miriam nodded. Papa had such a way with words and a love and understanding of God that had always astonished her. He saw the Lord's hand in everything—things others would have simply taken for granted.

"We need a good rain," Papa said as he took a seat on

the step beside Miriam.

"I suppose so, but it's making the air awfully muggy."

"Jah, well, we can put up with a little mugginess when the good Lord answers our prayers and brings the rain. The fields are in need of a good soaking."

Miriam couldn't argue with that. She knew how important the crops of alfalfa, corn, and wheat were to the Amish farmers in the area. She reached for Papa's hand. "How is it that you always see the good in things?"

"'For as he thinketh in his heart, so is he,' the Bible tells us in Proverbs 23:7."

Miriam wasn't able to dispute that, either. Perhaps the reason she was so unhappy was because she thought unhappy thoughts. But how could she make herself think pleasant thoughts?

She shuddered as a clap of thunder sounded close to the house.

"Is somethin' besides the storm troubling you?" Papa asked.

Of course something was troubling her. Something always seemed to be troubling her. She shook her head. "Just the storm. I hope the *wedderleech* doesn't hit anyone's house or barn."

"Lightning strikes are always uninvited. But if it should happen, then we'll simply rebuild." He smiled. "A good barn raising is always a joy."

"A joy? You mean, it's a lot of work, don't you?"

"That, too, but working together with your friends and family can be a happy time."

Miriam couldn't help but admire her father for his

optimistic attitude, but try as she might, she couldn't seem to emulate it.

That Sunday, church services were held at Andrew and Sarah's home. Their farm was only three miles away, so the ride by horse and buggy was rather short compared to some.

After Papa helped Mom down from the buggy, he and Lewis joined his two married sons, Jonas and Andrew, behind the barn where the horses had been put in the corral. Miriam and her mother made their way to the front porch to visit with Sarah, Crystal, and some of the other women who had already arrived. The twins were playing on the front lawn with their cousins, Rebekah and Simon, and several other small children.

"I'm going to step inside the kitchen for a drink of water before the service starts," Miriam whispered to Sarah.

Sarah, who was rocking baby Nadine, answered, "Help yourself. There's a pitcher of lemonade in the refrigerator if you'd rather have that."

Miriam shook her head. "Water will be fine, danki."

"Jah. Suit yourself."

When Miriam first entered the kitchen, she thought it was empty, but then she caught sight of someone across the room near the sink. Amos Hilty was bent over Mary Ellen, scrubbing her face with a wet washcloth. The child wiggled and squirmed, and she heard Amos say, "Mary Ellen, please stop *rutschich*."

"Sorry, Papa. I don't mean to do so much squirming." When the child spotted Miriam, she squealed and ran to her side. "Teacher Mim! You look schee today. Doesn't she, Pappy?"

Miriam looked down at her dark blue cotton dress with a white apron worn over the front. She wondered what there was about her that the child thought was pretty, and then she remembered Nick McCormick's comment about her being beautiful. Her gaze met Amos's, and he smiled.

"Your teacher's a fine-looking woman," he said, nodding at Mary Ellen.

Miriam made no reply.

Amos shifted his weight from one foot to the other. "Mary Ellen sampled some raspberries from Sarah's garden when we first arrived. She had sticky red juice all over her face."

Miriam nodded. "I came in for a drink of water. I'll get it and be out of your way."

Amos stepped away from the sink. "Help yourself. I've done about as well as I can with this little scamp's dirty face anyway."

Miriam hurried over to the cupboard and got out a glass; then she went to the sink and filled the glass with enough water to quench her thirst. She wished Amos would leave the room instead of standing there, watching her.

"Mary Ellen, why don't you run outside and play with some of your friends?" he said. "I want to speak with your teacher a few minutes."

The child gave him a questioning look, but obediently, she went out the back door, looking over her shoulder to flash Miriam a dimpled smile.

The last thing Miriam wanted was to be alone with

Amos Hilty. She looked around the room, hoping someone would come into the kitchen and rescue her.

Amos pulled out a chair and motioned her to sit down. Reluctantly, she obliged, and Amos took a seat directly across from her.

"Church will be starting soon," Miriam reminded.

Amos glanced at the battery-operated clock hanging on the far wall. "We still have some time yet. I wanted to discuss something with you."

"About Mary Ellen?"

"No, about us."

"Us?" Miriam's voice sounded high-pitched, even to her own ears.

"Jah. It–it's about our relationship."

Miriam looked into Amos's coffee-colored eyes to see if he was serious, while she cleared her throat to stall for time. She wanted to be sure her words were well chosen. "The only relationship we have is the fact that your daughter is one of my students. So, if this isn't about Mary Ellen, then what?"

Amos stood and began pacing the kitchen floor. "Miriam, surely you've been able to tell that I have an interest in you."

Her mouth dropped open. Amos had always seemed rather shy, and she hadn't expected such a bold declaration from him.

"I–I want to spend more time with you—to come calling at your home and court you. Yet every time I ask you to go someplace with Mary Ellen and me, you have an excuse why you can't. Whenever I try to engage you in conversation, you act as though you're trying to avoid me."

"I'm sure you mean well, Amos," Miriam replied, "but

I get the feeling that you're only looking for a mother for your little girl."

He looked stunned. "Oh, Miriam, I—"

"You needn't deny it. Everyone knows you're a widower without any family around to help you raise your daughter. It's understandable that you would want to find a wife to help care for her."

The room took on a distinctive chill, as Amos stared at the toes of his boots. "I. . .that is. . .I know Mary Ellen is quite taken with you. In fact, you're all she talked about when she returned from school every day last term. However, I do have some concerns about the type of influence you could have on her young mind."

"What's that supposed to mean?"

"You seem quite melancholy, and I had hoped if we started courting, you might find more joy in life and maybe even—"

"Do you think being courted by you would make me happy enough to have around your daughter? Is that what you're saying?" Miriam felt a trickle of sweat roll down her forehead, and she reached up to swipe it away.

"That. . .that's not what I meant to say at all." A crease formed between Amos's brows, and a pained expression crossed his face. "I—I think we could get along rather well if you'd only give it a chance."

Miriam stood and hurried across the room. When she reached the door, she halted and turned back to face him. "There are several available Amish women in the area, Amos. Some are a bit younger than me, but I'm sure if you use your charms on one of them, you might persuade her to be your wife."

"But I—"

Miriam rushed out the door without waiting to hear the rest of his sentence.

Amos stood staring at the back door and shaking his head. "She doesn't understand. She doesn't realize how much I care for her or that I would do my best to be a good husband. If only she would give me the opportunity to show her how things could be."

"You talkin' to yourself these days?"

Amos whirled around and was shocked to see one of Miriam's brothers standing in the doorway. "Andrew, I didn't realize you had come into the room."

"I was in the hallway and heard someone gabbin' away in here," Andrew replied with a crooked grin. "Don't tell me you're so desperate for conversation that you've taken up talkin' to yourself as a pastime."

"A few minutes ago, I was talking to your sister—at least, I was trying to—but she didn't stick around long enough to hear all of what I had wanted to say."

"She wouldn't listen, huh?"

"No. To tell you the truth, she doesn't seem to be interested in much of anything I have to say."

Andrew pulled out a chair and sat down. "Is there anything in particular you wanted her to hear? Maybe I could relay the message."

Amos took the seat opposite Miriam's brother. "I asked if I could court her, but she's obviously not interested."

"Did she come right out and say so?"

"Not exactly, but she said I should use my charms on some other Amish woman and try to get her to be my wife." Amos groaned. "If I have any charms, I sure don't know about 'em. Besides, I'm not interested in courting anyone but Miriam."

"How come?" Andrew scratched the side of his head. "I mean, if she's not interested—"

"She's my daughter's teacher, and Mary Ellen's quite taken with her." No way was Amos going to admit to Miriam's brother that he was in love with her and had been for a good many years.

"That's all well and nice, but it doesn't mean Miriam would make you a good wife, Amos."

"But she would make Mary Ellen a good *mudder*, I'm sure of it."

Andrew nodded. "You're probably right. Miriam's done well as a schoolteacher, and she would likely do as well as Mary Ellen's mother."

"Got any ideas how I can make her see that?"

"Guess you need to try harder, and don't give up, 'cause one thing I know for sure is my big sister has no other suitors." Andrew paused and scrubbed a hand down his bearded face. "So do you want me to put in a good word for you or what?"

"You—you would do that for me?"

"Sure thing, because I think you'd be good for my unhappy sister. Truth be told, I wouldn't mind havin' you as a brother-in-law, either."

Amos released a puff of air. "That would be great. I'll appreciate any help I can get on this."

"In case you don't know it, my mamm wants to see you and Miriam together, too."

"Really?"

"Sure. Why do you think she's had you for supper so many times?"

"Maybe I'll have a talk with Anna then, too."

"Might not be a bad idea." Andrew slid his chair back and stood. "A little prayer wouldn't hurt, either."

Heartless. . .heartless. . .heartless. . . The steady rhythm of the buggy wheels echoed in Miriam's ears as they traveled home that evening. The repetitive noise seemed to be calling out a reminder of the heartless way she had behaved toward Amos that morning.

She had probably hurt his feelings by letting him know she wasn't interested in him and thought he was only after her because of Mary Ellen. But he needed to realize there was no chance of them courting, much less of her agreeing to marry him. No matter how hard Miriam tried, she couldn't seem to get over the hurt and pain that lingered in her heart because of William's deception. Now Amos was hurting her even more by using his child to try and gain her favor. How foolish did he believe her to be? She'd been tricked by a man once, only to have her heart torn asunder. She would never allow herself to be hurt like that again.

As Papa pulled their buggy alongside the barn, Miriam pushed her thoughts aside, climbed down, and followed her mother up to the house.

"How about a glass of lemonade or some iced tea?"

Mom asked as they stepped into the kitchen a few minutes later.

Miriam tried to smile but failed. "I'm kind of tired. So if you don't mind, I think I'll head upstairs to my room."

Mom patted Miriam's arm. "Sleep well then, daughter."

"I will. Danki."

Miriam trudged wearily up the stairs, feeling like the weight of the world sat on her shoulders. If only there were some way to remove the heavy burden that made her feel like a prisoner.

CHAPTER

7

The following day after lunch, Anna and Miriam got busy cleaning up the kitchen. The men had gone back to the fields, leaving the women alone with a sink full of dirty dishes.

Anna filled the plastic dishpan with hot water and a touch of liquid detergent. "The men were sure hungry, jah?"

Miriam motioned to the bowl on the cupboard, full of watermelon rinds. "I think Lewis ate three or four pieces of watermelon himself."

"Our men do have some hearty appetites." Anna stepped aside so Miriam could wash the dishes while she dried. "Speaking of men, I was talking with Amos Hilty yesterday after the worship service. He asked me—that is, he was wondering if I would speak to you on his behalf."

Miriam dropped the dishrag into the soapy water so hard that it sent several bubbles drifting toward the ceiling. "Doesn't that man ever give up? I thought I had made myself clear when I spoke to him yesterday. Obviously my words fell on deaf ears."

"Now, Miriam, please don't be upset." Anna spoke in a

soothing tone, hoping to calm her daughter. "I've probably made a mistake by bringing this up, but Amos seemed quite upset after he talked with you yesterday."

"I'm sorry about that, but I was upset, too."

"He's afraid you may have the wrong impression of him—of his intentions, that is."

"Oh, his intentions are clear enough. At least, to me they are." Miriam's forehead wrinkled as she turned to face Anna. "Can't you see it, too, Mom? Amos cares nothing for me. He just wants a housekeeper and a mudder for Mary Ellen."

"I'm sure he wants more than that."

"Jah, he probably wants someone to darn his socks, scrub his floors, and cook his meals. Well, I'm sorry, but that someone won't be me."

Anna placed a gentle hand on her daughter's arm. "Miriam, is it so wrong for a man to want those things?"

"Then he ought to get a hired girl to help out. Please tell Amos the next time you see him that I want to be left alone."

"I believe he does have a hired girl who comes in part-time, and you know Amos has no relatives to call on. His parents are both deceased, and his two brothers have farms of their own to run. His in-laws live in another state, so—"

"I'm truly sorry about all that," Miriam interrupted, "but it's certainly not reason enough for me to marry Amos, and I don't appreciate him asking you to speak to me on his behalf."

A ray of hope shone in Anna's soul. "Has he asked you to marry him?"

"Well, no, he just asked if he could come calling."

"I think he only wants to establish a friendship with you for now. In time, you'll both know if there's a chance for love or marriage."

Miriam released a noisy sigh. "I can already tell you that there's no chance for either love or marriage. Not for me."

Anna handed Miriam a few dishes to wash. "Must you always be so negative? Can't you look for some things to be joyous about?"

"What is there to be joyous about?"

Anna nodded toward the open window. "There are so many reasons to smile—the pretty birds chirping and flapping their wings, a clear blue sky on a sunny day, warm apple dumplings with fresh whipping cream for dessert, freshly cut flowers to decorate the table." She smiled. "And of course, knowing one is loved and cherished."

Miriam shrugged and then moved across the room. She picked up the bulky ceramic bowl and headed for the back door. "I'm going out to the pasture to give these rinds to the cows."

Out in the pasture, the herd of dairy cows grazed contentedly, but they perked up their ears as Miriam approached. She dumped the watermelon rinds over the fence and watched as they ate greedily, nudging each other with their noses.

"You silly old cows. You carry on as though you haven't a thing to eat." She gestured to the field. "See here, you have a whole pasture of green grass to eat, so why all the excitement over a few watermelon rinds?"

Miriam lingered awhile, watching the doting mothers

with their young ones. She was in no hurry to get back inside to more of Mom's lectures, so she figured she may as well stay a bit longer. She longed for the day when school started in August, for she looked forward to teaching again. Being at home all summer gave her too much time to think. Even though there were always plenty of chores to do, it wasn't the same as keeping her brain busy. Besides, when she was around home so much, Mom seemed more tempted to meddle in her life.

Miriam leaned on the fence rail and watched with interest as a mother cow washed its baby with a big, rough tongue. For some reason it reminded her of the sight she had witnessed on Sunday when she'd stepped into Sarah's kitchen and found Amos scrubbing his daughter's face. The baby cow squirmed all around, just as Mary Ellen had done.

"I suppose all little ones need a mudder to care for them," she whispered.

Amos had just left his blacksmith shop and was heading to the house to get a jug of iced tea and to check on Mary Ellen, when Andrew Stoltzfus's rig came into the yard.

"*Wie geht's?*" Andrew called as he stepped down from the buggy.

"I'm doin' all right. How about you?"

"Can't complain." Andrew crossed his arms and leaned against the side of his buggy.

"Were you needing your horse shoed?"

"No. I actually came by to talk to you about my sister."

"Did you put in a good word for me like you said you

would?" Amos asked hopefully. If Andrew had achieved any measure of success, then maybe it was time for Amos to invite Miriam on another picnic.

Andrew shook his head. "My mamm spoke to her, but I'm afraid she didn't get very far, so I figured it would be best if I didn't stick my nose in where I'm sure it's not wanted."

"I see." Amos couldn't help but feel disappointed. If Anna hadn't been able to get through to her daughter, it wasn't likely that anyone else in the family could, either. "Maybe it would be best if I gave up on Miriam," he mumbled.

"Or maybe you should try a little harder."

Amos dug the heel of his boot into the ground. "I invited her to go on a picnic with Mary Ellen and me, but she said no. I sent some wild pansies to school with Mary Ellen, but your sister didn't seem to appreciate them. I even got up the nerve to tell Miriam I wanted to court her, but her response was that I should find someone else."

"My sister's not allergic to flowers, if that makes you feel any better," Andrew said with a slanted grin.

"The only thing that would make me feel better would be if I could see Miriam smile the way she used to do when we were kinner."

Andrew pulled his fingers through the end of his beard as his smile turned upside down. "I don't think I've seen her crack a full-fledged smile since William Graber ran off to Ohio and married some other girl, leaving Miriam with a broken heart and a horrible mistrust of men."

"She doesn't mistrust her daed or any of her bruders, does she?"

"I don't believe so. Of course, none of us has ever given her any reason to mistrust us."

Neither have I. If she had given me a chance instead of William when we were teenagers, she would have found out that I wouldn't have let her down the way he did. Amos kicked at a small stone with the toe of his boot. *Course she didn't know the way I felt back then, and she still doesn't know it. Probably wouldn't care even if she did.*

"You okay?" Andrew asked, taking a step toward Amos. "You're not taking it personally because Miriam's shown no interest in you, I hope."

Amos shrugged. "It's hard not to take it personally."

"I can still put in a good word for you if you think I should."

"It's probably better that you don't. No point in ruffling your sister's feathers any more than they already are. If it's meant for us to be together, then it will happen in God's time. I just need to pray more and leave things in His hands."

Andrew nodded and thumped Amos on the back. "Now that's good thinking."

※

As Nick sat at his office desk, studying the pictures he'd taken of several covered bridges in the area, he thought about Miriam Stoltzfus. He couldn't believe she had affected him so much that he'd willingly deleted those great shots he'd taken of her drying her hair by the stream. Even though she had explained the reasons for not wanting her picture taken, it made no sense to him. In fact, he didn't understand much about the Amish way of life, and he found

Miriam's reference to God and the Bible a bit irritating. Ever since Nick's dad had been killed in a car accident, Nick had made his own decisions about life, and he didn't need any religious crutches in order to deal with life's problems. He believed that a man could be anything he wanted to be, do anything he wanted to do, and deal with whatever came his way.

Sure hope I get the opportunity to see Miriam again, Nick thought. *I should have asked for her phone number so I could call once in a while.* He slapped the side of his head. *Dummy. Amish don't have phones in their homes, and those who do have phones for business reasons keep them in an outside building. It's not likely that Miriam has a phone, and if someone else in her family does, I'm sure they wouldn't appreciate her receiving calls from a nosy English reporter.*

The phone on Nick's desk rang, rousing him from his musings, and he quickly reached for it. "Nick McCormick here."

"Hi, Nicky. It's Aunt Nora."

"Hey there. How are you doing?" Nick was always glad to hear from his aunt. She was his only relative living in the area, and since he had moved here six months ago, he'd gotten to know her pretty well.

"I'm doing fine. All but one of my rooms is filled with boarders right now," she said. "I'd be happy to give that one to you if you'd like somewhere more peaceful and quiet to live."

"I appreciate the offer, but I like having an apartment in Lancaster because it puts me closer to the newspaper office."

"I understand." There was a short pause. "If you don't

have a date for next Friday evening, how would you like to come over for supper?"

"Are you fishing for information about my love life, Auntie?"

"Of course not. I'd never do something like that."

He snickered. "Yeah, right, and frogs walk on their hind legs, too."

"You would tell me if there was someone special, wouldn't you, Nicky?"

"Sure I would, but there's nothing to tell. I'm a contented bachelor and plan to stay one for as long as possible."

"You'll change your tune one of these days when the right woman comes along."

A vision of Miriam Stoltzfus leaped into Nick's mind, and he blinked several times, trying to dispel it. She wasn't the right woman for him; he knew that much. She couldn't be, because they were worlds apart.

CHAPTER 8

It was hard to believe it was August already and that today was the first day of school. Every year, the first day seemed a little hectic and unorganized, and today was certainly no exception. There were several new children in Miriam's class, and since they were first graders and knew only their Pennsylvania Dutch language, they needed to be taught English. This took extra time on the teacher's part, and it meant the older students must do more work on their own.

Mary Ellen Hilty was in the second grade and already knew her English fairly well, but she still lacked the discipline and attention span to work on her own for long. From her seat in the second row, the child raised her hand and called out, "Teacher Mim, I need your help."

Miriam tapped her foot impatiently and frowned. She was busy helping Joanna and Nancy with the letters of the alphabet and didn't want to be disturbed.

"Teacher!" Mary Ellen called again.

Miriam put her finger to her lips. "One minute, Mary Ellen. I'll be with you in a minute."

Mary Ellen nodded, folded her hands, and placed them on top of her desk.

When Miriam finished with her explanation to the younger girls, she moved across the room and squatted beside Mary Ellen's desk. "What is it you need?"

"I don't know what this word is." The child pointed to the open primer in front of her.

"That word is *grandfather*," Miriam answered. "You must learn to sound it out. Gr-and-fa-ther."

Mary Ellen looked up at Miriam, her hazel eyes round and large. "My grandpa and grandma Zeeman live far away. Grandpa and Grandma Hilty live in heaven with Jesus. So does Mama."

Miriam saw a look of sadness on the child's face she'd never seen before. Usually there was a light in Mary Ellen's eyes and a sweet smile on her lips. She felt pity for the little girl, knowing she had no one but Amos to look after her. No one but him to love.

The light came back to Mary Ellen's eyes as quickly as it had faded. "Danki—I mean, thank you for helping me, Teacher Mim."

Miriam gently touched the child's arm, pleased that she had remembered to use only English words in her sentence. "You're welcome."

Back at her own desk, Miriam found herself watching Mary Ellen instead of grading the morning spelling papers lying before her. The child never looked terribly unkempt, but her hair always showed telltale signs of not being secured tightly enough in the bun at the back of her head. Her face was always scrubbed squeaky clean, which came as no surprise to Miriam after watching Amos wash the child's face that one Sunday morning in Sarah's kitchen.

Miriam shook her head, bringing her thoughts back to the present. She had no desire to think about that day or to be reminded of the things Amos had said to her. Regardless of everyone's denial, she was convinced that Amos's interest in her was purely selfish. A mother for his little girl was what he wanted most. Though Mary Ellen was a dear child and Miriam did have a soft spot for her, it was certainly not enough reason to marry or even to allow the girl's father to court her. A woman should be in love with the man she planned to marry, and that possibility seemed seriously doubtful for her.

Mary Ellen looked up and offered a warm, heart-melting smile, and Miriam found herself fighting the urge to rush across the room and hold the child in her arms. For one brief moment, she wanted to tell Mary Ellen that she would marry her daed and be her new mamm—that she would love her and take care of her needs. Instead, she turned her attention back to the spelling papers. *What was I thinking? The idea of me marrying Amos is just plain* narrisch*—crazy. I don't love him, and he certainly doesn't love me.*

Miriam knew her students always looked forward to lunchtime, but she dreaded pulling the rope for the noon bell, because she would no doubt be caught up in a stampede as they made a mad dash for their brightly colored lunch buckets. Today was no exception, and she fumed as soon as she pulled the bell and was nearly knocked over by one of the older boys.

"Slow down at once," she scolded. "There's no need for

you to rush like that."

Kenneth Freisen grunted an apology, grabbed his lunch box, and walked slowly back to his seat.

It took only five minutes for the children to gobble down their lunches and scamper outside to play for the remaining twenty-five minutes of lunch break. Games of baseball, Drop the Hankie, and hopscotch could be seen being played around the school playground, while some of Miriam's scholars took turns on the swings and teeter-totters.

Miriam stood at the window, watching the children and wondering if the ache she felt between her temples would turn into another one of her pounding migraine headaches. The day was only half over, and already she felt physically and emotionally drained. At moments like this, she wondered if teaching was really her intended calling in life. She often ran out of patience, and when she felt as she did today, she wondered if her mother could be right about her needing to find a husband and get married.

What am I thinking? she chided herself. *Even if I did want to get married, which I don't, I'm not in love with anyone, and I'll never marry without love or trust—both of which I don't feel for Amos.* She shrugged, deciding that her mood was only because it was the first day of school. In a few days when everything became routine again, she would be glad she was teaching school.

When a ruckus broke out in the school yard, Miriam's thoughts came to a halt. She heard laughing and shouting, and when she went to the door, she saw several of the children standing in a circle.

Miriam hurried outside. "What's the trouble?" she asked

Kenneth Freisen, who stood nearby.

"The girls were blabbing again."

Miriam pulled two of the girls aside. That was when she noticed Mary Ellen standing in the middle of the circle. Tears streamed down the child's flushed cheeks, and she sniffed between shaky sobs.

"Mary Ellen, what is it?"

"It. . .it's all right, Teacher Mim. They didn't mean it, I'm sure." Mary Ellen managed a weak smile, even through her tears.

"Who didn't mean it? Did someone hurt you?"

"Aw, she's just a little crybaby." Kenneth wrinkled his nose like some foul odor had permeated the air. "She can't even take a bit of teasing."

Miriam eyed him with suspicion. "Who was doing this teasing?"

"It wasn't me, Teacher. It was the girls. Like I said before, they like to blab."

"Which of you girls was involved, and what were you teasing Mary Ellen about?" Miriam's patience was beginning to wane, and the pain in her head had increased. She feared the dizziness and nausea that usually followed would soon be upon her, as well.

The cluster of students remained quiet. Not one child stepped forward to announce his or her part in the teasing.

Miriam frowned and rubbed her forehead. "All right then, the entire class shall stay after school for thirty minutes."

"But, that's not fair! Why should we all be punished for somethin' just a few of the girls said?" Kenneth wailed.

"I didn't do nothin', and I'll be sent to the woodshed for

a *bletsching* if I come home late," Karen Lederach whined. "My daed don't like tardiness."

"My mamm has chores waitin' for me," Grace Schrock put in.

Miriam looked at Mary Ellen. "Won't you tell me now who's guilty and what they said?"

Mary Ellen shuffled her feet a few times and motioned for Miriam to come closer. When Miriam bent down, the child whispered in her ear, "I'll tell you in private what they said, but I can't say who said it 'cause that would be tattling, and Pappy don't like a *retschbeddi*. He's warned me against being a tattler many times." She smiled, but the expression never quite reached her tear-filled eyes. "He says the Bible tells us to do to others what we want done to us. I wouldn't want someone to get me in trouble."

Miriam took hold of Mary Ellen's arm and led her inside the school building. Looking at the little girl's sweet face brought a sense of longing to Miriam's soul. She felt an unexplainable need to protect this child, and it went way beyond teacher to student. "All right, Mary Ellen. Please tell me what that was all about."

Mary Ellen looked up at Miriam, and her chin trembled. "Some of the kinner noticed that I don't dress like them."

"What do you mean? You're wearing the same Plain clothes as the rest of the girls in class."

"Today I must have put my dress on backwards, and I never even knew it. That's why some of 'em were laughing." She bit her quivering lip. "But please don't punish anyone on account of me, Teacher Mim."

"I'll worry about that later," Miriam said, as she helped

the child out of her dress. *I should have noticed her dress was on backwards. What kind of teacher am I?*

Once the dress was put on correctly, Miriam held Mary Ellen at arm's length and scrutinized her. "You've set a good example for the entire class." She tucked some stray hairs into the bun at the back of the child's head. "I only wish the others would do the same."

"I always try to do what's right. It's what God wants me to do."

Miriam nodded, wondering how a child of Mary Ellen's age could be so full of love and forgiveness, when she, an adult, struggled every day with bitterness and an inability to forgive.

Pushing the thoughts to the back of her mind, Miriam returned to the school yard to speak with her other students while Mary Ellen waited on the porch. "I hope you've all learned something today," she said, shaking her finger. "No one will be required to stay after school this time, but if anything like this ever happens again, I will punish the entire class. I don't care if you all have to go to the woodshed for a spanking when you get home. Is that clear?"

All heads nodded in unison.

"Now get back to your play. Lunchtime will be over soon."

When Miriam stepped onto the porch, Mary Ellen smiled up at her. Miriam couldn't help but offer a smile in return. *She really is a dear little girl. Mary Ellen, the heartsome. Even in the face of difficulty, she still has a forgiving heart.*

❦

"It's good to get out of that blistering sun awhile," Henry

said as he washed up at the kitchen sink. "I was sweating buckets out there."

Anna placed a platter of sandwiches on the table, as he turned to reach for a towel hanging on the handle of the refrigerator door. "I'd figured you and Lewis would not only be hungry for lunch but needing some time away from the hot, humid weather."

"And speaking of lunch, I'm hungry enough to eat everything on the table," Lewis said, sneaking up behind his mother and giving her a squeeze.

She chuckled. "The Good Lord may have only blessed me and your daed with four kinner, but ever since you could eat solid food, you've been packing away enough for ten."

"That's a bit of an exaggeration, wouldn't ya say, Anna?" Henry asked, joining them at the table. "It might have been better to say that our youngest son was born with a hole in his leg."

"Puh!" Lewis waved a hand. "You're both exaggerating."

As soon as they were all seated, they bowed their heads for silent prayer. When Henry cleared his throat so the others would know he was done, Anna passed the platter of sandwiches around.

"I wonder how things are goin' for our daughter at the schoolhouse today," Henry said, snatching two bologna sandwiches off the plate, then handing it over to Lewis. "She seemed kind of naerfich today."

"Miriam's always a little nervous on the first day of school because she never knows how things will go with the scholars," Anna said, reaching for the pitcher of goat's milk and pouring some into each of their glasses.

Lewis bit into his sandwich and washed it down with a gulp of milk. "I remember when I was a boy attending the one-room schoolhouse. I always looked forward to the first day of school."

Henry shook his finger at Lewis. "That's because you couldn't wait to tease the girls." He reached for the bowl of cut-up vegetables and plopped two carrots and a handful of radishes onto his plate. "I'm surprised you haven't honed in on one of them girls and gotten married by now."

Lewis's face turned red as a tomato, but he said not a word. Anna had a hunch he'd already found that special girl and was probably secretly courting her. Of course Lewis wasn't likely to volunteer such information, and she wouldn't embarrass him by asking.

"Maybe being back to teaching will make our daughter feel happier," Henry said, bringing the subject back to Miriam again. "I hate seeing her so down-in-the-mouth all the time."

"It is hard to see her that way," Anna agreed. "Guess the best thing we can do is keep praying that God will heal her heart soon."

"And bring her a man to love," Lewis added around a mouthful of food.

CHAPTER

9

The days rolled quickly by, and Miriam fell back into her role as teacher. She still had moments of frustration and tension, leading to her now-familiar sick headaches, but at least she was keeping busy and doing something she hoped was worthwhile.

One morning, Miriam told her mother that she would pay a call on Crystal after school had been dismissed for the day. It had been awhile since they had taken the time for a good visit, and she was certainly in need of one now.

When Miriam pulled her horse and buggy to a stop in front of Jonas and Crystal's farmhouse, she saw Crystal outside removing her dry laundry from the clothesline. Miriam called to her, and Crystal turned and waved, then motioned for Miriam to follow her to the house.

Crystal deposited the laundry basket on a kitchen chair and pulled out another chair for Miriam. "It's good to see you. You've been on my mind a lot lately, and also in my prayers."

"Oh, really? Why's that?"

Crystal shrugged and began to fold the clothes, placing

them in neat stacks on the table. "I've been praying for your happiness."

"Maybe it's not meant for some people to be happy," Miriam said, feeling a deep sense of sadness surround her heart.

"I don't believe that for a single moment, and neither should you." Crystal shook her head. "We've been taught since we were kinner that life offers each of us choices. God gave us the ability to choose what we will think and feel. He expects the believer to make the right choices, and He wants us to be happy and content with our lives."

Miriam shrugged. "That's easy for you to say. You're happily married to a man you love deeply, and you have two beautiful little boys. How could you not be happy?"

Crystal dropped a towel into the basket, pulled out the chair next to Miriam, and sat down. "Please don't be envious of my life. You can have the same happiness, as well."

Miriam stood suddenly, knocking over her chair in the process. "How can you speak to me like that? I thought you were supposed to my friend."

"I—I am," Crystal stammered.

"Then please don't talk to me as though I'm a child."

"I wasn't. I mean, I don't think of you as a child. I was merely trying to tell you—"

"That I should marry someone? Were you thinking of Amos Hilty?" Miriam bent to pick up the chair, feeling more agitated by the minute. "Marrying Amos would not make me happy."

"How do you know that?"

"For one thing, he doesn't love me." She released a deep

sigh as she straightened. "I've said this before, and I'll say it again: All Amos wants is a mother for Mary Ellen and, of course, someone to do his cooking and cleaning. Furthermore, I don't feel any love for him."

"Sometimes one can learn to love."

"Did you have to *learn* to love my brother?"

"Well, no, but—"

"Can't we please change the subject and just enjoy each other's company?" Miriam went to the cupboard and removed a glass. She was beginning to feel another headache coming on and knew she should take some aspirin right away if she was going to stave it off.

"Of course we can change the subject," Crystal was quick to agree. "I'm sorry if I upset or offended you. It's just that I want you to be as happy as I am."

"Please, don't worry and fret over me. I'm doing fine without a husband, and who cares if I'm not truly happy anyway? I've come to accept the fact that life isn't meant to be a bowl of sweet cherries. I. . ." Miriam's voice trailed off when she heard a horse and buggy pull into the yard, and she glanced out the window.

"Who is it?" Crystal asked.

"It looks like Lewis. Mom knew I was coming by here on my way home from school, and she probably sent him over to let me know that she needs my help. It's getting pretty close to suppertime, you know."

Crystal glanced at the clock on the far wall. "You're right. I'm surprised the twins aren't up from their naps yet."

Heavy footsteps could be heard clomping on the porch. The back door flew open, and Lewis burst into the room.

Miriam couldn't remember ever seeing her youngest brother look so upset. "What is it, Lewis? You look as though you've seen something terrible."

Crystal pulled out a chair. "Maybe you'd better sit down."

Lewis shook his head. "There's no time. "We have got to go *schnell!*"

"Go quickly where?" Miriam questioned.

"To the hospital." Lewis's voice quivered, and he seemed close to tears.

"The hospital? Is someone *grank?*"

"No one's sick, Miriam, but I think Papa's in bad trouble."

"What kind of trouble? Did something go wrong in the fields?"

"He seemed fine when we went up to the house at noon, but later on while we were workin' in the fields, he turned really pale, clutched at his chest, and then toppled right over."

Miriam gasped, and Crystal waited silently as Lewis continued. "It took everything I had to get him into the wagon, and as soon as I got him up to the house, I went straight over to Ray Peterson's place so we could call 911 for help." He sucked in a deep breath and wiped the sweat from his forehead with the back of his hand. "The ambulance came soon after that and took Papa to the hospital. Mom rode with Vera Anderson in her van, and I went to let Andrew know and then came over here to tell you."

"Wh-what do you think is wrong with our *daed?*" Miriam asked with a catch in her voice.

"I thought at first it might be the heat, but the paramedics said they thought it was his heart."

"A heart attack?" Crystal's mouth hung open.

Lewis nodded. "Where's Jonas? He needs to know, too."

"He's still out in the fields with my daed, but they should be here anytime, I expect," Crystal said. "If you and Miriam want to get a ride and go ahead to the hospital, I'll send Jonas there as soon as he comes back to the house."

"We'd better head out to the field and try to find Jonas now. He can ride with us."

Miriam shook so hard, she could hardly stay upright. "I'll leave my buggy here and ride with Lewis, if–if that's all right," she stammered, looking over at Crystal.

"Of course. You can get your buggy later on this evening or tomorrow morning."

Lewis grabbed hold of Miriam's hand. "Andrew's on his way to the hospital already, and our other English neighbor, Alan Wiggins, said he'd drive us there, so we need to get Jonas and go now before it's too late."

"Too late? What do you mean, too late? Is Papa's condition that serious?" Miriam felt the blood drain from her face, and tears pricked her eyes.

Lewis nearly pushed her toward the door. "I really don't know, but Papa wasn't conscious when the paramedics arrived."

"Remember Papa in your prayers," Miriam called to Crystal over her shoulder.

"Jah, I surely will."

❧

Nick gripped the steering wheel as he squinted against the glare of the sun streaming through the front window of his sporty new car. He was heading to Lancaster General

Hospital to cover a story about an elderly man who had been beaten and robbed at a local mini-mart, and he wasn't looking forward to it one bit.

Ever since Nick's father had been killed after being involved in a five-car pile up on the interstate, Nick had avoided hospitals. He'd only been twelve years old at the time, and for the two days following the accident, Nick and his mother had spent nearly every waking moment at the hospital. It had almost killed Nick to watch Dad slip slowly away, as his body's organs failed from the multiple injuries he'd sustained. Even now, fourteen years later, Nick could visualize his father lying in that hospital bed, hooked up to all sorts of strange-looking machines that had done nothing to save his life. Just driving by a hospital caused Nick to feel nervous, and going inside made his blood run cold.

He had tried to get out of the interview, but his boss wouldn't take no for an answer. In fact, he had told Nick that if he didn't do the interview, he could look for another job. So Nick was on his way to the hospital now, giving himself a pep talk, which he hoped would help conquer his fear.

If you're afraid of something, then reach deep inside and face it head-on. Nick remembered his father reprimanding him for being afraid to ride his bike after he'd crashed and scraped up his knees. *"Grit your teeth and get back on that bicycle,"* Dad had instructed. *"You'll never conquer your fear until you do."*

Nick had spent the better portion of twenty-six years trying to be brave and attempting to do everything in his own strength. He'd pretty much succeeded at it, too, because not much caused him to fear. Except for hospitals, that is, and tonight, he was determined to combat that fear, as well.

He clenched his fingers around the steering wheel tighter and fought the wave of nausea that threatened to overtake him. "I can do this. I can reach inside myself and find the strength I need."

CHAPTER 10

Soon after Miriam and Lewis arrived at the hospital they learned that their father's condition was quite serious. The doctors confirmed that he had suffered a massive heart attack. Miriam, her mother, and her three brothers stood around Papa's bed as the doctor gave the shocking news that, because his heart was so weak, Papa would probably not survive the night, though they would do all they could for him.

"How can this be?" Mom cried. "My Henry has always been a strong, healthy man."

"Sometimes as we get older—" the doctor began.

"Older? My father is only fifty-seven. He's not old, and he isn't going to die." Miriam shook her head as her face heated up like hot coals.

"Try to calm down. Your outburst isn't helping anyone." Jonas put his arm around Miriam's waist and pulled her off to one side. "If it's the will of God, then Papa shall live. If not—"

"If not, then what? Do we all put on a happy face and go on living as though Papa had never been a part of us?"

"Miriam, don't do this," Mom said tearfully. "We need to remain calm. We need to pray for your daed."

"That's right," Lewis agree. "*Mir lewe uff hoffning*–we live on hope, so we need to remain hopeful."

Miriam's thoughts drew inward. How many times had she prayed over the last couple of years? How many of her prayers had God answered? Had He kept William from falling in love with someone else? Had He given William back to her? Had God made the pain in her broken heart go away?

Miriam was weary of praying and receiving no answers. Still, she knew that prayer was the only chance Papa had. So she would pray, and she would even plead and bargain with God. Perhaps He would trade her life for Papa's. If she were gone, she wouldn't be so greatly missed, but everyone in the family needed Papa, especially Mom.

"I'll be out in the waiting room," she whispered to Mom, feeling the need to be by herself and untangle the confusion that swirled in her head. "Send Lewis to get me if I'm needed or if Papa wakes up." She glanced once more at her father, lying there so still, hooked up to machines and IVs; then she rushed out of the room.

❧

"What's wrong with Miriam that she can't stay and face this with the rest of her family?" Andrew asked as he turned toward Anna with a pinched expression. "Does she think running away will make anything better?"

Anna shook her head. "I'm not sure what my daughter believes."

"Well, she'll be sorry if she's not here when Papa wakes up," Lewis put in. He moved toward the foot of his father's bed and stood with his head bowed and shoulders shaking.

Jonas stepped up to Anna and put his arm around her shoulders. "Each of us must deal with this in our own way, so it's not our place to judge Miriam."

She nodded, and tears sprang to her eyes. "I don't know what I'm going to do if your daed doesn't make it, but I'm sure God will see me through, just as He will minister to all my children."

" 'God is our refuge and strength, a very present help in trouble,' " Jonas quoted from Psalm 46. "He knows our every need and will help us through this time of trouble."

Lewis turned away from the bed and frowned. "You all talk like Papa has already died. Shouldn't we be praying for our daed's healing instead of talking about how we'll get through it if he dies?"

"Of course we should be praying," Anna was quick to say. She didn't want to see any of her sons at odds with one another, especially not when their father might be dying. *No matter what happens, I'll have to be strong,* she determined in her heart. *With God's help I will set a good example to all my children and keep trusting Him.*

***

The waiting room was empty when Miriam entered. She was glad for the chance to be alone. For the next half hour, she silently paced, going from the window to the doorway and back again, pleading with God to heal her father.

At one point, Miriam stopped in front of the window

and stared at the street below. She saw some cars parked along the curb. . . .several more driving past. Some children rode by on bicycles. A bird fluttered past the window and landed in a nearby tree. The world was still going about its business as usual. It was a world that she and her Amish family had chosen to be separate from based on the biblical teachings of nonconformity.

Yet now, due to unwelcome circumstances, they were being forced to accept the modern ways in order to provide her father with the best medical care available. But would modern medicine be enough? Could the doctors save Papa's life and bring him back to them? If by some miracle he did get well enough to come home, would he ever be whole and complete, able to work on the farm again?

The waiting room door suddenly swung open, interrupting Miriam's thoughts and halting her prayers. Jonas and Andrew stood in the doorway, their faces pale and somber. "Papa's gone," Andrew mumbled.

She stared at him numbly. "What?"

"He said, 'Papa is gone,' " Jonas spoke up. *"Er is nimmi am scharfe."*

Papa is gone. He's no longer breathing. The dreaded words resounded in Miriam's head like a woodpecker tapping on a tree. "Is it true?" she asked, looking back at Andrew.

He nodded. "Jah, *sis awwer waricklich so*—yes, it's really so."

Miriam clenched her fingers into tight little balls as she held her arms rigidly at her side. Yet again her prayers had gone unanswered. Once more her heart would ache with pain. It wasn't fair. Life wasn't fair! Without a word to either of her brothers, she dashed from the room.

Tears blinded Miriam's vision as she stumbled down the hospital corridor. Her only thought was to run away—to escape this awful place of death, though she had no idea where she was going. She passed the elevator and ran down two flights of stairs. She flung open the outside door and was about to step into the evening air, when she ran into a strong pair of arms.

"Hey, fair lady! You almost knocked me off my feet."

Miriam looked up into the deep blue eyes of Nick McCormick. They were mesmerizing eyes, and she had to force herself to look away.

"We seem to keep bumping into each other, don't we, Miriam?"

Knowing she needed to put some space between herself and the tall, blond-haired man who stood in front of her, blocking the exit door, she tried to skirt around him. "If—if you'll excuse me, I was on my way out."

"I can see that. You almost ran me over." Nick squinted as he took hold of her arm. "I didn't notice before, but I can see that you're upset. Is there something I can do to help?"

"I—I just need some fresh air."

"No problem." Nick moved to one side and opened the door so that Miriam could walk through.

Once outside, she took several deep breaths, allowing the cool air to fill her lungs and clear her head, then she hurried away.

"Slow down. What's your hurry?" Nick called as he quickened his steps to keep up with Miriam.

She halted and turned to face him. "I—I thought I was alone. I mean, I didn't know you had followed me."

"Do you mind?"

"Don't you have business at the hospital?"

Nick shrugged. "I was there to cover a story about an old man who was beaten and robbed at a mini-mart."

"Then maybe you should—"

"It can wait." Since Nick was in no hurry to begin his interview, he actually welcomed this little interruption. "I think maybe you need someone to talk to right now."

"Front-page headlines or a back-page article?" she asked in a sarcastic tone.

"You insult my integrity, fair lady. I have no intention of interviewing you, so you can delete that thought right now. I just figured you might need a shoulder to cry on and maybe a little heartfelt sympathy."

Miriam sniffed. "What makes you think I need any sympathy?"

Nick reached out and, using his thumb, wiped away the tears that had dripped onto her cheeks; then he reached into his pocket and retrieved a hankie. "You've obviously been crying," he said, handing it to her.

Miriam blew her nose on the hankie and handed it back to him. "My—my father just died of a heart attack."

"I'm sorry to hear that, but shouldn't you be with your family at a time like this?"

"Probably so, but I—I needed to be alone."

"You want to be alone in your misery, is that it?"

Miriam began walking briskly again, but Nick was not to be put off. Despite her claim of wanting to be alone, he was sure she needed some support, so keeping in step with her, he offered his arm.

She declined with a shake of her head.

"Let's go somewhere for a cup of coffee," he suggested. "It might help if you tell me what happened and talk about the way you're feeling right now."

"I told you already—"

"Yes, I know. You'd rather be alone. Maybe that's how you think you feel, but I'll bet if you searched your heart you would realize that what you really need is someone to talk to." Nick took hold of her arm. "I promise not to include our conversation in my next article on the Amish—and I definitely won't take any pictures."

She released a deep sigh and gave a quick nod.

*

The small café Nick chose was a few blocks from the hospital, and it was nearly empty when they stepped inside. They took a seat at a booth in the far corner, and Nick ordered them each a cup of coffee and a slice of apple pie.

Miriam declined the pie, saying she wasn't hungry, but Nick insisted that she needed the nourishment and said she would probably feel better if she ate something.

Miriam finally gave in and ate the pie, realizing that she was a bit hungry after all.

"Feeling better?" Nick asked, as he stared at her from across the table.

She nodded. "At least my stomach does. I had no supper tonight. After school let out, I stopped to see my sister-in-law for a few minutes. I planned to be home in plenty of time to help Mom with supper, but then my brother Lewis came by and told us that Papa had collapsed while he was at work in the fields. We rushed to the hospital, and—well, you know the rest."

Miriam blinked back tears and took a deep breath. It turned into a sob. She couldn't believe she was sitting here in a café with a man she barely knew, pouring out her heart to him. Maybe that was why she felt free to do it—because she didn't really know him. He had no expectations of her. He would make no demands on her emotionally.

Nick reached across the table and took her hand, and she made no effort to stop him. The comfort he offered felt good. It was something she hadn't felt in a long time.

"I think I understand how you're feeling right now," he said. "Several years ago, I lost my dad when his car was involved in an accident on the interstate. I was an only child, and Mom and I had it pretty rough for a while."

"How did you manage?"

"It was hard. We lived with my grandparents for a few years. They looked after me while Mom went back to school for some training. She became a nurse, and then she was able to support us by working at a hospital in Chicago. That's where I'm from." Nick stared out the window. "Those were tough times, but I think they helped to strengthen me."

"Where's your mother now?" Miriam asked.

"Still living in Chicago. When I was fifteen, she remarried. I never got along well with her new husband, so after I finished high school, I went off to college, majored in journalism, and worked at several small newspapers after I graduated. When the newspaper in Lancaster offered me a job, I took it." Nick winked at her. "And you know the rest of the story."

Miriam's cheeks warmed. It had been so long since any man had looked at her the way Nick was looking at her now, and she'd forgotten how pleasant it could feel. With her heart aching so, his attention was like a healing balm. Nick had actually made Miriam forget her grief for a few brief moments, and she appreciated it. "Do—do you live in Lancaster alone, or are you—?"

"Married?"

She nodded, wondering what had caused her to be so bold or why she cared whether he was married or not. She felt confused and frightened by the feelings he generated in her, and she quickly pulled her hand out of his, nervously reaching up to straighten her head-covering.

Nick laughed. "No, I'm not married. It's not that I have anything against the state of matrimony. Guess I've just never met a woman who captured my heart enough to make me want to settle down and start a family." He winked again. "Of course, any woman who could put up with me would have to be a real gem."

Miriam smiled in spite of her sadness over losing Papa. "I think I should get back to the hospital now. My family might think I've deserted them."

Nick nodded with a sympathetic expression.

"Thank you for your kindness. I do feel a little better after talking to you, but I know the days ahead will be difficult ones." She gulped as a new realization swept over her. "I—I don't know how we will manage without Papa."

"I suspect you'll get through it, Miriam. I don't know you well, but I get the feeling that you're a strong woman—one with a determined heart."

She nodded. "My three brothers will help out, and Mom won't have to support herself. Of course, I'll be there to help with some money, too."

"I don't imagine an Amish teacher makes much, though."

The magic of the moment was suddenly gone, and Miriam's mind came back into proper focus. This man was a reporter. He didn't care about her as a person. He probably just wanted to satisfy his curiosity. "I make enough," she muttered.

"I meant no harm in asking about your wages," Nick said, lifting one hand as though asking for a truce. "I was only trying to show my concern for your situation, and I was about to say that if there's ever anything I can do to help you or your family, feel free to call my office at the newspaper."

"It's kind of you to offer," Miriam said, her voice softening some, "but—"

"You're not willing to ask favors of a worldly English man?"

"It's not that—I do appreciate your offer," she stammered. "If I should ever need your help, I'll let you know."

Nick smiled as she stood. "Guess I'd better pay for our eats; then I'll walk you back to the hospital."

"Really, there's no need for that. I can find my own way."

"Have you forgotten that I have an interview at the hospital? I was going in as you were going out."

"Okay."

The walk back to the hospital was silent. When they entered the building, Miriam turned to Nick and said, "Thanks again for your kindness."

"It was my pleasure, Miriam." He turned toward the information desk, then looked back again. "Don't forget my offer of help should you ever need a listening ear. Just call the *Daily Express* and ask for Nick McCormick."

CHAPTER

11

The three days following Papa's death were difficult to get through. After the funeral director had done what was necessary to prepare the body for burial and had returned it to the Stoltzfus home, Miriam and her family dressed Papa in his burial clothes. For the next three days, friends and family came to the home for the viewing.

That had been difficult enough, but Miriam wondered how she would ever get through Papa's funeral. She had never lost anyone so close to her before. When Grandma Gehman died, Miriam had only been five years old. Grandpa Gehman, who had moved to Illinois shortly after his wife's death, had passed on nearly ten years ago, when Miriam was still a teenage girl. She had never been close to her maternal grandfather and didn't know him that well. Her paternal grandparents were still living, though their health had failed in the last few years. Miriam figured it wouldn't be long before they were gone, too.

Papa's somber funeral service began early in the morning and was held in the Stoltzfus home. Miriam, dressed all in black, as were the other family members, was relieved that she had managed to get through the ordeal without falling apart. She was determined to be strong for her mother and not give in to the tears pushing against her eyelids, for if Mom saw her daughter crying, she was sure to fall apart.

After the funeral was over, the procession to the cemetery followed, and a short time later, Miriam huddled with her family and friends to watch as Papa's plain pine box was taken from the horse-drawn hearse and set in place at the burial site. She squeezed her eyes shut, trying to block out the memory of her final look at Papa's face before the lid on the coffin had been closed. Though the local undertaker had done a fine job, Miriam's father no longer looked like himself, and the stark reality that Papa was gone was almost more than she could bear.

Why, Lord? Why? she asked, as unbidden tears slipped from under her lashes. *How could You have taken Papa from us?*

Miriam forced her eyes open and glanced to her right, where her mother stood, openly weeping as the bishop said the final words over her husband of thirty-five years. *Is Mom strong enough to make it without Papa? Will I be able to offer her the kind of emotional support she will need in the days to come? Do I have enough strength for the both of us?*

With a heavy heart and a firm resolve, Miriam decided that she must be determined. Through her own sheer will, she would do whatever it took to remain strong for Mom and the rest of the family.

When the graveside service concluded, everyone climbed into their buggies. Then, the buggy Miriam rode in with Mom and Lewis led the way back to their farm, where they would share a meal with those who had come to say good-bye to

Miriam's father and offer condolences to the family.

Miriam didn't feel the least bit hungry, but rather than draw attention to the fact that she wasn't eating, she put a sandwich, some dilled cucumbers, and a piece of gingerbread on her plate. Then she picked up a glass of iced tea and made her way to the stream, where she could be alone. Friends and family had been dropping by the house ever since the news of Papa's death, and today nearly everyone in their community seemed to be present. Miriam needed some quiet time away from all the sympathetic looks and consoling words.

As Miriam approached the stream, she noticed a change in leaves on the trees and realized that they were on the verge of being kissed by crimson colors as fall crept in. Something about the peacefulness of the water gurgling over the rocks and the gentle wind caressing her face caused Miriam to think about Nick McCormick. Perhaps it was only the fact that the two of them had visited in this same spot several months before that brought his name to mind.

Miriam's face flushed. Just thinking about how the obstinate man had sneaked up on her with his camera and how he had taken a picture with her hair uncovered and hanging down her back made her feel almost giddy. Now wouldn't that have made a fine photo for the *Daily Express?*

What was there about Nick that made her feel these unexplained emotions? She had only seen him on three occasions, and each time he had succeeded in making her angry, but he'd also made her smile.

William had been the only man with whom Miriam had ever shared her deepest thoughts and dreams, and when he left her for another woman, she had vowed never to get close to another man again. While she wasn't exactly close to Nick, for some reason she had let her guard down. Was it simply because he seemed easy to talk to, or was it because Nick was an outsider and she knew there was no threat of a possible commitment?

Miriam's thoughts were interrupted when a deep voice called her name. She looked over her shoulder and saw Amos heading toward the stream with a plate of food in his hand.

"I thought you might like something to eat," Amos said when he reached the spot where she sat near the stream.

She held up her half-eaten plate of food. "I haven't finished this."

Feeling more than a little self-conscious, Amos took a seat on the grass beside her. "I already had one helping, but I suppose I could eat another. All this tasty food sure does whet the appetite. I'm not the best cook, so I don't enjoy my own meals so much."

"Where's Mary Ellen?" Miriam asked, making no reference to his cooking. Was he hinting that he needed a wife to cook for him—maybe her, in fact?

"My daughter is playing little mudder to your twin nephews," Amos answered. "Since she's well occupied, I decided to sneak away and check up on you."

"What makes you think I need checking up on?" Miriam's tone was harsh.

"I. . .uh. . .know what it's like to lose someone close to you, and I thought—well, I might have some words of comfort to offer." Hesitantly, he touched Miriam's shoulder, wishing he didn't feel so tongue-tied whenever he was with her. "I—I'm sorry about your daed. He will be missed by everyone in our community, but I'm sure he will be missed by his family even more. Henry was a good man."

Miriam stood, brushing away the pieces of grass that clung to her dress. "I should be getting back to the house. Mom may need me for something." She offered him a quick nod. "Danki for your kindness, but I'm going to be fine. Life is full of hardships and pain, but each of us has the power within to rise above our troubles and take control."

"The power within is God," he reminded.

"It's up to me to help my family get through this time of loss."

"That's fine, but—but what about you? Who will help you in the days ahead?"

"I'll help myself." Miriam pivoted on her heels and darted away.

"When you need me, I will come," Amos whispered.

☙

As Nick left the dentist's office, where he'd gone for a checkup, he spotted a young Amish woman across the street. From this vantage point, she looked a lot like Miriam Stoltzfus.

The woman had just reached the crosswalk when she dropped her sack, tripped over a small red ball that had rolled out, and landed hard on the concrete.

Nick hurried across the street, barely taking the time to look for oncoming cars, and rushed to her side. "Miriam? Are you okay?"

The woman looked up at him, and her cheeks turned pink. "I–I'm not hurt, just skinned my knees a bit. And my name's not Miriam."

Nick was glad the woman hadn't been seriously injured, but he felt a keen sense of disappointment that she wasn't Miriam. He helped her to her feet and then bent down to retrieve the ball and a couple of books that had bounced onto the sidewalk when the sack slipped from her arms.

"I appreciate your help," she said, smoothing her dress and righting the small white cap perched on her head.

Nick handed her the paper sack with the items back inside. "I'm Nick McCormick, and I make it my duty to rescue fair ladies in distress," he said with a smile.

"It's nice to meet you. My name's Katie Yoder."

"Do you live around here?" Since the woman was willing to talk to him, Nick thought she might be agreeable enough to answer a few questions—in case he was ever asked to do another story on the Amish.

She shook her head. "I live in Mifflin County, north of here."

"Guess you must have hired a driver to bring you to Lancaster, huh?"

She nodded. "My brother lives not far from here, and since today's his son's birthday, I wanted to buy something to give the boy before I headed over to their place."

"Say, I've got an idea," Nick said. "Why don't we go have a cup of coffee someplace?"

Katie's dark eyes became huge, and the color in her face darkened. "I–I couldn't do that. I'm betrothed."

"You mean you're engaged to be married?"

She nodded. "Jah, in November."

His forehead wrinkled. "It's not like I'm asking for a date or anything. Just thought we could have a cup of coffee and talk awhile."

"I—I really can't. My driver's supposed to meet me on the next block, and I need to be on my way."

"I could drive you to your brother's house. That would give us time to talk."

"What did you want to talk about?"

"I'm a reporter for the *Daily Express*, and I—"

"You—you want to interview me?" Her voice raised a notch, and she blinked her lashes in rapid succession.

"Interviewing is what reporters do best."

She pursed her lips and stared up at him as though he'd said something horrible. "I have no interest in being interviewed for the English newspaper. Besides, my driver is waiting for me, and I wouldn't feel right about having coffee with you even if you weren't a reporter."

Wow! This little gal was as feisty as Miriam, although now that Nick had seen her up close, he realized she wasn't nearly as beautiful. Maybe Amish women weren't as passive as he'd thought them to be.

"Thanks for helping me, but I really must be going." Clasping the paper sack to her chest, Katie started walking at a brisk pace.

Nick was tempted to tag along but decided against it, figuring she might create a scene if he followed. So he sauntered back across the street where his car was parked as thoughts of Miriam filled his head. Something about her fascinated him. As strange as it might seem, he knew that if he were given the chance to pursue a relationship with her, he might just take it.

"How come we don't go over to Teacher Mim's house for supper no more?" Mary Ellen asked as Amos placed a sandwich on the table in front of her.

Amos didn't know quite how to respond. A few weeks ago Anna had invited him and Mary Ellen to join them for supper again, but he'd declined because he'd decided not to push so hard where Miriam was concerned. That meant not seeing her any more than necessary. Maybe if he gave her some time, she would see that he wasn't trying to force her into a relationship and might even come to him on her own.

"Pappy, did ya hear what I said?" Mary Ellen persisted.

He pulled out a chair and sat down beside her. "I've been real busy in my shop these last few weeks, and it's been easier just to eat at home."

"But I miss Teacher Mim."

"How can you miss her when you see her every day at school?"

"I just do, that's all." Mary Ellen lifted her chin and stared up at him with a peculiar expression on her face. "You think she might wanna be my mamm someday?"

Amos cringed. He wanted that, too. Wanted it more than he cared to admit. But unless God wrought a miracle, he didn't think it was likely that Teacher Mim would ever become his wife.

He patted Mary Ellen's arm. "Let's pray about it, shall we?"

She nodded eagerly. "I have been prayin', Pappy."

CHAPTER 12

The routine of life went on, even for those in mourning. With Papa gone, Lewis had to work twice as hard to keep up with the farm chores. The alfalfa fields needed one final harvesting before winter set in, and even with the help of their Amish family members and neighbors, the work was difficult and time-consuming.

Mom, too, kept busier than ever, working tirelessly from sunrise to sunset. While it was true everyone had more work to do now that Papa was gone, Miriam suspected the main reason her mother stayed so busy was so she wouldn't have to think about Papa so much and about how terribly she missed him. Often in the middle of the night, Miriam would be wakened by the sound of her mother crying. Her parents' marriage had been a good one, and she figured Mom would probably never get over Papa's untimely death.

If only there was some way to erase all the pain in one's life, Miriam found herself thinking as she put the finishing touches on a baby quilt she planned to give Carolyn Zeeman, the mother of one of her students. *God could wipe away all our tears if He wanted to. He has it in His power to keep bad things from happening.*

"What's wrong, Miriam? Did you stick your finger with the needle?" Mom asked, taking a seat in the other chair beside the quilting frame.

"No, I was just thinking."

"Whatever you were thinking about must have been pretty painful, because that frown on your face spoke volumes."

Miriam didn't want to respond. It would be too hurtful to remind Mom that God seemed to have abandoned them and could have saved Papa's life if He had wanted to. "It's nothing," she said, reaching for another spool of thread. "Nothing worth mentioning."

Anna sat beside Miriam for several minutes, watching her slender fingers move in and out of the brightly colored material, as she sewed straight, even stitches. Finally, when Anna could bear the silence no longer, she reached out and touched her daughter's arm. "Did you have a rough day at school? Have some of the kinner been saying unkind things about you again?"

Miriam shook her head, but Anna noticed the tears that had gathered in her eyes. "I–I'm just missing Papa tonight. That's all."

Anna swallowed around the lump in her throat. "I miss him, too. Guess I always will."

"That's understandable. You were married over thirty years."

"Jah, and I have much to be thankful for in that regard."

"What do you mean, Mom?"

"Your daed and I had a good marriage—one that was based on love not only for each other but for our heavenly Father, as well."

Miriam's gaze dropped to the floor, and she released a sigh. "Don't you feel angry that God took Papa away? Don't you want to shout at God for His unfairness?"

Anna gulped back a sob as she wrapped her arms around her daughter's trembling shoulders. "Oh, Miriam, please don't talk like that. Don't you know your daed's in a much better place, where there's no more sickness or dying, no more tears or toiling under a blistering sun?" She closed her eyes as a vision of Henry standing tall and handsome on their wedding day came to mind. "I can only imagine what it's like for him now, up there in heaven with Jesus. As much as I miss him, I take comfort in knowing he's safe and secure in our Father's arms. Why, if I know my Henry, he's running all over those golden streets, happy as a meadowlark in spring."

Miriam sat staring at the floor and breathing quick, shallow breaths like she couldn't get enough air.

"Maybe it would help if you wrote down your feelings," Anna suggested. "In the last article I wrote for *The Budget*, I expressed my deep hurt over the loss of your daed, and just writing it down helped to ease some of the pain."

Miriam looked up and shook her head. "I tried keeping a journal after William left for Ohio, and where did that get me?"

Anna wasn't sure what to say, so she closed her eyes and did the only thing she knew could help. She prayed that the Lord would release Miriam of her pain and help them all in the days ahead.

The fall harvest was finally complete, and everyone's work-load had lightened a bit. One afternoon in early November as Miriam dismissed her students at the end of the school day, she noticed that a storm seemed to be brewing. Angry-looking dark clouds hung over the school yard, and the wind whipped fiercely against the trees. Miriam figured a torrential rain was sure to follow, and she hoped everyone would make it home before the earth was drenched from above.

"I'll give you a ride," Miriam told her six-year-old niece.

"Okay." Rebekah smiled and gave Miriam a hug. "Are you ready to go now?"

"In a few minutes. I need to get the blackboard cleaned and gather up a few things before I leave. Then I'll head out to the corral and get my horse hitched to the buggy."

"Is it okay if I wait for you outside?" the child asked.

"Jah, but you'd better wait in the buggy because the clouds look like they're about to burst wide open."

Rebekah darted out the schoolhouse door. "I will," she called over her shoulder.

Miriam hurriedly erased the blackboard and was about to write the next day's assignment, when a clap of thunder rent the air, causing the schoolhouse to vibrate. It was followed by a loud *snap* and then a shrill scream that sent shivers spiraling up Miriam's spine.

She rushed to the door, and a sob caught in her throat when she saw Rebekah lying on the ground next to her buggy, pinned under a tree limb that lay across her back. "Oh, dear

God," Miriam cried with a muffled groan. "Please let her be all right."

Rebekah was unconscious when Miriam got to her. A gash on her head was bleeding some, but Miriam couldn't tell the full extent of her niece's injuries. She felt Rebekah's wrist for a pulse and was relieved when she found one, but the tree limb was heavy, and she couldn't lift it off the little girl's back.

She looked around the school yard, feeling helpless and alone. All the other children had already gone home. She knew Rebekah must be taken to the hospital, but she couldn't do that until the limb had been removed. There was a farm down the road, owned by an English couple, but if she went there to phone for help, she would have to leave Rebekah alone.

Miriam seldom found herself wishing for modern conveniences, but at the moment, she would have given anything if there had been a telephone inside the schoolhouse. "Oh, Lord, what should I do?" she prayed, as she wrapped a piece of cloth she'd torn from her apron around Rebekah's head. "I don't ask this for myself but for the dear, sweet child who lies at my feet. Please send someone now, or I must leave her alone and go for help."

Miriam heard the *clip-clop* of a horse's hooves and knew a buggy must be approaching. As soon as it entered the school yard, she realized it was Amos Hilty, who'd probably come to pick up his daughter because of the approaching storm.

"Oh, Amos, Mary Ellen has already gone home, and— and. . .a tree limb fell on my niece." Miriam pointed to the spot where Rebekah lay. "She's alive but unconscious, and I can't lift the limb off her back." Her voice shook with emotion, and her breath came out in short, raspy gasps.

Amos hopped down from his buggy and hurried over to the child. In one quick movement, he lifted the limb and tossed it aside. "Let's put Rebekah in my buggy, and we'll take her to the Andersons' place so we can call for help," he suggested.

"I don't think she should be moved. What if something's broken? What if—" Miriam choked on a sob, and she felt as if there was no strength left in her legs.

"You wait here then, and I'll make the call for help."

Miriam nodded. "Please hurry, Amos. She hasn't opened her eyes, and I think she might be seriously injured."

"I'll go as quickly as I can."

As Amos sped out of the school yard, Miriam feared his horse might trip and fall. *Please let Rebekah be all right, Lord,* she fervently prayed.

For the next twenty minutes, Miriam stood over Rebekah, praying that she would live and that Amos would return with help before it was too late. It seemed like hours until she finally heard the ambulance's siren, and she breathed a sigh of relief. The wind continued to howl, but the rain held off until Rebekah had been strapped to a hard, straight board and placed into the back of the ambulance.

"I need to go to the hospital with her," Miriam told Amos, who had returned to the schoolhouse to offer further assistance. "But someone needs to notify Andrew and Sarah."

"You ride along in the ambulance, and I'll go over to

your brother's place and tell them what's happened to their daughter before I head for home."

"My buggy. What about my horse and buggy?"

"I'll see that they get safely home for you." Amos touched her arm. "Try not to worry, Miriam. Just pray."

Miriam nodded and numbly climbed into the ambulance. As the vehicle pulled out of the school yard with its siren blaring, she looked out the back window and saw Amos climbing into his buggy. "I never even told him thank you," she murmured.

After numerous tests had been run on Rebekah, the doctor's reports were finally given, but the news wasn't good. Rebekah had a concussion and a bad gash on the back of her head where the tree limb had hit. However, the worst news of all was that her spinal cord had been injured, and if the child lived, she would probably never walk again.

Miriam clamped her lips together to keep from screaming, and Sarah sobbed. Andrew wrapped his arms around Sarah as tears coursed down his sunburned cheeks.

Why would God allow this to happen to an innocent young child? Miriam fumed as she clenched her fingers tightly. "I'm so sorry," she said, nodding at Andrew and Sarah. "If I just hadn't allowed Rebekah to wait outside for me. If only—" Her voice broke, and she bolted from the room.

As Miriam made her way down the hospital corridor, she was reminded of that terrible night she had fled the hospital after learning that Papa was dead. When she'd opened the door that led to the street, she half expected to see Nick standing on the other side, but he wasn't there this time to offer words of comfort and a listening ear. Suddenly, she remembered the last words he'd spoken to her. *"If there's ever anything I can do to help you or your family, feel free to call my office at the newspaper."*

Should I call? she wondered. *Should I be turning to an outsider for comfort and support?*

As Miriam turned the corner and headed for the telephone booth at the end of the block, she was relieved that the storm had subsided. She stepped inside and dialed the number of the *Daily Express*, but her fingers trembled so badly she feared she might be hitting the wrong buttons.

"Hello. May I speak to Nick McCormick?" she asked when a woman's voice came on the phone. "He's a reporter at your newspaper."

"One moment, please."

Miriam held her breath and waited anxiously. At least she had reached the newspaper office and hadn't dialed the wrong number.

"This is Nick McCormick. How may I help you?" she heard Nick say a few seconds later.

"It–it's Miriam Stoltzfus. You said I should call if I ever needed anything."

"Sure did, and it's good to hear from you again. What can I do to help?"

Miriam pressed the palm of her hand against the side of her pounding temple. She hoped she wasn't about to be sick. "I. . .uh. . .need to talk. Can we meet somewhere?"

"Where are you now?"

"About a block from Lancaster General Hospital."

"The hospital? Are you all right?"

"It's not me. It's my—" Miriam's voice broke, and she couldn't go on.

"Miriam, whatever's happened, I'm so sorry," Nick said in a reassuring tone. "Remember the little café where we had coffee a few months ago?"

"I remember."

"Meet me there in fifteen minutes. You can tell me about it then."

CHAPTER 13

Miriam found the café to be full of people when she arrived a short time later. A quick look at the clock on the far wall told her it was the dinner hour. Her eyes sought out an empty booth, but there was none. She stood feeling nervous and self-conscious, as everyone seemed to be looking at her. Was it the fact that she was wearing Plain clothes that made them stare, or was it her red face and swollen eyes?

"May I help you, miss?" the man behind the counter asked.

"I'm. . .uh. . .supposed to meet someone here, and we need a table for two."

"The tables and booths are all filled, but you can take a seat on one of the stools here at the counter, if you'd like."

Not knowing what else to do, Miriam took a seat as the man suggested and studied the menu he'd handed her. Nothing appealed. How could she have an appetite for food when her niece was lying in the hospital, unconscious, with the prospect of being crippled for the rest of her life? Rebekah was such a sweet child, easy to teach and always agreeable; she didn't deserve such a fate.

Miriam gritted her teeth and clenched her fingers around the menu so tightly that her knuckles turned white. *I should never have let Rebekah go outside without me when I knew a storm was brewing.*

A firm hand touched Miriam's shoulder, and she turned her head. "Nick! How did you get here so quickly?"

Nick lifted his arm and pointed to his watch. "It's been over thirty minutes since we talked, and I told you I'd be here in fifteen. So I'm actually late, fair lady, and I'm sorry to have kept you waiting." He looked around. "It's sure crowded in here. Was this the only seat you could find? It won't give us much privacy, you know."

"I've been waiting for one of the booths, but no one seems in much of a hurry to leave."

"Are you hungry?" he asked.

Miriam shook her head, one quick shake, and then another. "I could use something to drink, though, and maybe some aspirin." She rubbed the pulsating spot on her forehead and grimaced.

"Headache?"

She nodded. "I get bad migraines whenever I'm under too much stress, and I don't have any white willow bark herb capsules with me right now. They usually help."

"I'll get you some iced tea to go," Nick offered. "I've got a bottle of aspirin in the glove box of my car. How about if we go for a ride? We can talk better if we have some privacy, and I don't think we'll get any in here."

"I—I suppose it would be all right," Miriam said hesitantly. "But I shouldn't be gone too long. I left my brother and his wife at the hospital, and I didn't tell them where I was going or when I would return. They've got enough on their minds right now, and I don't want them to worry about me."

"I promise not to keep you out past midnight." Nick smiled and gave her a quick wink before turning to the waitress and ordering an iced tea to go.

Heat rushed to Miriam's face, and she tried to hide it by hurrying toward the door. She wasn't used to having a man flirt with her the way Nick did, and whenever he flashed her that grin, she felt as if her insides had turned to mush. Maybe he didn't mean anything by it. It might have been just a friendly gesture or his way of trying to get Miriam to relax.

She walked silently beside him across the parking lot until they came to a small, sporty-looking vehicle. He opened the door on the passenger's side and helped her in.

Miriam could smell the aroma of new leather as she slid into the soft seat. "You have a nice car," she commented after he'd taken his seat on the driver's side.

"Thanks. It'll be even nicer once it's paid for." Nick reached across Miriam and opened the glove box. He pulled out a small bottle of aspirin and handed it to her. "Here, take a couple of these."

"Thank you." As soon as Miriam had swallowed the pills with the iced tea Nick had purchased for her, he turned on the ignition and pulled away from the curb.

"Do you want to tell me what's bothering you now, or would you rather ride around for a while and try to relax and get rid of that headache?"

Miriam clutched the side of her seat with one hand while hanging on to her tea with the other. "Going at this speed, I'm not sure I can think well enough to speak, much less relax."

"How about if I pull over at the park so you can sit and relax while you tell me what's happened?"

"That—that would be fine, I suppose." Miriam pulled nervously on the ties of her *kapp*, where they dangled under her chin. Being alone with Nick made her feel a bit uneasy, since he had such an unsettling way about him. The strange way he kept looking at her stirred something deep within, too, and it made her feel giddy—like she used to feel when she and William had been courting.

Maybe it's just the shock of being told the extent of Rebekah's injuries that has me feeling so quivery, she told herself. *I'm sure I'll calm down once the aspirin takes effect and my headache eases.*

Thinking he might be able to read Miriam's thoughts, Nick glanced over at her and said, "Don't worry. You're safe with me. No harm will come to you, because you're a fair lady, and I'm your knight in shining armor."

Her cheeks flamed, but she silently turned her head toward the window.

Nick figured she probably needed some time to let the aspirin take effect and realize that he wasn't planning to take advantage of her. When they pulled into a parking place at the city park a short time later, he rolled down the window to let in some fresh air.

"Thanks for taking the time to meet me," she said. "I'm sure you're a busy man."

He shrugged. "I was about to call it a day anyhow. So, tell me what's happened. Why were you at the hospital again?"

"It is my niece Rebekah. She's been seriously injured, and I'm afraid it's my fault."

"What happened?" Nick asked as he reached for the notepad he kept tucked inside his window visor.

Miriam seemed to barely notice that he'd taken a pen from his pocket and was prepared to take notes as she continued her story.

"The storm was just beginning when my students headed for home. I told my niece I would give her a ride, and she asked if she could wait outside for me." She drew in a quick breath. "I asked her to get into the buggy and said I would be there soon, but I never thought about the fact that I'd parked my buggy under a tree this morning." She paused for another breath. "Then I heard this terrible snapping sound followed by a scream. I rushed outside and found Rebekah on the ground with a heavy branch lying across her back."

"A branch broke and fell on the child?"

She nodded, as tears pooled in her eyes.

"What happened next?"

Miriam sat up straight and blinked a couple of times as she pointed to his notebook. "You-you're writing this down?"

He nodded. "Please go on. It's a newsworthy item, and I think—"

"I will not go on! I didn't ask you to meet me so you

could write a story for your newspaper. When you offered to help before, I thought that included a listening ear."

"I have been listening. The thing is, reporting the news is what I do, so—"

"I think you'd better take me back to the hospital now. I can see what a mistake this has been. I should never have phoned or asked you to meet me."

"Don't get into such a huff." Nick placed the notebook on the seat and returned the pen to his shirt pocket. "I won't write down another thing, Miriam. I didn't think you were going to get so riled up about this. I'm a reporter, so it was only natural for me to take notes on something that seemed like a good story. I'm sorry if I've offended you."

Miriam stared at her hands, clenched tightly in her lap. "I'm not sure I believe you. Maybe you're not the one I should be talking to right now."

"Of course I am." He slipped his arm across Miriam's shoulder, thinking a quick hug might let her know he was sincere. "I'd like to be your friend, Miriam, if you'll let me."

Her lower lip quivered, and when he wrapped both of his arms around her, he felt hot tears against his cheek. "I—I appreciate that," she murmured, "because a friend is exactly what I need right now."

Amos sat at the kitchen table, watching Mary Ellen eat her bowl of vegetable soup while he struggled to eat his own. He had no appetite for food and dreaded having to tell his daughter about her friend's accident. But he knew she would learn about it when she went to school tomorrow, and he didn't want her to find out that way.

He cleared his throat a couple of times, searching for the right words. "There's. . .uh. . .something I need to tell you, Mary Ellen."

She placed her spoon on the table and stared at him with a quizzical expression. "What is it, Pappy? How come you look so *bedauerlich?*"

"I'm feeling a bit sad because one of your friends from school is in the hospital."

Her eyebrows lifted high on her forehead. "Who's in the hospital?"

"Rebekah Stoltzfus."

"How come? Is she sick?"

He shook his head. "After school let out and you and the rest of the kinner had already gone, Rebekah was hit by a tree limb while she waited for Miriam to give her a ride home."

The creases in Mary Ellen's forehead deepened. "Was Rebekah hurt bad? Is—is she gonna be okay?"

Amos groaned inwardly as he pictured Rebekah's still, small frame lying on the ground with a heavy limb pinning her down. He'd seen blood on her head and knew that wasn't good. How he wished he could think of something to tell Mary Ellen that might offer hope that her friend would be all right. But the truth was, it didn't look good for Rebekah Stoltzfus, and he feared she might not make it.

"Pappy?" Mary Ellen's voice quavered. "Rebekah won't die, will she?"

He reached across the table and took hold of her hand, squeezing it gently. "I haven't heard from anyone since they took her to the hospital, so I don't know how badly she was hurt."

Mary Ellen pulled her hand away and jumped up, nearly knocking over her chair. "I want to see her, Pappy. Can we go to the hospital right now so I can talk to Rebekah and find out how she's doin'?"

Amos shook his head. "Rebekah was knocked unconscious when the limb fell from the tree, and I'm sure the doctors are busy running tests on her."

Mary Ellen's eyes filled with tears, and several splashed onto her flushed cheeks. "Is—is Rebekah goin' to heaven, the way Mama did?"

"I don't know," Amos replied honestly. "But I do know that she's in good hands at the hospital, and I'm certain that the doctors and nurses are doing everything they can. We just need to pray."

"I prayed for Mama, and God took her from us anyway," Mary Ellen said tearfully. It was the first time since Ruth's death that the child had shown such emotion, and Amos was at a loss for words.

Mary Ellen's shoulders shook, and convulsing sobs wracked her little body. "If God takes Rebekah away, I don't think I'll ever forgive Him!" She rushed out of the room, and Amos heard her footsteps clomp up the stairs.

Dear Lord, he prayed, *please let Rebekah be all right, and if You choose to take her home, then I'm asking You to help my little girl in dealing with it.*

Chapter 14

"I can see that you really do need to talk, and I'm more than willing to listen," Nick assured Miriam. "No more note-taking, I promise."

She nodded slowly. "All right. As I was about to say, the tree branch broke, and it landed across Rebekah's head and back. Amos came along soon after, and he went to call for help."

"Who's Amos?"

"He's the father of one of my students. When the ambulance arrived, I rode to the hospital with Rebekah, and then Amos went to tell my brother Andrew and his wife, who are Rebekah's parents, what had happened."

"What's the child's prognosis—her condition?"

"I know what *prognosis* means," she said in a tone of irritation.

"Sorry. I didn't mean to sound condescending." He squeezed her shoulder. "Now, would you please continue with the story?"

She moistened her lips with the tip of her tongue. "The doctor said Rebekah has a concussion, and that's the reason she's still unconscious."

"Guess that's understandable."

"He also said there's some injury to her spinal cord." Miriam gulped. "Rebekah will probably never walk again."

"Doctors have been known to be wrong," Nick said, thinking his optimism might offer some hope.

"I'm praying for a miracle, but—"

"Oh, that's right, you Amish believe in all that faith stuff, don't you?" Nick wrinkled his nose. "I've never held much stock in any kind of religious conviction."

Miriam frowned. "Faith in God is biblical, Mr. McCormick. It's not just the Amish who believe God is in control of their lives, either."

"Come on now, Miriam. I don't agree with you on something, and now it's back to calling me Mr. McCormick. Is that how it is?"

"I think I was wrong in expecting you to help me sort out my feelings. You're just trying to confuse me."

"Not at all," Nick said with a shake of his head. "I admire you for your faith, but it's just not for me. I'm not one to put others down for their beliefs, but I don't want to rely on anyone but myself. I don't need God or faith."

Miriam stared at her cup of iced tea. "You must think I'm pretty old-fashioned—in appearance as well as in my ideas."

Nick took the iced tea from her and placed it in the cup holder on the dash. "I'm not trying to confuse you, but I'm afraid you have confused me."

"How have I confused you?"

Nick leaned close to her. "I find you to be quite fascinating, Miriam, yet your ways are a bit strange to me and hard to understand. I'd like to find out more about you and your Amish traditions."

"What would you like to know?"

"I know you're expected to remain separate from the rest of the world, but I don't grasp the reasons behind such a lifestyle."

"The Bible tells us that we must present our bodies as a living sacrifice, holy and acceptable to God. It also states that we are not to be conformed to this world, but rather that we be transformed by the renewing of our minds," Miriam said. "In 2 Corinthians it says that we are not to be unequally yoked together with unbelievers. Our entire lifestyle—our dress, language, work, travel, and education are the things we must consider because of this passage in the Bible. We must not be like the rest of the world. We must live as simply and humbly as possible."

"So, things like telephones in your homes, electricity, cars, and gas-powered tractors are worldly and would cause you to be part of the modern world?"

She nodded. "To some, it may seem as if our religion is harsh and uncompromising, but all baptized members are morally committed to the church and its rules."

"It sounds pretty hard to live like that, but I suppose if you're content and feel that your way of life makes you happy, then who am I to say it's wrong?"

Miriam was on the verge of telling Nick she was anything but happy and content, but she decided those words were best left unspoken. Besides, if she had discussed that issue

with him, she would have been forced to deal with the nagging doubts that so often swirled in her head.

"I really would like to help you, Miriam," Nick said.

"What kind of help do you have to offer?"

"It sounds to me like your niece is going to be in the
hospital for quite a while, and she will no doubt require a
lot of physical therapy and medical care."

Miriam nodded. "I suppose so."

"That will cost a lot of money."

"Jah, I suppose it will."

"If I wrote an article for the newspaper about the girl's
accident, I'm sure a lot of people would respond to it."

"Respond how?"

"With financial help."

"I'm sure you mean well, Nick, but the cost of Rebekah's
medical needs isn't my only concern. Our community has
a fund we use when someone has a need, and we will probably have some fundraisers to help, as well."

"I see."

"My mother will no doubt mention Rebekah's accident in
her next newspaper article, so my brother's family will probably receive money from some of *The Budget* readers, too."

"Sounds like the Amish take good care of one another."

"We do our best." Miriam grimaced. "I'm just sick about
the accident, and I blame myself for it."

"Come now. There was no way you could have known a
tree limb would fall on the child when she went outside to
wait for you. You can't blame yourself for a freak accident
caused by an act of nature." Nick touched his finger against
her trembling lips. "If you want my opinion, I think the

best thing you can do is face this situation head-on. In matters such as this, no amount of faith in God will get you through. I believe we all have the inner strength to deal with the problems life brings our way."

An unbidden tear slid down Miriam's cheek. Hadn't she decided awhile back that her own determined heart was all she could count on? Perhaps Nick was right. Had faith in God prevented Rebekah's terrible accident, kept Papa from dying, or stopped William from falling in love with another woman? Miriam had dutifully served God all of her twenty-six years, only to end up an old-maid schoolteacher with no father, no husband, and a crippled niece to remind her that God had let her down yet again.

She looked at Nick, so obviously sure of himself, and resolved that she, too, could face life head-on and find her own inner strength.

With a lift of her chin, Miriam said, "I'm ready to go back to the hospital now."

"Sure, okay." Nick smiled. "I've enjoyed being with you, Miriam. Maybe we can get together again."

Miriam returned his smile, feeling as if a special kind of friendship was taking root in her heart.

"Do you have a phone on your property like some Amish folks do?"

She shook her head. "Why do you ask?"

"I'd like to keep in contact—maybe call and check up on you." Nick started up the car. "Since you don't have a phone, I want you to promise to call me if you need more advice or just want to talk."

"All right. I will."

"Or how about this? Since I was on the back side of your property where the stream runs through, I have an idea where your house is, so maybe I can come by for a visit sometime soon."

Miriam shook her head as a sense of panic welled in her chest. "I—I don't think that's such a good idea." The last thing she needed was for Nick to drop by her house. How would she explain the sudden appearance of a good-looking English reporter to her family?

"Why not?"

"You know why, Nick. You're English; I'm Amish. My family might get the wrong idea if—"

"Oh, you mean they might think I was trying to woo you away from the Plain life? Is that what you're afraid of?"

Miriam was at a loss for words. She enjoyed being with Nick, and he made her feel so special, but she was sure no one in the family would believe he was just a friend.

As Amos sat in a chair beside his daughter's bed, he thought about his wife's untimely death and wondered how things would be if she were still alive. Ruth had been a good mother and had always given Mary Ellen the best of care. They'd wanted to have more children, but Ruth hadn't been able to conceive again after Mary Ellen was born. Yet she'd never complained because the Good Lord had only given them just one child. Amos knew that if his wife was still with them, this precious little girl he'd been left to raise wouldn't have to wear dresses that needed mending, put up with unruly hair, or eat slapped-together meals that weren't fit for any growing child.

What Mary Ellen needs is a mother, he thought as he reached out and touched her rosy, damp cheek. The poor little thing had cried herself to sleep after she'd learned about Rebekah's accident.

His thoughts turned to Miriam, as they always did whenever he reminded himself that his daughter should have a mother. If he only felt free to tell Miriam what was on his heart—that he loved her and wanted her to be his wife. It would be difficult to lay his feelings on the line when he knew the only thing she felt for him was irritation.

Amos pushed the chair aside and stood. Chores in the barn waited to be done. He leaned over and kissed Mary Ellen's forehead. *Bless this child, Lord,* he prayed. *And give her only sweet dreams tonight.*

Chapter 15

Get up at five in the morning, light the woodstove, head out to the chicken coop to gather eggs, slop the pigs, and milk the goats. Miriam knew the routine so well she probably could have done it in her sleep. It had been her routine ever since Papa died. This morning was like no other, except that the wind had picked up and it had begun to rain.

As she left the chicken coop and noticed how the wind whipped through the trees, she was reminded of the day Rebekah had been injured. Could it have only been a few weeks ago? It seemed like much longer. Perhaps that was because she kept so busy. Being busy seemed to keep her from thinking too much about the things that caused her heart to feel so heavy.

Rebekah was still in the hospital. She had regained consciousness, but the doctors were fairly certain she would never walk again.

Miriam shuddered. No matter how hard she tried, she couldn't convince herself that she wasn't partially to blame for the accident. She had made up her mind that the only way to deal with it was to seek her inner strength, as Nick had suggested. She must go on with the business of living, no matter how unhappy she was or how guilty she felt.

Today, after school let out, she planned to hire a driver and go to the hospital. She would take some books to Rebekah and perhaps some of her favorite licorice candy. Maybe she would call Nick and ask him to meet her for coffee again. That thought caused Miriam to quicken her step as she hurried back to the house, carrying a basket of bulky brown eggs. Her day was just beginning, and she still had plenty of inside chores to do before she left for school.

Amos had just left his blacksmith shop after shoeing one of his own buggy horses when he spotted Mary Ellen running across the yard with her lunch pail swinging at her side. "Can I walk to school by myself today?" she called.

"I think it would be best if I take you there," he said when she caught up to him.

Her lower lip jutted out. "Most of the other kinner are allowed to walk. Why can't I?"

Amos grimaced. He knew he was probably being over-protective, but ever since Rebekah's accident, he'd been afraid to let Mary Ellen walk to school by herself for fear that something might happen to her. There had been a couple of accidents on the road between their place and the schoolhouse in the last month, and some of those had involved Amish walking alongside the road. He'd already lost Mary Ellen's mother, and he couldn't risk losing her, too.

"I feel better taking you to school. It's safer that way, and it gives us more time to be together."

Mary Ellen seemed to be satisfied with that answer, and she smiled up at him. "I packed my own lunch again, and I'm ready to go whenever you are, Pappy."

"I need to run inside and wash my hands first." He held them up and wrinkled his nose. "Old Jake's hooves were pretty dirty."

"I'll wait for you in the buggy then." Mary Ellen headed in that direction but turned back around. "Say, I was wonderin'—"

"What were you wondering?"

"You said I could visit Rebekah soon. Can we go to the hospital to see her after school lets out?"

"Not today, daughter."

"But I made her a card last night, and I want to take it to her."

Amos didn't think going to the hospital and seeing Rebekah unable to stand or move her legs would be good for Mary Ellen. It might upset the child. "Why don't you give the card to your teacher? I heard that Miriam goes to the hospital often, so maybe she can give Rebekah your card."

Mary Ellen frowned. "But that's not the same as me seeing Rebekah. She might think I've forgotten her."

He shook his head. "I'm sure she won't think that. I believe it would be best if you wait 'til Rebekah comes home from the hospital to pay her a call."

"How come?"

"She'll be stronger and feeling better by then. Probably be more up to company comin' by."

"Jah," Mary Ellen said with a nod. "When she goes

home, I'll make another card and maybe give her one of the horseshoes I've painted."

❧

Not another headache, thought Miriam as she stood at the door, watching the last of her pupils leave the school yard. *Why must I always get a migraine when I have something important to do? Well, I won't let this one stop me from going to the hospital.*

Miriam crossed the room and opened the top drawer of her desk. Inside was a bottle of white willow bark capsules. She took two and washed them down with some cold water from her Thermos. She could only hope that today the herbals would work quickly. Was it the stress of knowing she was going to the hospital later, or was it the fact that John Lapp had given her a hard time in class today that had brought on the headache? *Probably a bit of both,* she decided. She was determined not to give in to the pain or stressful feelings. John had been punished for his shenanigans by losing his playtime during lunch, and she would force herself to go to the hospital no matter how much it distressed her to see Rebekah lying helplessly in her hospital bed.

❧

When Miriam arrived at the hospital later that day, she discovered that Rebekah wasn't in her room. She was informed by one of the nurses that the child had been taken upstairs for another CT scan and would be back in half an hour or so. Miriam could either wait in Rebekah's room or in the waiting room down the hall.

She left the candy and books on Rebekah's nightstand and made her way down the hall toward the waiting room.

Except for an elderly gentleman, the room was empty. Miriam took a seat and thumbed through a stack of magazines. Nothing looked interesting, and she was about to leave in search of a phone so she could call Nick when she noticed a copy of the *Daily Express* lying on the table in front of her. She picked up the paper and read the front page, then turned to page two. She stifled a gasp. Halfway down the page was a picture of a young girl lying in a hospital bed. It was Rebekah, and a four-column story accompanied the photo.

Miriam fumed as she read the reporter's name—Nick McCormick. "How dare he do such a thing! I had hoped I could trust him."

She read the entire story, pausing only to mumble or gasp as she read how Rebekah had been struck down by a tree limb during a storm that had swept through Lancaster County. The article went on to say that the little Amish girl would probably never walk again and that the hospital and doctor bills would be nearly impossible for her parents to pay. The story closed by asking for charitable contributions to the hospital on the child's behalf.

Miriam slammed the paper onto the table with such force that the elderly man seated across from her jumped. She mumbled an apology and stormed out of the room.

Miriam had nearly reached a phone booth at the end of the hall when she saw Andrew and Sarah heading her way.

"Miriam, we didn't know you were here," Andrew said. "We dropped Simon and Nadine off at Mom's, but she didn't tell us you were at the hospital."

"Mom doesn't know," Miriam answered. "Gladys Andrews drove me here after school let out."

"You look really upset. Is something wrong? Is it Rebekah? Is she worse?" Sarah's eyes widened, and deep wrinkles formed in her forehead.

"It's not Rebekah. She's having another CT scan, and I was waiting until she came out. It's what I found in the waiting room that upset me so." She lifted a shaky hand to touch her forehead. Her headache, which had previously eased, was back again with a vengeance.

"Miriam, you're trembling," Andrew said. "What did you see in that room?"

"A newspaper article with a picture."

"The news can be unsettling at times," Sarah interjected. "There are so many murders, robberies, and—"

"No, no, it's nothing like that. It's a story about Rebekah."

"Rebekah?" Andrew and Sarah said in unison.

Miriam nodded. "The article tells about her accident and how you won't have enough money to pay all the bills. There's even a picture of Rebekah lying in her hospital bed."

"What?" Andrew asked a bit too loudly. A nurse walking by gave him a warning look, but he didn't seem to notice.

"Who would do such a thing, and how'd they know about Rebekah's accident?" Sarah questioned.

"Let's go to the waiting room, and I'll show you the article." Miriam led the way down the hall.

The newspaper still lay on the table where she had angrily tossed it, and she bent down to pick it up, then handed it to Andrew.

"Who's responsible for this?" he asked, his dark eyes flashing angrily.

"I'm afraid I am." Miriam stared at the floor as a feeling of shame washed over her. She should never have gotten friendly with Nick or shared anything about her family with him. He'd pretended to be her friend, but he had only been using her as a means to get information for one of his newspaper articles.

Andrew raised his eyebrows. "You?"

She nodded. "I told the reporter about Rebekah's accident."

"You called the newspaper and asked them to write an article about our daughter?" Sarah's wounded expression revealed obvious hurt and betrayal.

Miriam placed a hand on her sister-in-law's arm. "Please don't think for one minute that I called the *Daily Express* or wanted anything like this to be printed."

"Then how did the reporter know about it?" Andrew asked.

Miriam suggested that they all sit down; then she told her brother and his wife everything except for the fact that she had nearly been taken in by Nick McCormick—even allowing herself to feel tingly and excited when she'd been with him. She would never have admitted that to anyone.

❧

Nick had just entered his office when his boss stormed in. "I wanted to talk to you about this," Pete said, tossing a folded newspaper onto Nick's desk.

Nick glanced at the article, recognizing it as the one he'd

written on Rebekah Stoltzfus, the child who had been hit by a tree limb that had left her legs paralyzed. "What about it? You did put your stamp of approval on it before it was released, remember?"

Pete nodded. "I just didn't realize you were going to include a close-up shot of the little Amish girl."

"I thought it would add more appeal to the story if the readers could see how pathetic she looked lying in her hospital bed, unable to walk."

"Maybe you should have thought more about how the girl's family would feel about the whole county seeing their daughter's face in the newspaper."

Nick could tell by the tone of Pete's voice that he was irritated, and the deep furrows in his forehead drove the point home.

"Have you had a complaint about this?" he asked. "Or did you simply become concerned that I might have offended someone?"

Pete pulled out the chair across from Nick and sat down. "The child's aunt phoned yesterday evening after you'd left to do that story about the drug bust on the other side of town."

"Miriam called? Did she ask for me?"

Pete nodded. "Fran took the call, but since you weren't in your office and the woman on the phone mentioned the article you had written, Fran forwarded the call to me."

"So what did Miriam say?"

Pete thumped the article with the tip of his pen and frowned. "She was upset and said you knew how the Amish feel about having their pictures taken, yet you sneaked into her niece's hospital room and snapped a picture of her anyway, without asking the family's permission." He gave the newspaper another quick tap. "I thought the article was well-written, but I'd like you to do a follow-up story and include an apology for that picture you used."

CHAPTER 16

As Miriam sat at the kitchen table, reading the newspaper one evening, she thought about Nick and how he'd let her down by writing that article on Rebekah and including a picture with it. Had she really been so naive as to believe he was different than other men? To think that she'd nearly phoned him to ask if they might meet again for coffee. She promised never again to allow her emotions to get in the way of good judgment.

Rebekah had been in the hospital for nearly three weeks already, and Miriam knew the medical bills were adding up. She had a little money put aside from her teaching position, which she would give to Andrew to use toward the mounting bills. She also planned to sell the beautiful quilts she had made for her hope chest at one of the firemen's benefit auctions, which were known as "mud sales" because they were held in the early spring when the ground was still muddy. Since Miriam never planned to marry, the quilts were useless to her, anyway. Tourists were always on the lookout for items made by the Amish, so she was sure she would have no trouble selling the quilts to the general store in town if they didn't sell during one of the mud sales.

Miriam was aware that several other Amish families had given money to help with Rebekah's hospital bills, and it made her thankful she belonged to a group of people who helped one another in times of need.

"I think I'll hire Gladys to drive me to the hospital tomorrow so I can see Rebekah again," Miriam said, glancing at her mother, who sat across the table, reading her Bible. "Would you like to go along?"

Mom looked up and smiled. "I appreciate the offer, but I went this morning with Sarah. Barbara Nyce, the Mennonite woman she usually hires, took us there."

Miriam frowned. "How come you didn't mention it earlier? I would think you would have wanted to give us a report."

"I did say something to Lewis about it when he came to the house at noon, but when you came home from school today, you said you had a headache and needed to lie down, so I didn't mention it."

"I see. How was Rebekah doing?"

"As well as can be expected. Her spirits are up, and that's a good thing."

Miriam released a heavy sigh. "How I wish the doctors had been wrong about her not being able to use her legs. It won't be easy for that sweet little girl to spend the rest of her life confined to a wheelchair, relying on others to do everything for her."

Mom clucked her tongue. "That's not true. There are many things Rebekah can do while she's sitting down."

Miriam opened her mouth to comment, but her mother rushed on.

"The child has a determined spirit, and I don't think she will let her handicap keep her from living life to the fullest."

Miriam folded her arms and leaned on the table. "Thanks to me being foolish enough to let her go outside, she'll only be living half a life."

Mom shook her head and looked hard at Miriam. "I wish you would stop being so negative."

"I'm not being negative; I'm just facing the truth."

"The truth is you have a lot to learn about how God wants us to live, and unless you allow Him to fill your heart with joy and love, I'm afraid you'll be living less of a life than my crippled granddaughter."

Mom's harsh words pricked Miriam's heart, but she would not allow them to penetrate the wall of defense she had built around her wounded soul. She pushed the newspaper aside and stood. "I'm going upstairs to bed. It's been a long day, and I'm awfully tired."

Long after Miriam left the room, Anna stayed at the table, reading her Bible and praying. She knew only one answer for her daughter's troubled spirit, and that was to open her heart to God's unconditional love and allow Him to fill her life with His joy and peace.

"Is there any of that good-tasting gingerbread cake left?" Lewis asked as he stepped into the kitchen, rousing Anna from her time of prayer and meditation. "I wouldn't mind a piece if there is."

"I think that can be arranged." Anna slid her chair back

and stood. "Would you like a glass of milk or some tea to go with it?"

He smacked his lips. "Ice cold milk sounds good to me."

"If you want ice cold, maybe you'd better take it outside," she said with a chuckle. "The weather's turned frigid this week, and I'm thinking that soon we'll be having some snow."

He took a seat at the table. "I believe you're right about that."

Anna placed a hunk of gingerbread and a tall glass of milk in front of Lewis; then she returned to her seat across from him.

"Aren't you having any?" he asked around a mouthful of cake. "This is sure tasty."

She shook her head. "I'm still full from supper, and I had a big lunch today after Sarah and I went to see Rebekah."

"You think she'll be goin' home soon?"

"I don't know. Her therapy sessions are going well, so maybe it won't be too long before the doctor says she's ready to leave the hospital."

"It's a good thing Miriam's been giving her a few lessons while she's there." Lewis took a swallow of milk. "Otherwise Rebekah would be way behind when she returned to school."

Anna drummed her fingers along the edge of the table. "It might be some time before Rebekah's up to going back to school. Even with Miriam giving her lessons to do at home, she's likely to have a lot of makeup to do."

"You think she may be held back and have to do this year over again?"

"Might could be."

Lewis reached for a napkin and wiped a spot on his chin

where some crumbs had accumulated. "I remember when I entered eighth grade and knew I'd be graduating that year. I wanted to be held back a year and even tried to fail just so Katherine Yoder wouldn't graduate me."

Anna's forehead wrinkled. "This is the first I've heard of that. Why would you have wanted to fail?"

His ears turned pink, and he stared at his empty plate. "You want the truth?"

"Of course."

"As you know, Grace Zepp is a year younger than me, and since I'd be leaving school after eighth grade and she still had another year, I didn't want to graduate yet."

"Ah, I see. You cared for Grace even back then?"

He nodded. "Of course, she made me see reason when I told her my plan to flunk all my tests that year so I wouldn't have to graduate."

"What did Grace say?"

"She reminded me that the sooner I learned a trade, the sooner I'd be ready to marry and begin a family." The color that permeated Lewis's ears spread quickly to the rest of his face. "I think I'm almost ready for that, Mom."

She smiled and reached across the table to touch his hand. "I think so, too."

Whenever Miriam went to the hospital to visit Rebekah, she always took a book to read, as well as some of the child's favorite licorice candy. Today was one of those days, but Miriam found herself dreading the visit. Would she ever stop feeling guilty whenever she looked at the sweet young child lying so helpless in her bed? Maybe Rebekah would be asleep when she arrived, and then she could leave the treat and book on the table by her bed and retreat to the protection and solitude of home.

As Gladys pulled her van into the hospital parking lot, Miriam thanked her. "I'll be ready to head for home in about an hour."

"That's fine," Gladys replied. "I'll run a few errands and meet you here at five o'clock."

"All right." As Miriam stepped out of the car, it started to rain, so she hurried toward the hospital's main entrance. Just as she was about to step inside, she collided with a man. When she looked up, she found herself staring into the familiar blue eyes of Nick McCormick. She trembled, fighting the urge to pound her fists against his chest.

Nick smiled, apparently unaware of her irritation. "Miriam, it's good to see you again. As usual, you look a bit flustered, but beautiful, nonetheless. Is there something I can do to help?"

Miriam clasped her hands tightly behind her back, trying to maintain control of herself. She had never been so close to striking anyone. Strangely, Nick seemed to bring out the worst in her, yet he also brought out the best.

"I have no patience with a liar," she mumbled.

"Excuse me?"

She lifted her chin and met his piercing gaze. "I'm referring to the fact that you promised not to do a story about my niece but then went ahead and did it anyway. Your word meant absolutely nothing, did it?"

Nick reached up to scratch the back of his head while

giving her a sheepish-looking grin. "Guess you caught me red-handed. When I wrote the article, I didn't think about how some Amish probably read the *Daily Express*."

"We're not ignorant, you know."

"I'm sure you're not."

"My people aren't perfect and don't claim to be, but we do strive for honesty, which is more than I can say for some."

"My, my, aren't you a feisty little thing today?" He chuckled. "I like spunky women—but I also like women who get their facts straight."

"What's that supposed to mean?"

"Fact number one: I never actually promised that I wouldn't do a story about your niece."

"But you said—"

"That I wouldn't do any more note-taking while you were talking to me. I kept true to my word and put away my paper and pen."

"But when you mentioned that you wanted to do an article about Rebekah's accident and include something about the cost of her medical bills, I asked you not to, and I assumed you would abide by my wishes."

He gave no reply, just staring at her in a most disconcerting way.

"And I certainly never thought you would sneak into her hospital room and take her picture," Miriam added, putting emphasis on the word *picture*.

"I did what I thought best—as a reporter and as your friend."

"What kind of friend goes behind someone's back and does something so sneaky?"

"The kind who believes he's doing the right thing." Nick pulled Miriam into the little waiting area across the hall. "Fact number two: I really do care about you, and I believed I was doing something helpful for your family. I apologize if it upset you or if you thought I had betrayed you." He sank into a chair. "If it makes you feel any better, I got a good chewing-out from my boss for including the picture I took of your niece, and that's why I wrote the apology letter that went into the paper a few days later. Did you happen to read it?"

She shook her head.

"Well, it's true. I didn't want anyone to think I had done anything to intentionally step on the Plain People's toes—especially not your pretty toes."

Miriam's anger receded some. It was hard to remain in control when she was in Nick's presence. And when he looked at her with such a tender expression, she could barely think or breathe. Did she really need acceptance so badly that she would go outside her Amish faith to get it? Despite her desires, she couldn't allow this man to deceive her into believing he actually cared for her.

"I need to go see my niece now," she said, starting for the door. "I appreciate your apology, but I would ask that you not see Rebekah again."

Nick stood and moved toward her, but before he could give a reply, she dashed from the room.

🙖

"That sure went well," Nick muttered under his breath. "I wait all this time to see Miriam again, and then I can't think of anything to say that might redeem myself and make her willing to spend time with me again."

He groaned. *If she knew why I'd come to the hospital today, she would really be mad. Maybe it's good that she left the room before I ended up telling her where I just came from and how I bribed her niece into letting me take her picture again.* He grabbed his camera bag, which he'd placed on a chair when they'd come into the room, and started for the door. *I didn't take any face-on shots of Rebekah this time, so at least I shouldn't catch any flak from Pete for doing it.*

As Nick left the waiting room, he glanced down the long corridor, hoping to catch a glimpse of Miriam. She was nowhere in sight. *It's probably just as well. After my next article comes out, she'll probably never speak to me again.*

⁂

When Miriam entered Rebekah's room, she found the child propped up on pillows. *So innocent, sweet, and helpless,* she thought.

"Aunt Miriam!" Rebekah smiled and reached her small hand out to Miriam.

"How's my best pupil and favorite niece today?" Miriam asked as she took the child's hand in her own.

"Better. My head don't hurt no more. Doctor said I can go home soon."

Miriam cringed at the thought of Rebekah returning to her family as a cripple. Rebekah had never made mention of it, though. Was it possible that she wasn't yet aware of the fact that she could no longer walk? How would the once-active child handle the probability of spending the rest of her days confined to a wheelchair?

"I'm glad you're feeling better," Miriam said, trying to make her voice sound light and cheerful.

"Did you bring me some licorice?" Rebekah asked with an expectant look.

"Jah, and another book to read for your English lessons, as well as a get-well card from your friend Mary Ellen." Miriam handed the card and candy to Rebekah; then she seated herself in the chair next to the bed. "Would you like to look at Mary Ellen's card before we start the lesson?"

Rebekah nodded and tore open the envelope. Her smile stretched ear to ear as she read the card:

> Dear Rebekah,
>   I miss not seeing you at school. Pappy says I can come visit when you get home. I pray for you every night— that God will make you well.
>
>   Your friend,
>   Mary Ellen

Tears welled in Miriam's eyes, and she blinked to keep them from spilling over. Rebekah was paralyzed and would never be whole again, so Mary Ellen's prayers were wasted. But she wouldn't tell Rebekah that; it would be too cruel.

"A man took my picture," Rebekah surprised her by saying.

"I know, but that man will never bother you again." It was then that Miriam noticed the teddy bear sitting on the table near Rebekah's bed. She picked it up. "Where did you get this, Rebekah?"

"The man gave it to me."

"When was that?"

"Awhile ago."

"What man?"

"The picture man."

Miriam's head started to throb, and she pressed her hands against her temples, trying to halt the pain. So Nick must have just come from Rebekah's room when she'd bumped into him at the hospital entrance. Had he come out of concern for the child? Was his gift one of genuine compassion, or had he used it to bribe Rebekah in order to take additional pictures? Now that Miriam thought about it, Nick had been carrying his camera bag when she'd first seen him, and he'd set it on a chair in the waiting room while they talked.

"Rebekah, did the man take more pictures of you today?"

The child nodded. "He gave me the bear, and then he asked me to turn my head to the wall, so's he could use his camera without makin' everyone mad."

CHAPTER 17

One month after Rebekah's accident, the doctors released her from the hospital. She would still need to return for physical therapy twice a week, but at least her days and nights could be spent with family.

On Rebekah's first day home, Mom suggested that she and Miriam ride over to see if they could help out. "Sarah's certainly going to have her hands full now," she said. "Just taking care of a *boppli* and two small *kinner* is a job in itself, but now this?"

"Since today's Saturday and there's no school, I have all day to help out." Miriam pulled her jacket from the wall peg. "I'll go out and feed the animals while you start breakfast. Then we can go."

"Jah," Mom agreed with a nod.

A blast of cold air greeted Miriam as she stepped onto the porch. It was early December, and a definite feeling of winter hung in the air. She shivered and pulled her collar up around her neck. "I hate winter!" The truth was, she was beginning to dislike all seasons. Perhaps it was life in general that she hated. *Is it all right for a believer to feel hate toward anything—even the weather?*

Another thought entered her mind. Maybe she wasn't a believer anymore. Her faith in God had diminished so much over the last several months. She got very little from the biweekly preaching services she attended with her friends and family. She no longer did her daily devotions, and her prayers were few and far between. When she did pray, she offered more of a complaint to God rather than heartfelt prayers and petitions. Where was God anyway, and what had happened to her longing to seek His face?

Miriam trudged wearily toward the barn and forced her thoughts onto the tasks that lay before her.

On her way back to the house half an hour later, she noticed a clump of wild pansies growing near the fence that ran parallel to the pasture. Pansies were hardy flowers, blooming almost continuously from early spring until late fall. The delicate yellow and lavender blossoms made her think of Mary Ellen and the day she'd given her the bouquet of heartsease. *Children like Rebekah and Mary Ellen are a lot like wild pansies,* she thought. *They're small and delicate, yet able to withstand so much.*

Thoughts of Mary Ellen made Miriam think about Amos. She'd seen him only a few times since the day of Rebekah's accident. Those times had been at preaching services. It seemed strange that he wasn't coming around anymore. He hadn't even come over for supper at Mom's most recent invitation. Perhaps he'd been too busy with his blacksmith duties or taking care of Mary Ellen. Or maybe he'd finally come to realize that Miriam had no interest in him, so he'd given up on his pursuit of her. Regardless of the reason, Miriam was glad he wasn't coming around anymore. The last thing she needed was an unwanted suitor. Her life was complicated enough.

She bent down and picked several of the colorful pansies. They would make a lovely bouquet to give Rebekah.

When they arrived at Sarah and Andrew's place, Anna noticed Sarah sitting on the front porch, with her head bent and shoulders shaking. She quickly got down from the buggy and rushed to Sarah's side, leaving Miriam to unhitch the horse. "What is it, Sarah? Why are you sitting out here in the cold?"

Sarah lifted her head. Tears coursed down her cheeks. "Oh, Anna, please remember me in your prayers."

"Jah, I surely will," Anna answered, taking a seat beside her daughter-in-law and reaching for her hand. "What has you so upset?"

"I'm happy to have Rebekah home again, but there isn't enough of me to go around." Sarah sniffed and dabbed at her eyes with the corner of her apron. "Simon's into everything, the baby always seems to need me for something, and taking care of Rebekah will be a full-time job. She's only been home half a day, and already I can't seem to manage."

"There, there," Anna comforted. She slipped her arm around Sarah's shoulders. "We'll work something out."

"Is there anything I can do to help?" Miriam asked as she joined the women on the porch.

Anna spoke before Sarah could reply. "Miriam, would you please go inside and check on the kinner while I speak to Sarah?"

"Jah. I want to give Rebekah the flowers I picked for her this morning," she said, holding the bouquet in front of her.

As soon as Miriam had gone into the house, Anna turned back to Sarah. "When I learned that Rebekah was coming home, I became concerned that her care would be too much for you to handle alone."

Sarah nodded and released a shuddering sigh. "I want to do right by all my kinner, but caring for Rebekah is going to take up so much of my time, and we really can't afford to hire a maad right now."

"There's no need for you to hire a maid," Anna said with a shake of her head. "I think I may have the answer to your problem."

When Miriam entered the kitchen, she spotted Rebekah sitting in her wheelchair next to the table, coloring a picture. The child looked up and smiled. "Hi, Aunt Miriam. Do you like my picture?"

"Jah, it's nice." Miriam placed the flowers on the table. "These are for you."

"Danki. They're very pretty."

"Where are Simon and baby Nadine?"

Rebekah pointed across the room.

Miriam gasped when she spotted three-year-old Simon sitting on the floor with a jar of petroleum jelly he had obviously rubbed all over his face and hair. The baby, who sat on the braided rug next to Simon, had some in her hair, as well.

"*Was in der welt*—what in the world? How did you get this, you little *schtinker?*" Miriam rushed across the room and grabbed the slippery jar out of his hands. "That is a no-no!"

Simon's lower lip trembled, and tears gathered in his big, blue eyes.

"Come over to the sink with me, and let's get you cleaned up. Then I'll tend to the *boppli.*"

Just as Miriam finished cleaning both children, Mom and Sarah entered the kitchen. Sarah's eyes were red and swollen, but at least she was no longer crying.

"Our help is definitely needed here today, and there's much to be done," Mom said with a nod in Miriam's direction. "So now, let's get ourselves busy."

By the time they reached home that evening, Miriam felt exhausted. The last thing she wanted to do was chores, but farm duties didn't wait, so she climbed down from the buggy with a sigh, prepared to head for the barn.

"If you don't mind, I'd like to talk before we have our supper," Mom said as she stepped down from the buggy. "When you go out to the barn, if Lewis is there, would you ask him to come up to the house with you if he's not busy? The matter I have to discuss pertains to both of you."

Miriam tipped her head in question, but when Mom gave no explanation, she nodded and started for the barn, wondering what her mother could have to talk about that would affect both her and Lewis.

She found her brother grooming one of their horses

when she entered the barn leading Harvey, her buggy horse. "Here's another one for you," she called. "When you're done, Mom wants to see you up at the house."

Lewis looked up from his job. "What's up?"

"She said she has something to discuss and that it pertains to both of us."

"Tell her I'll be there in a while," Lewis answered with a nod.

As Miriam left the barn a few minutes later, a chill ran through her body. She shivered and hurried toward the house. Was the cool evening air the cause of her chilliness— or was it the fear she felt in her heart? Fear that whatever Mom had to tell them was bad news.

By the time Miriam entered the house, Anna had steaming cups of hot chocolate waiting and a kettle of soup simmering on the stove. "Is Lewis coming?" she asked, after Miriam had removed her heavy black shawl and hung it over a peg near the back door.

"He said he'd be in when he's done with the horses." Miriam moved away from the door and took a seat at the table. When Anna offered her a cup of hot chocolate, she smiled and said, "Danki."

"You're welcome." Anna settled herself into the rocking chair near the stove and reached into a basket on the floor. She pulled one of Lewis's holey socks out and began to mend it as she made small talk with Miriam. "I figured I may as well keep my hands busy while the soup heats. After Lewis comes in and we've had our talk, we can make some sandwiches."

"Okay."

"Winter's in the air. Can you feel it?"

Miriam lifted the cup of hot chocolate to her lips. "Jah, I nearly froze to death this morning when I went out to do my chores. I suppose I'll have to get out my heavier jacket soon. A shawl sure isn't enough for these crisp, cold mornings and evenings."

"The hens aren't laying as many eggs, either," Anna said. "It's a sure sign that winter's here."

The back door creaked open, and Lewis entered the kitchen. "Yum. . .I smell hot chocolate. I'd recognize that delicious odor even if I was blindfolded and still out on the porch." He smiled at Anna. "Miriam said you wanted to talk to us?"

She nodded, laid the sock aside, and cleared her throat a couple of times. "I. . .uh. . .was wondering. . .that is, how would you two feel about me moving in with Andrew and Sarah? Could you manage on your own?"

Neither Lewis nor Miriam spoke for several minutes; then Miriam broke the silence. "For how long, Mom?"

"Indefinitely."

"Indefinitely?" Lewis echoed.

"Jah. Now that Rebekah's confined to a wheelchair and what with all the work the other two kinner will take, Sarah's going to need all the help she can get for a good long while."

"But Mom, how do you expect Lewis and me to manage here by ourselves?" Miriam asked in a shrill tone.

"You're both capable adults. I'm sure you can manage fine without me."

"I think we could do all right," Lewis said with a nod.

"I know that my moving out will cause some discomfort for you," Anna continued. "However, I'm sorely needed over at Andrew and Sarah's right now."

"What about Sarah's folks? Can't they help out?" Lewis questioned.

"Their place is several miles away. Besides, they still have young kinner living at home to care for."

"It's just like you to make such a sacrifice, Mom," Lewis said. "You have a heart of compassion."

Miriam left her seat at the table and knelt next to Anna's chair. "It should be me that goes. I'll quit my job teaching and care for Rebekah. After all, it was my fault she was injured."

Anna placed her hand on top of Miriam's head. "It was not your fault, and I wish you would quit blaming yourself. It was an accident, plain and simple. It was something bad that God allowed to happen. You are in no way responsible. You're a fine teacher, and you're needed at the school. Sarah and I talked things over today, and I've made my decision. I'll be moving to their place this weekend, and I hope I have your blessing on this."

Miriam rose to her feet. "If you're determined to go, then I'll abide by your decision."

"And we'll do our best to keep this place runnin'," Lewis added with a grin.

Anna smiled despite the tears running down her cheeks. How grateful she was to have such a supportive family during times of need.

CHAPTER 18

The winter months seemed to drag unmercifully. With all the work to be done, the days should have passed quickly, but Miriam's tired body and saddened soul made her feel as if each day were endless. The snow lay deep on the ground, which made the outside chores even more difficult. And the cold—Miriam couldn't remember a winter that had been as cold as this one. She wondered if it was because the temperatures often dipped below zero, or was it simply because her heart had turned so cold?

Valentine's Day was only a few weeks away, and she knew her pupils would expect to have a party, with refreshments and the exchange of valentine hearts with one another. The last thing she felt like was a party, but she would force herself to get through it somehow.

As Miriam returned home from school one afternoon and entered the quiet, lonely kitchen, she admitted to herself that she missed her mother terribly. She knew Mom was doing a good thing and that her help was needed at Andrew and Sarah's, but they hardly got to see Mom anymore, for she was too busy caring for Rebekah and her siblings.

Miriam had many chores to do, as well, and the foul weather made it difficult to travel. Only for those things that were necessary, such as school and church, did Miriam go out.

Lewis had begun to officially court Grace Zepp. He'd taken her to a couple of singings and more recently had begun to call on Grace at her home. Miriam worried about him because, ever since Papa's death, Lewis had been forced to do the work of two men. Of course, she was doing the work of two women, but she wasn't taking the time for courting. Maybe it was good that Lewis was young and obviously in love. How else could he have managed the extra activity of courting?

The scholars were full of excitement on the day of the Valentine's Day party. Nearly everyone brought goodies. There were cookies sprinkled with red sugar crystals; cupcakes frosted in pink icing; candy hearts; glazed, sugared, and powdered donuts; and a pink and white decorated cake. Miriam furnished a beverage of cold apple cider.

The party was held after lunch, and the children began by eating refreshments and followed their snack by playing some games. Finally, they exchanged valentine cards. Some of the cards were store-bought, but most of them had been made by hand, using construction paper and white paper doilies.

Every child had taken a cardboard shoebox and decorated it, then cut a hole in the top and placed it on their school desk. As Miriam sat at her desk, watching the proceedings, the scholars took turns walking around the room, placing their valentines into one another's special boxes. Miriam had instructed the class earlier in the week that each child was expected to give a card to everyone. That way nobody would be left out or go home with only a handful of valentines. She even thought to make a box for Rebekah, which she had placed on her own desk, reminding the class that Rebekah was unable to come to school right now because of her accident and would probably be studying at home for some time.

Miriam hoped some valentines, a cupcake, and a few cookies might cheer Rebekah, and she planned to deliver them after school today. It had been several weeks since she'd been over to Sarah and Andrew's, and she looked forward to a much-needed visit with Rebekah, Mom, and Sarah. The chores at home would have to wait.

Miriam forced her thoughts aside as Mary Ellen approached her desk. The child had a large valentine heart, and she handed it to Miriam. "This is for you, Teacher Mim. It's from me and Pappy."

Miriam nodded and tried to smile. "Danki, Mary Ellen. That was nice of you."

"And Pappy, too. He helped me make it and even wrote some words on it. I think Pappy likes you, Teacher."

Miriam placed the valentine on her desk. "Tell your daed I said danki for his thoughts, as well."

"Aren't you gonna read it, Teacher Mim?"

"I'll look at it later. Right now it's time for the class to begin cleaning up the room."

Mary Ellen's eyes were downcast, but she obediently returned to her seat.

Just when I thought Amos had forgotten about me, Miriam fumed inwardly. She placed the valentine on her desk along with a stack of papers she would be taking home to correct; then she turned her attention back to the class.

As Amos forked hay into his horses' stalls, he thought about Miriam and wondered what her reaction would be to the valentine card he and Mary Ellen had made for her last night. It was the first effort he'd made in a while to reach Miriam, and he hoped she wouldn't take it wrong or think he was being too pushy. He hoped that, by giving her some time and space, she might have reconsidered his offer to court her. Maybe receiving the valentine would soften her heart and make her willing to speak with him the next time he decided to broach the subject of them courting.

"And when will that be, Lord?" he asked, setting his pitch-fork aside and looking up at the rafters. "Will You let me know when the time is right to speak with Miriam again? Will You make her heart open to the idea of my courting her?"

No answer. Only the gentle nicker of the buggy horses could be heard.

Amos thought about a recent message their bishop had given on the subject of friendship. It had been based on Proverbs 18, verse 24: "A man that hath friends must shew himself friendly: and there is a friend that sticketh closer than a brother."

"Maybe that's all I need to do where Miriam's concerned," he murmured. "I just need to show myself friendly, so she will know I'm her friend."

Nick headed across the parking lot to his car, his feet slipping on the ice with every step he took. "Stupid weather!" he fumed. "I hate getting out in this slick stuff in order to conduct an interview." That afternoon, he was on his way back from a fire station across town, where he'd met with the fire chief about a benefit auction, called a "mud sale," that would be held later in the month.

Nick had learned that local people, both English and Amish, would turn out to support the volunteer firefighters by buying crafts, food, horses, farm equipment, buggies, washing machines, plants, furniture, livestock, and various handmade items like quilts and wall hangings. Part of the sale would be held inside the building, but much of the proceedings would take place outside, where the ground was churned into mud by the feet of hundreds of people. Thus the name "mud sale."

"I'll bet anything Pete will find the story I'm doing today so interesting that he'll want me to be there on the day of the sale so I can learn more and write up another article for the newspaper."

Nick blew out his breath and watched it curl into the air like steam pouring from a teakettle. *If Amish are going to be at this shindig, maybe there's a chance I'll see Miriam Stoltzfus there.* That thought brought a smile to his lips, and as he climbed into his car, he began to whistle.

CHAPTER

19

Snow was beginning to fall again as Miriam climbed into her buggy and headed for Andrew and Sarah's place. But today she didn't care. She wasn't going to let a little bad weather stop her from an overdue visit with her family. This was a special day—a day when folks showed others how much they cared.

She placed the stack of school papers on the seat next to her and was about to pick up the reins when she noticed the red and white valentine heart sticking out between two pieces of paper. "I suppose I may as well read it now," she murmured.

On the inside, something had been written on both sides of the card. She read the left side first. It was printed and obviously done in a child's handwriting:

Dear Teacher Mim,

I wanted to bake you some cookies, but I don't know how to bake yet. I think you're smart and pretty, too.

Love,
Mary Ellen

Miriam sighed. "What a sweet little girl." She turned her attention to the other side of the card. It was written in cursive writing:

Dear Miriam,
   I think of you often and wonder how you're doing. Let me know if I can be of any help to you or your family. I say a prayer for you every day.

                              Sincerely,
                              Amos Hilty

Miriam felt moisture on her cheeks and reached up to wipe it away. Had the snowflakes drifted inside the buggy? She thought all the windows had been closed, but then she felt a familiar burning in the back of her throat and realized she was crying. *But why?* she wondered. *Surely Amos has no real concern for my well-being. He's only worried about himself and his daughter.*

She drew in a deep breath and blew it out quickly. Maybe she had been too quick to judge Amos. Was it possible that he did care for her in some small way? He had experienced the pain of losing someone close to him when Ruth died. He might have been sincere in expressing his desire to help. Maybe it was time to let go of the terrible ache in her heart and move on with life.

Miriam sniffed. Even though her head told her to let go of her bitterness, it would mean she must risk being hurt again, and she couldn't take that chance.

"I don't care if Amos Hilty is sincere," she mumbled as she picked up the reins and got the buggy moving down the snow-covered road that would take her to Andrew's place. "I can't allow him to court me."

🙟

Anna was sitting at the kitchen table, writing her next article for *The Budget*, when Miriam showed up carrying a paper sack in her hand and wearing a disgruntled look on her face. Rather than make an issue of Miriam's obvious bad mood, Anna smiled and said, "It's good to see you, daughter. What brings you by on this snowy, cold afternoon?"

"I brought some valentine cards for Rebekah that her classmates made." Miriam placed the sack on the table, slipped out of her heavy coat, draped it over the back of a chair, and sat down with an audible sigh.

"What's wrong?" Anna asked. "Do you have another one of your headaches this afternoon, or are you feeling stressed because the roads are so icy?"

Miriam glanced around the room. "Where is everyone? I'd rather that no one else knows what is irritating me so."

Anna nodded toward the door leading to the hallway. "Sarah's upstairs with the younger ones, and Rebekah's on the sofa in the living room, reading a book."

"Where's Andrew?"

"He went out to the barn some time ago to check on the batch of pups his chocolate Lab had last week."

"I'll bet the kinner are excited about having new puppies around."

Anna nodded and poured Miriam a cup of tea from the pot that sat in the center of the table. She had a feeling her daughter was trying to avoid talking about what was bothering her.

"Danki. I can use a cup of warm tea about now."

"You're welcome." Anna waited until Miriam had taken a sip of tea and seemed a bit more relaxed before she asked, "Now what's got you looking so down in the mouth today?"

"I got a valentine card—from Amos Hilty."

"Oh?"

"Actually, it was from both him and Mary Ellen, but I have a hunch he had more to do with it than she did." She groaned. "The way he's pushing like this makes me kind of angry."

Anna clicked her tongue. "Miriam, Miriam, will you never learn?"

Miriam's forehead wrinkled as she set her cup down. "What do you mean, Mom?"

"I mean that you should not kick a gift horse in the mouth."

"You think Amos is a horse?"

"That's just an old expression, and you know it." Anna leaned forward, resting her elbows on the table. "I'm trying to tell you that you should stop questioning Amos's motives and enjoy the attention he's giving you."

"I might be able to do that if I didn't know that he has an ulterior motive."

Anna opened her mouth to reply, but Andrew stepped into the kitchen just then, interrupting their conversation.

"Brr," he said, briskly rubbing his hands together. "It's getting colder by the minute out there." He started across the room but halted when he saw Miriam. "I didn't realize you were here, sister."

"I came to bring Rebekah some valentine cards the scholars made for her."

"That's nice, but do you really think you should be out on your own this close to dark—especially with the roads being so icy?"

"I did fine on the way over here," she said, wrinkling her nose at him. "I'm sure I'll do fine going home."

"Maybe so, but being out alone after dark is not good. Too much could happen between our place and yours."

"Like what?"

"The horse could lose its footing on the icy pavement, or the buggy might slide off the road." He made a swooping gesture with his hand as though he thought she needed a picture drawn.

"Just because I'm a woman doesn't mean I'm helpless, and for your information, I think I'm doing rather well on my own."

Andrew removed his jacket and hung it on a wall peg. "I'm thinkin' what you need is a man in your life."

Miriam's face flamed, but before she could open her mouth to reply, Anna spoke up. "I'm sure Miriam wouldn't have driven over here if she didn't believe she could handle the horse and buggy in the dark or on the icy road," she said, coming to her daughter's defense.

"It's nice to know that somebody's on my side," Miriam said with a smug smile.

Anna held up her hand. "Only on that one issue." She nodded at Andrew as he took a seat at the table. "I must agree with your bruder on the other issue. When I was your age, I was happily married, and your daed and I had already begun our family."

Miriam's lips compressed into a thin line as her eyes

narrowed. "Isn't there anyone in this family who doesn't think I need a man in order to be happy?"

Andrew stared at his sister. "Can you honestly say that you're happy now?"

She shrugged.

"Miriam, why don't you take the valentines into the living room and give them to Rebekah? After you've visited awhile, you can join us for supper," Anna suggested.

"I'd be happy to follow you home in my buggy," Andrew put in.

Miriam shook her head. "I'll visit with Rebekah a few minutes, but then I'll be heading for home. Lewis will no doubt expect *his* supper to be waiting."

CHAPTER 20

The first sign of spring came on Saturday morning when Miriam, preparing to leave for the mud sale in Strasburg, discovered some yellow crocuses poking their heads between clumps of grass that were surrounded by patches of snow not far from the barn. How she wished the new life spring brought could give her a new life, too. She wanted to wake up every morning with a feeling of joy and peace. She wanted to find a reason to begin each new day with anticipation, knowing it truly was a day the Lord had created, and she wanted to enjoy every day to the fullest.

The sound of a horse and buggy plodding up the graveled driveway caused Miriam to turn away from the flowers. She shielded her eyes against the sun, wondering who would be coming by so early in the morning. As the buggy approached, she took a few steps toward it to get a better look.

When the buggy was a few feet away, it stopped, and Amos Hilty stepped down. He smiled at Miriam and said, "Guder mariye. It's a beautiful day, wouldn't you say?"

Her only reply was a quick nod.

"I know there's still snow on the ground in places, but

the sun's shining bright as a new penny, and there's a definite promise of spring in the air."

Miriam mumbled something about the crocuses she had just seen, then quickly added, "What brings you out here so early in the day, Amos? There's nothing wrong with Mary Ellen, is there?" She really did feel concern for the young girl who always seemed so determined to make "Teacher Mim" like her.

"Mary Ellen's fine. Since this is Saturday, and there's no school, I allowed her to spend last night with her friend Becky Weaver."

"I see. Then if it's not about Mary Ellen—"

"I came by to see if Lewis has any horses he might like to sell."

"If you're looking for a new horse, then why not ask Henry Yoder? He raises horses for the purpose of selling, you know."

"That's true, but I thought maybe Lewis could use the money."

"We are not destitute, Amos Hilty!"

"I–I'm sorry if I've offended you. I don't think you need charity. It's just that. . .well, with Lewis planning to get married in the fall, I thought he could probably use some extra money to put away. I'm in need of a couple of horses anyway, and—"

"Married? Who told you Lewis is planning to be married?"

"He did. I thought you knew." Amos looked flustered, and he shifted from one foot to the other.

"I know Lewis has been courting Grace Zepp, but he hasn't said anything to me about marriage in the fall," Miriam said, trying to gain control of her quivering voice.

"I–I'm sorry. I guess I shouldn't have said anything.

I think maybe I've put my big boot in my mouth."

"No, you were only telling me something you thought I already knew."

"I can't believe Lewis hasn't told you," he said with a shake of his head.

"Since the wedding is several months off, he probably figured it could wait awhile." Miriam frowned. "Or maybe he didn't want to upset me."

"Why would it upset you if Lewis married a nice girl like Grace?"

"I have nothing against Grace. It's just that our life has been full of so many changes in the last year or so. If Lewis marries Grace, it will mean more changes—especially for me."

"You mean because she'll be moving into your house?"

"I suppose she will. The farm is Lewis's now that Papa's gone, and Mom isn't likely to move back since she's needed at Andrew's to help with Rebekah." Miriam shrugged. "The only logical thing for me to do is move out before they get married."

"But where would you go?"

"I'm not sure. I just know I don't want to stay here once they're married."

"Two hens in the same henhouse? Is that it?" Amos asked with a crooked grin.

Miriam had to bite her lower lip to keep from smiling. She could almost picture Grace and her running around the kitchen, cackling and chasing each other the way the hens in the coop often did. "Grace and I would probably get on fine together," she said. "But it wouldn't be fair to the newlyweds to have Lewis's big sister hanging around all the time."

"That's considerate, Miriam. You're a good woman."

Miriam's face grew warm and she looked away, hoping Amos wouldn't notice. The truth was, the idea of living in the same house with Lewis and his new wife was too painful for her. It would be a constant reminder of what she would never have—a loving husband and the hope of children to raise someday. It would also mean giving up the control she had gained in the house since Mom had moved out, and that wouldn't be easy.

Amos could see that he had embarrassed Miriam, and impulsively he reached out and touched her arm. "I—I think I might have an answer to your problem."

"Oh?"

He nodded. "You could marry me and move to my place. Mary Ellen loves you, and—"

"Are you joking?"

"About Mary Ellen's feelings toward you?"

She shook her head. "Are you joking about me marrying you?"

"No, I. . .that is. . .I've been thinking on this for some time." Amos paused a moment to calm his nerves. "I'll admit that I do have some concerns because you don't seem to be as interested in spiritual things as you should, but from what I know of you in the past—"

"My spiritual life is none of your business." She squinted. "Besides, how would you know what I think or feel about God?"

Amos cleared his throat. "I-I've been watching you for

some time, and I've noted during our preaching services that you often stare out the window rather than concentrate on the sermons being preached. You don't even participate much during the time of singing. Are you bitter because of your daed's untimely death, or does the problem go back further, to when William Graber jilted you?"

"Why must you bring that up?" Miriam stared at the ground. "Are you trying to pour salt in my wounds?"

"Of course not. It's just that William and I used to be friends, until he—"

"My personal life is none of your business, and I think this discussion had better end now."

Gathering up a bit more courage, Amos took a step toward her, but she backed away, almost bumping into her buggy, which was parked next to the barn. "I-I'm sorry if I've taken you by surprise or said things that hurt you," he mumbled. "But I hope you'll at least give the matter of marrying me some deep thought. I believe we can work through your bitterness together."

She opened her mouth as if to say something, but he rushed on before he lost his nerve. "My main concern is for Mary Ellen. If we were to marry, I would hope you wouldn't let your attitude affect her. I don't want my child to have feelings of distrust toward God."

Miriam shook her head. "I would never do anything to hurt Mary Ellen's belief in God. She must draw her own conclusions as she matures and is dealt more of life's harsh blows. Now, regarding your proposal of marriage—you haven't said anything about love."

"I told you that Mary Ellen loves you, and—"

Miriam held up her hand. "You needn't say anything more, Amos, because I'm not in love with you, either."

Amos gave his beard a quick tug. Miriam's truthful words had stopped him from making a fool of himself, yet her announcement had hurt his pride more than he cared to admit. Even so, he was still willing to marry her in the hope that someday she might come to care for him the way he did her. For now, he would bide his time and keep praying for a miracle. He moistened his lips with the tip of his tongue and forced a smile. "There's. . .uh. . .still plenty of time before Lewis and Grace's wedding, so you don't have to give me your answer right now. But I hope you will at least pray about it."

Miriam looked dumbfounded, but she didn't say a word. He figured her silence probably meant she had no plans to change her mind about marrying him.

With a quick nod in her direction, Amos headed into the barn to find Lewis.

"Men," he heard Miriam mutter. "They would trade their heart in exchange for a live-in housekeeper."

Nick had never been to a mud sale before, and if he'd had his way he wouldn't be at this one, either. It was only ten in the morning, and already the ground outside the firehouse had been churned into mud by the hundreds of people milling around.

Despite the fact that he knew the Amish didn't like to have their pictures taken, Nick couldn't resist this chance to get some good shots of the Plain People buying and selling their wares while they interacted with others not of their faith. He spotted one teenage Amish boy pedaling furiously on an exercise bike. Two Amish girls stood in front of an English vendor's table, playing with the brightly colored plastic toys that were for sale, while a couple of young English boys pretended to shoot each other with plastic squirt guns. Adults stood around, conversing with one another and bidding on the merchandise being sold in the auction rings. Everything from plain, old-fashioned wringer washing machines to fancy, modern speedboats was available to buy or bid on. Nick noticed a tent had been set up to shelter the horses that would soon be auctioned off. He started toward that area but stopped when he spotted an Amish woman plodding through the mud, carrying a box in her arms. It was Miriam Stoltzfus.

"Miriam, wait up!" he called, slipping his camera back into the bag and trudging after her.

She halted and turned to look at him. "What are you doing here, Nick?"

"Came to cover the mud sale for an article I've been asked to do for the newspaper."

"I'm not surprised," she said with a sniff. "You seem to be good at doing stories that involve my people."

"You're still mad at me for writing that article about your niece, aren't you?"

"It wasn't what you said in the article; it was the picture you took of Rebekah that upset me so."

"I said I was sorry."

"Yes, but then you went back to her room again and bribed her with a stuffed animal so you could take more pictures."

Nick knew he was caught, so he decided to change the subject. "Are you here to buy or sell?"

Miriam nodded at the box in her arms. "I've brought a couple of quilts for the auction that will be held later on. The money will go to help with Rebekah's hospital bills." She started walking in the direction of the building again, and he followed.

"How's your niece doing? Is she getting along okay?"

She halted before they reached the door. "Rebekah's legs are paralyzed, and she's in a wheelchair. My mother has moved to my brother Andrew's house to help care for her."

"Does that mean you're living alone?"

She shook her head. "My brother Lewis is still at home, and he will continue to live there even after he's married in the fall."

Miriam's serious expression made Nick wonder if she might disapprove of her brother's choice for a wife. "Are you opposed to the idea of your brother getting married?" he asked.

Her lips compressed into a thin, straight line. "Of course not. It's just that things won't be the same for me after Grace moves into the house, and if I can find someplace else to live before the wedding, I may move."

"My aunt runs a boarding home not far from here," Nick said. "Want me to see if she has any spare rooms?"

"No, thank you. I'll find somewhere to go, and when I do, it will be within the Amish community." Someone opened the door to exit the building just then, and Miriam stepped quickly inside. "I need to get this quilt in for the auction before it's too late. I hope you get all you need for your mud-sale story," she called over her shoulder.

Nick chuckled as he watched her retreating form. "I think that woman likes me. She just doesn't know it."

CHAPTER
21

Miriam made her way to the house as though she were moving in slow motion. Her mind was filled with thoughts of the conversation she'd had with Nick at the mud sale, and she wondered what kind of hold he had on her that she always managed to tell him more than she wanted him to know about her personal life. What had she been thinking, blurting out that information about Lewis's marriage plans? She hadn't even told Lewis she knew, and since his plans to marry Grace hadn't officially been published during church yet, she had no right to tell anyone.

By the time Miriam reached the back porch, her thoughts took her in another direction as she remembered the marriage proposal she'd had from Amos that morning. She wondered if the man actually thought he'd be doing her a favor by marrying her, solving the problem of where she would live after Lewis's marriage to Grace and all. If she were to marry Amos, it would be her doing him the favor, not the other way around.

She entered the kitchen and tried to focus her thoughts on what she should be doing. Baking some muffins and making a pot of baked beans for tonight's supper—wasn't that what she'd planned to do after returning home from the mud sale? Maybe if she got busy, it would take her mind off Amos Hilty and Nick McCormick.

"How could Lewis keep something as important as his decision to marry Grace from me and yet tell Amos?" Miriam fumed as she pulled a tin of flour down from the cupboard. "Men are all alike. None of them can be trusted! I wonder who else Lewis has told, and how many other people have been hiding the truth from me. If people would talk behind my back about how William jilted me, then who knows what else they're saying?"

Miriam soon had her pot of beans cooking on top of the stove and had just put a pan of muffins in the oven when she heard the sound of heavy footsteps clomping up the porch steps. A few seconds later, Lewis entered the kitchen with a broken harness hanging over one arm. "Umm. . . something smells good," he said, sniffing the air.

"It's muffins and baked beans for supper," Miriam said.

Lewis dropped the harness to the floor, then pulled out a chair and sat down. "How'd the mud sale go today?"

"Fine. I sold both of my quilts, and that gives me a little more money toward Rebekah's hospital bills."

"That's good to hear."

Miriam stirred the pot of beans but said nothing more. She was afraid if she voiced the thoughts in her head, she and Lewis might end up in an argument.

He cleared his throat a couple of times. "Uh, Miriam, I think the two of us need to have a little heart-to-heart talk."

She turned down the burner on the stove and took a

seat at the table across from him. "If it's about you and Grace, I already know."

"Jah, Amos told me he'd let the cat out of the bag. I'm sorry you had to hear it secondhand. I was planning to tell you, but I was just waiting for the right time."

"Didn't you think I could handle the news? Don't you know by now that I can handle most anything that comes my way—even disappointments?" Miriam's voice sounded harsh even to her own ears.

"You're disappointed because Grace and I plan to be married?" Lewis shook his head. "I never expected you to be jealous."

It was true. Miriam was jealous, but she never would have admitted that to her brother. "This has nothing to do with jealousy. It has to do with the fact that you told Amos, who isn't even a family member, before you told me, your only sister." She paused for a breath. "With so many other changes having gone on in our lives lately, this news is a bit too much to take."

"What do you mean by that?"

"First, Papa dies, and then Rebekah gets injured. Next, Mom moves out of the house, and now I have to move out, as well."

"I don't expect you to move out. This is your home, too, and I want you to stay here as long as you like."

"I'm sure you're only saying that to be kind, Lewis. I would never dream of staying on here once you and Grace are married. It wouldn't be fair to either of you. And quite frankly, I'm not sure I would enjoy it much, either."

Lewis's forehead wrinkled. "Why not?"

"I've had complete control of the household for several months now, and another woman in the house would be a difficult adjustment. I have my own ways of doing things, and I'm certain Grace has hers, as well."

"But I'm sure Grace would be most understanding," Lewis argued. "Besides, she'll probably need your help with a lot of things."

Miriam shook her head. "For a time she might, but soon she would come to think of the house as hers and want to run it her own way. It's only normal that she would, and I won't stand in her way. Besides, you newlyweds will need your privacy. When is the wedding to take place? Have you set a date yet?"

"We're planning to be married on the third Thursday of November."

Miriam nodded stiffly. "Maybe I'll see if Mom's willing to move back home, and then I could move in with Andrew and Sarah when the time gets closer to the wedding."

"I suppose there's nothing I can say to change your mind?"

"No, nothing."

"I can't believe I was dumb enough to propose to Miriam this morning," Amos mumbled as he traveled down the road in his buggy toward the Weavers' place, where his daughter had spent the previous night and would be waiting for him to pick her up. "Now Miriam's really convinced that I only want to marry her for the sake of convenience."

He gave his horse the signal to trot, hoping a brisker ride might smooth the edges of his frayed nerves a bit. All day he had berated himself for everything he'd said to Miriam—first telling her about Lewis's plans to marry Grace; then asking her to marry him; and finally, allowing her to believe he didn't love her, but only wanted a mother for Mary Ellen. What a *dummkopp* he had been!

I do love Miriam and have for a long time, he thought ruefully. *But what good is that if she doesn't return my feelings?* Miriam had made it clear by her actions that she felt no love for Amos, and today, when she'd actually spoken the words, he had been crushed. At that point he would have made a bigger fool of himself if he had opened his heart to her, and he was sure her response would have only pierced him further by a firm rejection.

"Well, I won't ask again," he shouted into the wind. "If Miriam changes her mind, then she'll have to come to me."

On Monday after school let out for the day, Miriam went to Strasburg to do some shopping. As she passed a boardinghouse situated on a quiet street on the south side of town, she remembered Nick mentioning that his aunt ran a boardinghouse. Miriam thought this particular home, tall and stately, shaded by leafy elm trees, and surrounded by a white picket fence, looked like the perfect place to live. It would offer solitude, seclusion, and no more farm duties or household chores to take up her time. Living in a boardinghouse would probably mean that all of her meals would be provided, and her only real responsibilities would be to keep her room clean and, of course, continue to teach at the Amish schoolhouse.

Just think of all the free time I would have for reading, quilting, and visiting friends and family, she told herself. But of course, that idea was about as ridiculous as the thought of her marrying Amos Hilty. The boardinghouse wasn't run by anyone Amish, which was obvious by the electrical wires running to it. And Miriam was too committed to her family to do anything that would hurt them or get her shunned.

She moved on down the street but had only taken a few steps when she bumped into a man. Her mouth dropped open. "Nick!"

Nick couldn't believe his good fortune. He had run into Miriam twice in one week, and that pleased him more than he cared to admit. He smiled and winked at her. "It's good to see you again, Miriam. I've been thinking about you and wondering how you're doing."

"I'm managing."

"You're looking well—as beautiful as ever in fact."

Miriam wrinkled her nose. "Are you trying to flatter me?"

"Not at all." He took a step toward her. "So, what are you doing in this neck of the woods?"

"I was about to ask you the same question."

"My aunt lives here." He turned and pointed to the stately home Miriam had been admiring. "That's the boardinghouse she runs. Too bad you don't live in Strasburg. I come here frequently to see my aunt, and if you lived in Strasburg, we'd be able to see each other more often, too."

Miriam's cheeks turned pink, and she stared at the ground.

"If we saw each other more, we'd be able to find out if

we could ever see eye-to-eye on anything."

"I—I would like to move," Miriam said as she lifted her gaze to meet his. "But it won't be here."

"How come?"

"I'm sure you know why, Nick. An Amish woman's place is with her family."

"What if your family lived here? Then would you consider moving?"

"Of course, but I have no family living in Strasburg."

"What if I was your family?"

"Wh-what are you saying?" she croaked, her voice all but gone.

"I'm saying that you could marry me. I'm not getting any younger, and maybe it's time I settled down with a good woman—and a beautiful one at that."

Miriam's face turned even redder, and he noticed that perspiration had beaded up on her forehead.

"You're making fun of me, aren't you?" she asked in a near whisper.

"No, I'm not. Listen, I've surprised myself as much as I have you by popping the question, but now that I have, I kind of like the idea." Nick scrubbed his hand across his chin, realizing that he'd forgotten to shave that morning. "You know, I never thought I'd hear myself say this, but the thought of coming home at night to a good, home-cooked meal and a beautiful wife waiting for me is kind of appealing."

He took another step toward her and was glad when she didn't back away. "I know we're about as different as your buggy horse and my sports car, but maybe we could make it work. After all, we do seem to find one another easy to talk to, and there's a certain kind of chemistry between us. In fact, this could turn out to be the adventure of our lives."

"But. . .but—I would have to leave the Amish faith if I were to marry an outsider," she stammered. "I'd be excommunicated and shunned by my family and friends."

Nick reached for her hand and pulled her toward his car. "Let's go for a ride and talk this over."

At first, Miriam looked as if she might go with him, but then she halted and slowly shook head. "You've not said anything about love, Nick."

He shrugged and pulled his fingers through the back of his hair. "Who says there has to be love in a marriage? There's chemistry between us; you can't deny it."

"I could never marry without love, and leaving my faith to marry you is impossible." She turned on her heel and started to walk away, but he reached out and took hold of her arm so she was facing him again.

"If two people are as attracted to each other as I believe we are, then nothing else should matter."

Tears pooled in Miriam's eyes, and she pulled away. "I–I'm sure you meant well, asking me to leave my faith and marry you, but I can't. We hardly know each other, and even if we did, I think we both know that things could never work out between us. My faith has weakened in the last several months, but I won't let my family down by leaving our church for a relationship that's built on nothing more than a physical attraction."

"Is that your final word?"

"It has to be." She turned toward her buggy, parked across the street. "I need to go. I have chores to do at home."

Nick felt a strange mixture of relief and disappointment as he watched Miriam climb into her buggy. He didn't know what had come over him to pop the question like that, and now he felt kind of stupid. It wasn't his style to let his guard down like that or make himself so vulnerable. Asking Miriam to marry him, when they were so different, bordered on ridiculous. Maybe that was why he'd proposed—because he knew it would never work and that she would say no.

As Miriam was about to pull away from the curb, Nick gathered his wits and called, "I wish you the best, Miriam. If you ever need a shoulder to cry on or just want to talk, you know where to reach me."

Miriam sat up in bed and wiped the perspiration from her forehead. She'd been dreaming about three men. First there had been William Graber, smiling and waving at her as he drove away in his buggy with his new bride. Then Nick McCormick had come onto the scene, traipsing after her with his camera and calling her "fair lady." Miriam had pulled her dark bonnet down over her face, and when she removed it again, Nick was gone. Amos Hilty stood before her, holding a bouquet of pansies. *What did that strange dream mean?* she wondered. *Was there any significance to it?*

She glanced at the clock on the table by her bed and frowned. It was only four in the morning. She didn't have to get up for another hour, yet she was afraid to go back to sleep. What if her dream continued? She didn't want to think about William, Nick, or Amos. For that matter, it would suit her fine if she never thought of any man ever again!

CHAPTER

22

As the months flew by and Lewis's wedding drew closer, Miriam began to feel a sense of panic. Mom wasn't willing to move back home and allow Miriam to take her place at Andrew and Sarah's, so Miriam had about decided that she would have to stay at the house with Lewis and Grace after they were married. She hoped the newlyweds would understand and that she would be able to handle not being in charge of the house once Grace took over.

One morning on the way to school, Miriam passed Amos's rig. He and Mary Ellen were obviously headed for the schoolhouse. Mary Ellen leaned out the window and waved. "Hello, Teacher Mim!"

Miriam waved in response and urged her horse into a trot. She didn't think it would be right for any of her students to arrive at school before their teacher did.

As she pulled into the school yard a short time later, she was relieved to see that none of the other children were there yet. She halted her horse, climbed down from the buggy, and had just started to unhitch the mare when the Hiltys showed up.

Miriam watched as Amos got out and went around to help his daughter down. In spite of her mistrust of the man, she had to admit that he was a good father, and Mary Ellen obviously loved him very much.

Just as the child stepped down from the buggy, her foot snagged in the hem of her dress. She looked down and gasped. "It's torn! Pappy, please don't make me go to school today. The others will laugh at me; I just know they will."

The sympathetic look Amos first gave his daughter turned to obvious frustration. "I can't do anything about your dress right now, Mary Ellen. We'll take it over to Maudie Miller's after school lets out. She can mend it for you then."

Mary Ellen shot him an imploring look. "No, Pappy, please. I don't want to wait that long."

Feeling the child's embarrassment as if it were her own, Miriam stepped forward. "Let me get my horse put in the corral, and then we'll go inside the schoolhouse. I'll mend your dress before the others get here."

When Amos turned to face Miriam, he wore a look of astonishment. "Would you really do that for her? Do you have the necessary tools?"

Miriam gave a small laugh. "You needn't be so surprised, Amos. In spite of what some may say about me, I've actually been known to do a few acts of kindness."

"I–I didn't mean to say—"

"Never mind. Just go on your way, and Mary Ellen will be fine."

"Well, let me take care of your horse then."

"Danki." Miriam put her hand across Mary Ellen's back and guided her toward the schoolhouse; then she turned back and called to Amos, "Oh, and by the way—you don't use tools to sew, but I do keep a small kit full of sewing supplies in my desk for such an emergency as this."

Amos mumbled something under his breath and headed over to Miriam's buggy to unhitch the horse.

When Miriam entered the schoolhouse with Mary Ellen, she saw right away that the child's face was streaked with tears. The first thing she did was to dip a clean cloth into the bucket of water she kept nearby and gently wipe the little girl's face. "Now stand on this chair while I hem up your dress," she instructed.

"How come?"

"It would be quicker and easier if your dress was off, but some of the other kinner may arrive soon, and you wouldn't want to be caught without your dress on, would you?"

Mary Ellen shook her head. "No, Teacher Mim."

"Now, hold real still, and no rutsching."

"I'll try not to squirm, I promise."

Miriam threaded a needle and began the task of putting Mary Ellen's hem back into place. When the job was completed, Mary Ellen smiled happily and jumped down from the chair. "Danki, Teacher. You did a good job, and it looks real nice now."

"Gern gschehne—you are welcome," Miriam replied as the door opened and three of the Hoelwarth boys burst into the room.

She was glad the sewing job had been completed, because the Hoelwarths were all teases, and they would probably have taunted Mary Ellen if they'd seen her standing on a chair getting her dress mended.

All the way home, Amos thought about Miriam and how she had seemed so concerned about Mary Ellen's torn dress.

"Miriam has a lot of good in her, Lord," he said out loud. "Trouble is she doesn't seem to know it. So maybe what we need here is some way to bring out all that goodness."

Keeping his focus straight ahead, Amos guided his horse and buggy down the road, allowing his thoughts to wander back to the day when he and Miriam were still kinner in school. . . .

"Let's get a game of baseball going," Noah Troyer shouted when the school children were dismissed for morning recess.

Amos always enjoyed a good game of ball, so he eagerly grabbed the baseball glove from under his desk and headed outside to the playground. It was a hot, humid day, and before he joined the game, he made a quick trip to the pump around back for a drink of water. He came across Miriam and her youngest brother, Lewis, whose face was wet with tears. "I wanna play ball," the boy wailed, "but Noah says I'm too young, and he told me to go play on the swings with the girls."

Miriam dropped to her knees and wrapped her arms around her brother. "It's okay. You and I can have our own game of ball."

Lewis looked up at her, and a slight smile tugged at the corners of his lips. "Really?"

She nodded. "I was going to read for a while, but I'll go inside and get a ball from Teacher Leah."

Amos was tempted to ask if he might join in their game, but the shyness he felt whenever he was around girls prevented him from saying anything. So he gave the pump handle a couple of thrusts and took a big drink of water.

Miriam's got such a kind heart, he thought, as he headed over to the ball field a few minutes later. *Someday, if I ever get up the nerve, I'm gonna ask that girl to marry me.*

❧

"Well, I've finally asked her to marry me," Amos mumbled, as his thoughts returned to the present. "But unless God changes Miriam's heart, I'll never have the chance to show how much I love her."

A truck sped by Amos's buggy just then, causing the horse to spook and veer off to the left. Amos gripped the reins and shouted, "Whoa, there. Steady, boy!"

He struggled to gain control of the skittish animal, but it was too late. The buggy flipped onto its side as the horse broke free and took off down the road. Except for a couple of bumps and bruises, Amos was relieved that he had escaped serious injury. The last thing Mary Ellen needed was to lose another parent or to have him end up in the hospital.

He reached over and pushed the opposite door of the buggy open, then crawled out. "That's what I get for letting my mind wander and not paying better attention to my driving," he muttered. "Now I've got a buggy to repair, not to mention a runaway horse that needs to be found."

❧

The morning went by quickly, and soon it was lunchtime.

Miriam watched as Mary Ellen opened her metal lunch box. The child ate hungrily, but Miriam was appalled to see what Amos had given his daughter to eat. The contents of the lunch box revealed a biscuit, some dried beef jerky, a green apple, and a bottle of water.

Miriam wondered if Mary Ellen's father had been in a hurry that morning or was completely ignorant as to a child's nutritional needs. She had seen some of the pitiful lunches he'd made Mary Ellen in the past, but none of them had looked this bad.

Miriam shook her head and sighed, wishing she hadn't already eaten her own lunch, for she would have shared some of her sandwich with Mary Ellen. *That man really does need a wife, and Mary Ellen surely needs a mother.*

She looked away from the little girl and directed her gaze out the window. She had to get her mind on something else. She could feel one of her sick headaches coming on and knew she had to ward it off, so she reached into her desk drawer and retrieved a bottle of white willow bark capsules. The Thermos of water that normally sat on her desk was half full, so she popped two capsules into her mouth and swallowed them down.

Miriam was relieved when all the children had finished their lunches and filed outside to play. Now maybe she would have a few minutes of peace. But that was not to be. After only a brief time, a commotion outside ended her solitude.

When Miriam went out to investigate, she found a group of children gathered around Mary Ellen. This was not the first time she'd witnessed some of them picking on the child, and she wondered what the problem could be.

Mary Ellen lay crumpled on the ground, whimpering pathetically, while several of the older boys, including two of the Hoelwarths, pointed at her and jeered. John Hoelwarth held a long stick in his hand and was poking Mary Ellen with it. "Get up, baby Hilty. Quit your cryin'. You're such a little boppli!"

Angrily, Miriam grabbed the stick from John and whirled him around to face her. "What is going on here, and why are you poking at a defenseless little girl and calling her a baby?"

John hung his head as he made little circles in the dirt with the toe of his boot. "I was only tryin' to make her quit bawling. She sounds like one of my daed's heifers."

The children's laughter rang out, vibrating through Miriam's tensed body. "Quiet!" she shouted. "I want to know why Mary Ellen was crying, and why you've been teasing her again."

"Look at her hair, Teacher," Sara King said. "She hasn't got a mamm, and her daed can't fix it so it stays up the way it should. She looks pretty silly, don't ya think?"

Miriam bent down and gently pulled Mary Ellen to her feet. "Come inside now. I'll fix your hair and clean you up." To the other children, she said, "You may all stay outside until I call you. Then we'll discuss what's happened here." She turned and led Mary Ellen to the schoolhouse.

It took nearly half an hour for Miriam to get the child calmed down, cleaned up, and her hair put back in place.

"Try not to let the kinner's teasing bother you," Miriam said. "Some of the older ones like to make trouble. Everyone but you will be made to stay after school."

"It don't matter," Mary Ellen said with a shake of her

head. "They'll always tease me, 'cause I have no mamm. If Mama were alive still, she'd sew my dresses so the hems stayed up. She would fix me good lunches like the others have, and she'd do better with my hair then Pappy does. He tries real hard, but he can't do some things the way a mudder can." Mary Ellen sniffed deeply, although she did manage a weak smile. "Teacher Mim, I sure wish you was my mamm."

Miriam swallowed hard. There was no doubt about it. Mary Ellen needed her. For that matter, Amos probably did, too. And as much as she hated to admit it, she needed them—or at least their home to live in. She knew she could never give up her faith to marry Nick, and perhaps a marriage without love wouldn't be such a bad thing. If she married Amos, all concerned would have mutual needs met.

Heartrending though the decision was, Miriam knew what she wanted to do. She would tell Amos that she had changed her mind and decided to accept his proposal, and she must do it soon before she lost her nerve.

"I will not tease" had been written on the blackboard one hundred times by each of the boys who had tormented Mary Ellen, and Miriam had kept the entire class after school and given them a lecture on kindness.

It had been a long, emotionally exhausting day at school, and Miriam was glad it was finally over. Now she must ride over to the Hiltys' and speak to Amos before she lost her nerve. The decision to marry him had not been an easy one, and her mind was full of questions. Would he still want to marry her? Would Mary Ellen be happy about it? What would her own family think? Most of all, she wondered if she could really make herself go through with it.

Miriam poured herself a glass of water and swallowed the two white willow bark capsules she had put in her mouth. If she was going to face Amos, it had better not be with a pounding headache. With a sigh of resignation, she gathered up her things and headed out the door.

"I love you, Grandma," Rebekah said as she smiled up at Anna, her pale blue eyes gleaming in the sunlight that streamed through Anna's bedroom window.

Anna smiled in return and pushed Rebekah's wheel-chair closer to the African violets sitting on her window ledge. "I love you, too, child."

"I like the purple ones best," Rebekah said, reaching out to touch the tip of one leafy bloom.

"Jah, I agree."

Anna knew there weren't many things Rebekah could do without the use of her legs, but helping water and prune the plants was one thing she could do to make herself feel useful. Besides, Rebekah seemed taken with the pretty flow-ers and was always eager to help out whenever Anna said it was time for watering, pruning, or repotting some of the plants that had grown too big for their containers.

"I'm glad you came to live with us, Grandma. Otherwise, I would have had to come all the way over to your house to see your pretty houseplants." Rebekah sighed. "Of course, someone would have to drive me there, since I can't walk to your place the way I used to do."

A stab of regret pierced Anna's heart. She hated to see any of her family suffer.

"I'm glad I live here, too," she said, patting Rebekah on top of her head.

"Mama says you write stories about me sometimes for the newspaper," Rebekah said, changing the subject.

"Jah, that's true. I write about many things that go on in our community."

"Do you think I could write some stories for the paper?"

Anna smiled. "I don't see why not. In fact, someday after

I'm gone, maybe you can take over my column."

"I'd like that, but I don't want you to leave—not ever."

"If God allows it, I hope to be around for a long time yet."
Anna motioned to another one of her plants. "After all, who
would keep these pretty violets watered if I wasn't here?"

Rebekah giggled. "I guess I could water 'em, but it's a lot
more fun when we do it together, don't ya think?"

"Jah, everything is always more fun when you have someone to do it with." Anna's thoughts turned to Miriam, who
seemed to prefer being alone these days. *Or maybe she just
doesn't like me butting into her business.*

Anna closed her eyes and lifted a silent prayer. *Heavenly
Father, I've asked this before, I know, but I'm beseeching You to fill
my daughter's heart with peace, joy, and love. Oh, and would You
remind me if necessary that it's You who can work on Miriam's
heart, not me? Amen.*

Mary Ellen was sitting on the front porch, playing with a
fluffy white kitten, when Miriam pulled into the yard. The
child waved and ran toward Miriam as soon as she climbed
down from her buggy. "Teacher Mim, you came to visit!
Look, my hem's still in place," she said, lifting the corner
of her dress.

Miriam nodded. "I see that, and I also see that your hair
is in place yet."

Mary Ellen's grin stretched ear to ear. "You did a good
job with it. Don't tell Pappy I said so, but you're much better
at fixin' hair than he is."

Miriam smiled. She couldn't help but like the sweet

little girl. Mary Ellen obviously needed a woman to train her to do all the feminine things her father was unable to do. "Speaking of your daed," Miriam said, "where is he? I need to talk to him."

"He's out in his shop. I can take you there, if you want."

"Danki for offering, but I think it would be best if you stayed on the porch and played with your kitten. Your daed and I have some grown-up things we need to say to each other. We'll join you on the porch when we're done. How's that sound?"

Mary Ellen's eyes widened. "You're not gonna tell Pappy about those boys teasin' me today, are you?"

Miriam shook her head. "What I have to say to him has nothing to do with the Hoelwarth boys."

The child released a sigh of obvious relief. "I'll play 'til you're done talking. Then maybe we can all have cookies and milk."

"Jah, maybe so," she said, turning toward Amos's black-smith shop.

Miriam had never been inside his shop before, and when she entered the building a few minutes later, she saw no sign of Amos but was surprised at how neat and orderly everything looked. She noticed a large wooden table with several small compartments, each filled neatly with tools of all shapes and sizes. A stack of firewood stood along one wall next to a tall brick fireplace and an anvil. A large rack also rested nearby, with horseshoes of all sizes hanging from it. A metal desk, a few chairs, and a filing cabinet took up the corner area near the door, and a stack of magazines lay on a small table nearby. *Probably for customers to browse as they wait for their horses to be shod,* she thought. *Amos may not do such a good job of putting his daughter's hair in place, but he sure runs a neat, organized place of business.*

"Amos, are you about?" Miriam called, cupping her hands around her mouth.

A few seconds later, he stepped through the doorway of the smaller room that was attached to the main part of his shop. "Oh, it's you, Miriam. I—I was just cleanin' things up in the other room and didn't realize anyone had come in," he said, looking kind of red-faced and flustered.

"I just came in." Miriam made a sweeping gesture of the room. "This is quite impressive. There must be a lot of work involved in what you do."

He nodded. "Jah, always seems to be a lot of horses that need shoeing."

Feeling the need to stall for time, as her resolve began to weaken, Miriam decided to question him about his business. "How often do horses need to be shod?"

"You don't know?"

She shook her head. "Papa used to take care of that kind of thing, and now that he's gone, it's become Lewis's job to see that our horses are looked after."

"Well, most need shoeing every six to eight weeks on the average. In the summertime the pavement is softer because of the heat, so that can loosen the shoes." Amos leaned against his workbench and folded his arms. "Plus, the horses are stamping at flies all the time, and that action can wear down the shoes pretty good."

"Do they need to be shod that often during the winter?"

"Not usually. Most horses can go eight or even ten weeks

between visits to my shop during the colder months."

"I see." Miriam shuffled her feet a few times, wondering how best to broach the subject of his earlier marriage proposal.

"I want to thank you for mending Mary Ellen's dress this morning," Amos said, taking their conversation in a different direction.

"No problem. I was glad to do it."

"So what brings you out our way? Does your horse need new shoes or did you need to speak with me about Mary Ellen?"

"Neither one. Actually, I. . .uh. . .came to talk about your offer of marriage."

"Really?"

She nodded.

"Have you been thinking it over then?"

"I have, and if the offer's still open, then I've decided that I will marry you."

Amos dropped his arms to his sides and took a step toward Miriam. "I don't know what caused you to change your mind, but I'm glad you did. I think Mary Ellen will be real pleased about this, too."

"Mary Ellen is the reason I did change my mind," Miriam stated truthfully. No point in letting him think otherwise. "I've come to the conclusion that the child needs a woman's care." She paused for a quick breath, hoping she hadn't offended him. "It's not that you aren't doing a fine job with her, but—"

"I understand what you're trying to say. My daughter needs a mudder. She needs someone who can do all the feminine things I can't do for her. As you know, I do have some concerns about how your attitude might affect Mary Ellen, and if there's to be a marriage, I need your word that you won't let Mary Ellen see your bitterness. It's important that you help me train her in God's ways, and we both must set a good example for her." He reached out and touched her arm.

Miriam pulled away, feeling as if she'd been stung by a bee and wondering if she had done the right thing after all. Could she really keep from letting her bitter heart be noticeable to Mary Ellen? Could she set the child a good example?

"I—I promise to do my best by Mary Ellen," she finally murmured.

"Danki." Amos smiled. "I need you as well, Miriam. I need a wife."

She gulped. "Do—do you mean just for cooking and cleaning, or in every way?"

He shuffled his feet and stared at the concrete floor. "I. . . that is. . .of course I would like a physical relationship with my wife, but if you don't feel ready—"

"I'm not ready. I may never be ready for that, and if this will be a problem for you, then it might be best if we forget about getting married."

He shook his head. "No, please. I'll wait until you feel ready for my physical touch. Until then, we'll live together as friends and learn more about one another. Maybe as our friendship grows, things will change between us."

"I don't want to give you any false hope, Amos. I don't think I can ever love you," Miriam said as gently as she knew how.

"We'll see how it goes." Amos turned toward the door with his shoulders slumped. "Shall we go up to the house and tell Mary Ellen our news? I'm sure she will be glad."

"I—I hope so." Miriam could hardly believe Amos had accepted her conditions so easily. She figured he must be desperate for a housekeeper and a mother for his child. Of course, she'd had to agree to set a good example for Mary Ellen and teach her about spiritual things. She just hoped she wouldn't fall short of that promise.

Mary Ellen was still on the porch playing with her kitten when Amos and Miriam joined her a few minutes later. She looked up at them expectantly. "Can we have some cookies and milk, Pappy?"

He smiled down at her. "Jah. That sounds like a fine idea. Let's go inside, and we'll sit at the table, eat our cookies, and have a little talk. Miriam and I have something important we want to tell you."

When they entered the house, Miriam realized it was the first time she'd been inside the Hilty home since Ruth's funeral. The place wasn't dirty, just cluttered and unkempt. If there had ever been any doubt in her mind about whether Amos needed a wife or not, it was erased. The touch of a woman in the house was greatly needed.

Amos poured tall glasses of milk, while Mary Ellen went to the cookie jar and got out some cookies that were obviously store-bought. When they'd all taken seats at the table, Amos cleared his throat a couple of times and said, "Mary Ellen, how would you like it if Pappy got married again?"

The child tipped her head and looked at him with a quizzical expression. "A new mamm for me?"

Amos nodded. "And a *fraa* for me."

Mary Ellen turned to face Miriam. "Is it you, Teacher Mim? Are you gonna be Pappy's wife?"

"How would you feel about that?" Miriam asked.

"I'd like it very much." Mary Ellen gave Miriam a wide grin. "When can ya come to live with us?"

Amos chuckled. "Not 'til we're married, little one."

"When will that be?"

Amos looked at Miriam, and she shrugged. "As soon as possible, I suppose."

He nodded in agreement. "I'll speak to Bishop Benner right away."

CHAPTER 24

Miriam's family seemed pleased when she told them she was going to marry Amos—Mom most of all. Miriam was certain that everyone thought she was marrying Amos because she had changed her mind about him and perhaps had even come to love him. She had no intention of telling them otherwise.

However, Miriam had a hunch that Crystal hadn't been so easily deceived. She had acted a bit strange when Miriam gave her and Jonas the news, although she hadn't said anything more than a pleasant "congratulations."

I suppose I'll have to tell her the truth if she asks, Miriam thought as she cleaned up the kitchen after breakfast one morning. Crystal had always been able to see right through her, even when they were children and Miriam had tried to hide her feelings when she was upset about something.

Forcing her thoughts aside, Miriam finished her cleaning and had just decided to take a walk, when Crystal showed up.

"I came by to see if you'd like to go to town with me to do some shopping," she said, stepping into the kitchen.

"Right now?"

"Jah."

"I don't feel much like shopping today," Miriam said as the two of them took seats at the table. "But I appreciate you asking."

"Do you have other plans for the day?"

"Not really. Just the usual work around here." Miriam chose not to mention that she had planned to take a walk.

"Then let's get out for a while. It'll do us both some good. Ever since school let out for the summer, you've been staying around here too much."

"I like being at home. It feels safe, and I don't have to answer to anyone." Miriam's chin quivered as she sat on the edge of her kitchen chair, blinking back the tears that had gathered in her eyes. She felt Crystal's arm encircle her shoulders.

"What is it, Miriam? Why are you crying?"

"It–it's just that. . ." Miriam's voice faltered. "I'm not sure how things will go once Amos and I are married."

"You're already having second thoughts?"

Miriam's only reply was a quick nod.

"I was afraid of that, and your tight muscles are proof of it." Crystal massaged the knots in Miriam's neck and shoulders. "When you gave Jonas and me the news about you and Amos, I suspected that your heart wasn't in the decision. Why are you marrying him, Miriam? What changed your mind?"

"I only agreed to marry Amos because of Mary Ellen." Miriam sniffed deeply. "That sweet little girl needs a mother so badly." She wiped the tears from her face with the back of her hand. "I know I've said many times that I would never marry without love, but there will be love—Mary Ellen's love for me, and my love for her."

"I understand, but what about love for Amos?"

"He's a nice enough man, but I must admit that I don't love him."

"Then how can you marry him when there's no love between you?"

Miriam shrugged. "I can live without a man's love; I've done it for some time. My biggest concern has to do with trust."

"What do you mean?"

"I don't know if I can trust Amos."

"Trust him how?"

"He's agreed not to force a physical relationship on me, but men are selfish, and—"

"Miriam, all men are not like William Graber. Amos appears to be an honest and upright man. I don't believe he will hurt you the way William did. However, since you obviously feel no love for him and you say he doesn't love you, then—"

"He doesn't love me."

"Then maybe it would be best if you don't make a life-long commitment to him. As you know, divorce isn't an acceptable option among the Old Order Amish, and it isn't fair of you to expect Amos to enter into a relationship that won't be a real marriage."

"You think I should tell Amos I've changed my mind and call off the wedding?"

"I'm only saying that I feel you need to give the matter

more prayer and thought. I want to see you happy, and if you marry someone you don't love, how can you ever be truly happy?"

Miriam shrugged. "I've come to realize that life's not always so joyous."

"Until you get rid of your feelings of mistrust and allow God to fill your heart with peace, you'll never find love or happiness."

"I've learned to manage without those things." Miriam swallowed against the bitter taste of bile rising to her throat. "Besides, if I marry Amos, it will benefit others, as well."

"Like who?"

"First of all, I won't be living here with Lewis and Grace, so they'll be happier. Then there's Mom. I'm sure she will be pleased to see me married off. Mary Ellen will have a mother to care for her needs properly. And of course, Amos will have someone to cook and clean for him."

"What about your needs, Miriam? How will they be met?"

"My needs will be provided—I'll have a roof over my head and a child to help Amos raise." Miriam drew in a deep breath. "I hope that as my best friend, you will support me in this decision."

"Of course I support you," Crystal said with a nod. "I'll help with your wedding plans in any way I can. If you're doing what you feel your heart is telling you to do, then I'll support you with my love and prayers, too."

Miriam stared at a dark spot on the tablecloth. It was probably a coffee stain that would never come clean—just like the stain of William's deception that would never leave her heart. "I—I feel that this is the right thing to do."

"All right then; enough has been said." Crystal patted Miriam gently on the back. "Now, are you sure you won't go shopping with me?"

Miriam pushed her chair aside and stood. "I guess there are a few things I might need before the wedding. So, jah, I'll go along."

⁂

"How come you're staring at the newspaper and smiling, Grandma?" Rebekah asked, as she rolled her wheelchair up to the table where Anna sat. "Is there somethin' funny in that paper?"

Anna smiled. "I was reading an article written in our Amish newspaper by a woman who lives in Kentucky. She found a nest of baby mice in her box of wedding china."

Rebekah giggled. "I bet Aunt Miriam would scream if she found a baby *maus* in with her wedding dishes."

"You're probably right about that."

"I'm glad Aunt Miriam is gonna marry Mary Ellen's daed. That will make my best friend my cousin, jah?"

"I expect it will." *I just hope things turn out well between my daughter and Amos,* Anna thought. *I've got a feeling things aren't quite right between those two.*

⁂

The Country Store was Miriam's favorite place to shop, and today she found it unusually busy. Not only were there several Amish customers milling about, but a lot of tourists had crowded into the small building. Miriam disliked crowds, especially when she knew they were watching her and all the other Amish who often shopped here. Crystal had gone across the street to the quilt shop, and Miriam wondered if it was crowded there, too.

When she moved to the back of the store where the household items were kept, she spotted an oil lamp she wanted to look at, but it was too high to reach. She glanced around, hoping to find a store clerk to help, but none were in sight. She turned away, deciding to look at some other items instead.

"Are you in need of some help?"

Thinking one of the clerks had seen her and had come to help, Miriam replied, "Jah, I would like to see—" Her mouth fell open as she turned her head. "Nick! What are you doing here?"

He smiled his usual heart-melting smile. "I like to come here on weekends. I get lots of story ideas from watching the people."

"You mean *my* people, don't you?"

Nick gave her a playful wink. "The Amish are quite interesting. Especially you, fair lady."

Every nerve in Miriam's body tingled, and her cheeks grew warm. She'd always considered herself quite plain, but in Nick's presence, she almost believed she was pretty.

"You know, I wonder if this could be fate, us always running into each other." Nick brought his head close to hers. "Maybe we really are meant to be together, Miriam."

She leaned away. What if someone she knew saw her engaged in such a personal conversation with this man? "We're not meant to be together, Nick. I'm sure you know that."

"Yeah, you're probably right," he whispered. "But if you

weren't Amish, I might not have given up so easily on pursuing a relationship with you."

Miriam's hands felt clammy, and her heart beat fast against her chest. She had to get away from Nick as quickly as possible. Yet she didn't want to leave the store until she had completed her shopping. "If you'll excuse me, I must find a clerk for some assistance."

"What kind of help do you need?"

She pointed to the shelf above. "I'd like to see that kerosene lamp."

"No problem." Nick easily reached for the lamp and handed it down to her. "Here you go."

"Thank you."

"So, how are things with you these days?"

"Fine. I'm. . .uh. . .getting married in a few weeks."

Nick's eyebrows lifted in obvious surprise. "What was that?"

"I said, 'I'm getting married in a few weeks.' "

"Kind of sudden, isn't it?"

She stared at the floor for a few seconds, then finally lifted her gaze.

"Not really. I've been thinking about it for some time."

He grunted. "And who's the lucky fellow?"

"He–he's a nice Amish man."

"I didn't think he'd be anything but Amish. You made it pretty clear the day I proposed that you could never be happy with someone who didn't share your beliefs and traditions. So as much as I hate to admit it, you were right to turn down my offer of marriage. We both know it probably wouldn't have worked for us."

Nick lifted his shoulders in a shrug. "Besides, I'll be moving next week, and I doubt you'd have wanted to move to Ohio, much less become English."

Her mouth dropped open. "You're leaving Lancaster and going to Ohio?"

He nodded. "Got a job offer at the newspaper in Columbus, and I couldn't say no to the paycheck they're offering."

"I see."

"I won't be but a few hours from Holmes County, which I understand is where a large settlement of Amish is, so maybe I'll get the privilege of writing some more stories about your people."

"*The Budget* office is located in Sugarcreek, Ohio," Miriam said. "Maybe you can stop in there sometime and see how they put it together."

"That's not a bad idea. And if the job at the newspaper in Columbus doesn't work out, I could put in my résumé at *The Budget.*" Nick chuckled and leaned close to her again. "I don't suppose I dare ask for a kiss from the bride-to-be before we part ways?"

Miriam's face heated up as she shook her head and took a step back.

"Well, you can't blame a guy for trying." He winked. "Guess a word of congratulations would be more appropriate under the circumstances, huh?"

"Jah."

"Well, congratulations then."

Before Miriam could comment, he smiled and said, "Say, I'd like to do something for you, if you'll let me."

"Wh-what is it?"

"Let me buy that oil lamp. It will be my wedding present to you. Whenever you look at it, maybe you'll remember me and know that I'm happy you've found true love."

Miriam swallowed against the lump rising in her throat. How could Nick possibly know she hadn't found love at all but was only marrying Amos so she would have another place to live and Mary Ellen could have a mother? If she tried to explain things, would he understand? Probably not, since his way of life was so different than hers.

"Please, don't deny me the pleasure of giving you the lamp," he said in a pleading tone. "It would make me happy to do something special for you."

Miriam shrugged as she released a sigh. "I suppose it will be all right." After all, who was she to stand in the way of anyone's happiness?

CHAPTER

25

As Miriam's wedding day approached, she found herself feeling increasingly anxious. She wondered at times if she could make herself go through with the marriage or if she should cancel it and go back to teaching. But then she would think about how she really did want to find another place to live before Lewis married Grace. Besides, Mary Ellen desperately needed her. With those thoughts firmly in mind, Miriam determined in her heart to follow through with the commitment she'd made to marry Amos.

On the day of the wedding, Miriam awoke with a headache. "Oh, no," she groaned as she climbed out of bed. "Not today of all days!" She forced herself to get dressed and headed downstairs to the kitchen with a firm resolve that she could make it through the day without any regrets.

As she sat at the table, drinking a cup of peppermint tea, she reflected on her past. So many memories swirled around in her head. She'd been born here in this old farmhouse—upstairs in what used to be Mom and Papa's room. She'd grown up here and had never known any other home, but that was about to change. In just a few hours, Miriam would become Amos's live-in housekeeper and Mary Ellen's new mamm. Nothing would ever be the same.

She swallowed hard, trying to force that ever-familiar lump out of her throat. Oh, how she would miss this house filled with so many memories of her happy childhood, when things hadn't been nearly so complicated or painful as they were now that she was an adult.

"Guder mariye, bride-to-be."

Miriam turned and saw Lewis standing in the doorway, stretching both arms over his head as he yawned.

"Good morning," she mumbled.

"This is your big day. Are you feeling a bit naerfich?"

"Jah, I am a little nervous," she admitted.

Lewis smiled. "I'm sure I'll be naerfich when Grace and I get married, too."

"Grace is a special girl. The two of you should be quite happy living here together."

"I hope we can be as happy as Mom and Papa were for so many years." His smile widened. "I'm happy for you and Amos. You've both been through a lot and deserve some joy in your lives."

Miriam groaned inwardly, but outwardly, she managed a weak smile. She was glad her brother was happy about his upcoming wedding. She only wished she didn't feel so anxious on her own wedding day.

❦

Amos paced from his dresser to the bed and back again. He couldn't remember when he had been so nervous. Even on his and Ruth's wedding day, he hadn't felt this keyed up or suffered with such sweaty palms and shaky hands. Of course, he'd known that Ruth loved him and was marrying him for the right reasons. Not so with Miriam.

He moved over to the window and stared into the yard below. The morning had dawned with a clear, blue sky, and he spotted a cardinal sitting on a branch of the maple tree near the house, looking eager to begin its day.

I should be eager, too, he thought, as he opened the window and drew in a couple of deep breaths. *I hope I didn't make a mistake in asking Miriam to marry me, and I hope her agreeing to do so isn't a mistake. I know she doesn't love me, and even though I love her, I haven't been able to tell her, because I'm afraid it might drive her further away.*

He pressed his palms against the window ledge and inhaled again. *Dear Lord, please let me know when it's the right time to tell her how I feel, and I pray that You will bless our union, even though it's a marriage of convenience and will be in name only.*

🪶

Miriam, wearing a navy blue dress draped with a white cape and apron, grew more anxious by the moment as she sat rigidly in her seat, waiting to become Mrs. Amos Hilty. She glanced across the room where Amos sat straight and tall, wearing a white shirt, black trousers, and a matching vest and jacket. Did he feel as nervous as she did about this marriage? Was he having second thoughts, too? His stoic expression gave no indication as to what he might be thinking.

Should I have accepted Nick's proposal? Maybe I would have been happier being married to him. Miriam mentally shook herself. She wasn't marrying Amos so she could be happy.

She was doing it for Mary Ellen, so the child would have a mother and so that Miriam would have a home. Things wouldn't have worked out between her and Nick. Besides, she didn't love him, nor did he love her. The feelings she'd had for him had only been a silly attraction, and she would never have risked hurting her family or being shunned just to satisfy a need for affection or even a home. By marrying Amos, she would be gaining a daughter, and she wouldn't have to give up her family or the only way of life she had ever known.

The wedding ceremony, which was similar to a regular Sunday preaching service, began at 8:30 a.m. Miriam did all right during the first part of the service, but as the time drew closer for her and Amos to stand before the bishop and say their vows, she became increasingly apprehensive. Miriam knew that both men and women of the Amish faith took their wedding vows seriously. Divorce would not be an acceptable option if things didn't go well between her and Amos. Married couples were expected to work out their problems and, above all else, remain true to the vows they had spoken before God and man.

Though Miriam's intent was to remain married to Amos until death parted them, it would not be easy for her to promise to love him. She was sure she would never feel anything more than mutual respect for Amos, but for Mary Ellen's sake, she would go through with the wedding. No one but Miriam and Amos, and perhaps Crystal, would know this was not a marriage based on love. No one need know the reasons behind her decision to marry him.

When it was time for Miriam and Amos to stand before

the bishop, she pushed her nagging doubts to the back of her mind and took her place beside her groom.

If Bishop Benner knew about my lack of faith in God and the circumstances of my marriage to Amos, I'm sure he would never have agreed to perform the ceremony, she thought as a lump formed in her throat.

"Brother," the bishop said, looking at Amos, "can you confess that you accept this our sister as your wife, and that you will not leave her until death separates you? And do you believe that this is from the Lord and that you have come thus far by your faith and prayers?"

With only a slight hesitation, Amos answered, "Jah."

Bishop Benner then directed his words to Miriam. "Can you confess, sister, that you accept this our brother as your husband, and that you will not leave him until death separates you? And do you believe that this is from the Lord and that you have come thus far by your faith and prayers?"

Miriam cringed inside because of her deception, but in a clear voice, she answered, "Jah."

The bishop spoke to Amos again. "Because you have confessed that you want to take this our sister for your wife, do you promise to be loyal to her and care for her if she may have adversity, affliction, sickness, or weakness, as is appropriate for a Christian, God-fearing husband?"

"Jah."

Bishop Benner addressed the same question to Miriam, and she, too, replied affirmatively. He then took Miriam's right hand and placed it in Amos's right hand, putting his own hands above and beneath their hands. Offering a blessing, he said, "The God of Abraham, the God of Isaac, and the God of Jacob be with you together and give His rich blessing upon you and be merciful to you. To this I wish you the blessings of God for a good beginning, and may you hold out until a blessed end. Through Jesus Christ our Lord, amen."

At the end of the blessing, Miriam, Amos, and Bishop Benner bowed their knees in prayer. When they stood, he said, "Go forth in the name of the Lord. You are now man and wife."

Amos and Miriam returned to their respective seats, and one of the ordained ministers gave a testimony, followed by two other ministers expressing agreement with the sermon and wishing Amos and Miriam God's blessings.

When that was done, the bishop made a few closing comments and asked the congregation to kneel, at which time he read a prayer from the prayer book. Then the congregation rose to their feet, and the meeting was closed with a final hymn.

Miriam clenched her fingers as she blinked against stinging tears. It was done. There was no going back. She was now Amos's Miriam and would remain so until the day they were separated by death.

As several men began to set up tables for the wedding meal, Amos stole a glance at Miriam's three brothers, who stood off to one side, talking and laughing like this was a most joyous occasion.

And it should be, Amos thought painfully as he reflected on the somber expression he'd seen on his bride's face as they had each responded to the bishop's questions during their wedding vows. For many years before Amos had married Ruth, he had wished that Miriam could be his wife. Now that it had finally happened, it seemed bittersweet, for he knew she had only married him because of Mary Ellen's need for a mother, not because she felt any love for him.

Amos clenched his fingers until his nails bit into the palms of his hands. *Dear Lord, what have I done? I've married a woman who will never fully be my wife. I've given my word that I won't put any physical demands on her, and since we won't have an intimate relationship, we'll never have any kinner of our own. Miriam doesn't love me, and short of a miracle, she probably never will.*

CHAPTER 26

Miriam had only been living in Amos's house a few days, and already he wondered if he had made the biggest mistake of his life. Since today was an off-Sunday and there would be no preaching services, he hoped they could use this time together to discuss a few things concerning their marriage.

Mary Ellen, who was playing on the kitchen floor with her kitten, looked up at Miriam and smiled. "I'm glad you've come to live with Pappy and me. Can I call you Mama Mim from now on?"

Miriam smiled at the child. "If you like."

Amos's chair scraped against the linoleum as he pushed it away from the table and stood. He went over to the stove and removed the coffeepot, deciding that now might be a good time to say what was on his mind. "Mary Ellen, would you please go upstairs and play for a while?"

"Can I play outside on the porch instead?"

"Jah."

Mary Ellen looked at him with questioning eyes. "You and Mama Mim want to be alone, don't you, Pappy?"

If only that were true. I'm sure the last thing Miriam wants is to be alone with me.

"Miriam and I need to talk," he said, nodding at the child. "If the rain stops, maybe we'll go for a picnic at the lake later on."

"Really, Pappy? I love picnics!" Mary Ellen scooped the fluffy kitten into her arms and headed for the back door.

"Don't forget your jacket," Miriam called to her. "Since it's still raining, be sure you stay on the porch."

Mary Ellen grabbed her jacket from a low-hanging wall peg and bounded out the door.

"Do you think it was a good idea to get her excited about a picnic when it may not stop raining?" Miriam asked, turning to look at Amos with a frown.

"We'll see how it goes," he mumbled as he placed the coffeepot on the table.

She stood. "Well, I have dishes to do."

"Please, stay seated awhile. We need to discuss a few things."

She gave him a brief nod and sat down.

Amos poured coffee for them both and took the chair across from her. "I–I'm not sure what you believe about our marriage, but I want you to know that I. . .well, I think God brought us together." He wanted desperately to reach out and caress Miriam's cheek. Instead, he grabbed hold of the coffee mug and took a sip.

She opened her mouth as if to respond, but he held up one hand to silence her, knowing he needed to get this said while he had the chance and before he lost his nerve.

"I also think God will bless our marriage if we're faithful

to Him and to one another."

"I'll be faithful to our vows, Amos. Divorce will never be an option for me."

"Nor for me." He took another sip from his cup as he searched for the right words. "I know we have many adjustments to make, and some of them might take some getting used to on both our parts."

Miriam blew on her coffee. "You're right about that."

"As I'm sure you know, the Bible teaches us in Ephesians 5:23 that the man is to be the head of the house, just as Christ is the head of the church." Amos paused to gauge her reaction, but she just stared at the table. "So, while I may want to consult with you on certain matters," he continued, "I believe that the final decisions should always be made by me."

Miriam looked up and stared at him with her forehead wrinkled and her lips compressed. After a moment, she asked, "Are you saying that I must do whatever you tell me to do?"

"No, it's just that I need to know that you respect my opinion, and I—I have a need to—to be able to touch you, Miriam." Amos tentatively reached for her hand, but she quickly pulled it away as soon as his fingers made contact with her skin, as though repulsed by his touch.

"You—you promised our marriage wouldn't have to be a physical one. Are you going back on your word now, Amos?"

"No. No, I'm not." He pushed away from the table and began pacing the floor, wishing he could somehow ask or even insist that she be his wife in every respect, knowing that he couldn't. "I will keep true to my word, Miriam. We'll continue to sleep in separate rooms just as we've done since our wedding night."

"I—I appreciate that," she murmured, staring down at the table again.

Amos cringed as he reflected on their wedding night. It certainly hadn't gone the way he would have liked, but a promise was a promise, and he wouldn't go back on it no matter how much he wanted to make Miriam his wife in every sense of the word. He knew that if he was ever to win her heart, he would have to remain honest and trustworthy. And he must remember never to try to touch her again unless she let him know first that it was what she wanted.

Miriam sat silently as Amos paced back and forth across the kitchen floor, his face red and his breathing heavy. "Was there anything else you wanted to talk to me about?"

He gave a quick nod and returned to the table. "Jah. I have some things to say about Mary Ellen."

"What about her?"

"I would appreciate it if you didn't mother my daughter so much."

"What? I thought that's why you agreed to marry me—so she would have a mudder."

Amos pulled his fingers through the end of his beard. "I'm not saying you shouldn't be like a mother to her. I just don't think she needs smothering."

"Smothering? How am I smothering the child?"

"Making her put on a jacket when it's warm outside and reminding her to stay on the porch."

"But it's raining, Amos. Surely you don't want your daughter to be outside playing in the rain."

He took a long drink from his cup. "I played in the rain a lot when I was boy, and it never did me any harm."

Miriam clasped her fingers tightly around her mug to keep them from shaking. She could hardly believe they were having this conversation. "I'm only concerned for her well-being. It may still be summer, but it's kind of nippy outside this morning."

"If I thought my daughter needed to put on her jacket or stay on the porch, don't you think I would have said something?"

She pursed her lips. "Maybe so. Maybe not."

He gave his beard a quick pull. "I-I'm sorry if I upset you. It's just that I've been Mary Ellen's only parent for a year now, and—"

"If you didn't think Mary Ellen needed a woman's care, then why did you marry me?"

"Because I—" Amos broke off in mid-sentence, pushed his chair aside, and stood. He tromped across the room, snatched his straw hat from the wall peg, and went out the back door, letting it slam shut.

Miriam's throat constricted, and a tight sob threatened to escape her lips. In an effort to regain control of her emotions, she dropped her head into her hands and squeezed her eyes shut. *Being married is nothing like I imagined it would be when I thought William was going to marry me.*

So far nothing had gone right—from the wedding ceremony, where she had made promises she wasn't sure she could keep, to their wedding night, when she had slept alone in the room next to Amos's.

After tucking Mary Ellen into her own bed that evening,

Miriam had slipped quietly into the bedroom across the hall. For some time after she'd crawled into bed, she had heard Amos moving about in his own room next door. She had lain awake for most of the night, worrying that he might change his mind and come to her room, and wondering if she'd made the biggest mistake of her life by agreeing to marry him.

She was grateful Amos had been true to his word on their wedding night, but when he had reached for her hand a few minutes ago and said he wanted her touch, she'd become full of new doubts about whether he could be trusted.

She lifted her head and blinked a couple of times to chase away the tears in her eyes. "I will get through this. I'll reach deep inside myself and find the courage to face each new day. And despite what Amos says or thinks, I do know what's best for Mary Ellen."

A routine was quickly established at the Hilty home, and even though Miriam found herself adapting to it, she didn't think she would ever adjust to being Amos's wife. Her heart longed for something more than wifely chores to do, but without love, a real husband-and-wife relationship was out of the question. Being a stepmother to Mary Ellen helped to fill a part of Miriam that seemed to be missing, but she knew it would never completely fill the void in her heart.

She didn't want to admit it, not even to herself, but she found Amos's presence to be unnerving. It made her keenly aware of the emptiness in her life. In the past, she had managed to keep her life fairly uncomplicated because she'd forgotten what love felt like. But now she had the strange desire—a need really—to love and to be loved.

Longing for love doesn't bring love into one's life, she told herself one evening as she washed the supper dishes. *The best thing I can do is keep busy, and I've certainly been doing a good job of that since I came to live here.* Her jaw clenched as she forced herself to concentrate on the task at hand.

Soon after Miriam had put the last dish away, Amos picked up his Bible to read as he had done every night since they had married. At first, she'd been irritated by the practice, since she had long ago given up reading her Bible every day. But now she was able to tolerate the ritual he'd established. It was a time when the three of them sat around the kitchen table, reading God's Word as a family. Mary Ellen usually had questions, and Amos seemed to take pleasure in being able to interpret the scriptures for her.

"Tonight I'll be reading in Proverbs," Amos said as he opened the Bible. "'Whoso findeth a wife findeth a good thing, and obtaineth favour of the Lord.'" He looked up and smiled. "That was chapter 18, verse 22."

Does he think I'm stupid? Miriam fumed. *I may not have the kind of faith Amos has, but I'm well acquainted with the Bible.*

Mary Ellen gave her father's shirtsleeve a little tug. "Mama Mim's a good wife, isn't she, Pappy?"

"Jah, she is." Amos glanced over at Miriam and smiled.

His piercing gaze made her feel uncomfortable, and she looked away, hoping he hadn't seen the blush she was sure had come to her cheeks.

"Is there more in the Bible about Mama Mim?" Mary Ellen questioned.

"Let's see," Amos thumbed through the pages. "Here in

Proverbs 31, verse 27, it says, 'She looketh well to the ways of her household, and eateth not the bread of idleness.' "

The child gasped. "Pappy, do you mean that Mama Mim isn't supposed to eat any bread? Won't she get awfully hungry?"

Amos laughed, and Miriam did, too. It felt good to laugh. It was something she did so seldom.

Mary Ellen stared up at her father, her hazel eyes wide and expectant. Amos patted the top of her head. "The verse isn't talking about real bread, Mary Ellen. The bread of idleness refers to someone who's lazy and doesn't want to work."

Mary Ellen's forehead wrinkled as she frowned. "But Mama Mim's busy all the time. She ain't one bit lazy."

"Isn't, Mary Ellen," Miriam corrected. She glanced at Amos, hoping she hadn't overstepped her bounds.

To her surprise, Amos nodded and smiled. "You're right, daughter. Your new mamm is a hard worker." He pointed to the Bible. "The verse is saying that a good wife isn't idle or lazy, and it's speakin' about someone like Mama Mim. She looks well to our house and takes good care of us. She doesn't eat the bread of idleness, because she's not lazy."

Mary Ellen grinned, revealing cute little dimples in both cheeks. "I'm so glad we have Mama Mim livin' with us now."

Amos looked over at Miriam and smiled. "I'm glad, too."

Miriam's face grew warm again, and she wasn't sure how to respond. So she merely nodded and said, "I made some pumpkin pie today. Would anyone like a piece?"

"I do! I do!" Mary Ellen shouted.

Amos nodded. "Jah, that sounds real good."

CHAPTER

27

M iriam looked at the kitchen clock on the wall above her head. It was one thirty in the afternoon, and Mary Ellen wouldn't be home from school for a few hours yet. Amos was out in his blacksmith shop, and since he'd taken his lunch with him today, Miriam had been alone all morning. She found that no matter how busy she kept, the loneliness and sense of longing that had crept into her heart never went away. The longer she lived under Amos's roof, the more those emotions intensified.

A knock at the back door brought her thoughts to a halt. Surely it couldn't be Amos. He wouldn't knock on his own door.

The door creaked as Miriam opened it, and a ray of sun bathed the room with its pale light. She was surprised to see her mother on the porch, holding a basket draped with a cloth. "What a surprise! I didn't hear your buggy drive in, Mom."

"I left it parked in front of Amos's shop while he shoes my horse."

"Ah, I see." Miriam motioned to the table. "Have a seat, and let's visit awhile."

Mom set the basket on the table, then removed her dark shawl and hung it over the back of a chair. "I brought you a loaf of oatmeal bread," she said, lifting the cloth from the basket.

"It looks good. Should I slice a few pieces? We can have some with a cup of tea."

"Jah, that'd be nice."

Miriam took the bread over to the cutting board. "How are things at Andrew and Sarah's, and how did you manage to get away by yourself?" she asked as she sliced the bread and placed a few pieces on a plate.

"Things are going along okay, and I was given the day off because baby Nadine had a checkup at the doctor's today."

"Oh?"

"Jah, and Andrew and Sarah decided to take all the kinner along and make some time for shopping and a meal out after Nadine's appointment."

Miriam set the plate of bread on the table. "Didn't they invite you to go with them?"

"They did, but I turned them down because I thought they should have some time alone as a family without me tagging along. Besides, I needed to get my horse shoed, and I saw it as a good chance to come visit with you for a while."

Miriam smiled. It was nice to see her mother in the middle of the week. To be able to spend some time together over a cup of tea and some oatmeal bread made Miriam's day seem less gloomy. She poured them each a cup of tea from the pot she'd placed on the table a few minutes before Mom had arrived and took a seat. "I'm glad you're here. We don't get to see each other much anymore now that I'm married."

"That's true, but we didn't see each other much before you were married, either."

"There was a good reason for that," Miriam said. "Between my job teaching school and all the work you were doing at Andrew's place, we were both too busy to spend much time visiting."

Mom took a sip of tea. "I know how much you enjoyed teaching. Do you miss it now that you're a *hausfraa*?"

"I do miss it some," Miriam admitted as tears stung the back of her eyes. "But I'm learning to adjust to the role of being a housewife and a mother."

"Speaking of being a mother," Mom said, "I just found out yesterday that my sister Clara's daughter Ada is going to have her first boppli later this fall. Ada's due around the time of Lewis and Grace's wedding in November."

"That's nice," Miriam said, trying to make her voice sound as excited as possible. "I'm happy for Cousin Ada and her husband, Sam."

"What about you, daughter? When do you think you and Amos will be starting your own family?"

Miriam reached for a piece of bread and took a bite, wondering how to let her mother know that she would never have any children of her own. It was a touchy topic, to be sure. One Miriam would rather not talk about.

"Miriam, did you hear what I said?"

She nodded. "I—I already have a family. Mary Ellen's a good child, and—"

"I'm sure she is, but wouldn't you like some kinner of your own?"

Miriam's eyes flooded with tears, and she quickly looked

away so Mom wouldn't notice. How could she explain that her heart longed for a baby but that having a child with Amos wasn't possible because they didn't share the same bed? And that no matter how badly she might want a boppli, it simply wasn't meant to be.

"You and Amos haven't been married long, so there's still plenty of time for you to conceive. You just need to be patient, because kinner will come in God's time, not yours."

Miriam swallowed hard. "When you go out to Amos's shop to get your horse, please don't say anything to him about my not being pregnant yet. It might upset him."

"Of course not. I won't mention it to anyone, but I will be praying." Mom patted Miriam's arm. "My heart longs to be a *grossmudder* many times over, just as I'm sure your heart longs to be a mudder."

Miriam picked up her cup and took a drink. *If you only knew the truth about my so-called marriage to Amos.*

✦

Amos had just returned to his shop after shoeing Anna's horse and hitching him to her buggy, when she stepped into the room. "Done visiting already?" he asked.

She nodded. "I figured you'd probably be finished with Harvey by now, and I really do need to go back home and get supper started before the rest of the family returns from their day in town."

Amos smiled as he looked up from the metal desk where he sat. "I hope Andrew knows how fortunate he is to have such a caring mudder."

Anna's face turned a light shade of pink, and she waved

her hand like she was fanning herself. "Ah, I don't do anything so special. And if I thought I did, then I would be *hochmut*."

"There's nothing prideful about admitting that you work hard." He smiled. "And you do work hard, since you help care for Andrew and Sarah's kinner, do a multitude of chores around their place, and offer support and encouragement to Sarah whenever she feels down."

"You know about her bouts with depression?"

He nodded. "Andrew's shared a few things with me."

"It's not been easy for Andrew or Sarah to see Rebekah confined to a wheelchair, struggling to deal with her handicap, but Sarah has taken it the hardest." Anna sighed. "I try to spend as much time with the child as I can, and since I discovered that she's taken with the plants I have in my room, it gives us something we can do together—something Rebekah doesn't need much help with at all."

Amos leaned against his chair and folded his arms. "You've been as good for Andrew's Rebekah as Miriam's been for my Mary Ellen."

Anna smiled, and her blue eyes fairly twinkled. "From what I can tell, Miriam loves your little girl as if she were her own flesh-and-blood daughter. She seems devoted to caring for that child."

Amos couldn't argue with that. Many times he'd seen or heard Miriam do or say something that had let him know how much she cared for Mary Ellen. *If only she cared that much for me*, he thought, as a feeling of regret coursed through his body.

"Have I said something wrong?" Anna asked in a tone of

concern. "You look so solemn all of a sudden."

He was about to reply, when Bishop Benner entered the shop, saying he had a couple of horses he wanted shoed.

"I'd better be on my way home," Anna said. "It was good talking with you, Amos, and danki for hitching the horse up to my buggy again."

"You're welcome." Amos saw Anna out; then he turned to face the bishop. "Did you bring your horses with you, or do you need me to head out to your place to get the job done?"

The bishop motioned toward the door. "I brought 'em along."

"All right then. Guess I'd best get to it." Amos was glad he kept so busy these days. It helped take his mind off Miriam, who seemed to consume his thoughts more than ever. He knew that only the good Lord could change things between them, and he would continue to pray for such a miracle.

Miriam could hardly believe fall was behind them already and winter was well on the way. The month of November had been a busy one, with Lewis and Grace's wedding, and then Thanksgiving a week after that. Soon Christmas would be here, and that would mean the opportunity for her to spend more time with family and friends.

Not that Mary Ellen and Amos aren't family, she thought as she sat at the treadle sewing machine, preparing to make Mary Ellen a new dress for school. The child had grown so much in the last month, and everything she wore seemed much too short for her gangly body.

When Miriam had agreed to marry Amos, she hadn't realized how demanding the role of motherhood would be, but she found herself enjoying the responsibility of being Mary Ellen's mother, although it caused her heart to ache for a child of her own.

At times like now, she found herself thinking about William Graber and the love they'd once shared, knowing that if they had married, she might have one or two children by now.

Miriam shook her head to clear the troubling thoughts and reminded herself that it did no good to dwell on such things. The past was in the past, and now she had a new life to think about. Mary Ellen would be the only child she would ever be able to help raise, and being around the little girl had given Miriam a reason to laugh and smile again.

Miriam found that she was even becoming more relaxed around Amos. He was a soft-spoken man with an easy, pleasant way about him. Though he wasn't what she would consider handsome, he certainly wasn't ugly. Being near him didn't make her heart pound wildly the way it had when she'd been with William or Nick, but she did feel respect for Amos, which was something William certainly hadn't earned.

One evening as Amos opened the Bible, he announced to Miriam and Mary Ellen that he would be reading from Psalm 127:3–5. " 'Lo, children are an heritage of the Lord: and the fruit of the womb is his reward. As arrows are in the hand of a mighty man; so are children of the youth. Happy is the man that hath his quiver full of them.' "

"What's a quiver, Pappy?" Mary Ellen asked.

Amos stroked his beard and looked thoughtful. "A quiver is a case for carrying arrows."

"Do you have a quiver?"

He grinned. "I have no case full of arrows, but I do have a home, and God's Word is saying that men are happy when they have a home full of children."

Mary Ellen's forehead wrinkled. "You only have one

child, Pappy, so you must be awful sad."

Miriam cringed. Mary Ellen had hit a nerve, for Miriam knew she wasn't as happy as she could be, and one of the reasons was her deep desire for a baby.

Amos pulled Mary Ellen from her chair and into his lap. "I must admit, having more kinner would be nice, but I'm happy with just one."

Mary Ellen cuddled against his chest. "I hope God sends us a boppli sometime. I want a little bruder or *schweschder* to play with."

The tears that had formed behind Miriam's eyes threatened to spill over, and it took all her willpower to hold them at bay.

"If God wishes you to have a brother or sister someday, then it will happen, but it will be in His time," Amos told the child.

"Then I'll pray and ask God to hurry up," she said eagerly.

Amos looked as though he was about to say something more, but he closed the Bible instead, and then in a surprising gesture, he lifted his hand to brush away the tears that lay on Miriam's cheeks.

A deep-seated longing coursed through her body, and she quickly pulled back.

"Sorry. I—I didn't mean to offend you or go back on my word." Amos pushed away from the table. "There are a few things outside I must tend to."

As Miriam watched his retreating form, she felt relieved that he'd left the room, yet that sensation was mixed with disappointment. She didn't bother to analyze her feelings, but she knew one thing for certain—Amos Hilty, her husband in name only, was as miserable as she was right now.

Feeling the need to work off his frustrations, Amos grabbed an axe and a kerosene lantern from the woodshed and headed around back to the pile of logs he'd been planning to split for firewood.

"Miriam hates it whenever I touch her," he mumbled, placing the first hunk of wood on the chopping block. "I had promised her I wouldn't, yet I touched her anyway."

Crack! The axe came down hard, splitting the wood in two and sending both chunks into the air. They landed a few feet away, and Amos grunted as he bent to pick up another hunk of wood. He positioned it on the chopping block, raised his arms, and let the axe fall once more.

It seems like she always has to be moving—jumping up and down to check something on the stove, racing back and forth from the table to the refrigerator. She tries to keep busy so she doesn't have to talk to me, and when we do talk, there's either an invisible wall between us, or I say or do the wrong thing.

For the next half hour, Amos chopped wood with a frenzy as he thought about Miriam and how much he loved her. "I was a fool to marry that woman!" he shouted into the night sky. *Crack!* "Why can't she look at me with tenderness and love, the way she does Mary Ellen?" *Crack!* "How can I go on living with her when I can't touch her or let her know how much I love her?"

He swiped at the rivulets of sweat rolling down his forehead with the back of his hand and grabbed another piece of wood. Placing it on the chopping block, he gritted his teeth. "I don't think I can do this much longer. I can't stand not being able to touch Miriam when I love her so much. Oh, Lord, give me the strength to endure this test."

Crack! The axe came down hard, shattering the wood into several pieces and sending them flying. Amos ducked as one came his way, but it was too late. The wood smacked him in the head quicker than he could blink. At first, all he felt was a dull ache, but soon his head began to throb. He lifted his hand to touch the spot, and thick, coppery blood oozed out between his fingers.

"Dummkopp!" he mumbled. "I'm a dunce for thinking too much and not watching what I was doing."

Amos knew the cut needed to be looked after, and he hoped it wasn't so deep that it would require stitches. The last thing he needed tonight was a trip to the hospital. He leaned the axe against the chopping block.

Feeling very foolish and a bit woozy, he turned for the house. A few minutes later, he found Miriam and Mary Ellen sitting at the kitchen table, putting a puzzle together and eating popcorn.

"Pappy, your head's bleeding!" Mary Ellen shouted.

Miriam was immediately on her feet and rushing to his side. "Oh, Amos, what happened?"

"I was choppin' wood out behind the shed, and one of the pieces flew up and hit me in the head."

"Come, sit at the table and let me look at that." Miriam took hold of Amos's arm and led him across the room. As soon as he was seated, she leaned over and examined the wound, shaking her head and clicking her tongue.

Mary Ellen peered up at them with a worried expression. "Is Pappy gonna be okay?"

"The cut doesn't look too deep. I think it just needs to be cleaned and bandaged." Miriam hurried across the room and pulled a small towel from one of the cupboards. Then she went to the sink and wet it. She returned to the table and placed the towel against Amos's forehead. "Hold this here while I run upstairs and get some bandages."

When Miriam left the room, he smiled at Mary Ellen and said, "Now wipe that frown from your face, little one. I'm not hurt so much, and Mama Mim will be back soon to put a bandage on for me."

Mary Ellen's chin quivered, but she managed a weak smile. "I'm sure glad you married her, Pappy, 'cause I wouldn't know what to do if you came in here bleedin' like that."

Amos patted the top of his daughter's head. "Jah, I'm glad I married Mim, too."

Miriam's hands shook as she dabbed some antiseptic on Amos's wound and covered it with a bandage. What if the cut had been deeper? What if the wood had hit him in a vital spot?

She straightened and stepped away from him. "There. I think you'll be good as new."

"Pappy ain't old, Mama Mim." Mary Ellen stared at Miriam with a wide-eyed expression.

"I don't think that's what Miriam meant when she said I'd be good as new," Amos said before Miriam could reply.

Miriam touched the little girl's shoulder. "I guess I should have said that your daed will be fine and dandy now. The bleeding has stopped, and in a few days, the cut will be all healed up."

"I'm glad to hear it." Mary Ellen pivoted toward the table and pointed to the bowl of popcorn. "Now can we finish eatin' our snack?"

Amos chuckled, and Miriam felt herself relax. For the first time since she had become Mrs. Amos Hilty, she felt as if they were a real family. If only that feeling could last.

CHAPTER
29

The days moved on, bringing frosty cold mornings with plenty of snow on the ground. One afternoon in the middle of February, Miriam decided to leave a little early when she went to pick up Mary Ellen after school so she could pay a call on Crystal.

"Be careful today," Amos called to her from the door of his blacksmith shop. "The roads could be icy what with that snow we had last night."

"I'll watch out for it," she said as she climbed into her buggy. It was nice to know Amos was concerned, but she wondered if his apprehension over her driving on icy roads was because he cared about her welfare, or if he was merely worried that if something happened to her, he would have to find another mother for Mary Ellen.

She shook the thought aside and reached for the reins. At least Amos had kept true to his word and not tried to touch her again.

Half an hour later, Miriam guided her horse and buggy up her brother and sister-in-law's long driveway. She spotted Crystal right away, standing on the front porch, sweeping snow that had probably been blown in from the wind they'd had last night. When Crystal saw Miriam, she waved and set the broom aside. "It's good to see you," she called.

Miriam stepped down from her buggy and started toward the house, being careful not to slip on the icy path. "It has been awhile, hasn't it?"

Crystal nodded. "I've been wondering how you're doing on these cold, snowy days."

Miriam stepped onto the porch. "It's still kind of hard for me to take Mary Ellen to school each day, then turn around and go back home to an empty house. Teaching the scholars was a part of my life for several years, and I still miss it some."

Crystal opened the door and led the way into her warm, cozy kitchen. "But you have Mary Ellen to train and teach at home. The role of motherhood can be very rewarding. You'll see that even more once other kinner come along." She took Miriam's coat and hung it on a wall peg, then motioned to the table where a teapot sat. "Why, you'll be so busy changing *windle* and doing extra laundry, you won't have time to think about anything else."

"Other children? Changing diapers?" Miriam sank into a chair with a moan. "Have you been talking to Mom by any chance?"

"About what?"

"Me having a boppli."

"You're in a family way?" Crystal's face broke into a wide smile, and she leaned over to grab Miriam in a hug.

"I'm not going to have a baby," Miriam said. "Not now. Not ever."

Crystal clicked her tongue. "Miriam, it's only been six

months since you and Amos were married. You need to give it more time. It's God's time anyway, and it will happen when He's ready for it to."

Shortly before Miriam's wedding, she had told Crystal why she was marrying Amos, and she'd thought she had made it clear that there was no love between them. However, she hadn't spoken of the matter since that day, so she was sure Crystal didn't understand the extent of how distant things really were between her and Amos. Miriam felt ashamed to admit that she slept in her own room and Amos in his. There had been no physical union between them, so there would be no babies.

She drew in a deep breath and decided that, despite her embarrassment, maybe it would help if she confided in someone who might give her a little understanding and sympathy. "I'll never get pregnant," she whispered with a catch in her voice.

"Now, Miriam, good things come to those who wait."

Tears slipped out from under Miriam's lashes and splashed onto the front of her dress. "Amos and I—we haven't consummated our marriage."

Crystal's mouth fell open. "You mean—"

"We sleep in separate rooms. We're man and wife in name only." Miriam grabbed a napkin from the basket in the center of the table and wiped her eyes. She hated to cry and saw tears as a sign of weakness, yet she'd been giving in to weepiness a lot these days.

"Has Amos agreed to such an arrangement?" Crystal asked, staring at Miriam in obvious disbelief. "I know you only married him because of Mary Ellen, but I thought that by now you—"

"He knows I don't love him, and he feels no love for me. Our marriage is still one of convenience. He provides a home and food for me, and I cook, clean, and take care of his daughter."

Crystal placed a gentle hand on Miriam's arm. "Miriam, he could have simply hired a *maad* for those tasks. Surely Amos needs a wife and not just a housekeeper."

"Then he should have married someone else. Someone he could love and cherish. Someone who would love him in return." More tears dribbled down Miriam's cheeks, and she sniffed deeply. "I'm afraid I have ruined Amos's life—and mine, as well."

"How can you say that? You obviously care deeply about his daughter."

"I do," Miriam admitted. "Mary Ellen's a wonderful child, and I feel almost as if she's my own little girl." She sniffed again, nearly choking on the tears clogging her throat. "I've come to love her so much."

"You see," Crystal said with a nod. "You just said that you have *come* to love Mary Ellen. It didn't happen overnight. It happened gradually, so maybe you can learn to love Amos in the same way."

"But I–I'm afraid of being in love."

"I think you fear falling in love because you're afraid of losing control."

Miriam's throat burned, and she swallowed hard. She wanted to argue with Crystal, but she couldn't, because she knew her friend's words were true. She did like to be in control, and since she'd married Amos, she felt as if she'd lost control of everything.

Crystal took hold of Miriam's hand and gave it a gentle squeeze. "Please think about what I've said. Why don't you ask God to fill your heart with love toward the man you've chosen to be your husband? I feel certain that, with God's help, things can work out between you and Amos."

When Miriam left Crystal's house a short time later and headed for the schoolhouse, her heart was full of questions. She knew her friend cared for her and wanted her to be happy, and she wondered if Crystal might possibly be right. Could she learn to love Amos? Was love a feeling that was simply there? Or was it a matter of choosing to love some-one, as Crystal had said?

Miriam shook her confusing thoughts aside, knowing she needed to concentrate on the road ahead. The once-cloudless sky had darkened, and soon the heavens opened, dropping thick snowflakes that nearly blinded her vision.

She turned on the battery-operated windshield wipers and gripped the reins to hold the horse steady. She'd left Crystal's later than she had planned, and she was worried that she might be late picking Mary Ellen up from school.

As the snow came down harder and stuck to the road, the wheels of the buggy started to spin. Miriam strained to see the road ahead and fought to keep her rig on the road. The battery-operated lights on the front of the buggy did little to light the way.

Miriam found herself wishing she hadn't taken the time to stop and see Crystal. She would have been at the school-house by now, and she wouldn't have ended up telling her friend the truth about her and Amos. She was sure she could trust Crystal to keep the information she had shared to herself, but she didn't want Crystal's pity—and she wasn't sure she wanted her advice, either.

The buggy lurched as it hit a patch of ice, jolting Miriam's thoughts back to the task at hand. She shivered from the cold as well as from her fear of the near-blizzard-like conditions. Suddenly, the horse's hooves slipped, and the buggy lunged to the right. Miriam pulled back on the reins, calling, "Whoa, now! Steady, boy!"

The gelding whinnied and reared its head, jerking against the reins and causing the buggy to sway back and forth. It was dangerously close to the centerline, and when Miriam saw the headlights of an oncoming car, she gave a sharp tug on the reins.

The horse reared up, and before Miriam could think what to do, the buggy flipped onto its side, skidded along the edge of the road, and finally came to a halt.

She strained to see out the front window. The horse must have broken free, for it was nowhere to be seen. She pushed unsuccessfully against the door on the driver's side and winced in pain. Her side and shoulder hurt terribly, and she knew she must have a gash on her head. It not only stung, but she felt warm blood dripping down her face. She managed to rip a piece of her apron off and place it against her head to stop the bleeding.

In spite of Miriam's predicament, her first concern was for Mary Ellen. She knew the child would be waiting for her at the schoolhouse and might be frightened. *There must be some way to get out of here. Surely someone will see the buggy and stop to help. Oh, what about the horse? Is Amos's gelding all right?*

As Miriam's head continued to throb, making her feel helpless and dizzy, she was overtaken by a sense of panic, and she swallowed several times to keep from vomiting. She, who had always been so determined to solve her own problems, was now trapped inside the buggy, unable to find an answer to her dilemma. "Oh, dear God!" she cried. "Please help me!"

She squeezed her eyes shut and tried to think of scripture verses she had committed to memory. "Second Timothy 1, verse 7," she recited. "'For God hath not given us the spirit of fear; but of power, and of love, and of a sound mind.' Psalm 23, verse 4, 'Yea, though I walk through the valley of the shadow of death, I will fear no evil: for thou art with me; thy rod and thy staff they comfort me.' Mark 4, verse 40, 'And he said unto them, Why are ye so fearful? how is it that ye have no faith?'"

She drew in a deep breath and tried to calm down. Then a sudden sense of peace came over her like a gentle spring rain. She had been so far from God for such a long time, yet now she was keenly aware that she was not alone. She was confident that the Lord was with her now, and she had nothing to fear.

Amos glanced at the battery-operated clock sitting in the middle of his desk. It was four o'clock. Miriam and Mary Ellen should have been home by now.

He left the desk and moved to the window. It was snowing—large, heavy flakes swirling in the howling wind. Had she gotten stuck in the snow somewhere along the way? Had the buggy slipped on a patch of ice? Could she have been involved in an accident?

"If Miriam's carriage doesn't come into the yard in the next ten minutes, I'm going out to look for them."

For the next ten minutes, Amos paced to the window, keeping an eye on the worsening weather, and then back to his desk, where the clock reminded him with every tick that his wife and daughter were still not at home. Finally, he grabbed his jacket and hat from the wall peg near the door and left the blacksmith shop, his heart pounding with dread. It was time to go looking.

※

"Miriam, can you hear me? Are you hurt?"

Miriam's eyes snapped open, and she winced when she tried to sit up. Then she remembered that the buggy was tipped on its side. Had she been asleep? If so, for how long? Had someone called out to her?

The voice came again. "Miriam, please answer me!"

It was Amos, and he'd come to rescue her. Tears burned Miriam's eyes as she turned her head to the left. "I'm here. I'm hurting, but I don't think my injuries are serious."

"The door is jammed shut, and I can't get it open," Amos hollered. "I'll have to go for help. Can you hang on awhile longer?"

"I'll be fine."

"What was that?"

"I'll be fine, Amos," Miriam said, her voice all but gone. "I'm not alone any longer; God is with me." Her eyes closed, and she drifted off.

❧

"*I love you, Miriam. I love you, Miriam. . . .*" The resounding words ran through Miriam's mind as she struggled to become fully awake and focus on her surroundings. Where was she? Why were her eyes so heavy? Who had whispered those words of love to her? Her head pounded unmercifully. Was she having another one of her sick headaches? She tried to sit up, but a terrible pain ripped through her side.

"You'd better lie still," a woman's soothing voice said.

Miriam squinted against the invading light as her eyes came open. "Where—where am I?"

The woman, dressed in a white uniform, placed a gentle hand on Miriam's arm. "You're in the hospital. You were brought here when your buggy turned over in the storm."

Miriam frowned as the memory of the frightening ordeal rushed back to her. "I—I was so scared. The wind was howling, and the icy road must have spooked my horse. I knew I would be late picking up my daughter, and—"

Her daughter? Had she just referred to Mary Ellen as her daughter? Perhaps she was just a stepchild, but she was the only child Miriam would ever have, and she had come to love her as a daughter.

Miriam tried to sit up again. "Mary Ellen. Is my little girl all right?"

The nurse placed a firm but caring hand on Miriam's shoulder. "Your daughter's just fine. She and your husband are waiting in the visitor's lounge, and they are anxious to see you. Your family must love you very much."

The words "*I love you*" came back to Miriam. Maybe Mary

Ellen had said them. But if that were so, then why had Mary Ellen called her "Miriam" and not "Mama Mim"?

Miriam remembered being trapped inside the buggy. She heard Amos call out to her and say that he was going for help. Maybe she'd fallen asleep and dreamed the endearing words about love. Her heart was so full of questions.

"How did I get here?" she asked the nurse.

"You were brought in an ambulance."

"When can I go home?"

"Probably in a day or so. You have a concussion, and the doctor wants to monitor you for a few days."

Miriam moaned. "What other injuries do I have?"

"Some cuts and bruises, and a few of your ribs are broken. You're fortunate, though. Your injuries could have been much worse in an accident of that sort."

Miriam nodded. "I–I'd like to see my family now."

"Of course. I'll tell them you're awake." The nurse moved away from the bed and left the room.

Tears slipped between Miriam's lashes and rolled onto her cheeks. She had referred to Amos and Mary Ellen as her family, but she reminded herself that Amos was her husband in name only.

The door opened, and Amos and Mary Ellen stepped into the room.

"Mama Mim!" Mary Ellen cried. "Are you all right?"

"I'll be fine," she answered as the child rushed to her bedside.

"You're crying, Mama Mim. Does your head hurt bad?"

"A little." Miriam couldn't explain to Mary Ellen the real reason for her tears.

"We were awful worried; you gave us quite a scare," Amos said in a serious tone as he drew near the bed.

Miriam studied his face. He did seem to be concerned. "How—how did you find me?"

"I was a bit anxious when the snowstorm got so bad, and when you didn't return home with Mary Ellen on schedule, I began to worry. So I hitched up my rig and started for the schoolhouse. On the way there, I came across your carriage lying on its side. I stopped to see if you were okay; then I went to call for help."

"I do remember hearing your voice," Miriam murmured. "I must have dozed off, because I don't remember much after that."

Mary Ellen's chin trembled, and her eyes filled with tears. "I waited in the school yard for a long time. When you didn't come, I got real scared."

Miriam reached for the child's hand. "I'm sorry you were frightened, Mary Ellen."

Tears slid down the child's cheek. "When Pappy sent Uncle Lewis to get me, he said you'd been in an accident. I thought you were gonna die and leave me like my first mamm did." She gripped Miriam's fingers. "Losin' you would make me feel so sad."

"I'm going to be fine," Miriam murmured. "Jah, just fine."

Mary Ellen leaned over and pressed her damp cheek against Miriam's face. "I love you, Mama Mim."

"I love you, too, daughter."

CHAPTER

30

Miriam spent three days in the hospital, and during that time, she did a lot of thinking, praying, and soul-searching.

Amos hired a driver and came to visit her twice a day. His daytime visits were after he'd dropped Mary Ellen off at school, but in the evenings, he brought Mary Ellen along. Miriam knew he must be getting behind on his work, but she looked forward to each of his visits.

The pain in Miriam's ribs and head was beginning to lessen, but her last night in the hospital was the worst, as every muscle in her body felt rigid. She had trouble falling asleep and asked for a sleeping pill. While waiting for it to take effect, Miriam stared at the ceiling and thought about her life with Amos and Mary Ellen.

She finally drifted off, only to fall prey to a terrible nightmare. In the dream, Amos was driving the same buggy she'd ridden the day of her accident. Miriam stood helplessly by the side of the road and watched in horror as the horse reared up and the buggy rolled onto its side. When she'd called out to Amos and he didn't answer, her heart was gripped with fear that he might be dead. "Amos! Amos!" she shouted. "Come back to me, Amos."

"Wake up, Miriam. You're having a bad dream."

Miriam opened her eyes and saw the night nurse standing over her.

"I—I was only dreaming?"

The nurse nodded. "The medication you took earlier probably caused that. Here, take a drink of water and try to go back to sleep."

Miriam's throat felt dry, and her sheets were wet with perspiration. She drank the water gratefully, thankful that she had only been dreaming. The thought of losing Amos bothered her more than she cared to admit.

When Amos heard the patter of little feet outside his room, he set his Bible on the nightstand and rolled over in bed. A few seconds later, a soft knock sounded on the door.

"Pappy, are you awake?"

"Jah, Mary Ellen. Come in."

As the child entered his room, the hem of her long white nightgown swished across the hardwood floor. "I miss Mama Mim, and I couldn't sleep for worryin' about her."

He patted the patchwork quilt that covered his bed. "Lie down here awhile, and I'll take you back to your room after you're asleep."

"Really, Pappy? You wouldn't mind?"

He smiled and stretched his hand out to her. "Not at all. I would enjoy your company."

Mary Ellen settled herself against the pillows and released

a sigh. "I wonder if Mama Mim's lonely there at the hospital without us."

"I'll bet she's as eager to come home as you are to have her back."

"How about you, Pappy? Aren't you lookin' forward to her comin' home?"

"Jah. Things haven't been the same around here without Miriam," he answered honestly. The truth was, Amos missed his wife more than he cared to admit, and if nothing but friendship ever grew between them, he knew he would always love her.

"If Mama Mim stays away much longer, I'm afraid the kinner at school will start makin' fun of my lunches again."

His eyebrows shot up. "What's wrong with your lunches? Aren't you getting enough to eat?"

"I get plenty. It's just that the lunches you make aren't near as tasty as what Mama Mim puts together for me."

Amos couldn't argue with that. He'd been the recipient of Miriam's lunches himself, and she had always fixed flavorful, healthy fare that would please any man's palate. "I'll try harder to make you better lunches," he said, gently squeezing the child's arm.

"That's fine, but will Mama Mim be comin' home soon?"

"Tomorrow, if the doctor says it's okay."

"Oh, I'm so glad!" Mary Ellen closed her eyes. "Gut nacht, Pappy."

"Good night, daughter of mine."

❧

Miriam awoke the following morning, knowing it was the

day she would be leaving the hospital. She was anxious to go home but felt confused as she continued to ponder the strange, frightening dream about Amos that she'd had the night before.

She could feel the beginning of another headache coming on, and her hands trembled. "What's wrong with me, Lord?" she cried, turning her head into the pillow and giving in to the threatening tears despite her desire to remain in control of her emotions.

Finally, when Miriam had cried until no more tears would come, she dried her eyes and sat up. Amos would be here soon, and she didn't want him to know she'd been crying.

Miriam was dressed and sitting on the edge of her bed, reading the Bible she'd found in the drawer of her bedside table, when Amos entered the room carrying a pot of purple pansies. He took a seat next to her on the bed, and she self-consciously averted his gaze, knowing she must look a sight. Her eyes were swollen and sore from loosing pent-up emotions that had been long overdue for release.

"Miriam, these are for you." Amos placed the flowers on the nightstand beside her bed.

"Danki. They're beautiful."

"Before we go, I want to discuss something with you," he said in a most serious tone.

Miriam forced herself to look into his eyes. "Oh?"

With a hesitant look, Amos reached for her hand, and he smiled when she didn't pull away from him. "I-I've been wondering if you've thought about what I said to you the other day."

"What day was that?"

"The day of the accident—right before I left to get you some help." Amos cleared his throat. "I–I've been wanting to tell you the truth for some time, but I didn't know how to say it, and I wasn't sure you would believe me or how you would take it."

"The truth about what?"

"The way I feel about you. Until the day of your accident, I was afraid to say anything. But when I saw your buggy toppled over on the side of the road, I was scared I might lose you, so I blurted out the truth—that I love you and have ever since we were kinner."

Miriam gasped. "I do remember hearing those words, but I thought I had only dreamed them, and I wasn't sure who had spoken the words to me." A film of tears obscured her vision as she stared at his somber face. "I had no idea you cared for me when we were kinner, Amos."

"How could you know when William never kept his word?"

"William? What's William got to do with this?"

"He knew I cared for you and that I was too shy to say anything. When I gave him some pansies to give to you, he promised he would put in a good word for me."

"You—you were going to give me flowers?"

"Jah." Amos groaned. "William, my so-called friend, let you think the pansies had come from him, and he never said a word on my behalf."

Miriam opened her mouth, then closed it again. She could hardly believe William would have done something so deceitful. But then he had led her to believe he loved her and wanted to make her his wife, only to run off to Ohio and marry someone else. "Amos, I—I don't know what to say," she stammered.

He placed one finger against her lips. "It's all right. You don't have to say anything. I know you don't return my feelings, but I had to tell you anyhow. When I saw you injured, I was afraid that I'd never have the chance to tell you what I would have told you years ago if I hadn't been so shy."

"You must have gotten over your shyness," Miriam pointed out. "Otherwise, you wouldn't have asked Ruth to marry you."

He nodded. "That's true. I did."

"Did you love her, Amos?" Miriam hated to think that Amos had married another woman while he was still in love with her.

"Jah, I loved her," he said in a voice barely above a whisper. "But not in the same way I've always loved you."

She stared down at her hands clenched tightly in her lap. "I—I don't see how you could love me when I've had such a bitter spirit. I've wasted a lot of time feeling sorry for myself because of William, and I'm afraid it's made me anything but lovable."

"I saw the old Miriam—the one I fell in love with when I was a boy." Amos took both her hands and pressed them gently against his lips. "Knowing the woman you were capable of being kept me loving you."

Miriam couldn't speak around the lump lodged in her throat.

"Are you angry with me for speaking the truth?"

"No, Amos, I'm not angry. I only wish that—"

"It's all right. I need you, Miriam, and so does Mary

Ellen, but I've asked God to help me be patient, and if He wants us to be together as man and wife, then He will soften your heart toward me."

Miriam swallowed hard. "God is dealing with me, Amos, but I'm not ready to make a confession of love yet."

"I understand."

"No, I don't believe you do understand. Real love means a yielding of the heart to another person. It means commitment, loyalty, and trust. Since William's betrayal, it's been difficult for me to trust a man—or even God. My heart's been filled with bitterness because of William's betrayal."

Amos nodded. "I know, but you've kept your promise and not let it show to Mary Ellen. I thank you for that."

She sniffed. "I really do love her, Amos."

"Jah, I can tell. I also know that you and your family have been through a lot over the last few years. You've suffered a great hurt losing your daed, and then Rebekah's accident happened not long after that."

"Everyone in the family seems to have dealt with these things. Everyone—except for me." She leaned her head against Amos's shoulder and released a shuddering sob.

Amos lifted her chin and looked into her eyes with such love and compassion that she felt as if she could melt into his arms. "I understand your pain, Miriam. When Ruth died, I felt as if my world had been shattered. I even felt betrayed by Ruth for leaving me alone to raise our child. I blamed God for taking her. I was bitter and angry, and I didn't know if I could trust Him anymore. But I was reminded that His Word says, 'I will never leave thee, nor forsake thee.' I clung to the promise of that scripture verse, and one day I woke up and realized how much Mary Ellen needed me, and that I needed her."

Amos slipped his arm around Miriam's shoulders. "Life goes on, whether our hearts are filled with bitterness or love. Each of us must make the choice. We either choose to love, or we choose to harbor bitter, angry feelings. Hatred, anger, and bitterness are negative feelings that can make us ill. That's why the Bible says, 'A merry heart—' "

" 'Doeth good like a medicine,' " Miriam said, completing the verse. "Mom has quoted that passage of scripture to me many times. I'm ashamed to admit it, but I've chosen to ignore God's desire for my heart. Lying here in the hospital these past few days has given me time to think and pray. I want to yield to God's will, but I'm not sure I can. I'm afraid of failing and never finding happiness."

Amos ran his finger down Miriam's cheek, tracing a pattern where her tears had fallen. "I'm afraid, too, Miriam—afraid of being happy again. But I do love you, and I want to make you feel happy and loved, as well. I want you to be my wife in every way. I want us to have kinner and raise them in a way so they'll come to know God and trust in His Son as their Savior. I want our family to be full of God's love."

Miriam gulped on a sob. "I—I want those things, too, but I'm not sure I'm ready to have any kinner with you."

"I understand."

"Earlier this morning, I was reading in the Bible, and John 5:42 caught my attention. It said: 'But I know you, that ye have not the love of God in you.' That verse hit close to home, because I don't have God's love in my heart. You see, I've never completely yielded to Him—not even when

I was baptized and taken into church membership. I did it because it was expected of me, not because I truly had faith in God or His Son, Jesus."

She paused and drew in a shaky breath. "I–I've struggled and tried to do things on my own far too long, and I know that I need God's love in my heart in order to find peace and happiness for my troubled soul."

"If you'd like to speak to Him about that now, I'll sit here quietly with you."

Miriam nodded and bowed her head. "Heavenly Father, forgive me for the hate and bitterness I've allowed to take over my heart. I thank You for sending Jesus to die for my sins. I accept His gift of forgiveness right now. Amen."

When Miriam finished praying, she opened her eyes and looked at Amos. He smiled, but she noticed tears in his eyes, which let her know he must have felt the emotion of the moment as much as she had. He blinked, and as the wateriness cleared, his lips lifted in a smile that warmed the last frozen place in her heart. "What God doeth is well done," he murmured.

It was then that a new realization came to Miriam. Amos wasn't William Graber or Nick McCormick. He was a kind, caring man, and he loved her. She knew without reservation that with God's help, her yielded heart could now become a loving heart.

CHAPTER 31

Miriam took a seat at the kitchen table and took a bite of the scrambled eggs Amos had set before her. For the first time in a long while, she actually enjoyed eating. Her whole world had taken on a special glow. She felt like a freed prisoner must feel after years of confinement.

"Danki for fixing breakfast," she said as Amos took a seat beside Mary Ellen, who sat across the table from her. "You shouldn't have let me sleep so long. I'm perfectly capable of cooking, you know."

Amos grinned. "I rather enjoyed fixing the eggs. I haven't done much in the kitchen since we got married. Besides, I want you to get as much rest as possible for the next few days. The doctor's orders, you know."

Miriam smiled in return. "These eggs are *appeditlich*. My compliments to the cook on their delicious flavor."

"Can we have pancakes tomorrow, Pappy?" Mary Ellen asked. "Pancakes with maple syrup are my favorite thing for breakfast, and since tomorrow's an off-Sunday and there's no preaching, we'll have plenty of time to make pancakes."

Amos laughed. "We'll see, Mary Ellen."

When breakfast was over, Amos excused himself to go outside and finish the morning chores, reminding Miriam not to do anything strenuous.

"I won't," she promised as she took a seat at the table and opened her Bible. Having decided to have a personal time with God each day, she turned to 1 John, chapter 4: "There is no fear in love; but perfect love casteth out fear: because fear hath torment. He that feareth is not made perfect in love."

Miriam was glad she'd decided to quit fearing love and stop trying to be in control of everything. She could love and be loved in return. She had nothing to fear anymore because she had God's love, as well as Amos's. The storm that had caused her buggy accident might have battered her body, but the storm that had been in her soul for too long had battered her heart. She had sought God's forgiveness and found the peace that only He could give.

Miriam turned the pages in her Bible and read from Philippians, chapter 4, which said, "Rejoice in the Lord always: and again I say, Rejoice." Further down the page, she read verse 8: "Finally, brethren, whatsoever things are true, whatsoever things are honest, whatsoever things are just, whatsoever things are pure, whatsoever things are lovely, whatsoever things are of good report; if there be any virtue, and if there be any praise, think on these things."

"I've wasted so much time thinking about all the bad things that have happened to me that I couldn't see all the good things You've done for me," she murmured.

"Who are you talking to, Mama Mim?"

Miriam turned to see Mary Ellen standing in the

kitchen doorway. The child had put on her coat and boots after breakfast, saying she was going out to play in the snow, but apparently she'd changed her mind.

Miriam reached her hand out to Mary Ellen and pulled her onto her lap. "I was talking to God."

"But your eyes were open, and you were praying out loud."

Miriam chuckled. "I suppose they were open."

"I'm glad today's Saturday and there's no school," Mary Ellen said eagerly. "I get to spend the whole day with my mamm and my daed!"

"Should we do something fun together?"

"Let's bake cookies; then we can go to the Country Store; and after that, we can go out to the barn and play with Pappy's new piglets; and—"

"Whoa! Slow down some, daughter!" Amos called as he entered the room. "Mama Mim has only been out of the hospital a short time and needs to take it easy. If we do all those things in one day, we'll wear her clean out."

Miriam looked up at Amos and smiled. "I'm fine, really."

"You may feel fine, but I don't want you to overdo."

"I appreciate that, and I will be sure to get enough rest," Miriam promised. "But I'll rest after Mary Ellen and I bake some chunky chocolate peanut butter cookies."

Mary Ellen's face lit up. "Yum! They're my favorite kind."

Amos laughed. "I think all cookies are your favorite." He took a seat next to Miriam. "May I help, too?"

"Pappy, do you know how to bake cookies now?"

"Sure he does," Miriam teased. "He knows how to lick the bowl, and he's an expert at eating the cookies." She poked Amos playfully in the stomach.

He gave her a crooked grin. "It's good to have you home, Mim."

"It's good to be home." Her forehead wrinkled. "Say, what are you doing back in the house? I thought you had chores to do outside."

"That's true, but I got to thinking about you and thought I'd pop back inside to see how you were doing."

"I'm doing just fine."

Amos grinned and pushed away from the table. "Okay then. Guess I'll head back out to the barn, but I'll be back soon to try out a few of those cookies."

Miriam smiled as he left the room. She knew her physical injuries were not the only injuries that were healing. So was her heart. Since love was a choice and not just an emotion, she could choose to love Amos in the way a wife should love her husband.

She reached for the most recent copy of *The Budget*, which had been lying on one end of the table, and opened it, hoping to find her mother's most recent article. As she scanned the pages, she noticed the CARDS OF THANKS heading and decided to read a few submissions.

A sincere thank you for the cards, letters, visits, and money I received after my recent knee surgery.
        —Abe Byler, Strasburg, Pennsylvania

Thank you to all my friends and neighbors who brought me cards, cookies, and came by for a visit on my birthday last week.
        —Carolyn Kuhns, Seymour, Missouri

A heartfelt thanks to the special woman I liked to call "fair lady" for her friendship and for helping me to realize that I could find happiness with a woman. In fact, I've met another very special lady, and she's even talked me into going to church with her a few times. So maybe there's some hope for this stubborn man yet. Be happy, fair lady.

—Knight in Shining Armor, Columbus, Ohio

Miriam gasped as tears slipped under her lashes and rolled down her cheeks. That message was from Nick, she was certain of it, and he'd found happiness and wanted her to know it.

She squeezed her eyes shut and offered a silent prayer on her friend's behalf, asking God to bless Nick, and thanking Him for the happiness that she, too, had found.

Amos whistled as he did his chores in the barn. He couldn't help himself, for he was happier than he'd been in a very long time. Miriam was home from the hospital and recovering nicely, and she seemed more peaceful now that she'd committed her life to God.

"Maybe there's some hope that she will come to love me," he said aloud as he spread clean straw in one of the horse's stalls. "She's been friendlier toward me since I admitted that I'm in love with her." He shook his head. "Of course that doesn't mean she loves me."

"You talkin' to yourself or one of the horses?"

At the sound of a man's voice, Amos nearly dropped his

pitchfork, and when he whirled around, he saw Miriam's youngest brother standing a few feet away. "Lewis, you about scared the wits out of me. I didn't hear your horse and buggy. What'd you do, walk over to our place?"

"Nope. Parked my rig down by your blacksmith shop, figuring I'd find you there."

"Not today." Amos leaned the pitchfork against the wall and stepped out of the stall. "Miriam came home from the hospital yesterday."

"Jah, I heard the doctor might be lettin' her go soon. Mom will be happy to hear that news."

Amos nodded. "I figured it would be best if I stuck around the house, at least through the weekend, just to be sure Miriam doesn't do anything she shouldn't be doin'."

"Makes sense to me. My big sister has always been a hard worker, and she's not likely to let a little thing like a bump on the head and a few broken ribs keep her down for long."

"Which is why I'm not working today."

Lewis motioned to the bales of straw stacked along one side of the barn. "Looks like you're workin' to me."

Amos chuckled. "Well, the horses needed some clean bedding, and I hadn't planned on being out here that long." He motioned to the barn door. "Why don't we go inside so you can say hello to Miriam? That will give me another chance to make sure she's not overdoing."

"Sounds like a good idea." Lewis opened the barn door and stepped outside. Amos followed.

When they entered the house a few minutes later, they found Miriam and Mary Ellen in the kitchen, baking cookies.

"Umm. . .smells mighty good in here," Lewis said, stepping up to Miriam and giving her a pat on the arm. "Welcome home, sister. I'd hug you real good, but I know your ribs are probably still pretty sore."

"They aren't so bad." She held a cookie out to him. "Try one of these."

"Hey, where's my cookie?" Amos asked with a mock frown.

Miriam smiled and handed him three cookies. "Is that enough?"

He wiggled his eyebrows. "I think that will tide me over for a while."

Mary Ellen giggled. "Pappy, you're so *eefeldich*."

"Oh, you think I'm silly, do you? Why, I'll show you silly!" Amos chased his daughter around the table, laughing like a schoolboy and tickling her as he went.

Lewis and Miriam stood off to one side, shaking their heads. "Maybe I need a couple more cookies," Lewis said. "Then I'll be smiling like your high-spirited husband."

Amos scooped Mary Ellen into his arms and gave her a hug. He wouldn't admit this to Lewis, but the reason he was so happy had little to do with the cookies he'd eaten and everything to do with the woman who had baked them.

❦

Miriam had been home from the hospital for several days, and even though she said she was feeling stronger, Amos wouldn't allow her to drive the buggy yet. So every morning, he drove Mary Ellen to school and picked her up again each afternoon. One morning when he returned from the schoolhouse, he entered the kitchen and found Miriam making a pot of coffee.

"I was wondering if you'd have time for a little talk," she said as he slipped out of his jacket and hung it on the wall peg.

He rubbed his hands briskly together. "That sounds good if a cup of hot coffee goes with the talk. It's pretty cold out there this morning."

Miriam smiled. "I'll even throw in a few slices of gingerbread. How's that sound?"

"Real good." Amos smacked his lips in anticipation and pulled out a chair at the table.

"I've been thinking," Miriam began. "That is, I was wondering if it would be all right if I moved my things out of my room and into yours."

"Are you saying what I think you are?" Amos asked as hope welled in his chest.

She nodded. "I want to be your wife in every way as God intended it should be."

Amos pushed away from the table and crossed the room to where she stood at the cupboard cutting the gingerbread. He placed his hands on her shoulders and turned her around to face him. Miriam's eyes held a look of tenderness and something more, too. Did he dare believe she might actually love him?

"Are—are you certain about this? I don't want to pressure you in any way. I know we're getting closer, but—"

Miriam placed a finger against his lips. "I want to be your wife, Amos. With God's help, I want to love you as a wife should love her husband."

Amos wrapped his arms around her as every nerve in his body tingled with the joy of holding her. "I love you so much, Miriam."

She pressed her head against his chest, and he inhaled the sweet scent of her freshly washed hair. "I love you, too, Amos," she murmured.

"Really?"

"Jah, it's true."

The words Amos had so longed to hear poured over him like healing balm, and he lifted Miriam's face toward his and placed a gentle kiss against her lips.

She responded with a sigh, and he felt her relax against him as they kissed again. It was a kiss that told Amos how full of love his wife's heart truly was. It was an answer to his prayers.

CHAPTER

32

I f love was a choice, then Miriam had made the right choice, for she found the love she felt for Amos seemed to grow more with each passing day. His tender, gentle way had always been there, but before, she'd chosen to ignore it. Now she thanked the Lord daily for helping her see the truth.

Miriam hardly missed teaching anymore. Her days were filled with household duties she now did out of love. When Amos wasn't busy with his blacksmith duties, he helped her with some of the heavier housecleaning. They took time to read the Bible and pray together, which Miriam knew was the main reason they were drawing closer to one another and to God. Their evening hours were spent with Mary Ellen playing games, putting puzzles together, reading, or just visiting.

Miriam had a special project she was working on, and whenever she had a free moment, she would get out her cross-stitching, just as she had done tonight after she'd tucked Mary Ellen into bed.

"What are you making?" Amos asked as he stepped into the living room.

"It's a surprise for Mom." She patted the sofa cushion.

"Have a seat. You look tired."

He sank down beside her with a groan. *"Ich bin mied wie en hund–*I'm tired as a dog."

She reached over and took his hand. "I don't know of any dog that works as hard as you do, Amos."

He smiled. "I think you're right about that. I've had so much business in my blacksmith shop lately that I'm plumb wore out. If things keep on the way they are, I might have to hire an apprentice."

"Might not be a bad idea; I hate to see you working so hard."

He leaned over and kissed her cheek. "It's nice to know you care about me."

"Of course I care." She needled him in the ribs with her elbow. "If you wear yourself out, who's going to brush my hair for me every night?"

"Oh, so that's how it is, huh?" Amos tickled her in the ribs. "I'm just a convenience to have around whenever you need something, jah?"

"Be careful, or you might get stuck with this needle," she scolded, holding her handwork out of his reach.

He took the sampler from her and placed it on the coffee table. Then he pulled her into his arms and kissed her gently on the lips.

🧶

One Saturday afternoon, Miriam suggested they go for a buggy ride.

"Where would you like to go?" Amos asked.

"I think it's time to pay my family a visit. Let's stop and

see Lewis and Grace first. Then we can go over to Crystal and Jonas's, and finally, we'll call on Mom at Andrew and Sarah's. I want to give her the gift I've been working on."

Amos raised his eyebrows. "A little ride, I thought you said. It sounds to me like you're planning to cover the whole of Lancaster County." He smiled at Miriam and gave his daughter a playful wink.

Mary Ellen, who had been coloring a picture at the kitchen table, jumped up immediately. "Can I go, too?"

Amos bent down and lifted the child into his arms. "Of course, you may. It'll be a fun outing for the three of us."

Miriam gathered up the chunky chocolate peanut butter cookies she had made the day before and placed some into the plastic containers she'd set out. She planned to give one package to each of the families they visited.

The buggy ride was exhilarating, and the trees, budding with spring, were breathtaking. It felt good for Miriam to be out enjoying God's majestic handiwork again.

Mary Ellen, who sat in the seat behind Miriam and Amos, called out, "Oh, look—there goes a mother deer and her boppli. Isn't it lieblich?"

"Jah, Mary Ellen. All babies are adorable," Miriam answered.

"I wish I had a boppli of my own to play with," Mary Ellen said in a wistful tone.

"Someday when you're grown-up and married, maybe you will," her daed answered.

"But I'm still a little girl, and that's a long time off."

"Maybe Uncle Lewis still has some of those baby bunnies left."

"Really, Pappy? Can I have a baby bunny for my own?"

"If it's all right with Mama Mim, it's all right with me."

Miriam smiled. She rather liked the nickname Mary Ellen had begun when they were first married. "If Uncle Lewis still has some bunnies left, you may have one, but only on one condition."

"What condition?"

"That you promise to help care for the bunny."

"Oh, I will. I promise!"

Mary Ellen knelt in the hay next to her father. Uncle Lewis had taken all of the bunnies out of their cages so she could have a better look and could choose which one she wanted.

The rabbit Mary Ellen finally selected was the smallest of the litter, but it looked healthy and bright-eyed and was certainly playful. As they left Lewis's place and headed to Crystal and Jonas's house, Mary Ellen had quite a time keeping the bunny inside the box she'd been given.

Crystal and the twins were out in the yard when Amos pulled their buggy near the barn. The boys jumped up and down, obviously happy to see their cousin.

"I have a surprise!" Mary Ellen called to John and Jacob.

When Amos lifted Mary Ellen down from the buggy, she and the twins rushed off toward the barn.

"Jonas is in the barn working on his old plow," Crystal told Amos. "I'm sure he could use a friendly face about now."

Amos laughed. "Maybe it's time to retire that aged thing. Floyd Mast has some good buys on the new ones he sells."

"I know he probably should buy a new one," Crystal

agreed, "but Jonas is rather partial to the old one. It belonged to his daed, you know."

The mention of Papa caused a sharp pain in Miriam's heart. She still missed her father and probably always would. He'd been a devout Christian man, and someday she was sure she would see him in heaven.

"I'll go see Jonas and leave you two ladies to yourselves. I'm sure you both have plenty to talk about. Women usually do." Amos winked at Miriam and poked her playfully on the arm.

She lunged for him, but he was too quick. His long legs took him quickly out of reach, and soon, he disappeared inside the barn.

"It's good to see you looking so happy," Crystal said as she steered Miriam toward the house.

"I am happy—more than I ever thought possible."

"I'm glad to hear it."

"I brought you some chunky chocolate peanut butter cookies, and I'll tell you about my reason for being so happy over a cup of your great-tasting cider."

"You're lookin' a mite tired today," Jonas said soon after Amos stepped into the barn. "Is that sister of mine workin' you too hard?"

Amos chuckled and shook his head. "It's that business of mine that's wearing me out. I might have to find an apprentice."

Jonas grabbed a piece of straw from a bale nearby and stuck it between his teeth. "I'll spread the word if you want me to."

"I'd appreciate that."

"Other than being tired, how are things going?"

"Real well. Things are much better between Mary Ellen and the other kinner at school, and Miriam and I are happier than I ever thought possible."

Jonas thumped Amos on the back. "I'm glad to hear that, because you've both been through your share of trials, and you deserve all the happiness you can get."

The last stop of the day was at Sarah and Andrew's place. While Miriam was looking forward to seeing her brother and his family, she was most anxious to see Mom and give her the gift she had made.

The sun had been shining all morning, but now, as a light rain began to fall, it slipped behind the clouds. Amos hurried Mary Ellen out of the buggy.

"Wait, Pappy. My bunny's still in the box. I want to take Dinky in to show Rebekah."

"Oh, it's Dinky, is it?"

"Jah, I like that name."

"Okay then. I'll get Dinky for you." Amos grinned at his daughter. "You go on ahead with Mama Mim."

The warmth of the kitchen was welcoming, but the heat from the stove didn't warm Miriam nearly as much as the welcome she and Mary Ellen received from her family.

"What brings you by today?" Andrew asked.

"Jah, to what do we owe this pleasant surprise?" Mom questioned.

"Amos and I thought it would be nice to take Mary Ellen for ride."

"And I've got a surprise!" Mary Ellen hopped up and down in front of Rebekah, who had been wheeled into the room by her mother. "Pappy's gone out to the buggy to get it."

"What's the surprise?" asked Rebekah. "I love surprises."

"I think nearly everyone loves surprises," Miriam said, smiling down at her daughter. "I have one for Mom, too."

"Who wants to be the first to share their surprise?" Sarah asked as she pushed her daughter up to the kitchen table.

Miriam touched Mary Ellen's shoulder. "I'd better let you go first, since you can't seem to stand still."

"But Pappy isn't here yet."

Just then the door opened, and Amos stepped into the room with Dinky in his hands.

"*En gleener Haas!*" Rebekah squealed. "May I hold it, please?"

Mary Ellen reached for the small bunny. With a huge smile on her face, she sashayed across the room and placed the furry critter in Rebekah's lap.

Dinky's nose twitched as Rebekah stroked its floppy ear. "He's awfully cute. Where'd you get him?"

"From Uncle Lewis, and he still has three more, so maybe you'd like a bunny, too."

With an expectant expression, Rebekah looked first at her mother and then over at her father.

Andrew smiled. "If it's okay with your mamm, it's fine by me."

Sarah nodded. "I think it's a good idea, but you must help care for the bunny."

"Jah, of course I will."

"And you must share the bunny with your younger brother and sister," her daed reminded.

"I promise, Papa."

"Come, everyone. Sit awhile." Miriam's mamm motioned to the table. "I'll put water on the stove to heat, and we can have some hot chocolate."

"And I've brought along some chunky chocolate peanut butter cookies," Miriam said as Amos pulled out a chair for her.

When everyone was seated and the hot chocolate and cookies had been passed around, Miriam lifted the canvas tote bag from the back of her chair and reached inside.

"What's this?" Mom asked as Miriam pulled out a small package wrapped in tissue paper and handed it to her.

"I made this for you—to let you know how much I love you."

Mom took the gift, and she emitted a sob when she opened it. "Oh, Miriam, it's lieblich."

"What's lovely?" Sarah asked, craning her neck to see.

Mom held up the beautiful cross-stitched wall hanging Miriam had made. It read: "A merry heart doeth good like a medicine."

Miriam gave her mother a hug. "Those words from the Bible are true, Mom. You've been right all along, and I just couldn't see it. God wants His children to have merry hearts. It's my hope that anyone in our future generations who see this sampler will know that the only way to be truly healthy spiritually is to have a merry heart."

"This is a blessed surprise," Mom said tearfully. "And it's certainly an answer to my prayers to know that you finally understand the importance of having a merry heart."

"God had been calling to me for a long time. I only wish I had listened to Him sooner." Miriam looked over at Amos and smiled. "Would you like to tell them our other surprise?"

He shook his head. "I think we should let Mary Ellen tell 'em, don't you?"

Miriam nodded. "That's a fine idea. Mary Ellen, please tell everyone our other surprise."

Mary Ellen giggled; then in her most grown-up voice, she announced, "On the way here, Mama Mim and Pappy told me that I'm gonna be a big sister."

"Miriam, is she saying what I think she's saying?" Mom asked breathlessly.

Miriam nodded. "I'm expecting a boppli."

"Now that's wunderbaar news," Sarah exclaimed.

"I'm so happy for you." Mom gave Miriam a hug. "Oh, I wish the rest of our family were here for this joyful news."

"We've already seen Lewis and Grace, as well as Jonas and Crystal, so they've been told," Amos was quick to say.

"Congratulations!" Andrew said, thumping Amos on the back, then hugging Miriam.

Mom dabbed the corners of her eyes with a hankie. "If only my Henry could be here. He would be so pleased to see how happy our Miriam is now."

"Someday, we'll be reunited with Papa, but until then, he'll always be with us—right here." Miriam placed her hand against her chest. "I hope my own kinner and future kinskinner will grow up to love the Lord and have merry hearts, too."

MIRIAM'S CHUNKY CHOCOLATE PEANUT BUTTER COOKIES

Ingredients:
  ¾ cup margarine
  1 cup white sugar
  1 cup brown sugar
  ½ cup peanut butter
  2 eggs
  2 teaspoons vanilla
  2 ½ cups flour
  1 teaspoon baking soda
  ½ teaspoon salt
  1 (8 oz.) chocolate candy bar, chopped

Preheat oven to 350 degrees. Beat margarine, sugars, and peanut butter until light and fluffy. Blend in eggs and vanilla. Add the dry ingredients and mix well. Stir in chocolate pieces. Drop rounded tablespoons of dough onto ungreased cookie sheet. Bake 10-12 minutes or until lightly browned. Let stand a few minutes before removing from cookie sheet. Makes four dozen cookies.

LOOKING FOR A MIRACLE

Brides of Lancaster County

2

To my six wunderbaar *grandchildren,*
Jinell, Madolynne, Rebekah, Ric, Philip, and Richelle.
You are each one of God's special miracles.

Commit thy way unto the Lord; *trust also in him;*
and he shall bring it to pass.
Psalm 37:5

CHAPTER 1

Rebekah Stoltzfus sat on the sidelines in her wheelchair, watching with envy as the others who had come to the young people's singing played a game of volleyball.

Sixteen-year-old Harold Beachy zipped past Rebekah, nearly bumping into her wheelchair. "Oops, sorry."

Rebekah opened her mouth to reply, but Harold had already raced to the other side of the volleyball net to join the game. She sighed. "What's the use? No one seems to know I'm here anyway."

Self-pity was a common occurrence for Rebekah these days, as she struggled to deal with her insecurities and envy of others who could do all the things she couldn't do. Take her cousin, Mary Ellen Hilty, for example. Mary Ellen had lots of suitors and could probably have her pick of any of the young men if she wanted.

Rebekah and Mary Ellen had become cousins by marriage when Mary Ellen's father, Amos, had married Rebekah's aunt Miriam. The young girls had been friends before that, but after the joining of their families, they had become even closer, despite the fact that they were nothing alike.

Mary Ellen had dark brown hair and hazel-colored eyes, while Rebekah had light brown hair and pale blue eyes.

Mary Ellen, who had been teaching at the Amish one-room schoolhouse for the last year, was fun loving, self-assured, and outgoing, which was probably why all the young men admired her. Rebekah, on the other hand, was quiet, self-conscious, and certain that no one except her family could possibly love her. She lacked the confidence seen in most young women her age.

Rebekah hadn't always been shy, however. In fact, when she was a little girl, she used to be as outgoing as Mary Ellen was now. But thirteen years ago, everything had changed when a freak accident left her crippled.

Rebekah still remembered the details of the accident as though it had happened yesterday. A storm had come up just as Aunt Mim, who'd been the schoolteacher back then, had dismissed the class to go home after school ended for the day. Aunt Mim had promised to give Rebekah a ride home, and Rebekah had gone outside to wait in the buggy while Aunt Mim finished cleaning the blackboard. Rebekah had just reached the buggy, which had been parked under a tree, when she heard a terrible snap and was knocked to the ground.

The next thing she knew, she was in the hospital with doctors and nurses standing over her bed, looking ever so serious. Her distraught parents stood nearby, and Mom was weeping for all she was worth. When Rebekah had asked what was wrong, she'd been informed that a branch had broken from the tree and fallen across her back, knocking her unconscious. The blow had injured part of her spinal cord, and she would probably never walk again.

The reality didn't truly sink in until one month later when Rebekah was allowed to go home. It was then that she'd come to realize exactly what her limitations would be. She would be confined to a wheelchair, unable to walk, run, and play the way other children could do. Her grandmother Anna Stoltzfus had moved into their house in order to help care for Rebekah. That gave Rebekah a clue that she would always be a burden to those she loved. She would never be able to live a normal life—never marry, never have children of her own.

"Are you havin' fun?"

Rebekah's thoughts came to a halt when Emma Troyer skidded to a stop in front of her wheelchair, red-faced and panting for breath.

How can I have fun while I sit here on the sidelines watching you and the others play games? Rebekah kept her thoughts to herself and nodded in reply. After so many years of being left out of things, she had come to realize that there was no use in complaining, as it would do nothing to change her condition. She'd learned to suffer in silence and put on a brave front as though her handicap didn't matter. Trouble was it did matter because it singled her out as being different from the rest of her family and friends.

"We should be eating soon," Emma said, nodding toward the refreshment table.

"*Jah*, I expect so."

"Well, guess I'll go see if I can get in on the next game of volleyball." Emma patted Rebekah's shoulder, offering her a sympathetic-looking smile; then she hurried away.

Rebekah hated to see pity on anyone's face. It wasn't

their sympathy or pity she wanted. What she needed was a miracle. Some said she'd already had one miracle. Leastways, that's what everyone had called it when, after several months of physical therapy, Rebekah had been able to stand and even take a few steps on her own. Of course, in order to do it, she needed leg braces and a pair of special crutches strapped to her arms. Some miracle that was! It took a lot of effort to walk that way, so Rebekah spent most of her time in her wheelchair. One of the few things she did that she would consider useful was the monthly column she wrote for *The Budget*, an Amish newspaper. As one of the scribes for the paper, she often wrote about some of the major happenings in their area of Lancaster County, but that was nothing compared to what other people her age got to do.

Rebekah caught sight of Mary Ellen running through the tall grass across the yard with several young fellows right on her heels. Mary Ellen lifted her hand in a wave, and Rebekah waved back, wishing that she, too, could run through the grass with even one suitor following her.

It was obvious by the smile on Mary Ellen's face that she enjoyed all the attention she'd received this evening. And why wouldn't she? Rebekah was sure that any woman who had so many men interested in her would take pleasure in it, too.

She swallowed past the lump in her throat and squeezed her eyes shut, willing herself not to give in to the threatening tears. Crying wouldn't do her a bit of good.

Rebekah opened her eyes and wheeled herself back to the barn. She spotted the refreshment table inside the door and headed over to get something cool to drink, hoping it might help wash away that awful, familiar lump.

"Want some punch?"

Rebekah jerked her head to the right. There stood Daniel Beachy, one of the young men she had seen talking to Mary Ellen earlier this evening. "*Danki*, but I can get it," she muttered. "It's one of the few things I can do by myself."

"It's no bother. I was about to get something for myself anyway." Daniel ladled some punch into a paper cup, then handed it to Rebekah in spite of her refusal. "So, are you enjoying the singing?"

Rebekah smiled as she took the offered punch. "It's all right, but I wish we could do more singing and less game playing."

"Volleyball's a lot of fun, though."

Rebekah wondered if she should explain that the reason she enjoyed singing was because it was all she could do well. Game playing, at least the kind that required running and jumping, was out of the question for someone like her. However, she never got the chance to express those thoughts because Mary Ellen showed up.

"Rebekah, you should have heard some of the silly jokes Johnny Yoder told me," Mary Ellen said breathlessly. "I've laughed so much tonight, I don't think I'll have to laugh again for the rest of the month."

Rebekah feigned a smile as Mary Ellen related a couple of the jokes Johnny had shared. Her cousin's cheeks were bright pink, and her eyes shone with obvious enthusiasm. No wonder so many of the young Amish men wanted to court her. Rebekah couldn't be mad at Mary Ellen, though. It wasn't her fault she was so cute and such fun to be around.

If Rebekah had been able to join in the games, maybe others would like her more, too. Some of the boys might want to court her if she could run, jump, and laugh at their silly jokes.

Mary Ellen leaned over Rebekah's wheelchair and whispered in her ear, "Johnny's asked if he can give me a ride home in his courting buggy tonight. You don't care if I go with him, do you?"

"But you came with me and Simon."

"I know, but I'm sure your brother won't mind not having to drive me home." Mary Ellen smiled. "After all, he has to go to the same place as you're going, and if I go with Johnny, then Simon won't have to travel clear over to my house."

"Jah, sure. Go ahead and ride with Johnny." Rebekah wasn't about to make a fuss over Mary Ellen riding home with someone else. She might appear to be jealous.

She glanced over at Daniel. Was that a look of envy she saw as he shifted from one foot to the other and stared at the concrete floor? Maybe he'd been waiting for the chance to ask Mary Ellen if he could give her a ride home and was disappointed because now he wouldn't get that opportunity. If Daniel hadn't wasted so much time getting punch for Rebekah, he might have been able to seek Mary Ellen out. Then it would be his courting buggy she would be riding home in tonight, not Johnny Yoder's.

Why do I always feel so guilty about things? Rebekah fretted. After all, it wasn't as if she had asked Daniel to get her some punch or kept him here on purpose. She hadn't intentionally spoiled his chances with Mary Ellen. He should have realized he was missing out on his chance and gone looking for the girl he wanted to escort home.

Rebekah tried to shake aside her contrary feelings as she said in her most cheerful voice, "I'm getting kind of tired, so I think I'll go find Simon and see if he's ready to head for home."

"Johnny and I will be leaving soon, too, I expect," Mary Ellen said with a nod. "Probably after we've had something to eat."

"I'd better see when my sister, Sarah Jane, wants to go. My two brothers will probably have dates to take home." Daniel glanced down at Rebekah and smiled. It was the kind of smile she'd become used to seeing—one of pity, she was certain of it. "*Gut nacht*, Rebekah." He looked over at her cousin and nodded. "Gut nacht, Mary Ellen."

"Good night," Rebekah and Mary Ellen said in unison.

As Daniel walked away, Mary Ellen leaned close to Rebekah's ear again. "He's kind of *gutguckich*, don't you think?"

If you think he's so handsome, then why aren't you riding home with him instead of Johnny? "He seems to like you," Rebekah muttered.

Just then, Johnny rushed up to Mary Ellen and grabbed hold of her hand. "Come on. Let's play one more game of volleyball before we eat, and then we'll head for home."

"All right, Johnny." Mary Ellen gave Rebekah's arm a little pat. "See you in two weeks at preaching, if not before."

"Jah," Rebekah murmured as she wheeled away in search of Simon.

❧

As Mary Ellen walked away with Johnny, she couldn't help

but feel sorry for her best friend. She could tell by the dejected look she had seen on Rebekah's face that her friend was upset—probably because Mary Ellen wouldn't be riding home with her and Simon. As much as Mary Ellen wanted to please her cousin, she didn't want to give up the chance to ride home with Johnny tonight, knowing it could be the beginning of their courting days. At least she hoped it would be because Johnny was a lot of fun, and she really enjoyed his company.

Johnny squeezed Mary Ellen's fingers. "What's with the sour expression? I thought you enjoyed playing volleyball."

"I–I do. I was just noticing how glum Rebekah looks tonight, and I'm concerned about her."

"Ah, she always looks that way. How does she ever expect to get a man if she goes around lookin' like she's been suckin' a bunch of sour grapes all the time?" Johnny offered Mary Ellen a wide grin. "Sure am glad my girl likes to laugh and smile."

My girl? Did Johnny really think of Mary Ellen as his girl? Or was he only flirting with her the way so many of the other fellows had done tonight?

Mary Ellen thought back to the days when she'd been a young girl attending the one-room schoolhouse. None of the boys had showed any interest in her then—except to tease and taunt. Her mamm had died when Mary Ellen was still quite young, and many students had teased her due to her unkempt appearance.

But all that had changed after Pappy married Mama Mim. From that time on, Mary Ellen's dresses were mended and her hair put neatly in place. She'd felt a new sense of confidence, having both a mother and a father. Mama Mim had always taken good care of her, and Mary Ellen felt as though Pappy's new wife loved her as much as if she were her own flesh-and-blood daughter.

Now, as a young woman, Mary Ellen not only had more confidence, but she also taught at the one-room school-house she had once attended. She had a host of male admirers like Johnny, who seemed determined to win her affections. She just wished that at least one of those fellows would notice Rebekah. It might help her smile more if she knew someone had an interest in her, and it would surely boost her confidence.

"Are you gonna stand there all night watchin' the back-side of Rebekah's wheelchair, or did you plan to play volley-ball with me?" Johnny asked, breaking into Mary Ellen's contemplations.

She forced her lips to form a smile, knowing she needed to put on a happy face if she was going to keep fun-loving Johnny's attention. "Jah. I'm ready to play."

Rebekah's sixteen-year-old brother, Simon, pushed her wheel-chair up the wooden ramp Dad had built soon after her accident, and they entered the house through the back door. Rebekah spotted her parents right away, sitting at the kitchen table, playing a game of Scrabble.

Dad didn't seem to notice them as he tugged on his beard and studied the wooden letters on the tray in front of him.

However, Mom looked up right away and smiled. Her

eyes, much bluer and brighter than Rebekah's, seemed to dance in the light of the gas lantern that hung above the table. "Sit yourselves down and talk awhile. Tell us about the singing. Did you two have a good time?"

"Jah, it was great!" Simon pushed a lock of sandy brown hair off his forehead. "Just about every Amish teen we know was there." He opened the door of their propane-operated refrigerator, obviously looking for something to eat.

"And you, daughter?" Mom asked. "Did you have a good time?"

Rebekah shrugged. "It was all right, I guess."

"Just all right? It's been a good many years for me now, but as I remember, singings were always a lot of fun." Mom glanced over at Dad, who was still studying the Scrabble board as if his life depended on the next move. "It was right after a singing when your *daed* asked me to marry him, you know."

"Jah, well, I expect our family might be in for another wedding soon," Simon said, as he helped himself to a thick slice of apple-crumb pie and took a seat at the table.

Mom's eyebrows lifted. "Is there something you've been keeping from us, Rebekah? *Kumme*—come now—tell us your news."

Rebekah wheeled her chair closer to the table. "It's not me. I think Simon's referring to Cousin Mary Ellen."

"I see. So who's her lucky fellow?" Mom prompted. "Or aren't we supposed to know that yet?"

"It could be anyone. Mary Ellen's popular with several young men in our community. She can probably take her pick of whomever she pleases." Rebekah drew in a quick breath and released it with a moan. "I think Daniel Beachy is the one most in love with her, but Johnny Yoder won't give him a chance."

"Hmm. . ." Mom gave a slight nod of her head. "It sounds as if Mary Ellen might have to make a choice then."

"She'll pick Johnny," Simon said with his mouth full of pie.

"Really, Simon, didn't you get enough food at the singing? Sometimes I think all you ever do is eat," Mom scolded, though she was smiling when she spoke.

"Aw, leave the boy alone, Sarah. He's growin' so fast these days and needs all the nourishment he can get." It was the first time Rebekah's father had spoken since their arrival. Suddenly, he slapped the table and hollered, "My word is *zealot*! The *z*, which is normally worth ten points, is on a double letter square. The other letters are worth one point apiece. The *l* lands on a double word square, so my entire score is fifty!" He gave Mom a playful nudge on the arm. "I have only one letter left, so beat that if you can!"

Mom laughed and tickled Dad beneath his full beard, which had recently become sprinkled with a few gray hairs. "All right, Andrew, you've won the game fair and square, so now you're deserving of a reward. How about a piece of pie? If your growing son hasn't eaten it all, that is," she added with a wink.

"You two act like a couple of *kinner*," Rebekah said with a mock frown. "Watch out now, or you'll end up waking Nadine and Grandma Stoltzfus."

Dad chuckled. "Well now, we wouldn't want to do that, would we? Grandma might eat all the pie before any of us could make it to the refrigerator."

"Dad," Rebekah said with a snicker. "You know Grandma doesn't eat so much."

Dad bent down and tapped her under the chin. "That's true, but if Simon or little sister Nadine should decide to help her, then I might have to take on a second job just to pay for the grocery bills."

"You're such a tease," Rebekah said, as she propelled her chair quickly away from him.

"You're right, I am. That's why your mamm agreed to marry me. She loves to be teased." He turned his attentions on Mom again, tickling her in the ribs and under the chin.

She tickled him right back, and soon the two of them were howling and tickling so much that Rebekah was sure they really would wake Grandma or Nadine.

As Mom and Dad chased each other around the table, a pang of jealousy washed over Rebekah like the rippling creek running across the back of their farm. She couldn't help wondering how it would feel to laugh and run around with a young man—someone she loved as much as her folks obviously loved each other. *But that would take a miracle, and miracles only happened back in the Bible days, didn't they?*

A silent prayer for an honest-to-goodness miracle floated through Rebekah's mind as she directed her wheelchair toward her downstairs bedroom. What she really needed was to quit thinking about miracles and be alone for a while.

"I wonder what's wrong with Rebekah tonight," Andrew said to Sarah as they started another game of Scrabble. He squinted at the board and reached for two letters from his pile. "She sure didn't act like she enjoyed that singing so much."

"She didn't enjoy it at all," Simon chimed in before Sarah could respond. "You should have seen the way she sat there in her wheelchair watching the others play games with a big old scowl on her face. Guess she felt left out because she couldn't join in the fun, but I don't think that's any excuse for being such a stick-in-the-mud."

Sarah glanced over at Andrew. "I hate to see our daughter hurting so. Maybe it would be best if we didn't allow her to go to any more singings or young people's functions."

Andrew's eyebrows lowered as he frowned, causing deep wrinkles to form on his forehead. "We can't shield Rebekah from everything, Sarah. She's not a little girl anymore, and she needs to mingle with others her age, don't you think?"

"I—I suppose so, but—"

"It's time for her to grow up and realize that even though she can't do everything others can do, she's still a capable person and can do many things quite well." He added two of his letters to a word already on the Scrabble board, which gave him another ten points.

Sarah took her turn, making a five-letter word and racking up fifteen more points.

Simon chuckled. "You'd better watch out, Dad, or Mom might skunk ya on this game."

"Not if I can help it."

"Back to the subject of my moody sister," Simon said. "I read in the paper the other day that there's going to be a convention in Ohio next month. It's for Amish folks who are handicapped, like Rebekah. Maybe the two of you could hire a driver and take her there. That would give her the chance to be with some people she could relate to better, and maybe she'd even learn a few new things about how to cope with her disability."

Sarah opened her mouth to comment, but Simon rushed on before she could get a word out. "If you're worried about Grandma, Nadine, and me, I'm sure we can get along fine by ourselves for the couple of days you'd be gone."

Andrew squinted as he continued to study the board. "I read about that handicap convention, too, but I'm not sure I could get away from the farm that long, so your mamm might have to be the one to take her." He glanced up from the board and looked over at Sarah. "How do you feel about it? Do you think Rebekah would agree to go?"

"I don't know. I suppose we could ask her."

"You want to bring it up, or should I?"

"I'll mention it tomorrow," Sarah replied. "In the meantime, I'll be praying that she will be open to the idea."

Andrew nodded. "I'll do the same."

All the way home from the singing, Daniel thought about Rebekah—how cute she was, how sad she had looked sitting in her wheelchair all alone.

"It must be hard for her not being able to run around and play games like the other young people do," he muttered as he guided his horse and open carriage up the long driveway that led to his father's house and dairy farm. He had enjoyed his brief conversation with Rebekah tonight, even though she hadn't said all that much. He wished he'd been able to get up the nerve to ask if he could give her a ride home from the singing in his courting buggy.

Daniel pulled up to the barn and climbed down from the buggy. " 'Course it ain't likely that she'd have agreed to go," he mumbled as he kicked a couple of small stones with the toe of his boot. After all, there had been a lot more interesting fellows at the singing tonight than him—some with fancy buggies they'd fixed up to impress the girls, some with fun-loving personalities like Johnny Yoder. "Wish I could be more like him instead of being afraid I'll say the wrong thing or do something stupid."

He quickly unhitched his horse and led him toward the barn as a feeling of regret threatened to weigh him down. "Even if I had found the nerve to ask if Rebekah would take a ride in my rig, it ain't likely she would have been interested in riding home in my simple courting buggy with an ordinary fellow like me."

CHAPTER

2

When Rebekah awoke the following morning, she felt physically drained and out of sorts. She had lain awake for hours, thinking about her disability and all the restrictions she had to deal with. She wondered if there was some way she could possibly fit in with the other young people her age. Since she wasn't able to join most of their activities, she couldn't really blame them for ignoring her, but it hurt, nonetheless. She seemed to be more accepted by older people—especially Grandma. Maybe it was because Grandma couldn't do as much as the younger ones did. Most of her activities, though not as restricted as Rebekah's, were still a bit hampered.

Rebekah knew her parents and grandmother loved her and were dedicated to taking care of her needs, but she worried about what would become of her when they were gone. Would her younger brother or sister, or maybe a cousin or niece, be stuck caring for her? She didn't want to be a burden to anyone and wished there was some way she could provide for her own needs.

Rebekah pulled herself to an upright position, using the

wooden side rails on her bed to lend the needed support. *I know I'll never have a husband or children of my own, but if I could at least be financially independent, I would be less of a burden to everyone.*

Unbidden tears slipped out of Rebekah's eyes, rolling down her cheeks in little rivulets. What could one crippled young Amish woman do that would provide her with enough money to care for herself? Was it even possible, or was it just wishful thinking?

"I think what I need to do is commit this problem to prayer," she whispered. "Jah, that's what Grandma would say I should do."

Closing her eyes, Rebekah sent up a silent petition to God. *Heavenly Father, what I need is a miracle. If You still perform miracles, could You please give me some kind of a sign? I know I've done nothing to deserve a miracle, and I'm not asking You to heal my crippled body or give me a husband. I only want to support myself, so I'm not such a burden to my family. If You could show me how to do that, I'd be much obliged. Amen.*

Silence filled Rebekah's small, unadorned bedroom. Had she really expected God to answer her out loud? Hadn't the bishop and other ministers in their church shared some scripture verses proving that God talked to people's hearts? Sometimes He spoke through other believers or from His Holy Word. Rebekah had read herself how God had spoken out loud to some people in the Bible, but she figured they probably needed that type of thing back then. If there was any hope of her receiving a miracle, she felt it would only occur if she learned more patience, read her Bible regularly, and prayed every day.

As Rebekah wheeled into the kitchen, Sarah turned from the stove where she had been frying a slab of bacon. "*Guder mariye*, daughter," she said with a smile. She hoped after a good night's sleep Rebekah might be in a more cheerful mood.

"Good morning," Rebekah mumbled.

"Did you sleep well?"

"I slept okay."

Sarah could see by the solemn expression on her daughter's face that she still wasn't in the best of moods. Maybe now wasn't a good time to bring up the subject of the handicap convention. It might be better to wait until after they had eaten breakfast to talk about the possibility of the two of them going to Ohio. Maybe Rebekah would be in a better mood once her stomach was full of bacon and eggs.

Rebekah wheeled into the middle of the room and glanced around. "Where's Grandma? She's usually the first one to the kitchen every morning."

"Still in bed. When I came into the kitchen and realized she wasn't here, I went in to check on her."

"Is she all right?"

"Said she wasn't feeling well, so I told her we could manage and insisted that she stay in bed and rest awhile."

"She seemed to be feeling all right yesterday evening before Simon and I left for the singing." Rebekah's lips puckered as her forehead wrinkled with obvious concern. "Sure hope it's nothing serious."

Sarah flipped the bacon over in the frying pan. "She's

been a little tired the past few days, but other than that, she's made no complaints until this morning. I think sometimes she tries to do too much for a woman her age."

Rebekah nodded. "I know she does. Ever since Grandma came to live here, she's done the work of two women. It wonders me so how she can keep up like she does."

"Jah, but in the beginning, I think keeping busy helped her not miss Grandpa so much, and now she's just developed a habit of always being on the move."

"It was nice that Aunt Mim and Uncle Amos named their son Henry, after Grandpa Stoltzfus," Rebekah said, changing the subject.

"I know it meant a lot to Grandma at the time, and even now, whenever young Henry's around, I believe she thinks of your *grossdaddi*."

"Jah. She's often said that in many ways Henry reminds her of Grandpa." Rebekah glanced at Grandma's bedroom door, which was just across the hall and right next to her own room. "Do you think maybe she should see the doctor?"

"If she's not up and around and acting like her old self by this afternoon, I'll speak to your daed and see that he takes her to see Dr. Manney."

Rebekah nodded and wheeled toward the table. "What can I do to help with breakfast, and where's Nadine? She's not sick, too, I hope."

"No, she's feeling fine. I sent her out to gather some eggs a little while ago." Sarah piled the crispy bacon into a glass pan and popped it into the oven so it would stay warm until breakfast was served. "I'll be doing some baking later this morning, and since we're having eggs for breakfast, we might run short. I checked the refrigerator, and there aren't as many now as I remember."

"Simon probably ate them," Rebekah said. "Now that it's summertime and he has a lot more chores to do, he eats enough to feed ten boys his age."

Sarah was glad to see Rebekah relaxing a bit and making a joke—even if it had been at her brother's expense. "You're right. Simon can surely put away the food these days." She clicked her tongue. "I pity the poor woman my boy marries. She'll probably have to cook from sunup to sunset in order to keep his stomach satisfied."

"Maybe we should start alerting all the eligible women in our community right now. That way, if anyone should ever fall for my little *bruder*, she can't say she wasn't warned."

Sarah reached for a can of coffee from the cupboard. "Enough about Simon and his eating habits. How about if you scramble up some eggs while I get the coffee going?"

Rebekah frowned. "You know it's hard for me to reach the stove from my wheelchair."

Sarah turned to face her daughter and squinted. "I thought you might decide to wear your crutches and leg braces today. You can stand at the stove for a short time if you're using them."

"*Jah*, but it's so much trouble to put them on. Besides, the braces make my legs stiff like a doll's."

"I know they're awkward and uncomfortable, but they do allow you to stand and even walk a short ways. It's much more than we could have hoped for, since the doctors said you would probably never walk again."

"Okay, Mom, I'll go get the leg braces," Rebekah muttered

as she turned her wheelchair toward the door leading to the hallway.

"Better wait on that," Sarah called. "The menfolk will be in from their chores soon, and we need to get breakfast on as quickly as possible because I'm sure they'll be anxious to get out to the fields." She motioned to the table. "Why don't you set the dishes and silverware out? Nadine can cook up the eggs when she gets back. We'll have more eggs by then anyhow."

"Jah."

The back door opened with a *whoosh*, and Nadine burst into the room, all red-faced and wearing a smile that stretched ear to ear. Instead of her usual stiff white *kapp*, she wore a black kerchief over her pinned-up brown hair.

"How'd it go in the chicken coop?" Sarah asked.

"I got over a dozen eggs." Nadine lifted the basket she held in her hands and grinned. "I'm thinkin' those fat little hens must like summer nearly as much as I do." She placed the basket of eggs on the counter and went to wash up at the sink.

"I'm glad it went well, and it's a good thing they're laying so well," Sarah replied. "We're having scrambled eggs this morning, and I was afraid we might run out and I wouldn't have enough for the baking I want to do later." She stepped away from the stove. "Nadine, would you please scramble up the eggs?"

"Sure." Nadine moved over to the stove; then she glanced over at Rebekah, who had just placed some silverware on the table. "How was the singing last night, sister? Did you have a good time?"

"It was okay."

"Just okay?"

"Jah."

"Well, I can't wait until I'm allowed to go to one." Nadine cast a wistful look in Sarah's direction.

Sarah smiled. "You'll get there soon enough, like as not."

Rebekah wheeled over to the cupboard where the dishes were kept. "Going to a singing isn't that exciting."

"You must be joking. There are boys at those singings, right?"

Rebekah lifted her gaze to the ceiling. "Of course there are boys."

"Then I think it would be a lot of fun to go to one."

"Which is why you're not ready to go to any singings yet," Sarah said firmly. "In my opinion, a girl of fourteen shouldn't be so interested in the opposite sex, either."

"Oh, Mom," Nadine groaned. "I'll bet if you had your way, I'd grow up to be *en alt maedel* like Rebekah."

"Nadine Stoltzfus, that's an awful thing to say about your sister. Rebekah is not an old maid. She's only nineteen and still has plenty of time to get married. I think you should apologize to Rebekah for saying that, don't you?"

Nadine's youthful face reddened as she looked down at Rebekah with her eyebrows drawn together. "Well, I–I–"

"Go ahead," Sarah prompted. "Tell you sister you're sorry for what you said."

Rebekah held up her hand. "It's all right. Nadine spoke the truth. I am en alt maedel, and that's just the way of it."

"Such nonsense," Sarah said with a shake of her head. "When the right man comes along and captures your heart, you'll marry and start a family of your own."

Rebekah's gaze went immediately to her crippled legs. "Like this?" She touched one knee and then the other. "Would any man want a wife who looks like me?"

"There's nothing wrong with the way you look, Rebekah."

"But who would want someone who can't do all the things a normal wife should be able to do?" Tears slipped out from under Rebekah's dark lashes, and she blinked several times.

Sarah rushed to her daughter's side and dropped down beside her wheelchair. "Oh, Rebekah, please don't say things like that."

Rebekah leaned her head against Sarah's shoulder and wept. "It's true, and you know it. No one will ever want me. I'll never find a husband, and I'm nothing but a burden to my family."

"That's not so."

"Jah, it is, and no one understands how I feel about things."

Deciding that now might be a good time to bring up the handicap convention, Sarah patted Rebekah's back gently and said, "Simon mentioned last night that he'd read about a convention for Amish people who have handicaps like you. It's to be held next month in Ohio, and your daed and I thought maybe you and I could—"

"I don't want to go anywhere right now," Rebekah interrupted. "Especially not to some convention where I don't know anyone." She released a quiet moan. "I just want to be able to take care of myself."

"Oh, but you do. You've learned to dress and groom

yourself, and you can do so many other important things."

"What kind of important things?"

"The column you write for *The Budget* is one thing you do well." Sarah smiled. "If you went to the convention, you'd be able to write about it when you returned home. It might give someone else in your predicament the incentive to attend the next convention."

"I'm sure it's a good thing for some, but I'm really not interested, Mom."

"Won't you at least give it some thought?"

Rebekah's eyes filled with more tears. "Are you wanting to get rid of me for a while? Is that it?"

"Why, no. Of course not. I just thought you might benefit from going, and I had planned to go with you." Sarah sighed. "But if you're dead set against the idea, then I won't mention it again."

"Danki, I appreciate that."

Nadine stepped up to Rebekah and opened her mouth as if to comment, but her words were cut off when the back door flew open and Andrew and Simon rushed into the room. Their faces were as red as one of the heifers out in the pasture, and they huffed and puffed something awful.

"Your son is gettin' too good for me now, Sarah," Andrew panted. "We raced all the way from the barn, and Simon nearly beat me to the back door."

"Nearly?" Simon scrunched up his nose. "What do ya mean, nearly, Dad? My feet hit the porch steps at least six seconds before yours did."

Andrew's deep laughter bounced off the walls. "Well, what does it matter? I got to the kitchen first, and that's all that counts." He thumped Simon on the back a couple of times. "So now I get the first kiss!"

"The what?" Simon took two steps back and bumped into the table, clattering the silverware.

"Not you, boy. I was referring to your mamm." Andrew marched across the room, drew Sarah into his arms, and planted a noisy kiss right on her mouth.

"Andrew, really! What kind of example are you setting for the kinner?" Sarah bit back a chuckle as she shook her finger at him.

"I'm settin' a good example, I hope." With that, Sarah's playful husband bent down and kissed her soundly once more.

"Oh, yuk!" Simon shook his head and groaned.

"I think it's kind of romantic. Don't you, Rebekah?" Nadine asked with a girlish giggle.

Rebekah, who had been busy drying her tearstained cheeks with a napkin, gave only a quick nod in response.

"And I think it's time for all this silliness to end." Sarah motioned to the sink. "Breakfast is nearly ready, so if my men will get washed up, we can eat and get on with our day."

Get on with our day? Rebekah gripped the arms of her wheelchair. Today was just another day. Nothing to look forward to, that was for sure. When Rebekah was a child, her disability hadn't bothered her so much, but now that she'd become a young woman, things were different—she was different. *That must be why Mom wants me to go to the convention in Ohio—everyone there will be different, too.*

She glanced at the door leading to Grandma's room. *Maybe if I did something worthwhile today, I would feel better. As soon as breakfast is over, I think I'll fill a plate with eggs and bacon and take a tray into Grandma. Then maybe I can read to her for a while. Since she's not feeling well, it will give me a chance to minister to her for a change.*

After the men had washed up, everyone took their seats at the table. Following a short time of silent prayer, Mom passed the platter of scrambled eggs around the table, along with some biscuits and crispy bacon.

Rebekah only nibbled on her food, as her thoughts vacillated between Grandma not feeling well and Mom wanting her to attend the handicap convention in Ohio. Even if the convention did have some helpful things to offer, she didn't want to be away from home that long. She would miss her family too much—especially Grandma, who seemed to understand her needs more than anyone else.

"You've hardly touched your food, Rebekah," Dad said, breaking into her thoughts. "Has your appetite gone away this morning?"

She nodded. "I'm worried about Grandma."

"I'm sure she'll be fine after a few more hours of rest," Mom put in. "But as I said before, if she's not feeling better by this afternoon, we'll take her to see the doctor."

"That's right," Dad agreed. "Even if it means we have to tie her to the buggy seat in order to get her there."

"Now why would you have to do something like that to Grandma?" Nadine asked, tipping her head and looking at Dad as if he'd taken leave of his senses.

Simon, who sat next to Nadine, poked her arm and

snickered. "He's only kiddin', *dummkopp*."

"I am not a dunce," she shot back, giving him a jab to the ribs with her elbow.

Mom wagged her finger. "That will be enough, you two. Just eat your breakfast, and no more goading each other."

"I wasn't." Nadine's bottom lip jutted out. "Simon was the one who started it."

"It doesn't matter who's at fault," Dad said, his eyebrows drawing together in a frown. "Just do as your mamm says, or I'll give you both double chores to do for the next week or two."

Simon and Nadine fell silent, and Rebekah was glad for it grated on her nerves to have to listen to their senseless chatter.

When everyone had finished eating, the men excused themselves, saying they were headed out to the fields and would be back in time for lunch.

"Jah," Mom said as she pushed away from the table. "We'll be sure to have the noon meal ready on time."

"Do you want me to help with the dishes now, or should I take Grandma a tray with some breakfast first?" Rebekah asked her mother.

"You can go ahead and do up the tray while Nadine and I start the dishes."

Nadine looked over at Rebekah and scowled, but she grabbed a clean dish towel without a word of protest.

As soon as Rebekah had placed a plate of scrambled eggs with a biscuit and two strips of bacon on a tray, along with a cup of tea, she set it in her lap and wheeled out of the kitchen, being careful not to bump into anything along the way.

When she reached Grandma's door, she knocked softly. Hearing no response, she rapped a little louder. "Grandma, it's Rebekah. Can I come in?"

Still no reply.

Rebekah opened the door a crack and peered inside. She spotted Grandma lying in her bed with her long gray hair fanned out across her pillow. It was one of the few times Rebekah had seen her grandmother with her hair down. Of course, Grandma was usually up and dressed way before anyone else in the family, so her hair had always been done up in a bun with her kapp set in place by the time Rebekah came to the kitchen each morning.

"Grandma, are you awake?" Rebekah called softly. "We had scrambled eggs, bacon, and biscuits for breakfast this morning, and I have a tray for you." She pushed the door open more fully and wheeled into the room. Grandma Stoltzfus's eyes were shut, and her Bible lay open across her chest. She looked awfully still. A strange feeling crept over Rebekah. Why hadn't Grandma answered her call? Maybe she was sicker than she had let on. Maybe she was too weak to respond.

Rebekah wheeled closer to Grandma's bed, being careful not to jostle the tray. "Grandma, can you hear me?"

Grandma remained silent and unmoving.

Rebekah looked down at the open Bible and noticed a passage of scripture from Proverbs that had been underlined: "Trust in the LORD with all thine heart; and lean not unto thine own understanding. In all thy ways acknowledge him, and he shall direct thy paths."

One of Grandma's wrinkled hands lay across the open

page, so apparently she'd been reading her Bible sometime during the night or early this morning. Rebekah reached out to touch the dear woman's hand. Cold! It was ice cold!

"Grandma, wake up! Please open your eyes and look at me."

There was no response from Grandma Stoltzfus. None at all. Her body seemed lifeless like a sack of corn. She had obviously gone to her reward in heaven and wouldn't have to do another chore or suffer any of life's pains ever again.

Rebekah sat still for several seconds as she let the reality of the situation fully sink in. Then, with an anguished cry, she let her head fall forward and sobbed for all she was worth.

Mom stepped into the room a few seconds later. "Rebekah? What is it, daughter? I thought I heard you weeping in here."

Rebekah jerked her head up and gulped on a hiccup. "Sh-she's gone, Mom. I'm sure that Grandma is dead."

"What? *Ach*, that just can't be! I spoke to her but a few hours ago." Mom rushed over to the bed and picked up Grandma's hand, feeling for a pulse. Glancing at Rebekah, she slowly shook her head. Then she placed her hand in front of Grandma's mouth, and held it that way for several seconds. "Oh, Rebekah, I believe you're right. Grandma's gone home to heaven."

CHAPTER

3

*G*ood-bye, Rebekah. I'm leaving you now." Grandma held her hand out to Rebekah, but when Rebekah reached for it, Grandma shook her head, turned, and walked away.

"I need you, Grandma. Please don't leave me all alone." Rebekah tried to run after Grandma, but her legs wouldn't move. She glanced down at the ugly metal braces strapped to them and drew in a shuddering breath. "Come back, Grandma. Come back to me!"

Grandma was gone—vanished into some kind of a misty, thin air.

Tears streamed down Rebekah's face, and she trembled. "Please, please. . .don't leave me. I need you!"

"Rebekah, what's wrong? Why are you crying?"

Rebekah turned and saw her mother moving slowly toward her. She extended her arms, but Mom kept walking right past Rebekah, heading in the same direction as Grandma had gone.

"Mom, don't go. Wait for me, please." Rebekah struggled to lift her right foot, but it wouldn't budge. She gritted her teeth and tried to move her left foot, but it seemed to be stuck like glue. "Don't leave me! Don't leave me!" she shouted as Mom disappeared into the eerie mist.

"Calm down," Dad said as he trudged past her. "You'll wake

the dead if you keep on hollering that way."

"Something terrible is happening, and I can't seem to stop it." Rebekah *gulped in some air and almost choked on a sob. "Can't you make it stop, Dad? Can't you bring Grandma and Mom back to me?"*

He shook his head and kept on walking as though he hadn't heard a word she'd said.

"I need you!" Rebekah shouted to her father's retreating form. "I can't make it on my own. I need someone to love me and care for my needs."

Dad lifted his hand in a backward wave; then he disappeared into the misty vapor.

"Come back! Come back! Come back to me!"

❧

"Wake up, sister. Wake up. Do you hear me, Rebekah?"

Rebekah felt someone shaking her shoulder, and she struggled to open her eyes. Was it Grandma? Had the dear woman come back from the shadow of death to be with her?

She tossed her head from side to side and moaned. "Grandma. Grandma, don't leave me."

"Rebekah, calm down at once, and look at me."

It took great effort on Rebekah's part, but she forced her eyes open and squinted against the invading light. "Wh-where am I? What's happened to Grandma?" she asked as Nadine's face came into view.

"You're in your own bed. You must have been having a bad dream because I could hear you hollering all the way upstairs." Nadine's forehead wrinkled as she stared at Rebekah. "That must have been some nightmare you were havin'."

Rebekah nodded, noticing that her nightgown was sopping wet, and so were her sheets. "I—I dreamed that Grandma was with me, but she disappeared in a fog. Then Mom and Dad came along, and they vanished, too." Her voice caught on a sob, and she shuddered. "It—it was so real, and I—I was so scared."

Nadine patted Rebekah's shoulder. "You'll feel better once the funeral is over. Mom says it's easier to deal with the loss of a loved one once we see them buried and allow ourselves some time to grieve."

Grabbing the sides of her bed, Rebekah pulled herself to a sitting position. That's right. . .today was Grandma's funeral. No one could have foreseen that just three short days ago the dear woman would be taken from them, but she had slipped quietly away from her family, making her journey home to be with the Lord. It had been determined that she'd died of a stroke. As soon as the news of her death had gotten out, the entire Amish community had rallied to do whatever was necessary in order to help with the preparations for the funeral service and the meal afterward.

Rebekah supposed that was some comfort, but oh, how terribly she missed her dear grandma, and not just because the woman had taken care of Rebekah through so much of her childhood. Rebekah would miss everything about Grandma Stoltzfus—her kind, helpful ways; her soft-spoken words; and her sweet, tender spirit, which was a testimony of God's love in action.

꙳

As Rebekah rolled her wheelchair into the living room a

short time later, she caught sight of Grandma's coffin—a plain pine box with a split lid. The upper part of the lid was hinged so it could be opened for viewing the body. According to tradition among the Lancaster Amish, Grandma's dress had been covered with the same white cape and apron she had worn on her wedding day many years ago.

Grandma's funeral service would be held after breakfast, right here in the house, with a second service going on in the barn simultaneously if there were more people than the house could hold. For two days prior to the service, Grandma's body had been available for viewing, but after today, Rebekah would never look on the dear woman's face again—not until they met in heaven someday.

Rebekah gulped on a sob and guided her chair out of the room, knowing her help would be needed in the kitchen and hoping the action of doing something constructive would take her mind off the pain in her heart. She discovered Mom and Nadine scurrying around the kitchen as they made preparations for breakfast.

"Are you all right?" Mom asked, casting Rebekah a look of concern. "Nadine said you'd had a bad dream and seemed quite upset when she woke you."

Rebekah's only reply was a quick shrug. She didn't want to talk about the terrible nightmare that had left her nightgown and bed sheets drenched in sweat. Talking about it would do no good, and it certainly wouldn't bring Grandma back.

"Rebekah?" Mom persisted. "Are you okay?"

"I'm fine." Rebekah rolled her chair farther into the room. "Want me to set the table?"

"If you don't mind."

"I would have done it, but Mom's got me squeezing oranges for fresh juice," Nadine said from her place in front of the counter. "Simon says he's comin' down with a cold, and he seems to think the vitamin C he'll get from the oranges will lick it quicker than anything."

"Grandma used to drink a lot of orange juice whenever she had a cold," Rebekah said, swallowing hard in hopes of pushing down the awful lump that had lodged in her throat. She guided her chair quickly over to the silverware drawer, determined to keep her hands busy so her mind wouldn't dwell on the funeral service that would be starting in just a few hours.

Rebekah didn't know how she had made it through Grandma's service, but she had—and without breaking down in front of everyone. All too often, she got looks of sympathy or curious stares from others because of her handicap, and the last thing she needed today was anyone's pity. All she wanted to do was get through the graveside service, which would soon take place, mingle with their guests awhile during the afternoon meal, and retreat to the solitude of her room.

As Dad's horse and buggy pulled away from the barn, Rebekah glanced out the back window. In perfect procession, Grandma's close family members followed the simple horse-drawn hearse, with the other buggies coming up behind them. Single file, the Amish carriages wound their way down the Stoltzfus driveway and continued onto the narrow road. The mourners passed fields of growing corn, soon-to-be-cut alfalfa, and Amish farmsteads dotting the countryside. The long column turned down an even narrower road and finally came to a halt at a fenced-in graveyard.

The drivers got out first and tied their horses to the fence. Soon everyone was assembled at the graveside, and the pallbearers slid Grandma's coffin from the wagon and carried it to the grave that had been dug the day before. Right beside the new grave was the small, simple headstone of Grandma's husband, Henry Stoltzfus, who had preceded her in death some thirteen years ago.

Wooden poles with long straps extending the width of the grave had been placed across the hole for the coffin to rest upon. Rebekah's family mourned openly when the box was lowered into the ground and the hole was covered with dirt. Their beloved grandma was laid to rest. After the men had all removed their hats, Bishop Benner conducted the graveside service, which included the reading of a few verses from one of their Amish hymns. He closed the service by inviting those present to pray the Lord's Prayer silently with him.

Rebekah's stomach felt like it was tied in one big knot, and she fought to keep her emotions under control. She knew in the days ahead she would pine for the long talks she and Grandma used to have; for the board games they often played; the times spent together caring for Grandma's houseplants; and the meaningful hours she had listened to Grandma read the scriptures to her. There were so many precious memories of the dear woman.

Rebekah glanced at the somber faces surrounding her and knew she wasn't the only one in pain. Aunt Mim wept openly as she leaned against Uncle Amos's shoulder, and

Mary Ellen and her twelve-year-old brother, Henry, stood near their parents with tears streaming down their faces.

To the left stood Uncle Jonas and Aunt Crystal with their fifteen-year-old twin sons, Jacob and John, and eleven-year-old daughter, Maddie. Next to them were Uncle Lewis, Aunt Grace, and their children, Peggy, age twelve, and Matthew, who was seven. To the right stood Rebekah's own family—Mom, Dad, Simon, and Nadine. They were all shedding plenty of tears—everyone but Rebekah, who was determined to remain in control.

This was the first time Rebekah had lost someone so close to her. She'd only been six when Grandpa Stoltzfus died of a heart attack. She barely remembered him, and at the time of his death, she hadn't been so greatly affected.

Despite Rebekah's resolve, a few tears slipped out from under her lashes and splashed onto her cheeks. *Oh, God, why did you have to take my mammi? Why must life be so unfair?*

No answer. Just the whisper of the wind wafting through the trees overhead.

Rebekah wondered if God had even heard her prayer. She wondered if He cared about her at all.

❦

The funeral dinner was held at Rebekah's folks' place, and an array of food and beverages had been prepared and brought in by many of their friends and neighbors. Most of the adults had been served inside the house, but some of the younger ones decided to eat their meal at one of the picnic tables set up on the lawn since it had turned out to be such a warm day.

As Mary Ellen walked across the grass carrying two plates of food, she noticed Rebekah sitting in her wheelchair under the branches of a large willow tree. Her eyes were closed, and her mouth was pursed tightly as if an invisible drawstring had pulled her lips together.

"Are you sleeping?" Mary Ellen asked as she approached her cousin.

Rebekah's eyes snapped open. "No. Just resting my eyes."

"Sure is a hot, muggy day, isn't it?"

"Jah, but then that's typical summertime weather."

Mary Ellen held one of the plates out to Rebekah. "I brought you something to eat."

"Danki, but I'm not so hungry."

"Maybe not, but you need to keep up your strength."

"My strength? My strength for what—crying?" Tears seeped under Rebekah's long lashes and dribbled onto her flushed cheeks. "I—I was determined not to do that, yet here I am, giving in to my tears anyway."

Mary Ellen bent down to place both plates on the ground; then she leaned over Rebekah's wheelchair and gave her a hug. "We'll all miss Grandma, but you probably will feel the greatest loss. She lived with you and took care of your needs for a long time."

Rebekah nodded.

"God knows what's best for each one of us, so I'm sure He will give you the strength to get through this time of loss."

"It was best to take Grandma away?"

"Not better for us, maybe, but for Grandma, it surely was."

"She's dead, Mary Ellen."

"I know that, and I'll miss her, too. But remember that

the Bible says for a believer to be absent from the body is to be present with the Lord." Mary Ellen smiled as she looked up at the cloudless sky. "If we could only know what heaven is really like, I think we would all long to go there."

"Maybe so."

"Grandma's no longer confined in her aging body. She doesn't have to toil here on earth or feel any more physical pain. She's probably having the time of her life, walking all over heaven with Grandpa and Jesus right about now."

Rebekah nodded slowly. "I—I know you're right, but it's ever so hard to let go of my precious mammi because I miss her so much. Every time I go into her room or see something that reminds me of her, I feel as if my heart is breaking in two."

"Grieve if you must, Rebekah, but don't let your grief consume you. Grandma wouldn't want that."

"Last night I had a distressing nightmare about her leaving me. Mom and Dad were in the dream, as well, and they disappeared into the same foggy mist that Grandma walked into after she told me good-bye." Rebekah groaned and held her stomach as though she was in terrible pain. "Do you think that means they'll be leaving me soon, too?"

Mary Ellen shook her head. "Of course not. It was only a dream—a dream that most likely came about because you are grieving over the loss of our mammi."

"You're probably right, but it was so terrifying, and I—I'm afraid of what it might have meant."

"What do you mean?"

"Maybe it was a warning of things to come. . .a time when I'll be all alone with no one to care for me."

"That won't happen because you have plenty of family who will be around to help take care of your needs." Mary Ellen patted Rebekah's arm in a motherly fashion. "I'm sorry about the nightmare, but I'm sure it won't happen again, and you can't let anything steal your joy."

"How can I feel joy when I've just lost Grandma?"

"We all lost her, Rebekah. But life goes on, and we need to keep a positive attitude and look for things to be joyous about."

"It's not so easy for me to feel joy the way you do. You've always been able to smile, even in the face of difficulty. I remember when we were kinner and some of our classmates used to pick on you. Your loving, forgiving spirit was evident even back then." Rebekah slowly shook her head. "I don't know how you managed to stay so sweet and kind."

"My life hasn't always been easy. As you know, I lost my real mamm when I was young, and I had to make many adjustments. It was hard on Pappy, too, but he set a good example and taught me how to love and laugh. Then God brought Mama Mim into our lives, and she's been there for me ever since." Mary Ellen released a sigh. "There's always something for which to be thankful. Maybe you just need to count your blessings, consider all the beautiful things God has made, and focus on how much He loves us."

Rebekah nodded. "I know that's true, and I'll try to do as you suggested."

Mary Ellen lowered herself to the ground beside the wheelchair. She reached for Rebekah's plate and handed it to her. "We'd better eat before the ants find our food and decide to have themselves a little picnic of their own."

Rebekah's lips curved into a tiny smile. "I might be willing to share my food with one of my special aunts, but never with a bunch of picnic ants."

Rebekah's first bite of food tasted like cardboard, and she had trouble swallowing, but after a while, she found herself actually enjoying the meal. A short time later, Rebekah looked down at her plate and was surprised to see that it was empty. She'd been so busy visiting with Mary Ellen that she hadn't even realized she had eaten everything.

"Guess I'm done," she said, handing her plate to Mary Ellen.

"Good for you. I'm glad you ate something."

Rebekah caught sight of Daniel Beachy walking across the yard, and she was surprised when he joined them under the weeping willow tree. Maybe he'd decided this was a good chance to speak with Mary Ellen since Johnny wasn't around to hog the conversation.

"I'm sorry about your mammi," Daniel said, dropping to the ground on the other side of Rebekah's wheelchair. "I didn't know her as well as some in our community, but she seemed like a right nice woman."

"She was the best grandma anyone could ever want," Rebekah said with a nod.

"She wasn't my mammi by blood," Mary Ellen put in, "but she always treated me as such."

Daniel removed his straw hat, and with the back of his hand, he wiped away the rivulets of sweat running down his forehead. "Whew! Sure has turned out to be a mighty warm day. With so many folks here, it's nice that some of us could eat outside."

Mary Ellen nodded. "If June's this hot and sticky, I wonder what we can expect from the rest of our summer."

"Probably more hot, muggy days," he replied with a chuckle.

Mary Ellen joined him in laughter, but Rebekah just sat there, feeling as out of place as a June bug in December. *My cousin looks so cute whenever she laughs. I'm sure that's why all the fellows hang around her so much of the time. That and the fact that she's got two good legs and can join in their fun and games.* Rebekah glanced down at her lifeless legs. Two dead sticks, that's all they were. Sure weren't good for much. *I'd probably never look as cute as Mary Ellen, no matter how much I laughed or smiled.*

"Is this a private party, or can anyone join in?" Johnny Yoder asked in his usual, smooth-talking way. Rebekah looked on in surprise as he plunked on the grass beside Mary Ellen. He held a man-sized plate of peanut butter cookies in one hand, and the smile he wore could have melted a block of ice. "I've brought you some dessert," he said, extending the plate to Mary Ellen.

She reached out and snatched one off the plate. "Danki, Johnny. Peanut butter's my favorite, so I'm beholden to you now."

Johnny's smug expression reminded Rebekah of the way some of their barn cats looked whenever they brought a poor defenseless mouse up to the house to show off their catch.

Johnny nudged Mary Ellen's arm. "Since you're beholden to me, does that mean I'm welcome to join this group?"

"Of course you're welcome to join us. We're glad to have your company, aren't we?" Mary Ellen glanced over at Rebekah and then at Daniel.

Rebekah nodded. "It's fine by me."

Daniel only shrugged, and Rebekah was sure that his wrinkled forehead gave proof of his obvious disappointment. The poor fellow was probably irritated with Johnny for interrupting the conversation he'd been having with Mary Ellen. Rebekah couldn't fault him for that. It did seem as if Johnny always showed up just when Daniel had begun to make a bit of headway with Mary Ellen.

In no time at all, the cookies were gone, though the two young men had eaten most of them. Conversation didn't lag much, either—at least not between Johnny and Mary Ellen. Rebekah thought it most unfair that Johnny seemed to be hogging her cousin that way and hadn't given either her or Daniel a chance to say much.

"The funeral service was long, wasn't it?" Johnny asked, looking over at Daniel for the first time.

"Jah, they usually are." Daniel leaned back on his elbows and turned his face toward the cloudless sky. Apparently he wasn't any more interested in talking to Johnny than Johnny was in talking to him. Daniel was obviously put out because he hadn't been able to say anything to Mary Ellen since Johnny had showed up.

"The funeral was almost as long as a regular preaching service, and sometimes it's hard for people to stay awake that long." Johnny cast a sidelong glance at Mary Ellen. "Say, how about that time you fell asleep in church?"

Mary Ellen jumped up, planting her hands on her slender

hips. "What do you mean, Johnny? I never did such a thing, and you know it!"

"Sure you did," he teased. "You nearly fell right off your wooden bench that day."

"That's not so." Mary Ellen wrinkled her nose at him. "I always pay close attention during preaching."

"I think he's only kidding with you," Rebekah said. "I sure don't remember you ever falling asleep in church."

"Me neither," Daniel put in.

"Jah, well, maybe she wasn't sleepin'," Johnny admitted. "She might've been prayin' for a really long time." He leaned his head back and hooted until his face turned red and tears trickled down his cheeks. Then he jumped up and grabbed Mary Ellen's hand. "Say, why don't you take a little walk with me? We'll head on down to the creek, and maybe that'll help you cool off. A girl with a fiery temper needs a bit of coolin' down, don't ya think?"

Mary Ellen pulled away from him and folded her arms, although there was a tiny smile tugging at the corners of her mouth. "What makes you think I would be willing to go anywhere with you, Johnny Yoder?"

He blinked a couple of times and gave her a jab in the ribs with his elbow. "Because I'm irresistible, and if you don't agree to go with me, then I'll have to get down on my knees and beg like a *hund*. You wouldn't want me to do something that embarrassing, now would you?"

"Oh, all right," Mary Ellen conceded with a shrug. "I couldn't stand to see you beg like a dog." Her gaze fell on Rebekah; then it swung over to Daniel. "You're both welcome to come along."

"No, thanks," Rebekah declined. "I'd rather stay right here under this shady old tree." She glanced at Daniel, who now lay on his back, using his straw hat as a pillow. "You go ahead, if you want to, Daniel."

He crinkled his nose and waved a hand. "Naw, they don't need me taggin' along."

There's that look again, Rebekah noted. *Poor Daniel. He's so smitten with Mary Ellen that he doesn't know what to do. What with Johnny being around all the time, he has about as much of a chance at winning her over as a snowball does of staying frozen until the Fourth of July.*

Mary Ellen and Johnny said their good-byes, then walked away, giggling like a couple of kinner.

❦

"Why didn't you go with them?" Rebekah asked, as she looked down at Daniel. "I'm sure Mary Ellen would—"

"I'd rather not be a fifth wheel on the buggy." He pulled himself to a sitting position. "I'd have gone if you'd been willing, but no, not alone."

Rebekah shook her head. "If I had agreed to go along on the walk, I would have only slowed the rest of you down."

"I could have pushed you in your wheelchair. I've had lots of practice with the plow and my daed's mules, so we'd move along pretty fast, and we wouldn't have slowed anyone down."

Rebekah grunted. "I've never been compared to a team of mules before."

His face heated up, and he gave his earlobe a quick tug. "Sorry. Didn't mean it the way it sounded." *Why do I always seem to say the wrong thing?*

"That's all right. It's not important," she murmured.

"Have you written anything interesting for *The Budget* lately?" Daniel asked, taking their conversation in another direction and hoping to draw Rebekah out of her melancholy mood.

"Not really." She stared down at her hands, clenched tightly in her lap. "I–I'm not so sure I want to continue doing it now that Grandma is gone."

"How come?"

She shrugged.

"Do you think your mammi would want you to give up doing things just because she died?"

"I–I guess not. Knowing Grandma, she'd probably want me to keep writing for *The Budget*, the way she used to do before she turned her column over to me."

He nodded and smiled. "I think you're right about that."

"Well, I suppose I'd better go see if Mom needs me for anything." Rebekah motioned to the plates on the ground. "Would you please hand me those so I can take them inside?"

"Want me to take 'em there for you?"

She shook her head with a determined expression. "I can manage something that simple."

"Okay." Daniel placed the plates in Rebekah's lap, wishing there was something he could do or say that might help take away her pain.

"Danki."

"You're welcome."

Rebekah wheeled away, leaving Daniel alone and wondering why he could never seem to say the right thing when she was around.

CHAPTER

4

Grandma had been gone for nearly a month, yet the pain still lingered in Rebekah's heart. She missed the dear woman so much—especially the long talks they used to have. Grandma had always been full of good advice, and Rebekah often wondered where all that wisdom had come from.

Nearly every night since Grandma's death, Rebekah had dreamed about her, often having the same nightmare that involved others in her family being taken from her, too.

"Oh, Lord, what would I do if something happened to Mom and Dad? How would I manage on my own?" she mumbled one morning, as she entered Grandma's old room.

No answer. Like all the other times she had asked God before, He seemed to be ignoring her. Didn't God care how much she was hurting? Didn't He want to give her a miracle?

Rebekah drew in a deep breath and reached for the watering can sitting beside some pots of African violets on the dressing table. Grandma had died so unexpectedly, and Rebekah hadn't been able to do anything about it. Now she was determined to keep Grandma's plants alive and flourishing so she would have something to remember her by.

When Rebekah finished watering and pruning all the plants, she spotted Grandma's Bible lying on the small table next to the bed. The last time she'd seen it, it had been lying across Grandma's chest. Now it was closed just like Grandma Stoltzfus's life.

Rebekah rolled her chair up to the table and reached for the Bible, holding it close to her heart. Unbidden tears seeped under her eyelashes, and she sniffed deeply, trying to keep them from falling onto her cheeks. She had heard about the process of grieving for a loved one, but nothing had prepared her for this terrible, empty ache in her soul. She hadn't realized how much her grandmother had meant to her until she was gone. Now it was too late to tell Grandma all the things that were on her heart.

Why do folks always wait until it's too late to express their real feelings for one another? she wondered. *Why not tell them how much you care while they're still alive?*

She placed the Bible in her lap and opened it to a spot where a crocheted bookmark had been positioned. It was in the exact place where the Bible had been open when Rebekah found Grandma in the deep sleep of death.

"Mom must have put this in here," Rebekah whispered. "Maybe she wanted to save the place where Grandma had last read God's Word." Her gaze traveled down the page until it came to rest on the verses Grandma had underlined. "Proverbs 3:5 and 6," she read aloud. " 'Trust in the Lord with all thine heart; and lean not unto thine own understanding. In all thy ways acknowledge him, and he shall direct thy paths.' "

"Those are some good words to live by, don't you think?"

Rebekah turned her head and saw Mom standing inside

the doorway. She nodded but made no reply. If she spoke, she feared her voice would break and she would dissolve into a puddle of unstoppable tears.

Mom came the rest of the way into the room. She took a seat on the edge of the bed near the wheelchair and placed her hand on Rebekah's trembling shoulder. "It's all right to grieve for Grandma, but she would want you to go on with life and find happiness."

"Go on with life?" Rebekah sobbed. "What life, Mom? What kind of a life can a person with a handicap like mine ever have? What happiness awaits someone like me?"

"Oh, Rebekah, it is possible for you to have a meaningful life. Why, many people in the world have disabilities, and most of them live fairly productive lives." Mom squeezed Rebekah's shoulder. "You were always such a pleasant, easygoing child, and I thought you had come to accept your limitations. However, since you've become a young woman, I've noticed a definite change in your attitude, and I'm not sure I like what I see."

Rebekah sniffed deeply, swiping at the tears running down her cheeks. "When I was a little girl, you all spoiled me. Someone was always around to care for me or just sit and talk, the way Grandma often did. I thought there would always be someone available to provide for my needs. Now I know I'm really a burden, and someday I might not have anyone to care for me."

Mom moved from her place on the bed and knelt in front of Rebekah. She grasped her hands and held them tightly. "Losing Grandma has made us all aware of how fragile life is. None of us will live on this earth forever. Someday, every believer will join Grandma in heaven." She closed her eyes, as though searching for just the right words. When she opened them again, she was smiling. "We're a close family, and I'm sure that, even after your daed and I are both gone, someone will take over the responsibility of your care."

Rebekah nearly choked on the sob rising in her throat. "I—I don't want anyone to *have* to be responsible for me. I want to provide for myself—at least financially." She wiped her eyes with the backs of her hands. "I just don't know what someone like me can do to make enough money in order to accomplish that goal."

"You could sell eggs or do some handcrafts and take them to the farmers' market," Mom suggested.

"Doing small things like selling eggs or crafts wouldn't give me enough money." Rebekah felt as if Mom was treating her like a child, and it irked her just a bit.

"If it means so much to you, maybe you should pray about the matter and search God's Word for wisdom." Mom stood. "Why don't you keep Grandma's *Biewel?* I think she would have wanted you to have it. I know the scriptures gave her a lot of comfort, not to mention answers whenever she needed the Lord's guidance."

Rebekah thought about the underlined verses in Grandma's Bible. Maybe she would continue to search for other scriptures Grandma might have underlined or highlighted. Perhaps the miracle she was looking for could be found in one of those passages.

Sarah returned to the kitchen with a heavy heart, and she flopped into a chair at the table with a moan. If there was only something she could say or do to help her daughter accept her limitations and gain back the joy she had known when she was a child. As a toddler, Rebekah had been so adventuresome, always attempting new things, and full of laughter and smiles, even when she fell down or didn't get her way on something. The first few years after Rebekah's accident, she had been easygoing and seemed positive about her situation.

But things began to change when Rebekah started into puberty, and by the time she'd become a teenager, she had developed a completely different attitude. Things she used to shrug off or even laugh about now became issues. She seemed worried about being a burden to others, lacked the confidence of other young women her age, and sometimes succumbed to depression.

Since Grandma's passing, Rebekah's dismal attitude seemed to have gotten worse, and it concerned Sarah that she couldn't reach her daughter or help ease her despair.

Sarah glanced at the calendar hanging on the wall near the door and shook her head. The handicap convention had already taken place, and there wouldn't be another one until next year, so the idea of taking Rebekah there was certainly out. If only she had been willing to go. If only. . .

Feeling the need to pray, Sarah closed her eyes and lowered her head to the table. *Heavenly Father, please comfort Rebekah, and give me the strength to keep trying to be an encouragement to her.* She paused and swiped at the tears trickling down her cheeks. *If it's Your will for my daughter to become self-sufficient, then please show us the way.*

For the next several days, Rebekah spent every free moment looking through Grandma's well-worn Bible. On almost every page, she found a verse of scripture that had been underlined. In some places she discovered that Grandma had scrawled notes in the margin or at the bottom of certain pages, mentioning how some particular verse had spoken to her heart. There was no doubt in Rebekah's mind— Grandma Stoltzfus had lived and died by the truth of God's Word. Perhaps that's what Rebekah needed to do, too.

One morning after breakfast, Rebekah found herself alone in the house. Mom and Nadine were outside weeding the garden, and Dad and Simon were hard at work in the fields. She decided this would be a good time to read a few more scriptures from Grandma's Bible. Rebekah positioned her wheelchair at the kitchen table and set the Biewel and a glass of cold lemonade in front of her. A deep sense of longing encompassed her soul as she silently prayed, *What words do You have for me today, Lord? I need to know whether You have a special plan for my life.*

She opened the Bible to a place that Grandma had marked with a small piece of ribbon. As she studied the page, she spotted another underlined passage, Jeremiah 31:3-4. "The LORD hath appeared of old unto me, saying, Yea, I have loved thee with an everlasting love: therefore with lovingkindness have I drawn thee. Again I will build thee, and thou shalt be built."

Rebekah sat for several minutes, pondering the scripture. Deep in her heart she knew God loved her, but was

His Word saying He wanted to rebuild her? If so, did it mean rebuild her body? Now, that would take a huge miracle. No, she was fairly sure the scripture referred to being spiritually renewed and rebuilt, and she knew she was in need of that, especially where her lack of faith and tendency to fear the unknown were concerned.

For the next little while, Rebekah continued to seek out verses. She was pleased to discover several that dealt with the subject of fear. Psalm 34:4 in particular spoke to her heart: "I sought the LORD, and he heard me, and delivered me from all my fears." After Rebekah read the verse a couple more times, she had a deep sense that she must not be afraid of her dreams anymore or of being left alone. God would provide for her needs and calm her fears; she just needed to be faithful and learn to trust Him more.

With a feeling of peace she hadn't felt in many months, Rebekah closed the Bible, bowed her head, and offered a silent prayer. *Dear Father, thank You for reminding me that You love me with an everlasting love and want to build up my faith. Please draw me closer to You, and help me remember not to fear but to trust in You. And if it's Your will for me to support myself financially, then please show me how. Guide me, direct me, and prepare my heart for a true miracle from You. Amen.*

When Sarah finished her weeding and returned to the house, she was surprised to see that Rebekah was not in the kitchen where she had been earlier. Figuring her daughter might have gone to her room, she rapped on the door.

No answer.

"Rebekah, are you there?"

Still no response.

"Maybe she went to Grandma's old room." Sarah moved to the next room and knocked on that door.

"Come in."

She opened the door and spotted Rebekah sitting in her wheelchair, watering some of Grandma's African violets that had been placed on the window ledge. "I thought I might find you in here," she said, crossing the room to join her daughter in front of the window.

Rebekah turned her head and gave Sarah a questioning look. "Did you need me for something?"

"Not really, but I did want to talk to you about an idea I have."

"What idea is that, Mom?"

"Your daed's hired a driver to take us to the farmers' market tomorrow, where we plan to sell some of our fresh produce and a few other things. Since you seem so set on wanting to make some money of your own, I thought you might like to take some flowers from the garden or maybe a few of these houseplants to sell," she said, motioning to the violets.

"Sell off Grandma's plants?" Rebekah's eyebrows furrowed as she shook her head. "No, Mom, I could never do that. It wouldn't be right. No, not right at all."

"Why not?"

"Because the African violets were so special to her." Rebekah's smile never quite reached her eyes. "They help keep her memory alive, too."

"Grandma's memory will always be alive in our hearts," Sarah said. "We have many other things to remind us of her besides the plants, and I don't think Grandma would mind if you sold a few violets so you could have some money of your own."

"I do want to start making money, but selling off Grandma's plants? Sorry, but I just couldn't do that and feel good about it."

"Why not take cut flowers from the garden then? I'm sure those would sell, too."

"That would be all right, I suppose." Rebekah stared out the window with a wistful expression. Suddenly, she snapped her fingers and smiled. "I know! I could take some starts from Grandma's plants. All I need to do is put them in some pots full of good soil, and they'll soon become new plants of their own. It might even be good for the bigger plants to be thinned a bit. At least that's what Grandma used to say whenever I asked her why she was pinching some of the leaves off the violets and repotting them in smaller pots."

"I think that's a fine idea. If you want, I'll help you get the cuttings done today."

"Danki for offering, but if I'm to make the money from the plants, then I want to do all the work myself." She blinked a couple of times. "Besides, this is something I can do without any help at all."

"Okay." Sarah clasped Rebekah's shoulder and gave it a gentle squeeze. She turned to leave, but before she got to the door, Rebekah called out to her.

"Mom, there's one more thing."

"What's that, Rebekah?"

"I think I'm ready to start writing some things in my *Budget* column again."

"I'm glad to hear that. Maybe you can write up something about our trip to the farmers' market."

"Jah, maybe so."

"All right then. Tomorrow you can share our sales table at the market, and we'll see how everything goes." Sarah went out the door, feeling a little more hopeful about Rebekah. She knew full well how important it was for her daughter to feel independent, and she would do nothing to stand in the way of Rebekah doing something on her own.

CHAPTER
5

The farmers' market seemed unusually busy, and the proof was in the parking lot, nearly full of cars. "It must be all the summer tourists," Dad said to Mom as they began unloading their things from the back of Vera Miller's van.

She smiled. "Jah, business should be good today."

Rebekah sat in her wheelchair beside the van, holding a box of African violet cuttings in her lap. "I hope so," she put in. "All the pruning and potting I did yesterday had better pay off."

Nadine, who stood behind Rebekah, leaned over her shoulder. "Want me to push you inside the building?"

Rebekah nodded. She hated to ask for assistance, but if she let go of the box in order to manipulate her wheelchair, she would probably end up losing the whole thing.

A few minutes later, they headed for the market building, each carrying a box of their own.

Once Rebekah's father and brother got tables set up, they started making sales. Mom had some vine-ripened, juicy red tomatoes and baskets of plump, sweet raspberries from her garden; Dad had brought some of his delicious, quick-to-make root beer; Simon sold cartons of bulky brown eggs; Nadine had several batches of chocolate cupcakes and ginger cookies for sale; and Rebekah had her freshly cut flowers and starts from several of Grandma's plants.

By noon, nearly all of Rebekah's African violet starts had been sold and many of the cut flowers, as well. It was the first time she'd ever made so much money in such a short time, and she was pleased that she had finally done something that might prove to be financially productive if she had more plants to sell and could come to the market more often.

"How's business?" Mary Ellen asked as she stepped up to the table Rebekah shared with her two siblings.

Rebekah grinned. "Much better than I'd ever imagined it would be. I only wish I had more plants and flowers to sell. If the market was open six days a week, I believe I could actually make enough money to be self-sufficient."

Mary Ellen nodded. "That would be *wunderbaar*, all right."

"Even if it was open all week, I couldn't afford to hire a driver that often." Rebekah shrugged. "Oh, well. It was a nice thought, anyway."

"You really do like flowers and plants, don't you?"

Rebekah's head bobbed up and down. "Jah. Ever so much."

"And as you've said, you've discovered today that they sell quite well."

"Indeed! I've done real well."

Mary Ellen leaned close to Rebekah's ear. "Can you take a little break? I'd like to talk with you—in private."

"About what?"

"I think I might have a great plan for you."

"What is it? Can't you tell me now?"

"We'd probably be interrupted by a customer if we tried to talk about it here."

Rebekah nodded. "Okay. It's time for lunch anyway, so I'll ask Nadine to watch my end of the table, and then I'll get the box lunch my mamm prepared this morning. We were planning to eat in shifts, so I'm sure Mom won't mind if I take my lunch break with you."

Mary Ellen grinned. "Sounds good to me. We can eat under the shade of that old maple tree out behind the building."

Soon after Rebekah wheeled away from their table, Nadine spotted her friend Carolyn Weaver heading her way. A freckle-faced Amish boy who looked to be about Nadine's age walked beside Carolyn. Nadine didn't think she had ever seen him before, but she thought he was awfully cute.

When Carolyn and the boy reached the end of the table where Nadine sat babysitting Rebekah's plants, they came to a halt.

"Didn't expect to see you here today," Carolyn said, offering Nadine a wide smile.

"Didn't expect to be here, neither." Nadine's gaze went to the dark-haired boy who stood beside her friend. Wasn't Carolyn going to introduce him?

As if she could read Nadine's mind, Carolyn nodded at the boy and said, "Nadine, this is my cousin Melvin. He and his family live in Missouri, and they've come to Lancaster County to visit for a couple of weeks."

Nadine put on what she hoped was her best smile. "It's nice to meet you, Melvin." She glanced over to see what her folks were doing and was pleased to see that they were both busy with customers at the moment.

"Nice to meet you, too," he said with a friendly grin.

Nadine leaned her elbows on the table and stared up at him. "I've never been to Missouri before. What's it like?"

Melvin shrugged his broad shoulders. "The weather's not much different than it is here, but the community we live in is a whole lot smaller." He scrunched up his nose. "Not much to do around there—that's for certain sure."

"No big towns nearby?"

"Nope. Just Seymour, and that's a pretty small place. The closest big town is Springfield, but of course, I don't get to go there so often."

"Is there a farmers' market in Seymour?"

"Just during the summer, and it's nothing at all like this place." He made a sweeping gesture to the tables nearby. "Ours is held outside in a vacant lot across the street from the hamburger place, not in a big building such as this."

"Oh, I see."

"Have you had your lunch yet?" Carolyn asked, breaking into their conversation.

Nadine shook her head.

"Want to get a hot dog with me and Melvin?"

Of course Nadine wanted to go. Selling Rebekah's plants was boring, and it would give her a chance to get to know Carolyn's cousin a little better. "Let me ask my folks."

Nadine pushed her chair aside and moved to the other table, where Dad sat with his jugs of root beer, and Mom her mounds of produce. "Can I go have lunch with my friend Carolyn and her cousin?" Nadine asked, leaning close to her mother's ear.

Mom shook her head. "Not until Rebekah gets back. You're needed here right now."

"How come?"

"Someone needs to keep an eye on her flowers."

"But that's not fair. You let Simon go to lunch at the same time as Rebekah."

"And you shall go as soon as they get back."

"But why can't you and Dad watch Rebekah's table?"

"Because the market is really busy, and a lot of customers are heading our way," Dad interjected. "So put on your best smile, sell lots of your sister's plants while she's gone, and no sulking. You hear?"

Nadine grunted and moved back to her end of the table. "Sorry, but I can't go to lunch until my sister and brother get back." She kept her gaze fixed on one of the African violets, afraid if she looked at Melvin as she spoke he might see the tears that were stinging the back of her eyes and threatening to spill over.

"How long will they be gone?" Carolyn asked.

"Probably another half hour or so."

"I guess we could walk around awhile and come back for you then."

Hope welled in Nadine's soul, but before she could give a reply, Melvin spoke up. "I'm really hungry, so if it's all the same to you, I think I'll head over to the hot-dog stand right now."

"Jah, okay. Maybe we can visit some other time," Nadine mumbled.

As Carolyn and Melvin walked away, Nadine pushed one of Rebekah's plants closer to the front of the table and gritted her teeth. *Rebekah always gets to do what she wants. Sometimes I wish I were the one in a wheelchair.*

"It's another hot, sticky day," Rebekah remarked as Mary Ellen took a seat on the grassy patch beside her wheelchair. "I'm glad we have a nice shady place to help keep us cool."

Mary Ellen took a drink of her foamy root beer. "Umm. . . your daed sure makes some good soda. This helps put the fire out on a muggy summer day such as this."

Rebekah giggled when the end of Mary Ellen's nose became covered with the frothy white head of the root beer. "And you wear my daed's soda real well, too."

Mary Ellen reached into her lunch basket and retrieved a napkin; then she swiped it across her nose. "There. Do I look any better?"

Rebekah nodded. "But then, you always look good in the face. It's not hard to figure out why so many of the fellows we know act like silly kinner in order to seek your favor."

"There's only one man whose favor I seek."

"And who might that be?"

"I'd rather not say just yet. Not until I'm sure he likes me, too. Besides, you didn't agree to have lunch with me so we could talk about my love life. I want to discuss a possible business venture with you."

"Business venture?" Rebekah's eyebrows lifted high on her forehead. "You and me?"

"No, just you. I've got my teaching job at the school, remember?"

"Of course I do, but what business venture are you thinking about that would involve me?"

"You've been telling me for weeks that you want to be self-sufficient. Isn't that right?"

Rebekah nodded. "Right as rain."

"Then I think I have an idea that might work quite well for you," Mary Ellen said as a feeling of excitement welled in her soul. She did so want to see her cousin make some money of her own.

"What idea do you have?"

"You need to make money in order to be more independent, correct?"

"Right again."

"Today you found out that you have a product people will buy."

"Jah. The flowers and plants."

"And you enjoy working with them?"

"Very much so."

"Then all you have to do is get more plants and sell more plants."

"That sounds wunderbaar, but you've forgotten one important thing."

Mary Ellen pursed her lips. "What's that?"

"The farmers' market isn't open often enough, and even if it were, there's the problem of me being able to afford transportation to and from."

"I'm getting to that." Mary Ellen tapped her finger against the side of her head as the excitement of her plan continued to mount. "I was thinking if you had a greenhouse near the front of your property, you could sell your plants and flowers from there. News travels fast around here, so I'm sure folks—especially the tourists who come to our area—would soon find out about your business. In no time at all, you would probably have a stream of customers coming the whole year long."

Rebekah's forehead wrinkled in obvious confusion. "That sounds like an interesting business venture, but there's one big problem."

"What problem is that?"

"We have no greenhouse on our property."

"So you have one built," Mary Ellen said, reaching into her lunch basket to retrieve a sandwich.

"It-it's not that simple. Building a greenhouse would take time and money."

"Not if your family and friends did all the work. I'm sure my daed would be glad to help out, and so would your other uncles and cousins. Maybe some of the neighboring Amish men would come, too." Mary Ellen grasped Rebekah's hand and gave it a gentle squeeze. "You really must ask your folks about this."

"Well, I don't know—"

"I'm sure your family wants you to be happy and self-reliant. Won't you at least give my idea some thought and talk it over with them?"

Rebekah finally nodded. "I'll think about it and, of course, pray for some answers. If God wants me to do something like this, then He will have to show me how."

Mary Ellen smiled, pleased that her cousin liked the idea and even more pleased to see Rebekah so excited about something.

CHAPTER 6

The entire Stoltzfus family had been invited to a picnic at the Hiltys' place, and Rebekah looked forward to going. Family picnics were always fun, and it was a good time for the busy farmers and craftsmen to get caught up with one another's active lives. Since preaching services in their Amish community were biweekly and this was an off Sunday, it was a nice way to spend the afternoon.

Mom had insisted that Rebekah wear her leg braces for at least part of the day, reminding her that she needed to get out of that wheelchair once in a while and exercise the lower half of her body. As much as Rebekah disliked the cumbersome braces and the effort it took to walk, she didn't want to make a fuss about it, so with the aid of her crutches, she gritted her teeth and hobbled up the dirt path leading to the Hiltys' front porch.

Mary Ellen had been sitting on the porch swing, but when Rebekah approached, she jumped up and rushed toward her. "Oh, it's so good to see you walking today."

Rebekah frowned and shook her head. "This isn't really walking. I feel like one of those little metal robots I've seen in the toy section at the Wal-Mart store."

"Here, let me help you up the steps," Mary Ellen offered, ignoring Rebekah's negative comment. "We can sit on the swing and visit awhile."

Rebekah allowed her cousin to help her up the stairs, then over to the swing. "What's new in your life?" she asked, once she was seated.

"Not so much," Mary Ellen said with a shrug, but her hazel-colored eyes sparkled as though she could hardly contain herself.

"Are you sure about that? You look pretty happy about something."

Mary Ellen stood for a few seconds, rocking back and forth on her heels. Then her lips turned into a wide smile. "If you must know, Johnny has finally asked if he can court me."

Rebekah had mixed feelings about that bit of news. She was trying to be happy for Mary Ellen because she was her best friend and all, but she felt sorry for poor Daniel. Now that Johnny would be calling on Mary Ellen, Daniel's chances of winning her would be slim to none.

Rebekah plastered a smile on her face, although she really felt like crying. "It's nice to see you're so happy."

"Jah, I truly am." Mary Ellen's face fairly glowed as she took a seat beside Rebekah on the swing and reached out to clasp her hand. "How are things with you these days? Have you thought any more about my greenhouse idea?"

Rebekah nodded, glad for the change of subject. "I have. I even talked to Mom and Dad, and they think it's a good idea, too. Dad says he can begin building it sometime next week." She drew in a deep breath and let it out in a rush.

"Just think, I might actually be able to support myself if this business takes hold."

"That would be wunderbaar, all right." Mary Ellen squinted. "But what will you sell? Do you have enough plants and flowers?"

"Not yet, but with the money I made at the farmers' market, I'll be able to buy some of what I need to get started. I can use more starts from Grandma's plants, and there's always fresh-cut flowers from our garden to sell."

"Sounds like you've got it all figured out."

"I'm working on it. In the beginning, all my profits will have to go back into the business. I'll need to buy more plants, seeds, fertilizers, pots, and potting soil. After the first year or so, I'm hoping that I'll be able to start supporting myself."

Mary Ellen pumped the swing back and forth with her legs—legs Rebekah would have given nearly anything to have owned. "It's good to see you so cheerful. You've been acting kind of gloomy lately."

Rebekah sighed. "That's partly because of those awful dreams I kept having about Grandma dying and then others in my family leaving me, too."

"Are you still having the nightmares?"

"Not since I started praying more and committing to memory some scriptures on trusting God and not fearing the unknown."

"I'm glad to hear it. Which verses have you memorized?"

Rebekah was about to reply when Aunt Mim stepped onto the porch, interrupting their conversation. "I see you two have found my favorite swinging seat," she said, smiling brightly.

"Would you like to sit here?" Rebekah offered. "We can go someplace else to visit."

"You stay right where you are. I can't take time to sit just now, anyway. I have to see about getting some food set out for this family picnic of ours."

"Is there anything we can do to help?" Mary Ellen questioned.

Aunt Mim shook her head. "Maybe later. Sarah, Crystal, and Grace are here to help, so you two can sit right there for now and keep on visiting." With a wave of her hand, she hurried into the house.

"Aunt Mim's a sweet lady. She always seems so full of joy," Rebekah said, nudging Mary Ellen with her elbow.

"Jah. She may not be my real mamm, but she loves me like she is. I thank God for bringing her into our lives when I was a young girl—though she wasn't always so happy."

"What do you mean?"

"Don't you remember when she was our schoolteacher and some of the kinner used to call her en alt maedel with a heart of stone?"

Rebekah nodded. She wondered how many folks thought of her as an old maid. She knew her sister did because she'd already said so. Despite the fact that Nadine had apologized for her hurtful words, things hadn't been the same between them since their last disagreement.

"God can change hearts if we allow Him to," Mary Ellen said, waving her hand at a bothersome fly that seemed determined to buzz their heads.

"Do you think God still performs miracles?"

"Of course He does. Why would you ask such a thing?"

Rebekah's eyelids fluttered, then closed and opened again. "Sometimes I think I might be able to actually *feel* God's presence if He gave me an enormous miracle the way He did for folks back in the Bible days. In fact, I've been praying for such a miracle and trying to trust that He will answer that prayer."

"We don't need big miracles in order to see God. He performs small miracles in people's lives nearly every day." Mary Ellen took hold of Rebekah's hand and gave her fingers a gentle squeeze. "Often we don't see the small miracles because we don't have our eyes wide open."

"Are you talking about me?"

"Not in particular. I'm talking about believers in general. Even when clouds of pain seem to hide God's face, we're never hidden from His miracle of love and His tender mercies."

Rebekah studied Mary Ellen's pretty face. "Just how did a nineteen-year-old woman get to be so smart, anyway?"

Mary Ellen smiled, bringing to the surface her two matching dimples. "I think my wisdom comes from God, but I wouldn't be teaching school if I wasn't putting it into practice every day."

Rebekah nodded and released another audible sigh. "You're probably right. I'm praying that God will give me lots of wisdom, and I hope it's real soon. For as I'm sure you've heard some of the older folks say, 'we grow too soon old and too late smart.' "

※

Four large picnic tables had been set up on the front lawn

for eating, and two more were loaded with a variety of food and beverages. Rebekah noticed that everyone seemed to be in good spirits and had come with hearty appetites, for not only was a lot of visiting going on, but in no time at all, most of the food was gone, too.

When it appeared that everyone had finished eating, Rebekah's father stood and called for their attention. The hum of talking subsided as he clapped his hands together. "Those who work hard eat hearty, and you've all done right well. Now it's time to share some good news with you." He paused and glanced over at Rebekah. "I want you to know that my oldest daughter is about to become a businesswoman."

All eyes turned to Rebekah, and she felt the heat of a blush creep up the back of her neck and spread quickly to her face.

Dad laid his hand on her shoulder. "Rebekah wants to open a greenhouse that will be built near the front of our property."

Cheers went up around the tables, and everyone smiled at Rebekah—everyone except Nadine. She just sat stony-faced, staring at her empty plate, which only confirmed in Rebekah's mind that things still weren't right between her and her sister.

"If the greenhouse is to be built before summer ends, I'll need some help with the project," Dad continued. "Are there any volunteers?"

"You can count on me," said Uncle Lewis.

Uncle Jonas nodded. "Jah, me, too."

"I'd be more than happy to help," Uncle Amos put in.

"Same here." This came from Cousin Henry, whose eager

expression made Rebekah think he might like to begin building on her greenhouse right away.

"Don't forget about us," John and Jacob said in unison.

"I would help if I was bigger," seven-year-old Matthew piped up.

Dad laughed. "I'll not turn away any help. Danki, to all of you."

"I'm ever so grateful," Rebekah said, feeling tears of joy flood her eyes.

"What will you call this new business of yours?" Aunt Mim questioned.

Rebekah sniffed and wiped her eyes with the backs of her hands as a vision of Grandma Stoltzfus came to mind. "I'm thinking about calling it Grandma's Place. I'll be using lots of starts from her plants, and she loved flowers so much. It seems only fitting to name the greenhouse after her."

"I think it's a wunderbaar name," Aunt Mim said with a nod.

"I do believe we'd better move this conversation indoors," Mom interjected, "because I just felt something wet splat right on my nose!"

❦

Everyone scrambled to get the dishes cleared off the tables and into the house, but Nadine, arms folded, and chin tucked against her neck, remained seated. Why was it that everything always had to be about Rebekah? *Rebekah needs more understanding. Rebekah should sell plants at the farmers' market. Rebekah will soon be getting her own greenhouse.* Nadine was sick of her sister being the center of attention and getting to do all the fun things she was never allowed to do.

She thought back to the day at the farmers' market when she'd been denied the privilege of having lunch with Carolyn and her cousin Melvin. Rebekah had gotten back late from her lunch with Mary Ellen, and by the time Nadine was free to go, Carolyn and Melvin had already left the market.

It's not fair, she grumbled in silence as the rain continued to fall. *I'm always kept busy with chores, and I hardly ever get to do anything just for fun.*

"How come you're still out here in the rain? I thought you'd gone inside with the other women."

Nadine whirled around. Dad stood behind her with a disgruntled look on his face. At least he hadn't referred to her as a little girl. She supposed that was something to be thankful for.

"I was just sitting here thinking," she mumbled.

He lifted his hand and caught several raindrops in his palm. "You like thinkin' in the rain?"

She gave an exaggerated shrug.

"You'd better get into the house now. This storm is getting worse, and we'll be leaving as soon as we've had our dessert."

With a weary sigh, Nadine climbed off the picnic bench and trudged toward the house, feeling even more frustrated because she wouldn't be allowed the privilege of sitting in the rain by herself.

❧

"Dad, I wish we weren't heading for home already," Nadine complained from the back of their closed-in buggy. "That homemade ice cream Uncle Amos made was sure good, and I wanted a second helping."

"We left because of this storm," Dad called back to her. "It's getting worse all the time, and we need to be home to see that the livestock gets fed and put to bed."

It was obvious by the way their father gripped the reins that he was fighting to keep the horse under control. Jagged streaks of lightning zigzagged across the horizon, thunderous roars shook the sky, and the rain pelted to the ground in torrents.

"I'm scared," Nadine whined. "I hate *wedderleech* and *dunner*. I wish we could have stayed at Aunt Mim's house until the storm was over."

"Aw, a little lightning and thunder is nothin' to be scared of," Simon asserted. "This is just a typical summer storm."

Mom looked back at them over her shoulder. "There's nothing typical about this weather, and I think it would be wise if we all kept quiet so your daed can concentrate on his driving."

Rebekah leaned her head a little closer to Nadine, hoping to calm the girl's nerves. "We'll be home soon enough."

Another shuddering clap of thunder sounded, and the horse whinnied loudly. "Whoa there. Steady, boy," Dad said in a soothing voice.

They were nearing their farm, and as they turned up the gravel driveway, Mom let out a shrill scream. "Fire! Oh, Andrew, our barn's all ablaze!"

"It must have been struck by lightning." Dad urged the horse into a fast trot. When they reached their front yard, he halted the gelding and jumped down from the buggy.

"Go get help!" he called to Mom. "Simon, you and Nadine should start filling some buckets with water right away."

"What about me?" Rebekah asked, feeling helpless and frightened. Wasn't there something she could do to lend a hand?

"You can either go on up to the house or ride with me," Mom said over her shoulder.

Rebekah looked out the window and saw Dad running toward the water trough, with Simon and Nadine on his heels. It was obvious that none of them had the time to help her out of the buggy right now. "I'll ride with you, Mom," she replied, knowing full well that they couldn't afford to waste a single moment.

Mom nodded and quickly turned the buggy around. As they tore out of the yard, Rebekah grabbed the edge of her seat, fearing she might be thrown out. When she turned to look out the back window again, she saw Dad, Simon, and Nadine running frantically toward the barn, each carrying two buckets of water in their hands.

The rain soon turned to a trickle, but the wind continued to blow furiously. Rebekah was painfully aware that, unless the fire department could get to their place quickly, Dad would surely lose the whole barn.

The first stop Mom made was at their English neighbors' house, which was about two miles down the road. She asked them to call the county fire department; then she headed over to Jonas and Crystal's place to let them know what had happened.

Uncle Jonas and his boys left right away to help fight the fire, while Mom and Rebekah moved on to enlist the help of Uncle Lewis, Uncle Amos, and Henry.

Rebekah prayed and kept a close watch out the window to be sure there was nothing in Mom's way. By the time they got home, the wind had subsided, and two Lancaster County fire trucks were parked in the driveway, their red lights flashing this way and that. One look at the barn told Rebekah all she needed to know. The firefighters' efforts had been in vain—the barn had burned clean to the ground.

She glanced toward the corral and realized that Dad must have managed to save the livestock, because the cows and horses he kept inside the barn were now crowded into the corral. At least that was something for which to be grateful.

As the reality of the situation took hold, Rebekah's eyes stung with tears, and she nearly choked on a sob. "Ach my, what will Dad do now?"

Mom reached over the seat and took hold of Rebekah's hand. "He'll do just as all other Amish men do whenever they lose a barn. He shall have a barn raising."

Chapter 7

Rebekah figured the news had spread quickly about Dad's barn burning to the ground, for offers of help to rebuild came from far and wide, from both their English and Amish neighbors. It was a comfort to know that so many people cared about them.

"When is the barn raising going to be?" she asked Dad as the family sat around the kitchen table the following morning.

"Simon and I, and probably Amos, Jonas, and Lewis, will spend time today and tomorrow cleaning up the mess left from the fire. Many bales of hay were ruined, and those have to be disposed of, too. Then the foundation will need to be laid, and if all goes well, we should have the barn fairly well finished by next Saturday." He pulled his fingers through the end of his beard and grunted. "I'm sorry, Rebekah, but the building of your greenhouse will have to wait awhile longer. I hope you understand."

Rebekah felt a keen sense of disappointment, but she couldn't let Dad know that. He had enough on his mind. She wouldn't say anything that might cause him to feel guilty about something he couldn't prevent. "It's all right," she said, forcing a smile. "Getting the new barn up is more important than anything else right now."

"We'll all be busy during the next several days," Mom put in as she left the table and headed across the room to get the pot of coffee from the stove. "There will be a lot of food to prepare for the hungry crews and several errands to run as we get everything ready for the barn raising."

Nadine, who sat across the table from Rebekah, seemed to perk right up. "Will some of the boys my age come to help raise the barn?"

"I'm sure many of the young fellows will show up with their daeds," Dad replied. "There will be plenty of work to do, even for the younger ones."

"Maybe I can help by bringing nails and other supplies out to the workers," Nadine volunteered.

"She doesn't really want to work. She just wants to flirt with the boys." Simon reached across Rebekah and jabbed Nadine's arm with the end of his spoon.

"There'll be no time for flirting," Mom said with a shake of her head. "Nadine will be kept busy helping the women that day, not the boys."

"I always have to help the women," Nadine mumbled.

Simon wrinkled his nose. "Oh, quit with all the *gebrutz*."

"I'm not pouting."

"Sure you are," he said with a slow nod. "It seems like you're always pouting or complaining about something these days."

Before Nadine could respond, Dad shot them both a warning look, and they clamped their mouths shut real quick.

When Mom joined them at the table again, she touched Rebekah lightly on the shoulder. "I was thinking of hiring a driver to take me to Lancaster to do some shopping later today. If you'd like to go along, maybe we could stop by the garden center and pick out some plants for that new greenhouse of yours."

Rebekah's spirits lifted a bit. "Do you have time for that? I know you had planned to do some baking today."

"Oh, that can wait until tomorrow, I expect."

"Can I go, too?" Nadine asked with a hopeful expression.

"I'd rather you stayed home today," Mom said. "I have some wash that should be hung, and Dad and Simon will be cleaning up the mess from the old barn so they'll need someone here to make their lunches."

"Does that mean you're not gonna be home from Lancaster by lunchtime?" Nadine questioned.

Mom poured herself a cup of coffee and then one for Dad. "By the time Rebekah and I finish our shopping, it will no doubt be noon, so we'll probably eat someplace along the way."

Nadine crinkled her nose and leered at Rebekah. "That's not fair. She always gets to have all the fun. I wish that I were—"

"What? You wish you were like me? Is that what you were going to say, Nadine?"

Her sister shrugged. "Maybe."

"Come now. Would you really want to be trapped in my crippled body, limited to a wheelchair or those confining leg braces I sometimes must wear? Do you think that's anything to be jealous of?" Rebekah's voice had raised at least two octaves, and her hand shook as she pointed a finger at Nadine. "You don't even know what you're saying. Why, I'd gladly trade places with you or anyone else who could walk and run!"

Rebekah knew she was letting her emotions get the best of her, but she had already begun to say what was on her mind, and she wasn't about to stop until she'd gotten it all said. "Someday you'll grow up and fall in love. Then you'll get married and have kinner. Your life will be full and complete." She gulped on a sob. "I, on the other hand, will never marry or fall in love. So please don't envy me or anything I might be allowed to do, because I would give almost anything if I could do all the things you're able to do."

Nadine's face flushed, and without a word, she jumped up from the table and dashed out of the room.

Dad turned to Rebekah and said, "Don't let your sister upset you. She's young and doesn't understand what it's like to be in your situation. To her, it probably seems as though you get more attention and special favors, so it might help if you could be more tolerant of her, too."

Rebekah nodded, feeling foolish for allowing her temper to get the better of her. "Jah, Dad, I know, and I'll try to be more understanding of Nadine."

❧

As Rebekah and Mom rode to Lancaster in Vera's van later that morning, Rebekah put her nose up to the open window on her side to enjoy the clean, fresh smell. Sometimes after a summer storm had left its mark, the air would turn hot and muggy. Not today, though. Today was much cooler with hardly any humidity at all. For the benefit of the men who would be working on Dad's barn, she hoped it would stay like this until the job was done.

Rebekah's thoughts went to her sister, and she began to fret over the way Nadine always reacted whenever she wasn't allowed to do something Rebekah got to do. If there was only some way to make her sister understand the way things were. Rebekah wished she could be as close to Nadine as she was to Mary Ellen, but unless Nadine's attitude changed, they were unlikely to become good friends.

As they pulled into the town of Lancaster, Rebekah pushed her thoughts aside and allowed her emotions to soar. Opening a greenhouse of her own would be the most exciting thing she had ever done. She could hardly contain herself as Vera steered the van off the main road and into the parking lot at the garden center.

Mom and Vera went around to the back of the van to get Rebekah's wheelchair, and a short time later, Rebekah and Mom entered the store.

With a feeling of anticipation, Rebekah wheeled up and down the aisles, inspecting a variety of houseplants and outdoor foliage as she went along. "Oh, Mom," she said excitedly, "just look at how many plants and flowers there are to choose from."

Mom smiled. "Maybe someday you'll have nearly as many in your own place of business."

Rebekah sucked in a deep breath and released it quickly. "I could only wish for such a miracle."

"I believe miracles are to be prayed for, daughter, not wished for," Mom corrected.

Rebekah shrugged. "Well, you know what I mean."

"Are you looking for anything in particular?" one of the clerks asked, as he stepped up to them.

Rebekah smiled at the tall, gray-haired man. "I need several of your hardiest, most reasonably priced indoor and outdoor plants."

He chuckled. "I see we have a shrewd businesswoman here."

Rebekah felt the heat of a blush creep up her neck. She wondered if she looked old enough or smart enough to be a businesswoman. Or did the clerk only see her as a pathetic crippled girl in a wheelchair, who needed someone to say something nice to her so she would feel better?

"I think I do know a good bargain when I see one," she said. "So if you'll lead the way, as we go along, I'll decide what will best suit my needs."

Rebekah was thankful when Mom walked slowly behind and gave her opinion only when it was asked for. If this was going to be Rebekah's business venture, then she figured she should do as much of the decision making as possible.

It took about an hour for her to select all the plants she needed, and when Vera showed up, the clerk helped load all the boxes into the back of Vera's van. He even offered to help Mom with Rebekah's wheelchair.

"You did real good today," Mom said, as she assisted Rebekah into the back seat of the van. "You got quite a few plants for the amount of money you had. I would think if you took some starts from them, you could probably double—or even triple—your investment in no time."

Rebekah smiled and reached over to touch her mother's

arm. "You knew I was disappointed about Dad not being able to start building the greenhouse this week, didn't you?"

"Jah, I knew."

"And you thought this trip to town might make me feel better?"

"I hoped it would."

"Well, it worked, because I do feel better." Rebekah patted her stomach and grinned. "But I'd feel even better if we had something to eat."

Mom laughed. "Vera and I talked about that earlier. We'll have lunch somewhere on the way home, and right after that, I have one more errand I need to run."

"Oh? What errand is that?"

"It's going to be a surprise for someone."

"A surprise? You can tell me, Mom. I won't spill the beans, I promise."

Mom placed her fingers against her mouth. "My lips are sealed."

Rebekah was allowed to choose where they would eat lunch, and she picked a Pennsylvania Dutch restaurant near the town of Bird-in-Hand, telling Mom she never got tired of traditional Amish cooking. The three women were escorted to a long table where several other people sat. This was part of family-style dining, but Rebekah felt funny about sitting next to folks she'd never met before. She knew most of them were just curious tourists wanting to check out the Plain folks, but that didn't make her feel any less self-conscious.

"Could we have a small table by ourselves?" she asked her mother.

Mom turned to Vera. "Is that all right with you?"

"Whatever Rebekah's comfortable with is fine by me," Vera said with a nod.

Mom smiled at their Mennonite hostess and said, "Would you possibly have a separate table for the three of us?"

The young woman, who was dressed in plain clothes similar to what Rebekah and Mom wore, nodded and led them to a small table near the window, then handed them each a menu.

Rebekah maneuvered her wheelchair as close to the table as possible. It wasn't as easy as eating at home, where the big wooden table had plenty of leg room, but at least they would have some measure of privacy. "I'm just not up to people's curious stares today," she said to Mom and Vera when they'd taken their seats across from her.

"I don't think folks would be staring at us," Mom replied. "This is a Pennsylvania Dutch restaurant, remember? There are several Amish and Mennonite people eating here, too."

Vera smiled. "Most of the help are Plain People, as well."

"I know, but I was thinking more about them staring at me—my disability," Rebekah said with a grimace.

Mom reached across the table and patted Rebekah's hand. "Try not to worry so much about what other people think. Not everyone in the world stares at people with disabilities, you know." She shrugged. "Even if they should stare, how can it really hurt?"

Rebekah fingered her silverware, pushing her knife and

spoon together and then apart again. "It makes me feel uncomfortable when they look at me, that's all."

Another young Mennonite woman came to take their order. "We have two choices for the Dutch family-style lunch," she explained. "One is roast beef, which also comes with baked country sausage, mashed potatoes, green beans, chowchow, pork and sauerkraut, pepper cabbage, and homemade bread." She paused a moment, then added, "The other menu includes baked ham, fried chicken, bread filling, applesauce, pickled beets, noodles in brown gravy, sweet potatoes, creamed corn, bread-and-butter pickles, and homemade rolls." She stopped again and drew in a deep breath. "The beverages we have to offer are coffee, hot tea, iced tea, lemonade, and milk. The choice of desserts for both meals is the same: carrot cake, shoofly pie, cherry crumb pie, tapioca pudding, apple crumb pie, vanilla ice cream, German chocolate cake, and pumpkin roll."

"Ach! With either meal there's so much food to eat," Mom exclaimed. "It's a hard choice to make—that's for sure." She nodded at Rebekah. "What would you like?"

"I think I'd prefer the one that includes baked ham and bread filling. I could eat tasty filling until the cows come home."

Mom glanced at Vera. "Which meal appeals to you?"

"The second one is fine for me," Vera told the waitress.

As soon as the woman walked away, Mom leaned across the table and whispered to Rebekah, "You know, I may have to borrow that wheelchair of yours when we leave this place."

Rebekah squinted. "Huh?"

"They might have to wheel me out of here because I'll be too full to walk."

Rebekah giggled. It felt good to spend the day with Mom like this. She could understand why her sister might be a bit jealous, but Nadine got to do so many other things—things Rebekah couldn't do. She hoped by now that Nadine had forgotten about the little argument they'd had this morning and had found something to feel positive about. Knowing her little sister, she was probably daydreaming about some boy already.

In no time at all, the food started coming, and whenever one bowl emptied, the waitress was there to fill it up again. Rebekah ate until she couldn't take another bite, and as they left the restaurant, she figured none of them would need any supper that night.

"Where would you like to go while I'm on my secret errand?" Mom asked, helping Rebekah into the van.

Rebekah shrugged. "Oh, I don't know. Maybe the bookstore. I might find something there on caring for plants or possibly on business management."

"That sounds fine," Mom agreed. "We'll drop you off first; then Vera can take me to my errand. We'll be back in half an hour or so."

"Okay, Mom."

The bookstore was only a few blocks away, and soon they had pulled up to the brick storefront. Mom went around and got out the wheelchair; then she helped Rebekah into it, walked to the front of the bookstore, and held the door open. "See you soon, sweet daughter."

Rebekah waved and wheeled herself inside. There seemed

to be a lot of tourists milling around today, looking at all the books that had been written about the Amish and Mennonite people and their Plain lifestyle. She moved quickly away from the group of curious onlookers and found the shelf where the books about plants and flowers were kept. She spotted one on the second shelf entitled *Caring for Your African Violets.* Rebekah strained to reach it, but her arm wasn't long enough. She could attempt standing, she supposed, but she had tried that a time or two without the aid of her crutches, and usually ended up flat on the floor. Falling on her face at home was one thing, but making a fool of herself in front of an audience was not on Rebekah's list of things to do for the day.

She glanced around, hoping to catch the attention of one of the store clerks. They all seemed to be busy helping the English tourists.

"You are buying a *buch?*" The question came from a deep male voice.

Rebekah gave her chair a sharp turn to the left. Daniel Beachy stood looking down on her with his straw hat in one hand and a crooked grin on his face. "I'm surprised to see you here, Rebekah. Are you alone?"

"Mom's in town, but she's on an errand so I'm here buying a book." Rebekah's forehead wrinkled. "At least I would be if I could reach it."

"Which one is it? I'll get it down for you," he offered.

Rebekah pointed to the shelf above her. "*Caring for Your African Violets.*"

Daniel's long arm easily reached the book, and he handed it to her with another friendly looking smile. "Are you a plant lover?"

She nodded. "Oh, jah. Especially African violets. They were Grandma Stoltzfus's favorite plant, too." She placed the book in her lap. "I hope to open a greenhouse soon, so I want to learn all I can about how to run the business."

Daniel's eyebrows shot up. "A greenhouse, you say? Now that sounds like an interesting business venture. Where will it be located?"

"Near the front of our property. Of course, that won't be until Dad has time to build it. We lost our barn last night, so the greenhouse project will have to wait another week or two."

Daniel's dark eyes looked more serious than usual as he nodded. "I heard about that fire; such a shame it is, too. When is the barn raising going to be?"

"There's a lot of cleanup work that needs to be done, and then the foundation will have to be laid, so the building probably won't begin until at least next Friday or Saturday."

"Tell your daed he can count on my help." Daniel drummed his fingers against his chin. "Maybe I could help build your greenhouse, too. I'm pretty handy with a hammer and saw."

"Danki. I'll appreciate any help I can get."

Daniel shuffled his feet a few times and stared down at his boots. "Well, guess I'd best get going. I picked up some supplies for my daed, and he's probably wondering what's takin' me so long."

"I'm sorry for keeping you."

He patted his stomach. "Naw, it wasn't you. I spent way too much time eating my noon meal. They were serving roast beef at the Plain and Fancy today. I think I ate my share and enough for about five others, as well."

"Mom and I were at the Plain and Fancy, too, with our driver, Vera," Rebekah said. "I didn't see you there, though."

"I was at one of the long tables with a bunch of other folks over on the right side of the room."

"That's probably why we didn't see you, then. We three ate at a small table near the window."

Daniel turned toward the door; then as though he might have forgotten something, he turned back around. "Say, I hear there's going to be another singing in two weeks. It's supposed to be over at Clarence Yoder's place. Do you plan on being there, Rebekah?"

Rebekah thought about the last singing she had attended and remembered how out of place she'd felt. She shook her head. "I've got too much work to do if I'm going to get all my plants ready to open for business in August." A small sigh escaped her lips. "That is, if I have a greenhouse by then."

"The barn raising will only take a good full day if there's plenty of help," Daniel said. "We should have your building up in short order once the work on the barn is done."

"That would be nice."

"Well, I'd best go now. See you soon, Rebekah."

"Have fun at the singing," she called to his retreating form.

"Guess I won't go to this one, either," he mumbled before he disappeared out the door.

"Poor Daniel," Rebekah whispered. "He likes Mary Ellen so much he's probably not going to the singing because he can't stand to see Johnny flirting with her again." She clicked her tongue. "What a shame my cousin doesn't see how nice Daniel is."

As Daniel exited the bookstore, he couldn't get the image of Rebekah out of his mind. She'd looked kind of bewildered and had even acted a bit nervous when he'd first spotted her trying to reach that book. After he'd taken it off the shelf for her and they'd talked about the plans for her new greenhouse, she had seemed to relax some. But then when he'd mentioned the singing, Rebekah had acted kind of distant again.

Maybe some ice cream would cheer her up, he thought as his gaze came to rest on the ice-cream store across the street. *Think I'll get a couple of cones and take one over to her.*

A short time later, Daniel left the ice-cream store holding two double-dip strawberry ice-cream cones in his hands. He had just started up the sidewalk and was almost ready to cross the street, when a young Amish boy riding a scooter whizzed past.

Daniel jumped out of the way just in time to keep from being knocked off his feet, but in the process, the ice-cream cones toppled over, landing on the sidewalk with a *splat.*

"Sorry," the boy mumbled, but he kept on going.

"Jah, me, too." Daniel bent to pick up the smashed cones, tossed them into the nearest trash can, and headed back to the ice-cream store.

A short time later, holding two more double-dip cones securely in his hands, he made his way across the street and into the bookstore. At first glance he saw no sign of Rebekah, so he walked up and down every aisle, looking for her.

"May I help you?" the middle-aged Englishman who ran the bookstore asked as he stepped up to Daniel.

"I–I'm looking for a young woman in a wheelchair. She was here a few minutes ago, looking at a book about African violets."

The man nodded. "She bought the book and then left the store right after that."

"Well, wouldn't ya just know it?" Daniel started for the door but turned back around, lifting one of the cones in the air. "Say, would you like an ice-cream cone?"

The man smiled but shook his head. "Thanks anyway, but I'm a diabetic so I have to watch my sugar intake."

"Jah, okay." Daniel shuffled his way to the front of the store and headed out the door. "Should have never bought any ice cream at all," he grumbled. "Guess I'm gonna have to eat both of these cones now so they don't go to waste."

CHAPTER 8

Friday morning, Rebekah awoke to the piercing sound of pulsating hammers pounding nails into heavy pieces of lumber, and the grating of saws cutting thick pieces of wood. She had slept well the night before and had even had a very pleasant dream about her future greenhouse, where she'd become quite successful.

She grabbed hold of the bed rails, pulled herself upright, scooted to the edge of the bed, and dropped into her wheelchair. Her arms were strong, and she had become quite adept at this morning ritual. It wasn't an easy task, but it was better than bothering someone else to come help.

Rebekah wheeled herself over to the window so she could look out at the side yard and see what was going on. From her downstairs bedroom, she had the perfect view of the spot where the new barn was going to be.

She lifted one edge of the dark shade a bit and took a peek. She was surprised to see so many men and boys scurrying about the place. Why, nearly two hundred of them had come to help out. Some were already laying the floor beams and planks, while others had paired off in groups to prepare the panels, beams, and rafters.

Rebekah caught sight of one of the younger men looking her way, and she quickly turned her chair away from the window. From this distance, she couldn't be sure who had been watching her, but she didn't need anyone's curious stares or pitying looks this morning. Besides, she knew she should hurry and get dressed so she could see about helping with breakfast and whatever else needed to be done.

Aunt Mim, Aunt Crystal, Aunt Grace, and Mom were already in the kitchen when Rebekah made her entrance a short time later. Nadine and their cousins Peggy, Maddie, and Mary Ellen were also helping out. The room was warm and smelled of sweet cinnamon buns, reminding Rebekah of Grandma, who had always liked to bake. A pang of regret shot through her, but it was quickly replaced with a sense of peace. She still missed Grandma and probably always would, but Rebekah had finally come to grips with her loss, taking comfort in the fact that Grandma was in a much better place.

"Why'd you let me sleep so late?" Rebekah asked, as she wheeled up to her mother. "I didn't know anyone was here until I woke up to the racket of all those noisy hammers and saws."

"You must sleep pretty sound. They've been at it for nearly an hour already," Aunt Crystal said with a wink.

"Don't worry about it," Mom said. "As you can see, I have plenty of help. I thought it would do you good to sleep a little longer this morning. Ever since our trip to the garden center in Lancaster, you've been busy cutting and repotting all those plants you bought and studying that book on African violets."

"Your mamm was telling us more about your new business venture," Aunt Mim said as she made a place at the table for Rebekah to park her wheelchair. "It sounds exciting—hopefully prosperous, too."

Rebekah reached for a sticky cinnamon bun and smiled. "I sure hope so."

"Rebekah's going to use some starts from Grandma Stoltzfus's plants in her greenhouse," Mary Ellen put in.

Aunt Mim smiled. "That sounds like a good idea."

"Grandma was real special, and she taught me to appreciate flowers and plants," Rebekah said, reaching for a glass and the pitcher of cold milk, also on the table.

The back door flew open just then, and Rebekah's fifteen-year-old twin cousins, Jacob and John, rushed into the kitchen. "We need somethin' cold to drink!" Jacob wiped his sweaty forehead with the back of his arm. "It's already hot as an oven out there."

John nodded in agreement, his brown eyes looking ever so serious. "That's right, and when a body works hard, a body deserves a cool drink!"

Aunt Crystal nodded. "I think these boys are real workers. We should give them some iced tea. Better send some of it out for the other men, too."

"There are several jugs in there," Mom said, pointing to the refrigerator. "Just help yourself and take the rest outside. I think there are some paper cups on the picnic table."

John stared at the plate of sticky buns sitting on the table. "You wouldn't happen to have enough of those so we could have some, would you, Aunt Sarah?"

She laughed. "There's more on the counter behind you. Help yourself and take some out to the other workers, as well."

The boys piled some of the cinnamon rolls onto a plate, grabbed some jugs of iced tea, and headed back outside.

As soon as Rebekah finished eating her breakfast, she rolled her wheelchair over to the sink, where her mother stood washing dishes. "What can I do to help?"

"Why don't you and Mary Ellen shell some peas for the salads we'll be having with our noon meal? You can go outside on the porch to do it, if you like."

"Okay," Rebekah said with a nod.

Mary Ellen gathered up two hefty pans and a paper sack full of plump peas, and Rebekah followed her out the back door.

Mary Ellen found a metal folding chair that had been propped against the side of the house near the door and pulled it up next to Rebekah's wheelchair. She placed one of the pans in Rebekah's lap and put the other in her own. Then she distributed the peas equally between them.

"How's the courtship with Johnny going?" Rebekah asked as she picked up a handful of pea pods and began to shell them lickety-split.

Mary Ellen's face broke into a wide smile. "It's going real good. He's been over to our place to see me nearly every night for the past week."

"Do you like him a lot?"

"Jah, I do. He's so much fun and pretty good-looking,

too, don't you think?"

Rebekah wrinkled her nose and emitted a noise that sounded something like a cat whose tail had been stepped on. "That's not for me to be saying. Johnny might not take kindly to me making eyes at him."

"I'm not asking you to make eyes at him, silly. I only wondered if you think he's good-looking or not."

Rebekah shrugged her slim shoulders and grabbed another handful of pea pods. "I suppose he's all right. He's just not my type, that's all."

"Who is your type, might I ask? Is there something you're not telling me? Do you have your heart set on anyone special?"

Rebekah shook her head.

"I'll bet it's Daniel Beachy. I've seen the way you steal looks in his direction whenever you think no one's paying any attention."

Rebekah's face turned crimson. "I have no interest in any man, and none have interest in me."

"Maybe they do have an interest, and you're just too blind to see it."

"Don't you think I would know if someone cared for me?"

"Maybe so. Maybe not."

"What's that supposed to mean?"

"It means that you might not be paying close enough attention."

Rebekah made no further comment on the subject, and Mary Ellen decided it was probably best to drop the subject. No point in embarrassing her cousin any further; she had enough to deal with.

"Sure is a hot one today," Rebekah complained. "I don't envy those poor men working out there in the sweltering sun all day."

"Jah, but I'm sure they—" Mary Ellen's sentence was interrupted when a man's heavy boots thudded up the porch steps.

"*Wie geht's*, you two?" Daniel asked with a nod in their direction.

Rebekah waited to see if Mary Ellen would respond, but when her cousin made no comment, she smiled up at him and said, "I'm doing okay. How's the work on my daed's barn coming along?"

Daniel yanked off his straw hat and wiped the perspiration from his forehead with the back of his hand. "It's going well enough. Whew! Today's sure hot and humid, don't you think?" His question was directed at Rebekah, and she swallowed hard as his serious dark eyes seemed to bore straight into her soul.

"Jah, I was just saying that to Mary Ellen before you showed up," she murmured, feeling another flush of warmth, but excusing it as coming from the heat of the day.

"I've talked to your daed about helping with the greenhouse," Daniel said, shifting his weight from one foot to the other. "He said he hopes to begin working on it sometime next week."

Rebekah swallowed again. Why was Daniel being so nice, and why did he keep looking at her in such a strange way? It wasn't a look of pity, she was sure of that much, but she couldn't decide what his tipped head and lips curved slightly upwards meant. "I—I really appreciate the offer of help," she said. "I'll be grateful to anyone who helps build my new greenhouse."

Daniel stared down at his boots, rocking back and forth on his heels as if he might be feeling kind of nervous all of a sudden. Then he cleared his throat a couple of times and looked up at her again. "Well, guess I. . .uh. . .had better get back to work before my daed comes lookin' for me and accuses me of sloughin' off."

He turned and was about to step off the porch when Rebekah called out to him. "Did you get some cold tea yet?"

Daniel lifted his hat over his head and waved it at her. "I had some, danki." He took the steps two at a time and actually ran back to the job site, leaving Rebekah to wonder about his strange behavior. Had he been nervous because Mary Ellen was sitting there beside her and hadn't said one single word to him? Had he wanted to say something to her but not been able to work up the nerve? Jah, that was probably the case, all right.

"You could have at least said hello to Daniel," Rebekah said, squinting at her cousin, who had seemed intent on shelling peas the whole time Daniel had been on the porch, rather than joining in on their conversation.

Mary Ellen's eyebrows drew together. "I figured if he had something he wanted to say to me, he wouldn't have been talking to you."

"Maybe the reason he was talking to me was because you just sat there, shelling peas like there was no tomorrow and never taking part in the conversation at all."

Mary Ellen merely shrugged in response, but a few seconds later, she poked Rebekah with her elbow and whispered, "Daniel seems like a nice person, don't you think?"

Rebekah nodded but kept her focus on the pan of peas in her lap. *If you think he's so nice, then why aren't you giving the poor fellow a chance?* she silently fumed. *If I had someone like Daniel Beachy interested in me, I sure wouldn't be wasting my time on the likes of that juvenile Johnny Yoder.*

Daniel kicked at a hefty stone with the toe of his boot as he ambled across the yard toward the new building that was rapidly going up. Had he made a fool of himself during his conversation with Rebekah? She'd been friendly enough, he supposed, but she had acted kind of nervous, too. And her cousin Mary Ellen hadn't said a single word the whole time he'd been on the porch—just sat there shelling peas as though he didn't exist.

Does Mary Ellen disapprove of me? Maybe she thinks I'm not good enough for Rebekah. She might have even said some things against me to her.

Daniel didn't have a fancy way with words like Johnny did, and he sure wasn't nearly as funny or persuasive. But he was a hard worker, and he cared about Rebekah—so much so that it actually hurt. He figured that ought to count for something.

He kicked another stone and grimaced. *Maybe I'm just too unsure of myself. Maybe I ought to come right out and tell Rebekah what's on my mind and be done with it. At least then I'd know where I stand with her. If she doesn't care for me at all,*

I should at least give her the chance to say so.

"Hey, Daniel, are you comin' back to work anytime soon, or did you plan to stand there all day kickin' at stones?" Daniel's father shouted from where he knelt on one of the rafters of the new barn.

Feeling a rush of heat cover his face, Daniel cupped his hands around his mouth and hollered back, "I'm on my way, Pop!"

CHAPTER

9

As Nadine stood in front of the kitchen sink, drying the dishes Rebekah had washed earlier, she stared out the window at Dad's new barn. It was now fully erected and had been filled with hay and animals soon after its completion. The men who had helped out had been hardworking and faithful, in spite of the fact that they all had their own chores waiting to be done at home.

Dad said he didn't feel he could ask any of them to return the following week to begin building Rebekah's greenhouse, and even though the uncles said they were still willing to help with the greenhouse, he had turned them all down.

"It wouldn't be fair," Nadine had heard him tell Rebekah last night after supper.

However, with the help of Simon and Daniel, who had insisted on lending a hand no matter what Dad had said, the building would go up, even if it would take a little longer than expected.

Nadine suspected the main reason Daniel had insisted on helping with the greenhouse was because he had an interest in Rebekah. Too bad her older sister seemed too blind to see it.

A knock at the back door drove Nadine's thoughts aside, and she went to answer it. She was surprised to see Daniel standing on the porch holding a large clay pot with an equally large Boston fern inside. She stood in the door-way staring at him and wondering what the plant was for, and he stood staring back at her with a red, sweaty face.

"I'm. . .uh. . .here to help build Rebekah's greenhouse," he mumbled. "Is she at home?"

Nadine nodded and stepped away from the door, motion-ing him into the kitchen. She pointed to where Rebekah sat at the table, drinking a cup of tea and writing on a tablet. "You've got company, sister."

Rebekah swiveled her wheelchair around. "Guder mariye, Daniel. What brings you by so early this morning?" She eyed the plant he held but made no mention of it.

"This is for you," Daniel said, hurrying across the room and placing the fern in the center of the table. "It's for your new greenhouse—to keep, not sell."

She smiled. "It's beautiful, and I wouldn't think of sell-ing it. Danki, Daniel."

Nadine went over to the sink to finish up the dishes but glanced over her shoulder to see what Daniel would do next. He shifted from one foot to the other, looking kind of embarrassed.

"Is. . .uh. . .your daed still planning to begin work on the greenhouse this morning? I've come prepared to work all day if he is."

"I think so," Rebekah replied, looking rather embarrassed

herself. "Dad's out in the new barn right now, so if you want to talk to him about it, you'll have to go out there."

"Naw, that's okay. I'll stick around here for a while yet." Daniel removed his straw hat and went to hang it on a wall peg. Then he shuffled back toward Rebekah, wearing a silly grin.

Nadine lifted her gaze toward the ceiling, thinking how goofy Daniel was acting and wondering why he wasn't more assertive.

"Say, what's that you're workin' on there?" Daniel asked as he peered over Rebekah's shoulder.

Rebekah smiled, and her cheeks turned pink. "Well, I was writing my latest column for *The Budget,* but that's about done so now I'm ready to begin working on the inventory for my new greenhouse."

"Mind if I take a look-see?"

"No, no, not at all."

Those two are just sickening, Nadine thought as she grabbed another dish to dry. *It's obvious to me that Daniel has his eye on my sister, so why doesn't he quit thumpin' around the shrubs and just come right out and say so?* She pivoted away from the sink and turned toward the table. "Would you like some coffee or a glass of milk, Daniel?"

"Jah, that'd be fine."

Nadine planted both hands on her hips and glared at him. "Well, which one do you want? Milk or coffee?"

"I'll have whatever Rebekah's havin'," Daniel said, barely looking at Nadine.

She shook her head and muttered, "She's drinkin' tea; can't you see that?"

"Okay. Tea's fine for me then." Daniel pulled out a chair beside Rebekah's wheelchair and took a seat. "Do you mind if I see what you have written there?"

"Sure, go ahead." She pushed the tablet toward him.

He studied it intently, commenting with an occasional, "Hmm. . .ah. . .I see now. . . ."

When Nadine thought she could stand it no longer, Rebekah asked, "Well, what do you think? Does it seem like I have enough plants to open for business?"

Daniel scratched the back of his head. "I suppose it'll all depend on how many customers you have at first—and on what they might decide to buy. Sometimes one certain flower or plant seems to be everyone's favorite, so that might sell rather quick."

"How is it that you seem to know so much about flowers and plants?" Rebekah asked.

Before Daniel had a chance to respond, Nadine moved over to the table and set a cup of hot lemon-mint tea and a hunk of shoofly pie in front of him.

"Danki," Daniel said, never taking his eyes off Rebekah. "My uncle Jake lives in Ohio, and he owns a greenhouse. I spent some time there one summer, and I helped him in the greenhouse for a bit."

Rebekah's eyebrows lifted. "Really? Then you could probably give me all kinds of good advice."

He bobbed his head up and down and grinned. "I would be happy to help out. That is, if you really want my suggestions."

Nadine gritted her teeth. "Of course she does, silly. Why else would she have said what she did?" Listening to the way those two carried on was enough to make her wonder why she was so anxious to start courting.

"Nadine's right. I do want your suggestions," Rebekah said. "Of course, that's only if you have the time. I know you keep busy helping your daed with those dairy cows of his."

"I do get some free time, and my brothers, Harold and Abner, help Pop out, too, so I'm sure I can manage to find the time." Daniel stared at his cup of tea as though he might be puzzling over something.

Unable to stand the suspense, Nadine was on the verge of asking him what he was thinking about, but he spoke first. "I wonder sometimes if workin' with dairy cows is what I want to do for the rest of my life. I believe God's given us all special abilities, and I'd sure like the chance to use mine."

Rebekah tipped her head and stared at Daniel. "I know exactly what you mean."

"I would think running a dairy farm would be kind of interesting," Nadine spoke up. "What's it like, Daniel? Can you tell us a little about the operation?"

He nodded. "Well, I guess I'm lucky in that my daed uses diesel-generated milking machines rather than doing the milking by hand the way some dairymen in other Amish communities still do."

Nadine pursed her lips, as she shook her head. "Dad makes either me or Simon milk our two goats twice a day, and I don't enjoy it one little bit."

"Even with the use of mechanical milkers, refrigerated coolers, and battery-operated agitators, dairy farming is still a lot of work." Daniel wrinkled his nose. "I especially don't like the job of cleaning the barn and disposing of all the cow manure."

"Do you do that by hand?" This question came from Rebekah.

"Nope. We use our horses to pull metal devices through the manure trenches. The manure then goes into a tank, which is later pumped into a spreader."

Unable to listen to any more talk about smelly manure, Nadine went back to the sink to finish drying the dishes. A short time later when she had put the last dish away in the cupboard, she moved back to the table. "I'm done with the dishes now, so I think I'll go outside and see if Mom needs help hanging up the wash."

"What?" Rebekah pulled her gaze away from Daniel and angled her wheelchair toward Nadine.

"I said I'm done here. I'm going out to help Mom."

"Okay then."

Nadine headed out the door, but she was sure that neither Rebekah nor Daniel had even noticed. "When I'm old enough to start going to singings," she mumbled under her breath, "I'll be looking for a fellow who at least knows how to speak his mind."

❦

Rebekah and Daniel went back to talking about her greenhouse, and they stayed deeply engaged in conversation about her future plans for nearly an hour. Finally, Daniel looked up at the clock on the opposite wall and whistled. "Wow, it's later than I thought. Guess I'd better get outside and see if your daed's ready to go to work on the greenhouse." He smiled kind of sheepishly. "If he hasn't already gotten half of it built while I've been in here yappin' away and boring you with all my silly notions."

Rebekah shook her head. "You haven't been boring me at all. I appreciate all of your good ideas."

Daniel's chair made a scraping sound as he pushed it away from the table and stood. "Feel free to ask me for help of any kind once you open for business. I enjoy being around plants and would be more than happy to come by and help out whenever I'm able." His gaze dropped to the floor. "Well, I–I'd better get going."

"Don't work too hard," Rebekah called as he went out the door.

For the next several minutes, she sat staring at the list she and Daniel had made for the things she might need in her greenhouse and thinking about how nice it was of him to offer his assistance and how interesting she found him to be. While Daniel couldn't be considered handsome the way Johnny was, his dark chocolate eyes always looked so sincere. His slim, angular nose and full lips made him seem rather appealing, too. At least Rebekah thought so.

Mom and Nadine came into the kitchen just then, each carrying an empty wicker basket in their hands.

Rebekah smiled. "Guess what, Mom?"

"What's that?"

She tapped the notebook with her pencil and grinned. "Turns out that Daniel knows a lot about greenhouses, and he helped me add some more items to my list."

"That's good to hear." Mom set her basket on the floor and moved over to the table where Rebekah sat. "I saw Daniel outside. He and your daed, as well as your brother, were getting ready to work on your greenhouse."

Nadine placed her basket on the end of the counter and rushed over to the table. "Say, Mom, did you know that Daniel's sweet on Rebekah?"

Rebekah's face heated up, and she shook her head vigorously. "No, he's not. He's got his eye on Mary Ellen and has for some time."

Nadine snickered. "Jah, well, you should have seen the way he hovered over Rebekah, stumbling over every word and making cow eyes at her the whole time."

"That's not so!" Rebekah whirled her wheelchair around to face her sister. "And you shouldn't have been spying on us."

"I wasn't spying," Nadine said in a defensive tone. "I was just dryin' the dishes, and it's not my fault I could hear every word that was being said." She clicked her tongue. "And it didn't take me long to realize that you're as sweet on Daniel as he is on you."

Rebekah wanted to deny her sister's accusation, but she couldn't. The truth was, she did care for Daniel, but she would never have admitted that to Nadine or Mom. Especially when she knew nothing could come from her feelings for him. She was painfully aware that, even if by some miracle Daniel returned those feelings for her, they could never have a future together.

❦

With Dad, Simon, and Daniel working on the greenhouse, it took a little more than two weeks to complete the project. The day after the greenhouse was completed, Mom and

Dad hosted a picnic in honor of the official opening of Grandma's Place. All the family had been invited, as well as Daniel since he had done so much of the work.

The picnic supper was served on the lawn out back, and soon everyone was heaping their plates with barbecued burgers and hot dogs, potato salad, coleslaw, homemade soft pretzels, baked beans, pickles, olives, and carrot sticks. For dessert, they served homemade ice cream with both chocolate and strawberry toppings.

When it appeared as if everyone had finished eating, Dad stood and called for their attention. "As you all know, the greenhouse is finally done, so I'd like to offer my thanks to two very helpful people. First of all, my son, Simon, who worked as hard as any man could." He reached over and ruffled Simon's hair, and Simon grinned up at him. Then he nodded at Daniel, who sat on the end of a bench beside Rebekah's wheelchair. "A special thanks goes to Daniel, who came over for several hours nearly every day and did more than his share of the work."

Rebekah couldn't help but notice how red Daniel's face had become as he stared at his empty ice-cream bowl. "Aw, it was nothin'," he mumbled. "I was glad to do it."

"Daniel not only helped build the greenhouse, but he also assisted Rebekah in setting out all the plants and flowers she will sell. I appreciate the fact that Clarence Beachy was so willing to loan out his son," Dad went on to say.

Rebekah stifled a giggle behind her hand. Just thinking of Clarence loaning out his son made it seem as if Daniel was some piece of farm equipment instead of someone's grown son.

"Now my wife has a little something she would like to give to the new owner of Grandma's Place." Dad nodded at Mom, and she stood.

"This is for you," she said, bending down and pulling a large paper sack from under the table.

Rebekah sat staring at the sack Mom had just handed her.

"Well, go ahead and open it," her brother prompted. "We'd all like to see what's inside that sack."

With trembling fingers, Rebekah tore open the bag. When she reached inside and withdrew a large wooden plaque, she gasped. Inscribed in bold, block letters were the words GRANDMA'S PLACE–OWNER, REBEKAH STOLTZFUS.

"Oh, Mom, it's wunderbaar! Danki, so much."

Mom fairly beamed, obviously quite pleased with herself for keeping such a special secret. "It's that surprise I was working on when Vera took us shopping a few weeks ago. You see now why I couldn't tell you where I was going?"

Rebekah nodded and wiped away the tears that had dribbled onto her cheeks despite her best efforts to hold them at bay.

"And now," Dad said in a booming voice, "let's all go down to the new greenhouse and hang up the sign, because Rebekah Stoltzfus is officially in business!"

As everyone stepped inside the greenhouse, Rebekah was filled with a sense of awe. Even though she had been inside plenty of times during the building of it, she was still pleased with how nice it looked and excited about the prospect of making her own money. Grandma's Place was everything

Rebekah could have hoped for. The building was a wooden structure with glass panels set in the middle section. Dad had built a wheelchair ramp up to the door so she could easily come and go on her own. The front of the building, which was divided by a partition, had a long counter where people could place their purchases. A battery-operated cash register, a calculator, several stacks of notepaper, and some pens had been placed on the end of the counter where Rebekah would wait on her customers. Several gas lanterns would light this section of the building, and a small woodstove would heat the building during the chilly winter months.

"This is nice," Uncle Amos said with an enthusiastic nod. "Jah, really nice."

"It's much bigger than I thought it would be," Aunt Mim put in.

"We wanted to make it big enough for expansion in case Rebekah should ever need more space," Dad said, looking rather pleased with himself.

"Let's go into the next area of the greenhouse and check that out now. It's where all the glass panels are set." Rebekah rolled her wheelchair in that direction, and the others followed, chattering as they went.

"See, here," she said, motioning to a row of low-hanging shelves. "These are for me to set some of the plants on." She pointed up. "And those large hooks hanging from the rafters are so other plants can be secured from wire or chains that will be operated by a pulley." Rebekah smiled up at Daniel, who stood near her wheelchair. "Daniel figured that out for me. The hanging chains will make all the plants more accessible for me, and at the same time, the customers will be able to see everything I have for sale."

"Makes good sense to me," Uncle Lewis put in. "Daniel's a right smart fellow."

Daniel's face turned even redder than it had earlier when Dad had made such an issue over how helpful Daniel had been. Rebekah knew it wasn't right to feel *hochmut*, but she couldn't help feeling a little pride at how well this special greenhouse had turned out.

"Due to the glass panels, the building will be well-lit during daylight hours, and it should stay quite warm in here," Dad spoke up. "There's also a small propane heater, which will supplement the sun's natural heat on colder days." He thumped Daniel on the back. "And this young man also suggested that we install several small screens that will be set in place of the glass windows during warmer weather. They'll provide the necessary cross draft that will help keep the room at a more even temperature."

Several others commented about how nice the greenhouse was and what a good job the men had done. Then Rebekah asked everyone to follow her to the back room, where she showed them a small area where she could work on repotting plants and arranging bouquets of cut flowers. It had a long, low table, as well as a small cot where she could rest awhile if she felt the need.

"See here," Rebekah said, motioning to a door not far from the cot. "Dad even plumbed in a small bathroom for me, which is powered by a gas generator. There's also a sink; a compact, propane-operated refrigerator; and a small cookstove, which is also operated on propane." She grinned as a sense of pure joy bubbled in her soul. "Why, I could spend the whole day here if I had a mind to."

"Of course she won't," Mom put in. "She'll be too busy selling all her flowers and plants to friends, neighbors, and eager tourists to be lazing around her private little room all day."

Everyone laughed. Everyone except for Nadine, that is. She stood off to one side with her arms folded and a grim expression on her face. It was then that Rebekah realized her sister hadn't said one nice thing about her greenhouse. Nadine hadn't said anything at all, not even during the picnic supper.

Under different conditions, Rebekah might have been put out by her sister's poutiness and lack of interest, but not today. This was Rebekah's moment to share the joy of owning her own business with her family and friends, and she wasn't going to let anyone or anything spoil it for her.

"In the wintertime, my store hours will be shorter," she said. "But the greenhouse should stay plenty warm and cozy, even on the coldest of days."

"That might be a good time for you to start seeds that could be ready to repot and sell in the spring," Daniel said, as they started back toward the other room.

Rebekah smiled up at him. "Jah, that's what I was thinking, too."

Soon after they returned to the main entrance, Aunt Mim leaned over Rebekah's wheelchair and gave her a hug. "It looks like you've thought of everything, dear girl."

"Actually, it was Dad and Daniel who thought of most of the things I would need in the greenhouse." She extended her hand to her father. "And I'm ever so grateful."

He gave her fingers a gentle squeeze. "I'll bet you'll settle into this greenhouse like it's always been your home."

Rebekah nodded, feeling as if her miracle might be just round the corner. Now all she needed was some paying customers.

CHAPTER

10

The first official customer to visit Grandma's Place was Johnny Yoder. It was Tuesday morning, and Rebekah had just hung the OPEN sign on the front door of the greenhouse.

When Johnny rang the bell, which hung on a rope outside the door, Rebekah called, "Come on in!"

The door swung open, and Johnny sauntered into the room, holding his straw hat in one hand, while his white shirttail hung out of his dark trousers as if he hadn't even bothered to check his appearance. "Guder mariye. Are you to home?"

Rebekah wheeled her chair toward him, laughing. "Of course I'm here. I just told you to come in, didn't I?"

"Jah, you sure did." Johnny grinned and tipped his hat in her direction.

"Can I help you with something?" Rebekah asked, ignoring his immature antics.

He moved slowly about the room as though he might be checking everything out. "Say, you wouldn't happen to have any cut flowers, would ya?"

"This is a greenhouse, Johnny, so of course I have flowers." Johnny had always been such a kidder. Rebekah figured all his joking around might be why Mary Ellen enjoyed his company so much. It probably made her feel good to be around someone so lighthearted and spirited.

He chuckled as he jiggled his eyebrows up and down. "Jah, I reckon that's true enough. Don't know what I was thinkin', askin' such a silly question as that."

"Are you needing some flowers for any particular reason?"

Johnny nodded, and his face turned the color of ripe cherries. It was a surprise to see him blush that way since he never seemed to let things bother him much. "Uh, they're for your cousin Mary Ellen. I've been courtin' her here of late."

"So I've heard." Rebekah motioned him to follow as she wheeled into the part of the greenhouse where the flowers and plants were kept. "Did you have anything special in mind?"

He shrugged. "Not really. I thought you might have a suggestion, seeing as to how you're in the business of sellin' flowers and whatnot."

If Rebekah had known exactly how much Johnny planned to spend, it might have helped in her selection of a bouquet. However, she didn't feel it would be proper to come right out and ask such a question. Instead, she discreetly said, "I have several bunches of miniature roses. They sell for ten dollars apiece. I also have some less expensive gladiolas—or maybe some pink carnations would be more to your liking."

"I think roses would be best," Johnny said, his green eyes twinkling like fireflies doing their summer dance. "I want the gift to be really special—somethin' that will let Mary Ellen know how much I care."

"I think a bouquet of pink and white roses will do the trick." Rebekah moved over to select the flowers and then proceeded to wrap the stems tightly together with a rubber band. A bit of tissue paper gathered around the bottom completed the arrangement. "If you're not going to give these to her right away, maybe you should put them in some water," she said, handing Johnny the flowers.

Johnny grinned, looking as excited as a first-grade scholar. "We're goin' on a picnic today, so I'll see her real soon, I expect." He reached into his pants pocket and pulled out a ten-dollar bill, then handed it to Rebekah.

"Danki," she replied. "I hope you enjoy your picnic, and I hope Mary Ellen likes the flowers."

Johnny started toward the door, but before his hand touched the knob, he swiveled back around. "You know, it looks mighty nice around here. I hope your new business is a huge success." He left the building, tossing his hat in the air and whistling like a songbird on the first day of spring.

Rebekah smiled to herself as she placed the money from her first sale into the drawer of the cash register. Had it not been for the fact that she was so excited about her new business venture, she might have felt a twinge of jealousy hearing that her best friend had a picnic date. While running the greenhouse gave her a feeling of satisfaction, it didn't take the place of love or romance. Maybe if the business made a go and she could fully support herself, she wouldn't miss courting so much.

By the end of August, news of Rebekah's greenhouse had spread throughout much of Lancaster County. She averaged at least twenty customers a day, sometimes even more. Her inventory was quickly receding, and she knew she would either have to restock soon or put a CLOSED sign on the door.

Dad and Simon had been busy harvesting the corn-fields, so Rebekah asked Mom if she would schedule a ride with Vera to take her to town in order to buy some more plants.

The following morning, they set out right after breakfast. This time, Nadine was allowed to accompany them. She seemed excited about the trip, and as she sat behind Rebekah's seat in Vera's van, she giggled and talked nonstop about all sorts of silly stuff. Rebekah tried to be patient with her sister's prattling, but her mind was on other things—things more important than how cute Eddy Shemly was or who had recently gotten a new pair of rollerblades.

Rebekah was mentally trying to add up the estimated cost of what she might be able to purchase during this trip. Cut flowers weren't a problem since they still had several varieties in their garden at home. What she needed most were more plants and some seeds.

When Nadine finally took a breath between sentences, Rebekah seized the opportunity and leaned over to her mother, who sat beside her. "Say, Mom, you know I've made a fairly good profit during the last few weeks."

"That's wunderbaar."

"Well, I'm wondering how much of that profit to put back into the business and how much I should save."

"Never borrow, for borrowing leads to sorrowing. Spend less than you earn, and you'll never be in debt. That's the true motto of every good businessman—or woman, in your case," Mom said with a wide smile.

Rebekah bobbed her head up and down. "That's good advice, and I'll try to remember it." She paused but not for long, because she knew if she didn't speak quickly, she would probably be interrupted by Nadine's small talk again. "I've been wondering about something else, too."

"What might that be?"

"Do you think I really can make enough money to support myself? I mean, will things work out all right if I work extra hard in the greenhouse?"

" 'And we know that all things work together for good to them that love God, to them who are the called according to his purpose,' " Mom quoted from Romans 8:28. "I know you love God, Rebekah, so you must learn to trust Him more."

Rebekah fell silent. Trust. That was the hard part. When things were going along fine and dandy, it was easy to put one's trust in God. But when things became difficult, it was hard not to waver in one's faith. She would need to keep Grandma's Bible handy in the days to come for she needed to bathe herself in God's Word every day in order not to give in to self-pity or start fretting about the future.

A short time later, they pulled into Lancaster and had soon parked in front of the garden center. Once inside, it didn't take Rebekah long to select a good supply of plants as well as numerous packets of seeds. She concentrated on indoor plant varieties since winter would be coming soon and people would most likely want something to bring a bit of color and cheer into those dreary days.

The back of Vera's van was nearly full when they left the nursery, but Rebekah still had some money left over. She felt good about the purchases she had made and smiled, thinking that she had Daniel to thank for all the good suggestions he'd given her before the greenhouse had been built.

When they left Lancaster, Vera drove them to the farmers' market in Bird-in-Hand, where Mom planned to buy some whole grains and dried beans that one of her friends was selling there. As soon as they were inside the building, Nadine asked if she could wander around by herself for a while. Much to Rebekah's surprise, and probably Nadine's, Mom agreed. So Rebekah wheeled off by herself, as well, leaving Mom and Vera to visit with Ellie Mast and purchase some of her dried goods.

Rebekah hadn't eaten anything since their early morning breakfast, and she felt kind of hungry. She knew they would be going to lunch soon after they left the market, but she decided that a little snack right now might not be such a bad idea.

She wheeled over to a table where they were selling everything from homemade candy to fresh salads. She wasn't in the mood for anything as sweet as candy, but a small fruit salad sure looked refreshing. She bought one and had begun to maneuver her wheelchair to the corner of the room where she could be out of the way when a teenage English boy bumped into the front of her chair.

"Why don't you watch where you're going?" he grumbled, giving the chair a quick shove.

Another English boy, about the same age, grabbed the handle and swung the wheelchair completely around.

Rebekah's head spun dizzily, and she gripped the armrests, hanging on for all she was worth. "Please, stop it," she pleaded. "You're making me dizzy."

"Hey, Joe, we've got ourselves one of those Plain little gals, and she's in a wheelchair!" the first boy hollered. "She bumps right into my leg and then has the nerve to tell me to stop it. Can you believe the gall some folks have these days?"

The one named Joe let out a hoot and gave Rebekah's chair another hefty shove. She was close to tears for in all the time she'd been crippled, nothing like this had ever happened before, and she didn't have a clue what to do about it.

"How about a ride in your wheelchair?" the first boy asked, wiggling his dark eyebrows up and down. "You wouldn't mind scooting over and letting me sit next to you, now would you, honey?"

Rebekah shook her head, and he pushed the wheelchair in the direction of his friend again. It rolled with such force that the bowl of fruit salad flew out of Rebekah's lap and landed upside down on the floor with a *splat*.

"Now look what you've gone and done, Ray," Joe hollered, shaking his finger in his friend's face. "The poor little gal has lost her lunch." He leaned close to Rebekah, and when he squinted his eyes, it reminded her of a newborn pig. "Say, tell me somethin', honey—why do you Amish women wear such plain-looking clothes?"

Before Rebekah could find her voice, Ray wrinkled his

freckled nose and said, "Yeah, and how come you eat all that healthy food?" He poked his friend on the arm. "You know, Joe, I hear tell that many Amish folk still grow a lot of their own food, just like the pioneers used to do." He stared right at Rebekah. "Is that true, little missy? Is it, huh?"

Rebekah swallowed around the bitter taste of bile rising in her throat, fearing she might be about to get sick. She looked around helplessly, knowing she was completely out of her element and hoping someone would see what was happening and come to her aid. However, the closest table was several feet away, and the people who ran it were busy with customers and never even looked her way.

"I–I've got to find my mom," she squeaked. Her shaky voice was laced with fear—the gripping kind that finds its way to the surface, then bubbles over like boiling water left unattended on the stove.

"Now isn't that sweet," Joe taunted. "The little lady wants her mama." He gave the wheelchair a good yank toward his friend. It wasn't Ray who caught it by the handles this time. It was someone much bigger than either one of the boys. Someone who wore a stern look on his face.

Rebekah felt as though all the air had been squeezed clean out of her lungs. Daniel Beachy's serious brown eyes stared down at her. Since the Amish were pacifists, she knew he wouldn't be apt to fight the young men who had been taunting her, but he sure looked like he might. Daniel's eyes narrowed into tiny slits, and he pursed his lips. Rebekah drew in a deep breath and waited expectantly to see what would happen next.

"I think you fellows owe this woman an apology, and

also some money to buy another salad." Daniel motioned to the mess on the floor. As his gaze went back to the boys, Rebekah noticed that his face had turned bright red and a muscle on the side of his neck twitched like a cow's tail when a fly had buzzed it.

"Aw, we were just having a little fun. We didn't hurt her none," Ray mumbled.

Joe shuffled his feet a few times. "Come on, Ray. She's probably his girlfriend, so we'd better leave 'em alone to do their lovebird crooning."

Daniel moved his body to block the boys. "What about that apology and some money for the salad?"

"It's all right, Daniel," Rebekah said in a pleading voice. "Just let them go, okay?"

Daniel planted his hands firmly on his hips and stared hard at the boys. "Jah, well, I don't want to see you two around here again. Is that clear?"

Rebekah had never seen this side of Daniel before, and his response surprised her almost as much as seeing Joe and Ray tear out of there as fast as their long legs could take them.

Daniel dropped to his knees beside Rebekah's wheelchair, obvious concern etched on his face. "Are you okay? They didn't hurt you, did they?"

Rebekah trembled, closer to tears now than ever. "I—I appreciate you stepping in like that, Daniel. I don't know what would have happened if you hadn't come along when you did." Her eyes stung, and she blinked rapidly to hold back the tide of threatening tears.

Daniel's fingers brushed hers, and their gazes locked. "I

couldn't let 'em hurt you, Rebekah. You're a special girl, and you sure as anything don't deserve to be taunted that way."

Rebekah looked away, hoping to hide the blush she knew must have come to her cheeks. "Danki, Daniel. Danki, so much."

"You're welcome." Daniel remained on his knees for several more seconds. Then he finally stood.

"Oh, there you are, Rebekah. Do you know where Nadine is?"

Rebekah lifted her gaze and saw Mom heading in their direction, waving her hand.

"Please don't say anything about my encounter with those English boys," she whispered to Daniel. "Sometimes my mamm can be a bit overprotective. If she thought letting me go off by myself had put me in any kind of danger, she might have second thoughts about letting me be alone in my greenhouse so much of the time."

Daniel nodded. "I won't say a word."

"Hello, Daniel," Mom said, as she approached. "How's your family these days?"

He smiled. "Oh, fair to middlin'. I'm in town picking up a new harness for one of my daed's plow mules. I thought I'd stop by the market to see what's doin', and I was just figuring on going somewhere to get a bite of lunch pretty soon."

Mom's face seemed to brighten. "Would you like to join me and the girls at the Plain and Fancy Restaurant? If we can ever find Nadine, that is."

"I haven't seen her, Mom," Rebekah said. "Not since we separated earlier."

Daniel motioned across the room. "I saw her over at Kauffmeirs' root-beer stand. She was talkin' to a couple of fellows about her age." He gave Rebekah a crooked grin. "I'd be happy to join you for lunch. The Plain and Fancy is one of my favorite eating spots."

"Well then, let's see if we can round up that stray daughter of mine, and we'll go eat ourselves full," Mom said with a nod.

CHAPTER 11

As Nadine followed the others to a table at the Plain and Fancy, she wondered why she had been scolded by Mom for talking to Luke and Sam Troyer over at the root-beer stand and yet Rebekah had been allowed to bring Daniel Beachy to the restaurant with them. As usual, everything went her sister's way, and it didn't seem fair that Rebekah was so spoiled. *Luke and Sam must think I'm still a little girl who has to check in with her mamm every few seconds,* she fumed.

She looked over at Daniel, who had taken a seat beside Rebekah's wheelchair. *He likes her. I don't care what Rebekah says. And I'm sure she likes him, too, even though she's too stubborn to admit it.* Nadine glanced at Rebekah, who wore a smile on her face, and she was sure the satisfied look wasn't just because they were about to eat lunch at her favorite restaurant.

"Is everyone as hungry as I am?" Vera asked, as she took a seat between Mom and Nadine. "I didn't take time to eat much breakfast this morning, and I think it's finally caught up with me."

"I know I'm hungry," Daniel said, giving his stomach a couple of thumps. " 'Course my mamm says I've been hungry since the day I was born."

"What's wrong, sister?" Rebekah asked, glancing across the table at Nadine. "You look like you might not be feeling so well."

"It's nothing. I'm fine."

"Probably drank too much root beer at the farmers' market," Mom put in. "That is where I found her, after all."

"I didn't drink any root beer at all," Nadine said with a frown. "I never got the chance because you dragged me away from there, saying it was time for lunch."

"I didn't *drag* you anywhere, Nadine." Mom clicked her tongue. "How you do exaggerate sometimes."

Vera cleared her throat. "If I might change the subject. . ."

"Certainly," Mom said, giving their driver a pleasant smile. "What did you want to talk about?"

"Well, I subscribe to *The Budget*, and when I was reading it the other day, I noticed that there's going to be a barbecue next week for the volunteer firemen in our area and their families. I know that two of Andrew's brothers are volunteers, so I was wondering if you would all be going to that."

"I'd like to go," Nadine spoke up before Mom could open her mouth to reply. "My friend Carolyn went to the one last year, and she said—"

"We'll have to wait and see how it goes," Mom interrupted. "We might be busy with other things that day."

"I'll bet if Rebekah wanted to go, you'd say it was okay."

"Not if we had other plans, I wouldn't."

Nadine was about to say something more on the subject,

but Mom put her finger to her lips and shook her head. "We'll talk about this later."

Rebekah glanced over at Daniel and noticed that he seemed to be staring at the place mat underneath his silverware. Was he thinking about that incident at the market with the English fellows? He might be wondering if he should tell her mother about it, after all.

Rebekah hoped he wouldn't go back on his promise because it had been stressful enough to go through that ordeal without having Mom in some kind of a stew over what could have happened to Rebekah had Daniel not come along when he did.

"How's your new business going?" Daniel asked suddenly, breaking into Rebekah's thoughts.

"It's doing real well," she said, feeling a sense of relief that he wanted to talk about something on a more positive note. "We went to the garden center in Lancaster this morning, so I could buy more plants and some packets of seeds that I can start during the winter."

Daniel's eyes seemed to brighten. "I think spending all day around plants and flowers would be wunderbaar. I wish I could do something more enjoyable like that. I've got a love for flowers that just won't quit, but my daed says being a dairyman is important work." He crinkled his nose. "My uncle Jake—the one I told you about who lives in Ohio—has invited me to move out there and help in his greenhouse."

"Why don't you go then?" The question came from Nadine, who leaned her elbows on the table and looked intently at Daniel. "Or is something keeping you here?"

Daniel shrugged. "I've thought about his offer, but Ohio's kind of far from my family and friends, and I'm afraid I'd be lonely out there." He glanced over at Rebekah, but she averted her gaze.

"Living near one's family can be important in times of need," Mom put in. "None of my immediate family lives close, but I appreciate having Andrew's family to call my own. They've always been there for us—through the good times and the bad."

Rebekah's thoughts drifted back in time—back to when she'd had her accident. She still remembered how everyone in the family had rallied with food and money for the hospital bills. That's when Grandma had decided to move in with them. She had a heart full of love and wanted to help out.

"When I marry someday, I hope to teach my kinner the value of a loving family," Daniel said with a note of conviction.

If you married Mary Ellen, you'd be getting a wonderful family, Rebekah thought ruefully. *What a shame she's passing up someone as good as you, Daniel. Maybe when I see Mary Ellen at church on Sunday, I'll tell her that, too.*

⁂

Daniel enjoyed the Pennsylvania Dutch meal they had been served, which consisted of fried chicken, meatloaf, buttered noodles, potato filling, homemade rolls, chowchow, and green beans, but he didn't enjoy watching the disagreeable looks Nadine kept shooting at Rebekah. Had their mother noticed it—or even Vera, the English driver Sarah had hired today? If so, what must they be thinking?

Had something happened between Rebekah and her sister earlier in the day, or was Nadine taking out her frustrations on Rebekah because her mother had caught her flirting with the Troyer boys? Whatever the reason, Daniel could tell that Nadine wasn't happy, and her sulky attitude seemed to put a damper on everyone's meal. For the last ten minutes, Rebekah hadn't said more than two words to Daniel, and he figured it might be because she was upset with Nadine. Either that or she was still fretting over the incident with the rowdy English fellows at the farmers' market.

Daniel clenched his teeth. It had been hard for him to control his temper and not give in to the temptation to punch those two in their snooty noses. But that wasn't the Amish way, and he was pleased that he'd been able to run them off by his words. He could understand why Rebekah didn't want her mother to know about the unpleasant episode. If Sarah was upset because one of her daughters had run off to flirt with some Amish boys, he could only imagine how she would have reacted to Rebekah being tormented by those rude Englishers.

He glanced over at Rebekah again and watched as she ate the piece of apple-crumb pie their waitress had just brought. "This is pretty tasty, jah?" he commented, after he'd taken a bite of his own piece of pie.

She smiled and nodded but gave no other reply.

"If you need some help setting out those plants you bought this morning, I'd be glad to come over later today and assist."

"That's nice of you, Daniel, but I'm sure there are things at your place that need to be done, and I wouldn't want to impose."

"It's no imposition. I'd be glad to help in whatever way I can."

"Well, if you really want to, I won't turn down the help."

He nodded enthusiastically. "I'll go straight home after I've finished my dessert, drop off the harness I picked up for my daed, and then head on over to the greenhouse."

"Danki," Rebekah said with a heart-melting smile. "I really appreciate that."

"Danki for runnin' to town for me this morning," Daniel's daed said, when Daniel entered the barn and handed him the harness he'd picked up at the harness shop near Bird-in-Hand.

"You're welcome."

"Did you make it by the farmers' market to get some of that fresh-squeezed apple cider your mamm likes so well?"

Daniel nodded. "Picked up a couple of jugs when I first got there and put 'em in my buggy while I looked around for a bit."

"So that's why you're late gettin' home, huh?" Pop placed the harness on a shelf inside one of the horse's stalls and turned back to face Daniel. "I thought maybe you might have gone out to lunch at your favorite restaurant."

Daniel's face heated up. "Actually, I did—after I left the market."

Pop nodded and gave Daniel a thump on the back. "That's no reason for ya to be lookin' so embarrassed. I know you've got a hole in your leg that has to be kept filled up."

Daniel chuckled. Pop always had liked to tease about his ravenous appetite.

"So, where'd you eat? At the Plain and Fancy?"

"Jah. I shared a table with Sarah Stoltzfus and her daughters. Her English driver was with 'em, too."

"Ah, I see. Did you run into them at the restaurant then?"

"Actually, I saw Rebekah along with her mamm and sister at the market, and Sarah—well, she invited me to go with 'em for lunch, and I said I would."

Pop moved toward the barn door. "Sarah's a good woman, and she's had a lot on her hands since Rebekah got hurt and ended up in a wheelchair."

Daniel nodded as he followed his father out the door. "Speaking of Rebekah—I was wondering if it would be all right if I went over to her greenhouse this afternoon. I want to help her set out the plants she bought in Lancaster this morning."

Pop shook his head and kept right on walking. "I'm needin' your help here. Got a fence that needs mending in several places, and your brothers are already out there workin' on one section of it."

"How long is it gonna take? Couldn't I go over to the greenhouse after I'm done?"

"From the looks of things, we'll be workin' on fences at least until suppertime, and then we'll have the milkin' to do after that."

Daniel felt a keen sense of disappointment all the way to his toes. He'd been counting on seeing Rebekah again today, and he'd as much as promised that he would go there and help out. What would she think if he didn't show up?

"Can I at least drive over there and tell her I'm not comin', so she won't think I went back on my word?"

Pop halted and turned to face Daniel. "You should never have given your word in the first place. You knew when you left here this morning that there would likely be some kind of chores waiting when you got home."

"But Pop—"

"Enough said. Now grab a hammer, and let's get busy."

Would you like me to stay and help with those?" Mom asked Rebekah after she and Vera had finished hauling the plants into the greenhouse for her.

Rebekah smiled but shook her head. "I appreciate the offer, but Daniel said he'd be coming by soon to help."

"That's awfully nice of him. He seems to have taken an interest in you, daughter."

Rebekah was glad Nadine had gone up to the house. If she'd heard what Mom had just said, she would have probably put in her two cents' worth and insisted that Daniel was sweet on Rebekah.

"He's interested in flowers, Mom," Rebekah said, maneuvering her wheelchair over to the table where her plants had been put. "There's nothing more to it than that."

Mom gave her a knowing look, shrugged, and then headed for the door. "I'll ring the bell when supper's ready."

"Jah, okay." Rebekah was glad Dad had thought to build a ramp leading up to the front door of her greenhouse. That way she didn't have to bother anyone to help her get to and from her place of business. When it was time for supper, she just wheeled herself right out the door and up to the house.

As soon as the door closed behind Mom, Rebekah grabbed the ledger she kept on the shelf under the front counter and got busy recording the names and prices of all the plants she had bought. By the time she finished that job, she hoped Daniel would have arrived.

Sometime later, Rebekah glanced at the clock on the far wall and frowned. It was almost three and still no Daniel. *I wonder what could be keeping him?*

She rolled her chair across the room and peered out the window. No sign of Daniel's rig. She pressed her nose up to the glass. No sign of any buggies going by on the road, either. Had Daniel forgotten about coming, or had he changed his mind and decided not to come after all?

"Jah, that must be it," she muttered, a keen sense of disappointment threatening to weigh her down. She should have known better than to let herself get so worked up about the idea of spending a few hours this afternoon with Daniel in the greenhouse.

She sighed and rolled her wheelchair away from the window. "Guess I'd better get busy and set these plants out myself, because it surely won't get done otherwise."

CHAPTER

12

The preaching service that week was held at Uncle Amos and Aunt Mim's house. It was the first Sunday of September, and the weather was still unbearably hot, feeling stickier than the flypaper hanging from the rafters in Dad's barn. All the doors and windows were flung wide open, but Rebekah thought it was still much too uncomfortable to be inside with a bunch of warm-bodied folk today.

She maneuvered her wheelchair next to the backless bench where Nadine sat with several girls her age. Her eyes scanned the other benches on the women's side of the room, searching for Mary Ellen. She wasn't in her usual place, and Rebekah worried that she might have gotten sick and wouldn't be in church at all today.

"I wonder where Mary Ellen is," Rebekah whispered to her sister.

Nadine shrugged. "How should I know?"

"I hope she isn't sick," Rebekah said, choosing to ignore Nadine's curt words.

"I don't think so." Nadine pointed to the door. "Here she comes."

Rebekah wished she had been able to talk to her cousin before church started, but she guessed what she had to say could wait until the service was over. She had lain awake for several hours last night, rehearsing what she would tell Mary Ellen about her decision to let Johnny court her. She had planned to suggest that Mary Ellen give Daniel a chance, but after he'd promised to show up at the greenhouse the other day and hadn't followed through, Rebekah wondered if it might be better for Mary Ellen not to get involved with Daniel, either, because apparently he couldn't stick to his word.

"And now, before we close our service for the day," the bishop said, "I'd like to announce some upcoming weddings that will be held in our community. The marriage of Johnny Yoder and Mary Ellen Hilty will take place on the second Thursday of November."

Rebekah's mouth fell open, and she sat in her wheelchair too stunned to move. She was so shocked by Bishop Benner's announcement that she didn't hear the other names he published before the congregation.

What on earth was Mary Ellen thinking? How could she have agreed to marry Johnny without consulting her best friend about it first? Surely she would have wanted to get Rebekah's opinion on something as important as this. In the past, they had always talked things over whenever either one of them had a big decision to make. Rebekah had discussed her plans to open a greenhouse with Mary Ellen, so it made no sense that Mary Ellen would become betrothed to Johnny without mentioning it to Rebekah.

Maybe their friendship wasn't as strong as it used to be.

Maybe Mary Ellen cared more about Johnny than she did Rebekah.

Of course, Rebekah reminded herself, *when a person falls in love, no one else matters so much anymore. Once Mary Ellen and Johnny become husband and wife, they'll put each other first, and I guess that's the way it should be.*

When the service was finally over and the people had been dismissed, Rebekah drew in a deep breath and forced herself to move her wheelchair toward the front door. Mary Ellen would probably expect hearty congratulations from her family and friends—especially her best friend. But how could Rebekah offer such congratulations when she felt so betrayed? She knew it was the right thing to do, but it wouldn't be easy.

Rebekah swallowed against the burning sensation pushing at the back of her throat and wheeled onto the front porch. Was the pain she felt because she hadn't been told about the engagement, or was it the fact that she was intensely jealous? She and Mary Ellen had shared nearly everything up until now. When they were young girls, Mary Ellen had gotten a rabbit, and she'd made sure that Rebekah had one, too. When they were a few years older, Grandma had given Rebekah a faceless doll. Immediately, she had asked Grandma to make one just like it for Mary Ellen.

Things had begun to change of late, however. Mary Ellen was moving on with her life in a direction Rebekah was sure she could never take. She also knew it wouldn't be fair to expect her cousin to give up love, marriage, and a family of her own because Rebekah couldn't have those things, but it hurt, nonetheless. If Mary Ellen thought

Johnny was the best choice for a husband, then who was Rebekah to say otherwise? She would simply have to accept it. Maybe Johnny would settle down once he and Mary Ellen were married. It might turn out that his playfulness would be exactly what his wife would need during times when things didn't go so well.

Rebekah scanned the yard and caught sight of Mary Ellen walking across the grass with Johnny. With a sense of determination to do the right thing, she glided the wheelchair down the ramp Uncle Amos had built for her sometime ago and headed in the direction of the young couple.

As Rebekah drew near, she reminded herself to be happy for her best friend no matter how much her heart was breaking. She had nearly reached the spot where Mary Ellen and Johnny stood when she was greeted by yet another surprise.

"Have ya heard the news about Aunt Grace and Uncle Lewis?" her cousin John asked as he and his twin brother, Jacob, walked beside her.

Rebekah shook her head. "What news is that?"

"She's in a family way. They're gonna have a *boppli*," Jacob put in.

"Really? I hadn't heard."

"Their boy, Matthew, is already seven years old, and I'll bet he's gonna think a little *bruder* or *schweschder* is a real bother." John's forehead wrinkled as his eyebrows drew together. "I can still remember when our little sister was born. It seemed like Maddie cried all the time."

Rebekah chuckled despite her dour mood. "Kumme now, John. You and Jacob were only four when Maddie joined your family. You weren't much more than a baby yourself, so I doubt you can remember much about it at all."

"Jah, I can," Jacob asserted. "All Maddie ever did was eat, sleep, cry, and wet her *windle. Bopplin* are such a bother!"

"When you get married and start a family of your own, you'll change your mind about babies," Rebekah said.

John chuckled and thumped Jacob on the back. "That might be true, but I doubt my brother will ever like anything about dirty diapers."

"That will never be a problem because I ain't never gettin' married." Jacob shook his head with such vigor that his hat fell off.

"Jah," John agreed, "Jacob and I have decided that we're gonna stay single for the rest of our lives."

Rebekah smiled and grasped the wheels of her chair. "If you two will excuse me, I've got to congratulate the happy couple." She rolled away quickly before she lost her nerve.

Rebekah found Mary Ellen and Johnny surrounded by several well-wishers, so she stayed off to the side, awaiting her turn. She would be glad to be done with this so she could get off by herself for a while to think things through. When the others finally cleared away, she maneuvered her wheelchair close to the smiling couple.

"Congratulations, you two." She tried to make her voice sound cheerful, even though her heart ached something awful. "You're full of surprises; that's for sure."

Mary Ellen's smile widened, and Johnny nodded enthusiastically. "It was a surprise to most, but surely not to you, Rebekah," he said. "You're Mary Ellen's best friend so she must've told you about our plans."

Mary Ellen's smile faded, and she stared at the ground. "No. I—I didn't tell Rebekah you had asked me to marry you."

"You didn't? Why not?" Johnny's tone was one of surprise, and his eyebrows lifted high on his forehead.

Rebekah looked over at her cousin, wondering the same thing.

"Could we speak privately for a minute?" Mary Ellen asked, bending down to whisper in Rebekah's ear.

Rebekah glanced up at Johnny for his approval.

"Jah, sure, go ahead. It's fine by me," he replied with a shrug.

"Let's go down by the pond," Mary Ellen suggested. "I don't think anyone else is there right now since everyone's waiting to eat."

"Shouldn't we help the other women get lunch on?"

"We won't be gone long, and there are plenty of others here to help so we probably won't even be missed."

"Well, okay then." Rebekah wheeled off in the direction of the pond, and when they reached the taller grass, making it hard for her to maneuver the chair, Mary Ellen took over pushing.

A couple of ducks on the water dipped their heads up and down and flapped strong wings as if they didn't have a care in the world.

"They look so happy," Mary Ellen said, dropping to a seat on the grass.

"Almost as happy as you and Johnny seem to be," Rebekah mumbled.

"Oh, we are," Mary Ellen's voice bubbled like a sparkling stream, but when she looked up at Rebekah, her dreamy expression turned suddenly sorrowful. "I'm sorry for keeping our betrothal from you. It's just that—well, I was afraid you might be upset."

"Upset? Why would you think I'd be upset?"

"We've always done everything together. If I got a bunny, you got one, too."

"If I got a doll, so did you."

Mary Ellen nodded. "But this time, I was afraid you would be hurt that I was getting married and you weren't."

"That's just the way of things," Rebekah said flatly. No use telling Mary Ellen how she really felt. "There comes a time when little girls must grow up. I've come to realize that I can't have everything my friend has."

"Oh, but you can." Mary Ellen touched Rebekah's shoulder. "Well, maybe not at the exact same time as me, but someday you'll fall in love and get married."

Rebekah groaned. "We've had this discussion before. I'm not able to get around like you, and I doubt that any man would want to be stuck with a handicapped wife."

"Other women—some much worse off than you—get married and even have children."

"It doesn't matter because no one is in love with me." Rebekah shrugged. "Besides, I have my new business now, and if I can become self-supporting, then I won't have need of a husband."

"Love can change all that."

"As I said, there's no one to love."

" 'Commit thy way unto the Lord; trust also in him; and he shall bring it to pass,' " Mary Ellen recited the verse from Psalm 37.

Rebekah gave her wheelchair a sharp turn to the left. "We'd better get back. I'm sure they're probably getting ready to serve up the noon meal by now, and we should be there to help."

Mary Ellen looked like she might want to say something more, but instead, she grabbed the handles of Rebekah's wheelchair and directed it toward the house.

※

Many of the families lingered for most of the day, enjoying the good food and the fun of being together. It was a time for laughter and games, stories to be told and retold. No one seemed in a hurry to return home to the evening chores that waited to be done.

But Rebekah wasn't anxious to stay around the Hilty farm and be reminded of her cousin's happiness. Even the news about Aunt Grace expecting a baby had sent a pang of regret to her tender, aching heart. She knew it was wrong to harbor feelings of jealousy, and she also knew she had been unkind to Mary Ellen earlier. Since her family had no plans to leave early, the noon meal was over, and everyone seemed occupied, she decided it would be a good time for her to find a place of solitude and talk to God about a few things.

Rebekah wheeled off toward Aunt Mim's garden, where an abundance of flowers and herbs grew. Maybe after some time in the beauty of colors and fragrances that only God could have created, she might find forgiveness for her attitude and could return to the yard feeling a bit more sociable.

A firmly packed dirt path ran through the middle of the

garden, and Rebekah had no trouble navigating it with her wheelchair. She rolled right between two rows of pink roses and stopped to drink in their delicious aroma.

Closing her eyes and lifting her face toward the warming sun, Rebekah sent up a silent prayer. *Dear God: Help me to be a gracious friend and accept the fact that Mary Ellen will soon be a married woman even though I'll always be single. Help my business to do well so I can keep busy and make a good living. Amen.*

Even after Rebekah had finished her prayer, she kept her eyes closed, allowing her imagination to run wild. *Wouldn't it be like heaven to stand in a garden like this one and whisper words of affection to a man who had pledged his undying love to me?* She could almost feel his sweet breath on her upturned face as she envisioned the scene in her mind. She could almost hear his steady breathing as he held her in his arms, whispering words of endearment.

"The roses are sure beautiful this time of year, *jah*?"

Rebekah's eyes flew open, and she whirled her chair in the direction of the deep voice that had pulled her from the romantic reverie.

Daniel stood a few feet away, hands in his pockets and a peculiar expression on his face. "I'm sorry if I scared you. I could see that you were probably meditating, but I figured you would have heard me come into the garden." He grinned, causing the skin around his eyes to crinkle. "My mom always says my big feet don't tread too lightly."

Rebekah had to smile in spite of her melancholy mood. "You're right. I was meditating." She chose not to mention what she had been meditating on or that she was still a little put out with him for not coming over to help set out the greenhouse plants as he'd said he would do.

As if he could read her mind, Daniel knelt on the grass beside her wheelchair. "I'm sorry about not comin' over to the greenhouse the other afternoon. My daed needed me to help fix some broken fences, and I couldn't get away."

"I figured you were either too busy or had changed your mind about coming," she said, staring down at her hands, clasped tightly in her lap. "It took me awhile, but I finally got all the plants set in their proper place."

Daniel shook his head. "I didn't want to be too busy, Rebekah. I really wanted to help you, and I would have come over to let you know I wasn't able to help out, but Pop wouldn't let me leave." He drew in a deep breath and blew it out with a puff of air that lifted the ties on Rebekah's kapp. "I'll be glad when I'm out on my own and don't have to answer to my daed anymore."

Rebekah wasn't sure how to respond to that comment. It wasn't like Daniel to speak out against either of his folks, but she figured he was probably talking out of frustration.

"Have you gotten any starts from your aunt's rose garden?" Daniel asked, taking their conversation in a different direction.

She shook her head. "I've never thought to ask."

"Mim seems to like you a lot. I'm sure she wouldn't mind sharing some of them with you."

"Maybe I'll talk to her about it."

"I was surprised when I showed up here and found you sitting all alone. I figured you'd be up on the lawn, joining in the young people's celebration."

"Mary Ellen and Johnny's betrothal?"

He nodded, and Rebekah was sure that same look she'd seen on his face a few times before had cast a shadow of sadness on it now. The bishop's announcement must have jolted Daniel like it had her. He was probably hurting every bit as much as she, only for a different reason. She was jealous because she would never have the kind of happiness Mary Ellen was experiencing. Daniel probably wished it had been him, not Johnny, who had won Mary Ellen's heart.

Rebekah swallowed hard, struggling for words that wouldn't be a lie. "Celebrations are for those who can run and play games. I'd much rather be enjoying these *lieblich* flowers."

"They are lovely," Daniel said. "But don't tell my daed I said so 'cause he might think I was *ab im kopp* for caring so much about flowers and plants." He grunted. "All Pop ever thinks about is those cantankerous dairy cows of his."

Again, Rebekah didn't know how to respond. She didn't think Daniel was off in the head, but she certainly didn't want to criticize his father so she sat there quietly, drinking in the delicious aroma of Aunt Mim's flowers and enjoying this special time alone with Daniel.

Daniel stood and moved toward her like he might be about to say something. Then he stared down at his boots a few seconds and slowly raised his gaze to meet hers. "Would ya like me to push your wheelchair? We can walk around the rest of your aunt's garden if you like."

Rebekah's first thought was to decline. She didn't need anyone's help pushing her wheelchair, and she certainly didn't need Daniel's pity. She hesitated only a moment as pride took a backseat and a desire to spend more time with

Daniel took the front seat. "Danki, I'd like that," she finally murmured.

Daniel smiled and stepped behind her wheelchair. "You'd better hang on tight, Rebekah Stoltzfus, because I've been known to be a reckless driver!"

CHAPTER 13

The days sped by with a delicate shifting of summer to fall. A few tourists still visited Rebekah's greenhouse, but most of her customers now were Amish or English people who lived in the area.

Rebekah began to fret over the possibility that her business might fail and had to remind herself frequently to pray, trust God, and search the scriptures for more of His promises. Her faith was still weak, and she knew it.

One Friday since she had no customers at the moment, she decided to lie down on the cot in the back of her store to rest awhile and seek God's will. *Heavenly Father,* she prayed, *I'm still looking for a miracle. I really need to be able to support myself because I don't want to be a burden to others. Please bring in more customers, and show me what to do to make the business more successful.*

The sharp ringing of the bell outside the greenhouse pulled Rebekah from her prayer. "Come in!" she called.

As she struggled to a sitting position, she heard the door creak open. "Rebekah? Are ya here?"

Rebekah recognized the familiar male voice, and she had

to take several deep breaths in order to quiet her pounding heart. Why did Daniel make her feel so giddy? She knew he only cared for her as a friend, but she couldn't seem to stop thinking about him and wishing for more. Daniel's kind face flashed before her eyes as she remembered that Sunday afternoon at the Hiltys' when he'd pushed her wheelchair through Aunt Mim's garden. They'd laughed and talked so easily then, and he had actually made her forget the pain over hearing the news about Mary Ellen's plans to be married.

Rebekah forced all thoughts to the back of her mind as she called, "I'm back here, Daniel. Just trying to get my crutches strapped to my arms."

Daniel poked his head around the partition, and his wrinkled forehead let her know he felt concern. "Are you all right? Why aren't you in your wheelchair? Were you lyin' down?"

Rebekah laughed. "So many questions, Daniel. And don't look so poker-faced. I'm wearing my leg braces today and using the metal crutches that help me stay upright." She dropped one stiff leg to the floor. "Mom hollers at me if I spend too much time in the wheelchair, so I'm trying to humor her today." The other leg followed the first, landing on the floor with a thud. "I was only lying down to rest awhile, but sometimes getting up again isn't so easy."

Daniel moved closer to the cot. "Need some help?"

Rebekah swallowed hard. There it was again. That "I feel sorry for you" look on Daniel's face. She winced, wishing he could see her as a woman and not some *elendich*—pitiful—handicapped girl. She didn't need his pity.

"Are you hurting?" he asked, dropping to his knees in front of her.

She drew in a deep breath. "I'm fine, really." Her crutches were propped against the wheelchair, next to the cot. She reached for one and bumped the other, sending it crashing to the floor. "Always trouble somewhere," she muttered.

Without waiting to be asked, Daniel lunged for the crutch. "Trouble usually has an answer, though," he said, handing it to her with one of his heart-melting smiles.

Rebekah's eyes misted. She hated to be dependent on others, but receiving help from someone as thoughtful as Daniel made it almost a pleasure. "You always seem to be around whenever I need something," she murmured.

"Jah, well, that's what friends are for." Daniel looked Rebekah right in the eye. "I only wish we could be more than friends."

More than friends? What was Daniel saying? Did he actually see her in some other light—something that would involve more than friendship? Rebekah wasn't sure what to say or do next. "You. . .you want to be more than friends?"

He nodded.

"What are you really saying, Daniel?"

He adjusted his weight from one foot to the other. "I'm sayin' that if it were possible, I'd like to be your partner."

"Partner?" Rebekah could barely get the word out.

To her surprise, he touched her arm, sending a jolt of electricity all the way up to her neck. "Jah. I'd like to be your business partner."

Business partner. The words echoed in Rebekah's head like a woodpecker thumping on the side of Dad's barn. She drew in a long, steady breath, hoping to calm her nerves. She should have known Daniel wasn't asking her to be his marriage partner. What a dunce she was for even letting such a ridiculous notion pop into her head. She and Daniel weren't courting, and he'd never shown the slightest interest in her in a romantic sort of way. In fact, she was still sure he was in love with Mary Ellen. How could she have been so stupid as to misread his intentions?

With the aid of her crutches, now strapped to her arms, Rebekah pulled herself to a standing position. "Why would you want to be my business partner?" she asked, once she had found her voice.

Daniel frowned, looking as though it almost pained him to say the words. "I've told you before that I have a love for flowers. Running a greenhouse would be the most exciting thing I could imagine. I envy you, Rebekah."

"Envy me? How could anyone envy a woman with a handicap such as mine?" Tears gathered in the corners of her eyes, and she squinted, hoping to keep them there.

"I–I'm very sorry. I didn't mean to upset you," Daniel sputtered.

With both crutches securely in place, Rebekah plodded across the room. When she stepped into the area where the plants and flowers were kept, she came to an abrupt stop, turned, and almost bumped into Daniel. "Oh, I didn't know you were there."

"Followed you out," he mumbled.

Rebekah glanced around the room, feeling suddenly self-conscious. "I love these green-leafed, blossomed creations God made, so I do understand why you'd want to run a greenhouse." She clicked her tongue. "There are two small problems, though."

He scrunched his forehead until it wrinkled. "Two problems? What would they be?"

"First of all, my greenhouse is a new business. I've been open only a few months, and it's not showing enough profit to support two people. I'm not even sure if it's going to support me."

"And the second problem?"

"Probably the most obvious problem is my parents. They'd never allow such a thing."

"Why not?"

"We'd be spending many long hours together—alone—with no chaperones."

"We're both adults, Rebekah." A slight smile tugged at the corner of Daniel's lips, and a twinkle danced in his usually serious brown eyes. "Of course, my daed don't always see me that way."

Why must Daniel look at me like that? Especially when he sees me as nothing more than a possible business partner? "If we were both the same sex, then maybe it wouldn't be a problem."

"I see what you mean." Daniel shrugged. "Besides, I doubt my daed would want me to quit helping with the dairy business."

"If it were possible," she said with feeling, "I'd actually consider becoming partners. You know a lot about flowers, and you've proved to be pretty handy to have around."

Her words brought a smile to Daniel's face, and when he gave her a surprising wink, her heart fluttered so much she had to will it to stop. "So, what brings you here today? I'm sure it was for something more than to retrieve my crutch."

He chuckled. "I'm here to buy a plant for my mamm. Her birthday's tomorrow, and I want to give her a gift that will last awhile."

"How about a purple African violet?" Rebekah suggested, moving over to the area where all the violets were kept. "I have a beautiful one that came from a start off one of Grandma Stoltzfus's plants."

Daniel bent over and scrutinized the plant in question. "I'll take it."

She giggled. "You haven't even asked the price."

He shrugged. "Well, what does it matter? I like the plants, my mamm needs a gift, and you probably can use the money."

Rebekah gave him a mock frown. What should she do with the likes of Daniel Beachy?

❦

A few days later, Daniel decided to pay Rebekah another visit. "Back so soon?" she asked as he stepped inside her greenhouse. "Did your mamm not like the plant you bought her? I can exchange it for something else, if you like."

Daniel shook his head. "She liked it just fine." He glanced around the room, feeling kind of nervous and wondering how Rebekah would take to the idea he hoped to present.

Rebekah turned her wheelchair toward him. "Then what can I help you with?"

Daniel nodded in her direction as he gathered up his courage. "I was hoping I could help us both."

She lifted her chin to stare up at him. "What are you talking about?"

He shuffled his feet a few times while sticking his thumbs under the edge of his suspenders. "I know I can't work with you here every day, but I think I've come up with a way we can make some extra money, and we'll be doin' exactly what we both enjoy." He wiggled his eyebrows, hoping the playful act might give him an edge the way it seemed to do for Johnny whenever he wanted Mary Ellen to agree with him on something.

Rebekah tipped her head as though she was studying him. Did she think he was joking with her?

"I really do have a good idea," he said, moving closer to her. "Can I tell you about it?"

"If you like," she responded with a shrug.

"All right then. I'll be right back." Daniel spun on his heels and rushed out the front door. A few minutes later, he returned with a large cardboard box. He placed it on the floor, dropped to his knees, and lifted the flaps.

Rebekah wheeled her chair closer as he pulled out several wooden bird feeders, a few whirligigs for the lawn, and some homemade flowerpots.

"Daniel, those are so nice," she exclaimed. "Did you make them yourself?"

He grinned up at her. "In my free time, I like to do a bit of woodworking."

"You do a fine job. However, I don't see what it has to do with—"

"You can try to sell these things here in your greenhouse. I could leave 'em on consignment, and we'd each get a percentage of the profit when they sell."

Rebekah clicked her fingernails against the armrest of

her wheelchair. "Do you think folks coming here would buy items like these?"

"I'm sure they would. My uncle in Ohio sells all kinds of things in his greenhouse. It helps bring in more customers—especially the tourists. They all seem to want something that's been made by one of us Plain People, you know." Daniel paused and moistened his lips. "So, what do you say, Rebekah? Shall we give 'em what they want and make a profit for both of us, as well?"

"It might work. Jah, I suppose it's worth a try."

Daniel grinned, as a new sense of hope welled in his chest. "Silent partners then?"

She nodded. "Jah, silent partners."

Daniel made two more trips over to the greenhouse that day bringing several more boxes filled with bird feeders, bird-houses, flowerpots, and lawn ornaments. With Rebekah's permission, he placed them around the greenhouse in various locations. He also put a few outside the building, saying he hoped to entice more customers into the store. After setting the prices for each item, he and Rebekah reached an agreement that she would get 25 percent of all the money collected from Daniel's handiwork.

"I need to get home now," Daniel said later that afternoon, "but I wanted to make a suggestion before I go."

"Oh? What's that?"

"I was thinking maybe you could also stock vegetable and flower seeds, potting soil, and fertilizers to sell. Since winter will be coming soon, I thought maybe you should get some small holly bushes and several poinsettia plants, too."

Rebekah nodded and followed him to the door in her wheelchair. "You sure do have some good ideas, Daniel."

His smile stretched from ear to ear. "Here's another one of my ideas. What would you think about taking out an ad in *The Budget*, as well as in our local Amish paper, *Die Botschaft*?"

She tipped her head in contemplation. "Hmm. . ."

"I think it would help get things going here even more, and I'd be happy to put up several flyers around town to advertise Grandma's Place."

"Jah, okay. I'll put the add in *The Budget* the next time I send in some information for my column, and I'll do the one for *Die Botschaft* tomorrow morning." Rebekah smiled. Things were looking more hopeful for her business, and she was gaining a kind of self-confidence she had never known before. Having to deal with customers helped her feel less self-conscious, and opening the greenhouse seemed like an answer to prayer. It just might be that miracle she had been looking for.

CHAPTER 14

"I hope Mary Ellen likes this quilt," Rebekah told her mother as the two of them sat in front of their quilting frame, stitching on the dahlia-patterned quilt they planned to give Mary Ellen as a wedding present.

"I'm sure she will be very pleased," Mom said. "You do real well with a needle and thread, and you're doing a fine job with this lovely quilt."

Rebekah smiled. "I've always liked quilts—even when I was a kinner."

"Jah, I know. I remember when you and Mary Ellen were barely old enough to walk, the two of you used to like to crawl underneath the quilting frame at whoever's house the quilting bee was being held. I think you thought none of us women could see you under there."

"Maybe we thought it was a tent and were playing that we'd gone camping."

Mom chuckled. "I doubt that since you weren't even out of diapers yet and had never been on a camping trip."

Rebekah thought about the camping trip Dad had taken Simon on last summer, when they'd done some fishing.

Simon had come home dirty, tired, and plenty sunburned, but he'd had a good time and said he couldn't wait until the next camping trip. Rebekah had felt a little envious of her brother, wishing that she, too, might have gone camping. But with her being so limited in what she could do, it would have been difficult on her as well as Dad if he'd tried to take her camping.

"I wish Nadine had shown some interest in helping us make this quilt," Mom said, breaking into Rebekah's reflections. "That girl doesn't seem to want to do anything these days unless it has something to do with boys."

Rebekah nodded. "Jah, she has become pretty interested in the opposite sex, but maybe she'll calm down once she finds a boyfriend and starts courting."

"Let's hope so, although I'm in no hurry for my boy-crazy daughter to begin courting." Mom's needle flew in and out of the material, and she never missed a stitch as they continued to visit.

"I think it's just as well that you let Nadine go over to visit her friend Carolyn today," Rebekah said. "She's never been able to sew a straight stitch, and I don't want anything to ruin Mary Ellen's wedding quilt." She released a sigh. "Besides, if my little sister had stayed around, the two of us would have probably ended up in another disagreement. Seems like every time we're in the same room together, something is said or done that causes Nadine to become upset with me."

Mom stopped sewing and reached over to take Rebekah's hand. "She's having a hard time understanding why you get to do some things she can't."

"Me?" Rebekah's voice raised a notch, and she drew in a deep breath to calm herself. "She's the one who gets to do all the things I can't do. Doesn't she realize how much I envy her for being able to walk around normally, run, skip, jump, or take the stairs two at a time? Can't she see how hard it is for me to sit back and watch others without limitations and not feel sorry for myself?"

"She's young and headstrong," Mom said quietly. "Give her some time to mature and come to a place where she has more compassion and understanding."

"If she listened to the sermons being preached during our church services, she would already know about compassion and understanding." Rebekah tied a knot in her piece of thread and cut the end with the scissors. "There are so many places in the Bible that speak of having consideration for others and being accepting and supportive."

Mom nodded. "That's right, and God's words aren't just for your sister. You need to take them to heart, too."

Rebekah blinked a couple of times as her mother's words registered. Was Mom saying she wasn't kind or understanding? Did she think Rebekah was as selfish and self-centered as Nadine?

"I'm not saying you're inconsiderate," Mom said. "I'm just saying you need to be a little more understanding of Nadine and look past her immaturity—maybe try to set the example for her rather than casting judgment or arguing with her all the time."

A lump formed in Rebekah's throat, and she swallowed hard, trying to push it down. She did want to be a good example to her sister and to everyone she knew. It was just that sometimes when Nadine accused her of being spoiled or always getting her way, Rebekah became irritated and a bit defensive. "I'll try harder where Nadine's concerned," she murmured. "I'll ask God to give me more understanding, too."

Mom smiled and resumed her sewing. "I'm pleased to hear that. Jah, very pleased indeed."

The days of fall moved along quickly, and soon it was time for Mary Ellen's wedding. She had asked Rebekah to be one of her *newehockers* along with Lena, another close friend. The day before the wedding, the two bride's attendants and some who would be table waiters showed up at Mary Ellen's house to help out, as did several aunts, uncles, and close neighbors.

The bench wagon was brought from the home church district to the Hiltys' along with another bench wagon from a neighboring district because they would need a lot more seating at the wedding than during a regular Sunday church service. Much of the furniture had been removed from the house and stored in the cleaner outbuildings, while smaller items were placed in the bench wagons after the men had unloaded the benches, unfolded the legs, and arranged them in the house.

Many hands were needed in the kitchen that morning, preparing the chickens that would be served at the wedding meal, as well as fixing mounds of other food items. The four couples assigned as "roast cooks" divided up the dressed chickens and took them home to roast in their ovens. Mama

Mim had asked Aunt Crystal, who was her best friend and a very good baker, to make most of the doughnuts. Some of the other women relatives had made a variety of cookies.

Mama Mim and Mary Ellen were already hard at work in the kitchen when Aunt Sarah, Rebekah, and Nadine showed up. Mary Ellen grabbed hold of Rebekah's wheel-chair and pushed her into the kitchen and up to the table, where she had a pot of tea waiting. "Oh, Rebekah, I'm get-ting such butterflies! I wonder if I'll be able to eat anything at all between now and tomorrow morning." She extended her trembling hands. "Just look at me—I'm shakin' like the branches of a maple tree on a windy day."

Rebekah reached up and took Mary Ellen's hands in her own. "Try not to think about it. That's what Mom always tells me whenever I'm anxious about something."

Mary Ellen grunted. "That's easy enough for you to say. You're not the one getting married tomorrow."

Rebekah recoiled as if she'd been stung by a hornet.

"Oh, Rebekah, I'm so sorry," Mary Ellen quickly apolo-gized. "I didn't mean—"

"It's okay," Rebekah interrupted with the wave of her hand. "You're right. I'm not the one getting married, and I don't even presume to know what you're feeling right now. I was only trying to help quiet your nerves."

"I know, and I appreciate it." Mary Ellen took a seat at the table and blew on her tea before taking a tentative sip. "I never thought I could be this happy. I love Johnny so much, and I know we're going to be content living together as husband and wife."

"I'm truly happy for you," Rebekah said. "And I'm glad

you asked me to be one of your newehockers."

Mary Ellen felt as if she could burst with the excitement she felt coursing through her veins. "Jah, well, who else would I ask to be one of my attendants but my very best friend?"

Rebekah smiled. "What do you need me to do today?"

"Let me check with Mama Mim. She's the one in charge of things around here."

After consulting with her stepmother, Mary Ellen asked Rebekah, Lena, and Nadine to cut, wash, and dry the celery pieces.

"Sounds easy enough," Rebekah said. "At least it's something I can do from a seated position."

For the next little while, Rebekah sat at the kitchen table, blotting the celery stalks dry with a clean towel after Nadine and Lena had cut and washed them. As she methodically worked, her thoughts went to her greenhouse business, which was doing better than she had ever expected it would. Daniel's wooden items were selling almost as fast as he could make them. She had taken his advice and purchased potting soil, fertilizer, and seeds, not only to use in the business, but to sell, as well. She'd also placed an order for several Christmas cacti, holly plants, and poinsettias to offer her customers during the winter months.

Rebekah's musings about the greenhouse turned naturally to a more personal nature. She always seemed to be thinking about Daniel, especially when she thought of her flowers and plants. If she were truly being honest, she thought of him other times, too. Daniel's kind face was never far from her thoughts. She couldn't understand this attraction because she felt sure it was one-sided. Truly, even if it weren't, there was no hope for any kind of a future for them as a couple.

"You look like you're a million miles away," Mary Ellen said, handing Rebekah another batch of celery to dry.

Rebekah looked up and smiled. "I was thinking about my business." She chose not to mention the part that included Daniel. Why give Mary Ellen something to goad her about?

"Is the greenhouse doing well then?"

Rebekah nodded. "It truly is."

"I'm glad to hear it." Mary Ellen pursed her lips. "I haven't been over in quite a while, what with all the wedding preparations and whatnot, but I've heard from some others that you've made some changes there."

"Daniel Beachy brought several of his handmade wooden items over to sell. The bird feeders are going real fast—probably because everyone likes to feed the birds during the fall and winter months. Daniel does good work, and most of his things sell nearly as quickly as he can make them." Rebekah grinned. "He seems to like flowers and plants as much as I do, and he's given me some helpful suggestions about re-potting, taking cuttings, and which plants need more water than others. He's been a real help."

Mary Ellen poked Rebekah's arm. "So has he started calling yet?"

"Daniel comes over to the greenhouse at least once or twice a week. He likes to see if I need any more items to sell or whether I want help with anything," Rebekah answered as she took up another piece of celery to pat dry.

"No, no, not calling at your greenhouse. Is he calling at your home? Are you two courting, or am I not supposed to ask?"

Rebekah dropped the celery with a thud, and it nearly rolled off the table. "Is that what you think—that Daniel and I are a courting couple? Do you suppose others think that as well?"

Mary Ellen shrugged. "I can't say what others are thinking, but I for one have noticed that he seems to hang around you a lot. I've seen the way you look at him, too."

"Of course he comes around. I just told you, he brings things over to sell at the greenhouse." Rebekah grabbed another hunk of celery out of the pile. "Furthermore, I don't look at him in any special way. He's a good friend, nothing more."

Mary Ellen took an apple from the bowl in the center of the table and bit into it. "All right then. Whatever you say."

Thursday morning dawned bright and clear, a cool, crisp, November day. But the birds were singing, and the sun had rolled over the horizon like a giant ball of fire. It was the perfect day for a wedding. Rebekah figured Mary Ellen had probably been awake since sunup, beside herself with anticipation of her special day. And who could blame her? She was, after all, marrying the man of her choice.

Rebekah sat at her bedroom window, watching two turtledoves in the old maple tree. *Mary Ellen's so happy with Johnny, but I'll never love—leastways not like a woman loves a man.* She groaned, knowing full well that self-pity had stolen into her heart again. Yet she seemed powerless to stop it.

A knock on the door caused her to jump, and she lifted a hand to wipe away the tears rolling down her cheeks. "Come in."

"You didn't show up when I called for breakfast," Mom said, poking her head inside the door. "I was hoping you weren't still asleep. We must hurry if we're to get to the wedding on time."

Rebekah turned the wheelchair toward Mom and forced a smile. "I'm up and, as you can see, even dressed. I guess I was too busy with my thoughts to hear you calling."

Mom moved swiftly across the room, falling to her knees in front of Rebekah's chair. "Is something troubling you this morning? You look so sad."

Rebekah shrugged. Something was troubling her all right, but she didn't want to talk about it. What was the point? Nothing could be changed by talking about it. "I'm fine. I just need a little time for thinking and dreaming."

Mom smiled. "I agree. Without dreams and goals, our lives would never move forward. I believe God has a plan for each of us, but we must be open to His will in order to discover what that plan is."

Rebekah wondered if Mom was trying to tell her something specific. It made her feel so *verhuddelt*. "I guess we'd better get to breakfast," she said, forcing a cheerful voice and ignoring her confused emotions. "After all, this is my best friend's wedding day."

❦

While Rebekah and Nadine washed and dried the breakfast

dishes, Sarah hurried outside to speak with Andrew. She found him in the buggy shed, hitching their horse to the carriage they would ride in.

"What is it, Sarah?" he asked in a tone of concern. "You look like you might be worried about something."

She nodded and took hold of his arm. "I'm concerned about Rebekah. She's not acting right this morning."

His eyebrows arched high on his forehead. "Is she feeling *grank*?"

"No, I don't think she's sick. At least not in a physical sense."

"What is it then?"

"I think she's having a hard time dealing with the fact that her best friend is getting married today."

"Is that all?" Andrew snickered and gave his horse's flanks a couple of pats. "Did you remind her that couples have been gettin' married for hundreds of years?"

Sarah grimaced. "I'm sure she knows that. I just think it's hard for her not to have a suitor of her own."

"That will happen in God's time."

"Maybe so, but Rebekah has told me often enough that she doesn't think anyone would want to marry her because of her disability."

"*Puh!*" He waved a hand. "That's just plain *lecherich*."

"You may think it's ridiculous, but our daughter is convinced she will be en alt maedel for the rest of her life."

"She'll only be an old maid if she closes her mind to love." Andrew's eyebrows drew together. "Maybe I should ask my sister to have a little talk with her because Miriam knows firsthand what heartache that kind of thinking can bring."

"But Mim's happily married now."

"That's just the point. She used to be en alt maedel, but she finally woke up and realized she could be happy being married to Amos."

Sarah shook her head. "Need I remind you that it wasn't so in the beginning of their marriage? It took some time before Mim allowed herself to fall in love with Amos."

"You're right, which just goes to show that given a little time, Rebekah might fall in love with some lucky fellow, too."

"Any idea who that could be?"

He shrugged. "I might have a clue or two."

"You think it's Daniel Beachy?"

"Could be. From what I've noticed whenever he's around Rebekah, I'd say he's got more than a passing interest."

"Can you think of any way we can get the two of them together?"

Andrew let go of the harness and drew Sarah into his arms. "I think we need to leave that matter in God's hands, don't you?"

"I guess you're right," she said, nestling against his muscular chest. "But it wouldn't hurt for us to pray about the matter."

"No, of course not."

"And maybe a little talk with Mim about this wouldn't hurt, either."

"If I don't forget, I'll mention it to her."

Sarah stood on tiptoes and kissed the end of her husband's nose. "I love you, Andrew Stoltzfus."

"And I love you," he said, kissing her upturned mouth.

CHAPTER 15

When Rebekah and her family arrived at the Hiltys' for Mary Ellen and Johnny's wedding, she noticed right away that already there were several gray-topped buggies lined up in the yard, along with a few of the black, open courting buggies. Some of their English friends and neighbors were also present because a couple of vans and several cars were parked nearby, too.

As soon as Dad had parked their buggy and unhitched the horse, they were greeted by one of the six teenage boys, known as the "hostlers," whose job it was to lead the horses away and tie them in the barn.

Their hostler, Paul Troyer, greeted them with a smile. "Looks like there's gonna be a lot of people here today. Guess my biggest job will be to help feed all the horses around noontime."

Dad nodded. "That will be quite a job all right, but I'm sure you boys are up to the challenge."

"Jah, and because there ain't enough room to tie all the horses on the lower level of the barn where they'll be fed, the horses from the upper level will have to trade places with the others when it's their turn to eat," Paul said as he grabbed hold of Dad's horse. "That will make it an even bigger job."

Dad nodded; then he smiled down at Rebekah. "Guess we'd better get you inside. Since you're one of Mary Ellen's newehockers, you'll need to get yourself in place soon, I expect."

Rebekah returned his smile, even though her stomach was doing little flip-flops. She would be losing her best friend to Johnny Yoder today, which was hard enough to deal with, but knowing she would never have the privilege of becoming a bride herself was almost too painful to bear.

The wedding began promptly at eight thirty with the chant-like singing of a song from the Amish hymnal, the *Ausbund.* As the people began the third line of the hymn, the ministers stood and made their way up the stairs to a room that had been prepared for them on the second floor. Mary Ellen and Johnny followed, but their attendants waited downstairs.

Rebekah sat in her wheelchair, fidgeting with the corner of her apron and wondering what was being said to the bride and groom in the room above. She nearly broke into tears when she glanced over at Daniel and saw his somber expression. Surely his heart must be broken because Mary Ellen had chosen Johnny and not him.

When the wedding couple returned to the main room and had taken their seats again, the congregation sang another song. The ministers reentered the room during the final verse and also sat down. Abe Landis, one of the ministers, gave a message, which was followed by a period of silent prayer and scripture reading. Then, Bishop Benner rose and began the main sermon.

Rebekah glanced at Daniel again, and he must have

caught her looking at him, for he flashed her a grin. Rebekah's heart did a silly little dance, and she averted his gaze. She figured he was only being friendly, but oh, how she wished it could be more.

The truth hit Rebekah with such force she felt like one of Dad's bulls running at full speed had slammed into her. She was in love with Daniel Beachy. The problem was she couldn't do anything about it. Daniel didn't share her feelings of love, and even if he did, her disability would stand in the way of them being together.

The bishop asked the bride and groom to stand before him then, and Rebekah's attention snapped to the front of the room.

Mary Ellen, looking happy and more beautiful than ever, wore a blue cotton dress draped with a white cape and apron. Johnny looked quite dashing, too, in his white shirt, black trousers, black vest, and matching jacket.

Rebekah listened attentively as the young couple answered each one of Bishop Benner's questions, asking if they would be loyal to one another in sickness or adversity and stay together until death separated them. When the bishop placed Mary Ellen's right hand in Johnny's left hand and pronounced the blessing, Rebekah's eyes stung with tears. She squeezed them shut, hoping to keep the dam from bursting wide open. *Why do I have to be handicapped? Why can't I be like the other young women I know?* She swallowed hard, struggling against the sob rising in her throat. *Dear God, please fill my life in such a way that I won't miss having love or marriage. Give me peace in my heart, like only You can give.*

Rebekah opened her eyes in time to hear the bishop say,

"Go forth in the name of the Lord. You are now man and wife." Johnny and Mary Ellen seemed to radiate a blissful glow as they returned to their seats. In a short time, the wedding feast would begin, and so would Mary Ellen's new life as Mrs. Johnny Yoder.

After the tables had been set up to replace the benches that had been used during the wedding service, and then each of them covered with tablecloths, the eating utensils were put in place. From the temporary kitchen located in the basement, to the eating areas in the living room and upstairs kitchen, foot traffic was heavy and continuous. Food for all courses was soon placed on the tables, beginning with the main course, which included roasted chicken, bread filling, and mashed potatoes. Creamed celery—a traditional wedding dish—coleslaw, applesauce, pies, doughnuts, fruit salad, pudding, bread, butter, jelly, and coffee finished out the meal.

As soon as everything was ready, the bridal party made its entrance, with the bride, groom, and their attendants entering single file.

When Rebekah wheeled her chair in behind Mary Ellen and Johnny, she noticed the jars of select celery she'd dried the day before, which had been spaced at regular intervals on each of the tables so that the leaves formed a flowerlike arrangement. She was pleased to see that the two bouquets of flowers Mary Ellen had selected from her greenhouse were also on the tables.

A special tablecloth from the bride's hope chest adorned the *eck*, the corner table where the bride and groom would sit. On this table sat three cakes that had been made by some of Mary Ellen's friends. A more elaborate cake that had been bought from a bakery in town bore the words, "Congratulations, Johnny and Mary Ellen," across the top in yellow icing.

Also on the eck were pretty dishes filled with candy, nuts, and fancy fruits, as well as some platters full of lunch meats, crackers, and dips.

After each of the tables had filled with the first group of guests, everyone paused for silent prayer. Then, as the people ate, the waiters and waitresses scurried about supplying more food and tending to everyone's needs. When they had all eaten their fill, another silent prayer was said, and the tables were quickly vacated so the next group could be fed.

After the meal, the young folks had some free time to mill around and visit. Mary Ellen invited several of the young women to go upstairs with her and look at some of the wedding presents she'd received, while Johnny went out to the barn to visit with some of his friends.

Rebekah, feeling the need for some fresh air and not wanting to put anyone through the trouble of carrying her upstairs, declined Mary Ellen's offer to view the gifts and said she wanted to go outside for a while.

"You do look flushed," Mary Ellen said with a note of concern. "Are you feeling all right?"

"I'm fine. It's just a bit too warm and stuffy in here for me."

Mary Ellen leaned over and gave Rebekah a hug. "All right, then. See you a little later."

Rebekah wheeled out the door and down the ramp.

As soon as she was on the lawn, she caught sight of Daniel standing under a leafy maple tree with one of his brothers. He smiled and nodded as he clasped Harold's shoulder.

Rebekah turned her wheelchair toward Aunt Mim's garden, wondering how Daniel could appear so happy when he had just lost the girl he loved to Johnny. As she reached the edge of the garden, she noticed a few late-blooming chrysanthemums and geraniums, as well as several kinds of flourishing herbs. Their pungent aroma drifted on the wind, and Rebekah sniffed deeply, drinking in the serenity of it all. "A garden is my favorite place to be," she murmured.

"Jah, mine, too."

Rebekah jerked at the sound of Daniel's deep voice. "I—I didn't realize anyone else was here."

"I saw you come out and thought I'd join you. That is, if you don't mind my company."

"Of course not."

Daniel grabbed the handles of her chair and pushed it down the wider path. They moved in silence for a time, until he stopped and stepped in front of the wheelchair. "What did you think of the wedding, Rebekah?"

"It was very nice, and I ate more than my share of the good food we were served."

He grinned and nodded in agreement. "Do you think God brought Johnny and Mary Ellen together?"

"I believe Mary Ellen and Johnny would say so."

"They do seem to be very much in love, don't they?"

"Jah." Rebekah was tempted to ask if Daniel was terribly disappointed that he hadn't been Mary Ellen's choice for a husband, but she didn't think that would be a fitting thing to say. Besides, if Daniel was grieving, the reminder might make him feel worse than he already did.

Daniel went back to pushing her chair until he came to a wooden bench. He stopped next to it and took a seat. "I was wondering," he said, looking straight ahead.

"What were you wondering?"

"There's going to be another singing this Sunday night over at the Yutzys' place. Do you plan to go?"

Rebekah shook her head. "I don't think so."

He stole a quick glance at her. "I thought I might go to this one. They'll be having a bonfire with a hot-dog roast and marshmallows. It might be kind of fun, and it may be the last time we can have an outside gathering such as this before the snow flies."

Rebekah pursed her lips as she stared down at her hands, folded in her lap.

"What's wrong?"

"It's just that—well, it's hard for me to go to singings and such when I can't do much of anything but sit and watch from the sidelines."

"I understand, but—"

"No, you don't understand! You're not stuck in a wheelchair like me. No one with a pair of good legs understands what it's like to be confined in this chair or to be forced to walk with stiff leg braces and cumbersome crutches."

Tears welled in Rebekah's eyes, and she was powerless to stop them from dribbling onto her cheeks. She sniffed and reached up to wipe them away.

Daniel sat for several seconds, staring at the garden foliage. Finally, he turned to Rebekah and said, "Okay, so I don't understand what it's like to be in your place, but I don't think you should let your handicap keep you from living."

"I–I'm not. I own a greenhouse now, and that keeps me plenty busy. If that's not living, then I don't know what is."

"You do keep busy working, but what about having fun?"

She nearly choked on the lump in her throat and had to swallow a couple of times before she could respond. "I–I enjoy playing games and putting puzzles together with my family. That's fun. And of course, I still have the column I write for *The Budget*. It's fun whenever someone tells me something humorous that has happened to them."

"That's all well and good, but don't you think you should spend more time with other young people your age?"

"I do. Sometimes. I mean, I spend time with my sister and brother, and of course, Mary Ellen."

"Jah, well, I think you should go to the singing next Sunday, because I'll be there—and it wouldn't be the same without you."

Hope welled in Rebekah's soul. Was Daniel asking her to meet him at the singing, kind of like a date? If she went, was there a chance that he might ask if he could take her home in his courting buggy afterward? She wanted that more than anything, even if they couldn't have a future together. It would be so wonderful to experience what other young women did when they got to ride home with some special fellow—if only just once.

Throwing her doubts and fears aside, Rebekah looked over at Daniel and smiled. "Jah, okay. I'll try to be at the singing."

Chapter 16

Now that the time had come to go to the singing, Rebekah had second thoughts about attending. However, the idea of seeing Daniel again won out, and she and Simon were on their way to the Yutzys' in his open courting buggy. The wind whipped against Rebekah's face and stung her nose like a swarm of buzzing bumblebees, but she didn't mind. The sky was clear and full of twinkling stars, and the air was as cool and crisp as a tasty winter apple. To her way of thinking, this was perfect weather for a bonfire—and the perfect night for what she hoped would be her first ride in Daniel's courting buggy.

It will seem odd not to see Mary Ellen there tonight, Rebekah thought regrettably. Now that Mary Ellen and Johnny were married, they would no longer be attending any of the young people's activities. Mary Ellen's days of flirting with the boys and running around looking so cute had come to an end because she was now a *hausfraa.*

Rebekah moaned softly. *I wonder what it would be like to be a housewife with a home of my own to manage? Even a house right next door to Mom and Dad or one that was built on the same property as theirs would make me feel so thankful and independent. Maybe if I become financially self-reliant, Dad will build me a small house. It would have to be near family, of course—in case of an emergency.*

Rebekah supposed she would always need someone in the family to look out for her unless she could make enough money to hire a maid to do the things she couldn't do for herself. But since she couldn't be sure how well the greenhouse would do in the days ahead, there were no guarantees of that, either.

"Now what's that old frown about?" Simon asked, nudging Rebekah's arm with his elbow. "We're on our way to a singing, and there's bound to be lots of good food, fun, and games, so you should be smiling, not frowning like some old sourpuss. Are you feeling sad about something, sister?"

Rebekah managed a weak smile, knowing if she didn't, he would probably needle her all the way to the singing. "I'm not really sad. I was just thinking about something, that's all."

"Like what?" he asked, flicking the reins a couple of times to get the horse moving faster.

"It was nothing important, and I'd rather not talk about it, if you don't mind." She wasn't about to tell her brother that she was nervous about seeing Daniel tonight or that she'd been fretting over whether she might be able to support herself. He would just accuse her of being a worrywart, and he'd probably tease her about Daniel, too.

"Well, if you want to be an old stick-in-the-mud, then suit yourself. I'm really looking forward to tonight, and I plan on havin' fun whether you do or not."

"I wouldn't think of standing in the way of your good time." Rebekah glanced down at her stiff legs. "Make that, sitting in the way of your good time."

🎵

Daniel had just hitched a horse to his courting buggy and was preparing to head out to the singing, when his father called out to him. "Where do you think you're goin', son?"

"To the singing over at Yutzys' place."

"Not before we get the milking done. You know that don't wait."

Daniel released a groan. He had been in such a hurry to see Rebekah that he'd plumb forgotten about milking the cows. "Okay, Pop. I'll be right there," he called.

A few minutes later, Daniel entered the milking barn, where his two brothers were already hard at work on one end of the room. His father owned a diesel-operated milking machine so they didn't have to milk all the cows by hand, but even so, the job would take more of his time than he wanted it to.

Sure hope I don't have to do this for the rest of my life, he thought as he squatted down by one of the cows in order to get her hooked up to the milking apparatus. *I'd much rather be raising plants and flowers than milking a bunch of moody old cows.*

A large, annoying horsefly buzzed Daniel's head, and he reached up to swat it away. The fly kept on circling and buzzing, flitting from Daniel's head to the cow's hind end and then back again. The nervous cow mooed, twitched her tail, and then sidestepped, making Daniel feel more exasperated by the minute.

Finally, when he thought he had everything ready to go, the cow let out a raucous *moo-oo*, kicked out her back leg, and slammed her foot into Daniel's leg with such force that he was thrown against the wall behind him. Searing pain shot through his leg, and when he tried to stand, he knew without question that his leg had been broken.

"Pop!" he shouted. "You'd better come on over here 'cause my leg is busted."

<hr />

It seemed to Rebekah as if all the young people in her community were at the singing. Everyone had crowded into the Yutzys' barn to play games and sing, and as usual, she sat on the sidelines in her wheelchair, listening to the lively banter and watching the door for some sign of Daniel.

I wouldn't think he would want to miss out on all the game playing. Could he have changed his mind about coming? Of course, something might have come up to detain him.

Knowing it would do no good to worry or fret, Rebekah forced her attention onto the game of kickball several of the boys were playing on the other side of the barn. Simon was among those involved, and he was running around, trying to get control of the ball as if his life depended on it. Several young women sat on the sidelines, cheering the fellows on, but Rebekah couldn't muster up the enthusiasm for cheering. If Daniel didn't show up tonight, then she had come to the singing for no purpose whatsoever.

She sighed, and her eyes drifted shut as an image of Daniel's kind face came to mind. If she thought hard enough, she could almost feel his warm breath on her upturned face—could almost sense him looking at her.

"Rebekah, are you awake?"

Her eyes snapped open, and she sat up with a start. Someone *had* been breathing on her, but it wasn't Daniel. Harold Beachy, Daniel's sixteen-year-old brother, stood in front of her with his head bent down so his face was a few inches from hers.

Rebekah drew in a deep breath, trying to calm her nerves. "Don't scare me like that, Harold."

"Sorry, but I need to speak with you about my brother."

"Daniel?"

"Jah. He had a little accident in the milking barn awhile ago."

"Wh–what happened?"

"A nervous cow kicked him real good."

Rebekah's heart slammed into her chest. "Oh, no! Was he hurt bad?"

Harold nodded. "From the looks of things, I'd say his leg was broke."

"I–I'm so sorry to hear that."

"Our daed called 9-1-1 from the phone he keeps in the shed because of his business, and now Daniel and our folks are on their way to the hospital in our neighbor's van."

"How come you're not with them?"

"Daniel asked me to come here and let you know what happened. He was worried that you might think he'd changed his mind about comin' to the singing." Harold gave her a crooked grin. "Don't tell him I said anything, but I think he was planning to give you a ride home tonight in his courtin' buggy."

Under different circumstances, hearing that Daniel had planned to take her home after the singing would have made Rebekah's heart sing, but learning that his leg was probably broken made her feel sick all over.

"Well, I'd better get going," Harold said. "My driver's waiting out front to take me and Abner to the hospital so we can see how Daniel's doing."

She nodded soberly. "Tell Daniel I'm real sorry about his leg and that I'll be praying for him."

Harold gave a quick nod, turned, and sprinted out of the barn.

Rebekah closed her eyes as she fought to keep the tears behind her burning lids from spilling over. She didn't want to be here any longer. All she wanted to do was go home, where she could be alone to read her Bible and pray for Daniel.

❧

"I hope Daniel will like the plant I picked out for him," Rebekah said to her mother as the two of them headed down the road in their buggy toward the Beachys' place. The morning after the singing, they had received word that Daniel's leg was badly broken and he would have to spend a few days at the hospital, since he might require surgery. Word now had it that he was doing as well as could be expected and had been home from the hospital for two days. Rebekah was most anxious to see how he was doing and hoped that her visit might help cheer him up because he was no doubt in a lot of pain.

Mom smiled and reached across the seat to touch Rebekah's arm. "I'm sure Daniel will like the plant you chose."

Rebekah glanced at the cactus sitting in a cardboard box at her feet. "Sure is too bad about him getting kicked by that cow. He probably won't be able to help his daed in the dairy barn for some time now that his leg is broken."

"Maybe there are some things he can do from a seated position, same as you're able to do."

"Jah, but the kinds of things I do in my greenhouse aren't the same as what Daniel's expected to do with those ornery old dairy cows."

"I'm sure he and his daed will work something out. And Clarence does have the help of his other two sons, so they'll probably manage okay even without Daniel's help."

Rebekah nodded and leaned her head against the seat, trying to relax. As she closed her eyes, a vision of Daniel popped into her head. If it weren't for her handicap, maybe someone as nice as him might want to court her. But under the circumstances, she couldn't allow herself the privilege of even hoping for love or romance. She would have to be satisfied with Daniel's friendship. After all, it was better than nothing.

Daniel was lying on the sofa with his leg propped on two pillows when Rebekah came rolling into the living room in her wheelchair holding a cactus with red blossoms in her lap. "It's good to see you," he said, as he started to sit up.

She shook her head. "Stay where you are. No need to sit up on my account."

He dropped his head back to the pillow and grimaced. "I sure hate bein' laid up like this."

"I can understand that." Rebekah wheeled up to the table near the sofa and set the plant on one end. "This is for you, Daniel."

"Danki, that was nice of you." Just seeing Rebekah was a gift in itself, but her thoughtfulness made Daniel realize why he'd come to care for her so much. "Is it from your greenhouse?"

"Jah. It's a Christmas cactus."

"I thought so. I've never tried raising one before, but I hear they can be kind of tricky."

"Not really. Just be sure you water it once in a while—but not too often," she added with a smile.

"I'll do my best not to kill it." He grunted. "Until I can be up and around more on my crutches, there isn't much for me to do, so havin' a plant to care for will be something at least." Daniel knew his limitations were temporary, but it frustrated him not to be able to do the things he was used to doing. Even milking the cows would seem like fun compared to lying around on the sofa all day with his leg propped up on pillows.

Rebekah just sat staring at the cactus with a tiny smile on her face.

"Sorry I missed the singing the other night. Sure was lookin' forward to seeing you."

"Same here."

"So how'd it go? Did you have a good time?"

"Not really. Since I can't play any of the games that require two good legs, it's not so much fun to sit and watch." She lifted her gaze to meet his, and her cheeks turned rosy red. "After your brother came by to let me know about your accident, I asked Simon to take me home."

Hope welled in Daniel's soul. Had Rebekah left because of him not being there? Or had she simply gotten tired of sitting on the sidelines watching the festivities? He was about to ask when his mother stepped into the room with a tray of cookies and two glasses of milk.

"Sarah and I are having tea in the kitchen, and I thought maybe you two would like some refreshments," she said, placing the tray on the table beside the cactus.

"Danki, that'd be real nice." Daniel grabbed the sides of the sofa cushion and pulled himself to a sitting position. "I'm always in the mood for some of your good cookies."

Mom chuckled and ruffled his hair. "I've got a hunch you're only telling me that so I'll keep making more." She smiled at Rebekah. "How about you? Are you hungry enough to eat a little snack?"

Rebekah nodded and patted her stomach. "Jah, I've got the room."

As soon as his mother returned to the kitchen, Rebekah handed Daniel a glass of milk and a napkin with four cookies on it.

"So when's the next singing, do you know?" he asked, placing the napkin in his lap.

"In a few weeks. I think it's supposed to be over at the Hiltys' place."

He bit into a cookie and washed it down with a gulp of milk. "Maybe by then I'll be able to go. In fact, I'm countin' on it."

Rebekah nibbled on the end of a cookie.

"How about you?" he persisted. "Will you go if I do?"

"I—I suppose I could."

He grinned and chomped down the rest of his cookie. "That's good news, Rebekah. It'll give me somethin' to look forward to until then."

She smiled, and the light from the gas lamp nearby reflected in her eyes. "Jah, me, too."

Chapter 17

I'm sorry to be so late," Daniel apologized as he hobbled into the Hiltys' barn on his crutches. "I hope you didn't think I wasn't comin'."

Rebekah, who sat in her wheelchair near the door, stared up at him. "I wasn't sure. I thought maybe your leg might be hurting, so you had decided not to come to the singing."

"I told you I'd be here, and I wasn't about to stay home because of my leg." Daniel glanced around the room. "Have I missed much?"

She shook her head. "Not really. Just some songs and a few games. We haven't had anything to eat yet, but some of the men started the bonfire awhile ago, so we should be having the hot-dog roast soon, I expect."

"Now that is good news because I'm a hungry man." Daniel propped his crutches against the wall and lowered himself to a bale of straw near Rebekah's wheelchair.

Rebekah smiled. Daniel made her feel so lighthearted. The sense of peace she felt while sitting with him made her wish the feeling could last forever. But she knew she needed to prepare herself for the day when Daniel would meet someone, fall in love, and get married. Then Rebekah and Daniel's special friendship would be over.

"How's the Christmas cactus doing?" she asked. "Is it still thriving?"

He nodded. "Haven't killed it yet, and it sure is pretty. Makes me think of you every time I look at it."

Rebekah's face heated up. Surely Daniel hadn't meant that he thought she was pretty. He probably had meant that seeing the cactus made him think of her because they both liked flowers and plants.

"Would you like to go out by the fire?" Daniel asked. "Maybe if some of us wander out that way, the Hiltys will get the hint and set out the food."

Rebekah nodded. "You could be right."

Daniel stood and grabbed his crutches. Then, following Rebekah in her wheelchair, they left the barn and headed across the yard to the bonfire.

The cool night air was chilly, and Rebekah suppressed a shiver.

"Are ya cold?" he asked in a tone of concern. "We can move closer to the fire, or I could get a quilt from my buggy."

She shook her head. "I'm fine. I think my shawl will be enough." She pulled the heavy woolen cloak a bit tighter around her shoulders.

"Rebekah, there's something I'd like to ask you," Daniel said in a most serious tone.

She looked up at him expectantly. "Oh? What's that?"

"Well, I was wondering—"

Daniel's words were chopped off when a group of young people rushed out of the barn, laughing and hollering like a bunch of schoolchildren. Karen Sharp along with several other young women began setting food on a nearby table. Then someone yelled, "God is good, and it's time to eat!"

Rebekah glanced over at Daniel and smiled. "I guess this is what we've been waiting for."

He nodded. "Would you like me to get you a hot dog and a stick for roasting?"

"Don't bother. I can get it."

"It's no bother." Daniel hobbled off and returned a few minutes later with two long sticks and a couple of hot dogs. "Would you like me to roast yours for you?"

"Roasting a hot dog is one of the few things I can manage to do for myself." Rebekah knew her words had sounded harsh, and she quickly apologized. "Sorry. I—I didn't mean to sound so ungrateful."

He handed her one stick and a hot dog. "It's all right. Since my accident, I've come to understand a little better how you must feel about not being able to do many things."

"It is hard to rely on others so much of the time." Rebekah rolled her wheelchair closer to the fire so she could reach the stick into the sizzling coals. Her stomach rumbled as she thought about eating some of the delicious food that awaited them. Besides the hot dogs and buns, there was potato salad, coleslaw, potato chips, sweet pickles, baked beans, chocolate cake, and, of course, plenty of marshmallows for roasting.

Since Rebekah had two free hands, and a lap to hold

a plate, she dished up some food for Daniel and handed it to him after he'd found a seat on a bale of straw. Then she went back to the food table and filled her own plate. She had just returned to the spot where Daniel sat when Simon sauntered up to her.

"Rebekah, I need to talk to you," he whispered.

"What? I can hardly hear you, Simon."

"I need to talk to you!"

"What do you want?"

"I've asked Karen Sharp if I can give her a ride home in my buggy."

"That was nice of you. I'm sure we can make room for her."

Simon shook his head. "I don't think you understand. I want to take her home—alone. So I was wondering if you might be able to find another ride."

His words and the implication of their meaning finally registered, and Rebekah grimaced. The last thing she wanted to do was beg someone for a ride home.

"I can give Rebekah a ride," Daniel said before Rebekah had time to think of a reply.

"I'd sure appreciate that." Simon grinned and thumped Daniel on the back. Then he walked away quickly before Rebekah could say a word.

Her heart sank. Little brother was growing up—about to begin his own courting days. It wouldn't be fair to hold him back. It wasn't right to hold Daniel back, either. She studied him as he sat perched on the bale of straw, with his broken leg extended in front of him. She wondered how he must be feeling right now, having been put on the spot by her brother like that. She had hoped Daniel might ask to take her home tonight but not because he felt forced to do it.

"You're not obligated to see that I get home, Daniel. If you'd planned to ask someone else, then it's—"

Daniel held up a hand as he swiveled around to face her. "I didn't agree to take you home as a favor to your brother, Rebekah. I was plannin' to ask you anyways."

Rebekah blinked a couple of times. "You. . .you were?"

"I was." He smiled at her so sweetly she thought her heart might burst wide open. "So how about it? Will you accept a ride home in my courting buggy?"

Rebekah's common sense said she should probably say no, but the desire deep in her heart won out. "Jah, Daniel," she said with a nod. "I would like a ride home in your buggy tonight."

"Your horse is so *gross*," Rebekah commented once she and Daniel were settled inside his open buggy.

Daniel chuckled. "Toby's a big one, all right. He handles well, though, and we get along just fine."

"Your buggy's real nice, too."

"Danki. I was pretty excited about getting it when I turned sixteen. I've had this buggy over four years now, and I still think it looks pretty good."

"I can see that you take great care with it," she said, letting her hand travel over the black leather seat, so smooth and shiny.

Daniel answered with a smile and a nod as he took up the reins and moved the horse forward.

They rode in silence for a while, with the only sounds being the steady *clip-clop, clip-clop* of the horse's hooves and the rhythmic rumble of the carriage wheels bumping against the pavement.

Rebekah felt such joy being in Daniel's courting buggy on this beautiful, star-studded night. *It's almost like a real date,* she thought wistfully. But then she reminded herself that it was merely one friend giving another friend a ride home from the singing. There was no meaning attached, and she didn't dare to hope that there was, either.

"Do you ever drive any of your daed's buggies?"

Daniel's sudden question pushed her thoughts aside. "Dad's taught me how, but he never allows me to take the horse and buggy out alone," she answered. "He says it would be taking too much of a chance because something unexpected might occur."

"Some unpleasant things have been known to happen, all right. Why, just the other day a buggy was run off the road by a bunch of rowdy teenagers speeding down Highway 6 in their fancy sports car." Daniel shook his head and grunted. "I guess some of those English fellows don't care about our slow-moving buggies. They probably think we're just a nuisance who like to get in their way."

"It does seem so," Rebekah agreed.

"We need to be especially careful when we're out at night. Even with our battery-operated lights and reflective tape, cars don't always see us so clearly."

"I remember once my aunt Mim got caught in a snowstorm and lost control of the buggy, causing it to flip over. She was trapped inside for some time until Uncle Amos came along and rescued her."

"Those two stories are reason enough for your daed not to let you drive alone," Daniel said with a note of conviction. "None of us would want anything to happen to you; that's for certain sure."

Rebekah's heart did a flip-flop at Daniel's thoughtful words. Did "none of us" include him? Was he trying to tell her that he would care if something bad happened because he had romantic feelings for her? She shoved the thought aside, sternly reminding herself that Daniel was only a friend, nothing more.

The ride to Rebekah's house was over much too soon. She'd been having such a good time that she wished it could go on forever.

When they pulled up near the house, Daniel climbed down from the buggy, using the aide of his crutches. "I'll be right back."

"Where are you going?"

"To ask for some help in getting you down."

Rebekah watched as Daniel hobbled up to the steps. Just as he was about to knock on the door, her father stepped onto the porch.

"I spotted your buggy pulling in," she heard Dad say. "Do you need some help gettin' my daughter out of your buggy?"

Daniel nodded. "If it weren't for my bum leg, I'm sure I could manage fine on my own, but under the circumstances, I will need your help."

"No problem." Dad stepped off the porch and hurried out to the buggy. He removed Rebekah's wheelchair first, then lifted her down with ease and placed her in the chair as though she weighed no more than a child.

"I appreciate the ride home," Rebekah said to Daniel as Dad pushed her wheelchair up the ramp and onto the porch.

Daniel smiled and leaned against the porch railing as if he was in no hurry to leave. "I'm glad I could do it."

Rebekah felt relief when Dad grabbed hold of the doorknob and said, "I'm sure you two would probably like to visit awhile, so I'll just go inside now and see what your mamm's up to." He gave Rebekah a sly grin, opened the door, and stepped into the house.

As soon as the door shut behind Rebekah's father, Daniel moved to the front of her wheelchair and leaned over so his face was close to hers. The full moon sent a shaft of light shimmering down from the starry sky, and Daniel's mahogany-colored eyes seemed to dance in the glow of it. "Rebekah, I was wondering something."

"What's that?"

"Well—could I maybe come calling on you one night soon?"

Daniel's whispered words made Rebekah's head feel kind of woozy. Was he asking if he could court her? Oh, surely not. He must mean—

"Rebekah, did you hear what I said?"

Her chin quivered slightly. "What was it, Daniel?"

"We have so much in common, what with our love for flowers and all, and I want to court you."

The rhythm of Rebekah's heartbeat picked up. She hadn't misunderstood him after all. He really did want to court her. It was almost too much to comprehend. "Daniel, I'm honored that you would ask such a thing, but I don't—"

He looked away, and his shoulders slumped. "You don't care for me? Is that it?"

Rebekah felt the sting of hot tears at the back of her eyes, and she blinked a couple of times. "That's not the problem. I. . .well, aren't you in love with Mary Ellen?"

"Mary Ellen?" he sputtered.

She only nodded in reply.

"But Mary Ellen's a married woman, for goodness' sake!"

Rebekah gritted her teeth. What was wrong with Daniel? Did he think she was verhuddelt? "I know my cousin's married, but before she and Johnny started courting, it seemed as though you were quite smitten with her."

"Now why would you think that? What have I ever done to make you believe such a thing?"

"You were always hanging around her."

He chuckled. "And you didn't know why?"

Rebekah didn't see what was so funny. It irked her that he would laugh about such a serious matter as this. "I—I thought you, like so many other fellows, had your eye on my cute, outgoing cousin."

"The only thing my eyes have ever wanted to look at is you, Rebekah Stoltzfus. I only hung around Mary Ellen because you were usually with her. I wanted to be near you, but I never had the courage to say so before."

Rebekah swallowed against the lump in her throat, and despite her best effort, several tears dribbled onto her cheeks. "Oh, Daniel, I'm flattered by your words, but I—I can't agree to let you court me."

"Why not?" His poker face couldn't hide his obvious surprise at her response. "I think I've made it clear that I'm not in love with Mary Ellen, so there shouldn't be a thing wrong with us courting—unless you don't care for me."

Rebekah's eyelids fluttered. "That isn't the problem, Daniel."

"What is the problem?"

"Courting for us would be pointless."

"Pointless? What could be pointless about two people who enjoy each other's company and have so much in common agreeing to court?"

Rebekah drew in a deep breath and reached up to swipe at another set of tears. "For most couples, courting often leads to a more permanent commitment."

"What's wrong with that? Love and marriage go well together, you know," he said with an impish smile.

Rebekah smiled, too, in spite of her tears. Daniel was everything a woman could want. He was all she wanted; that was for sure. She felt certain that any normal girl would never have considered turning down his offer.

However, that was the problem. Rebekah was not any normal girl. She was crippled and always would be. To her way of thinking, her handicap didn't make her a good candidate as a wife. There were many things she couldn't do without the use of two good legs. And children—she wanted to be a mother so badly. Daniel probably wanted to be a father, too. But it was unlikely that she would ever conceive, and even if by some miracle she could get pregnant, how would a mother in a wheelchair or walking stiff-legged with cumbersome crutches ever care for a baby?

The very thing Rebekah wanted most—to be courted by a man—particularly this man, was being offered to her right now. As much as it hurt, she knew she had to turn it down. She gazed into Daniel's serious brown eyes and blinked rapidly. "I'm a cripple, and I'll always be one."

"I know that already."

"But you don't understand what it's like for me."

"I do understand, Rebekah." He lifted one crutch and nodded at his broken leg.

"But your handicap is only temporary. Once your leg heals, you'll throw those crutches away and walk like a normal man again." She pushed her wheelchair toward the door. "Our relationship could never go any further than just the fun of courting, and as much as it pains me to say this, my answer has to be no."

Daniel stepped between Rebekah and the door and stood for several seconds, staring at her like he didn't quite believe what she'd said.

"Gut nacht, Daniel." Rebekah opened the door and wheeled into the house without another word.

CHAPTER 18

It had been four weeks since Daniel asked if he could court Rebekah, but the pain she felt over her decision made it seem like only yesterday. She dreaded facing Daniel at the preaching service again today, but there was no way she could get out of going because church was to be held in their home this time.

"Oh, you're up," Mom said as Rebekah rolled her wheelchair into the kitchen. "We must hurry and get breakfast on if we're to be ready in time."

Rebekah glanced out the kitchen window. Huge snowflakes fell like powdered sugar from the sky. "It's starting to snow," she said. "Maybe no one will come."

Mom smiled. "It's not coming down so hard. Besides, a little bit of snow isn't likely to keep any of our people from worshiping God."

"I suppose you're right." Rebekah sighed and wheeled away from the window. "What can I do to help?"

"You can set the table and cut the breakfast pie. I'll have Nadine get out some cereal and milk when she comes in from collecting eggs."

As if on cue, Nadine opened the back door and hustled into the kitchen. Her cheeks were pink from the cold, and she stamped snow off her feet. "Brrr. . .it's sure chilly out there. I think winter's definitely on the way." She set the basket of eggs on the counter, slipped out of her jacket, and hung it on a wall peg. "Soon I can get my sled out of the barn, and I'm sure it won't be long until the ponds in the area will be frozen over. Then we can all go ice skating."

Winter, with its drab, gray days and bitter chilling winds always makes me feel sad, Rebekah thought. *Sledding and ice skating for me are out of the question, and Nadine knows that. Is she trying to rub vinegar on my wounds or start another argument with me this morning? Oh, if only. . .*

"Rebekah, are you going to the singing at the Rabers' tonight? Will your beau be bringin' you home again?" Nadine asked suddenly.

Rebekah nearly dropped the plate she'd been about to place on the table. "My what?"

"Your boyfriend. We all know Daniel Beachy gave you a ride home in his courting buggy last month, and I saw him leaning real close to you after Dad came inside, so I'm guessing he's pretty sweet on you, sister."

Rebekah's face heated with embarrassment. She hadn't said a word to anyone in the family about Daniel's offer to court her, and with good reason. "You don't know what you're talking about, Nadine. Furthermore, you shouldn't go around spying on people."

"I wasn't spying. I just happened to be looking out the living-room window when Daniel's buggy pulled into the yard." Nadine puckered her lips. "I'll bet he even kissed you when he thought no one was looking."

"He did no such thing!" Rebekah's voice shook with emotion. So much for her resolve to get along better with Nadine and have more understanding.

"I'll bet you're just too embarrassed to admit it."

Rebekah was about to offer a comeback, when Mom spoke up.

"Nadine, this little discussion has gone on long enough. Stop bothering your sister now. Rebekah will decide when to let us know what's going on with her and Daniel, and she doesn't need your teasing."

Rebekah's eyes filled with tears, clouding her vision. "The simple fact is that there'll never be anything going on between me and Daniel except friendship. Now, can we get on with breakfast?"

Mom gave Rebekah a sympathetic look. "Jah, it's on the way."

All during breakfast, Nadine sulked, barely able to eat anything she had put on her plate. It didn't seem fair that Mom always took Rebekah's side on things, but it had been that way ever since Nadine could remember. She'd only been a baby when Rebekah had lost the use of her legs, so she had no memory of her sister ever walking in a normal way. Nadine had grown up watching her folks, especially Mom, treat Rebekah as if she was someone special—someone who always needed to be stuck up for and sheltered.

"Anything wrong with your eggs?" Dad asked, tapping Nadine on the shoulder.

She shook her head. "I'm not so hungry this morning."

"You're not feeling grank are you?" Mom asked with a look of concern. "If you are, then you'd better get upstairs and into bed."

"I'm not sick."

"Then why the sour face?" Simon asked, giving her arm a nudge.

First Dad and then her little brother. Nadine wished she had sat in another chair.

"I think she's put out with me," Rebekah spoke up before Nadine had a chance to respond.

"Why would that be?" Dad questioned.

"Because I got upset with her for spying on me and Daniel when he brought me home from the singing four weeks ago."

Dad shook his finger in Nadine's face. "You know better than to spy on your sister. What were you thinkin' of, girl?"

"I wasn't spying. I can't help it that I happened to be looking out the window when Daniel and Rebekah were on the porch."

"You were looking out the window so you could see what was going on." Rebekah squinted at Nadine from across the table.

"No, I wasn't trying to see what was going on. I was just—"

Mom held up her hand. "I've heard this once already, and I'm not in the mood for another go-round." She pointed to Nadine's plate. "Now hurry and finish your breakfast so we're all ready when the others show up for church."

Nadine's stomach clenched as she picked up her fork and stabbed a piece of egg. Rebekah had won again.

As Rebekah rolled her wheelchair into the living room, she noticed that everything was in place and ready for the church service. The large hinged doors that separated the living room from the rest of the house had been flung open wide, and the furniture had been replaced with the traditional backless benches used in their worship services.

Soon everyone began to file into the house. The women and girls took their seats on one side of the room, while the men and boys sat on benches across from them.

Rebekah spotted Daniel sitting on a bench between his brothers, Abner and Harold, and she was pleased to note that the cast on his leg had been removed. When he smiled and nodded at her, she felt her face flame so she averted her gaze, hoping no one had noticed. There was no point in giving Daniel any reason to believe she might have changed her mind about them courting, and she certainly didn't want to give anyone the impression that she was interested in him. It was bad enough that Nadine believed it to be so.

The three-hour service seemed to take longer than usual, and the room grew hot and stuffy, despite the cold day. Rebekah fidgeted in her wheelchair, wishing she could be someplace where there was some fresh air to breathe. In spite of the fact that the padded seat of her wheelchair was a lot more comfortable than the hard, wooden benches, she was getting tired of sitting and felt relief when the service was finally over and she could wheel into the kitchen to help with the noon meal.

Several tables were set up throughout the house, and

the guests ate a nourishing lunch of soup and sandwiches, followed by cookies and plenty of hot coffee and apple cider.

The men and boys were fed first, and Rebekah made certain that the group she helped serve were the ones farthest away from the table where Daniel and his brothers sat. Nadine had been assigned to that table, and Rebekah was grateful.

When the men and boys were done eating, they headed outside to the barn. Then the women and girls sat down to their meal. It was during this time that Rebekah was able to visit with Mary Ellen.

"How's it going with being a full-time wife and not teaching school anymore?" she asked.

Mary Ellen shrugged as she offered Rebekah a wide smile. "I'm getting used to it now. Besides, being married to Johnny makes me happy."

Rebekah didn't know quite how to respond. She wanted to express happiness for her friend. She would have liked to say that she, too, was in love and hoped to be married. However, she said neither, for she was sure she would never marry or find that kind of joy.

"I hear you and Daniel Beachy have begun courting," Mary Ellen said suddenly.

"What?" Rebekah's mouth fell open. "Where did you ever hear such a thing?"

"Someone who attended the last singing said Daniel took you home." Mary Ellen grinned at Rebekah. "I always did think he had an interest in you."

"So he says."

"Then you've agreed to begin courting?"

"I told him no."

"You what?" Mary Ellen's wide-open eyes revealed her obvious surprise. "Oh, Rebekah, why? Don't you care for Daniel at all?"

Rebekah nodded. "I care very much for him."

"Then why won't you let him court you?"

"You, of all people, should know the answer to that. You've been my friend a long time, and I've shared many things with you."

"It's about your handicap, right?"

Rebekah nodded, her eyes filling with tears. "I care for Daniel, but if we started courting, he might want marriage—and later, kinner. I can't give him those things, and you know it."

"I know of no such thing, and neither do you. If you'll just trust God and give yourself half a chance—"

"A chance to do what? I'm not a complete woman. I could never make Daniel happy."

"Don't say that."

"Don't say what?" Nadine asked as she joined the women at their end of the table.

Rebekah's head snapped up. "Nothing. It was nothing important."

"I think you two must have been talkin' about boys. Everyone always closes up like a star tulip whenever I come along. Mom especially does that. She thinks I'm too young to be thinkin' about boys." Nadine clicked her tongue. "It's just because I'm the boppli of the family—that's all."

Mary Ellen squeezed Nadine's arm. "Just hold on a bit longer, for your time is coming. Sooner than you think, you'll end up like me—an old married woman."

Nadine shook her head. "You're not old, Mary Ellen, but you sure are pretty. No wonder Johnny wanted to marry you." She glanced over at Rebekah. "My sister has a boyfriend, too, only she won't 'fess up to it."

Rebekah slammed her empty coffee cup down with such force that she thought it might be broken. When she realized it wasn't, she gave it a little shove, then pushed her wheelchair away from the table. "I'm going outside for some fresh air!"

As Rebekah left the room, Mary Ellen looked over at Nadine and shook her head. "I wish I knew what's gotten into your sister today. She sure seems upset."

"Rebekah's always upset about something." Nadine grunted. "Of course, she gets away with it because of her handicap."

"What do you mean by that?"

"Mom's always taking Rebekah's side, and she favors her over me."

"Your mamm has always taken good care of Rebekah, but from what I've seen, she's not treated her any different than you or Simon."

"*Humph!* You don't live at our house, and you don't see how Mom takes Rebekah's side on every little thing. Why, just this morning, Rebekah and me were having a disagreement about her relationship with Daniel, and Mom told me to quit bothering Rebekah." Nadine folded her arms. "Why doesn't she get after Rebekah for her negative attitude instead of always scolding me?"

"I don't know the answer to that, but I do know that it must be hard for your sister to be confined to either her wheelchair or those rigid leg braces and crutches she sometimes uses." Mary Ellen studied Nadine's serious face. "I know it's not easy for you, but maybe you should try a little harder to have more understanding for Rebekah instead of arguing with her about things that don't really matter or feeling resentful because she receives a little more attention than you do at times." She paused a moment to gauge Nadine's reaction, but the young woman just sat staring at the table.

"Your folks love you and Simon as much as they do Rebekah," Mary Ellen continued. "And I'm sure it hurts them when any of their kinner has a disagreement. So won't you try a little harder to get along with your sister and be more understanding?"

Tears welled in Nadine's eyes, and she nodded slowly. "I'll try, but I promise you, it won't be easy."

"I'll be praying for both you and Rebekah," Mary Ellen said.

"Danki." Nadine scooted off the bench. "Guess I'll go visit with some of my friends for a while."

A few minutes after Nadine left, Mary Ellen noticed that Mama Mim was heading her way. Maybe she would have a talk with her about Rebekah's gloomy mood and see what she had to say.

CHAPTER

19

Rebekah sat on the front porch, wrapped in a heavy shawl and breathing in the crisp, cool, afternoon air. The sun peeked out between fluffy white clouds, casting a golden tint on the gently rolling hills. A light dusting of powdery snow rested on most of the trees.

A group of boys played tug-of-war in the driveway, and a few men stood on the lawn, visiting. *The rest of the men must be out in the barn,* Rebekah decided. She was glad Daniel wasn't among those who were still outside, for she didn't want to face him.

She released the brake on her wheelchair and rolled down the wooden ramp. Up the path leading to her greenhouse she went, feeling the need for some solitude. A time to think and enjoy all the plants might help get her mind off Daniel.

When Rebekah entered the greenhouse a few minutes later, she lit a gas lantern so she would have more light. It was chilly in the first section of the building, so she added a few logs to the burning embers inside the woodstove, thankful that Dad had placed them within easy reach.

Once the fire was going well, Rebekah moved into the glassed-in section of her greenhouse. Between the kerosene heater and the solar panels, this area was always plenty warm. She rolled her wheelchair up and down the aisles, drinking in the rich colors and fragrant smells coming from the variety of plants.

"If this is the only miracle You ever give me, Lord, then I'll learn to be content," Rebekah whispered. Even as she said the words, a feeling of emptiness settled over her like a heavy fog. Was the greenhouse really enough? Could she learn to be content?

She reached for a lacy-edged, pink African violet and held the pot as though it were a baby. She thought about Aunt Grace, who would be holding a real baby in just a few months, and about Mary Ellen, recently married. Unlike her aunt or cousin, Rebekah's fingers might often caress a delicate plant but never a husband's bearded face. Like as not, her hands would change potting soil, not dirty diapers. As much as she enjoyed working with plants, they weren't the same as a living, breathing human being, who could offer love in return.

Rebekah startled when she heard the front door of the greenhouse creak open, then snap shut. "Who's there?" she called out, drawing in a quick breath.

"It's me, Rebekah—Aunt Mim."

Rebekah expelled her breath, feeling a sense of relief that it wasn't Daniel.

"I'm back here!"

Aunt Mim poked her head through the doorway and smiled. "I haven't been in here since your opening day. I see you've made quite a few changes."

Rebekah nodded. " I'm selling more items now. Daniel Beachy gave me plenty of good ideas, and all the wooden items you see are his handmade creations."

"So your business is doing well then?"

"Better than I ever expected." Rebekah placed the African violet back on the shelf. "Of course, winter's almost here, and I won't have nearly as many customers now as I did in the summer."

"No, I suppose not," her aunt agreed. "But then, a young woman can certainly find other ways to fill the long winter hours."

Rebekah shrugged. "I suppose I can always quilt or do some other type of handwork. And there's the column I write for *The Budget*. That keeps me busy."

Aunt Mim gave her a wide smile and moved closer to the wheelchair. "It wasn't sewing or writing news about our community I had in mind, Rebekah."

"What did you have in mind for someone like me?" Rebekah asked with a catch in her voice.

Aunt Mim pulled out a wooden stool and sat down beside her. "I was thinking more about courting. I hear you have a suitor these days."

"Mary Ellen Hilty—I mean, Yoder. You are such a blabbermouth!"

"Don't be so hard on Mary Ellen," Aunt Mim said softly. "She only cares about your happiness."

"Jah, well, she can care without meddling. I suppose she saw me come in here and asked you to have a talk with me."

Aunt Mim shook her head. "She shared her concerns,

but it was my idea to speak with you." She placed a gentle hand on Rebekah's arm. "I believe I can help. I think you should hear my story."

"Your story?"

"Jah."

"You used to read me stories when I was a kinner. Why do you think I need to hear one now?"

"Because, sweet niece, I think my story might teach you something."

Rebekah leaned her head against the back of her wheelchair and closed her eyes. "I'm ready to hear your story."

"Once there was a young woman named Miriam Stoltzfus. She fell in love with her childhood sweetheart, and he broke her heart when he moved away and married someone else. Miriam became bitter and angry. She didn't trust men and resolved never to marry. Miriam even blamed God for all her troubles. Her pupils at the one-room school-house often talked behind her back, saying she had a heart of stone."

Rebekah nodded. She remembered hearing such talk.

"And so," Aunt Mim continued, "the bitter old-maid schoolteacher decided she could do everything in her own strength. She even forgot how to pray.

"Then one day after school had been dismissed, she told her young niece that she would give her a ride home. A few minutes later after the child had gone outside to wait for her, Miriam heard a clap of thunder, then an awful, ear-piercing snap, followed by a scream. She rushed outside, only to find her favorite niece lying on the ground with the limb of a tree lying across her back."

Aunt Mim paused a moment as though it pained her to relive the past. After inhaling a deep breath, she finally continued. "The doctor said Rebekah's spinal cord had been injured and that she would probably never walk again. Miriam's heart was broken, and she blamed herself for the tragic accident."

Rebekah's eyelids fluttered. "You—you blamed yourself? I never knew that."

Aunt Mim nodded, her eyes brimming with tears. "I'm the one who said you could wait outside, and I felt responsible for what had happened."

"I never faulted you at all, Aunt Mim." Rebekah's vision blurred with her own tears. It nearly broke her heart to think that her aunt had blamed herself.

Aunt Mim touched Rebekah's shoulder. "I know you didn't. As a young girl, you were always so happy and accepting of your limitations. However, as you grew, I saw a change come on. You began to withdraw and seemed unsure of yourself." She made a sweeping gesture at the room. "When you opened this new business, I thought things might be different. I was hoping you would see that your handicap couldn't keep you from reaching your goals. I prayed that God would send the right man into your life so you would find the joy of being in love, too."

Rebekah slowly shook her head. "I couldn't put the burden of my handicap on Daniel. It wouldn't be fair."

Aunt Mim's forehead wrinkled. "I think we'd better get back to my story."

"All right then. I'm all ears." Rebekah leaned her head back again, but this time she kept her eyes open.

"Well, Miriam Stoltzfus almost made a huge mistake. She met an English man, and after a while, he tried to talk her into leaving the Amish faith."

Rebekah's mouth fell open. "An English man? He asked you to leave the faith?"

"Jah. Do you remember when a reporter came into your hospital room shortly after the accident?"

"The picture man?"

"Right. The one who took your picture and put it in the English newspaper."

Rebekah squinted. "He's the one who asked you to leave the faith?"

Aunt Mim nodded. "We'd become friends, and there was a certain magnetism between us." She sighed. "But despite my attraction to Nick, I knew I could never give up my Amish way of life—although I still wasn't right with God at that time."

"So what did you do?"

"I made the wisest decision of my life. I married Amos Hilty." Aunt Mim crinkled her nose a bit. "When he first asked me to marry him, I turned him down."

"Didn't you care for him?" Rebekah could hardly imagine such a thing. Aunt Mim and Uncle Amos seemed to be so much in love.

Aunt Mim shrugged. "I didn't give myself a chance to find out whether I cared or not. I was so certain that Amos would let me down just as my first beau had done. I didn't think I could trust God to bring happiness into such an empty, bitter life as mine."

"But you did marry Uncle Amos, and you seem to be very happy."

Aunt Mim's eyes filled with another set of tears, and she sniffed deeply as she swiped them off her cheeks. "Jah, I'm happy and have been for a good many years. You see, one day God showed me something very important."

"What was that?"

"He let me know that my bitterness and blaming myself for so many things was of my own doing. He showed me that I could shed all my doubts and hurts from the past. God can do that for you, too, Rebekah. He wants you to be happy, and if you'll only trust Him, He can work a miracle in your life, just as He did mine."

A *miracle*. Wasn't that exactly what Rebekah had been looking for—an honest-to-goodness, true miracle from God? But could she take a leap of faith toward love and possibly marriage? She wanted to—more than anything—but she was afraid of failing.

"Well, I think I'd better stop now. Stories from my past are good, but Rebekah, you'll never know what God can do until you give Him the chance. If Daniel loves you, then he will accept you—imperfections and all."

Rebekah blinked back a fresh set of tears. "I'll try to take the step of faith I need to find love. Will you pray that I'll have the strength to do it?"

Aunt Mim bent down and gave Rebekah a hug. "I'll be praying, and may the Lord be with you, sweet niece."

❦

Rebekah's wheelchair rattled down the path toward the barn. She could only hope that Daniel and his family hadn't left for home yet. If she could just have the chance to speak with him alone for a few minutes, it might be that they could talk things out. If he hadn't changed his mind about them, maybe she would allow him to come calling on her after all.

When Rebekah reached the barn, she pushed open the side door and peered inside. Several clusters of men and boys filled the area—some talking, some playing games. She didn't see any sign of Daniel or his family, though.

Dad spotted her and came over to the door. "What's up, Rebekah? Did you need something?"

She shook her head. "I was looking for Daniel Beachy, that's all."

"I saw him leave with his folks awhile ago, and his brothers and sister left even before that."

"Do you know where Simon is, then?"

"I think he's outside. He and some of the other fellows his age were planning to get a game of corner-ball going."

"Okay, danki." Rebekah wheeled into the chilly air again. She knew what she had to do, but she'd better do it before she lost her nerve.

Dad had been right. She spotted Simon and a group of boys playing ball—in the snow, of all things. Rebekah sat on the sidelines until Simon looked her way; then she motioned for him to come over.

He kept playing a few more minutes but finally ambled her way. "What do you want, and why are you sittin' out here in the cold? Don't you know it might start snowing again?"

"Jah, I know it's cold, but I—I need your help." Rebekah clung desperately to her brother's arm.

"What do you need my help for?"

"Could you please hitch one of our more gentle horses to the buggy and help me get inside?"

His eyebrows lifted high on his forehead. "Inside the buggy?"

"Of course, inside the buggy. What else would I be talking about?"

"Where are you going, and who's going with you?"

"I–I'd rather not say. I just need to go, that's all."

Simon's mouth dropped open. "I hope you're only jokin' about this, sister."

"No, I'm not. I need to go someplace, and I know Dad won't allow me to head out alone so I'm asking for your help."

"You want me to go with you?"

She shook her head. "I need to do this alone. I just want you to get the buggy ready and help me inside. I'll leave my wheelchair in the buggy shed."

"Oh, sure, so I can be the one Dad hollers at? You know I'll be in big trouble if he finds out I helped you do such a stupid thing."

"Then we'll have to be sure that he doesn't find out."

Simon grunted. "All right, then, but you'll owe me big for this one."

CHAPTER 20

Any other time, Rebekah might have been nervous about driving the buggy alone. But at the moment, she was too excited about the prospect of seeing Daniel and telling him she had changed her mind about them courting to think of the possible dangers involved. Dad had taught her how to handle the horse, and just because she had no one with her didn't mean she should be afraid. After all, the Beachys' farm was only a few miles up the road, and it wouldn't take long to get there.

One thing Rebekah hadn't counted on was bad weather. She'd gone about a mile or so when a heavy snow began to fall, making it more difficult to see. The road quickly turned slippery, and it became harder to maintain control.

Rebekah gripped the reins a little tighter and talked soothingly to the horse. She knew it was important for her to remain calm and stay focused on the road ahead, or she could end up in trouble. She snapped on the switches for the battery-operated windshield wipers and the lights. With icy snow pelting her windshield, she had to be sure she could see well enough, not to mention the need to alert any oncoming cars that her buggy was on the road.

Rebekah might not have been scared when she'd started this little trip, but she sure felt nervous now. What if she lost control and her horse and buggy skidded off the road and into a ditch? The buggy could overturn and end up on its side. *Who would help me then?* she worried.

Rebekah drew in a deep breath, hoping to steady her nerves, then did what she should have done at the start of her ride. She prayed. Prayed for all she was worth. *Heavenly Father, I know I was wrong for taking the horse and buggy out alone and without Dad's permission. I probably don't deserve Your help, but I'd be obliged if You would get me to the Beachy farm safely. When I get back home, I promise to tell Mom and Dad what I've done and accept responsibility for my reckless actions. Amen.*

Rebekah was almost to the cross street leading to the road where the Beachy farm was located when she saw another Amish buggy. It was lying on its side along the shoulder of the road. The windows were all steamed up, and she couldn't see inside. With her heart pounding and hands so sweaty she could hardly hold the reins, she pulled up beside the wreck and opened her door. "Is anyone there? Are you hurt?" she called, her voice carrying in the crisp, cold air.

"We're okay, but the door's jammed," a man responded. When she recognized Daniel's voice, her heart slammed against her chest.

"Daniel, it's Rebekah. What happened?"

"We hit a patch of ice. Our horse broke free and bolted. Me and the folks are trapped inside my daed's buggy!"

She lifted a trembling hand to still her racing heart. "Is anyone hurt?"

"We're all okay; just can't get out is all."

"What can I do to help?"

"Is Andrew with you?" Clarence Beachy spoke, and he sounded almost desperate.

"No, I'm alone," Rebekah replied in a shaky voice.

"Rebekah Stoltzfus, what are you doing out by yourself in this horrible weather?" Daniel scolded.

"I was heading for your place. I needed to speak with you."

"Could you possibly go for help?" This question came from Daniel's mother, Frieda, whose high-pitched voice gave clear indication that she was quite agitated. "It's cold in here, and I'm uncomfortable in this awkward position."

"I'll turn around and head back home right away."

"Be careful now," Daniel called.

"I will."

"I'll be praying for you."

"I'll be praying for you, too." Rebekah choked on a sob, and after turning her buggy around, she started back down the road. "Please, God," she fervently prayed, "I need You to guide me safely home. The Beachys are in trouble, and I seem to be their only source of help right now."

❧

Sarah had just set a fresh pot of coffee on the table and was about to serve some apple pie to Miriam, Amos, and Henry Hilty, who had stayed on to visit after the other guests had gone home, when Simon entered the kitchen. His face was bright red, and his jacket was covered with snowflakes.

"Where's Rebekah?" Sarah asked. "Is she in the barn?"

Simon shook his head as he flicked some snow off his jacket.

"I hope she's not sitting out on the porch. It's way too cold for her to be outside this evening."

"She's not on the porch."

Andrew, who was getting ready to pour them all a cup of coffee, looked up at their son and frowned. "Do you know where Rebekah is?"

Simon shuffled his feet a few times and stared at the floor. "Jah, but. . .uh. . .I'd rather not say."

A muscle on the side of Andrew's neck quivered as he set the coffeepot down on the table. "What do you mean, you'd rather not say?"

"I. . .uh. . .kind of led her to believe I wouldn't snitch on her."

"Snitch on her?" Sarah moved over to stand beside her son. Their guests sat quietly, but curiosity covered their faces. "What could Rebekah have done that she wouldn't want us to know about?"

Simon kept his focus on the floor and mumbled, "She's headin' over to the Beachy place to see Daniel."

"How could she be heading to Daniel's when we're all here and the horse and buggies are in the shed?" Andrew asked before Sarah had a chance to respond.

Simon lifted his gaze and turned to face his father. "I got one of our easygoing horses out and hitched it to a buggy so—"

"You did what?" Andrew's fist came down hard on the table, clattering his cup, and nearly spilling the pot of coffee. He jumped up and stormed across the room, shaking his finger in Simon's face. "If anything happens to Rebekah, you'll be to blame for it, is that understood?"

Sarah, fighting to keep her tears at bay, left the table and took hold of her husband's arm, hoping to calm him down. "Yelling at Simon won't solve anything, Andrew. What you need to do is go after Rebekah."

Andrew nodded, then pointed to the door. "Simon, run out to the barn and get a horse hitched to one of our other buggies."

"We'll come, too," Amos said as he and Henry both pushed away from the table.

"Should I get Rebekah's wheelchair?" Simon asked. "We left it in the buggy shed."

"I'll see to it," Andrew said.

Mim and Nadine joined Sarah at the window, and they watched as the men headed out into the snow. "It'll be all right," Mim murmured. "We just need to pray."

Sarah nodded, tears filling her eyes. "Prayer is always the best thing."

※

"That was a good church service we had today, jah?" Johnny asked as he took a seat on the sofa next to Mary Ellen.

She smiled and nodded. "To me, they're always good."

"Jah." Johnny took a drink from the cup he held in his hands and smacked his lips. "This is real tasty. Hot cider always hits the spot on a cold winter's night."

"I agree." Mary Ellen reached for her own cup, which she had placed on the low table in front of the sofa. "Are you hungry? Should I fix us something to eat?"

"Might have a piece of apple-crumb pie after I get all the animals fed and bedded down for the night." Johnny glanced out the window. "I see it's started to snow real hard. Looks like we might be in for a storm."

"Oh, I hope not," she said with a sigh. "It's not so easy to get around when the roads are icy."

"That's when it's time to bring out the sleigh." He reached over and patted her knee. "Always did enjoy goin' on a sleigh ride with my best girl."

She smiled and took hold of his hand. "Always have liked riding in one, too."

He wiggled his eyebrows and grinned. "Lots of snow means we can have a snowball fight if we want to."

"Oh, Johnny, you're such a tease."

He lifted her hand to his mouth and kissed each one of her fingers. "And that's what you love about me, right?"

"Jah, that's exactly right."

They sat in companionable silence for a while, drinking their cider and holding hands. Then Johnny set his empty cup on the table and stood. "As much as I hate to leave your good company, I'd best get myself out to the barn. The animals won't feed themselves, that's for sure."

"Okay. I'll have a hunk of pie and another cup of cider waiting when you come back inside."

He grinned down at her. "I'm gonna hold you to that, *fraa*."

When Mary Ellen heard the back door open and click shut, letting her know that Johnny had left the house, she leaned her head against the back of the sofa and closed her eyes. An unexpected vision of Rebekah popped into her mind, and she shivered. Was something wrong with her best friend? Was she in some kind of trouble and in need of prayer?

Heavenly Father, Mary Ellen silently prayed, *I don't know why Rebekah's face has come to mind at this time, but I feel it necessary that I pray for her. Wherever Rebekah is, whatever she's doing, please bless her, guide her, and keep her safe from all harm. Amen.*

The snow fell harder, the chilling wind swirled in a frenzy, and the light of day quickly faded into darkness. With sheer determination and lots of prayer, Rebekah managed to keep the horse and buggy on the road. "Steady, boy," she coaxed. "Together we can do this. We have the Lord on our side." A verse from the Old Testament book of Nahum popped into her mind: "The LORD is good, a strong hold in the day of trouble; and he knoweth them that trust in him."

A sense of peace settled over her like a mantle of calm, and she knew instinctively that everything would be all right.

A short time later, Rebekah pulled up in front of her house. "Dad! Dad, come quickly," she hollered when she spotted him standing on the front porch with Uncle Amos and Cousin Henry. She also noticed that her wheelchair was sitting on the porch.

"Rebekah, we were getting ready to come looking for you. What on earth possessed you to take that buggy out alone?" he bellowed.

"I don't have time to explain things right now!" she cried. "The Beachys' buggy overturned not far from their house, and they're trapped inside. Your help is needed right away!"

"Go get some rope," Dad called to Simon, who was heading for the barn; then he raced over to Rebekah's buggy, jumped in, and gently pushed her into the passenger's seat. "You really should get into the house where it's warmer."

She shook her head with a determined expression. "I want to go along. I need to see with my own eyes that Daniel and his family are okay."

"All right then, but we'll be talkin' about this shenanigan of yours when we return home," he admonished.

Rebekah didn't argue. She knew Dad was right. It was a shenanigan she had pulled, and they needed to talk, even if she was in for a strong tongue-lashing.

Simon came running out of the barn just then. Holding a rope in one hand, he jumped into the backseat of their buggy. Uncle Amos and young Henry climbed into their own buggy.

Dad nodded and moved the horse forward. Uncle Amos's horse and buggy followed.

Rebekah's cheeks burned hot, and her hands shook so badly that she had to clench them in her lap in order to keep them still. "They're going to be all right, aren't they, Dad?"

With eyes straight ahead, he answered, "I hope so. Did they say if any of 'em were hurt?"

"Daniel said they weren't, but it's so cold, and what if a car comes along and doesn't see them there? They might be hit, and then—"

"Now don't you go borrowing trouble," Dad said in a calming voice. "If you want to make yourself useful, then you'd better start praying."

"I have been praying, and I won't let up until everyone's safely out of that buggy."

"Sure wish our other three kinner hadn't gone home so much earlier than we did," Daniel's father said as he tried unsuccessfully to open the door on his side of the buggy. "If we'd all left at the same time, they would have seen our rig tip over and been able to help. As it is, they don't even know we're in this situation."

"I'm sure after a time either Abner, Harold, or Sarah Jane will become worried, and then they'll come looking for us," Daniel's mother said.

Daniel shook his head. "Why would they? None of 'em knew what time we planned on leaving the Stoltzfuses' place. For all they knew, we were planning to hang around there until evening."

"Well, whatever the case, Rebekah's gone for help now, and we should be out of this buggy soon," said Daniel's father.

"I hope Rebekah will be all right," Daniel's mother put in. "It's not good for her to be out alone in this kind of weather."

How well Daniel knew that, and if it were up to him, she never would have taken her father's buggy out in the first place. But then, if she hadn't, how long might it have been before someone spotted their overturned buggy?

"I'm sure Rebekah will be fine," Daniel's father said. "We're all praying for her, so we need to trust God to get her home safely and bring us some help."

Daniel squeezed his eyes shut, remembering that Rebekah had said she'd been heading for his place because she needed to speak with him. He hadn't thought much about it until now, but he wondered what she could have wanted to talk to him about that would cause her to take her father's buggy out in the snow alone. Had she changed her mind about them courting? He prayed it was so—and he prayed God would guide her safely home to get them some help.

CHAPTER 21

Rebekah and her father and brother traveled in silence until they came upon the accident a short time later. "There it is. I see their rig!" Simon shouted.

"I see it, too." Dad pulled his buggy as far off the road as possible, and Uncle Amos did the same with his buggy. "Get out and set up some flares, Simon. They're in my toolbox behind your seat."

Simon did as he was told, and Dad climbed down, reaching for the rope Simon had put in the buggy. He handed the reins over to Rebekah. "Hold the horse steady while I get the rope tied around the Beachy buggy."

Rebekah's hands trembled as she held the reins firmly, and her heart pounded so hard she thought it might explode any minute. *Please let them be all right, Lord.*

She strained to see out the front window. Dad, Uncle Amos, and Henry had tied a rope to the back of the overturned buggy. When it was secured, Dad climbed back inside while Simon joined the other men to help stand the Beachy carriage upright. Uncle Amos, Henry, and Simon put their full weight against the buggy as Dad backed up and pulled on the rope until it was taut. It took several tries because the slippery road made things difficult, but the buggy finally righted itself. The men undid the rope and then tied it to the front of the other buggy.

Rebekah's father drove around until he was in front of the Beachy buggy; then the rope was tied to the back of Dad's buggy. In this manner, he towed the Beachy family safely to their farm.

When they arrived, Dad pulled on his reins and said, "Whoa now, boy!" Uncle Amos, who had been following, stopped his buggy, too.

Everyone got out except for Rebekah, who sat with her nose pressed against the window, waiting to see if Daniel and his parents were really all right. She felt so helpless and wished there was something she might do to assist.

"Your door is surely stuck," Dad called to the Beachys after he pulled on the handle and nothing happened. "Are you all okay?"

"We're fine," Clarence Beachy responded. "We'll push on this side of the door, and you can pull. If it still won't open, then you might want to look for a crowbar in my barn, so you can pry it open."

It took two tries, but the door finally opened, nearly spilling all three of the Beachys onto the snow-covered ground.

"Danki," Clarence said, pounding Rebekah's father on the back.

"We're just glad everyone's all right." Dad glanced over at his own buggy then. "Actually, it's Rebekah who deserves the biggest thanks, for she's the one who found you and drove home to give us the news."

As soon as Daniel's feet touched the ground, he hurried around to Rebekah's side of the buggy and flung open the door. "Rebekah Stoltzfus, I should be furious with you for driving the buggy by yourself—and in the middle of a snowstorm, no less."

"It wasn't snowing so badly when I left home," she said.

Lifting Rebekah into his arms, he held her close. "You're an angel of mercy, and even though you did take a chance doing what you did, I thank you for being so reckless."

"I only did what I had to do."

"You might have saved our lives," he said in a voice raw with emotion. "Who knows what could have happened if some car had come along and hit our rig while it was tipped on its side?"

"I know. That's what I was so worried about."

"What were you doin' out there on the road, anyhow?"

"I was driving over to tell you that if you still want to court me, I'm willing."

"Really? You mean it, Rebekah?"

She nodded. "If you still want to, that is."

Daniel's lips curved into a smile. "Of course I still want to. What happened to change your mind?"

Rebekah opened her mouth to reply, but Daniel's sister and brothers came rushing out of the house just then.

"What happened?" Sarah Jane cried when she caught sight of their mangled buggy.

"Has anyone been hurt?" Abner and Harold hollered at the same time.

"We're all fine, thanks to Rebekah and her family." Mom stepped up beside Daniel and nodded at Rebekah, who was still held securely in his arms. "It's getting colder by the minute, so you'd better bring her inside to warm up awhile before she and her family have to start for home."

"There's some coffee and hot chocolate on the stove," Sarah Jane said. "And I'll get one of my brothers to make a batch of popcorn so everyone can have a little snack before they head out."

"I could definitely use a cup of coffee." Uncle Amos clasped Henry's shoulder and grinned. "And I'm sure my growing son wouldn't turn down an offer to eat popcorn, now would ya, boy?"

Henry snickered and started walking toward the house. Everyone else followed.

"How are your arms holding up?" Rebekah asked, looking up at Daniel. "I'm probably getting kind of heavy."

"To me, you're light as a feather, but I do want to get you in out of this cold." He wondered how it looked to the others to see her being held in his arms in such a familiar way, but she had to get inside somehow, and he wanted to be the one to get her there.

Rebekah leaned her head against Daniel's shoulder, and he enjoyed the feeling as he carried her across the yard, up the steps, and into the house.

Soon, everyone had gathered around the kitchen table, and Mom poured cups of coffee for the men and hot chocolate for the young people. Harold got a batch of popcorn going while Sarah Jane sliced huge pieces of spicy gingerbread for the hungry crew.

Daniel placed Rebekah in one of the empty chairs; then he pulled out the one next to it for himself.

"Well, Rebekah, I would have to say that you're the heroine of the day," Daniel's father said, looking over at her with a grateful smile. "We're mighty thankful that God sent you along to find our overturned buggy when you did."

"My daughter took the horse and buggy out without my permission." Andrew gave Rebekah a brief frown, but then his lips curved into a smile. "Still, she did something meaningful today, and it was all on her own. While it may have been rather foolish, it was a brave thing to do, and I'm grateful she was able to bring help to those of you who were trapped in the buggy."

"Jah, and we truly thank you," Daniel's mother said as she handed Rebekah a cup of hot chocolate.

Rebekah blushed, and Daniel figured she wasn't used to being the center of attention—at least not this way. He knew the recognition she usually got was because of her handicap.

"I was pretty scared when the snow started coming down real hard, making it difficult for me to see," Rebekah said. "I know I shouldn't have been driving the buggy alone, but I thank God for watching over me so I could get you some help."

"And I thank God that you changed your mind about us," Daniel whispered in her ear.

❦

"Shouldn't Rebekah and the menfolk have come back by now?" Nadine asked her mother as the two of them stood by the living-room window, looking out at snow that seemed to be coming down harder all the time. "I'm gettin' kind of worried."

Mom draped her arm across Nadine's shoulder and gave it a gentle squeeze. "I'm sure they'll be all right. We just need to pray."

"That's right," Aunt Mim chimed in from across the room, where she sat in the rocker holding a cup of tea.

"I wish Rebekah had thought to ask me to go with her when she went after Daniel in the first place." Nadine swallowed around the lump in her throat. "But then I guess she wouldn't have wanted her little sister taggin' along when she was going to see her boyfriend. Especially since the two of us haven't seen eye to eye on much of anything lately."

Mom offered Nadine a sympathetic look. "Why do you think that is, daughter?"

"I—I suppose it's my fault because I'm always accusing her of being a *verdarewe* child."

"Is that what you really believe, Nadine—that your sister is a spoiled child?"

Tears welled in Nadine's eyes, blurring her vision, as she nodded.

"I've tried to explain things to you many times before," Mom said, taking hold of Nadine's shoulders and turning her around so she could look directly at her. "But you still refuse to understand that Rebekah is not our favorite child, nor do we intentionally spoil her."

Nadine opened her mouth to comment, but Mom rushed over to the front door and pulled it open. She stepped onto the porch, grabbed the handles of Rebekah's wheelchair, and pushed it into the living room. "Have you ever tried to put yourself in your sister's place, imagining what it would be like to be stuck in this chair, unable to walk normally or do all the fun things you're able to do?"

Nadine shook her head.

Mom grabbed a blanket off the sofa and threw it over the wheelchair, which Nadine knew must be cold from setting outside all this time. "Have a seat, Nadine."

"Huh?"

"I said have a seat."

Nadine hesitated a moment but finally did as Mom asked. "Now what?"

"I want you to pretend that you can't use your legs and that you're stuck in that chair. Imagine that a group of young people are having a skating party on one of the frozen ponds in the area, and you want to go with them. Would you be able to go ice-skating from your wheelchair?"

Nadine shook her head.

"And how about if I asked you to go into the kitchen and get the jar of cookies sitting on top of the refrigerator? Could you do it?"

"No, Mom."

"Now do you understand a little of what your sister goes through?"

"I—I think I do."

"Would you like to be in her place, unable to do so many things that you take for granted?"

"No, I wouldn't like it at all." Nadine's voice faltered, and she drew in a shaky breath. "I guess if I had to pick between gettin' more attention and bein' able to do everything I can do,

I'd choose bein' me."

"I'm glad to hear it." Mom smiled. "So do you think you can try a little harder to get along with Rebekah?"

"I guess it's my fault that Rebekah gets so annoyed. If I was a better sister, she might not get so exasperated with me." Nadine released a little sob. "If somethin' bad happens out there in the storm, I'll never forgive myself for not makin' things right with her before it was too late."

Aunt Mim stepped up to the window then, and motioned Nadine to join her.

Nadine looked to her mother for approval, and when Mom nodded, Nadine left the wheelchair and went to stand beside her aunt.

Aunt Mim slipped her arm around Nadine's waist. "Did Rebekah ever tell you that I used to blame myself for her handicap?"

Nadine's mouth dropped open. "How come?"

"Because I allowed her to wait outside for me while I cleaned up the schoolhouse. If I'd made Rebekah stay inside with me, she wouldn't have been standing beneath that tree branch when it broke."

"But you had no way of knowin' the branch would break and fall on Rebekah. It's not right that you should have blamed yourself for something that was nothing more than an accident."

"You're right about that, and I finally came to the same conclusion." Aunt Mim gave Nadine's waist a gentle squeeze. "I'm sure Rebekah and the others will be fine, but it will do you no good to blame yourself for not making things right with her before she left. The important thing now is for us all to pray, and when Rebekah gets back home, you need to talk things out between you."

Nadine nodded. "I know."

"Both of you need to show more patience and understanding with one another, but blaming yourself, or even your sister, will do neither of you any good at all."

"Guess I need to ask God to help me be a better sister," Nadine said tearfully. "Jah, with His help, I'll do my best."

All the way home from the Beachys' place, Rebekah thought about Daniel and how she had agreed to let him court her. She was pleased that he was still willing, but she had a few misgivings yet. Would they find enough things to do together—things that Rebekah was capable of doing? Would Daniel eventually become bored with her and find someone else to court? And what if he wanted something she couldn't give him—marriage and children?

Psalm 34:4, which she had committed to memory, popped into her mind: "I sought the LORD, and he heard me, and delivered me from all my fears." Then she thought of Psalm 37:5: "Commit thy way unto the LORD; trust also in him: and he shall bring it to pass." She'd found that passage in Grandma's Bible and had quoted it often as a reminder that she should trust the Lord in all things, while she committed her way unto Him.

She leaned her head against the seat and closed her eyes, resolving to have more faith and allow God to work things out between her and Daniel.

Winter had definitely come to Lancaster County, as the thick blanket of pristine snow lying on the ground proved. All the trees were dressed in gleaming white gowns, and every pond in the area was frozen solid. Many Amish families exchanged their buggies for sleighs in order to accommodate the dangerously slick roads.

Rebekah loved riding in an open sleigh, especially when it was with Daniel. At least that was something she could do, since she sure couldn't join the other young people in their area who had gone sledding and ice-skating a few times already. Now that she and Daniel were courting and had found some things they could do together, she didn't feel so left out and didn't miss many of the things others her age were able to do that she couldn't.

In spite of the wintry weather, Daniel and Rebekah had managed to go to several more singings, and Daniel called on Rebekah at her home as often as he could. They played board games, worked on puzzles, or just sat by the fire eating popcorn, drinking hot chocolate, and talking for hours on end.

Sometimes in the late afternoons, Daniel would come over to the greenhouse with his sister, Sarah Jane, who had taken over the job as schoolteacher right after Mary Ellen had gotten married. The three of them would repot plants, take cuttings off larger ones, or start flowers from seeds.

Rebekah and Daniel seemed to be drawing closer, and she had gotten to know Sarah Jane better, too. She was tempted to write something in her column for *The Budget* about the times she spent with Daniel, but she didn't feel it would be appropriate. The readers wanted to know about significant events such as births, deaths, and birthday celebrations, as well as community events, visitors from other states, hospitalizations, accidents, illnesses, and weather conditions.

One evening in late February, Daniel stopped by Rebekah's house for a visit. Everyone else in her family had already gone to bed, so he and Rebekah sat in the kitchen, looking through a stack of nursery catalogs that had recently come in the mail and discussing what she might order for her greenhouse in the months ahead.

After they'd been sitting there awhile, Rebekah looked up from her studies and saw Daniel looking intently at her. "What's wrong?" she asked. "You're looking so thoughtful all of a sudden."

"Nothing's wrong. I was just thinking how lucky I am to have you as *mei aldi*," he answered with a smile. "My girlfriend," he repeated. "You're so kind and sweet."

"Me, sweet?" She averted her gaze as heat flooded her face. "I never thought anyone would think of me as sweet."

Daniel reached out and took hold of her hand, sending a warm sensation traveling all the way up her arm. "Why not? You have a most generous spirit, and your expression is always so sincere. I find everything about you to my liking, Rebekah."

"Even my stiff, crippled legs?" She hated to spoil the moment by bringing up her disability, but she felt the question needed to be asked.

"Your legs only serve to remind me that you haven't

allowed your handicap to stop you from doin' good things with your life." Daniel stroked the back of her hand gently with his thumb. The light of the lantern hanging above the table lit his dark eyes. "I want to spend the rest of my days with you, Rebekah," he whispered. "I want you to be my wife."

Rebekah stared at the table, thinking she must have misunderstood what he'd said and wondering if he might have been joking.

Daniel lifted her chin, so she was looking directly at him. Such a serious expression she saw on his face. It let her know that she hadn't misunderstood, and she felt sure he wasn't joking. "Would ya be interested in marryin' me come fall?"

Rebekah felt like all the air had been squeezed out of her lungs—like when she was little and had taken a tumble from the hayloft. She had known she and Daniel were getting closer, but a proposal was the last thing she'd expected to hear tonight.

When she opened her mouth to reply, nothing came out but a little squeak.

"So what's your answer?" Daniel prompted. "Will you agree to be my wife?"

Tears sprang to Rebekah's eyes, clouding her vision and stinging her nose. She had never known such joy before Daniel came along. He made her feel whole and alive—so much so that she couldn't think clearly when he was looking at her in such a sweet way. Maybe that was the reason she was able to find her voice and didn't hesitate to answer, "Jah, Daniel, I would be honored to be your wife."

Daniel leaned his face close to hers until their lips nearly touched. Rebekah closed her eyes and waited expectantly for the kiss she felt was forthcoming. She had never been kissed by a man before. Not in the real sense of the word, anyway. Hugs and quick pecks on the cheeks didn't count, and those had only come from family and close friends.

The gentle kiss Daniel placed on her lips didn't last long, but it took Rebekah's breath away. When Daniel pulled back a few seconds later he was grinning from ear to ear. Rebekah suppressed a giggle, and without a word, she picked up the seed catalog they had been looking at. Except for the gentle hissing of the gas lantern above the table, all was quiet, and Rebekah felt more at peace than she'd ever thought possible.

CHAPTER

22

Winter melted into spring, and spring blossomed into summer. Everyone's life was busy as usual, and the new season was full of changes. Aunt Grace had given birth to a baby boy toward the end of March. About the same time, Mary Ellen announced that she, too, was expecting a baby, due in November.

Rebekah was happy for her cousin, but hearing the news put an ache in her heart for a child of her own. It also caused her to have second thoughts about whether marriage for her was such a good idea. What if she didn't make Daniel happy? What if she could never conceive? What if she got pregnant but couldn't take care of their baby? She determined to keep those nagging doubts hidden from Daniel, who seemed to be anxiously awaiting their wedding day set to occur on the third Thursday of November.

"How would you two young women like to drive over to Lewis and Grace's place with me later this morning?" Mom asked as Rebekah and Nadine helped to clean up the kitchen after breakfast.

"I'd like to go," Nadine said in an excited tone. "Last

Sunday after church was over, Uncle Lewis told me that one of his rabbits had given birth to ten little *haaslin*. It will give me a chance to see 'em."

Mom clicked her tongue. "We're not going over to see the baby bunnies, Nadine. We'll be making the trip to see Aunt Grace and Uncle Lewis's growing boppli." She smiled. "Wouldn't you like to spend some time holding your little second cousin?"

Nadine wrinkled her nose. "I'd much rather hold a *haasli*. At least they don't wet their *windles* and spit up all over the place."

Rebekah, who had been drying the dishes, spoke up for the first time. "Baby bunnies may not spit up on you, but since they don't have the protection of a diaper, they can sure make a mess."

"Jah, well," Nadine said, grabbing a broom from the closet, "I'll take my chances holding a haasli any old time."

As Rebekah sat in Grace's living room, with baby Timothy nestled in her arms, her eyes stung with tears. He was such a beautiful baby—dark hair, like his mother's, and a turned up nose like his father's.

If Daniel and I could have children, I wonder what they would look like. Would their hair be light brown like mine or dark like Daniel's? Would their eyes be blue, brown, or a mixture of the two?

"Would you like to hold the boppli for a while?" Aunt Grace asked, looking over at Nadine, who sat next to their mother on the sofa.

"I don't think so. He might spit up on me or somethin'."

"I have a burp cloth you can drape over your shoulder."

"He's a bundle of sweetness," Rebekah said, smiling down at the baby.

Nadine shook her head. "No, thanks." Then she looked over at Mom and said, "Can I go out to the barn to see the haaslin now?"

"I suppose if you don't get to hold one of those bunnies today, we'll have to hear about it all the way home."

"Danki, Mom." Nadine stood and rushed out the door.

Aunt Grace smiled at Rebekah. "How are things with you these days?"

Rebekah shifted the baby from her lap up to her shoulder. "Okay."

"Things are going well in Rebekah's greenhouse," Mom spoke up. "Word of mouth and a few newspaper ads have helped her business, and she's getting more customers all the time."

"That's good to hear."

"As I'm sure you know, she and Daniel will be getting married this fall, so Rebekah has a lot to do between now and then to get her dress made and do everything she wants done before the wedding."

"I can imagine how excited you must be, Rebekah," Aunt Grace said. "I remember when Lewis and I were betrothed—I was just counting the days until we got married."

Rebekah nodded as a rush of heat covered her face and neck. "I am excited," she admitted. "And a whole lot *naerfich*, too."

"There's no reason to be nervous," Aunt Grace said with a wave of her hand. "It'll all be over with sooner than you thought, and then you'll settle into the routine of being a hausfraa and probably a *mudder* soon after that."

"I'm not so sure about me being a mother," Rebekah mumbled. "The doctor said I may never be able to have any bopplin."

"Doctors have been known to be wrong," Mom interjected. "After they said you'd always be in a wheelchair and would probably never be able to stand on your legs, who'd have guessed that you could walk again?"

"Walk?" Rebekah looked down at her crippled legs and frowned. "What I'm able to do with those rigid leg braces and crutches isn't really walking, Mom."

"It's more than we could have hoped for, and it does get you out of that wheelchair for a time."

Rebekah shrugged. Walking with the leg braces was a chore, but rather than say anything, she thought it best to keep her opinion to herself. "Is it okay if I write something about little Timothy in my next article for *The Budget*?" she asked her aunt.

"Jah, sure. That'd be real nice."

The three women sat awhile. Mom and Aunt Grace sipped from their glasses of iced tea, and Rebekah snuggled the baby in her arms. The warmth of his soft skin and his sweet baby smell made her long all the more for a boppli of her own.

❧

It was already mid-August, which left only three short months until the wedding, and Rebekah knew if she didn't do something about her doubts and apprehensions soon, she might not be able to go through with her marriage to Daniel. She still loved him—probably more with each passing day. However, fear of the unknown was paralyzing her soul, causing more discomfort than the partial paralysis of her lower body.

What's wrong with me? Rebekah silently moaned as she sat in her wheelchair, repotting a spider plant that had grown too large for its container. *I thought I had all this settled in my mind. I believed I could take the step of faith necessary for love and marriage. When I agreed to marry Daniel, I thought it was God's will. I'd decided that He had brought the two of us together, yet now I'm not so sure.*

She patted some fresh potting soil around the roots of the plant, feeling downright jittery inside. "I need to stay busy, that's all. If I keep my mind occupied, I won't have time for second thoughts."

Rebekah's self-talk was cut short when a customer rang the bell and entered the greenhouse. She wheeled herself out to the front section of the building and was greeted by Johnny Yoder. As a married man, he now sported a full beard, and for the first time since they had become adults, she thought he actually looked mature.

"Guder mariye," she said.

"Good morning, Rebekah." Johnny took off his straw hat and wiped his forehead with the back of his hand. "Ach, my! It's hot out there. Only ten o'clock and already it's over eighty degrees."

Rebekah nodded. "Another hot and humid summer, that's for sure."

"I think the only critters who like this kind of weather

are the lightning bugs," Johnny said with a deep chuckle.

Rebekah nodded and smiled. "So what brings you here today?"

"I thought I'd get a nice plant for Mary Ellen. It might make her feel better."

"She's still not feeling well?"

"It's that awful morning sickness. Doc Manney says it should go away soon, but she's already in her sixth month, and still she fights it." Johnny shook his head. "Her back hurts somethin' awful, too, and the poor thing can't stand or sit long, neither."

Rebekah clicked her tongue. "That must be hard. I'll try to get over and see her soon."

Johnny nodded "You're Mary Ellen's best friend, and I'm sure a visit would do her some good."

"What kind of plant did you have in mind?" Rebekah asked, bringing the subject back to the reason for Johnny's visit. "Something for the flower garden or an indoor plant?"

He scratched the back of his head and squinted. "I'm not sure. Maybe something for the porch. Mary Ellen spends a lot of time outdoors in the shade there, since it's been so hot inside."

Rebekah smiled. Johnny did seem to care about Mary Ellen's needs. She was glad he had made her cousin so happy. "Let's go on back to where my plants are kept. I think I have a nice pot of mixed pansies she might like."

Johnny followed as she rolled into the other room, and a short time later, he was at the cash register, paying for a large pot of yellow, white, and purple pansies. As he opened the front door, he nearly bumped into Daniel, who was just coming into the greenhouse.

"That's a beautiful bunch of pansies you've got there," Daniel said, as he hung his straw hat on one of the wooden wall pegs near the door.

"Jah, and they're for a beautiful wife!" Johnny waved and was gone before Daniel could open his mouth to respond.

"Marriage seems to agree with him," Daniel said, smiling at Rebekah. "I think he's excited about becoming a daed, too."

Rebekah nodded but made no comment.

Daniel knelt next to her wheelchair and reached out to take both of her hands. "Is something wrong? You look kind of down in the mouth this morning."

Rebekah was about to reply when the doorbell rang again. Two English couples entered the greenhouse. "I've got to wait on those people," she whispered to Daniel, then wheeled away.

"May I help you with something?" she asked the two young couples who stood looking around the room.

"We were wondering if you might sell anything cold to drink," one of the women said. "It's so hot out today, and we're all thirsty."

Rebekah shook her head. "I don't sell any beverages, but I do have some cold water in the back room." She looked over at Daniel. "Would you mind getting the pitcher, along with some paper cups?"

"Sure, I can do that," he responded with a nod.

The group of English looked grateful and offered their thanks when Daniel reappeared a few minutes later with a pitcher of water and some paper cups.

"What do you sell here?" one of the young men asked Rebekah.

"Plants, flowers, and all garden-related items." Rebekah had to wonder why these people didn't know what things were sold in a greenhouse. They were obviously city folk.

"You could probably triple your profits if you sold some food and beverages, especially during the hot summer months," the other man said.

"Maybe so."

The tourists finished their water, then turned to leave. They were about to exit the building when one of the women spotted a wooden whirligig shaped like a windmill. "Look at this, Bill. Isn't it cute? I'd like to have it for our backyard."

The man reached into his pants pocket and handed his wallet to her. "Here, help yourself." He grinned, then turned to Rebekah. "We're newlyweds, and I can't seem to say no."

Rebekah just rolled her wheelchair over to the cash register.

"This is so nice," the woman said. "You should offer more handmade items for sale. Almost anything made by you Amish would probably sell well."

Rebekah smiled and muttered her thanks.

As soon as the customers left, Daniel moved over to stand beside her. "Those English tourists might have a good point about you sellin' more things in here."

Rebekah wrinkled her nose. "It wouldn't be much of a greenhouse if I sold all sorts of trinkets and souvenirs just to please the tourists."

"It would still be a greenhouse, Rebekah. It would simply have a few added items for sale, is all." His brown eyes fairly sparkled. "I sure can't wait until we're married. Then we'll finally be business partners. Why, I have all sorts of new ideas I'd like to put into practice here."

Rebekah felt like a jolt of lightning had shot through her. Was that all Daniel wanted—a business partner? Had he proposed marriage so he could become part owner of Grandma's Place?

"And what if there is no partnership, Daniel?" she asked pointedly.

He squinted. "No partnership? What do you mean? Two heads are better than one, ya know."

"That may be true, but what if I change my mind, and we don't get married after all?" The words seemed to jump right off her tongue, but there was no taking them back now.

"You're teasin' me, aren't you?"

She shook her head. "Here of late, I've been having some serious doubts about marriage, and what you just said only confirms my thinking."

"What? You can't mean that." Daniel bent down and took hold of her shoulders. "Please say you don't mean it."

She swallowed past the lump in her throat. "I—I do mean it. I'm thinking maybe you only want me for this business. Could be that the greenhouse is the only reason you ever showed any interest in me at all."

"Jumpin' frogs, Rebekah, I never thought anything of the kind! I care about you. Surely you can see that."

She bit her bottom lip so hard she tasted blood. "I'm not sure what I see anymore, but I know one thing—I can't be a normal wife, and I'm pretty sure I can't have babies. I also know that—"

Daniel stopped her rush of words by placing his finger against her lips. "Please don't say those things. We've talked about this stuff before—all except me wanting to be your business partner more than your marriage partner. I do want to be your business partner; I won't deny that, Rebekah. I've wanted it for a long time, but—"

Rebekah jerked her wheelchair to one side, cutting him off in midsentence. "I've heard enough, so please don't say anything more. It's over between us, and it's best that you go home and forget you ever knew me."

Daniel's face was red as a cherry. "Can't I have my say on this?"

She shook her head vigorously. "There's already been too much said. I should have never let things go this far. My answer to your proposal should have been *no* from the beginning."

Daniel shuffled his feet a few times, then jerked his straw hat off the wall peg and marched out the door.

CHAPTER 23

"Nadine and I have to go into town today. Would you like to go along?" Mom asked Rebekah the following morning as they prepared breakfast. "We're going to eat out afterward, so that might help lift your spirits."

"I don't need anything in town right now, but I would appreciate a ride over to Mary Ellen's," Rebekah answered, making no reference to her spirits. She'd already broken the news to her family about Daniel and her not getting married, and it was bad enough just doing the telling. No use sulking about it or trying to make herself feel better with food from the Plain and Fancy or some other restaurant. Rebekah figured the best thing she could do was go calling on her friend. "Get your eyes off your own problem, and help someone else with theirs"—that's what Grandma Stoltzfus often used to say.

"Taking you by Mary Ellen's won't be a problem because we're only going into Bird-in-Hand today, and it's right on the way," Mom said, cutting into Rebekah's thoughts. "Are you sure you wouldn't rather go with us? You can always visit your cousin some other time."

Rebekah shook her head. "Mary Ellen's not feeling well. I think a visit with her is more important than shopping or going out to lunch."

"What's wrong with Mary Ellen?" Nadine asked when she entered the kitchen.

"She's still having some morning sickness, and Johnny said that her back's hurting, too," Rebekah answered.

Nadine wrinkled her nose. "I think bein' pregnant must be the worst thing any woman could ever go through. I'm not gonna have any children when I get married."

Mom smiled and gave Rebekah a knowing look. "When you do get married, Nadine, children will come in God's time, not yours. And God will give you the strength to get through it, too."

"Jah, well, maybe I won't get married, then." Nadine folded her arms and frowned.

Rebekah smiled, even though her heart ached like crazy over her breakup with Daniel. "You? My boy-crazy little sister, not ever get married? That's about as silly a notion as thinking the robins won't come back in the spring."

"Don't make fun of me," Nadine mumbled. "I don't like to be laughed at."

Rebekah sobered. "I'm sorry, sister. No one likes to be laughed at. I should know that better than anyone."

Nadine moved over to the table where Rebekah sat buttering a stack of toast. "I'd never laugh at you, Rebekah. I admire you too much."

Rebekah looked up at Nadine with tears obscuring her vision. "You do?" Things had been better between her and Nadine of late, but she'd never expected her sister to say something like that.

"Of course. You've done so much with your life. Running a business of your own is something to feel good about."

"Nadine's right," Mom put in from her place at the stove. "If anyone should ever laugh at you, then they truly don't know you at all."

Rebekah's mind pulled her back to that day at the market when the two English boys had taunted her. They'd laughed in her face and made fun of her, not caring in the least how she felt. Those fellows hadn't known her. She hadn't really known herself until she'd begun to search the scriptures for answers and had taken a huge leap of faith by opening the greenhouse.

Rebekah had never mentioned that incident at the market to her folks, nor was she willing to admit to them that breaking her engagement to Daniel had nearly broken her heart. Despite them encouraging her to reconsider, she was convinced that she had made the right decision. With God's help, she hoped to get through this horrible letdown and move on with her life—without Daniel.

She added another piece of toast to the plate she'd already started and said, "We'd better finish getting breakfast ready and call Dad and Simon in to eat. I'm anxious to see Mary Ellen."

"It's sure nice to have you back workin' full-time with the cows," Daniel's father said as the two of them mucked out the horses' stalls. "For a while there, I was afraid I'd lost you to Rebekah's greenhouse since that's where you seemed to be spending all of your free time."

Daniel grimaced. Just the mention of Rebekah's name sent a pang of regret coursing through his body. If only she hadn't broken their engagement. If only she'd let him explain how things were.

"You okay, son? You're lookin' kind of peevish today. Aren't ya feelin' to rights?"

"I'm okay, Pop. Just feelin' a bit down and wishin' some things could be different is all."

Pop stopped scooping and set his shovel aside. "What's the trouble?"

Daniel leaned against the wall with his arms folded and his shovel wedged between his knees. "I can't accept Rebekah's decision not to marry me. We've been so happy together these past few months, and it makes no sense that she would call off the wedding now and wouldn't even let me have my say on things."

Pop scrubbed a hand down the side of his bearded face and squinted. "Maybe it's for the best, Daniel."

"How can you say that?" Daniel felt his defenses rise. Didn't Pop care how much he was hurting? Didn't his daed realize how much he loved Rebekah?

"Think about it, now. Rebekah's pretty much stuck in that wheelchair of hers, and her handicap could make for a difficult marriage."

Daniel shook his head. "No way! I know Rebekah has limitations, but I'm willing to do more than my share of the work in the greenhouse and around our home, too."

"That may be true, but what about kinner? Do you even

know if Rebekah's able to have any bopplin?"

"Well, no, but—"

"And even if she could get pregnant, how would she care for a baby when she can barely take care of herself?"

Daniel stared at the floor as he contemplated his father's words. Maybe Pop was right. Maybe Rebekah couldn't have any kinner, and maybe it would be difficult for both of them if they were to get married. Still, the thought of spending the rest of his days without the woman he loved by his side left Daniel feeling as if life had no meaning at all.

"I don't have any answers, Pop," he finally said, "but I do know that I love Rebekah with all my heart, and if we were to get married, I would do everything in my power to make her happy."

Pop thumped him lightly on the back. "Well then, be a man, boy! If ya love the girl, you'd better go after her."

"It's not that easy," Daniel mumbled. "Rebekah's made up her mind that I only want to marry her so I can get my hands on her business. I don't think I can say anything to make her think otherwise, either."

"Hmm. . .guess you'd best be prayin' about the matter."

"I have been prayin', and I've decided that if God wants Rebekah and me to be together, then He'll have to pave the way." Determined to get his mind off Rebekah and the void she had left in his soul when she'd called off the wedding, Daniel grabbed the shovel from between his knees and resumed his work.

Mary Ellen and Johnny's home was set on the back side of

Uncle Amos and Aunt Mim's property. It had been built by both of their fathers and was a two-story house with white siding and a long porch wrapped halfway around the building. Johnny had hung a two-seater swing under the overhang of the porch, and it was there that Rebekah discovered Mary Ellen. She held a glass of iced tea in one hand and was swinging back and forth, with her head leaning against the wooden slats.

After helping Rebekah down from the buggy and making sure she was secure in her wheelchair, Mom climbed back into the driver's seat. "If you see Mim, tell her I'll be over for a visit one of these days soon," she called before pulling out of the driveway.

"Jah, okay." Rebekah waved and propelled herself up the wheelchair ramp.

Mary Ellen smiled. "What a nice surprise. I'm so glad to see you today."

"Johnny was by the greenhouse yesterday and said you were still feeling poorly. I thought maybe a little visit might do us both some good."

"Johnny and Pappy are out in his shop. Pappy's getting way more work than he can handle these days, and Henry's help just isn't enough." Mary Ellen motioned toward the blacksmith shop on the other side of their property. "So Johnny helps him when he's not busy farming with his daed."

"Ah, I see."

"Would you like me to call Mama Mim and see if she can help you into the swing?"

"That's not necessary." Rebekah eyed Mary Ellen's protruding stomach. "You're getting kind of big around the middle these days. I think maybe you might need the swing all to yourself."

Mary Ellen grimaced. "Do I look that big?"

"Jah, just like one of Dad's draft horses!" Rebekah giggled. "But you're still as pretty as ever. I think being in a family way becomes you. You look almost radiant, in fact."

"My radiance comes from being much too warm, I'm afraid," Mary Ellen said, as she held the glass up to her flushed cheeks. "This late summer weather's sure getting to me, and my back—oh, it hurts something awful!"

"Johnny said you're still fighting the morning sickness, too."

Mary Ellen nodded. "It comes and goes, but when it comes, it can get pretty bad."

"Are you drinking plenty of peppermint tea to help with the nausea?"

In response, Mary Ellen lifted her glass. "Several glasses a day."

"Then all you can do is pray that the sickness goes away soon."

Mary Ellen sighed. "I hope the boppli comes in plenty of time before your wedding. I wouldn't want to miss that big occasion."

Now it was Rebekah's turn to sigh. "There will be no wedding; I called the whole thing off."

"You what?" Mary Ellen's raised eyebrows showed her obvious disbelief, and her mouth hung slightly open.

"I told Daniel we weren't getting married." Rebekah's vision blurred with unshed tears, and she looked away, hoping Mary Ellen wouldn't notice.

"You didn't really say that, did you?"

"Jah, I did. I was beginning to have some doubts as to whether I could be a good wife to Daniel anyway."

"Because of your concerns about whether you can ever conceive?"

Rebekah nodded in reply.

"What does the doctor say?"

"He doesn't really know. He said that in some cases of spinal cord injury, a woman can never conceive, but—well, some have actually been able to get pregnant and carry the baby to term."

"You might be one of those women." Mary Ellen tapped her fingernails against the side of her glass, making a clicking sound. "That's surely no reason for calling off the wedding."

Rebekah's forehead knitted into a frown. "Oh, Mary Ellen, I do so want to be a wife and mother. God's already given me one miracle, so I don't know if I dare ask for yet another."

"Of course you can ask. The Bible tells us in Luke 11:9: 'Ask, and it shall be given you; seek, and ye shall find; knock, and it shall be opened unto you.' Our heavenly Father wants to give us good things."

Rebekah sniffed. "Sometimes I think I'm not deserving of the things God gives to others."

"You are so," Mary Ellen said in an earnest tone. "All God's children are deserving of His love. He doesn't always give us everything we ask for, but He does give us what He knows is best for us."

"My own capabilities aren't the only problem," Rebekah finally admitted.

Mary Ellen tipped her head. "What else is there?"

"It's Daniel."

"Daniel? How could Daniel be the problem? He's so much in love with you that it's downright sickening."

"I thought so, too—until yesterday."

"What happened yesterday?"

Rebekah quickly related her and Daniel's conversation about him wanting to be her business partner and the fact that she was certain it was the only reason he wanted to marry her.

"I hope he set you straight on that one," Mary Ellen said.

"He tried to deny it, but in the process, he admitted to wanting the greenhouse real bad. That fact alone is unsettling to me."

"Sometimes we draw the wrong conclusions because we want to."

"What are you saying? Do you actually think I want to believe such things about Daniel?" Rebekah's voice raised at least an octave, and her cheeks felt flushed.

Mary Ellen shifted on the swing as she held up her hand. "Please, don't get defensive on me. I only meant that since you were already having some doubts about being a wife, maybe Daniel's comment was misunderstood. Maybe you were looking for a way out of what you felt wouldn't work."

"Now, listen, Mary Ellen—"

"Wie geht's, Rebekah?" Aunt Mim asked as she stepped up to the porch.

"I–I'm fine, danki."

"It didn't sound to me as if you were all that fine. You sounded pretty upset about something a moment ago."

"Rebekah thinks Daniel only wants to marry her so he can become her partner at the greenhouse," Mary Ellen was quick to say.

Rebekah nodded. "It's true. He sweet-talked me for months just so he could get his hands on my business."

"Do you have time to hear another one of my little stories?" Aunt Mim asked, squeezing in beside Mary Ellen on the swing. "I think it might give you some insight on a few things concerning you and Daniel."

"I guess so. I'll be here until Mom picks me up later this afternoon." Rebekah moved her wheelchair closer to the swing, ready to hear her aunt's story, although she couldn't imagine what it would have to do with her and Daniel. "By the way, Mom says she'll drop over for a visit sometime soon."

Aunt Mim nodded, then began her story. "A long time ago, when Miriam Hilty was still Miriam Stoltzfus, she thought that a certain Amos Hilty wanted to marry her for reasons other than love."

"Really? I never knew that, Mama Mim," Mary Ellen said with wide eyes. "What other reasons might Pappy have had?"

Aunt Mim patted Mary Ellen's hand. "Well, I thought your daed only wanted a mudder for his little girl." She shrugged. "I figured he probably wanted someone to do all his cooking and cleaning, too. It wasn't until well after our marriage that I finally woke up and realized that Amos cared deeply for me. What he really wanted all along was a companion and helpmate."

Aunt Mim motioned to Rebekah. "I've observed you and Daniel plenty of times, and I daresay he loves you very much. While it might be true that Daniel desires a partnership in your business, I'm convinced that he wants you as his wife even more."

Rebekah nibbled on her bottom lip. "I do appreciate your sharing another story with me. Only thing is, it doesn't change anything where Daniel and I are concerned."

"Why not? It seems a shame for you to give up on love and marriage, dear girl," Aunt Mim said, shaking her head.

"Daniel doesn't love me. He never even said he did, for pity's sake!"

Mary Ellen's eyebrows raised high on her forehead. "You're kidding, right?"

Rebekah shook her head. "Nope, and he only wants my business. I know it, sure as anything—and we're not getting married."

Chapter

24

Rebekah moved restlessly about the kitchen on her crutches. She felt so fretful and fidgety this morning. She stopped pacing a few moments, and when she glanced out the window, she spotted a sparrow eating from one of Daniel's handcrafted feeders. *Oh, Daniel, why'd you have to go and break my heart? Didn't you know how much I loved you? I was so hoping things would work out between us.*

It had been two weeks since their breakup, and the pain was no less hurtful now than it had been on that terrible day when she'd discovered that her intended had only been using her to acquire a business selling flowers. Seeing Daniel at the preaching service last week hadn't helped any, either.

Rebekah thought, maybe even hoped, that he might try to win her back. She squinted and then blinked a couple of times so the tears wouldn't give way. *Not that I'd ever consider taking him back.* No, she was through with men and all their sweet-talking, conniving ways. God had given her a business to run, and this summer it had done real well for her. If things kept going as they had been, she would be self-supporting in no time. That was the miracle she had been waiting for, wasn't it?

She trembled slightly as she thought about Daniel sitting across the room from her during church. He hadn't even looked her way, let alone said anything to her after the noon meal. It just proved what she had known as a fact—Daniel didn't love her now, and he never had.

Rebekah leaned her full weight against the windowsill. "God takes care of the little bitty birds, so He will most assuredly take care of you"—Grandma's words tumbled around in her mind like the clothes in Mom's old wringer washer on laundry day.

"I think what I need is a breath of fresh air," Rebekah said aloud, though no one was in the kitchen to hear but her. Mom had gone outside to hang some freshly laundered clothes, Nadine was in the barn playing with a batch of new kittens, and the menfolk were out working in the fields.

Rebekah thought about casting off her leg braces and taking the wheelchair outside, but it was such a job to get them unhooked. Besides, as Mom always said, "The exercise will do your whole body some good."

With the crutches fastened securely to her arms by leather straps, Rebekah grabbed a light shawl from a wall peg and headed out the back door.

Mom seemed to be struggling with a sheet the wind had caught in the clothesline, and she didn't notice when Rebekah plodded past her and down the path toward the creek.

A definite nip was in the air this morning, and Rebekah knew fall would be coming soon. Autumn. The time for most Amish weddings here in Lancaster County. Her own wedding was supposed to be in November. If only. . .

She shoved the familiar ache aside once again and attempted to pick up her speed just a bit. Walking stiff-legged was such a chore, and she was beginning to wonder if she had made a mistake by leaving the wheelchair parked in the kitchen. Already she was huffing and puffing, and she was only halfway there. At this rate, how was she ever going to make it all the way to the creek?

" 'I can do all things through Christ which strengtheneth me,' " she quoted from the scriptures. If she could just go another fifty yards or so, she would be at the water's edge and could hopefully find a log or something to sit on. Trips to the creek in the past had always been made in her wheelchair, which meant finding a place to sit and rest had never been a problem.

Rebekah lifted one foot, then the other, guiding herself along with the aid of her metal crutches. She could hear the water gurgling over the rocky creek bottom. The melodic sound soothed her nerves and gave her the added incentive to keep walking.

Soon, the rushing water came into view, meandering gracefully through a cluster of red maple and white birch trees. Rebekah scanned the banks, looking for something to use as a bench. She felt a spasm in her back, and the muscles in her arms had become tight. Even her legs, which normally had little feeling in them, felt kind of tingly and prickly-like.

With great relief, she spotted a fallen tree, its branches stretched partway across the water and the trunk lying on dry land. A few more determined steps, and she was there. Drawing in a deep breath for added strength, Rebekah lowered herself to the stump. The bumpy surface offered little comfort for her backside, but at least she was sitting and could finally catch her breath. Even her hands trembled, she noticed.

The trek from the house had nearly been too much. Oh, how she wished she had told someone where she was going. What if she couldn't make it back to the house on her own strength? The way she felt right now, she wasn't sure she could even stand up again.

"What a dunce I was for thinking I could be so independent and go traipsing on down here without my wheelchair," Rebekah chided herself. "It was just plain *kischblich* of me. I should know better than to be so silly." She wrapped her shawl tighter around her shoulders and shivered—not so much from the chilly morning, but from all her energy being used up.

The rustle of fallen leaves caught Rebekah's attention. She glanced to the right and saw Brownie, their mixed-breed farm dog, running for all he was worth. Out in front of him was something fuzzy and small. A white ball of fur, that's what it looked like.

Rebekah squinted, trying to get a better look. What in the world? Brownie was chasing one of those new baby kittens! Along the bank of the creek, the poor critter ran, with the old dog right on its tail.

"Run, kitty, run! Go quickly!" Rebekah cried. She knew the kitten couldn't understand what she was saying, so she turned her attention toward Brownie. "Bad dog! You come here and leave that poor cat alone!"

Brownie cocked his head as though he might actually be listening, but then he forged right ahead and kept on with the chase.

"Dumb dog," Rebekah mumbled. "You never did know when to hearken." She watched helplessly as the exhausted kitten began to lose ground. Brownie was about ready to pounce when the unthinkable happened.

Plop! Right into the cold water the poor kitty sailed. Rebekah gasped, and Brownie, apparently surprised, slammed on his brakes and nearly ran straight into a tree.

Rebekah stared in horror as the white ball of fur turned into a soggy little mass that resembled something akin to a roll of cotton when it had been drenched in alcohol. Tiny paws began to flail helplessly about, making trivial headway through the swirling waters holding it in its grip.

"It's not strong enough to swim yet," Rebekah moaned. "The poor little critter will drown sure as anything." She couldn't just sit there and watch it happen. She had to do something to save the kitten's life.

Rebekah grasped the crutches tightly and pulled herself up with a grunt. "Hang on, little one. I'm coming!"

Down the creek bank she went, inch-by-inch, step-by-step. At the water's edge, she let go of one crutch. Since it was strapped to her arm, it dangled precariously as she attempted to lean across the current in hopes of rescuing the perishing cat.

Brownie was at her heels now, swishing his tail from side to side and barking like crazy. It only seemed to frighten the pathetic little fur ball that much more. With eyes open wide and claws splashing against the water, it was swept farther downstream. Rebekah saw the poor critter take in a mouthful of water. Then down it went.

In a state of near panic, she took a few more steps. The creek water rose over the top of her sneakers. No doubt it was stinging cold, but her unfeeling legs knew no pain. Further into the creek she trudged, lifting first one foot, then the other. The swift-moving current made it more difficult to navigate, and soon she felt winded and emotionally spent.

"Help me, Lord," she prayed. "Allow me to reach the kitten in time." A few more steps, and she was almost there. A slight bend at the waist, a hand extended, and then. . . *splash!*

Facedown in the chilling water, Rebekah landed. She gurgled and gasped as her nose and mouth filled with unwanted fluid. She thrashed about with her arms and nearly smacked the side of her head with one of the crutches. All thoughts of the stranded kitten vanished from her mind. All she wanted to do was save herself. The more she flailed against the creek's rapid flow, the deeper her body seemed to be sucked under.

Rebekah had never learned how to swim, and even if she had, her crippled legs would have been useless. If her arms had been stronger, maybe she could have paddled her way to the grassy banks. But no, she had used all her strength just getting down to this silly creek. The panic she felt rising in her throat kept all clearheaded thinking away. She couldn't pray, she couldn't swim, and she couldn't think of any way to get back on her feet.

As Daniel cut through the fields bordering the Stoltzfus place, he wondered if it was such a good idea for him to try and see Rebekah today. His father had told him to be a man and go after her, but he didn't think he could deal with it if she rejected him again. Still, he had to at least try.

Normally Daniel drove his horse and buggy whenever he went to the greenhouse, but he'd decided that a good long walk might be what he needed, so he had headed out from his place on foot, walked up the road a ways, and then taken a shortcut through the cornfields near the Stoltzfus property.

"Sure hope Rebekah's willing to listen to what I have to say this time," he mumbled. "I need to make her understand the way things are and how I feel about her."

Daniel pulled an ear of corn from one of the drying stalks and peeled it back. The kernels were hard and dried up, just like his heart would be if he had to spend the rest of his days on earth without Rebekah.

He took a few more steps and halted when he heard a muffled scream. He tipped his head and listened. There it was again—a little louder this time. He dropped the corn and sprinted across the field toward the sound.

A few minutes later, the creek bordering the Stoltzfus property came into view.

"Help! Somebody, help me, please!"

Daniel's heart leapt in his chest when he saw Rebekah lying in the water, her arms splashing like crazy, and her head bobbing up and down as she gasped for air.

With only one thought on his mind, he sprinted down the slippery bank and dashed into the water. "Rebekah, I'm coming!" he hollered. "Here now, grab my hand!"

Rebekah turned her head to the right, taking in another murky mouthful of water in the process. She blinked rapidly, trying to clear her vision. Was she dreaming? Was there someone standing over her? No, it couldn't possibly be.

She opened her mouth to cry out, but nothing more than a pitiful squeak came from her cold lips.

"Rebekah, listen to me now," the deep voice said sternly. "Quit your floundering and take hold of my hand." Daniel's concerned-looking face was mere inches from hers, and she knew for certain that it wasn't an apparition after all.

She lifted one arm, but the weight of the crutch seemed to be working against her. Daniel's firm hand grasped hers, pulling with all the strength of an able-bodied man. Still, she couldn't seem to right herself, and instead of coming to her feet as she had hoped she would, Rebekah fell backwards, dragging Daniel into the water with her.

He came up spitting and sputtering, with a look of sheer bewilderment spread over his dripping wet face.

"Well, Rebekah Stoltzfus," he said, shaking his head and sending rivulets of water flying everywhere, "you had better have a mighty good reason for this."

Daniel swept Rebekah into his arms and carried her over his shoulder as if she were a sack of grain. He plodded through the murky, swirling waters until he reached dry land. Then he placed her in a sitting position on the grassy bank and dropped down beside her. "Are you okay, Rebekah? What were you doin' in that creek? How come you're all alone and without the wheelchair?" The questions seemed to pour out of him until Rebekah finally interrupted with a raised hand.

"Don't you think you should ask only one question at a time?" She coughed a few times and reached up to pull her soggy head-covering off. Her damp hair came loose from its usual bun, and long, thoroughly saturated hair tumbled down around her shoulders.

Daniel lifted his hand to her cheek and swiped at a splotch of mud. "You look like a drowned pup, you know that?"

Rebekah sniffed deeply and glared at him. "Jah, well, you don't look so good yourself."

Daniel's lips twitched. Then he burst into laughter. "No, I don't guess I do!" His face sobered after the laughter subsided. "So are you gonna tell me why you're down here all alone, and how you ended up in that water or not?"

"I w-went for a walk," she replied, her lips trembling like a leaf caught in the wind. Her whole body had begun to shake, and she wrapped her arms around her middle, trying to warm herself. "I was sitting on a fallen tree when I noticed our dog chasing one of Gretta's new kittens." She paused for a breath. "The helpless little critter couldn't outrun the mutt, so the poor thing ended up falling into the creek."

Rebekah and Daniel both turned their heads toward the swiftly moving water. "I—I can't believe it!" Rebekah pointed across the creek bank. On the other side, sitting in a patch of grass, was one waterlogged kitten, licking its tiny paws as if it didn't have a care in the world. The yapping dog that had caused all the trouble was nowhere to be found.

"Can you believe that?" Rebekah groaned. "I nearly drowned myself to save that silly creature, and there it is just fine and dandy."

"I'm so glad you didn't drown. I don't think I could stand it if something bad happened to you."

Rebekah jerked her head toward Daniel. "What are you doing here, anyway, and how'd you know I was in trouble?"

"I was out for a walk, and I heard a scream. When I ran through the fields and saw you splashing around in the creek, I thought my heart was gonna stop beating." Daniel grinned, looking kind of self-conscious. "To tell you the truth, I was on my way to the greenhouse to see you."

She blinked several times, as she stared at him. "You—you were?"

He nodded. "I thought it was time we got things aired out between us. I. . .well, I've been actin' like a mad dog these last few weeks, and I'm sorry to say that a bit of hochmut got in my way or I would have come to see you sooner." He paused a few minutes, searching for the right words. "I just can't stand the idea of facing another tussle with you, Rebekah, so I hope you'll hear me out this time."

Rebekah dropped her gaze to the ground. "You hurt me bad, Daniel. I thought you cared for me, but then—"

"I'm sorry for hurting you and for letting you think things that weren't true." He lifted her chin so she was forced to look directly into his eyes. "I love you, Rebekah Stoltzfus. I will always love you, now and forever."

Stinging tears flooded Rebekah's eyes, and she gulped back a sob. "Oh, Daniel, you've never said that to me before."

"Never said what? That I'm sorry?"

"No. That you loved me."

"I—I haven't?"

She shook her head.

He hung his head sheepishly. "I'm sorry about that. Guess I was a dumb old *kuh*."

"You're not an old cow, Daniel. You just don't always know the right words to say."

"Jah, well, I kind of figured you knew how I felt."

"I—I didn't."

"Well, you do now I hope."

"Jah."

He took hold of her hand. "So is everything okay between us again?"

She shrugged. "But what about being partners? You did say you couldn't wait until you could help run the greenhouse, and—"

Daniel stopped her flow of words by planting a surprisingly warm kiss on her mouth, despite their encounter with the chilly creek water. When he released her, Rebekah felt as though she could barely catch her breath. Daniel had kissed her before, but never like that!

"If you would have just listened to me that day at the greenhouse instead of jumpin' to conclusions about my feelings and all, I would have told you that even though I wanted to run a greenhouse, that was never the reason for me wanting to marry you."

"It wasn't? But I thought—"

"I know what you thought. You thought I was just using you so I could get my hands on that business of yours, am I right?"

She nodded. "That is what I believed."

"Well, it just isn't so, Rebekah. I've been in love with you ever so long. Way back when we first started going to singings, and you would sit there in your wheelchair, so sweet and sincere." He touched his chest. "I felt a stirring deep in my heart. Why, it was all I could do to keep from rushing right up to you and declaring my love."

Rebekah stifled a giggle. She could hardly imagine Daniel announcing his love that way; he had seemed so shy back then.

Daniel pulled her into his arms and held her real close, as though his life depended on it. "Please say you believe me, Rebekah. I want you to be my wife, honest I do. It truly isn't for the business, neither." He patted her gently on the back. "If it will help anything, I'll even agree to let you run the greenhouse by yourself. I won't be co-owner of Grandma's Place at all. I'll just keep on workin' at the dairy farm with my daed and brothers. Jah, that's what I'll do."

Rebekah swallowed hard and nearly choked on a sob. "Oh, sweet Daniel, I couldn't ask you to do that. I know how much you love flowers. Your love for cows in no way compares to that."

"That's right, but my love for flowers is nothin' compared to what I feel for you. So don't send me away again, for I just couldn't bear it. Will you marry me, Rebekah, and love me forever?"

Daniel's eyes glistened with unshed tears, and it tore at

Rebekah's tender heart to see him show his emotions like that. She stroked his clean-shaven face and sighed. "Oh, Daniel, I do love you so much. I'm sorry for doubting your intentions and not giving you the chance to explain."

"Does that mean you're willing to become my wife?"

She nodded. "I'd be honored."

CHAPTER 25

R ebekah was awakened by the sound of someone knock-ing on her bedroom door. "Who is it?" she called grog-gily into her pillow.

Mom opened the door a crack and poked her head in-side. "You're still in bed? Such a sleepyhead. I thought you'd be up with the chickens on your wedding day."

Rebekah yawned and grabbed the sides of the bed in order to pull herself into a sitting position. "I was having such a nice dream, I guess I must have not wanted to wake up."

"That's good," Mom said with a smile. "All brides should have pleasant dreams." She entered the room and poured fresh water into the basin on Rebekah's dresser. "It's time to rise and shine, though. Breakfast is waiting, and it won't be long before the first of our guests begin to arrive."

"But Mary Ellen probably won't be one of them."

"Now you don't know that." Mom handed Rebekah a damp washcloth. "Mary Ellen still hasn't gone into labor, so why wouldn't she be here for your special day?"

Rebekah shrugged. "She might not feel up to coming. I can't speak firsthand, of course, but I hear that women are pretty miserable when they're this close to delivering."

Mom nodded. "That's true enough. At least it was for me. However, some women carry on as usual, right up to the beginning of their labor."

"Then I guess I can only hope Mary Ellen's one of them who can carry on as usual, because I'll be mighty disappointed if she isn't here today."

※

"Good morning, wife," Johnny said, as he stepped into the kitchen.

Mary Ellen had been standing at the counter, cracking eggs into a bowl, and she turned around to face him, forcing a smile. "Morning, husband."

"Did you sleep all right last night?" he asked, moving over to stand beside her.

"Oh, so-so."

"You were actin' kind of restless for a while there, shifting back and forth from one side to the other and scrunching up your pillow like you couldn't find a comfortable position."

Mary Ellen gave her protruding stomach a little thump and smiled. "You try carrying this weight around for a while and see how comfortable you are."

Johnny chuckled and leaned down to kiss her on the cheek. "Did you finally get some good sleep then?"

Her only reply was a brief shrug.

"Are you feelin' okay? You're lookin' kind of done in this morning." He tipped his head and stared at her with a look of obvious concern. "Maybe you ought to stay home from the wedding and rest all day."

She shook her head. "I'm fine, and I won't miss Rebekah's wedding."

"I'm sure she would understand."

"Well, I wouldn't. Rebekah was there for our wedding, and I'm going to be there for hers."

He gave her shoulder a gentle squeeze. "All right then, if you're sure you're up to going."

"I'll be okay. Just feeling a bit tired, is all." The truth was Mary Ellen had been having a few pangs through her middle ever since she'd gotten out of bed, but she was certain they were nothing to be concerned about. Probably just a little indigestion. Jah, that's all they were. She'd feel right as rain once they got to the wedding and she saw how pretty and happy Rebekah was on her special day.

Rebekah sat straight and tall on a wooden bench directly across from her groom. She had chosen to wear her leg braces today so she could stand for her wedding vows, rather than sit in the confining wheelchair. She wore traditional Amish bridal clothes—a plain blue cotton dress draped with a white cape and matching apron, and a white kapp on her head. Daniel was dressed in a white shirt, black trousers, black jacket, and a matching vest.

Rebekah glanced over her shoulder and smiled at Mary Ellen, who sat two rows behind. She knew from the expression on her friend's face that she was probably not feeling her best, but she cared enough to be here, and that meant a lot.

At eight thirty sharp, the service began with singing from the *Ausbund*. A lengthy sermon from Bishop Benner followed, covering all aspects of the Christian marriage. Then he read several scripture passages, including one from Colossians that said, " 'And whatsoever ye do in word or deed, do all in the name of the Lord Jesus, giving thanks to God and the Father by him.' "

In a booming voice and with a most serious expression, he quoted from yet another passage. " 'Wives, submit yourselves unto your own husbands, as it is fit in the Lord. Husbands, love your wives, and be not bitter against them.' "

Rebekah looked at Daniel and smiled, feeling kind of shy all of a sudden. He nodded and graced her with a heart-melting smile of his own. His serious brown eyes, filled with obvious adoration, told her all she needed to know. He loved her with all his heart, and if her disability didn't matter to him, then she wouldn't worry about it, either. Her life was in God's hands, and He would see that her needs were met. She would just keep trusting Him.

When the Bible reading was done, two of the ministers spoke awhile. Rebekah fidgeted nervously, wondering if they would ever finish. Finally, Daniel and Rebekah were ushered into Grandma Stoltzfus's old room for counseling from the bishop. Rebekah's attendants, Nadine and Sarah Jane, Daniel's sister, waited in the other room with the guests, along with Daniel's two brothers, Harold and Abner, who were his attendants.

The counseling session consisted of several more scripture references and a long dissertation from Bishop Benner on the importance of good communication, trust, and respect in all areas of marriage. He reminded the couple that divorce was not an acceptable option among those of their faith, and he emphasized the need to always work through their problems.

When they finally emerged from the bedroom, Rebekah released an audible sigh. Even though she had been allowed to sit during the counseling session, she felt all done in and a bit shaky.

Returning to the main room, Rebekah and Daniel sat on their original benches while the bishop gave a rather lengthy prayer. At long last, he motioned them to step forward and stand in front of him.

Rebekah's heart pounded like one of Dad's hammers when he'd worked on the new barn. It seemed as if this had been the moment she'd been waiting for her whole life. She was about to repeat her wedding vows before family and friends, and most importantly, before her heavenly Father.

Daniel gave a reassuring smile, and she steadied herself with the crutches strapped to her arms, waiting for Bishop Benner to begin.

Finally the bishop turned to Daniel and asked, "Can you confess, brother, that you accept this, our sister, as your wife, and that you will not leave her until death separates you?"

Without any hesitation, Daniel answered in a clear voice. "Jah, I do."

"And do you believe that this is from the Lord and that you have come thus far by your faith and prayers?"

"Jah."

Then it was Rebekah's turn. Her quiet voice quavered as she answered each of the bishop's questions, taking the meaning fully to heart.

A rustling noise on the women's side of the room drew Rebekah's attention. Out of the corner of her eye, she caught sight of Mary Ellen leaving the room, assisted by Aunt Mim and Aunt Crystal. *Maybe she's tired from sitting so long,* Rebekah reasoned. *Or could be it's too warm in here. There are nearly two hundred people crammed into our house today. Maybe this is a bad sign. Maybe. . .*

"Because you have confessed, brother, that you want to take this our sister for your wife, do you promise to be loyal to her and care for her if she may have adversity, infirmities that are among poor mankind—as is appropriate for a Christian, God-fearing husband?"

Rebekah jerked her thoughts back to the present as Daniel answered affirmatively to Bishop Benner's last question. Then, when the elderly bishop asked the same question of Rebekah, she answered, "Jah."

Placing Rebekah's hand in Daniel's, the bishop pronounced the blessing. "The God of Abraham, Isaac, and of Jacob be with you both and give you His rich blessings for a good beginning, a steadfast middle, and may you hold out until a blessed end. In the name of Jesus Christ. Amen."

Rebekah and Daniel returned to their respective benches as husband and wife.

As soon as the closing prayer was said, everyone who wasn't helping with the cooking or serving went outside to wait for the wedding meal. Tables were quickly set up in the living room and adjoining room, and the benches that had been used during the ceremony were placed at the tables.

"We need to take our place at the eck soon," Daniel whispered to Rebekah.

She nodded. "I know, but I want to check on Mary Ellen first. She left the room during our vows, and I think something might be amiss."

"All right then. We'll meet at the corner table as soon as you come back." Daniel gave Rebekah's arm a gentle squeeze, and she hobbled out to the kitchen. She found Mom and several other women there, scurrying about to get all the food dished up.

"Frieda, do you think these children of ours can keep house?" Mom asked Rebekah's new mother-in-law.

"Well, if you raised Rebekah as well as I raised Daniel, I believe it will go," Frieda replied with a laugh.

"Do you know where Mary Ellen is?" Rebekah asked Mom, as she stepped between the two women. "She left during the ceremony, and I'm a bit worried."

"Mary Ellen's water broke," Mom explained. "I hear tell she's been in labor for several hours already. They've taken her upstairs because there's no time to get to the hospital now."

Rebekah's mouth dropped open. "Why did she come to the wedding, then? She should have insisted that Johnny take her to the hospital right away when her labor first started."

"Mim said Mary Ellen didn't want to miss your wedding. She thought, this being her first baby and all, that the labor would be a long one."

Tears welled in Rebekah's eyes, and she blinked a couple of times. "Oh, Mom, if anything happens to Mary Ellen or the baby, I'll never forgive myself."

Mom draped an arm around Rebekah's shoulders and led her to a chair at the kitchen table. "Don't go talking such foolishness, now. You can't take the blame for something like this. Mary Ellen had a choice to make. You didn't force her to come to the wedding today."

"I know, but she knew how much I wanted her to be here," Rebekah argued. "If only she would have had that boppli on schedule. She's over two weeks late, and—"

"Hush, now," Mom said, interrupting Rebekah's rush of words by placing a finger against her lips. "Nothing we say or do will change the fact that the baby was late or that Mary Ellen's here now. The best thing would be to carry on with the wedding meal so our guests don't go hungry. Women have been having babies for thousands of years, and we just need to pray that everything will be all right in the birthing room upstairs." Mom nodded toward the steps. "I'm sure Mim and Crystal are capable of helping with the delivery, but Johnny's ridden into town to get Doc Manney, in case any problems should occur."

Rebekah's hand trembled as she wiped a stray hair from her face. She bowed her head and silently petitioned the Lord for both Mary Ellen and the baby.

The wedding meal consisted of roasted chicken, mashed potatoes, bread filling, creamed celery, coleslaw, applesauce, fruit salad, bread, butter, jelly, and coffee.

Rebekah sat at the corner table with Daniel while they ate and visited with their guests, but she kept thinking about the new life that was about to be brought into the world. This was Daniel's and her special day. She should be laughing and enjoying all the jokes and stories people were telling.

She ought to be savoring the delicious foods and the love she could feel radiating from her new groom. Instead, she worried and prayed, until Mom finally came into the room and announced, "Mary Ellen's just given birth to a baby girl. Dr. Manney is with her right now, and the report is that both mother and daughter are doing well."

A cheer went up around the room, and Rebekah choked back a sob. With tears in her eyes, she turned to Daniel. "Would you mind if I slipped out for a moment so I can see the new boppli and her mamm?"

Daniel shook his head. "Of course not. You need to find out all the details so you can include them in your next *Budget* column." He squeezed her hand. "Would you like me to come along? Someone will have to carry you up the stairs."

"Why don't you stay and enjoy our guests? I'll ask Dad to take me up."

Daniel smiled and shrugged. "Okay then, do as you like."

With the aid of her crutches, Rebekah made her way out of the crowded room. Soon Dad carried her upstairs, and she found Mary Ellen lying on the bed in Nadine's room. In her arms, she cradled a small bundle of pure, sweet baby.

Mary Ellen's cheeks were flushed, and her voice filled with emotion as she whispered, "I'm sorry I missed the end of your wedding."

Rebekah hobbled over to the bed, then leaned over to give her friend a kiss on the forehead. "You had a pretty good excuse, I'm thinking."

"Why don't you say hello to your cousin Martha Rose?" Mary Ellen murmured.

Rebekah's eyes clouded with tears, and she stroked the baby's downy head. "It's soft as a kitten's nose." A small sigh escaped her lips, as she blinked back tears. "Today's been such a perfect day. I'm married to a wunderbaar man, and now I'm looking on a true miracle from God."

"Jah," Mary Ellen agreed. "God has surely blessed us with this sweet baby girl."

Rebekah nodded. "God is truly the God of miracles."

EPILOGUE

Rebekah closed the drawer of the cash register as an English man and his two small children left the greenhouse, carrying a pot of petunias. It had been a good year for her and Daniel's business and for them as a married couple, as well.

Their home, built by Rebekah's and Daniel's fathers, was connected to her parents' house. It gave them a place of their own, yet they were near enough to family to have help available should it be needed.

Rebekah smiled to herself. She and Daniel had been married a little over a year now, and their love seemed to grow stronger with each passing day.

Daniel no longer helped his father in the dairy business. He was too busy helping out at the greenhouse or building wooden gadgets to sell. He had added weather vanes, wind chimes, and lawn furniture to the other items he sold in the store. Rebekah had also begun selling wicker baskets and plant stands for her flowers and plants.

In the summertime, they sold bottles of Dad's quick homemade root beer and some of the tasty shoofly pies

Mom often baked. In the wintertime, they offered coffee and hot chocolate and several kinds of cookies.

They were making enough money to live comfortably. Their meat and milk were supplied by Daniel's father in exchange for fresh vegetables from the garden Daniel tended in the summer months. Mom saw that they had plenty of fresh eggs and chicken meat whenever they needed it, too. Setting her pride aside, Rebekah had learned to accept help from all available sources. She'd proven to herself that she could be financially self-sufficient, but it was no longer so important. What truly mattered was the love of family and friends, and especially, God's love.

Rebekah was jolted by the shrill sound of a baby crying. She left the cash register and wheeled quickly into the back room. Next to Rebekah's cot sat a wooden cradle, hand-made with love by the little one's father.

Reaching into the cradle, Rebekah picked up her month-old baby daughter. "Little Anna, are you hungry?" she crooned. The baby nestled against her mamm's breast and began to nurse hungrily. "If your namesake, Grandma Anna Stoltzfus, could only have seen you," Rebekah whispered, "I'm sure she would have loved you as much as we all do." She stroked the soft, downy hair on top of her baby's small head and closed her eyes.

"She's sure a miracle, sent straight from God, jah?"

Rebekah's eyes flew open, and she stared up at her tall, bearded husband. Blinking away the tears of joy that had crept into her eyes, she said, "She certainly is. I never dreamed God would be so good as to give us a child of our own. Someday I hope little Anna and her cousin Martha

Rose will have a special friendship like Mary Ellen and I have had for so many years."

Daniel bent down and touched his warm lips to Rebekah's mouth, causing little shivers to spiral up her arms. She never got tired of his kisses, nor of the look of love that so often crossed his face.

"Your faith has become strong, and God has given our girl a blessed gift having you as a mudder." Daniel kissed Rebekah again. "I thank God for baby Anna and for the love we share."

Rebekah wiped more tears from her eyes and murmured, "I thank God for all of His miracles."

Recipe for Andrew's Quick Homemade Root Beer

Ingredients:
  2 cups white sugar
  1 gal. lukewarm water
  3 tsp. root beer extract
  1 tsp. dry yeast

Mix all ingredients well and pour into jars. Cover and set in the sun for 4 hours. Chill before serving the next day.

PLAIN & FANCY

Brides of Lancaster County

3

In loving memory of my friend, Sharon Hanson,
whose love for her "special" child was an inspiration to all.

And this is his commandment,
That we should believe on the name of his Son Jesus Christ,
and love one another, as he gave us commandment.
1 JOHN 3:23 KJV

CHAPTER 1

Laura Meade opened her laptop, entered the correct password to put her online, and began the e-mail she had been meaning to write for the past week:

Dear Shannon,

I'm finally settled in at the Lancaster School of Design. I think I'm going to like it here. Not only is the college rated in the top ten, but the area is beautiful, and the Amish I've seen are unbelievable! I haven't met any of them up close and personal, but from what I've seen, the women wear simple, dark-colored dresses, with little white hats on their heads. The men wear cotton shirts, dark pants with suspenders, and either a straw or black felt hat with a wide brim. They drive box-shaped, closed-in buggies pulled by a horse.

Tomorrow, I'm going to the farmers' market. I hear it's a great place to get good buys on handmade Amish quilts. I may even be able to acquire some helpful decorating ideas there.

I hope you're doing well and enjoying your new job.

I'm looking forward to seeing you at Christmas and
hearing about those preschoolers you teach.

Your friend,
Laura

Laura thought about sending an e-mail to her parents, but she had talked to them on the phone just an hour ago, so there wouldn't be much to write about now. Moving away from the desk, she picked up a brush from the dresser and began her nightly ritual of one hundred strokes through her long, thick tresses.

She glanced around the room with disdain. Even the smallest room at home was bigger than this dinky dorm room. Fortunately, she would only be here two years. Then she could return to Minneapolis and redecorate to her heart's content—starting with her own bedroom at home.

"It's stifling in here." Laura dropped the hairbrush onto the bed and went to open the window. A slight breeze trickled through the screen, but it did nothing to cool the stuffy room. Here it was the first week of September, and the days were still hot and humid. To make matters worse, the air-conditioning wasn't working right and probably wouldn't be fixed until later in the week, according to what she'd been told.

Fall had always been Laura's favorite time of year. Someday, she hoped to decorate her own home with harvest colors. The kitchen windows would be outlined with sheer yellow curtains. The living-room, dining-room, and bedroom floors would be covered with thick, bronze carpets. She wanted to decorate with Early American furniture and to hang plenty of paintings from that era on the walls.

Mom and Dad had allowed her to travel halfway across the country to attend the Lancaster School of Design, despite the fact that several good schools were closer to home. When Laura had heard about this one so near to the heart of Amish land, she'd known she had to come. She'd read about the interesting culture of the Plain People on a few Web sites and was sure she could gain some unique decorating ideas here in Lancaster County.

Laura glanced at the photo of Dean Carlson, set in a gold frame on top of her dresser. Dean was the newest member of her father's law firm, and he had given her the picture soon after they'd started dating three months ago. Dean hadn't been too happy about her moving to Pennsylvania, even though she had assured him it would only be for a couple of years. She wasn't sure if his reluctance to see her go was because he cared so much or if he might be worried that she would find someone else and end up staying in Pennsylvania.

A loud knock jolted Laura out of her musings. With an exasperated sigh, she crossed the room and opened the door.

A young woman with short, curly blond hair stood in the hallway. "Hi. I'm Darla Shelby. I have the room next to yours."

Laura smiled. "I'm Laura Meade."

"Nice to meet you. Where are you from?"

"Minneapolis. How about you?"

"I grew up here in Lancaster, moved to New York with my folks when I was sixteen, and came back here again to attend this school." She grinned. "But my favorite place to be is Philadelphia. In fact, since tomorrow's Saturday,

I thought I'd drive into Philly and do some shopping. Would you like to go along?"

"So you must have your own car?"

Darla nodded. "It's a little red convertible—got it for my birthday last year."

Laura thought about her own car parked in the garage at home. She wished she could have driven it here, but her parents had insisted that she fly to Pennsylvania and lease a car during her stay.

"I realize we've only just met," Darla continued, "but I figure what better way to get acquainted than during a shopping spree."

Laura leaned against the doorframe as she contemplated the tempting offer. "I appreciate the invitation, and I'd love to go with you some other time, but I had planned to go to the farmers' market at Bird-in-Hand tomorrow. I understand some of the Plain People go there to shop and sell some of their wares."

Darla nodded. "Those Amish and Mennonites are quite the tourist attraction around here."

"Why don't you go to the market with me, and we can do some shopping there?"

Darla wrinkled her nose. "No way! I'd rather be caught in the middle of rush-hour traffic on the turnpike than spend the day with a bunch of farmers."

Laura giggled. "Those farmers do look pretty interesting."

"Maybe so, but they're not interesting enough for me to give up a day of shopping in Philly." Darla turned toward her own room, calling over her shoulder, "Whatever you do, Laura, don't let too much of that Amish culture rub off on you."

As Eli Yoder left Strasburg, where he worked at a store that made handcrafted Amish furniture, he thought about the conversation he'd had with Pauline Hostetler after church last Sunday. He had made the mistake of telling her that he planned to rent a table at the farmers' market this Saturday to sell some of the items he'd created in his wood shop at home.

"Oh, Eli," he could still hear her say, *"I was planning to go to the market on Saturday, too. Maybe the two of us could meet at noon and eat lunch together."*

"Pauline's after me to court her," Eli mumbled, as he headed down the road toward home in his buggy.

His horse whinnied as if in response and perked up his ears.

"Are you sympathizing with me, boy?" Eli chuckled and flicked the reins to get his horse trotting a bit faster. It was fun to ride in his open buggy and go a little faster than usual. It made him feel free and one with the wind whipping against his face.

I won't be free for long if Pauline has anything to say about it. I think she's in cahoots with Mom to see me join the church so I can get married and settle down to raising a family. Eli frowned. It wasn't that he didn't want to get married someday. He just hadn't found the right woman yet, and he was sure it wouldn't be Pauline. He was in no hurry to be baptized and join the church until he felt ready to settle down. So Mom would have to learn to be patient.

"Why'd I agree to meet Pauline for lunch?" Eli fretted. "She's likely to take it to mean I have an interest in her, and then she'll expect me to start officially calling on her."

He gripped the reins a little tighter. "I'll have lunch with her on Saturday because I promised I would, but I'll have to figure out some way to let her know there's no chance of us having a future together."

A ray of sun filtered through the window, causing Laura to squint when she opened her eyes. She peeked at the small clock on her bedside table. It was nearly nine o'clock. She had slept much later than she'd planned.

Jerking the covers aside, she slipped out of bed and headed for the shower. A short time later, as Laura studied the contents of her closet, she had a hard time deciding what to wear. She finally opted for a pair of blue jeans and a rust-colored tank top. She pulled her long, auburn hair into a ponytail and secured it with a navy blue scrunchie.

"Nothing fancy, but I'm sure I look good enough to go to the farmers' market," she said to her reflection in the mirror. "Amish country, I hope you're ready for me because here I come!"

Mary Ellen Yoder had just begun supper preparations when her husband, Johnny, stepped into the kitchen, holding a pot of pansies in his hands. He grinned at her and placed the pot on the counter. "These are for you. I got 'em from the Beachys' greenhouse."

She turned from her job of cutting vegetables for a stew and smiled. "Such a thoughtful husband I have. *Danki*, Johnny."

His smile widened, and he leaned over to kiss her cheek. "I still remember the first bouquet of flowers I bought for my special girl. Do you?"

She nodded. "That was way back when you were doing everything you could to get me to allow you to come courting."

He slipped his arm around her waist and gave her a squeeze. "And it worked, too, didn't it? We not only started courting, but you agreed to marry me, and now we've got ourselves four of the finest *kinner* around."

"*Jah*, I agree." Mary Ellen smiled and resumed cutting her vegetables.

"And let's not forget that spunky little *kindsbuh* our daughter gave us a few years back."

"Now if we can just get our three *buwe* married off so they can add more grandchildren to our family," Mary Ellen said.

"I think the chances of Lewis and Jonas finding wives might be pretty good since they've already joined the church, but Eli's another matter."

Mary Ellen sighed and glanced at Johnny over her shoulder. "It's hard for me to understand why he keeps saying he's not ready to settle down when he's got a fine woman like Pauline Hostetler interested in him. Eli's twenty-three years old already and has gone through his *rumschpringe* long enough. Wouldn't you think he'd be eager to end his running-around years and start courting a pretty girl?"

Johnny shrugged. "I don't want to get your hopes up, but I heard Eli talking to Jonas last night, and he mentioned that he's got plans to meet Pauline for lunch on Saturday when he goes to the farmers' market to sell some of his handmade wooden items."

Despite her husband's warning, Mary Ellen's hopes began to soar. "Really? You heard that?"

"Heard it with my own ears, so it's not just say-so."

She smiled. "Now that is good news. Jah, the best news I've had all day."

When Laura stepped out of her air-conditioned car, a blast of heat and humidity hit her full in the face. She hurried into the market building and was relieved to find that it was much cooler than the outside air had been.

The first table Laura discovered was run by two young Amish women selling an assortment of pies and cookies. Both wore their hair parted down the middle, then pulled back into a tight bun. They had small, white caps perched on top of their heads, and their long-sleeved, dark blue dresses were calf-length, with black aprons and capes worn over the front. One of the women smiled and asked Laura if she would like to sample something.

She stared longingly at a piece of apple pie. They did look delicious, but she'd had breakfast not long ago and didn't think she needed the extra calories.

"No thanks. I'm not really hungry right now." The truth was Laura was always counting calories, and she figured one bite of those scrumptious pastries would probably tip the scales in an unfavorable direction. She moved on quickly before temptation got the better of her.

The next few tables were run by non-Amish farmers. The items they offered didn't interest Laura much, so she found another table where an elderly Amish woman sold handmade quilts.

"Those are gorgeous. How much do they cost?" she asked.

The woman showed her each one, quoting the prices, which ranged from four hundred to nine hundred dollars.

"I'm definitely going to buy one," Laura said without questioning the price. "I don't want to carry it around while I shop, though. Can you hold this one for me?" She pointed to a simple pattern that used a combination of geometric shapes done in a variety of rich autumn colors.

"Jah, sure. I can hold it."

"Great. What's this one called, anyway?"

"It's known as 'Grandmother's Choice.' " The Amish woman's fingers traveled lightly over the material.

Laura smiled. "I like it very much. I'll be back for it before I leave, but I can pay now if you'd like."

"Pay when you come back; that'll be fine." The woman placed the quilt inside a box, then slipped it under the table.

It was getting close to lunchtime, so Laura decided to check out one more table, then look for something nonfattening to eat.

The next table was loaded with a variety of hand-carved items. Laura glanced around for the person in charge but didn't see anyone. She picked up one of the finely crafted birdhouses and studied the exquisite detailing. When a young Amish man popped up from behind the table, she jumped, nearly dropping the birdhouse. He held a box filled with more birdhouses and feeders. His sandy brown hair was cut in a Dutch-bob, and a lock of it fell across his forehead. His deeply set, crystalline blue eyes met Laura's gaze with such intensity it took her breath away. Her cheeks grew hot, and she quickly placed the birdhouse back on the table. "I—I was just admiring your work."

A hint of a smile tweaked the man's lips, revealing a small dimple in the middle of his chin. "I'm a woodcarver and carpenter, and I'm thankful God has given me the ability to use my hands for something worthwhile."

Though Laura had been to church a few times in her life, she wasn't particularly religious. In fact, the whole church scene made her feel kind of nervous. Nibbling on the inside of her cheek, she merely nodded in response to the man's giving credit to God for his abilities.

"Are you looking for anything special? I also have some wooden flowerpots and ornamental things for the lawn." He lifted one for her inspection.

Laura stared at the small, decorative windmill in his hand, and her gaze traveled up his muscular arm. Below his rolled-up shirtsleeve, his tanned arms were feathered with light brown hair. She moistened her lips and brought her wayward thoughts to a halt. "I. . .uh. . .live in a dorm room at the Lancaster School of Design, so I really don't have a need for birdhouses or whirligigs."

His dark eyebrows drew together. "Don't think I've ever heard of that school."

"I'm learning to be an interior decorator," she explained, drawing her gaze to his appealing face, then back to the items on the table.

When he made no comment, she looked up again and saw that he was staring at her with a questioning look.

"My job will be to help people decorate their homes in attractive styles and colors."

"Ah, I see. So do you live around here, then?"

She shook her head. "I'm from Minneapolis, Minnesota. I've already studied some interior design at one of our local community colleges, and I'm here to complete my training."

There was an awkward silence as they stood staring at one another.

"Eli, well, there you are! I thought we were supposed to meet for lunch. I waited outside, but you never showed up so I figured I'd better come looking."

A young, blond-haired Amish woman, dressed similarly to the Plain women Laura had seen earlier, stepped up to the table.

"I'm sorry, Pauline," he said. "I got busy talking with this customer and forgot about the time." He considered Laura a moment. "Is there anything you're wantin' to buy?"

"No. I. . .uh. . .was just looking."

"Eli, if you're finished here, can we go have lunch now?" Pauline took a few steps closer, brushing her hand lightly against Eli's arm.

"Jah, Pauline." Eli glanced back at Laura. "It was nice chatting with you, and I wish you the best with your studies and all." He turned away, leaving his wooden items unattended.

Laura shook her head. *That man is sure trusting. And how in the world could someone as simply dressed as him be so adorable?*

⁂

As Eli and Pauline exited the building, he glanced over his shoulder. The young English woman still stood beside his table. *She's sure a fancy one. Fancy and very pretty. I wonder why someone like her would be interested in birdhouses?*

"Eli, where do you want to eat lunch?"

Pauline's question and her slight tug on Eli's shirtsleeve brought his thoughts to a halt.

"I thought you carried a picnic basket," he said peevishly.

591

"I did, but I wasn't sure where you wanted to eat it."

He shrugged. "It makes no difference to me."

"Let's go to the picnic tables out back."

When Eli gave no response, she grabbed his sleeve again. "What's wrong? You're acting kind of *naerfich*."

"I'm not nervous. I've just got a lot on my mind."

Pauline slipped her hand through the crook of his arm. "After you've had a few bites of fried chicken, you won't be thinking about anything but my good cooking."

Eli feigned a smile. "Kissin' wears out, but cookin' don't." Truth be told, he wasn't really in the mood to eat just now, but he was sure Pauline had worked hard making the picnic lunch, and he'd promised to eat it with her. Besides, a few drumsticks and a plate of potato salad would probably make him feel a whole lot better.

Pauline smiled and set the wicker basket she'd filled with chicken, baked beans, cut-up vegetables, and chocolate cake on the picnic table. "You're right about cooking never wearing out. My *mamm* and *daed* have been married twenty-five years, and Dad's still complimenting Mom on her great cooking."

Eli's only reply was a quick shrug. Then he bowed his head, and she did the same. When their silent prayer was over, Pauline opened the basket and set out the food, along with paper plates, napkins, and plastic silverware. "I brought a jug of water for us to drink," she said. "I hope that's okay."

"Jah, sure; it's fine for me." Eli helped himself to a couple of drumsticks and some baked beans, and Pauline followed suit, only she added some cut-up carrots to her plate.

"I was sorry to learn that you hadn't taken the membership classes this summer so you could be baptized and join the church a week from Sunday," she said.

He gave a noncommital grunt and kept on eating.

"Will you take the classes next summer?"

"Maybe. It all depends on how I feel about things by then."

Pauline pursed her lips. "You're twenty-three years old already. Haven't you had enough rumschpringe by now? Don't you think it's past time for you to join the church and settle down?"

"Now you sound like my mamm." Eli frowned. "Maybe one of the reasons I haven't made the decision yet is because she's always hounding me about it."

Pauline flinched, feeling like he'd thrown cold water in her face. Eli obviously thought she was hounding him, too.

Eli reached into the plastic tub filled with chicken and retrieved another drumstick. "Don't get me wrong. I'm not refusing to join the church because I have any ideas about leaving the Amish faith. I just can't see the need of joining when I'm not ready to get married yet."

Pauline felt as if her heart had sunk all the way to her toes. If Eli wasn't ready to get married, then he obviously had no thoughts of marrying her. But he'd taken her home from a couple of singings, and he'd agreed to meet her for lunch today. Didn't that mean anything at all? Wasn't that a ray of hope worth clinging to? Pauline knew she would have to be careful not to push Eli too hard, but if she had her way, by this time next year they'd be planning their wedding.

When Laura returned to her dorm room later that afternoon, she placed the Amish quilt she'd purchased on her bed, making it a definite focal point in the room. For some reason, the quilt reminded her of the young Amish man who had been selling wood-crafted items. As Laura sat at her desk, trying to study, she found herself wishing she had bought one of his birdhouses.

She drummed her fingers restlessly across the desktop. As ridiculous as it might seem, she'd been attracted to the man. It was stupid, because she knew they were worlds apart. Besides, the young woman he'd been with had seemed awfully possessive, and Laura figured she might be Eli's girlfriend or even his wife.

Fighting the urge to fantasize further, she forced herself to concentrate on the monochromatic swatches of material on her desk. It wouldn't be good to get behind in her studies because of a passing fancy with someone she would probably never see again.

CHAPTER

2

For the next several weeks, Laura was kept busy with classes and what seemed like never-ending homework. She hadn't ventured into Amish land since her trip to the farmers' market, but since it was Saturday and most of her homework was done, she had time to have fun.

Since Laura was so fascinated by the Plain People, she decided to check out a few gift shops in one of the nearby Amish communities. This time she made sure she brought her camera along.

Laura drove the small car she had leased for the months she would be living in Pennsylvania and headed to the town of Paradise. The first store she entered was a gift shop filled with excited tourists. It had numerous shelves full of Pennsylvania Dutch trinkets and a rack of postcards with photos of Amish and Mennonite farms, Plain People, and horse-drawn buggies. Laura bought several with the intent of sending them to family and friends back home.

Her next stop was a variety store, which was stocked with more gift items, groceries, and snack foods.

Laura wandered toward the back of the store. To her amazement, the shelves were lined with oil lamps, bolts of plain cotton material, women's black bonnets, men's straw hats, boxes of white handkerchiefs, and several pairs of work boots. Another section was stocked with various-sized shovels and other gardening tools, as well as a variety of flower and vegetable seeds.

The Amish must do some of their shopping here, she thought. *I wonder if I'll see any of them come into the store while I'm here.*

Laura hung around for a while, looking at various items and keeping an eye out for Amish people. She soon got tired of waiting, so she bought a few more postcards and left the store.

Outside on the sidewalk, she spotted two little Amish girls walking hand in hand behind their mother.

They're so cute—I just have to get their picture. Laura pulled her digital camera from her purse, focused it on the children, and was about to snap the picture when someone grasped her shoulder.

"Would you mind not taking that picture?"

Laura spun around. A pair of penetrating blue eyes bore down on her, and her heart skipped a beat. It was the same Amish man she'd met at the farmers' market a few weeks ago.

"I remember you. You were at the market, looking at my birdhouses, right?"

Laura nodded and offered him what she hoped was a pleasant smile. "Why did you stop me from taking those little girls' pictures?"

"The Amish prefer not to have their pictures taken."

"Oh? How come?"

"We believe it's a form of pride, and some in our church say it goes against Bible teachings reminding us not to make any graven images."

"What about all the pictures on postcards?" She withdrew one from her purse. "Isn't that an Amish man working in the fields?"

"Some folks don't care how we feel about being photographed, and they just snap pictures of us anyway," he said without even glancing at the postcard. "And some people use close-up lenses so they can take pictures without us knowing. I'm sure the man in the postcard didn't actually pose for the picture."

"Well, you don't have to worry about me offending anyone." She slipped the camera back into her purse, then held out her hand. "I'm Laura Meade."

He seemed kind of hesitant at first, but then he shook her hand and smiled. "My name's Eli Yoder."

"It's nice to meet you, Eli." She laughed, feeling suddenly self-conscious. "I guess we did meet before—just no formal introductions."

He motioned toward a wooden bench in front of the building. "Would you want to sit awhile? I'll take my birdhouses inside; then we can have a cup of cold root beer. That is, if you'd like one."

Laura nodded eagerly. Of course she would like a root beer—especially when it would give her more time to talk to this good-looking Amish man. She dropped to the bench and leaned forward with her elbows resting on her jean-clad knees, as she watched Eli head to the parking lot, where his horse and buggy stood waiting. He made two trips into the store, shouldering large cardboard boxes. When he emerged for the last time, he held two Styrofoam cups full of root beer. He gave one to Laura and sat down beside her.

"I noticed your buggy is open—sort of like a carriage,"

she remarked. "Most of the Amish buggies I've seen are closed and kind of box-shaped."

Eli grinned. "That's my courting buggy. My daed gave it to me on my sixteenth birthday."

"Your *daed*?"

"Jah, my dad."

"Oh. So what's a 'courting buggy'?"

"English boys get a driver's license and sometimes a car when they turn sixteen. We Amish get an open buggy so we can start courting—or dating, as you Englishers like to call it."

She smiled. "Have you been dating very long?"

"Are you wanting to know my age?"

Laura felt the heat of embarrassment creep up her neck as she nodded. She did want to know how old he was—and a whole lot more besides.

"It's okay. I don't mind you asking. I'm twenty-three, and my folks think I ought to be married already." Eli lifted the cup of root beer to his lips.

So, he's single and just a year older than me. Laura wasn't sure why, but that bit of information gave her some measure of satisfaction. "How come you're not married?" she ventured to ask.

"For one thing, I haven't joined our church yet, and that's a requirement before marriage." Eli shrugged. "I haven't met the right woman yet, either."

Laura thought about the Amish woman who had been with Eli at the market. She'd seen the way that Plain girl had looked at him.

Eli smacked his lips. "*Umm*. . .this is sure good root beer. Thomas Benner, the store owner, makes it himself."

Laura took a sip. "Yes, it is very good." Her gaze traveled

across the parking lot. "Your buggy's sure nice-looking. Does it ride well?"

Eli rewarded her with a heart-melting smile, and his seeking blue eyes mesmerized her. "Would you like to find out?"

"Oh, I'd love that!" Laura jumped up; then, thinking he might have only been teasing, she whirled around to face him. "Would it be all right? It's not against your religion or anything?"

Eli's smile widened, causing the dimple in his chin to become more pronounced. "There are some other Plain sects who offer buggy rides to tourists. So if someone should see us, they'll probably just think you hired me for a ride."

Eli helped Laura into the left side of the open buggy; then he climbed up on the right and gathered the reins. With a few clucks to his faithful horse, they were off.

A slight breeze caught the ends of Laura's golden bronze hair, whipping them around her face. Eli's chest constricted. *This English woman is sure appealing. Why, it's almost sinful to be so beautiful. I'm wondering why she would want to be seen with someone as plain as me.*

Eli felt a twinge of guilt for allowing himself the pleasure of admiring her beauty, but he couldn't quit thinking how much fun it would be to get to know her better.

"This is so awesome! I never would have dreamed riding in a buggy could be so much fun." Laura's tone revealed her excitement, and her green eyes lit up like a sunbeam.

He glanced over at her and grinned. "Jah, it's wonderful good."

When they had gone a short distance, Eli turned the buggy down a wide, dirt path, where there were no cars, just a carpet of flaxen corn on either side.

"Where are we going?"

"There's a small lake down this way." Eli flashed her another smile. "I think you'll like it there."

Laura leaned back in her seat, breathed deeply of the fresh air, and drank in the rich colors of the maple trees lining both sides of the dirt road. "I think the temperate hues of autumn make it the most charming, loveliest time of the year," she murmured.

Eli raised his dark eyebrows. "Such fancy words you're using."

She laughed. "Should I have said it's 'wonderful good'?"

"Jah, sure." Eli pulled the horse to a stop in a grassy meadow near the small lake. "Here we are."

"You were right. It is beautiful here."

Eli grinned like a child with a new toy. "In the summer, it's a great place for swimming and fishing. We like to skate on the lake when it freezes over in the wintertime, too."

"It looks like the perfect place for a picnic."

"My family and I have been here many times." Eli glanced over at Laura. "Would you like to get out and walk around?"

"That sounds nice, but I rather like riding in your courting buggy." She released a sigh of contentment. "Can't we just keep driving?"

"Sure, we can." Eli got the horse moving again.

As they traveled around the lake, Laura began to ply him with questions about his way of life. "Can you tell me why the Amish people wear such simple clothes?"

"We feel that wearing plain clothes encourages humility and separation from the world. Our clothes aren't a costume, like some may believe, but they're an expression of our faith."

"I see." A gentle breeze rustled the trees, and Laura's heart stirred with a kind of excitement she had never known before. She wasn't sure if it was the fall foliage, the exhilarating buggy ride, or the captivating company of one very cute Amish man that made her feel so giddy. One thing was for sure: A keen sense of disappointment overcame her when Eli turned the buggy back to the main road.

"Do you like wearing men's trousers?" he asked suddenly.

She glanced at her blue jeans and giggled. "These aren't men's trousers. They're made for a woman, and they're really quite comfortable." When Eli made no comment, she decided it was her turn to ask another question. "What's your family like?"

"I have a wonderful family. There's Pop and Mom, and I have an older sister, Martha Rose. She's married to Amon Zook, and they've got a three-year-old son. I also have two younger brothers who help Pop on the farm while I'm working at the furniture shop near Strasburg."

"I think it would be interesting if I could see where you live." The unexpected comment popped out of Laura's mouth before she had time to think about what she was saying.

When Eli's brows drew downward and he made no response, she wondered if she had overstepped her bounds. As much as she would like it, she knew she would probably never get to see Eli's house, meet his family, or have another opportunity to ride in an Amish buggy.

It seemed like no time at all before they were pulling into the variety store's parking lot. Eli jumped down and came around to help Laura out of the buggy. When his hands went around her waist, she felt an unexpected shiver tickle her spine. "Thanks for the ride," she said breathlessly. "If I live to a ripe old age, I'll never forget this day."

Laura started across the parking lot and was surprised to see Eli walking beside her. They both stopped when they reached the sidewalk, and Laura glanced at her watch. "I'd better call my friend. We're supposed to meet for supper soon." She pulled her cell phone from her purse.

"Your friend is some lucky fellow."

She smiled. "It's not a man I'm meeting for supper. It's just a girlfriend from school."

"Ah, I see." Eli stared at the ground for a few seconds, then looked back at her. "Say, I was wondering—would you be interested in going back to the lake with me next Saturday? We could take a picnic lunch along, and if you have more questions about my way of life, I'll have a little more time to answer them."

Laura could hardly believe her ears. Had he really asked her on a date? Well, maybe not a date exactly, but at least it was another chance to see him.

"That would be nice," she said, forcing her voice to remain steady. "What should I bring?"

"Just a hearty appetite and a warm jacket. I'll ask Mom to fix the lunch, because she always makes plenty of good food."

"It's a date." Laura felt the heat of a blush creep up the back of her neck and spread to her cheeks. "I mean—I'll look forward to next Saturday. Should we meet here in front of the store, around one o'clock?"

"That'll be fine," he answered with a nod.

"Until next Saturday then." Just before Laura turned toward her car, she looked back and saw him wave as he was walking away. She lifted her hand in response and whispered, "Eli Yoder, where have you been all my life?"

CHAPTER 3

As Laura drove back to Lancaster, all she could think about was Eli. She pictured his twinkling blue eyes, sandy brown hair, and the cute little chin dimple that made him look so irresistible. Eli was full of humor and had a fresh, almost innocent way about him. It was something she'd never seen in Dean Carlson, who had a haughty attitude and seemed to think he was every woman's dream.

She clenched the steering wheel until her knuckles turned white. *What am I thinking here? I can't allow myself to fantasize about Eli or start comparing him to other men. He's off-limits—forbidden fruit for a modern English woman like me.* She grimaced as she pulled up to a stop sign and spotted a closed-in Amish buggy with two little tow-headed boys peeking out the back. *Then why am I reflecting on the time we had together today? And why did I agree to go on a picnic with him next Saturday?*

As hard as Laura tried, she seemed unable to squelch the desire to see Eli one more time. She could learn a bit more about the Amish; they would enjoy a nice picnic lunch and soak up the beauty of the lake; and it would be over. They'd probably never see each other again. She would have pleasant memories of the brief time she'd spent with an intriguing Amish man, and her life would return to normal. It would be a wonderful story to tell her grand-children someday. She smiled and tried to visualize herself as a grandmother, but the thought was too far removed. The only thing she could see was the face of Eli Yoder calling her to learn more about him and his Plain way of living.

All the way home, Eli thought about Laura and the conver-sation they'd had on their way to and from the lake. She had asked a lot of questions about his way of life, but he hadn't asked that many about hers. He would have to do that next Saturday, because there were so many things he wanted to know. How long would she be in Lancaster studying at the interior design school? How old was she? Did she have any brothers or sisters? Did she have a boyfriend? That was the one thing he wanted to know the most, and it troubled him deeply, because it shouldn't matter so much.

He could still picture Laura sitting in his buggy, her long auburn hair glistening in the sun like golden shafts of wheat. *I shouldn't be thinking about her, much less worrying over whether she has a boyfriend. Probably shouldn't have invited her to have a picnic with me next Saturday, but I just want to see her one more time. I'd like the chance to answer a few more of her questions and ask a few of my own.*

The family-style restaurant where Laura was to meet Darla seemed crowded, and after checking her watch, Laura knew she was late. She stood in the clogged entryway, craning her neck to see around the people in front of her. Was Darla already in the dining room? Sure enough, she spotted her sitting at one of the tables.

When the hostess seated Laura, she couldn't help but notice Darla's impatience as she tapped her fingernails against her place mat and squinted with obvious displeasure. "It's about time you got here."

"Sorry. I tried to call, but you must have had your phone turned off." Laura pulled out a chair and sat down.

"Were you caught in traffic, or do you just like to make people wait?"

"I went for a ride in an Amish buggy this afternoon, and I guess we lost track of time."

Darla's pale eyebrows furrowed. "I wouldn't think any buggy driver would lose track of time. I mean, they charge you a certain amount, and when the time's up, it's up."

Laura shook her head. "I didn't take a commercial buggy ride. I was with Eli Yoder."

"Who?"

"Eli's that cute Amish guy I met at the market a few weeks ago. I'm sure I mentioned it."

Before Darla could comment, Laura rushed on. "I had such a good time today. The fall colors at the lake were gorgeous." She glanced down at her purse and frowned. "I had my camera with me the whole time, but I forgot to take even one picture."

Darla stared out the window a few seconds; then she looked back at Laura. "I can't believe what I'm hearing."

"What do you mean?"

"You're obviously starstruck, and I hope you realize that you're making a huge mistake."

"What are you talking about?"

"I can see you're infatuated with this Amish guy, and you'd better not tell me that you plan to see him again, because it can only lead to trouble."

"I'm not *infatuated* with him!" When Laura noticed several people staring, she lowered her voice. "I did enjoy his company, and the buggy ride was exciting, but that's all there was to it. I hardly even know the man."

"Well, good. That means you're not planning to see him again then, right?"

"We did talk about going on a picnic next Saturday." Laura shrugged. "But it's no big deal."

"No big deal? Laura, do you have any idea of the trouble that could come from an Amish man dating an English woman?" Darla leaned across the table. "Don't do it. You need to cancel that date."

Laura's mouth dropped open. "It's not a real date. It's just an innocent picnic. Besides, I can't cancel. I don't have his telephone number, so I have no way of getting in touch with him." She grabbed her menu, hoping this discussion was finally over.

"Some Amish do have telephones now," Darla said, "but usually only those who have businesses. Do you realize that the Plain People live almost like the pioneers used to? They don't use electricity, or drive cars—"

Laura held up her hand. "I get the picture. Can we change the subject now?"

Darla's voice lowered to a whisper. "I want to say one more thing."

Laura merely shrugged. Darla was obviously not going to let this drop until she'd had her say.

"I told you before that I used to live in this area before

my folks moved to New York, so I know a little something about the Amish."

"Such as?"

"They don't take kindly to Englishers dating their children, and I'll bet Eli's folks don't know he was with you today, do they?"

Laura hated to be cross-examined. None of this was Darla's business. "I don't know what Eli told them when he went home, but today was the first time we've done anything together."

"The Amish are private people. They live separate, plain lives. They don't like worldly ways—or worldly women for their men." Darla shook her head. "You'd be smart to nip this in the bud before it goes any further."

Laura remained silent. She didn't need Darla's unwanted advice, and she knew exactly what she was doing.

⁂

"Say, Mom, I have a favor to ask," Eli said, when he stepped into the kitchen and headed toward the table where Mary Ellen sat tearing lettuce leaves into a bowl.

She smiled, thinking her oldest boy looked happier than usual this evening. "Oh? What favor is that?"

"I'm going on a picnic to the lake next Saturday, and I was wondering if you'd mind packing a picnic lunch for me to take along."

"How much food did you need?"

He grinned. "As much as you want to fix, I guess."

"For how many people, Eli?" she asked with a groan. *Johnny's silly ways must be rubbing off on our son. He thinks he's a practical joker now.*

"Uh. . .there will be two of us, Mom," Eli mumbled, his face turning red.

She nodded, feeling quite pleased with that bit of news. Eli obviously had a date, and she figured it was probably Pauline, since he'd gone to lunch with her awhile ago when they'd met at the farmers' market. "Anything special you'd like me to fix?"

He shrugged. "Just the usual picnic things, I guess."

"All right, then. I'll put together something that I'm sure both you and your date will like."

The color in Eli's face deepened, and he looked away. "Danki, Mom. I really appreciate that."

When Wesley Meade entered the living room, he found his wife curled up on the couch, reading a book. "Hi, hon. How was your day?" He bent down to kiss her forehead.

"It was all right, I suppose," Irene replied without looking up from her novel.

He set his briefcase on the coffee table and took a seat in the recliner across from her. "Did you do anything special?"

"Helen and I went shopping at the mall, got our nails done, and had lunch at Roberto's. Then on the way home, I stopped at our favorite catering place and ordered the food for the hospital guild's annual charity dinner."

Wesley's gaze went to the ceiling. It seemed all his wife did anymore was shop for new clothes she didn't need and flit from one charity organization to another, planning dinners, parties, and elaborate balls. Not that there was anything wrong with charities. He knew that most of the organizations she was involved with did a lot of good for those in need. However, Irene's emphasis seemed to be more on the social side of things rather than on meeting the needs of people who were hurting or required financial or physical help.

"I got an e-mail from Laura today," he said, changing the subject to something he hoped might interest her.

"Really? What did she have to say?"

"So you didn't check your e-mail?"

Irene's hand fluttered as if she was swatting a fly. "Wesley, you know I rarely use the computer you bought me for Christmas last year."

"Why not? It's got all the whistles and bells anyone could want."

"Maybe so, but every time I go online, I end up either getting booted off or everything freezes on me." She sighed. "I don't think that computer likes me."

He chuckled. "You just need to go on it more. Practice makes—"

"I know. I know. If I practiced more, I'd have it mastered." She swung her legs over the sofa and sat up. "So tell me. . .what did our daughter have to say in her e-mail?"

"She said she's getting settled in at the school and thinks she's going to like it in Lancaster County, where she can study the interesting Amish people."

Irene's perfectly shaped eyebrows drew together, and she reached up to fluff the sides of her shoulder-length auburn hair. "Amish people? Our daughter didn't go to Lancaster to study Amish people; she went to learn how to be an interior designer."

"Laura thinks she can get some design ideas from the Plain People."

She clicked her tongue. "That's ridiculous. From what I know of the Amish, they live very simply, without any decorations in their homes that don't serve some sort of purpose. So I don't see how studying the Amish can help Laura with her studies."

"Knowing our enterprising daughter, she'll figure out something about their way of life that she can use in her decorating classes." Wesley stretched his arms over his head and yawned. "Think I'll head upstairs and change into something more comfortable before we have dinner. It'll be a relief to get out of this suit." He undid his tie and slung it over his shoulder as he stood. "Never did like wearing a suit. Wish I could get out of putting one on every day."

She clicked her tongue again. "What kind of lawyer would you be if you didn't wear a suit?"

"A comfortable one."

Irene opened her mouth as if to say something more, but he hurried out of the room. He'd become a lawyer just to please her anyway, and if wearing a suit made her happy, then he'd probably end up wearing one until the day he died.

CHAPTER

4

Laura had been sitting on the wooden bench in front of the variety store for nearly an hour. *Still no sign of Eli. Where is he? Maybe he isn't coming. Maybe Darla's right and he's decided it's best not to have anything to do with a "worldly" woman. I'll give him another five minutes; then I'm leaving.*

She scanned the parking lot again. Several Amish buggies sat parked there, but they were all the closed-in type. Eli's courting buggy was nowhere in sight. She watched as an Amish family went into the store. *I wonder how those women deal with wearing long dresses all the time. If Eli ever shows up, I'll have to remember to ask him why they wear those little white caps on top of their heads.*

She glanced at her watch again—1:45.

Finally at 1:50, his buggy pulled into the parking lot. Laura felt such relief, she was no longer angry. She waved and skittered across the parking lot.

Eli climbed down from the buggy. "Sorry to be so late. I had to help my daed and brothers with some chores at home, and it took longer than expected."

"It's okay. You're here now; that's all that matters."

Eli gave her a boost up into the buggy, then went around

and took his seat. He glanced up at the sky. "There's not a cloud in sight, so it should be a fine day for a picnic." He grinned at Laura, and her heart skipped a beat. "Did you bring a jacket? Even though the sun's out, it's still kind of chilly."

Laura shook her head. "I'm wearing a sweater, so I'll be fine."

Eli picked up the reins and said something in Pennsylvania Dutch to the horse.

"What'd you say just then?"

His face turned crimson. "I told him I was taking a beautiful young woman on a ride to the lake so he'd better behave himself."

Laura's heart kept time to the *clip-clop* of the horse's hooves. "Thank you for such a nice compliment."

Eli only nodded in response.

They traveled in silence the rest of the way, but Laura found being in Eli's company made words seem almost unnecessary.

The air snapped with the sharpness of autumn, and soon the lake came into view. If it was possible, the picturesque scene was even more beautiful than it had been the week before. Maple leaves lay scattered about, reminding Laura of the colorful patchwork quilt lying on her bed. The sun cast a golden tint against the surrounding hills, and a whippoorwill called from somewhere in the trees. Laura relished the sense of tranquility that washed over her like a gentle spring rain.

As Eli helped her out of the buggy, she slid effortlessly into his arms. Raising her gaze to meet his, her breath caught in her throat at the intensity she saw on his face. Her pulse quickened, and she grabbed her camera, hoping the action would get her thinking straight again. She photographed the scenery, being careful not to point the camera in Eli's direction, but it was a sacrifice not to snap a few pictures of his handsome face. How fun it would be to download them to her laptop and send them on to her friend Shannon back home. Shannon would probably get a kick out of seeing how cute Eli looked wearing a pair of dark trousers, a pale blue shirt peeking out from a dark jacket, and a straw hat.

Eli pulled a heavy quilt and a wicker basket from under the buggy seat. After they'd stretched the quilt on the ground, they both took seats. When Eli opened the lid of the basket, Laura was shocked to discover more food than two people could possibly eat. She figured she would have to count calories for the rest of the week.

Eli spread a tablecloth over the quilt, then set out several containers that held fried chicken, coleslaw, dill pickles, wheat bread, Swiss cheese, baked beans, and chocolate cake. He smiled as he handed Laura a glass of iced tea, some plastic silverware, and a paper plate.

"Thank you."

"You're welcome." His face turned a light shade of red. "Uh. . .will you bow your head with me for silent prayer?"

She gave a quick nod, and Eli immediately bowed his head. Having never believed much in prayer, Laura sat quietly, waiting for him to finish.

When he opened his eyes again, she smiled. "It was nice of your mother to prepare this. Especially since she doesn't know me."

Eli's face turned even redder as he reached for a drumstick. "I. . .uh. . .didn't tell Mom about you."

"Why not?"

He removed his straw hat and placed it on the quilt. "Even though I'm still going through my rumschpringe, my folks wouldn't take kindly to the idea of me seeing someone outside our faith."

"Rumschpringe? What's that?"

"Rumschpringe means 'running around.' It's a time in the life of an Amish young person before he or she gets baptized and joins the church. It's a chance for him to explore the outside world a bit if he chooses."

"Ah, I see."

"My folks think I'm too old to be running around still, and as I mentioned last week, they've been pressuring me to join the church and get married."

She gave him a sidelong glance. "If you didn't tell your mother about me, then why did she pack such a big lunch?"

"I told her I was going on a picnic, but I'm sure she thought it was with someone else." Eli reached for another piece of chicken. "Is there anything more you'd like to know about the Amish?"

Laura sighed. Apparently Eli wasn't that different from other men. If he didn't like the way the conversation was going, he simply changed the subject. "When did your religion first begin?" she inquired.

"Our church got its start in the late sixteen hundreds when a young Swiss Mennonite bishop named Jacob Amman felt his church was losing some of its purity," Eli began. "He and several followers formed a new Christian fellowship, later known as 'Amish.' So, you might say we're cousins of the Mennonites."

Laura nodded as Eli continued. "The Old Order Amish, which is what my family belongs to, believes in separation of church and state. We also expect Bible-centeredness to be an important part of our faith. A peaceful way of life and complying with all nonworldly ways are involved, and we believe it's the way Christ meant for the Church to be."

"Life among your people sounds almost idealistic."

He shook his head. "It may seem that way to outsiders, but underneath the joys and blessings of being Amish lie special challenges and the hardship of keeping separate in an ever-changing world."

"I guess that makes sense." Laura ate in silence for a time, savoring the delicious assortment of food and trying to absorb all that Eli had shared. She knew about some Protestant religions and had attended Sunday school a few times while growing up. The Amish religion was more complex than anything she knew about, but she found it rather fascinating.

"Now it's your turn to answer some of my questions," Eli said suddenly.

"What do you want to know?"

He shrugged. "Guess you can start by telling me how old you are and whether you have any brothers or sisters."

"I'm twenty-two, and I'm an only child."

"How long will you be staying in Lancaster County?"

"Just until I finish my studies, which should take no longer than two years. Unless I mess up and flunk some classes, that is," she added with a frown.

"You seem real smart to me. I'm sure you'll do okay."

"Thanks, I sure hope so." She smiled. "Anything else you'd like to know?"

Eli's ears turned pink as he stared out at the lake. "I imagine a pretty woman like you has a boyfriend—maybe more than one, even. Am I right about that?"

Laura snickered. "You're really direct and to the point, aren't you, Eli?"

"My folks would say so." He turned back to look at her and chuckled.

She toyed with the edge of the quilt a few seconds, then stared into his seeking blue eyes. "I've dated several men, but none have ever captured my heart." *At least not until you came along.*

Was that a look of relief she saw on Eli's face? No, it was probably just wishful thinking on her part.

The wind had picked up slightly, and Laura shivered, pulling her sweater tightly around her shoulders.

"You're cold. Here, take my coat." Eli removed his jacket and draped it across her shoulders.

Laura fought the impulse to lean her head against his chest. The temptation didn't linger, because the sound of horse's hooves drew her attention to an open buggy pulling into the grassy area near their picnic spot.

A young Amish woman, wearing a dark bonnet on her head and an angry scowl on her face, climbed down from the buggy. Laura thought she recognized the girl, and her fears were confirmed when Eli called, "Pauline, what are you doing here?"

"I was looking for you, Eli. I stopped by your farm, but Lewis said you had gone to the lake for a picnic. I couldn't think who you might be with, but now I see who has taken my place." Pauline planted both hands on her hips as her frown deepened. "I'm mighty disappointed, Eli. How could you bring this Englisher here?"

Eli jumped up and moved toward Pauline. He placed one hand on her shoulder, but she brushed it aside. "She's that woman you were showing birdhouses to at the market, isn't she?"

Eli glanced back at Laura, his face turning redder by the minute. "Pauline, this is Laura Meade."

Pauline's lips were set in a thin line, and she glared at Laura as though she were her worst enemy.

Laura didn't feel much like smiling, but she forced one anyway. "It's nice to meet you, Pauline."

"You're involved in something you shouldn't be, Eli," Pauline said without acknowledging Laura's greeting. "*Wann der gaul dod is, drauere batt nix.*"

Eli grunted. "You're being ridiculous, Pauline."

"I don't think so, and you'll see what I mean if you don't wake up soon and join the church."

"That's my business, not yours."

Pauline turned away in a huff. "And to think, I came all the way out here for this! I deserve much better." She rushed back to her buggy and scrambled inside. "Enjoy your *wunderbaar schee* picnic!"

"Jah, I will," Eli called back to her.

Laura sat too stunned to speak and struggled to analyze what had just happened.

Pauline drove out of sight, leaving a cloud of dust in her wake. She was obviously Eli's girlfriend.

❦

As Pauline drove away, she clamped her teeth together so tightly that it caused her jaw to ache. *How could Eli have made plans for a picnic with that Laura person, who isn't even of our faith? I thought Eli and I were drawing closer. After two rides home in his courting buggy following singings and having had lunch together recently at the farmers' market, I thought we were officially courting.*

She snapped the reins and got the horse moving faster. Maybe some wind in her face would help her think more clearly.

What I should do is drive over to Eli's place and see if his folks know where he is right now. I'll bet they have no idea he's having a picnic with a fancy English woman who wears sweet perfume and way too much makeup.

Pauline continued to fume as she drove down the road, but by the time she neared the cross street that would take her to Eli's place, she had calmed down enough to think things through a bit more. *If I run tattling to Eli's folks, Mary Ellen will probably say something to Eli about it, and then he'll be angry with me. If that happens, I might never have a chance at winning his heart.*

She shook her head and directed the horse to keep going past the road to Eli's house. If she was ever to win Eli over, she would have to find some other way to do it.

∝

As Eli dropped to the quilt, Laura offered him a tentative smile. "Guess I owe you an apology."

"For what? You did nothing wrong."

"I caused a bit of a rift between you and your girlfriend."

Eli shifted on the blanket. "Pauline's not my girlfriend, although I think she'd like to be. We've been friends since we were kinner."

Laura tipped her head. "Kinner?"

"Children."

"If you've been friends that long, then it's obvious to me she was jealous."

"How do you know that?"

"You saw how upset she got. Only a woman in love shoots sparks the way she did."

Eli shrugged. "I'm sorry if she's jealous, but I've done nothing wrong, and neither have you."

"Nothing but have a picnic with an Englisher. I couldn't understand the Pennsylvania Dutch words you two were speaking. What were you saying?"

Eli fiddled with the end of the tablecloth. "Let's see. . . . She said, 'Wann der gaul dod is, drauere batt nix.' That means, 'After the horse is dead, grieving does no good.' "

"I don't get it."

"I think she meant that I made a mistake in asking you to have a picnic with me and that it will do no good to grieve once I find out how wrong it was."

Laura wrinkled her nose. "Is having a picnic with me really so wrong?"

"In Pauline's eyes it is." Eli grunted. "My folks would probably think so, too."

"She said something else I didn't understand. I think it was 'wonderbar' something or other."

He nodded. "Wunderbaar schee. It means 'wonderful nice.' "

"It's obvious that Pauline doesn't like me."

He frowned. "How can you say that? She doesn't even know you."

"That's true, but she knows you, and she's clearly in love with you. I think she's afraid I might be interested, too."

The rhythm of Eli's heartbeat picked up speed. "Are you?"

"Yes, I am interested. You're different from any other man I've ever met." Laura scooted across the quilt and stood.

"I don't want to make trouble for you, so maybe it would be better if we say good-bye and go our separate ways." She took a step back and tripped on a rock. The next thing Eli knew, Laura had a face full of water.

As Laura sputtered and attempted to sit up, Eli rushed forward, reaching for her hand and helping her stand.

"I—I can't believe I did that." She stared down at her soggy, wet clothes and grimaced. "Look at me. I'm a mess!"

Eli's lips twitched as he struggled not to laugh. "You are pretty wet, and you might get sick if you don't get your clothes dried soon." He nodded toward his buggy. "How about I take you to my place so you can get dried off?"

"Are. . .are your folks at home?" Laura's teeth had begun to chatter, and goose bumps erupted on her arms.

"Probably so—at least Mom."

"How do you know your family won't disapprove of you bringing me there?"

Eli shrugged. "Guess there's only one way to find out."

Laura held her stomach and took a deep breath, as though she were having trouble getting enough air.

"Are you okay? Did you swallow some water?"

She nodded. "A little, but I'm more worried about meeting your mother than anything else. What if she doesn't like me? What if she throws me off your property or disowns you because you brought me there?"

Eli snickered. "I hardly think either of my folks would throw you off the property or disown me." He motioned to the food. "Let's put the leftovers away and head over to my place before you freeze to death."

"Okay. I—I think I do need to get warmed up a bit."

CHAPTER
5

As they traveled down the road in Eli's buggy, Eli explained that his father's farm was situated on sixty acres of dark, fertile land, and as they approached the fields he spoke of, he mentioned that they had been planted in alfalfa, corn, and wheat.

"They remind me of a quilt—rich, lush, orderly, and serene," Laura said, as she snuggled beneath the quilt Eli had wrapped around her before they'd left the lake.

Eli smiled. "You sure do have a way with words, you know that?"

She shrugged. "I'm just expressing the way I see things."

An expansive white house came into view, surrounded by a variety of trees and shrubs, while an abundance of autumn blooms dotted the flower beds. Laura spotted a windmill not far from the home, turning slowly in the breeze as it cast a shadow over the tall, white barn directly behind the house. There were no telephone or power lines on the property, she noted, but a waterwheel grated rhythmically in the creek nearby, offering a natural source of power. There was also a huge propane tank sitting beside the house. Laura assumed it was used for heat or to run some of the Amish family's appliances.

"This is it," Eli said with a sweeping gesture. "This is where I live."

Laura's gaze traveled around the neat-looking farm. Sheep and goats stood inside a fenced corral, and chickens ran about in a small enclosure. On the clothesline hung several pairs of men's trousers, a few dark cotton dresses, and a row of towels pinned in orderly fashion.

"Here you go; this should help." Eli grabbed a towel from the line for Laura and led her around the house and up the steps of a wide back porch.

When they entered the kitchen, Laura's mouth fell open. She felt as if she'd entered a time warp and had stepped back in time. The sweet smell of cinnamon and apples permeated the room, drawing Laura's attention to the wood-burning stove in one corner of the room. No curtains hung on the windows, only dark shades pulled halfway down. Except for a small, battery-operated clock and one simple calendar, the stark white walls were bare.

A huge wooden table sat in the middle of the kitchen, with long benches on either side, and two straight-backed chairs, one at each end. A gas lantern hung overhead, with a smaller kerosene lamp sitting in the center of the table. Against one wall stood a tall, wooden cabinet, and a long counter flanked both sides of the sink. Strategically placed near a massive stone fireplace sat a sturdy-looking rocking chair.

Eli motioned to the stove. "Why don't you stand over there? The heat from the stove will help your clothes dry."

Like a statue, Laura stood as close to the stove as she dared. "Do all Amish live this way?"

Eli moved across the room. "What way?"

"So little furnishings. There aren't any pictures on the walls and no window curtains. Everything looks so bare." Laura rubbed her arms briskly with the towel and then did the same with her stringy, wet hair.

"The Old Order Amish believe only what serves as necessary is needed in the home. Although I must admit that my folks live more simply than some in our community."

This home was like no other Laura had ever seen. Here was a group of people living in the modern world yet having so little to do with it.

Eli looked a bit uncomfortable when a slightly plump Amish woman entered the room. Her brown hair, streaked with a bit of gray, was parted down the middle and worn in a bun at the back of her head. A small, white head covering was perched on top of her head, just like all the other Amish women Laura had seen in the area. The woman's hazel-colored eyes held a note of question when she spotted Laura.

"Uh. . .Mom, I'd like you to meet Laura Meade." Eli motioned to Laura, then back to his mother. "This is my mamm, Mary Ellen Yoder."

Eli's mother gave a quick nod in Laura's direction. Her forehead wrinkled as she looked back at Eli. "What in all the world?"

She doesn't like me. The woman's just met me, and she's already decided that I'm the enemy. Laura forced a smile. "It's nice to meet you, Mrs. Yoder."

Mary Ellen grunted and moved toward the stove, where she began to stir the big pot of simmering apples. "Do you live around here, Laura?"

"No, I. . .uh. . ."

"Has your car broken down, or are you lost and in need

of directions?" She stared at Laura and squinted. "And why are your clothes all wet?"

"Laura's from Minneapolis, Minnesota, Mom," Eli said, before Laura had a chance to respond. "She attends a designer school in Lancaster, and she fell in the lake while we were—"

Mary Ellen whirled around to face Eli. "You know this woman?"

"We met at the farmers' market a few weeks ago. Laura was interested in my birdhouses, and I've been showing her around."

Mary Ellen's gaze went to the wicker basket in Eli's hand. "You two have been on a picnic at the lake?"

"Jah."

"It's beautiful there," Laura put in. "The lunch you made was wonderful."

Before Eli's mother could respond, the kitchen door flew open, and two young Amish men sauntered into the room. They spoke in their native tongue but fell silent when they noticed Laura standing beside Eli and Mrs. Yoder near the stove.

"These are my younger brothers, Lewis and Jonas." Eli motioned to the rowdy pair. "Boys, this is Laura Meade. We met at the farmers' market, and I took her on a picnic today, but she ended up falling in the lake."

Lewis removed his straw hat, revealing a thick crop of dark, Dutch-bobbed hair. Then he nudged Jonas and chuckled. "It looks mighty nice around here, jah?"

Jonas nodded and removed his hat as well. "It sure does."

Laura felt their scrutiny all the way to her toes, and she knew the heat of a blush had stained her cheeks. "It's nice to meet you."

Turning to his mother, Jonas said, "Pop will be right in. Have you got any lemonade? We've worked up quite a thirst out there in the fields."

Mary Ellen nodded and moved across the room to the refrigerator.

Jonas, who had light brown hair and blue eyes like Eli's, pulled out one of the benches at the table. "Why don't you set yourself down and talk awhile, Laura?"

Laura glanced at Eli to see if he approved, but he merely leaned against the cupboard and smiled at her. His mother was already pouring huge glasses of lemonade, while her two youngest boys hung their hats on wall pegs and took seats at the table.

Laura would have expected Eli's brothers to have reacted more strongly to a stranger in wet clothes standing in their kitchen, but maybe they were used to having uninvited guests show up out of the blue.

She had the distinct feeling that Mrs. Yoder would be happy to see her leave, however, and she was about to decline the invitation when Eli spoke up. "I think Laura could probably use something hot to drink, and some of those ginger cookies you made yesterday would be nice, too, Mom."

With a curt nod, Mary Ellen scooped several handfuls of cookies from a ceramic jar, piled them on a plate, and brought it over to the table. Then she poured some coffee from the pot at the back of the stove into a cup and handed it to Laura without even asking if she would like some cream or sugar.

"Thank you."

"Welcome."

Lewis and Jonas dropped to one bench, and Laura sat

beside Eli on the other one. Her hair and clothes were somewhat drier now, and since the table was near the stove, she figured she would be nearly dry by the time she finished her coffee.

Eli made small talk with his brothers about the weather and their work in the fields, and occasionally Laura interrupted with a question or two. She was getting an education in Amish culture that rivaled anything she had ever read about or seen on any postcard.

They were nearly finished with their refreshments when the back door swung open, and a tall, husky man with grayish-brown hair and a full beard lumbered into the room. He slung his straw hat over one of the wall pegs near the door, then went to wash up at the sink. All conversation at the table ceased, and Laura waited expectantly to see what would happen next.

The older man dried his hands on a towel, then took a seat in the chair at the other end of the table. He glanced at Laura but said nothing. Maybe he was used to seeing strangers in their house, too.

Eli decided he needed to break the silence. "Laura, this is my daed, Johnny Yoder. Pop, I'd like you to meet Laura Meade."

Laura nodded. "Hello, Mr. Yoder."

Pop gave a quick nod, then turned to Mom, who was now chopping vegetables at the kitchen counter. "What's to eat?"

Mom's face was stoic as she replied in Pennsylvania Dutch, "Our guest is having coffee, and the rest are having lemonade and cookies. What would you like?"

Pop grunted. "Coffee, please."

Mom brought the coffeepot and cup to the table and placed it in front of Pop.

"Danki," he muttered.

Eli turned to his father again. "Laura's from Minneapolis, Minnesota. She's attending some fancy school in Lancaster, and I've been showing her around the area."

"The wisdom of the world is foolishness," Pop grumbled in his native language.

Eli grimaced. "There's no need to be going rude on my guest."

"Ah, so the Englisher can't understand the *Deitsch*. Is this the problem?" Pop asked with a flick of his wrist.

"What kind of fancy school do you go to, Laura?" Lewis questioned.

"I'm learning to be an interior decorator."

"It's so she can help folks decorate their homes," Eli interjected.

Mom placed another plate of cookies on the table. "It wonders me so that anyone could put such emphasis on worldly things."

"As I said before, Laura and I went to the lake for a picnic," Eli said, changing the subject to what he hoped was safer ground. "It's sure beautiful there now. Some of the leaves are beginning to fall."

"I'll be glad when wintertime comes and the lake freezes over," Jonas added. "I always enjoy goin' ice-skating."

Eli noticed that Laura's hand trembled as she set her cup down. He wasn't the least bit surprised when she hopped off the bench and announced, "Eli, my clothes are drier now, so I think I should be going."

He sprang to his feet. "I'm gonna drive Laura back to

Paradise so she can pick up her car. I'll be home in plenty of time for chores and supper."

When no one responded, Eli opened the back door so he and Laura could make a hasty exit. "That didn't go so well, did it?" he mumbled a few minutes later, as he helped her into the buggy.

"No, it didn't, and I'm sorry for putting you through all that. Your parents obviously don't approve of me."

"Don't worry about it. We're just friends. I'm sure they know that."

Laura twisted the ends of her purse straps, biting down on her lower lip. "Maybe it would be better if you never saw me again."

"No," Eli was quick to say. "I want to be your friend, and I'll be glad to show you around more of the area whenever you like."

"Even if your parents disapprove?"

He shrugged. "Pop and Mom are really fun-loving, easygoing folks, and since we're not courting or anything, there's nothing for them to be concerned about."

Laura looked a little disappointed. Was she hoping they could begin courting? No, that was about as likely as a sow giving birth to a kitten.

"How about next Saturday?" she asked. "Could you show me around then?"

He nodded. "Jah, I think I could."

❧

As the door clicked shut behind Eli, Mary Ellen turned to Johnny and frowned. "This isn't good. Not good at all."

Johnny glanced at Lewis and Jonas, then nodded toward

629

the living room, across the hall. "Why don't you two go in there awhile? Your mamm and me need to talk."

Jonas grabbed a handful of cookies and his glass of lemon-ade, then headed out of the room. Lewis did the same.

"Now let's talk this through," Johnny said, turning his chair to face Mary Ellen.

She moaned and let her head fall forward into her hands. "What are we going to do about Eli and that fancy English woman?"

"Since Eli's not joined the church yet, I doubt there's much we can do except look the other way."

Mary Ellen lifted her head. "We can't just stand by and let him be led astray."

Johnny reached over and took hold of her hand. "Now don't go borrowing trouble. Maybe Eli has just been showing Laura around, like he said. Might not be anything more to it than that."

"I hope you're right. It would break my heart if any of our kinner were to leave the Amish faith."

Eli returned home an hour later, just in time for supper. He was glad when neither of his parents brought up the subject of Laura, but just as they were finishing with the meal, Jonas spoke up.

"That English woman you brought home is sure pretty, Eli. Too bad she isn't Amish, because if she was, I'd be tempted to court her."

Mom let out a little squeal and pushed away from the table, and Pop just sat there with his eyes squinted, looking kind of befuddled.

"She's not trying to make you go fancy, is she, Eli?" The question came from Lewis, and it was followed by a jab to Eli's ribs.

"Of course not. Laura's just a friend who wants to know a little something about the way we live. I only brought her home after her fall in the lake so she could get dried off a bit."

"You play with fire, and you're bound to get burned," Mom mumbled from across the room, where she stood in front of a sink full of soapy water. "There's always trouble somewhere, and that Englisher had trouble written all over her pretty face."

Eli shook his head. "I'm old enough to make my own decisions, don't you think?"

Jonas grinned. "I'm thinkin' my big brother might be in *lieb*."

"I'm not in love! As I've already said, Laura and I are just friends, and I don't see how it could hurt for me to spend a little time showing her around the countryside and sharing a bit about our ways."

"Why would she need to know our ways?" Mom asked.

"She's just curious about our lifestyle, and I think—"

"A few questions here, and a few trips around the country there, and soon that woman will be trying to talk you into leaving the faith."

Eli felt his face heat up. "No way, Mom!"

"I'm sure our son is secure in his faith," Pop interjected. "He needs some time to think about what he's doing. If I know my boy right, he'll soon realize that it's time to get baptized, join the church, and find a nice Amish wife." He thumped Eli on the back. "Ain't that right, son?"

Eli swallowed the last bit of food in his mouth before he answered. "Are you forbidding me to see Laura again?"

Pop shook his head. "No, you have the right to choose, and since we haven't raised any *dummkepp*—dunces—I'm sure you'll choose wisely."

Eli pushed away from the table and stood. "I think I'll go out to my shop awhile." He made a hasty exit out the back door before anyone could respond.

Laura collapsed onto her bed. She felt as if she hadn't slept in days. By the time Eli had dropped her off in front of the variety store where she'd left her car, all her energy had been zapped. The thrill she had felt earlier when she'd been alone with Eli at the lake had diminished some, too.

Until today, Laura had usually been able to charm anyone she met. Not only had she not charmed Eli's parents, but she was quite sure that she'd probably alienated them. If they had known that she was hoping to see Eli again and had even fantasized about asking him to leave the Amish faith and join her in the modern English world, she was sure they would have told her to leave their home at once.

Laura looked forward to her date with Eli next Saturday, but she knew she would have to take things slow and easy. She didn't want to scare Eli off by making him think there was more to their relationship than friendship. That's all there was at this point, but she was hoping for more—so much more.

CHAPTER

6

Saturday dawned with an ugly, gray sky and depressing, drizzling rain. Laura groaned as she stared out the window of her dorm room. She figured Eli probably wouldn't show up for their rendezvous now. If they went for another buggy ride, they would be drenched in no time, and she doubted that he would want to pass the time sitting in some restaurant or wandering through a bunch of tourist-filled souvenir shops with her. They weren't supposed to meet until two o'clock, so with any luck, maybe the rain would be gone by then.

Laura turned from the window and ambled over to her desk, fully intending to get in a few hours of study time. Her mind seemed unwilling to cooperate, however, so she pushed the books aside and painted her fingernails instead.

By noon, the drizzle had turned into a full-fledged downpour. Laura could only hope Eli wouldn't stand her up.

She hurried downstairs and was almost to the door, when Darla showed up in the hallway.

"From the way you're dressed, I'd say you're going out. What I'd like to know is where you're heading on a crummy day like this."

Laura offered a brief smile and held up her green umbrella. "I'm going to Paradise."

Darla's forehead wrinkled. "I figured you would be up in your room studying for that test we'll be having on Monday."

Laura shrugged. "I can't concentrate on schoolwork today. Besides, I'm supposed to meet Eli at the variety store."

Darla's frown deepened. "Are you chasing after that Amish fellow?"

"Of course not. Eli and I are just friends, and he's offered to show me around the area. That's all there is to it."

"Yeah, right."

"It's the truth."

"Well, do whatever you want, but don't come crying to me when you get your toes stepped on."

Laura turned toward the door. "I've got to go. See you later, Darla."

※

"Where are you heading?" Mary Ellen asked as Eli started for the back door. "Out to work in your shop?"

He turned to face her. "Thought I'd go to the farmers' market today."

"Did you rent a table again?"

"Nope. Figured I'd just browse a bit. See if there's anyone else selling handmade wooden items and maybe pick up an idea or two."

Mary Ellen motioned toward the refrigerator. "We're about out of root beer. If you see some of the good homemade kind, would you pick up a couple of jugs?"

"Jah, sure. Anything else you'd like me to get?"

She contemplated a moment, then shook her head.

"Guess not, but knowing me, I'll think of something after you've gone."

He chuckled and headed out the door. "I'll be home by suppertime, Mom. See you then."

Mary Ellen moved over to the sink with the last of the breakfast dishes. She would let them soak while she drank a cup of coffee and read the Amish newspaper. "Sure hope that boy of mine isn't meeting the fancy English girl he brought over here last week," she muttered as she ran water into the sink. "The last thing this family needs is for Eli to fall in love with someone outside our faith and decide to leave."

As Pauline stepped onto the Yoders' back porch, she had second thoughts about her decision to see Eli. What if he became irritated with her for coming over? Would he still be angry because she'd interrupted his picnic at the lake last Saturday? She had to know. She had to work things out with Eli. She needed to make him realize that she was right for him, not some Englisher who probably wanted to try and change him.

Drawing in a deep breath, Pauline opened the door and stuck her head inside. "Anyone to home?"

"I'm in the kitchen," Eli's mother called in return.

Pauline stepped into the kitchen and spotted Mary Ellen sitting at the table with a newspaper spread out before her and a cup in her hand. "Are you busy?"

"Just reading *The Budget* and having a cup of coffee. Come join me." Mary Ellen smiled and motioned Pauline to take a seat.

Pauline pulled out a chair across from Eli's mother and sat down.

"It's good to see you. Did you come to visit with Eli or me?"

Pauline's cheeks warmed. Apparently Mary Ellen knew she had an interest in her son. "I came to see Eli. Is he here?"

Mary Ellen shook her head. "Left a few minutes ago for the farmers' market."

"Does he have a table again today?"

"Not this time. Said he just wanted to browse around."

"I see. Did he go there alone?"

"He left here by himself, but I'm not sure what happened after that." Mary Ellen's eyebrows drew together. "I may be speaking out of turn, but I'm a bit *bekimmere* about my son, and I'm thinking maybe you can help."

Pauline leaned forward, her elbows resting on the table. "How come you're concerned, and how can I be of help?"

Mary Ellen's voice lowered to a whisper, although Pauline didn't know why, since they were alone in the kitchen. "Eli has an English friend. He brought her here last Saturday."

"Does she have long reddish brown hair and a pretty face?"

"Jah."

"Her name's Laura, and Eli met her at the farmers' market a few weeks ago. She was at his table looking at birdhouses when I went there to see if he was ready to have lunch." Pauline nibbled on her lower lip as she contemplated whether to tell Eli's mother about her encounter with Eli and Laura at the lake. As she thought it through, she came to the conclusion that if Mary Ellen had already met Laura and had some concerns, she might already know about the picnic.

Pauline sat up straight. "I saw Eli with Laura at the lake last Saturday. They were having a picnic."

Mary Ellen nodded. "He told us about that, and I wasn't pleased with the news. When I fixed a picnic lunch for him that morning, I figured he was taking you to the lake."

"I had thought Eli and I were drawing close—that we were officially courting." Pauline swallowed around the lump that had lodged in her throat. "Now I'm afraid I might be losing him to that fancy English woman."

Mary Ellen reached across the table and patted Pauline's outstretched hand. "We can't let that happen. If we work together on this, I believe we can get my son thinking straight again." Her lips curved into a smile. "Are you willing to help me?"

"Jah, sure." Pauline would walk across the country and back again if it meant getting her and Eli together.

Laura stepped out of her car just in time to witness a touching scene. Eli stood in front of the variety store, holding a black umbrella over his head. The minute he spotted Laura, he stepped forward and positioned the umbrella over her.

She smiled up at him, her heart pounding with expectation. "I'm surprised to see you."

"I said I'd meet you here."

"I thought the rain might keep you from coming."

"We Amish don't stay home because of a little rain." Eli steered her across the parking lot. "I brought one of our closed-in buggies today, but if you'd rather we take your car, that's okay, too."

Laura's heart beat a staccato rhythm, and when she felt the warmth of his hand on her elbow, she realized his touch was something she could easily become accustomed to. "The buggy's fine with me."

Eli helped her into the left side of the gray, box-shaped buggy, then went around to the driver's side.

"Where are we going?"

"The farmers' market is open today. I thought maybe we could go there."

"That sounds like fun." Laura glanced over at Eli. Her heart felt light, and she was content just being with him, so it didn't really matter where they went.

"How come you're not selling your wooden things there today?"

"Because I'm here with you." He grinned and gathered up the reins. "I don't rent a table every week, and it will be fun just to look around."

She smiled. "Maybe I'll get some more decorating ideas, too."

When they entered the farmers' market a short time later, Laura noticed a host of people roaming up and down the aisles. "The rain didn't keep anyone at home today, did it?" she whispered to Eli.

"Nope, it sure didn't." He motioned to a table on their left. "Let's start over there."

Laura noticed several people staring at them. *What a strange-looking couple we must make: Eli dressed in his plain Amish clothes, and me wearing designer blue jeans and a monogrammed sweatshirt.* "Well, let them stare," she murmured.

"What was that?" Eli asked, as he moved close to a table where a man sold small wooden windmills.

"Nothing. I was talking to myself."

Eli let out a low whistle as he picked up one of the windmills. "Finely crafted—jah, very nice."

"It is nice," Laura agreed.

"Are you hungry? Want something to eat or drink?" he asked when they finally moved on.

"No, but if you're hungry, I'll drink a diet soda and watch you eat."

Eli gently pinched her arm. "A diet soda for someone so skinny?"

"I am not skinny. I'm merely trying to keep my figure."

Eli's ears turned red as he looked her up and down. "Your figure looks fine to me."

Laura giggled self-consciously. "Thanks for the compliment, but for your information, this shape doesn't come easy. I have to work at staying slender, and that means watching what I eat."

Eli raised his dark eyebrows as he continued to study her. "One so pretty shouldn't be concerned about gaining a few pounds. Mom's pleasantly plump, and Pop says he likes her that way."

"You'll never catch me in any kind of plump state—pleasantly or otherwise."

"Someday you'll meet a great guy, get married, and have a whole house full of kinner. Then you probably won't even have a figure, much less have to worry about keepin' it." Eli chuckled and steered her toward the snack bar at one end of the market.

"I told you, I'm not hungry."

"Oh, sure you are." He sniffed the air. "Don't those hot dogs and sausages smell good?"

She wrinkled her nose. "They smell fattening to me."

"If you ask me, you're way too concerned about your weight."

"I don't recall asking you."

Eli jerked his head as though he'd been slapped. "Maybe today wasn't such a good idea after all. Might be better if I take you back to Paradise."

"No, I don't want to go back." Laura clutched at his shirtsleeve. "I'm sorry if I sounded snappish."

They had reached the snack bar, and Eli turned to face her. "Our worlds are so different, Laura. I'm plain, and you're fancy. I see things differently than you do, and I'm afraid it will always be so."

Laura shook her head, her eyes misting with tears. "We're just getting to know each other. It will take some time for us to understand one another's ways." She smiled up at him. "I can teach you things about my way of life, and you can teach me more of the Amish ways."

"I already know all I need to know about the English ways, but if you're still wanting to know more about the Amish way of life, I'm willing." Eli motioned to the snack bar. "Can I interest you in a glass of root beer and a giant, homemade pretzel?"

Laura nodded and released a sigh. "Oh, all right. I guess I can count calories some other time."

Pauline wandered up and down the aisles inside the market building, searching for Eli. There was no sign of him anywhere, and she wondered if he had even come here today. Maybe he'd just told his mother he was going to the farmers' market, when in fact he'd made plans to meet that English woman again. Maybe they'd gone on another picnic at the lake.

She shook her head. No, that wasn't likely since it had been raining all morning.

"*Wie geht's*—how are you, Pauline?" Anna Beachy asked as she strolled up to her.

"I'm fine. And you?"

"Oh, fair to middlin'. Are you here alone, or did you come with your folks?"

"I'm alone. Came by to see if I could find Eli Yoder. Have you seen him around the market anywhere?"

Anna nodded. "Saw him over at Amos Hilty's root-beer stand about ten minutes ago. He was with some English woman, which I thought was pretty strange."

"Did you speak to him?"

"Just long enough to say hello, but then before I had a chance to say anything more, Eli said he was on his way out. He grabbed two jugs of root beer and rushed off like he was in a big hurry."

Pauline felt as if her heart had sunk all the way to her toes. Not only had she missed seeing Eli, but her fears had been confirmed—he was with Laura again.

"I was just heading over to the snack bar to get a German sausage," Anna said. "If you haven't had lunch yet, maybe you'd like to join me."

Pauline shook her head. "Thanks anyway, but I'm not so hungry." She turned toward the exit door as a feeling of defeat threatened to weigh her down. At the rate things were going, she would never get Eli to marry her.

That evening, Laura lay on her bed, replaying the events of the day. As strange as it might seem, she was glad she and Eli had experienced the little disagreement about her weight. Despite the dissension it had caused, for the remainder of the day, Eli had been quite compromising.

A knock on the door stirred Laura from her musings. "Who is it?"

"Darla."

Laura crawled off the bed and opened the door. "If you've come to give me another lecture, you can save your breath."

Darla shook her head. "I wanted to apologize and see how your day went."

Laura motioned her inside. "Actually, it went well. Eli and I drove to the farmers' market in Bird-in-Hand, and I got a few more decorating ideas while we were there."

Darla flopped onto the bed. "The Amish don't believe in fancy decorations or adornments in their homes, Laura."

"That's what makes it so unique."

"I don't follow."

Laura dropped down next to Darla, and her fingers trailed across the edge of the quilt covering her bed. "Take this, for example. It's plain, yet strikingly beautiful. A quilt such as this is in high demand, which is why it was so costly."

Darla shrugged. "To be perfectly honest, Amish decor doesn't do much for me. Neither do Amish men."

Laura clenched her jaw. She had a feeling this conversation might lead to another argument, and she wasn't in the mood for one. "It's been a long day, and I'm tired. Besides,

I think it's time to end this little discussion."

"Sure, okay." Darla stood and started for the door. "Oh, I almost forgot—you had a phone call while you were out exploring Amish land."

"Who was it?"

"Mrs. Evans took the call, and she just told me it was some guy asking for you."

"Hmm. . .maybe it was Dad. But then why wouldn't he have called on my cell phone?"

"I really couldn't say, but I think Mrs. Evans left a note in your mailbox."

"I'll go check." As soon as Darla disappeared into her own room, Laura ran down the steps and found the note in her mailbox. It read:

> A man named Dean Carlson called around two o'clock. He said he had tried to call your cell phone several times and only got your voice mail. He wants you to call him as soon as possible.

Laura sucked in her breath. *Is Dean really missing me, or is he just checking up on me? Should I call him first thing in the morning or make him wait a few days?*

※

"You ought to keep your cell phone charged and check your voice mail once in a while, Laura. I tried for two days to get you and finally had to call your school and leave a message."

Laura held the cell phone away from her ear and grimaced. She knew she had made a mistake calling Dean so early in the morning. She should have remembered he was a bear before his third cup of coffee. "Well, you've got me on the phone now, so you don't have to make such a big deal of it."

"Yeah, okay."

"What did you want, Dean?" she asked, tapping her foot impatiently.

"I thought that I'd come to Lancaster to see you next weekend."

"What?" Laura's mouth went dry. "Coming here is not a good idea."

"Why not?"

"I'm busy, that's why."

"But I miss you, Laura, and I—"

Laura lifted her gaze to the ceiling. She and Dean had only begun dating a few months before she'd left Minneapolis to come here, but he acted like they were practically engaged. "It's not that I don't want you to come. It's just that—well, I'll be coming home for Christmas soon, and—"

"Christmas? That's three months away!"

Laura could almost see Dean's furrowed brows and the defiant lift of his chin. He was a handsome man with jet black hair that curled around his ears, and eyes as blue as a summer sky, but he was way too possessive. "It would be nice to see you, Dean, but I always have a lot of homework to do on the weekends."

"Were you studying when I phoned yesterday?"

Laura knew she couldn't tell Dean about her Saturday date with Eli Yoder, but she didn't want to lie to him, either. "I went to the farmers' market."

"What's that got to do with homework?"

"I was researching the Amish culture."

"Sounds real interesting." Dean's tone was sarcastic, and it irritated her.

"Actually, it's very interesting. I've been studying their quilts and getting some ideas for my next design project." *I've been studying a fascinating Amish man, too.*

Dean cleared his throat. "How about next weekend? Can I come or not?"

Laura chewed on her lower lip. She liked Dean. . .or at least she had when they were seeing each other socially. So why was she giving him the runaround now? It took only a few seconds for her to realize the answer. She was infatuated with Eli and wanted to spend her free time with him. Dean would only be a distraction, and if Eli found out about her English boyfriend, it might spoil her chances with him.

"Laura, are you still there?"

Dean's deep voice drew Laura back to their conversation, and she sighed. "Yes, I'm here."

"What's it going to be?"

"I'd rather you didn't come."

"Is that your final word?"

"Yes, but as I said before, I'll be home for Christmas, so I'm sure we'll see each other then."

Dean grunted and hung up the phone without even saying good-bye. Laura breathed a sigh of relief.

CHAPTER 7

Over the next several weeks, Eli saw Laura as often as possible. In fact, he could hardly get her out of his thoughts. The vision of her beautiful face, smooth as peaches and cream, inched its way into his mind on more than one occasion. When he'd told his folks he was still seeing Laura, the news hadn't gone over so well, especially with Mom.

"She'll try to change you," she admonished one Saturday as Eli hitched the buggy for another trip to meet Laura. "Why, the first thing you know, that woman will be asking you to leave the faith."

"*Ach*, Mom, you worry too much. No one could ever talk me into something I don't want to do."

His mother pursed her lips. "I wouldn't be so sure about that. Love does strange things to people."

Eli's eyebrows shot up. "Love? Who said anything about love? Laura and I are just friends."

Mom gave him a knowing look. "I've seen the face of love before. Every time you come home after being with that fancy woman, I can see the look of love written all over your face, and it scares me, son."

Eli's face heated up. He would never admit it, especially

not to Mom, but he was beginning to wonder if his fascination with Laura might be more than curiosity or friendship. What if he were actually falling in love with her? If she felt the same way about him, would she expect him to leave the faith? Since he hadn't yet been baptized or joined the church, the decision to stay or leave was still his to make. However, there were too many things about his way of life that he would miss if he left home and became English. Besides, there were too many things in the modern world that he didn't particularly care for.

"You have no call to be worried or scared," he said, giving her arm a quick pat. "I know exactly what I'm doing."

"I hope so."

Eli climbed into the buggy and gathered up the reins. "See you later, Mom."

"Say, Eli. . .I was wondering if you could do me a favor."

"What's that?"

"Selma Hostetler has been laid up with a bad back for the last couple of days."

"Sorry to hear that. Nobody likes back pain."

Mom nodded. "I baked some zucchini-banana bread yesterday, and I thought maybe you could drop a loaf by to her. It might help cheer her some."

"Can't Lewis or Jonas do it? I don't want to be late meeting Laura."

Mom's eyebrows drew together. "They're both out in the fields with your daed, which is where you really ought to be, don't you think?"

Eli shook his head. "This is my day off from work, and even though I sometimes help Pop on my day off, he said he didn't need me this morning."

"I see. Well, can you drop off the bread to Selma then?"

"Jah, I suppose, but—"

"I'll go get it now." Mom rushed off before Eli had a chance to say anything more.

A few minutes later, she was back wearing a smile that stretched ear to ear. She handed him the bread, which she had enclosed in some plastic wrap. "Danki, son."

"You're welcome."

As Eli clucked to the horse, his mother waved and called, "Don't be too late for supper tonight. And remember that I love you."

"I love you, too."

When Pauline heard a horse and buggy pull into the yard, she hurried to the back door, not wanting her mother to be disturbed. Mom had taken some aspirin for the pain in her back and had returned to her bed soon after breakfast was over.

When Pauline saw Eli step down from one of their closed-in buggies, her heart skipped a beat. Had he come to see her—maybe invite her to go someplace with him today? She waited on the porch with sweaty palms and shaky legs as he headed to the house. When he reached the porch, he stopped and held out a loaf of bread.

"Mom asked me to deliver this to your mamm. I hear her back's been acting up."

Pauline nodded as a sense of disappointment flooded her soul. She took the bread and mumbled, "Danki. That was thoughtful of your mamm."

Eli shuffled his feet a few times as he stared at the ground. "Well, I—"

"Would you like to come in for a cup of coffee?" She motioned to the door. "I just made a fresh pot, and it might help take the chill out of your bones on this frosty morning."

"I. . .uh. . .appreciate the offer, but I can't stay."

"Are you working today?"

"No, it's my day off."

"Then surely you have time for a quick cup of coffee."

He shook his head. "I'm meeting a friend in Paradise, and I'm already late, so I'd better go."

Pauline clenched her teeth. *I'll bet it's that fancy English woman Eli's meeting. Should I come right out and ask?* She was about to, when Eli turned toward his buggy and started walking away.

"See you at church tomorrow," he called over his shoulder.

"Jah, see you then," she muttered as she went back into the house. *Will I ever get through to Eli? Will he ever see me as anything more than a friend?*

❧

"I'm sorry I was late picking you up," Eli said as he helped Laura into his buggy. "I had to make a delivery for my mamm."

"That's okay. You're here now, and that's all that counts." Laura drew in a deep breath. "It feels and smells like winter is coming, doesn't it?"

Eli nodded. "It's a lot warmer inside my daed's closed-in carriage, but I sure do miss my courting buggy."

"Don't you use it in the winter months at all?"

He shrugged. "Sometimes on the milder days, but it's much nicer inside this buggy today, don't you think?"

"Jah." She giggled and flipped the end of her ponytail.

Eli grinned. "You look real schee today."

"Nice. You said I look nice today, right?"

He nodded. "You're catching on fast to the Deitsch.

Laura's heart fluttered. "Thanks for the compliment."

Eli only nodded again and made the horse go a bit faster.

"Where are you taking me today?" Laura asked.

"I thought you might like to see one of our schoolhouses."

"Schoolhouses? You have school on Saturdays?"

He chuckled. "No, but Saturday's the best day for a tour of the schoolhouse. There won't be any kinner about, and no teacher wearing a stern look or carrying a hickory switch."

"Eli Yoder, you're such a tease." Laura reached across the short span between them and touched his arm. "Maybe that's why I like you so well."

"Because I like to kid around?"

"Yes. I find your humor and wholesome view on life rather refreshing. It's like a breeze on a sweltering summer day."

Eli scrunched up his nose. "I don't believe I've ever been compared to a breeze before."

She withdrew her hand and leaned back. "I've learned a lot from you."

"Is that good or bad?"

"It's good, of course." Her voice lowered to a whisper. "I could teach you a lot about English ways, if you'd let me. We could take in a movie sometime, or—"

Eli held up his hand. "No, thanks. I think I know more than enough about the fancy life."

"How can you say that? Have you ever given yourself a chance to find out what the modern world really has to offer?"

"I'm not blind, Laura," he muttered. "I see what's out there in the world, and even though I haven't felt ready to join the church, I'm not all that interested in electrical gadgets, fancy clothes, or thinkin' I don't need God."

Laura's mouth dropped open. "Who said anything about not needing God?"

"I'm sure lots of English folks do love God," Eli said. "But I've seen many people who seem too self-centered to give Him anything more than a few thoughts, and then it's only when they're in need of something."

"Where did you hear that?" she asked, her voice edged with irritation. Was this going to turn into a full-fledged disagreement? If so, she wasn't sure it was a good idea to give her opinion. After all, she was trying to appease, not aggravate, Eli.

He shrugged. "It doesn't matter where I got the notion. The important thing is, I'm happy to be a child of God, and I don't need any worldly things to make me complete."

"My father says religion is a crutch for weak men, and I'm inclined to believe him." The words were out before Laura had time to think, and she could have bitten her tongue when she saw the look of irritation on Eli's face.

Eli pulled sharply on the reins and eased the horse and buggy to the shoulder of the road. "Are you saying I'm a weak man, Laura?"

She turned to face him. "No, of course not. I just meant—"

"Maybe we've come too far," Eli said, his forehead wrinkling.

"Too far? You mean we missed the schoolhouse?"

He shook his head. "Too far with this friendship we probably shouldn't be trying to build."

Laura's heart began to pound, and her throat felt like she'd eaten a bunch of hot peppers. If Eli broke things off now, there would be no chance for them. She couldn't let that happen. She would not allow him to stay angry with her for something so ridiculous as a difference of opinion on religious matters.

She touched his arm and was glad when he didn't pull away. "Eli, I respect your religious beliefs, but can't we just agree to disagree on some things?"

"It's kind of hard to have a friendship with someone when we keep arguing."

She nodded. "I know, so let's not argue anymore. In fact, if it would make you feel better, I'll just sit here and listen to you narrate. How's that sound?"

He reached for the reins and gave her a sidelong glance. "You're a hard one to say no to, you know that?"

Laura smiled. "That's what my father says, too."

***

"Your wife called five times while you were in court today and left messages for you to call her back as soon as you could," Wesley's secretary told him when he entered the reception area of his office.

"Did she say what she wanted?"

"No, just that it was important and she wanted you to call as soon as you could."

"I can imagine how important it was," he grumbled as he headed to his office. "Probably some major crisis over a broken fingernail."

Wesley had no more than taken a seat behind his desk, when his phone rang. He picked it up on the second ring, recognizing the caller ID. "Hello, Irene. I heard you called a few times while I was in court."

"Yes, I did, and I'm very upset."

His gaze went to the ceiling. Irene was always upset about something it seemed. "What's the problem?"

"It's Laura. I got an e-mail from her today, and she's in real trouble."

Wesley's heart began to race. "Is she sick? Has she been hurt?"

"No, no. She's all right physically, but I think she's taken leave of her senses."

He shifted the receiver to his other ear. "What's that supposed to mean?"

"Our daughter's been seeing some Amish man. She's gone out with him several times, and—"

"Whoa! Hold on a minute, and calm down. You're not making any sense."

"Laura's e-mail said she's involved with an Amish man named Eli. I think his last name is Yoder, or something like that. She said they've gone on a couple of picnics, to the farmers' market, and for rides in his buggy." After a brief pause, Irene released a shuddering sob. "We've got to put a stop to this right away, Wesley. Can you fly out to Pennsylvania and speak to her about this?"

"Me? Why can't you go? I'm tied up in court for at least another week, and then I've got—"

"I can't go, either. I'm involved with that benefit dinner I'm helping plan for the historical society, and then there's the country club luncheon I'm in charge of."

"So you're not that worried about Laura, are you?"

"Of course I am."

"Well, you needn't be. Our daughter is old enough to make her own choices about whom she sees and when. I think if we try to interfere, it will only make things worse." Wesley reached for the cup of coffee his secretary had just placed on his desk and took a drink. "Besides, Laura will be home for Christmas in a few weeks. I'll talk to her about this Amish fellow then, and if I think she's in over her head, I'll try to dissuade her."

"All right. I guess that would be best. Oh, I've got a call on the other line. I'll see you when you get home." Irene clicked off without saying good-bye.

Wesley shook his head. "Like mother, like daughter."

CHAPTER 8

It was only the first week of December, but Lancaster County had been hit with a heavy blanket of snow. Laura figured it would mean the end of her enjoyable rides with Eli. . .at least until spring. She would be going home for Christmas soon, so that would put an end to their times, anyway.

Leaving Eli, even for a few weeks, wasn't going to be easy. However, she had promised her parents and friends that she'd be coming home for the holidays, and she didn't want to disappoint them. Besides, even if she stayed in Pennsylvania, Eli would spend Christmas with his family, and she, the fancy English woman, would not be included in their plans.

Laura stared out her dorm-room window at the falling snow. If only she had some way to get in touch with Eli. If they could just meet somewhere for lunch before she had to leave.

She finally curled up on her bed with a romance novel, surrendered to the fact that this Saturday would be spent indoors without Eli.

Laura had only gotten to the second page when a loud knock drove her to her feet. "Who's there?"

"Darla. Are you busy?"

Laura opened the door. "What's up?"

Darla was dressed in a pair of designer jeans and a pink sweater. A brown leather coat was slung over one arm, and a furry little cap was perched on top of her short, blond curls. "I thought I'd drive into Philadelphia. I still have some Christmas shopping to do, and only the big stores will have what I want."

"You're going shopping today?"

Darla nodded. "I was hoping you'd come along."

"In this weather?" Laura gestured toward the window. "In case you haven't noticed, there's a foot of snow on the ground."

Darla shrugged. "I'm sure most of the main roads have been cleared." She nudged Laura's arm. "I'll treat you to lunch."

"I'm on a diet."

"So, order a salad."

Laura released a sigh. "Oh, all right." It wasn't the way she wanted to spend the day, but she figured it would be better than being cooped up in her room all day.

"I'm going out for a while," Eli said, as he left the kitchen table and slipped into his heavy woolen jacket.

"Where you heading?" Lewis called to him.

"I've got some errands to run. . .not that it's any of your business, *schnuppich* brother." Eli plopped his black felt hat on his head and closed the door, curtailing more comments from his snoopy sibling.

Mary Ellen clicked her tongue against the roof of her mouth and turned to face Johnny. "Seems like our oldest boy is hardly ever home anymore."

Johnny shrugged. "Guess that's his choice."

"I'll bet he's sneakin' off to see that English woman again," Jonas said as he grabbed a hunk of shoofly pie.

"Don't you ever fill up?" Johnny's eyebrows drew together. "That's your third piece now, isn't it?"

"He's probably lost count," Lewis said with a chuckle.

Jonas smacked his lips. "Shoofly is my favorite breakfast pie. Never have been able to get enough of it."

"No, but you sure have tried." Mary Ellen pushed her chair away from the table and gathered up some of the dishes. As she placed them in the sink, she glanced out the window and caught sight of Eli hitching his horse to the sleigh. She couldn't help but wonder if Jonas was right about Eli meeting Laura today. He hadn't said much about her lately, but Mary Ellen knew from her last conversation with Selma Hostetler that Eli sure wasn't courting Pauline.

On more than one occasion, Mary Ellen had tried putting in a good word for Pauline, and from what she'd heard, Pauline had made several attempts at getting Eli to invite her somewhere. So far all efforts had failed, and Mary Ellen knew all she could do was pray—and she'd been doing a lot of that lately. If enough prayers went up on Eli's behalf, he might see the light and quit spending time with Laura. Or she might get bored with him and find a nice English man to take her places. Better yet, maybe the fancy English woman would leave Lancaster County and never return.

The ride to Philadelphia went well. They took the main highway, and just as Darla had predicted, it had been plowed and treated. The bad weather hadn't kept many people home, for the stores were crowded with holiday shoppers.

Laura and Darla pushed their way through the crush of people and fumbled through the racks of clothes and stacks of gift items until they'd both purchased enough Christmas presents for everyone on their lists. Everyone except for Eli. Laura wanted to get him something special, but since he lived a much simpler life than she did and was opposed to most worldly things, she couldn't find anything that might be suitable.

They had a late lunch and left the city around four o'clock, and by the time they reached the turnpike, it was snowing again.

"I know it's a little out of the way, but would you mind stopping at the variety store in Paradise on our way home?" Laura asked Darla.

"What for?"

"I want to get a Christmas present for Eli. I couldn't find anything appropriate in Philadelphia, but I'm sure I can find something there."

Darla squinted. "I don't mind stopping, but I do mind what you're doing."

Laura looked away. "What are you talking about?"

"I can see that no matter how much I've warned you about this, you've decided to jump into the deep end of the pool without even looking."

"Huh?"

"Don't be coy, Laura. I've warned you about getting involved with that Amish man, and you've forged ahead anyway. It doesn't take a genius to realize you're head over heels in love with this Eli fellow."

"In love? Don't be ridiculous! Eli and I are just friends."

Darla gave the steering wheel a few taps with her gloved fingers. "Sure. . .whatever you say."

When they arrived at the store in Paradise, no cars or buggies were in the parking lot, and it appeared to be deserted. However, the sign in the window said they were open, so Darla parked her car, and Laura went inside.

She soon realized that choosing a gift for an Amish man, even in a Plain store, wasn't going to be easy. Shelves were full of men's black felt hats, suspenders in all sizes, and a large assortment of white handkerchiefs. Laura wanted something more special than any of these things. It had to be a gift that would cause Eli to remember her whenever he looked at it.

She was about to give up, when she spotted a beautiful set of carving tools she was sure Eli could use. She paid for them and left the store feeling satisfied with her purchase. Now if she could only get the gift to Eli before she went home for Christmas.

As Laura returned to Darla's car, her foot slipped on the walkway, and she realized the snow had begun to freeze.

"This isn't good," Darla complained as they pulled out of the parking lot a few minutes later. "I should have gone directly back to Lancaster and stayed on the main roads."

Laura grunted. "I'm sure we'll get back to the school in time for your favorite TV show."

"I wasn't thinking about TV. I'm concerned about staying on the road and keeping my car intact."

No sooner had she spoken the words than they hit a patch of ice. The car slid off the road, coming to a stop in the middle of a snowbank.

"Oh, great!" Darla put the car in REVERSE and tried to back up. The wheels spun, but the car didn't budge. She tried several more times, but it was no use. They were stuck, and it was obvious that there was nothing either of them could do about it.

"Maybe I should get out and push," Laura suggested with a weak smile.

"I'd better make a call for help." Darla reached into her purse for the cell phone and started to dial but dropped it to the seat with a moan.

"What's wrong?"

"The battery's dead. I forgot to charge it last night." Darla opened the car door and got out. Laura did the same.

"Now we're really in a fix." Darla kicked at the front tire with the toe of her boot. "I should have checked my phone before we left Lancaster this morning."

"I guess it's my fault. If I hadn't asked you to go to the variety store—"

Laura stopped speaking when she heard the *clip-clop* of horse's hooves approaching. "Do you need some help?" a man's voice called out.

She whirled around, and her heartbeat quickened as Eli stepped down from an open sleigh. "Are we ever glad to see you!"

Eli joined them right away, and Laura introduced Darla. Then, offering Eli a wide smile, she asked, "Would it be possible for you to give us a ride to the nearest town? We need to call a tow truck to get Darla's car out of that snowbank."

Eli surveyed the situation. "I think I can pull you out with my horse."

Darla shook her head. "You've got to be kidding."

"My horse is strong as an ox."

"Okay," Darla said with a shrug. "You may as well give it a try."

Laura and Darla stepped aside as Eli unhitched the horse and hooked a rope around the animal's neck, then fastened the rope to the back bumper of Darla's car. He said a few words in Pennsylvania Dutch, and the gelding moved forward. The car lurched and was pulled free on the first try.

"Hooray!" Laura shouted with her hands raised.

Darla just stood with her mouth hanging open.

"Why don't I follow you back to the main road where it's cleared?" Eli suggested. "That way I can be sure you don't run into any more snowbanks."

"Thank you," Darla murmured, as though she could hardly believe her car had been freed by a horse.

Laura turned to Eli. "Would it be okay if I rode in your sleigh for a while? I've always wanted to ride in one." She touched his arm. "Besides, I have something for you."

His brows arched upward. "You do?"

She nodded. "I'll get it from Darla's car and be right back." Laura raced off before Eli had a chance to reply. When she grabbed Eli's gift from the car, Darla, already in the driver's seat, gave her a disgruntled look but said nothing.

Laura made her way back to where Eli waited beside the sleigh. After he helped her up, she pulled the collar of her coat tightly around her neck. "Brr. . . It's sure nippy out."

Eli reached under the seat and retrieved a quilt. He placed it across her lap, and she huddled beneath its warmth, feeling like a princess on her way to the ball.

As they followed behind Darla's car, Laura snuggled

closer to Eli and said, "I'm glad you came along when you did. I'm leaving for Minneapolis in a few days, and I didn't think I'd get the chance to see you before I left."

"I went to the variety store in Paradise this morning," Eli said. "You weren't there, so I thought maybe you'd already gone home for the holidays."

Laura frowned. If she'd had any idea Eli was going to venture out in the snow just to see her, she would have moved heaven and earth to get to Paradise this morning. "I guess fate must have wanted us to meet today after all."

Eli raised one eyebrow. "Fate? You think fate brought us together?"

She nodded. "Don't you?"

He shook his head. "If anyone brought us together today, it was God."

"I have something for you," Laura said, feeling a bit flustered and needing to change the subject. She lifted the paper bag in her hands, and her stomach lurched with nervous anticipation. "Merry Christmas, Eli."

"You bought me a gift?"

She nodded and smiled.

"But, I—I don't have anything to give you."

"That's okay. I didn't buy you a present so I would get one in return."

Eli's eyebrows lifted and almost disappeared under the brim of his black hat. "What is it?"

"Why don't you open it and find out?"

"If it's a Christmas present, shouldn't I wait 'til Christmas to open it?"

She shook her head. "I'd like you to open it now, so I can see if you like it or not."

"All right then, but let's wait 'til we get to the main road and have stopped so you can get back in your friend's car again."

Laura felt a bit disappointed, but she didn't want to start an argument, so she merely shrugged and said, "Okay."

They rode in silence until Darla's car slowed and came to a parking lot. Eli guided his horse and sleigh in behind her.

"Here you go." Laura handed the sack to him.

Eli opened it and pulled out the carving set. He studied it a few seconds before he spoke. "It's a nice gift—much better than the carving set I use now." He fidgeted kind of nervously, and Laura was afraid he was going to hand it back to her.

"What's wrong? Don't you like it?"

"It's very nice, but I'm not sure I should accept such a gift."

"Why not?" she asked, looking deeply into Eli's searching blue eyes.

"It doesn't seem right, since I have nothing to give you in return."

Laura reached for his hand and closed her fingers around his. "Your friendship is the only present I need this Christmas. Please say I'm one of your special friends."

Eli swallowed so hard she saw his Adam's apple bob up and down. Several seconds went by; then he finally nodded and offered her a smile that calmed her fears and warmed every inch of her heart.

CHAPTER 9

Laura's first few days at home were spent visiting with her parents and thinking about Eli. When she closed her eyes, she could visualize his friendly smile, little chin dimple, and those clear blue eyes calling her to him.

Ever since Laura had returned, her mother had been trying to keep her occupied. "Why not join me for lunch at Ethel Scott's this afternoon?" she suggested one morning.

Laura was lying on the couch in the living room, trying to read a novel she had started the day before. She set it aside and sat up. "I need to get my Christmas presents wrapped."

Mom took a seat next to Laura. Her green eyes, mirroring Laura's, showed obvious concern. "I'm worried about you, dear. You haven't been yourself since you came home for the holidays." She touched Laura's forehead. "Are you feeling ill?"

Laura shook her head. "I'm fine. Just a bit bored. I'm used to being in class every weekday."

"That's precisely why you need to get out of the house and do something fun while you're here." Mom tipped her head, causing her shoulder-length auburn hair to fall across one rosy cheek. Even at forty-five, she was still lovely and youthful looking.

"Ethel's daughter, Gail, is home from college, and I'm sure she would be thrilled to see you," Mom continued. "In fact, she'd probably enjoy hearing about that boring little town you're living in now."

Laura moaned. "Lancaster isn't little, and it sure isn't boring."

"The point is you've been cooped up in this house ever since you got home. Won't you please join me today? It will be better than being home by yourself."

"I won't be alone," Laura argued. "Foosie is here, and she's all the company I need." She glanced at her fluffy, ivory-colored cat sleeping contentedly in front of the fireplace. "After I'm done wrapping gifts, I thought I might try to call Shannon again."

Mom stood. "I would think it would be Dean Carlson you'd be calling." She shook her finger at Laura. "Dean's called at least four times in the past two days, and you always find some excuse not to speak with him."

Laura drew in her bottom lip. How could she explain her reluctance to talk to Dean? She sure couldn't tell her mother that she had been comparing Dean to Eli. "I'll be seeing him on Christmas Day. That's soon enough."

Mom finally shrugged and left the room.

Laura puckered her lips and made a kissing sound. "Here, Foosie, Foosie. Come, pretty lady."

The ball of fur uncurled, stretched lazily, and plodded across the room. Laura scooped Foosie into her lap and was rewarded with soft purring when the cat snuggled against her. "I've missed you. Too bad cats aren't allowed in the dorm rooms at school. If they were, I would take you back with me."

The telephone rang and Laura frowned. "Just when we were getting all cozy." She placed the cat on the floor and headed for the phone that was sitting on a table near the door. "Meade residence."

"Laura, is that you?"

"Yeah, it's me, Shannon."

"When did you get home?"

"Last Saturday. I've tried to call you a couple of times, but you're never home."

"I've been busy planning my preschoolers' Christmas party and the program they'll put on for their parents. My answering machine isn't working right now, either, so I'm sorry you couldn't leave a message."

"That's okay. I've been busy, too." *Busy thinking about Eli and wishing I could spend the holidays with him.*

"Is it all right if I come over?"

"Sure, I'd like that."

After Laura hung up the phone, she headed for the kitchen. She had two cups of hot chocolate ready by the time her friend arrived.

"Have a seat, and let's get caught up," Laura said, handing Shannon a mug.

Shannon sniffed her drink appreciatively. "Do you have any marshmallows?"

Laura went to the cupboard to look, while her friend placed her mug on the table, then took off her coat.

"I think it's going to be a white Christmas," Shannon commented. "We usually have some snow by now, but I'm sure it's not far off, because I think I can actually smell snowflakes in the air."

Laura tossed a bag of marshmallows on the table and took the seat across from Shannon. "We've already had a good snowstorm in Lancaster."

"Really? Were you able to get around okay?"

"Oh, sure. In fact, I—"

"Say, you haven't said a word about my new hairstyle." Shannon pulled her fingers through her bluntly cut, straight black hair. "Do you like it?"

Laura feigned a smile as she searched for the right words. "You. . .uh. . .look different with short hair."

Shannon blew on her hot chocolate, then reached inside the plastic bag and withdrew two marshmallows. She dropped them into the mug and grinned. "I like my new look, and so do my preschool kids."

"I'm surprised you cut your hair. I thought you would always keep it long."

Shannon shrugged, then took a sip of her drink. "Long hair is too much work, and it takes forever to dry." She set the cup down and snapped her fingers. "Why don't you get your hair cut and styled while you're home for Christmas?"

"I don't think I could ever cut my hair. It took me too long to grow it."

Shannon poked at the marshmallows with the tip of her finger. "Have you met any cute guys out there in Lancaster County?"

"Eli Yoder. I sent you an e-mail about him."

"You mean that Amish fellow?"

"He's the one."

"I thought that was just a passing fancy. Surely you're not seriously interested in this guy."

Laura felt the heat of a blush creep up the back of her

neck and spread quickly to her face. "I've been fighting my attraction to Eli, but I'm afraid it's a losing battle." She drew in a deep breath and let it out in a rush. "To tell you the truth—and I can't believe I'm actually saying this out loud—I think I might be in love with him."

Shannon nearly choked on her hot chocolate. "You can't be serious!"

"I am."

"Does he know how you feel?"

"I don't think so. We've agreed only to be friends, and I don't see how it could work for us to have a romantic relationship."

Shannon nodded. "Makes sense to me."

"Eli's family is really religious, and we're worlds apart, with him being a plain kind of guy and me being a fancy English woman." Laura laughed dryly. "At least that's how Eli sees me."

Shannon drummed her fingers along the edge of the table. "Hmm. . ."

"What?"

"Maybe he will leave the Amish faith and become fancy."

"I've thought about that—even hoped for it," Laura admitted. "Eli's religion and his plain lifestyle seem very important to him. I doubt he would be willing to give it up, though I might ask—when I get up the nerve."

Shannon reached across the table and patted Laura's hand in a motherly fashion. "This is a fine fix you've gotten yourself into. Maybe you'll end up going over to the other side before it's all said and done."

Laura's eyebrows furrowed. "Other side? What are you talking about?"

"I was thinking you might join the Amish faith. People have done a lot stranger things in the name of love."

Laura's frown deepened. "I don't think I could do that, Shannon. It would be hard to give up everything I've become used to, and—"

The kitchen door opened just then, and Laura's father entered the room, carrying an overstuffed briefcase. From the way his shoulders sagged and the grim look he wore, Laura figured he must either be exhausted or agitated about something.

Her father was a small, thin man, with dark brown hair and a matching mustache. His mahogany eyes looked unusually doleful as he shuffled across the room and collapsed into a chair.

"Dad, is something wrong?" Laura asked, feeling concern. "You look so tired."

"It's just this fast-paced world we're living in," he answered, lowering his briefcase to the table. "On days like today, I wish I could pull a magic handle and make everything slow down. Maybe the pioneer days weren't so bad. Life in the fast lane is pretty hectic, but I suppose I'll survive." His forehead wrinkled as he looked at Laura. "Whatever you do, young lady, never let 'all work and no play' become your motto."

"I'll try not to, Dad."

"By the way, your mother mentioned that you've become friendly with an Amish man, and I've been meaning to talk to you about it."

Laura nodded and swallowed hard. Was her father going to give her a lecture about Eli in front of Shannon?

Dad smiled. "Well, if you ever see that fellow again, be

sure to tell him that I envy his simple lifestyle." He glanced over at Shannon then. "Nice to see you."

"It's good to see you, too, Mr. Meade."

He turned his attention back to Laura. "Where's your mother?"

"She was supposed to have lunch with her friend Ethel today, and I think they planned to do some shopping afterward." Laura released a sigh of relief. Maybe Dad wasn't opposed to her seeing Eli. Maybe there would be no lecture.

"I can only imagine what kind of unnecessary things she'll bring home this time." He shook his head. "Your mother spends more time shopping than any other woman I know."

Laura nodded. "She does like to shop—when she's not busy with all her charity functions."

"There's nothing wrong with helping out, but the kinds of things she does make me wonder if she's more interested in making herself look good rather than helping others." He grunted. "I doubt that your mother knows how to relax anymore, she's so busy flitting from one charity benefit to another. What we both really need is a vacation from the rat race of city life."

"Maybe you should take a trip to Hawaii or go on a cruise to the Bahamas," Laura suggested.

"Maybe so." He moved across the room toward the door leading to the hallway. "Guess I'll head out to the living room and unwind a bit before your mother gets home."

"Okay."

"Your dad seemed pretty uptight, didn't he?" Shannon said after Laura's father had left the room.

"Yes, he did, and I was surprised he didn't lecture me about seeing Eli."

Shannon laughed. "Parents. Who can figure them out?"

"Not me." Laura took a drink of her hot chocolate as she reflected on her father's words. The things he'd said about wanting to slow down had made her think of Eli and his Amish family. They worked hard, but they weren't really a part of the fast-paced world. From all Eli had told her, she knew that he and his family took time out for fun and relaxation. She wondered if Dad were given the chance, whether he might trade in his briefcase for a hoe and the quiet life among the Plain People. She chuckled softly. *No, that could never happen.*

Wesley wandered into the living room, leaving his briefcase in the kitchen, along with his cares of the day. He had a splitting headache and wanted to spend the rest of his day relaxing and not thinking about anything that pertained to his latest court case.

Wesley discovered Laura's lazy cat lying in front of the fireplace, but the minute he took a seat in his recliner, the cat was in his lap.

"You've got life made, you know that, Foosie?"

The cat responded with a quiet *meow.*

He reclined the chair and closed his eyes as he allowed his mind to wander back to the days when he'd been a boy growing up on his dad's farm in Montana. Life had been so much simpler then. They had worked plenty hard on the farm, but they'd always taken the time to enjoy the simple things in life, and their focus had been on family and friends, not "things."

Wesley had given up that life to please Irene, and now

he felt as if he were caught in a trap from which there was no escape. Someday when he retired, maybe he would sell this place and move to the country again, where he could raise some chickens, a few pigs, and some cats. . .lots of cats.

Eli meandered toward his woodworking shop at one end of the barn. He didn't know why, but he wasn't in the mood to carve or build a single thing.

When he reached his workbench, he looked down at the woodworking set Laura had given him and groaned. He wished she hadn't presented him with such a fine, expensive gift. In fact, he wished she hadn't bought him anything. He'd given her nothing in return, and accepting Laura's present only made it that much harder to distance himself from her, which he knew he must do if he was ever going to join the church.

He thought about Pauline and wondered if he could have been content to court her if Laura hadn't come along when she did. It was hard to explain, but being with her made him feel alive and whole.

Eli sank to the metal folding chair by his workbench and leaned forward until his head rested in the palms of his hands. "If only I hadn't started seeing her. If I could just stop the feelings I have whenever we're together. It just isn't right."

"What isn't right?"

Eli jerked upright at the sound of his younger brother's voice. "Jonas, what do you think you're doing, sneakin' up on me that way?"

Jonas chuckled and sauntered over to the workbench. "I

thought you came out here to work on a Christmas present, not talk to yourself." He gave Eli's shoulder a couple of thumps.

Eli frowned. "I was planning to finish up the planter box I'm making for Martha Rose, but I can't seem to get in the mood to work on it right now."

Jonas pushed a bale of straw over to the bench and plopped down on it. "Christmas is only a few days away. How do ya think our big sister will feel about not gettin' a gift from you?"

Eli grabbed the planter in question, along with a strip of sandpaper, and began sanding it with a vengeance. "It'll be done on time."

Jonas touched Eli's arm. "Take it easy. Now you're gettin' all worked up."

"I'm not worked up," Eli snapped, as he continued to run the coarse paper over the edges of the wooden box.

Jonas eyed him intently. "Is that so? Well, ya sure could've fooled me."

"Quit your staring."

"I was just checkin' to see if my big brother is in lieb."

Eli slapped the sandpaper down on the bench and stood, nearly knocking over his wooden stool. "I'm not in love! Now, if you don't have anything sensible to say, why don't you go bother someone else?"

"It's that fancy English woman, isn't it? You're all worked up over her, I'm guessing."

Eli's forehead beaded with sweat, and he knew it wasn't from heat, for there was at least a foot of snow on the ground. If only he could get Laura out of his mind.

"You're not denying it, so it must be true," Jonas persisted. "She's gotten under your skin, huh?"

Eli whirled around to face his brother. "Laura and I are just friends." His right eyelid began to twitch. "Even if I wanted it to be more, it could never happen."

"How come?"

"She's English."

"I know, but—"

"There are no buts." Eli felt his patience begin to wane. "I don't want to leave our faith, and I sure couldn't ask Laura to become one of us."

"Why not?"

Eli folded his arms and drew in a deep breath. He was getting frustrated with this ridiculous conversation. "Let's put it this way—would you throw a newborn *bussli* into the *seischtall?*"

Jonas tipped his head and looked at Eli as if he'd gone daffy. "Huh? What's a little bitty kitten and a pigpen got to do with Laura Meade?"

Eli shook his head. "Never mind. You're probably too *verhuddelt* to understand."

"I'm not confused! Just say what ya mean, and mean what ya say!" Jonas's forehead now dripped with sweat.

"Calm down. This is a dumb discussion we're having, and I say we drop it."

Jonas stuck out his chin. "Want to know what I think?"

Eli blew out his breath and lifted his gaze toward the rafters. "No, but I'm sure you won't scram 'til you've told me."

"I think you're in love with Laura, but you know she's not good for you. I'm thinkin' the best thing for everyone is for you to hurry and get baptized, and then join the church so you can marry Pauline Hostetler."

Eli clenched his fists. If Jonas didn't leave soon, he

couldn't be sure what he might do. "Just go now before I drag you outside and push your face into a pile of snow."

"Jah, right."

"I mean it, little brother."

"You think you're big enough?" Jonas planted his hands on his hips and stared at Eli as though daring him to make a move.

Eli didn't hesitate. He lunged for Jonas, and Jonas darted for the door. When they bounded into the snowy yard, all thoughts of Laura vanished as Eli focused on catching his nosy brother and giving him a good face washing in a mound of frigid snow.

CHAPTER

10

Christmas Day turned out to be pretty much the way Laura had expected it to be. Her father had invited several people from his law firm to dinner, and most of them spent the whole time talking about trial dates, briefs, and who they thought might get out of going to jail.

Dean Carlson was among the guests, seated next to Laura. She studied him as he droned on about the new computer system they'd recently installed at the office. There was no denying it—Dean was one of the most handsome men Laura had ever met. The funny thing was Laura used to enjoy Dean's company. Now he seemed superficial and self-absorbed. She kept comparing him to Eli, whose warm, sincere smile could melt her heart and whose infectious laughter seemed genuine, not forced like Dean's. She didn't know why she'd never seen it before, but Dean's whole mannerism was brash, and he was certainly the most egotistical man she had ever met. Eli, on the other hand, was gentle and genuinely humble.

"Laura, are you listening to me?" Dean nudged her arm.

She managed a weak smile. "I think Dad may have mentioned the new computer system."

"You *weren't* listening. The computer system was not the last thing I said."

She blinked. "It wasn't?"

"I was asking if you'd like to go to the New Year's Eve office party with me."

Laura stared at Dean. How could she even consider dating a man like him? Oh, sure, he had money, a good education, great looks, and a prestigious job, but he simply wasn't Eli Yoder.

"I want to take you to the party," Dean said again. "Will you go with me or not?"

Every fiber of Laura's being shouted *no!* She reached for her glass of water and took a few sips, hoping to buy some time.

When Dean began tapping the side of his glass with the tip of his spoon, she finally answered. "I appreciate the offer, but I hadn't planned on going to the party."

"Why not?"

Laura wasn't sure how to respond. She really had no legitimate reason for staying home. "I. . .uh. . .I'm leaving for Pennsylvania the day after New Year's, and I need to get packed."

Dean leaned his head back and roared. It was the first genuine laugh she'd heard out of him all day, but it didn't make her smile. "You have a whole week between now and the party. Surely that's time enough to pack a suitcase."

When Laura made no reply, he reached for her hand. "Come on, honey, please say you'll go with me. After all, I do work for your dad, and I'm sure he would approve."

Laura inwardly groaned. She knew she was losing this battle, and she didn't like it one bit.

Dean leaned closer, and she could feel his warm breath against her ear. "If you don't have a wonderful time, I promise never to ask you out again."

She finally nodded in defeat. "Okay, I'll go."

All during dinner, Wesley kept glancing across the table at Laura. She looked uncomfortable, as if she would rather be anyplace else but here. Didn't she enjoy being with her family and friends? She'd always seemed to before. Surely she wasn't anxious to get back to her studies in Pennsylvania. Maybe she was just tired.

He looked over at his wife, sitting so prim and proper at the other end of the table. She seemed to be in her glory—chatting, smiling, soaking up every compliment that had come her way. He didn't know why. She really couldn't take credit for any of it. The meal had been catered. The house had been cleaned by their housekeeper. Irene's flowing, peach-colored dress had been bought at one of the most expensive shops in town. Her hair and nails had been done by her beautician. She hadn't done much of anything to prepare for this meal except tell others what to do.

Wesley inwardly groaned. It was all superficial. There probably wasn't a person sitting at this table who gave a lick about the person next to them. Except maybe Dean, who kept nuzzling Laura's neck and whispering in her ear. Could Dean be the reason Laura seemed so fidgety today?

"Wesley, did you hear what I said?"

He looked over to his wife again. "What was that, dear?"

Irene smiled sweetly. "I asked if you were still planning to host your office's New Year's Eve party at the country club.

Ethel wanted to know."

"Yes, it will be there again this year." Wesley forced a smile. He would never have admitted it to his wife, but the truth was, he would much rather stay home on New Year's Eve and watch TV or read a good book instead of dishing out the money for a party that no one would remember the following day. But he knew it was expected of him, and the gleam in Irene's eyes was a reminder that at least one of them was looking forward to the gala affair.

※

"What are you doing out here in the cold?" Eli's sister, Martha Rose, asked, as she stepped out the back door and joined him on the porch.

Eli shrugged and leaned against the railing. "It was getting kind of stuffy in the house, so I decided to get some fresh air."

Martha Rose shivered and pulled her heavy shawl around her shoulders. "This air is downright frigid—that's what it is."

He smiled. "So what are you doing out here in it?"

"Same as you—getting some fresh air." She nudged him playfully with her elbow, but then her face sobered. "You've been quiet all day, and I was wondering if there's something bothering you."

Eli pulled his fingers through the back of his hair. Of course there was something bothering him. Ever since he'd met Laura, he had been bothered. He'd been thinking about her off and on all day, wondering how she was spending her Christmas, wishing they could be together, and fretting because he was having such thoughts. He was tempted to share his feelings with Martha Rose, because the two of them had always been close, but he wasn't sure she would understand. She might even reprimand him, the way Mom had done when she'd learned he was seeing Laura—a fancy Englisher.

"I'm feeling kind of down today," he finally mumbled.

"On Christmas?"

He nodded, keeping his focus on the snowy yard, because he knew if he looked right at Martha Rose, he was likely to give himself away.

"Mom's worried about you, Eli."

"I'm fine. A little chilly weather never hurt anybody."

She touched his arm. "She's not worried about you being out here in the cold."

His only reply was an exaggerated shrug.

"She's worried that you might be thinking about leaving the Amish faith."

Eli bristled and whirled around to face his sister. "Did Mom send you out here to try and talk some sense into me? Is that it?"

Martha Rose shook her head. "Coming out here was my idea. I've seen how sullen you've been all day, and I was worried that it might have something to do with the English woman you've been seeing lately."

"Laura and I are just friends. Mom has nothin' to worry about."

"It might help ease her concerns if you got baptized and joined the church."

"I don't think calming Mom's fears is a good enough reason to become a member of the church, do you?"

"Well, no, but—"

"I've told Mom and Pop, too, that I'm not leaving the faith, and there's nothing serious going on with me and

Laura." Eli grunted. "So everyone, including you, can quit hounding me about this."

Martha Rose winced as though she'd been slapped. "I–I didn't mean to sound as if I was trying to tell you what to do. I only want your happiness."

"Sorry. I shouldn't have snapped at you that way."

She gave him a hug. "I want you to know that if you ever need to talk, I'm willing to listen, and I promise not to be judgmental."

Eli smiled and patted her on the back. "Danki. I appreciate that."

"Are you too full from dinner to finish your dessert?" Pauline's mother motioned to the half-eaten piece of pumpkin pie on Pauline's plate.

Pauline shook her head. "Not really. I'm just not so hungry right now."

Dad wrinkled his forehead. "You barely ate any dinner. As a matter of fact, you've been actin' kind of sulky all day. What's the problem, daughter?"

"Nothing. I'm fine."

"She's probably wishing she could be with her boyfriend today," Pauline's younger sister, Susan, piped up.

"I have no boyfriend. Not anymore."

"I thought you and Eli Yoder had been courting," Dad said, reaching for another slice of mincemeat pie.

"I thought so, too, but I was wrong." Pauline couldn't keep the bitterness out of her voice.

Mom poured herself a cup of coffee from the pot sitting in the center of the table. "I was talking to Eli's mamm a few weeks back, and she seemed concerned because he's not joined the church yet."

"He hasn't joined because he's seeing some fancy English woman with long, auburn hair," Sam, Pauline's brother, interjected.

Pauline glared at him. "Can't we talk about something else?"

He shrugged his broad shoulders and smiled. "Guess we could talk about Joseph Beachy. He's had a crush on you ever since we were kinner."

Pauline wrinkled her nose. "Joseph's three years younger than me, for goodness' sake."

Dad chuckled. "So what of it? Your mamm's a whole year older than me."

Mom shook her head as she lifted her gaze to the ceiling. "And you're never gonna let me live that down, are you, Ben?"

He grinned and tickled her under the chin. "Nope, but it don't make me love you any the less."

She reached for his hand. "I love you, too, even if you are just a big kid."

Feeling the need to be alone, Pauline pushed away from the table. "I'm kind of tired, so if you don't mind, I think I'll go upstairs to my bedroom."

"Sleep well," Mom called as Pauline started out of the room.

"Danki." Pauline trudged up the stairs, and with each step she took, she felt more discouraged. Even if Eli did quit seeing the Englisher and decided to join the church, she feared he might never be interested in her. And if she couldn't have Eli, then she didn't want any man.

Chapter 11

Mom had insisted that Laura buy a new dress for the New Year's Eve party. Laura couldn't understand what all the fuss was about, but she decided she might as well enjoy the pampering. After all, she would be leaving soon. Then it would be back to the grindstone of school, homework, and. . .Eli. She hoped she would be able to see him again.

Standing before her full-length bedroom mirror, Laura smiled at the lovely young woman looking back at her. *If Eli could only see me now, maybe he'd be tempted to go "fancy."*

Mom stood directly behind her, and she smiled into the mirror, as well. "You look exquisite. I'm glad you decided to buy this beautiful silk gown. That shade of green brings out the color of your eyes so well."

Laura merely shrugged in response. She knew she looked nice, but her heart wasn't in going to the party tonight or in spending the evening with Dean.

"I'm sure your date will be impressed," her mother continued. "Dean seems like such a nice young man."

"I suppose—just not my type."

"Not your type?" Mom's eyebrows furrowed. "How can

you say that, Laura? Why, Dean is nice looking, has plenty of money, and—"

Laura turned away from the mirror. "Do you think my hair looks all right this way, or should I have worn it down?"

"Your hair looks lovely in a French roll," her mother responded. She gave Laura's arm a gentle squeeze. "I'm sure Dean will think so, too."

The New Year's Eve party was already in full swing by the time Dean and Laura arrived a little after nine o'clock. He'd been nearly an hour late picking her up, which had put her in a sour mood right from the beginning.

They had no sooner checked their coats, than Dean pulled Laura into a possessive embrace. "You look gorgeous tonight. I'm glad you decided to come."

Laura wished she could reciprocate with a similar remark, but the truth was she wasn't glad to be here. In fact, she felt a headache coming on, and if it didn't let up soon, she knew she would have a good excuse to leave the party.

"Would you like something to drink before we check out the buffet?" Dean asked, pulling her toward the bar.

She merely shrugged in response.

"What can I get for you?"

"Nothing, unless they have some diet cola."

"You're not driving," Dean reminded. "And if you're concerned about me drinking and driving, you shouldn't worry your pretty little head. I won't have more than a few drinks, and I can handle those with no problem at all."

Laura gnawed on her bottom lip until it almost bled. If

Dean was planning to have a few drinks, she could only imagine how the evening might end. She had to do something to get away from him now. "There's my friend Shannon," she said, motioning across the room. "I'm going over to say hello."

"Okay, I'll get our drinks. I'll meet you at the buffet table in a few minutes." He sauntered off toward the bar like he owned the place.

Laura saw Shannon carrying her plate to one of the tables, and she hurried over to her. "I'm glad to see you here." She pulled out a chair and took a seat beside her friend.

"Why wouldn't I be? Need I remind you that my boyfriend works for your dad?" Shannon glanced at the buffet table and smiled. "Clark's still loading up on food, but he'll be joining me soon."

Laura shrugged. If Shannon's comment was meant to chase her away, it wasn't going to work. "Listen, can you do me a favor?"

"Sure, if I can."

"If you see my folks, would you tell them I came down with a headache so I called a cab and went home?"

Shannon's eyebrows lifted high on her forehead. "What about your date?"

"When Dean comes looking for me, which I'm sure he will, would you tell him the same thing?"

"You can tell him yourself. He's heading this way right now." Shannon pointed across the room, and Laura groaned.

"What's wrong? Did you two have a disagreement?"

"Something like that." Laura decided it would be pointless to tell her friend the real reason she wanted to get away from Dean. She wasn't just worried about his drinking. She didn't like the gleam she'd seen in his eyes when he picked her up tonight. She was sure he wanted more than she was willing to give, and her best line of defense was to leave now—alone.

"Here's your diet cola." Dean handed Laura the cold drink and nodded at Shannon. "How's it going?"

Shannon smiled. "Fine. How's everything with you?"

Laura set her glass on the table and tuned them both out as they engaged in small talk. Her thoughts turned to Eli, and she couldn't help wondering how he was spending his New Year's Eve. Did the Amish celebrate with a party, or would tonight be just like any other night for Eli and his family?

Laura cringed when Dean pulled her to his side and whispered, "Tonight's going to be a great evening." When he stroked the back of her neck with his thumb, she stood up so quickly, she knocked her soft drink over, spilling some of it down the front of her new dress. "I—I'm not feeling well, Dean. I'm going to call a cab and go home."

Obvious surprise registered on Dean's face, and his eyebrows furrowed. "You can't be serious. We just got here, and I haven't had a chance to eat yet, much less show you off to my friends."

I don't want to be shown off, and I don't want to be with you. Laura thrust out her chin and stared up at him. "I'm going home."

Dean set his drink on the table and steered her toward the coat closet. "Sure, no problem. I'll get my car."

"I'm calling a cab. There's no point in both of us missing the party. You stay and have a good time."

His eyes clouded over. "If you're dead set on going, then

I may as well collect that stroke-of-midnight kiss." Before Laura could say anything, Dean bent his head and captured her lips in a kiss that would have left most women reeling with pleasure.

Laura drew back and slapped his face.

"What was that for?" He grimaced as he touched the red mark she had left on his cheek. "I thought you wanted that kiss as much as I did. Always did before."

Laura's face was so hot she felt as though she were the one who had been slapped. She wasn't in control of her emotions tonight, and that really bothered her.

"I'm sorry, Dean," she apologized. "Your kiss took me by surprise."

Dean's eyelids fluttered, and he backed up a few steps. "I don't know what's come over you, Laura, but you haven't been the same since you returned to Minneapolis after attending that stupid school in Pennsylvania for a few months. If I were your father, I would never have allowed you to go there, and I would have insisted that you finish your design courses right here in town."

Laura's hands trembled as she held them at her sides. If Dean kept goading her, she was liable to let him have it on the other cheek. "Good night, Dean," she said through her clenched jaw. "Don't bother walking me out."

❦

The day after New Year's, Laura said good-bye to her parents at the airport. She was more than anxious to be on her way. It wasn't that she hadn't enjoyed being with them, but she wanted to get back to her studies. . .and she hoped to see Eli again.

Mom and Dad had no idea she'd fallen in love with an Amish man, only that she'd gone out with him a few times. She had no intention of informing them, either. At least not today.

Laura hugged her parents and thanked them for the beautiful leather coat they'd given her for Christmas. Then, without so much as a backward glance, she boarded the plane, welcoming the butterflies doing a tap dance in her stomach.

Her time on the plane was spent thinking about Eli. She couldn't decide if she should be straightforward and tell him that she'd come to realize how much she loved him or if she should try to draw a declaration of love from him first.

By the time the plane landed in Harrisburg, Laura was a ball of nerves. As soon as she picked up the car she had leased, she headed for the main road, knowing the drive to Lancaster would be slow since snow still covered the ground.

When she got back to the school, it would be dark and too late to try and find Eli's house. But come tomorrow, she hoped to see him and bare her soul.

CHAPTER 12

Laura awoke in her dorm room the following morning with a pounding headache. A warm shower and a cup of tea helped some, but when she knocked on Darla's door to see if her friend would like to ride with her to Eli's farm, Laura's headache worsened.

"I have other plans today," Darla said with a scowl. "Besides, I wouldn't consider being a party to you ruining your life."

"How can seeing Eli again ruin my life?" Laura had hoped Darla would be willing to go with her. She needed the added courage.

Darla opened the door wider and motioned Laura inside. "Have a seat, and I'll see if I can explain things a little more clearly."

Laura pulled out the desk chair, and Darla sat on the edge of her bed.

"I know you've got a thing for this guy, but the more you see him, the further your relationship will develop." Darla pursed her lips. "One of you is bound to get hurt, and I'm guessing that you're going to be the one."

"What makes you think I'll get hurt?"

"We've been through this before. You and Eli are from completely different worlds, and even if one of you were willing to try the other's way of life, it most likely wouldn't work."

"How do you know?"

"Trust me on this," Darla asserted. "You're living in a dream world if you think you can get Eli to leave his faith."

"Why is that so impossible? People change religions all the time."

"Has Eli joined the Amish church yet? Because if he has and he decides to leave the faith, he'll be shunned. Do you understand what that means, Laura?"

She nodded. "Eli's told me quite a bit about the Amish way of life, but this isn't a problem because he hasn't joined the church yet."

Darla's eyebrows drew together. "Even so, if he were to leave, it would be a difficult adjustment for him."

"I'll help him adjust."

Darla shrugged. "Whatever. But think about this: Maybe he doesn't want to leave. Then what?"

"I—I don't know. I suppose I'll have to convince him that he does want to leave." Laura stood. "So are you going to help me find the Yoder place or not?"

Darla shook her head. "I'm afraid you'll have to do this on your own."

"Fine. I will."

Laura spent the next couple of hours driving around the back roads near Paradise, searching for Eli's house. Since she'd only been there once before and hadn't paid close attention to where Eli was going, she wasn't sure she was heading in the right direction.

Suddenly, she spotted a one-room schoolhouse. It was the same one Eli had pointed out on one of their rides. *I've got to be getting close to his house.*

Laura continued up the road another mile or so until she spotted a mailbox with the name Yoder on it. She drove up the driveway, and the minute she saw the house, she knew it was Eli's. She stopped the car, turned off the engine, and stepped out.

Walking carefully up the slippery path, she headed for the Yoders' front porch. She was almost to the door when a sense of panic gripped her like a vise. What if Eli wasn't home? What if he was home but wasn't happy to see her?

She thought about turning around and heading back to Lancaster, but the desire to see Eli won out, so she lifted her hand and knocked on the door.

A few moments later, Eli's mother answered. She held a rolling pin in one hand, and with the other hand, she swiped at a wisp of hair that had fallen loose from her bun. Laura couldn't read Mary Ellen's stoic expression, but the woman's silence was enough to remind her that she was on enemy territory.

"Is. . .uh. . .Eli at home?"

Mary Ellen stood quietly a few minutes before she finally answered. "He's out in the barn in his woodworking shop."

Laura nodded and forced her lips to form a smile. "Thanks." She stepped quickly off the porch before Eli's mother had a chance to say anything more. If the older woman's sour expression was meant to dissuade her, it hadn't worked. She was here now and even more determined than ever to speak with Eli.

Eli was bent over his workbench, hammering a nail into the roof of a small birdhouse, when he heard the barn door open. He didn't think much of it, knowing his brothers were still busy with chores, but when a familiar female voice called out to him, he was so surprised, he smashed his thumb with the hammer.

"Laura! How'd you get here?"

She moved slowly across the room until she stood directly in front of him. "I drove."

"When did you get back from Minnesota?"

"Last night."

Eli wished she would quit staring at him. It was hard to think. Hard to breathe. He swallowed a couple of times. "How. . .how was your holiday?"

"It was okay. How was yours?"

"Good." *Though it would have been better if you'd been here.* Eli shook his head, trying to get himself thinking straight again.

"I've missed you," Laura said, leaning toward him. "Did you miss me?"

A warning bell went off in Eli's head, but it was too late. Laura touched his arm, as she gazed into his eyes in a way that made his heart slam into his chest. How could he tell this beautiful woman that it wasn't right for her to be here?

Eli couldn't voice any of his thoughts. He couldn't even think straight with her standing so close and smelling so nice. He took a step back and bumped into his workbench, knocking a hunk of wood to the floor. He bent to retrieve it, feeling more frustrated by the minute.

"So this is where you make your birdhouses, huh?"

He nodded. "And many other wooden items, as well."

She glanced around the small room, as if she were scrutinizing it. "How can you do this kind of work without the aid of electricity?"

"Some time ago, my daed installed a diesel engine that not only provides power for some of my saws and planers but also powers the compressed air pump that brings water to our house." Eli pointed to a small drill lying beside a handsaw. "Of course I do many things by hand, too."

"I see." Laura took a step closer to him. "Have you been back to the lake lately?"

"The lake's completely frozen over now." He tipped his head as an uncensored thought popped into his mind. "Say, would you like to go ice-skating?"

She pointed to her boots. "Ice-skating? Eli, in case you haven't noticed, I have no skates."

"I think my sister, Martha Rose, left her skates here in the barn when she married Amon Zook, and I'm sure she wouldn't mind if you wore them."

"If your sister's skates fit, I'd be happy to go ice-skating with you."

Eli nodded and smiled. So much for his resolve to keep Laura at a distance.

❧

"Always trouble somewhere," Mary Ellen muttered as she returned to the kitchen, where Johnny sat at the table with a cup of coffee in his hands.

"What's the problem? Who was at the front door?"

"That English woman."

"Which English woman? There are several living nearby, you know."

Mary Ellen dropped into the chair beside her husband with a groan. "I'm talking about Laura Meade. She was looking for Eli."

"What'd you tell her?"

"Said he was out in the barn, in his shop." She pursed her lips. "Couldn't hardly lie now, could I?"

Johnny shook his head. "No, but you could have sent her packing."

"I'd like to think Eli will tell her to leave, but I'm not holding my breath on that one, either."

Johnny set his cup down and reached for her hand. "We need to keep on praying and trusting that God will open our son's eyes."

She nodded. "Jah, but that's easier said than done."

When Eli pulled his sleigh into the open area near the lake, Laura was surprised to see that it was covered with a thick layer of shimmering ice. She thought it was even more appealing than it had been in the fall, and she drank in the beauty of the surrounding trees, dressed in frosty white gowns and shimmering in the morning sun like thousands of tiny diamonds.

They took a seat on a fallen log, and Eli helped Laura into his sister's skates, which were only a tad too big.

"If I ever get the chance to meet your sister, I'll have to be sure and thank her for the use of these skates."

"I'll thank her for you." Eli grinned. "You'd like Martha Rose. She's the best sister any fellow could possibly want, and we've been good friends since we were kinner." He stood and held out his hand. "Should we give those skates a try?"

"Jah, let's do."

Hand in hand, they made their way slowly around the lake. After a time, Eli set off on his own, doing fancy spins and figure eights.

Laura shielded her eyes against the glare of the sun as she watched in rapt fascination, realizing with each passing moment how much she really had come to love Eli. She tried skating by herself, but it was hard to concentrate on anything except the striking figure he made on the ice.

Her heart hammered in her chest when Eli waved and offered her a flirtatious wink. He wore a pair of black pants, a light blue shirt, and a dark gray woolen jacket. He had removed his black felt hat, and his sandy brown hair whipped against his face as he appeared to become one with the wind.

Laura decided to try and catch up to Eli, hoping she could convince him to take a break so they could talk. She needed to tell him what was in her heart.

Pushing off quickly with her right foot, she lost her balance and fell hard on the ice. Eli was at her side immediately, his blue eyes looking ever so serious. "Are you okay? You didn't break anything, I hope."

"My knee hurts, but I don't think my leg's broken."

Laura shivered as Eli pulled up her pant leg and gently probed her knee. "It looks like a bad sprain. You probably should put some ice on it."

She giggled. "I think I just did."

Eli helped Laura to her feet and put his arm around her waist as she hobbled over to the sleigh. "I'd better get you back to my place so you can rest that knee and get out of the cold."

Impulsively, Laura gripped Eli's shoulders with both hands and kissed him on the cheek.

His face flushed, and he smiled at first, but then he jerked back like he'd been stung by a bee. "Wh–why'd you do that?"

"Just my way of saying thanks for being such a good friend."

His gaze dropped to the ground, and an awkward silence followed as Eli helped her into the sleigh. She wondered if she had said or done something wrong.

"I–I think it would be best if we didn't see each other anymore," he mumbled as he picked up the reins.

"Why? Haven't you enjoyed yourself today?"

He nodded soberly. "That's the problem: I had too good of a time."

Her hand trembled as she touched his arm. "I don't see how enjoying yourself can be a problem."

"I told you once that I wanted to be your friend, but now things have changed."

"How?" Her voice rose, and her heart started to pound. "Why?"

"I can't be your friend because I've fallen in love with you, Laura." He didn't look at her, just stared straight ahead.

"Oh, Eli, I love you, too!" She buried her face in his jacket, relishing the warmth and his masculine smell.

"What we feel for each other isn't right," he mumbled.

"It feels right to me."

"It won't work for us. I think we need to end this before we both get hurt."

"Nothing could hurt worse than never seeing you again," Laura said with a catch in her voice. "We can be together if we want it badly enough."

He eased her gently away. "I don't see how."

"You could leave the Amish faith. You're not a member yet, so you won't be shunned, and when we both feel ready for marriage—"

Eli's eyebrows arched. "Marriage? Are you saying you want to marry me?"

Laura swallowed hard. Was that what she was saying? Did she really love Eli, or was he simply a prize she wanted and thought was out of her reach?

"After we've dated awhile, we might be ready for marriage," she amended.

Eli sat there several seconds, staring at the reins in his hands. "The only reason I haven't joined the church yet is because I was waiting until I felt ready for marriage."

"Wh-what are you saying?"

"I'm saying that despite my feelings for you, I don't believe I could be happy living and working as an Englisher."

"Why not?"

"To my way of thinking, a newborn calf, freshly plowed soil, and the ripening of grain are all manifestations of God's power. Farming to many Amish men in this area isn't just a job, it's a way of life blessed by God and handed down from one generation to another. If I left the Amish faith or moved away from God, I wouldn't feel like a whole person anymore."

She grasped the collar of his jacket and gazed at his handsome face. "I'm not asking you to leave God. You can worship Him in any church. I'm only asking you to give up your Plain lifestyle so we can be together."

"Could you give up your modern way of life to become Plain?"

She shook her head. "I—I don't think so. It would be too hard for me to adjust."

"Exactly. While it is possible for outsiders to join the Amish community, it seldom happens because it would be too big of a change." Eli leaned away from her. Snapping the reins, he shouted, "Giddap there, boy. It's time to go!"

Laura's eyes stung with unshed tears. As the horse moved forward and the sleigh began to glide across the snow, she felt as though her whole world had fallen apart.

Why wouldn't Eli listen to reason? What had gone wrong with her plan?

Eli gripped the reins so hard his fingers ached. *I wish I'd never met Laura. I should have never invited her to take that first ride in my courting buggy. I was stupid for asking her to go skating with me this morning, too. It only made both of us hope for the impossible.*

As much as Eli hated to admit it, he had come to care for Laura, but he didn't think he could give up his way of life in order to marry her. At the same time, he knew it would be impossible for her to give up the only way of life she had ever known to be with him.

They rode in silence all the way back to his house, and when Eli guided the sleigh into the yard, Laura leaned close to him, sending shivers up the back of his neck. "Won't you at least think about what I said earlier? Maybe there's a reason you haven't joined the church yet. Maybe we're supposed to be together."

Eli shook his head as he swallowed around the lump in his throat. "We've let this go on too long, Laura. You and I both know that neither of us could be happy living in the other person's world. So the best thing is for us to say good-bye now, before one or both of us get hurt."

Tears filled Laura's eyes, and Eli was tempted to pull her into his arms and kiss them away. Instead, he stepped out of the sleigh and skirted around to the other side to help her down. Laura leaned down and picked up Martha Rose's skates. "Tell your sister I said thanks for giving me the opportunity to spend a few hours with you before we had to say good-bye."

"Jah, I will."

"And you were right, Eli. It wouldn't have worked for us."

Before Eli could respond, she hopped down without his assistance and limped toward her car. Every fiber of Eli's being screamed at him to go after her, but reason won out. He turned his attention toward the horse, vowing that no matter what it took, he would forget he had ever met a fancy English woman named Laura Meade.

CHAPTER

13

January and February were cold. . .so cold and dreary Laura thought she would die. It wasn't just the weather making her feel that way, either. Her heart was broken because Eli had rejected her. If he really cared, he should have agreed to leave his world and join hers.

Two months had passed since their final good-bye, but Laura still longed for something she couldn't have. Visions of the happy times they had spent together danced through her mind. Losing Eli hurt so much, and she couldn't seem to do anything to ease the pain. Shopping for new clothes didn't help. Throwing herself into her studies made no difference. Even an occasional binge on hot-fudge sundaes and chocolate milkshakes did nothing to make her feel better. The barrage of e-mails and phone calls from Dean Carlson didn't soothe Laura's troubled spirit, either. She cared nothing for Dean, and she told him so.

As winter moved into spring, Laura finally began to move on with her life. At least she thought she was moving on until one of her teachers gave the class an assignment, asking each student to decorate a bedroom using something handmade by the Amish as a focal point.

Laura had her Amish quilt. . .the one she'd purchased at the farmers' market the first day she'd met Eli. However, when she and Eli broke off their relationship, she had boxed up the quilt and sent it home, unable to look at it any longer. She supposed she could call Mom and ask her to mail it back, but the assignment was due early next week, and there wasn't enough time for that. There was only one logical thing to do—go to the farmers' market and buy another quilt.

"If you can spare a few minutes, I'd like to talk to you about Laura."

Wesley halted in front of his office door and turned to face Dean. "What about her?"

Dean nodded toward the office. "Can we talk in there?"

"I guess so." Wesley stepped into the room and motioned to one of the leather chairs near his desk. "Have a seat."

Dean sat down, and Wesley took a seat in the larger chair behind the desk. "Now what did you want to say about my daughter?"

"I was wondering if you'd heard anything from her lately."

"Laura calls at least once a week, and we get e-mails nearly every day. Why do you ask?"

Dean rubbed his fingers along the edge of his chin and grimaced. "She won't answer my phone calls or any of my e-mails."

"Any idea why?"

"She turned off to me the night of the New Year's Eve party and wouldn't even let me take her home when she said she wasn't feeling well."

Wesley leaned forward with his elbows on the desk. "So you've had no contact with her since she went back to Pennsylvania?"

"Just one phone call, and she told me she didn't want to see me again."

"Then I guess you'd better take Laura at her word. She's a lot like her mother in many respects."

"How so?"

"Once my daughter makes up her mind about something, there's no changing it."

"Has she found someone else? Is that the problem?"

Wesley shrugged. "You'll have to ask her that question." He motioned to the door. "Now if you don't mind, I have work to do, and I'm sure you do, as well."

Dean stood. "The next time you talk to Laura, would you give her a message for me?"

"That all depends on what the message is."

"Tell her I'm not giving up on us, and when she finally comes to her senses, I'll be here waiting."

Before Wesley could respond, Dean sauntered out of the room.

"I'll give Laura a message all right," Wesley mumbled. "I'll tell her the best thing she ever did was drop you flat on your ear." He tapped the end of his pen against the desk a couple of times. "If you weren't such a crackerjack lawyer, I'd drop you flat, too."

❦

As Eli headed to the farmers' market in his horse and open buggy, he kept thinking about Laura and how interested she'd seemed in his birdhouses that first day when he'd met her at the market. It had been two whole months since they'd said good-bye after their ice-skating date, and a day hadn't gone by that he hadn't thought about her.

He glanced over at his date sitting in the seat beside him. *Here I am with Pauline again. Is it fair to lead her on? Is it possible for me to learn to love her?* It wasn't a case of Pauline not being pretty. She just wasn't as pretty as Laura. It wasn't that he didn't enjoy Pauline's company. She simply wasn't as much fun to be around as Laura. But Eli had decided to give Pauline a chance, thinking it might help him forget Laura, and knowing it would please his folks if he settled down, got baptized, joined the church, and took a wife. He just wasn't sure that wife could be Pauline.

"Spring's just around the corner, jah?" Pauline said, cutting into Eli's private thoughts.

He nodded. "Many of the trees have blossoms already, and some flowers are poking their heads through the soil."

She sighed. "Won't be long and it'll be warm enough for picnics."

"Jah."

"If this warm weather holds out, maybe we could go to the lake next Saturday."

"We'll have to see how it goes."

She reached over and touched his arm. "Guess I'll have to pray for sunshine."

He gave no reply as he guided his horse and buggy into the market parking lot.

§

Laura was glad Darla had agreed to go with her to the farmers' market. She didn't relish the idea of going there alone.

Too many painful memories lived inside that building. Too many reminders of the day she'd met Eli.

They had taken Darla's car this morning, and as soon as it was parked, Laura hopped out and headed for the building. She knew from what Eli had told her that Saturdays were always busy at the market, and she didn't want to miss out on the best deals.

"Hey, wait for me," Darla shouted.

Laura halted. "Sorry. Guess I'm in too big a hurry to look at those beautiful quilts."

"I might just buy one myself this time."

They stepped into the building, and Laura led the way.

"I'm beginning to see why the country look fascinates you so much," Darla commented, as they browsed through a stack of colorful quilts. "The vibrant hues and various shapes in these are actually quite pretty."

Laura nodded as she fingered a monochromatic blue quilt with a Double Wedding Ring pattern. The middle-aged Amish woman selling the quilts mentioned that it was an old patchwork design, and that as the name implied, two rings interlocked with each other.

"Some quilters use their scraps of material for the Double Wedding Ring because the pieces are quite small." She smiled and lifted one edge of the quilt. "Others plan their quilt with great care, alternating light and dark rings."

"I think I'll buy this one," Laura said. "I love the variance of colors and the interlocking rings."

"And I believe I'll keep looking awhile." Darla chuckled. "No sense picking the first one I see."

When Laura didn't answer, Darla poked her in the ribs. "Did you hear what I said?"

Laura stood frozen in her tracks. Her heart pounded like a pack of stampeding horses, and her throat felt so dry she could barely swallow.

"Laura, what's wrong? You look like you've seen a ghost."

"It's. . .it's Eli. . .and that woman." Laura's voice cracked. "I—I had no idea he would be here today. If I'd known, I wouldn't have come."

Darla craned her neck. "Where is he, and what woman are you talking about?"

"She seems really possessive and thinks she's Eli's girlfriend—and maybe she is now that I'm out of the picture. They're right over there." Laura pointed toward the root-beer stand several feet away. "I shouldn't be surprised to see them together, but it hurts, nonetheless."

Darla grabbed hold of Laura's arm. "Come on. We've got to get you out of here right now."

Laura jerked away. "I'm not going anywhere. This is a free country, and I have as much right to be here as they do."

"I'm sure, but you don't want Eli to know you're here. Do you?"

Laura dropped her gaze to the floor and shrugged. "Maybe."

"What? The guy threw you over for someone else, and you want to grovel in the dirt in front of him?"

"He didn't throw me over, and I wasn't planning to grovel. I was just thinking I should probably say hello."

"Now that's a real brilliant idea." Darla turned back toward the stack of quilts. "You can do whatever you like, but I came here to look at handmade Amish items. That *was* our assignment, you know, not saying hello to some cute Amish guy."

Ignoring her friend's comment, Laura took a deep breath

and marched straight up to the root-beer stand. "Hello, Eli. How are you?"

"Laura? What are you doing here?" Eli's eyes were wide, and his mouth hung slightly open.

"I'm looking at quilts," she answered, fixing her gaze somewhere near the center of his chest. "I—I have an assignment to do, and—"

"Come on, Eli, let's go."

Laura turned her gaze to Pauline. She stood beside Eli with one hand on his arm in a possessive gesture, and she offered Laura an icy stare.

Laura's legs felt like rubber, and tension pulled the muscles in her neck. She had a deep sense that she had done the wrong thing when she'd asked Eli to leave his Amish faith, and she couldn't ignore it a moment longer. She took a guarded step forward. "Eli, could we talk? I need to tell you something." Her mouth went dry with trepidation as she stared into his blue eyes and recognized hesitation.

A few seconds ticked by. Then he shrugged. "I guess it would be all right." He glanced over at Pauline. "Could you wait for me at the hot dog stand? I won't be long."

Pauline scrunched up her nose. "Are you kidding me?"

He shook his head. "I'll just be a minute."

She glared at Laura, then stalked off, muttering something in Pennsylvania Dutch.

Eli turned back to Laura. "Should we go outside?"

She nodded and followed as he led the way to the nearest exit. When they stepped outside, he motioned to a wooden bench near the building.

Once they were both seated, Laura felt a bit more comfortable. At least now she could gulp in some fresh air, which she hoped might tame the brigade of bumblebees marching through her stomach.

"What did you want to talk to me about?" Eli asked.

"Us. I wanted to talk about us."

"There *is* no *us*, Laura. I thought you understood that I'm not going to leave my faith. In fact, I've decided to—"

"I do understand, and I'm sorry for asking you to give up your way of life."

"Thank you for understanding. Someday you'll meet the right man, and—"

Laura lifted her hand and covered his mouth with her fingers. "I've already found the right man."

His eyebrows raised in obvious surprise. "You have? That's good. I wish you all the best."

She compressed her lips in frustration. Was Eli deaf, dumb, and blind? Couldn't he see how much she wanted to be with him? She grasped both of his hands and gave them a squeeze. "The man I've found is you. I want no other, and I never will."

"But, Laura—"

"I know, I know. You won't leave the Amish faith and become a fancy Englisher." She swallowed hard and drew in a deep breath. "That doesn't mean we can't be together, though."

He tipped his head and looked at Laura as if she'd lost her mind. "It doesn't?"

"No, it doesn't. Not unless you've found someone else." She leaned closer to him. "Have you, Eli? Are you in love with Pauline?"

He shook his head. "We're still just friends, but—"

"Do you still have feelings for me?"

"Jah, but you know—"

"Well, good. I can solve our problem by coming over to the other side."

A deep frown creased Eli's forehead. "I'm afraid I don't get your meaning."

"I'll join the Amish faith and become Plain."

"What?"

"I said—"

Eli held up his hand. "You don't know what you're saying, Laura. A few folks have joined our faith, but not many. It's not all cakes and pies, you know, and there would be much to learn—classes to take."

"I'm sure it wouldn't be an easy transition, but I can do it, Eli. I can do anything if I set my mind to it."

❧

Eli couldn't believe Laura was offering to join his faith. During the time they had been seeing each other, he'd often found himself wishing for just such a turn of events, but after she'd asked him to join her world, he was certain she would never consider becoming Amish. Now she suddenly wanted to become Plain? It made no sense at all. He studied her intently. She seemed sincere, but truth be told, Laura didn't have any idea what she was suggesting.

"I do love you," he admitted, "but—"

"I'm glad to hear that." She leaned her head on his shoulder. "I was afraid you might turn me away."

Eli breathed in the strawberry scent of Laura's hair and reveled in the warmth of her touch. How could he make her understand, yet how could he say good-bye to her again?

"These last few months have been awful," Laura said with

a catch in her voice. "I need to be with you."

"But you might not be happy being Amish, and then what? As I said, it would be a hard thing to change over and give up all the modern things you're used to having. You would have to learn our language and accept our religious views."

She nodded. "I know it won't be easy, but with your help, I can do it. You will help me, won't you, Eli?"

Eli filled his lungs with fresh air as he struggled to make a decision. He lifted Laura's chin with his thumb and stared into her sea green eyes, hoping to find answers there. He wanted to be with her more than anything. Yet he didn't see how it could ever work out.

When she smiled at him the way she was now, it was hard to think. Hard to breathe. Hard to know what was right and what wasn't.

"Eli, what's your answer?"

Pushing the niggling doubts aside, he finally nodded. "You'll need time to adjust, but I'll help you in every way I can."

CHAPTER

14

Once Laura made her decision to become Amish, the purchase of a second quilt was completely forgotten. The first order of business was to find Darla and tell her what she planned to do. Then she would need to go back to the interior design school and withdraw. After that, she would call her parents. That was going to be the hardest part, because she was sure they wouldn't understand. Eli's job was to tell Pauline the news, and also his parents, and she was sure that wouldn't be easy, either.

Eli stood from the bench where they had been sitting. "As soon as I leave the farmers' market, I'll head over to my sister's place and see if she would be willing to let you live with her."

Laura stood, too. "Do you think she would do that?"

"Jah. Martha Rose and I are close." He chuckled. "It's always been hard for her to tell me no, and I'm sure she would be a big help in teaching you everything you'll need to know about our way of life."

Laura gripped his arm. "I'm a ball of nerves, Eli. What if Martha Rose says I can't stay there? What if your folks don't accept me? What if—"

Eli held up his hand, halting her words. "Tomorrow I'll hire a driver to pick you up at the school in Lancaster, and we'll drive over to Amon and Martha Rose's place so you can meet them."

"That's okay," she said. "I'll need to turn in the car I'm leasing, so I'll have someone from the rental company drop me off in front of the variety store in Paradise. You can pick me up there, if that's all right."

"Jah, sure." He smiled, and it gave her a sense of reassurance. "I'm sure everything will work out okay."

"I still can't believe what you're planning to do," Darla said, as she and Laura drove back to their school. "Don't you realize what you'll be giving up? Don't you know how hard the transition from English to Amish will be?"

Laura nodded. "I know it won't be easy, but I can do it. I can do anything if I want it badly enough, and this is something I really want."

"You want to live the Plain life, without all the modern conveniences you've become used to?"

"Well, I—"

"Think about it, Laura. You won't be able to use your computer to send e-mails anymore. You won't be allowed to wear makeup, jeans, or any fancy clothes. You'll have to trade in your leased car for a horse and buggy."

Laura shrugged. "I'm sure it won't be easy, but I can do it for Eli—because I love him and hope to be his wife someday."

"Can't you talk him into leaving the Amish faith? You told me once that he's not joined the church yet, so he wouldn't be shunned if he were to become English."

"I did ask him about leaving once, and it wasn't long after that he said we should go our separate ways." Laura clenched her fingers tightly together in her lap. "I was miserable those months we were apart, and I won't let Eli walk out of my life again, no matter how many sacrifices I might need to make."

Darla gave the steering wheel a couple of taps. "Suit yourself, but don't come crying to me when things don't work out."

"I won't. You can be sure of that."

※

As Pauline waited near the root-beer stand for Eli to return, she became increasingly anxious. What had that English woman wanted to speak with Eli about, and why had he agreed to talk to her? She hoped he hadn't given up his plans to take membership classes this summer and join the church in the fall. Surely he wasn't thinking about leaving the Amish faith and going English.

"Oh, good, I'm glad you're still here. I need to speak with you."

Pauline whirled around at the sound of Eli's voice. She felt relief to see that the English woman wasn't with him. "Is everything all right, Eli? You look kind of flushed."

He drew her away from the table and over to one corner of the room. "I need to tell you something."

"What is it?"

Eli stared at the concrete floor as he shifted his weight from one foot to the other. "I—I've tried to tell you this before, but there's really no way it could work for us to be together."

Her forehead wrinkled. "Why not? We've been courting for a couple of months now, and I thought we've been getting along fairly well."

He lifted his gaze to hers. "There's no easy way for me to say this, but I'm in love with Laura."

"The Englisher?"

"Jah."

"You're going to leave the Amish faith to be with her?"

He shook his head. "Laura wants to become Plain."

Pauline tried to let Eli's words register in her brain while fighting the tears pushing against her eyelids. This couldn't be true. It had to be some kind of horrible joke. No one just up and decided to join the church—to her knowledge very few ever had.

"You're a nice person, and I'm sorry if I've led you on or hurt you in any way." Eli touched her arm. "I thought I could forget about Laura and move on with my life, but after seeing her today, I realized that she's the one I love and want to be with."

Pauline shrugged his hand away. "It won't work, Eli. That fancy woman will never become one of us. I doubt she could last one week as an Amish woman." Pauline's heart felt like it was breaking in two, but there was no way she would admit to Eli how much he had hurt her, or that she'd hoped to become his wife someday. She lifted her chin and stared right into his blue eyes. "You're verhuddelt if you think things are going to work out for you and Laura, but if she's what you want, then don't expect any sympathy from me if things go sour." Pauline turned on her heels and stalked off.

"Where are you going? Don't you need a ride home?"

She shook her head and kept on walking. She would

find her own way home, even if it meant phoning one of their English drivers for a ride.

𝔜

As Eli left his sister's place and headed down the road toward home with his horse and buggy, he reflected on the conversation he'd had with Martha Rose and felt relief that she'd agreed to let Laura stay with her and Amon while she took her training to become Amish. Martha Rose had also been willing to instruct Laura in cooking, sewing, and many other things she would need to know in order to become part of the Amish community.

Eli was sure that once his sister met Laura in person and saw how nice she was and realized that she wanted to become Amish, everything would work out fine and dandy. Now all he had to do was break the news to Mom and Pop.

𝔜

Mary Ellen was just putting lunch on the table when she heard a horse and buggy come into the yard. She glanced out the kitchen window and saw that it was Eli. "I wonder what he's doing home so soon," she said to Johnny, who had just finished washing up at the sink. "I thought he and Pauline were going out to lunch after they left the market, and I figured he would be gone most of the day."

Johnny shrugged. "Guess there must have been a change of plans."

"I hope they didn't have a disagreement. Eli can be kind of headstrong sometimes."

Johnny chuckled and flicked a little water in her direction. "Wonder where he gets that trait from?"

She wrinkled her nose. "Maybe you'd best look in the mirror."

"Ha! I'd say we both tend to be a bit headstrong at times."

"I guess you're right about that." She glanced out the window again. "Eli's putting his horse away, so he'll probably be in shortly. Did Lewis and Jonas say when they were coming inside?"

Johnny dried his hands on a towel before answering. "They had a couple of things to do in the barn, but I'm sure they'll be in soon, too."

"I'll go ahead and serve up the soup. By the time they come in, it will probably be cool enough to eat."

"Makes sense to me." Johnny kissed Mary Ellen's cheek, then ambled across the room and took a seat at the table.

A few minutes later, Jonas and Lewis entered the kitchen, followed by Eli, whose face was all red and sweaty.

Mary Ellen felt immediate concern, and she placed the ladle back in the pot of soup and rushed to his side. "Is there anything wrong, son? You look kind of flushed."

"That's what Pauline said right before I told her the news." Eli flopped into a chair and let his head fall forward into his hands.

Pop reached over and touched Eli's shoulder. "What news is that? What's got you so worked up?"

Eli looked up and blew out his breath. "There's something I need to tell you."

"Are you and Pauline gettin' hitched?" The question came from Lewis, who had also pulled out a chair and sat down.

Eli shook his head. "I think it might be good if everyone took a seat. What I have to say will probably be quite a shock."

Mary Ellen's heart slammed into her chest. Was Eli going to announce that he'd decided not to join the church in the fall, after all? With a sense of dread, she took the chair closest to him.

"So, tell us what's on your mind," Johnny said, after Jonas took his seat.

"You all remember Laura Meade, right?"

"The pretty redheaded woman you brought by the house a few months back?" Lewis asked with a grin.

Eli nodded. "The thing is—I saw Laura today, and she wants to join the Amish church."

"What?" Mary Ellen could hardly believe her ears. Eli hadn't mentioned the English woman in some time, and this made no sense at all.

"I've just come from Martha Rose's place, and she's agreed to let Laura stay there."

"She'll be staying with Martha Rose and Amon?"

"Jah, Mom."

"It just doesn't seem right, her being so fancy and all," Jonas said with a shake of his head.

"Jah," Lewis agreed. "It's not gonna be easy for Laura to give up all the modern things she's been used to and start livin' as we do."

"If Laura stays with Martha Rose, she can teach her all the things she'll need to know about being Amish, and Laura and I can both take the membership classes this summer. Then by fall, we'll both be baptized and join the church."

"Whose idea was this?" Johnny asked, leaning his elbows on the table.

"The part about joining the church was Laura's idea, but I'm the one who thought of asking Martha Rose to help her." Eli scrubbed a hand down his clean-shaven face. "Laura wants it, and so do I. She knows what she's giving up, and it's her decision to do this. So won't you please give her a chance?"

"It will take a lot of gumption for her to make all the sacrifices needed to join the church," Johnny put in. "If she can do it, then I'm willing to give her a chance."

"How about the rest of you?" Eli looked around the table.

Lewis and Jonas both nodded, but Mary Ellen couldn't seem to find her voice. If Laura wanted to join the church, and Eli wanted them to take classes and be baptized together, then in all likelihood, he had plans of marrying the girl soon after that. Mary Ellen didn't like the idea, but she knew if she voiced her concerns it might drive Eli away. They had waited a long time for him to reach a decision about joining the church, and she wouldn't do anything to discourage him. She finally nodded and forced her lips into a smile. "I'll give Laura a chance, too."

As soon as Laura returned to the school, she went straight to the admissions office and told them she would be withdrawing and would try to move her things out in the morning. Then she went to her room to call her parents.

She felt relief when Dad answered the phone, because she was sure the news of her decision would be harder for Mom to handle. "Hi, Dad, it's me," she said, drawing in a quick breath for added courage.

"It's good to hear from you, Laura. How are things going with your studies?"

She shifted the phone to her other ear. "I. . .uh. . .need to tell you something."

"Oh? What's that?"

"Starting tomorrow morning, I'll be done with school."

"Done? What do you mean? You haven't even finished your first year there yet."

"I'm. . .uh. . .not planning to finish, Dad."

There was a pause, then, "Irene, you'd better pick up the phone in the kitchen. Laura's on the line."

Laura held her breath as she waited for her mother to come on. Maybe it was better this way. She could tell them both the news at the same time and be done with it.

"Hello, Laura. How are you, dear?"

"I—I'm okay."

"Our daughter has some news she wants to share with us," Dad said before Mom could add anything more.

"What news is that?"

"I've withdrawn from school, and tomorrow morning, I'll be moving in with Eli's sister so I can join the Amish church."

"What?" Mom and Dad shouted in unison.

"I'm planning to join the Amish church."

"This is not April Fool's Day, Laura," Dad said with a chuckle. "Now quit fooling around."

"I'm not kidding. I'm in love with Eli Yoder, and the only way we can be together is if I join his faith."

"Why can't he leave the Amish faith and join our world?"

"Because, Mom, his roots are deep, and he's committed to his family as well as to his religion."

"Oh, and you're not committed to your family?"

"I am, but you and Dad have your own busy lives, and

you've raised me to be independent and make my own decisions." Laura paused as she groped for the right words. "This is the decision I've chosen to make."

"Laura, do you know what you're saying?" Mom's voice had risen at least an octave, and Laura had to hold the phone away from her ear. "I'm catching the next flight to Pennsylvania so I can talk some sense into you."

"You may as well save your money, because nothing you can say will make me change my mind. Besides, by the time you get here, I'll be moved out of my dorm room and into Martha Rose's house, and you don't know where that is." Laura sucked in her bottom lip. The truth was, she had no idea where Eli's sister lived, either. For that matter, she wasn't even sure Martha Rose would agree to take her in. What if the woman had said no to Eli's request? What if Laura had quit school for nothing and now had no place to go?

She shook her head, trying to clear away the troubling thoughts. It would all work out. It had to work out. Eli had said it would.

"What about Dean?" Mom asked. "I thought the two of you were—"

"It was over between me and Dean months ago. The last time we talked, I told him so, too."

"Laura, your mother and I want you to be happy," Dad said. "But is giving up the only way of life you've ever known and becoming Amish really going to make you happy?"

"Being with Eli will make me happy, and if I have to make a few sacrifices along the way in order for it to happen, then I'll learn to deal with it."

"She's got a determined spirit, this daughter of ours, and it took a lot of courage for her to make a decision such as this. I think we should give her our blessing."

Laura knew Dad was talking to Mom now, so she waited to hear what her mother's response would be.

"I don't see how you can expect me to give Laura my blessing when I know she's making the biggest mistake of her life. She won't be happy living without electricity and many other modern conveniences. She might think she's in love with this Amish man, but a few months from now, she'll change her mind; mark my words."

Laura released an exasperated sigh. "I've got to go now. I need to pack. I'll give you a call on my cell phone after I get moved so I can give you my new address. Maybe you can send me that quilt I bought at the farmers' market. It would be nice to have it in my possession again."

Mom released a couple of sobs and hung up.

"If you change your mind about this or ever need anything, don't hesitate to call," Dad said.

"Thanks, I'll remember that."

"Be happy, and please keep in touch."

"I will, Dad." Laura clicked off her cell phone and flopped onto the bed. Mom had reacted to the news pretty much the way she'd expected her to, but her father's reaction had been a complete surprise. Had he been so compliant because he wanted her to be happy, or was it possible that some part of Dad could actually identify with Laura's desire to go Plain?

CHAPTER 15

As Laura sat on a bench in front of the variety store in Paradise, she began to worry. She had turned in all of her books at the school, sent everything home that she didn't think she would need in her new life, and dropped off her rental car. Now she was waiting for Eli to pick her up. But what if he didn't show? What if he'd changed his mind about asking his sister to take Laura in? Maybe his folks had talked him out of his plans. Or maybe his sister had said no to his request.

She drew in a deep breath and tried to calm her nerves. The last time she'd waited on this bench for Eli and had been worried he wouldn't show, he'd only been running late. That was probably the case this time, too. At least she hoped it was.

She leaned her head against the wall behind her and tried to focus on something else. It was useless. All she could think about was Eli and how much she wanted to be with him. If he didn't show up, she would be devastated, and she'd never be able to face Darla again.

Darla had tried again this morning to get Laura to change her mind about joining the Amish faith. She'd reminded her of how hard it was going to be and said that Laura needed to give it more thought.

Ever since the day Laura had met Eli, he'd never been far from her thoughts. She dreamed about him at night, compared him to Dean during the day, and imagined what it would be like to be Mrs. Eli Yoder.

The *clip-clop* of horse's hooves drew Laura's attention to the parking lot, and a feeling of relief flooded her soul. Eli was here. He had come for her just like he'd promised. Everything would be okay now.

As Eli led Laura up the steps to his sister's home, her insides quivered with anticipation. She'd been relieved when Eli had told her that Martha Rose had agreed to let her stay, but that was only half the battle. Laura still had lots to learn, and she worried about whether she would be accepted among Eli's friends and family.

"Don't be nervous now," Eli whispered as he opened the back door. "You'll like it here, I promise."

Laura forced a smile. "I–I hope so."

When they entered the kitchen, they were greeted by a tall, large-boned woman with a flawless complexion, hair the color of chestnuts, and dark brown eyes. She offered a warm, friendly smile. "You must be Laura."

Laura's only reply was a quick nod.

"I'm Eli's sister, Martha Rose."

Laura extended her hand. "It's nice to meet you, and I appreciate your letting me stay here."

Martha Rose glanced over at Eli and smiled. "I'd do most anything for my little brother."

Eli chuckled. "Should I bring in Laura's things while you show her around?"

"Jah, sure." Martha Rose motioned toward the door leading to a hallway. "Why don't we start with the upstairs, since that's where Laura's bedroom will be?"

Eli disappeared out the back door, and Laura followed Martha Rose up the stairs.

"This will be yours," Martha Rose said, opening the door to the second room on the left. "It's right across the hall from the bathroom."

Laura breathed a sigh of relief. At least this Amish farm had indoor plumbing, and for that she felt grateful. Darla had told her that most Amish in the area used diesel or propane-operated generators, so they had indoor bathrooms with hot and cold running water, but a few homes still used outhouses.

As Laura stepped into the bedroom where she would soon take up residence, a shockwave spiraled through her. It was even smaller than her dorm room at the school had been. Plain. . .so very plain. There was a double bed, a chest of drawers with a washbowl and pitcher sitting on top, and a small cedar chest at the foot of the bed. Dark shades hung at the two windows, and except for a small, braided throw rug, the hardwood floor was bare. Instead of a closet, a row of wooden pegs was connected to a narrow strip of wood lining one wall.

"Here are a few dresses you can wear." Martha Rose handed Laura two long, cotton frocks. One was navy blue, the other a dark shade of green. "You're a bit shorter than me, so they might be kind of long." She grinned. "Better too long than too short."

Laura was too dumbfounded to even speak. In her excitement to join the Amish faith and win Eli's heart, she had almost forgotten that she would be expected to wear such plain, simple clothing.

"I have a white head covering for you. And you'll need a dark bonnet to wear over it when you go out at certain times."

Laura nodded mutely as she was given the rest of her new wardrobe. *What have I gotten myself into? Can I really exchange my jeans and T-shirts for long, plain dresses?* She inhaled deeply, reminding herself that she could do this and that it was for a good cause. Her determination and love for Eli would see her through.

"We'll go to the boot and harness shop tomorrow and buy you some black leather shoes for church and other special occasions," Martha Rose said. "If you already own a pair of sneakers, you can wear them for everyday." She looked down at her bare feet and smiled. "Of course, most of us just go barefoot around home, especially during the warmer weather. It saves our shoes, and it's much cooler."

Laura shifted from one foot to the other. Barefoot? Sneakers and black leather shoes? Were those her only choices? "Don't your feet get dirty and sore, running around barefoot?"

"Jah, but they toughen up, and I always wash my feet before going to bed."

Laura shrugged. What could she really say? She'd gotten herself into this predicament, and it was of her own choosing that she had decided to go Plain. She would simply draw from her inner strength and do whatever was necessary in order to convince Eli and his family she was worthy of being part of their clan.

The next few weeks were busy. . .busier than Laura ever imagined. She had so much to learn about cooking, sewing, baking, and doing laundry and other household chores, not to mention the outside jobs. Gathering eggs, slopping the hogs, and cultivating the garden were all things she had never done before. It was dirty, backbreaking work, and she made so many foolish mistakes at first.

One morning after breakfast, as Laura was in her room getting ready for a date with Eli, she glanced at herself in the hand mirror she'd found in the drawer and dug underneath her underwear for the satchel of makeup she had stashed away. She knew Amish women didn't wear makeup, but she wasn't ready to part with those things, so she hadn't mailed them home with all her clothes.

Today was Saturday, and Eli would be coming soon to take her for a buggy ride. They planned to go into Paradise and do some shopping, then stop for a picnic on the way home.

Laura stared longingly at the tube of lipstick she held in her hand. *What would it hurt to apply a little color to my pale lips so Eli will find me attractive? I wouldn't want him to lose interest in me and go back to Pauline.*

Laura blended the coral lipstick with the tips of her fingers, then reached inside the makeup case for some blush. A little dab blended on each cheek made her look less pale. She added a coat of mascara to her eyelashes and filled in her brows with a soft cinnamon pencil.

"There now," she whispered to her reflection. "I almost look like my old self—not nearly so plain." She glanced down at her plain green dress and scowled. "What I wouldn't give to put on a pair of jeans and a T-shirt." She slipped her head covering on and sighed. "Guess I'd better get used to this if I'm ever going to fit in here."

Downstairs in the kitchen, Laura found Eli's sister and his mother sitting at the table, drinking a cup of tea and eating shoofly pie. Just the smell of the molasses-filled pastry made Laura's stomach churn. She didn't think she would ever acquire a taste for this particular dessert.

"*Guder mariye,*" Martha Rose said cheerfully when Laura joined them.

"Good morning," she responded with a slight nod. Learning Pennsylvania Dutch was another challenge for Laura, along with studying the Bible and learning the church rules, which the Amish called the *Ordnung.* She glanced over at Eli's mother. "I didn't realize you were here, Mary Ellen."

"Came to help Martha Rose do some baking." Mary Ellen studied Laura intently, making her feel like a bug under a microscope. "What's that you've got on your face?"

Laura shrugged and reached for an apple from the ceramic bowl sitting in the center of the table. "Just a little color to make me look less pale," she mumbled as she bit into the succulent fruit.

"Makeup's not allowed. Surely you must know that."

Laura blinked a couple of times as she stared at Mary Ellen. "What harm is there in trying to make myself a bit more attractive?"

" 'Favour is deceitful, and beauty is vain: but a woman that feareth the Lord, she shall be praised,' " Mary Ellen quoted.

Laura squinted her eyes. "Where'd you hear that?"

"It's in the book of Proverbs," Martha Rose answered,

before her mother had a chance to respond.

Mary Ellen looked right at Laura. "Face powder may catch some men, but it takes baking powder to hold them."

Martha Rose giggled, and her mother chuckled behind her hand, but Laura sat stony-faced. She didn't see what was so funny. Besides, she had the distinct impression these two Plain women were laughing at her, not at the joke Eli's mother had just shared.

Laura felt foolish for doing something she knew was wrong, but it irritated her that Mary Ellen had made a joke at her expense. She was sure the woman didn't like her. With a sigh of frustration, she pushed her chair away from the table and stood. "Sorry about the mistake. I'll go wash the makeup off my face now."

Eli whistled as he hitched his horse to the open buggy. He was looking forward to his date with Laura, but he still couldn't believe she had actually agreed to become Plain. She was beautiful, talented, and smart. He was sure she could have any man she wanted, yet it was him and his way of life she had chosen. It almost seemed too good to be true.

"I'll make her happy," he said aloud. The horse whinnied and nuzzled the back of Eli's arm.

"At least *you* aren't givin' me a hard time. If Mom and Pop had their way, I'd be married to Pauline by now, not courting Laura."

Eli knew his parents had his best interests at heart, but they didn't understand how much he loved Laura. Even though his folks had agreed to try and make her feel welcome, he was sure it was only to please him. Deep in his heart, Eli felt they were just waiting for Laura to give up and leave so they could say, "I told you so."

He was glad Martha Rose seemed to be on his side and had agreed to let Laura stay there. It was a comfort to know his sister was willing to mentor his fancy English woman who wanted to become Plain. Mom and Pop were another matter. They were no more thrilled about the idea of Laura joining the Amish faith than they had been about Eli seeing her when she was still English. It was hard to understand how Mom, who normally was so pleasant and easygoing, had seemed almost rude to Laura when she'd first visited their home. Even now, as Laura prepared to become Amish, there was a coolness in the way his mother spoke to Laura. He hoped things would change once Laura took her training and was baptized into the faith.

Eli climbed into the driver's seat and gathered up the reins. He knew Mom had gone over to Martha Rose's this morning so she would see Laura before he did.

He clucked to the horse, and it moved forward. "Let's hope things went well between Laura and Mom, for if they didn't, I'm likely to have a cross woman on my hands for the rest of the day."

When Laura greeted Eli at the back door, he thought she looked like she'd lost her best friend. "What's wrong? Aren't you happy to see me this morning? Do you still want to go to Paradise and then on a picnic?"

"Of course I want to go."

"Would you like to come in and have a piece of shoofly pie?" Mom asked.

Eli glanced at his mother, who sat at the kitchen table with Martha Rose. "Jah, sure."

"I think we should be on our way," Laura said, stepping between Eli and the table.

He frowned. "What's your hurry?"

"I've got quite a bit of shopping to do, and we don't want to get to the lake too late." She rushed past him, pulled a dark blue sweater from the wall peg by the back door, and grabbed the wicker picnic basket sitting on the cupboard.

Eli looked at Laura standing by the door, tapping her foot. He glanced back at the table, and his mouth watered just thinking about how good a hunk of that pie would taste.

As though sensing his dilemma, Martha Rose said, "Why don't you take a few pieces along? You and Laura can have it with the picnic lunch she made."

Eli shrugged. "I guess I can wait that long to sample some of your good cooking, sister."

He reached for the pie, but Martha Rose was too quick for him. She had already begun slicing it by the time he got to the table. "If you really want to help, get some waxed paper from the pantry," she instructed.

He did as he was told, not caring in the least that his big sister was bossing him around. He'd grown used to it over the years. Besides, she really didn't mean to sound so pushy. Martha Rose had always been a take-charge kind of person. She was pleasant and kind, so he could tolerate a little ordering about now and then.

"You two have a good day," Martha Rose said as Eli and Laura started out the back door.

"Jah, and be sure to be home in time for chores and supper," Mom called.

"I will," Eli said, closing the door behind them.

Laura stopped at the bottom of the stairs, and Eli nearly ran into her. "What'd you stop for? I could have knocked you to the ground."

She scowled at him. "You're henpecked. Do you know that?"

His eyebrows furrowed. "You don't know what you're saying, Laura."

Her nose twitched as she blinked rapidly. "Those two women have you eating out of the palms of their hands."

Eli started walking toward his open buggy. "They do not. I just happen to like pleasing them, that's all. I love Mom and Martha Rose, and they're both mighty good to me."

"Well, they're not so good to me."

Eli whirled around to face Laura. She looked madder than one of his father's mules when a big old horsefly had taken a bite out of its ear. "How can you say they're not good to you? Martha Rose took you in, didn't she?"

Laura opened her mouth, but before she could respond, Eli rushed on. "She gave you some of her dresses to wear, took you shopping for shoes and the like, and both she and Mom have taken time out of their busy days to teach you about housekeeping, cooking, Bible reading, and so many other things you'll need to know before joining the church."

Laura's lip protruded as she handed Eli the picnic basket. "I should have known you wouldn't understand. You're one of them."

"What's that supposed to mean?" Eli asked, as he climbed into his rig and took up the reins.

Laura stood on the other side of the buggy with her

arms folded. "It means you're Amish and I'm not. I'm still considered an outsider, and I don't think anyone in your family will ever accept me as anything else."

"Of course they will." He glanced at her out of the corner of his eye. "Are you getting in or not?"

"Aren't you going to help me?"

He groaned. "I might have, if you hadn't been naggin' at me. Besides, if you're going to be Amish, then you'll need to learn how to get in and out of our buggies without any help when you're going someplace on your own."

Laura was so angry she was visibly shaking. If she hadn't been sure she would be expected to help with the baking, she would have turned around and marched right back to the house. It would serve Eli right if she broke this date!

"Time's a-wasting," Eli announced.

She sighed deeply, lifted her skirt, and practically fell into the buggy.

Eli chuckled, then snapped the reins. The horse jerked forward, and Laura was thrown against her seat. "Be careful! Are you trying to throw my back out?"

Eli's only response was another deep guffaw, which only angered her further.

Laura smoothed her skirt, reached up to be sure her head covering was still in place, then folded her arms across her chest. "I'm glad you think everything's so funny. You can't imagine what I've been through these past few weeks."

"Has something bad happened?" Eli looked over at her with obvious concern.

She moaned. "I'll say."

"What was it? Did you get hurt? How come I didn't hear about it?"

She shook her head. "No, no, I wasn't hurt. At least not in the physical sense."

"What then?"

"I've nearly been worked to death every day since I moved to your sister's house. It seems as though I just get to sleep and it's time to get up again." She frowned. "And that noisy rooster crowing at the top of his lungs every morning sure doesn't help things, either."

"Pop says the rooster is nature's alarm clock," Eli said with a grin.

How can he sit there looking so smug? Laura fumed. *Doesn't he care how hard I work? Doesn't he realize I'm doing all this for him?*

"In time, you'll get used to the long days. I bet someday you'll find pleasure in that old rooster's crow."

"I doubt that." She held up her hands. "Do you realize that every single one of my nails is broken? Not to mention embedded with dirt I'll probably never be able to scrub clean. Why, the other morning, Martha Rose had me out in the garden, pulling weeds and spading with an old hoe. I thought my back was going to break in two."

"You *will* get used to it, Laura."

She scrunched up her nose. "Maybe. If I live to tell about it."

CHAPTER 16

Laura's days at the Zook farm flew by despite her frustrations. As spring turned quickly into summer, each day became longer, hotter, and filled with more work. Instead of "becoming used to it," Laura found herself disliking each new day. How did these people exist without air-conditioning, ceiling fans, and swimming pools? How did the women deal with wearing long dresses all summer instead of shorts?

Laura and Martha Rose had gone wading in the creek near their house a few times, while Amon taught little Ben how to swim. The chilly water helped Laura cool down some, but she missed her parents' swimming pool and air-conditioned home.

Another area of Amish life Laura hadn't become used to was the three-hour church service held every other Sunday in a different member's home. She had gone to church only a few times in her adult life—mostly on Easter and Christmas—but she'd never had to sit on backless, wooden benches or been segregated from the men. The Amish culture still seemed strange to her and very confusing. She couldn't visit with Eli until the service was over, lunch had been served, and everything had been cleaned up. If Laura had ever thought life as an Amish woman was going to be easy, she'd been sorely mistaken. She couldn't even keep her cell phone charged because Amon's farm had no electricity. On days like today when she was hot and tired, she wondered if she had made a mistake by asking to join the Amish church.

"It's not too late to back out," she muttered as she set a basket of freshly laundered clothes on the grass underneath the clothesline that extended from the porch into the yard. "I can go back to the school in Lancaster or home to Mom and Dad in Minneapolis. At least they don't expect me to work so hard."

A pathetic *mooo* drew Laura's attention to the fence separating the Zooks' yard from the pasture. Three black-and-white cows stood on the other side, swishing their tails and looking at her.

"Just what I need—a cheering section. Go away, cows! Get back to the field, grab a hunk of grass, start chewing your cuds, then go take a nice, long nap." She bent down, grabbed one of Amon's shirts, gave it a good shake, then clipped it to the clothesline. "At least you bovine critters are allowed the privilege of a nap now and then. That's more than I can say for any of the humans who live on this farm."

"*Kuh,*" a small voice said.

Laura looked down. There stood little Ben, gazing up at her with all the seriousness of a three-year-old. He'd said something in Pennsylvania Dutch, but she wasn't sure what he was talking about. She'd been studying the Amish dialect for a few months, but she still encountered many unfamiliar words.

"Kuh," the child repeated. This time he pointed toward the cows, still gawking at Laura like she was free entertainment.

"Ah, the cows. You're talking about the cows, aren't you?" She dropped to her knees beside the little boy and gave him a hug.

Ben looked up at her and grinned. He really was a cute little thing, with his blond, Dutch-bobbed hair, big blue eyes, and two deep dimples framing his smile. He studied the basket of clothes a few seconds as his smile turned to a frown.

"*Loch,*" he said, grabbing one of Amon's shirts.

Laura smiled when she realized the child was telling her about his father's shirt with a hole. She patted the top of Ben's head. "No doubt that shirt will end up in my pile of mending."

Ben made no comment, but then, she knew he didn't understand what she'd said. He would be taught English when he started school. With an impish grin, the boy climbed into the basket of wet clothes.

Laura was about to scold him, but Ben picked up one of his mother's dark bonnets and plunked it on top of his head. She sank to her knees and laughed so hard that tears ran down her face. The cows on the other side of the fence mooed, and the little boy giggled.

Maybe life on this humble, Amish farm wasn't so bad after all.

❦

Pauline sat on the front porch, staring at the flowers blooming in her mother's garden but not really seeing them. She'd been miserable ever since Eli had told her they had no future together and had begun dating that fancy English woman. Not that Laura looked so fancy anymore. She wore the same plain clothes as the other Amish women in their community, but there was something about the way she walked, talked, and held her body so prim and proper that made her seem out of place among the other women in their district.

Every time Pauline saw Laura at church or some other community event, it made her feel sick to the pit of her stomach. She didn't know if she would ever get over the bitterness she felt over losing Eli to someone outside their faith.

She won't be outside the faith once she's baptized and joins the church, Pauline reminded herself. *She'll be one of us, and I'll have to accept her as such, no matter how much it hurts.*

"What are you doing sitting out here by yourself?" Pauline's mother asked as she seated herself on the step beside Pauline. "I figured you'd be anxious to get some baking done before it gets too hot."

"I don't feel much like baking today. Can't it wait for another day?"

"I suppose, but we're almost out of bread, and you know how much your daed likes those ginger cookies you make so well."

Pauline made no comment; she just sat there breathing in and out, feeling as though she couldn't get enough air.

"Are you okay? You look kind of peaked this morning."

"I'm fine. Just tired is all."

Mom laid a gentle hand on Pauline's arm. "Still not sleeping well?"

"Not since. . ." Pauline couldn't finish the sentence. It

pained her to think about Eli, much less speak his name.

"You've got to put your broken relationship with Eli Yoder behind you, daughter. You can't go through the rest of your life pining for something that's not meant to be."

Pauline released a shuddering sob. "It was meant to be, until *she* came along and ruined things. Eli and I were getting closer, and I was sure he would ask me to marry him after he finished his membership classes at the end of summer." Tears slipped from her eyes and rolled down her cheeks. "It's not fair, Mom. It's just not fair."

"Many things in life aren't fair, but we must learn to accept them as God's will and move on."

"I'm not sure I can do that. Not when I have to see Eli and that woman together all the time."

"Maybe you should go away for a while."

Pauline wiped her eyes with the backs of her hands and turned to face her mother. "Go away? Where would I go?"

"Maybe you could stay with your daed's sister, Irma, in Kidron, Ohio."

"I'll have to think about it."

Mom patted Pauline's hand. "You do that. Think and pray about the matter."

Laura sat at the kitchen table, reading the Bible Martha Rose had given her. Why did it seem so confusing? She had been to Sunday school and Bible school a few times when she was a girl. She'd even managed to memorize some Bible passages in order to win a prize. Why couldn't she stay focused now?

"You've been at it quite awhile. Would you like to take

a break and have a glass of iced tea with me?" Martha Rose asked, pulling out a chair and taking a seat beside Laura.

Laura looked up and smiled. She really did need a break. "Thanks, I'd like that."

Martha Rose poured two glasses of iced tea and piled a plate high with peanut butter cookies.

"Are you trying to fatten me up?" Laura asked when the goodies were set on the table.

Martha Rose chuckled. "As a matter of fact, you are pretty thin. I figured a few months of living here, and you'd have gained at least ten pounds."

"Your cooking is wonderful, but I'm trying to watch my weight."

"You need to eat hearty in order to keep up your strength." Martha Rose pushed the cookie plate in front of Laura. "Please, have a few."

Laura shrugged. "I guess two cookies wouldn't hurt."

"How are your studies coming along? Has little Ben been staying out of your way?"

"He's never been a problem. Your little boy is a real sweetheart."

"Jah, well, he can also be a pill at times." Martha Rose shook her head. "This morning I found him playing in the toilet, of all things. Said he was goin' fishing, like he and his daed did last week."

Laura laughed. "Where's the little guy now?"

"Down for a nap. I'm hoping he stays asleep awhile, because I've got a bunch of ripe tomatoes waiting to be picked. Not to mention fixing lunch and getting a bit more cleaning done. Church will be here this Sunday, you know."

"I'd almost forgotten. Guess that means we'll have to

do more cooking than usual." Laura reached around to rub a tight muscle in her back, probably caused from standing long hours at the stove.

"Not really. I'm just planning to fix a pot of bean soup and some sandwiches."

"Isn't the weather kind of hot to be having soup?"

"We enjoy soup most any time of the year, and my daed always says, 'A little heat on the inside makes the outside heat seem cool.' " Martha Rose chuckled. "Dad has lots of sayings like that, and plenty of jokes to tell, too."

Laura bit into a cookie and washed it down with a sip of cold tea. She hadn't really seen a humorous side to Eli's father and wondered if he held back because of her. She had a feeling Mary Ellen wasn't the only one in Eli's family who didn't care for her, and she had to wonder if she would ever truly feel a part of them.

"How's the Pennsylvania Dutch coming along?" Martha Rose asked. "Do you feel like you're understanding the words better yet?"

"I can figure out what many words mean, but I'm still having trouble speaking them."

"Practice makes perfect. I think it might help if we spoke less English to you."

Laura nearly choked on the second bite of cookie she had taken. "You're kidding, right?"

Martha Rose shook her head. "I think you need to hear more Deitsch and less English. It will force you to try saying more words yourself."

Laura groaned. Wasn't it enough that she had to wear plain, simple clothes, labor all day on jobs she'd rather not do, conform to all kinds of rules she didn't understand,

and get along without modern conveniences? Must she now be forced to speak and hear a foreign language most of the time?

As if she could read her thoughts, Martha Rose reached over and patted Laura's hand. "You do want to become one of us, don't you?"

Tears gathered in Laura's eyes, obscuring her vision. "I love Eli, and I'd do anything for him, but I—I didn't think giving up my way of life would be so hard."

"You say you love my brother, but what about your love for God? It's Him you should be trying most to please, not Eli."

Laura swallowed hard. How could she tell Martha Rose that, while she did believe in God, she'd never really had a personal relationship with Him? She wasn't even sure she wanted one. After all, what had God ever done for her? If He were on her side, then wouldn't Eli have been willing to leave his religion and become English? They could have worshiped God in any church.

"Laura?" Martha Rose prompted.

She nodded. "I do want to please God. I just hope He knows how hard I'm trying and rewards me for all my efforts."

Martha Rose's forehead wrinkled as she frowned. "We should never have to be rewarded for our good deeds or service to God. We're taught to be humble servants, never prideful or seeking after the things of this world. There's joy in loving and serving the Lord, as well as in ministering to others."

Laura thought about that. The Amish people she was living among did seem to emanate a certain kind of peaceful, joyful spirit. She couldn't figure out why, since they did without so many things.

Martha Rose pushed away from the table. "I think we should end this discussion and get busy picking in the garden, don't you?"

Laura eased out of her chair. While she had no desire to spend the next few hours in the hot sun bent over a bunch of itchy tomato plants, at least she wouldn't have to listen to any more sermons about God and what He expected of people.

A short time later, as Laura crouched in front of a clump of rosy, ripe tomatoes, she thought about home and how she'd never had a fresh out-of-the-garden tomato until she'd come here. Yesterday, she'd gone over to the Petersons, who were Martha Rose's closest English neighbors, to call her parents. Dad had been gone on a fishing trip, which was a surprise since he rarely did anything just for fun; and Mom had mentioned that she would be hosting a garden party this weekend and was having it catered.

Probably won't have anything this fresh or tasty to eat, Laura thought as she plucked a plump tomato off the vine.

Her thoughts went to Eli. Martha Rose had told Laura that Eli liked homemade tomato ketchup, which Laura hadn't learned to make yet. There were so many things she still didn't know, and even though she disliked many of the chores she was expected to do and still hadn't gotten used to wearing a dress all the time, she never got tired of spending time with Eli. The more they were together, the more she was convinced she had done the right thing when she'd decided to become Amish. Despite the fact that Eli could get under her skin at times, he treated her with respect—nothing like Dean had done when they were dating.

Laura wasn't looking forward to another long church

741

service this Sunday, but the promise of attending a singing that night gave her some measure of joy. It would be held in the Beachys' barn, and Eli had promised to take her. Since he would be coming to Amon and Martha Rose's for the preaching service, he would probably stick around all day, then later escort Laura to the singing. If things went as planned, she should be baptized into the Amish church by early fall, and she hoped she and Eli could get married sometime in November. Of course, he needed to propose to her first.

Eli felt a mounting sense of excitement over his date with Laura, and even though he'd told her awhile back that she should learn to get into the buggy herself, he helped her in this time, not wishing to cause another rift between them. Truth be told, Eli worried that Laura might not like the Amish way of life well enough to stay, and he didn't think he could deal with it if she decided to return to her old life.

"I've been looking forward to tonight," Laura murmured as she settled against the buggy seat.

"Jah, me, too." Eli glanced over at her and smiled. "You're sure pretty, you know that?"

Laura lifted her hand and touched her head covering. "You really think so?"

He nodded. "I do."

"But my hair's not long and beautiful anymore."

"Your hair's still long. You're just wearing it up in the back now."

"I know, but it looks so plain this way."

He reached over to gently touch her arm. "You may become one of the Plain People, but you'll never be plain to me."

When they arrived at the Beachy farm a short time later, the barn was already filled with young people. The huge doors were swung open wide, allowing the evening breeze to circulate and help cool the barn.

Soon the singing began, and the song leader led the group in several slow hymns, followed by a few faster tunes. There were no musical instruments, but the young people's a cappella voices permeated the air with a pleasant symphony of its own kind. Laura got caught up in the happy mood and was pleasantly surprised to realize she could actually follow along without too much difficulty.

When the singing ended, the young people paired off, and the games began. Laura was breathless by the time she and Eli finished playing several rounds of six-handed reel, which to her way of thinking was similar to square dancing.

"Would you like a glass of lemonade and some cookies?" Eli asked as he led Laura over to one of the wooden benches along the wall.

She nodded. "That sounds wunderbaar."

Eli disappeared into the crowd around the refreshment table, and Laura leaned her head against the wooden plank behind her. She caught a glimpse of Pauline Hostetler sitting across the room with her arms folded. She appeared to be watching her, and not with a joyful expression.

It was obvious to Laura that Pauline wasn't fond of her. In the months since Laura had been part of the Amish community, Pauline hadn't spoken one word to her. *I'm sure she's jealous because Eli chose me and not her, and I guess I can't really blame her.*

"Here you go." Eli handed Laura a glass of cold lemonade. "I was going to get us some cookies, but the plate was empty. I didn't want to wait around 'til one of the Beachy girls went to get more."

"That's okay. I ate a few too many of your sister's peanut butter cookies earlier this week, and I don't want to gain any weight."

Eli frowned. "I think you could use a few extra pounds."

Do you want me to end up looking like your slightly plump mother? Laura didn't vocalize her thoughts. Instead, she quietly sipped her lemonade. They would be going home soon, and she didn't want to say anything that might irritate Eli or provoke another argument.

CHAPTER
17

I f you're ready to go home now, I'll get the horse and buggy," Eli told Laura after they had finished their refreshments.

She smiled up at him. "I'm more than ready."

"I won't be long. Come outside when you see my horse pull up in front of the barn. There's no point in us both getting bit up by all the swarming insects tonight." He strolled out the door, leaving Laura alone by the refreshment table. She caught sight of Pauline, who had exited the barn only moments after Eli.

"I hope she's not going after him," Laura muttered under her breath.

"What was that?"

Laura whirled around and was greeted with a friendly smile from a young woman about her age, whom she'd seen before but had never personally met.

"I was talking to myself," Laura admitted, feeling the heat of a blush creep up the back of her neck.

The other woman nodded. "I do that sometimes." Her smile widened. "My name's Anna Beachy, and you're Laura, right?"

Laura nodded. "I'm staying with Martha Rose Zook and her family."

"I know. Martha Rose and I are friends. Have been since we were kinner, but I don't see her so much now that she's married and raising a family." Anna's green eyes gleamed in the light of the gas lamps hanging from the barn rafters. "Our moms were friends when they were growing up, too."

Laura kept on nodding, although it was a mechanical gesture. While this was interesting trivia, and Anna seemed like a nice person, she was most anxious to get outside and see if Eli had the buggy ready. What was taking him so long, anyway?

"Our families have been linked together for quite a spell," Anna continued. "Martha Rose's mamm, Mary Ellen, is the stepdaughter of Miriam Hilty. The dear woman's gone to heaven now, but Miriam, who everyone called 'Mim,' was a good friend of Sarah Stoltzfus, Rebekah Beachy's mamm. Rebekah's my mamm, and she's partially paralyzed. She either uses a wheelchair or metal leg braces in order to get around. Has since she was a young girl, I'm told." Anna paused a moment, but before Laura could comment, she rushed on. "Now, Grandma Sarah is living with my aunt Nadine, and—"

Laura tapped her foot impatiently, wondering how she could politely excuse herself. "I see," she said in the brief seconds Anna came up for air. "It does sound like you have a close-knit family." She cleared her throat a few times. "It's been nice chatting with you, Anna, but Eli's outside getting his horse and buggy ready to take me home. I'd better not keep him waiting."

"Jah, okay. Tell Eli I said hello, and let him know he

should inform his big sister that she owes me a visit real soon."

"Since I'm staying with Martha Rose, I'll be sure she gets the message." Laura hurried away before Anna could say anything more.

Once outside, she headed for the long line of buggies parked alongside the Beachys' barn. She stopped short when she saw Eli talking to Pauline.

When Pauline reached out and touched Eli's arm, he took a step back, bumping against his buggy. What was going on here? This didn't set well with him. Didn't Pauline know he was courting Laura?

"That English woman will never make you happy," Pauline murmured. "Take me home tonight, and let her find another way."

Eli brushed Pauline's hand aside. "I can't do that. I brought Laura to the singing, and I'll see that she gets home." He sniffed. "Besides, I love her, and as soon as she and I join the church, I'm planning to ask her to be my wife."

Pauline's pinched lips made her face look like a dried-up prune. "You're not thinking straight, Eli. You haven't been right in the head since that fancy woman came sashaying into your life."

"You have no right to say anything about Laura," Eli defended. "You don't even know her."

"I know her well enough to know she's not right for you."

Eli glanced toward the barn and spotted Laura heading out the door. "I need to go. Laura's waiting for me to give her a ride home."

Tears pooled in Pauline's eyes, and her chin trembled. "I—I thought there was something special between us. I thought—" She choked on a sob and fell into his arms.

Eli just stood there, not knowing what to do, but before he could think of anything, Laura showed up, and he knew right away that she was hopping mad.

"What's going on here?"

Pauline pivoted toward Laura. "What's it look like? Eli was hugging me."

Eli's face heated up. "Pauline, that isn't so, and you know it." He could see Laura's face in the moonlight, and it was nearly as red as his felt. How could he make her understand what had really happened? He knew she was a bit insecure in their relationship, and he was sure that seeing Pauline with her arms around him hadn't helped any.

"I should have known you were chasing after Eli when I saw you leave the barn." Laura's voice shook as she stood toe-to-toe with Pauline.

Pauline didn't flinch, nor did she back down. "All I did was say a few words to Eli, and it's not my fault he decided to give me a hug."

Eli touched Pauline's arm, and she whirled back around to face him. "I know you're not happy about me and Laura, but lying isn't going to help."

Pauline shrugged his hand away. "You'll be sorry you chose her and not me. Just wait and see if you're not." She wrinkled her nose and stalked off.

⁂

Laura was fit to be tied. Did Eli really make the first move, or had Pauline deliberately hugged him just to stir up trouble?

Even if it broke her heart, she needed to know what had transpired. She had to know the truth.

"Are you ready to go home?" Eli gave her a sheepish look.

"I was ready half an hour ago. And don't go thinking you can soft-soap me with that cute, little-boy look of yours, either."

"You remind me of *en wiedicher hund*," Eli said with a chuckle. "You've got quite a temper, but seeing how you acted when you saw me and Pauline together lets me know how much you really love me."

Laura folded her arms and scowled at him. "I'm beginning to know a lot more of your Pennsylvania Dutch language, and I'll have you know, Eli Yoder, I do not look like a mad dog."

He tickled her under the chin. "You do love me though, right?"

"You know I do. That's why it always makes me angry whenever I see that woman with you." She leaned a bit closer to him. "Tell me the truth, Eli. Did she hug you, or was it the other way around?"

Eli pursed his lips. "She hugged me. Honest."

"Did you encourage her in any way?"

He shook his head. "She knows I love you, Laura, and she's jealous, so she wants to make you think there's something going on with us." He helped Laura into the buggy. "Think about it. Who's the woman I've been courtin' all summer?"

"As far as I know, only me."

Eli went around and took his own seat, then picked up the reins and got the horse moving. "Let's stop by the lake on the way home."

Laura gazed up at the night sky. It was a beautiful evening, and the grass was lit by hundreds of twinkling fireflies. The buggy ride should have been magical for both of them. Instead, Pauline had thrown a damper on things.

Laura knew she was probably being paranoid where Pauline was concerned, but she couldn't seem to help herself. "I'm not much in the mood for love or romance right now, so I think it would be good if we just head straight to your sister's house."

Eli moaned. "Maybe our next date will go better."

"Jah, let's hope so."

Laura felt closer to Eli's sister than she did the rest of his family. Martha Rose had patiently taught her to use the treadle sewing machine; bake shoofly pies; and given her lessons in milking, gathering eggs, and slopping pigs. It was none of those things that made Martha Rose seem special, however. It was her friendly attitude and the way she had accepted a complete stranger into her home. Laura wasn't sure if it was Martha Rose's hospitable nature or if she was only doing it to please her brother, but living with this young woman and her family for the past few months had helped Laura understand the true meaning of friendship.

Having been raised as an only child in a home where she lacked nothing, Laura knew she was spoiled. The Amish lived such a simple life, yet they seemed happy and content. It was a mystery she couldn't explain. Even more surprising was the fact that on days like today, she almost felt one with the Plain People. Their slow-paced, quiet lifestyle held a certain measure of appeal. Although Laura still missed some modern conveniences and the freedom to dress as she pleased, she also enjoyed many things about being Amish.

Little Ben was one of the things she enjoyed most. He often followed her around, asking questions and pointing out things she had never noticed before. He was doing it now, out in his mother's herb garden.

"*Guck emol datt!*" the child said, pointing to a clump of mint.

Laura nodded, knowing Ben had said, "Just look at that." She plucked off a leaf and rubbed it between her fingers, the way she'd seen Martha Rose do on several occasions.

Ben sniffed deeply and grinned. "*Appeditlich!*"

"Jah, delicious," Laura said with a chuckle. She was amazed at the little boy's appreciation for herbs, flowers, and all the simple things found on the farm. Most of the English children she knew needed TV, video games, and electronic toys to keep them entertained.

In spite of Laura's fascination with little Ben, she had no desire to have any children of her own. If she ever were to get pregnant, she would lose her shapely figure and might never regain it. If she had children, she might not be a good mother.

❧

The baptismal ceremony and introduction of new members was scheduled for early September. Laura kept reminding herself that she needed to be ready by then, since most Amish weddings in this area were held in late November or early December after the harvest was done. If she wasn't able to join the church before then, it would probably be another year before she and Eli could be married. Of course, he hadn't actually proposed yet, but she was hopeful it would be soon.

For that matter, Eli still hadn't kissed her. She worried he might have lost interest in her. Maybe he was in love with Pauline and just wouldn't admit it. If only she could be sure.

Laura saw more of Eli's sister than she did him these days. His job at the furniture store kept him busy enough, but now he was also helping his father and brothers in the fields. Over the last month, she'd only seen him twice, and that was on bi-weekly church days.

"So much for courting," Laura complained as she trudged wearily toward the chicken coop. "If I weren't so afraid of losing Eli to Pauline, I'd put my foot down and give Eli an ultimatum. I'd tell him either he'd better come see me at least once a week, or I'm going home to Minnesota."

There was just one problem. Laura didn't want to go home. She loved Eli and wanted to be with him, no matter what hardships she had to face.

The day finally arrived for Laura and Eli, as well as several other young people, to be baptized and join the church.

Laura was nervous as a cat about to have kittens. She paced back and forth across the kitchen floor, waiting for Amon to pull the buggy out front.

Little Ben jerked on his mother's apron while she stood at the sink, finishing with the dishes. "*Boppli*," he said, pointing to her stomach.

Laura stopped pacing and whirled around to face Martha Rose. "Boppli? Are you pregnant, Martha Rose?"

Martha Rose nodded. "I found out for sure a few days ago."

"How is it that Ben knew and I didn't?"

"He was there when I told Amon. I planned to tell you soon."

"Oh," was all Laura could manage. Maybe she wasn't as much a part of this family as she had believed.

Amon stuck his head through the open doorway and grinned at them. A thatch of blond hair hung across his forehead, and his brown eyes seemed so sincere. "All set?"

"Jah." Martha Rose smiled at Laura. "Let's be off then, for we sure wouldn't want to be late for Laura's and Eli's baptisms."

Eli paced nervously across the front porch of their farmhouse. Today's preaching service would be held at their home, and he could hardly wait. This was the day Laura would become one of them. This was the day they would both be baptized and join the church. He was sure that, even before he'd met Laura, she was the reason he'd held off joining the church, because they were meant to be together.

The sight of Amon Zook's buggy pulling into the yard halted Eli's thoughts. He skirted around a wooden bench and leaped off the porch, skipping over all four steps.

Laura offered him a tentative-looking smile as she stepped down from the buggy. He took her hand and gave it a squeeze. "This is the day we've both been waiting for, Laura."

She nodded, and he noticed there were tears in her eyes.

"What's wrong? You aren't having second thoughts, I hope."

"No, I'm just a bit nervous. What if I don't say or do the right things today? What if—"

He hushed her words by placing two fingers against her lips. "You went through the six weeks of biweekly instructions just fine. Today's only a formality. Say and do whatever the bishop asks. Everything will be okay; you'll see."

"I hope so," she whispered.

The service started a few minutes after Eli and Laura entered the house. He took his seat on the men's side, and she sat with the women.

The song leader led the congregation in several hymns, all sung in the usual singsong fashion, and the baptismal rite followed two sermons.

When Bishop Wagler called the candidates for baptism to step forward, Laura's legs shook so hard she feared she might not be able to walk. The deacons provided a small pail of water and a cup, and the bishop told the twenty young people to get on their knees. He then asked them a question. "Are you willing, by the help and grace of God, to renounce the world, the devil, your own flesh and blood, and be obedient only to God and His church?"

Laura cringed. If she were to answer that question truthfully, she would have to say that she wasn't sure. But she couldn't let anyone know how weak her faith was or that she had no real understanding of God's grace, so along with the others, she answered, "Jah."

"Are you willing to walk with Christ and His church, and to remain faithful through life and until death?"

"Jah."

"Can you confess that Jesus Christ is the Son of God?"

Numbly, as though her lips had a mind of their own, Laura repeated along with the others, "I confess that Jesus Christ is the Son of God."

The congregation then stood for prayer, while Laura and the others remained on their knees. Bishop Wagler placed his hands on the first applicant's head, while Deacon Shemly poured water into the bishop's cupped hands and dripped it onto the candidate's head.

Laura awaited her turn, apprehensive because she wasn't sure she believed the things she had said, and trembling with joy at the prospect of hopefully receiving a marriage proposal from Eli soon. As water from the bishop's hands trickled onto Laura's head and down her forehead, she nearly broke down in tears. She would have plenty of time to think about her relationship with God. Right now, all she wanted was to be with Eli. Her love for him was all that mattered.

Chapter 18

When the service was over, Laura felt relief as she stepped outside into the crisp fall air. It was official. She was no longer a fancy English woman. For as long as she chose to remain Amish, she would be Plain.

Most of the women were busy getting the noon meal set out, but Laura didn't care about helping. All she wanted to do was find Eli. It didn't take her long to spot him, talking with Deacon Shemly over near the barn.

Are they talking about me? Is Eli asking the deacon if he thinks I'm sincere? Laura grabbed the porch railing and gripped it until her knuckles turned white. *What if one of the deacons or Bishop Wagler suspects that I'm not a true believer? What if he's counseling Eli to break up with me?*

"We could use another pair of hands in the kitchen," Martha Rose said as she stepped up behind Laura. "The menfolk are waiting to eat."

Laura spun around to face her. "Why don't the menfolk fix the meal and wait on us women once in a while?"

Martha Rose poked Laura's arm. "You're such a kidder. Everyone knows it's a woman's duty to serve the men."

Laura opened her mouth, fully intending to argue the

point, but she stopped herself in time. She had just joined the Amish church. It wouldn't be good to say or do anything that might get her in trouble. Especially not with Eli out there talking to Deacon Shemly. She might be reprimanded if she messed up now.

"What do you need help with?" Laura asked, stepping into the house and offering Martha Rose a smile.

"Why don't you pour coffee?" Martha Rose motioned to a table nearby. "The pitchers are over there."

Laura shrugged and started across the room. "Jah, okay."

As Pauline began to serve the men their meal, she tried to keep her mind focused on what she was doing and not on the terrible pain chipping away at her heart. She didn't know how she had made it through the baptismal service. It was so hard to see the joyful look on Laura's face when she was greeted with a holy kiss and welcomed into the church by Alma, the bishop's wife.

Pauline knew full well that the ritual of baptism placed Laura into full fellowship, with the rights and responsibilities of adult church membership. From this day on, she would have the right to partake of the elements during the Communion services held twice a year. She would be free to marry Eli, too, and Pauline was fairly certain he would propose to Laura as soon as possible now that they were both part of the Amish church.

She glanced across the room and spotted Laura serving the table where Eli sat. She could barely stand to see the happy expression on Eli's face, not to mention Laura's smug look. She knew it was wrong to harbor such bitterness, and it had been wrong to lie about Eli hugging her after the singing, but she couldn't seem to help herself. *Why can't Eli love me? Why can't he see how much better I would be for him than Laura?*

She squeezed her eyes shut. *Oh, God, please help me learn to deal with this.*

❧

Lunch was finally over, and everyone had eaten until they were full. Laura was just finishing with the cleanup when she saw Eli heading her way.

"Come with me for a walk," he whispered, taking Laura's hand and leading her away from the house.

"Where are we going?"

"You'll see."

A few minutes later, they stood under a huge weeping willow tree out behind the house, away from curious stares. Eli's fingers touched Laura's chin, tipping her head back until they were staring into each other's eyes. "You're truly one of us now," he murmured.

She nodded, feeling as though her head might explode from the anticipation of what she felt certain was coming. "We're both officially Amish."

Eli bent his head, and his lips touched hers in a light, feathery kiss. She moaned softly as the kiss deepened.

When Eli pulled away, she leaned against him for support, feeling as if her breath had been snatched away. It seemed as though she had waited all her life to be kissed like that. Not a kiss of passion, the way Dean had done, but a kiss with deep emotion. Eli loved her with all his heart; she was sure of it now.

"I can finally speak the words that have been in my heart all these months," Eli said, gazing deeply into her eyes. "I love you, Laura, and I want you to be my wife."

Tears welled in her eyes and spilled over onto her cheeks. "Oh, Eli, I love you, too." She hugged him tightly. "Jah. . .I will marry you."

"I just spoke with Deacon Shemly," Eli said. "If it's all right with you, we can be married on the third Thursday in November."

"It's more than all right." Laura blinked away another set of tears. "I can't wait to call my parents and give them the news."

Eli thought his heart would burst from the sheer joy of knowing Laura would soon be Mrs. Eli Yoder. She loved him; he was sure of it. Why else would she have given up her old life and agreed to become Plain? He wanted to shout to the world that he was the luckiest man alive and had found a most special woman to share the rest of his life with.

While he wasn't able to shout it to the world, Eli knew he could share his news with the family. Grabbing Laura by the hand, he started to run.

"Where are we going?"

"To tell my folks our good news."

Laura skidded to a halt. "Do you think that's such a good idea? I mean, can't you wait and tell them later. . .after you go home?"

Eli grimaced. "Now why would I want to wait that long? The family deserves to hear our news now, when we're together."

"They may not want you marrying a foreigner," Laura argued. "Your mother doesn't like me, and—"

Eli held up his hand to stop her words. "You're not a foreigner anymore, and I'm sure Mom likes you just fine."

Laura drew in a deep breath and released it with a moan. "Okay. Let's get this over with then."

Eli spotted his folks sitting in chairs on the porch, visiting with Martha Rose and Amon. Little Ben played at their feet, dragging a piece of yarn in front of an orange-colored barn cat's nose.

Eli led Laura up the steps and motioned her to take a seat in one of the empty chairs. He pulled out another one for himself and sat beside her.

"Today's baptism was good." Mom smiled at Eli. "We're glad you finally decided to join the church."

He grinned. "And Laura, too. She's a baptized member now, same as me."

Mom nodded and looked over at Laura. "We welcome you into our church."

"Jah, you're one of us now," Pop agreed.

"Danki." Laura offered them a smile, but it appeared to be forced.

In an attempt to reassure her, Eli took her hand. "Laura's agreed to become my wife. We'd like to be married the third Thursday of November."

Mom and Pop exchanged glances, and Eli was afraid they might say something negative about his plans. Much to his relief, Mom gave a nod in Laura's direction. "We hope you'll be happy being Amish, Laura, and we hope you will make our son happy, as well."

"Eli's a fine man with much love to give," Pop put in. "He'll make a good husband and father; just you wait and see."

Martha Rose left her seat and bent down to give Laura a hug. "Congratulations. Soon we'll be like sisters."

Amon thumped Eli on the back and then added his well-wishes.

Eli grinned. "I think Laura was a bit naerfich about telling you, but I knew you would all share in our joy."

Laura shot him an exasperated look, and he wondered if he'd said too much. Maybe he shouldn't have mentioned that she felt nervous.

He was trying to think up something to say that might make her feel better, when Pop spoke again. "Say, Eli, if you're gonna marry this little gal, then don't ya think you should try to fatten her up some?"

Eli looked at Laura, then back at his father, but before he could open his mouth to reply, she said, "Why would Eli want to fatten me up?"

"I've seen you at some of our meals, and you don't hardly eat a thing. Why, you'll waste away to nothing if you don't start eatin' more."

Laura stood so quickly, she nearly knocked over her chair. "I have no intention of becoming fat, Mr. Yoder!"

Pop tipped his head back and howled. "She's a feisty one, now, isn't she, Eli?" When he finally quit laughing, he looked at Laura and said, "If you're gonna marry my son, then don't ya think you should start callin' me Johnny? Mr. Yoder makes me feel like an old man." He glanced over at Mom and gave her knee a few pats. "I'm not old yet, am I, Mary Ellen?"

Mary Ellen grunted as she pushed his hand aside. "Go on with you, now, Johnny. You've always been a silly boy, and I guess you always will be."

Mom and Pop both laughed, and soon Martha Rose and Amon were chuckling pretty good, too.

Laura tapped her foot against the porch floor, and Eli figured it was time to end it all before she said or did something that might embarrass them both.

He stood and grabbed her hand. "I think Laura and I should take a walk down to the creek. She needs to get cooled off, and I need to figure out how I ended up with such a laughable family."

Two weeks before the wedding, Laura's and Eli's names were officially published at the close of the preaching service, which was held in the Zook home.

Laura's heart bubbled with joy as she helped her future sister-in-law and several other women get lunch served after church had let out. Everyone had a job to do, even Anna Beachy's mother, Rebekah, who sat at the table in her wheelchair, buttering a stack of bread.

Martha Rose handed Laura a jar of pickled beets. "Would you mind opening these?"

Laura glanced at the other four women, but they all seemed focused on their job of making ham-and-cheese sandwiches. She shrugged and took the jar over to the cupboard, wondering why no one had said anything about her upcoming marriage. Were they displeased with Eli's choice for a wife? Would they have rather heard Pauline's name published with Eli's?

She held her breath as she forked out the beet slices and placed them in a bowl. She disliked the smell of pickled beets. If she lived to be a hundred, she would never figure out what anyone saw in those disgusting, pungent things. She had just finished putting the last one in the bowl, when Pauline entered the kitchen.

"The tables are set up in the barn." Pauline glanced over at Martha Rose. "Do you have anything ready for me to carry out there?"

"You can take this plate of sandwiches." Mary Ellen held up a tray, and Pauline took it from her, never once looking Laura's way or acknowledging her presence.

Pauline was almost to the door when Martha Rose spoke. "Laura, why don't you go with Pauline? You can take the beets, then stay to help pour beverages."

Laura drew in a deep breath and let it out in a rush. The last thing she needed was another close encounter with her rival. She didn't wish to make a scene, however, so she followed Pauline out of the room without a word of protest.

They had no more than stepped onto the porch when Pauline whirled around and faced Laura. "You think you've won Eli's heart, don't you? Well, you're not married yet, so there's still some hope for me. You may have fooled Eli, but I can see right through you."

Laura took a few steps back, wanting to get away from Pauline, and wondering if the young woman really did know she wasn't being completely honest with Eli. Sure, she loved him and wanted to get married. She had become Amish, too. But deep down inside, she didn't think she needed God and was sure she could do everything in her own strength.

"I'm sure Eli will come to his senses soon," Pauline continued to rant. "He's blinded by romantic notions right now, but one of these days he'll realize you're not really one of us and can't be trusted." She gazed into Laura's eyes, making her feel like a child who had done something wrong.

Laura's mind whirled as she tried to figure out some kind of appropriate comeback. All she could think to do was run—far away from Pauline's piercing gaze. She practically flew into the barn, dropped the bowl of beets onto the nearest table, and sprinted off toward the creek.

When Eli looked up from the table where he sat with his brothers and saw Laura dash out of the barn, he knew something wasn't right. He was about to go after her, but Pauline stepped between him and the barn door. "Let her go, Eli. I'm sure she just needs to be alone."

Eli's forehead wrinkled. "What's going on, Pauline? Did you and Laura have words?"

Pauline placed the plate of sandwiches on one of the tables and motioned him to follow her out of the barn. When they were out of earshot and away from scrutinizing eyes, she stopped and placed both hands on Eli's shoulders.

He shrugged them away. "What's this all about?"

"That English woman will never make you happy. She's an outsider and always will be. She doesn't belong here, so you'd better think twice about marrying her."

Eli's face heated up. "I love Laura, and she's not an outsider. She's a member of our church now and has agreed to abide by our Ordnung."

Pauline squinted. "You're blinded by her beautiful face and smooth-talking words, but I know what's in her heart."

"What gives you the right to try and read someone else's mind?"

"I didn't say *mind*, Eli. I said *heart*. I have a sixth sense about things, and my senses are telling me—"

"I don't care what your senses are telling you." Eli drew in a deep breath to steady his nerves and tried to offer her a smile. "Look, Pauline, I'm sorry things didn't work out between us, but if you'll search your own heart instead of trying to see what's in other people's hearts, I'm sure you'll realize that we could never have been anything more than friends."

Pauline's blue eyes flashed angrily. "We could have been more than friends if she hadn't come along and filled your head with all sorts of fancy English ideas."

Eli was trying hard to be civil, but he'd had as much of Pauline's meddling as he could stand. He had to get away from her. He needed to be with Laura.

"I never meant to hurt you," he said sincerely, "but I love Laura, and she loves me. She gave up being English so we could be together, and nothing you say is going to change my mind about her."

Pauline's eyes filled with tears, making Eli feel like a heel. He was sorry for hurting her, but it didn't change anything. He didn't love her now and never had. Even when they'd been courting, he'd only seen her as a friend.

Eli gently touched her arm. "I pray you'll find someone else to love." He walked away quickly, hoping she wouldn't follow. His life was with Laura, and she needed him now.

❧

Laura sank to the ground and leaned heavily against the

trunk of a tree as she gazed at the bubbling creek. *Maybe I made a mistake thinking I could become part of a world so plain and simple. Maybe Eli should have chosen Pauline.*

She sucked in her bottom lip, and a fresh set of tears coursed down her cheeks. Could Pauline really see through her? Did the accusing young woman know Laura was only pretending to be a follower of God?

But how could she know? No one knew what was in Laura's heart or mind. She'd taken her biblical training classes, studied the Amish language, and learned how to cook, sew, and keep house. She wore plain clothes and no makeup and had learned to live without electricity or many other modern conveniences. What more was there? Why would Pauline think she couldn't be trusted?

"Because you can't," a voice in her head seemed to taunt. *"You're lying to Eli, and you're lying to yourself."*

Laura dropped to the ground and sobbed. She knew what she wanted out of life—Eli Yoder. She wanted him more than anything. If she had to pretend to have a relationship with God in order to join the Amish faith so she and Eli could be married, what harm had been done?

Laura jerked her head when someone touched her shoulder. She looked up and saw the face of the man she loved staring down at her.

"What's wrong? Why are you crying?" he asked, helping Laura to her feet.

"I—I had an encounter with your ex-girlfriend." She sniffed and reached up to wipe the tears from her face. "Pauline doesn't like me, and she's trying to come between us."

"No, she's not. I just spoke with Pauline, and I put her in her place but good."

"You did?"

He pulled her into his arms. "I told Pauline it's you I love, and nothing she says will ever change my mind."

"You mean it?"

"Jah, I do. Pauline and I have never been anything more than friends, and she knows it. I don't understand why she's bent on making trouble, but don't worry, because I'll never stop loving you, Laura." Eli bent to kiss her, and Laura felt like she was drowning in his love. Everything would be all right now. It had to be.

Laura was excited about the wedding and pleased that her parents would be coming soon. She was anxious for them to meet Eli. Her friend Shannon wouldn't be coming, because she had gone to California to visit her grandmother who was dying of cancer. Darla wouldn't be coming, either, because she had to work. But that was all right with Laura. She knew Darla didn't approve of her becoming Amish. The last letter she'd received from Darla had said that she'd finished school and was working in Philadelphia, designing windows for one of the big department stores.

Laura had asked Anna Beachy and Nancy Frey, the schoolteacher, to be her attendants, and the ceremony would be held at Amon and Martha Rose's house, since Laura lived with them.

"When are your parents arriving?" Martha Rose asked as she and Laura sat at the table, putting the finishing touches on Laura's wedding dress.

Laura snipped a piece of thread and smiled. "Their plane was supposed to get into Harrisburg late last night, and they were going to rent a car and drive out here as soon as they'd had some breakfast this morning, so I expect they should be showing up soon."

"They're more than welcome to stay with us. We have plenty of room."

"I know you do, and it's a kind offer, but Mom and Dad are hotel kind of people. I don't think they would last five minutes without TV or a microwave."

Martha Rose pursed her lips. "You're managing."

"Jah." Laura smiled. "I'm anxious for them to get to know all of you before the wedding on Thursday."

"It will be nice to meet them, as well."

"Since tomorrow will be such a busy day for us, what with getting things ready for the wedding and all, I figured it would be best if they weren't in the way."

Martha Rose's eyebrows lifted in question. "Why would they be in the way? If they'd like to help, I'm sure we can find plenty for them to do."

"The Amish lifestyle is quite different from what they're used to, and Mom's idea of work is a full day of shopping or traipsing around town trying to drum up donations for one of her many charity functions." Laura sighed. "I just hope they don't try to talk me out of marrying Eli."

"Why would they do that? I'm sure you've told them how much you love my brother."

"Oh, yes, and Dad said if I was happy, then he was, too. I think it gives him pleasure to see me get what I want."

"Having one's way is not always of the Lord," Martha Rose admonished. "We're taught to be selfless, not self-centered. Surely you learned that from your religious training prior to baptism."

"Certainly. I just meant when I was younger and didn't

know much about religious things, I was rather spoiled."
She shrugged. "Dad still thinks of me as his little girl, but I
know he and Mom both want my happiness."

"So, you're happy being Amish?"

"Of course. Why wouldn't I be?"

Martha Rose opened her mouth as if to answer, but
their conversation was interrupted when a car came up the
graveled driveway, causing their two farm dogs to carry on.

Laura jumped up and darted to the back door. "It's
them! My folks are here!" She jerked the door open and ran
down the steps.

Her father was the first to step from their car, and the
bundle of fur in his hands brought a squeal of delight from
Laura's lips. "Foosie!" Her arms went around Dad's waist,
and she gave him a hug.

"Your mother and I thought you might like to have your
cat, now that you're about to be married and will soon have
your own home."

Mom stepped out of the car and embraced Laura. "It's
good to see you." She frowned and took a few steps back.
"Oh, dear, you've changed, and you look so tired. What
happened to our beautiful, vibrant daughter, and why are
you dressed in such plain clothes?"

Laura had expected some reservations on her parents'
part, but her mother's comment took her by surprise. If she
wasn't beautiful anymore, did that mean she was ugly?

"Laura is still beautiful. . .in a plain sort of way, and you
should know enough about the Amish to understand why
she's dressed that way." Dad raised his eyebrows at Mom,
then handed the cat over to Laura. "Here you go, sweetie."

Laura rubbed her nose against Foosie's soft fur and

sniffed deeply. "I—I don't think I can keep her."

"Why not?" Mom asked.

"Eli and I will be living with his parents until our own house is complete." Laura stroked Foosie's head. "Since it will be several months before it's done, Eli's folks might not appreciate having an inside cat invade their home."

"But I thought Amish people liked animals." Dad gazed around the farmyard and pointed to the cows in the field. "See, there's a bunch of animals."

"Don't forget about those dreadful dogs that barked at us when we pulled in," Mom added.

Laura shook her head. "Those are farm animals. They're not pampered pets."

"Be that as it may, I would think your husband would want you to be happy," Mom said as she fluffed the sides of her windblown hair.

Before Laura could respond, Martha Rose was at her side, offering Laura's parents a wide smile. "I'm Martha Rose Zook. And you must be Laura's folks."

Mom nodded, and Dad extended his hand. "I'm Wesley Meade. This is my wife, Irene."

"I'm glad to meet you," Martha Rose said, shaking his hand.

"This is a nice place you've got here. I've always had a fondness for the country life," Dad said in a wistful tone.

Martha Rose motioned toward the house. "Won't you please come inside? It's kind of nippy out here in the wind, and I've got some hot coffee and freshly baked brownies waiting."

"Sounds good to me." Dad's wide grin brought a smile to Laura's lips. He looked like an enthusiastic child on Christmas morning.

Everyone followed Martha Rose to the house. When they stepped onto the back porch, Laura halted. "Uh, what would you like me to do with my cat?"

Martha Rose blinked. "Ach! I didn't realize you were holding a cat. Where'd it come from?"

"We brought it from Minnesota," Dad answered. "Foosie is Laura's house pet."

Laura rocked back and forth on her heels. What if Martha Rose made her put Foosie out in the barn? She knew the cat would never get along with the farm cats. Besides, she might get fleas.

"Bring the cat inside," Martha Rose said, opening the door. "I'm sure Ben would love to play with her awhile."

Once Laura's parents were seated at the kitchen table, Laura placed Foosie on the floor beside Ben. He squealed with delight and hugged the cat around the neck.

"Now don't *dricke* too hard," Martha Rose admonished her son. She quickly poured mugs of steaming coffee, and Laura passed around the plate of brownies.

"What's a dricke?" Mom asked.

"It means 'squeeze,' " Laura explained.

"Schee bussli," Ben said, as Foosie licked his nose.

"Ben thinks Foosie is a nice kitten," Laura said, before either of her parents could raise the question.

Martha Rose handed Laura's father a mug. "Laura says you plan on staying at a hotel in Paradise while you're here."

He nodded. "That's right. We made our reservations as soon as Laura phoned and told us about the wedding, and that's where we stayed last night when we got in."

"You're more than welcome to stay here. We have plenty of room."

Dad's eyes brightened. "Really? You wouldn't mind?"

Mom shook her head while smiling sweetly. "That's kind of you, Martha Rose, but I think it would be less hectic if we stay at the hotel."

Dad shrugged, but Laura didn't miss the look of disappointment on his face. "Whatever you think best, dear," he mumbled.

"I made my own wedding dress." Laura held up the pale blue dress she'd been hemming earlier.

Mom's mouth dropped open. "Oh, my! It doesn't look anything like a traditional wedding gown."

"It's a traditional Amish dress," Martha Rose stated.

"I see."

Laura could see by the pinched look on her mother's face that she was anything but happy about this Plain wedding. For that matter, she was probably upset about Laura marrying an Amish man. Mom most likely thought her only daughter had lost her mind.

Laura turned to look at her dad. He was grinning like a Cheshire cat and obviously enjoying the homemade brownies, for he'd already eaten three.

"Eli and his parents are coming over for supper," Laura said, changing the subject. "I'm anxious for you to meet him."

Martha Rose nodded. "Eli's excited about meeting your folks, too."

❧

Eli opened the Zooks' back door and stepped inside, along with his folks and two brothers. Laura, who had been standing near the kitchen sink, rushed to his side. "My parents are here, and I'm so glad you came!"

Eli grinned and squeezed her hand. "I'm glad, too."

Introductions were soon made, and Eli knew right away that he was going to like Laura's father. He wasn't so sure about her mother, though. Irene seemed to be scrutinizing everything in the room, and she had said very little to either Eli or his family.

Soon everyone took their seats at the table. Laura and Martha Rose had made a scrumptious-looking supper of ham, bread stuffing, mashed potatoes, green beans, coleslaw, and homemade bread.

All heads bowed in silent prayer, and Eli noticed that Laura looked relieved when her parents followed suit.

"Laura tells me you work in a law office," Eli said as he passed Laura's dad the platter of ham.

"Sure do. In fact, I have several other lawyers working for me." Wesley grinned and forked two huge pieces of meat onto his plate. "Umm. . .this sure looks tasty."

"Pop raises some hogs," Lewis spoke up. "He's always got plenty of meat to share with Martha Rose and Amon."

Eli's father nodded and spooned himself a sizable helping of bread stuffing. "I'm not braggin' now, but I think I've got some of the finest hogs in Lancaster County."

Mom reached over and patted Pop's portly stomach. "Jah, and some pretty good milking cows, too."

Laura moved the fork slowly around her plate, and Eli noticed that she hadn't taken more than a few bites of food since they'd sat down.

Pop glanced over at Laura's father and frowned. "Say, I'm wonderin' just how much influence you have on that daughter of yours."

Wesley gulped down some milk before he answered.

"I'm not altogether sure. Why do you ask?"

Pop pointed a finger at Laura's plate. "She eats like a bird. Just look at her plate. Hardly a thing on it!"

Laura's face blanched, then turned red as a cherry. "I eat enough to sustain myself. I just don't think one needs to become chubby in order to prove one's worth."

The room became deathly quiet, and Eli could almost feel her embarrassment. It wasn't like Laura to blurt something out like that, and he had to wonder what had gotten into her. Was she nervous because her fancy English parents were here? Did she feel embarrassed for them to be sitting at the same table with a bunch of Plain folks?

"I. . .um. . .meant to say, I prefer to watch my weight," Laura quickly amended. "If others choose to overeat, that's their right."

"Laura, what are you saying?" Eli whispered. "Are you trying to make some kind of trouble here tonight?"

She shook her head. "I–I'm sorry. I don't know what came over me."

"I think our daughter might be a bit nervous." Irene offered a pleasant smile as she patted Laura's arm. "It isn't every day she introduces her father and me to her future husband and in-laws."

Martha Rose nodded. "Laura's been jittery as a dragon-fly all day. Haven't you, Laura?"

Laura's only reply was a quick shrug.

"In fact, Laura did most of the work today, just to keep her hands busy," Martha Rose added.

"I did work pretty hard, but that's because I wanted Martha Rose to rest." Laura glanced over at her mother. "Martha Rose is in a family way."

Irene's eyebrows furrowed. "Family way?"

"She's pregnant, hon." Wesley chuckled. "I haven't heard that expression since I was a boy growing up on the farm, but I sure can remember what 'being in a family way' means."

"Your folks were farmers?" The question came from Pop, who leaned his elbows on the table as he scrutinized Laura's father.

Wesley nodded. "My parents farmed a huge spread out in Montana, but my father sold the farm several years ago since none of us boys wanted to follow in his footsteps." His forehead wrinkled. "Sometimes I wonder if I made the wrong choice, becoming a fancy city lawyer instead of an old cowhand."

Little Ben, who up until this moment had been busy playing with the bread stuffing on his plate, spoke up for the first time. "*Maus!*" He pointed to the floor, disrupting the conversation.

"Maus? Where is it?" Martha Rose was immediately on her feet.

"*Schpringe,* bussli!" Ben bounced up and down in his chair.

"What on earth is going on?" Irene's high-pitched voice held a note of concern.

"Aw, it's just a little mouse, and Ben's tellin' the kitty to run," Jonas said with a chuckle. "I'll bet that fluffy white cat will take 'em in a hurry."

"Fluffy white cat?" Mom's eyes were wide. "When did you get an indoor cat, Martha Rose?"

Martha Rose gave no reply, just held a broom in her hand and ran around the kitchen, swinging it this way and that. It was a comical sight, and Eli laughed, right along with the rest of the men.

Foosie dodged the broom and leaped into the air, as the tiny, gray field mouse scooted across the floor at lightning speed. By now, everyone at the table was either laughing or shouting orders at Martha Rose.

"Open the door!" Amon hollered. "Maybe it'll run outside."

Laura jumped up and raced for the door. "No, don't open that door! Foosie might get out, and I'd never be able to catch her once the dogs discovered she was on the loose."

Foosie was almost on top of the mouse, but just as her paw came down, the critter darted for a hole under the cupboard, leaving a very confused-looking cat sitting in front of the hole, meowing for all it was worth.

Laura's father was laughing so hard that tears rolled down his cheeks. "Well, if that doesn't beat all. In all the years we've had that cat, I don't believe I've ever seen her move so fast." He wiped his eyes with a napkin and started howling again.

Laura planted both hands on her hips. "I don't see what's so funny, Dad. Poor Foosie has never seen a mouse before. She could have had a heart attack, tearing around the kitchen like that."

Another round of laughter filled the room. Even Martha Rose, who moments ago had been chasing the mouse with her broom, was back in her seat, holding her sides and chuckling as hard as everyone else.

Eli stood and moved to Laura's side. "I think you were nervous for nothing. The cat and mouse game got everyone in a happy mood."

"So what did you think of Eli and his family?" Wesley asked his wife as they drove back to their hotel in Paradise later that evening.

She shrugged, a small sigh escaping her lips. "They seemed like nice enough people, but I don't understand how our daughter thinks she can ever fit in with them."

He drummed his fingers along the edge of the steering wheel. "She's already one of them, Irene. Laura has joined the Amish church and is about to marry an Amish man."

"I know that, Wesley, but Laura is used to nice things— modern conveniences, pretty clothes, makeup, and pampering. It doesn't seem right to see her dressed so plainly or watch her washing dishes over a sink full of hot water the way she did tonight after we ate dinner."

"Have you heard her complain?"

"Not in so many words, but you saw how tired she looked, and I sensed her unhappiness." She paused and released another sigh. "And what of that comment she made tonight about not wanting to get fat?"

"She was feeling nervous about us meeting Eli and his folks. You mentioned that yourself."

"Maybe so, but I've got a feeling our daughter will be making a mistake by marrying Eli, and I'm afraid she won't realize it until it's too late." She glanced over at him and shook her head. "The Amish don't believe in divorce, you know. Laura mentioned that in one of her letters."

He shrugged. "I think you worry too much. It was obvious to me by the way Laura and Eli looked at each other that they're very much in love. If our daughter loves a man so much that she can give up her fancy way of life and become Plain, then I say more power to her."

She clicked her tongue noisily. "If I didn't know better, I would think *you* had a desire to join the Amish faith."

Wesley shook his head. "You needn't worry about that. I like my favorite TV shows too much." He grinned over at her. "It would be nice to live our lives at a little slower pace, though, don't you think?"

Irene leaned her head against the seat and closed her eyes. "Dream on, dear. Dream on."

CHAPTER 20

"Today's the big day," Martha Rose said when Laura entered the kitchen bright and early Thursday morning. "Did you sleep well last night?"

Laura yawned, reached into the cupboard for a mug, and poured herself some coffee from the pot sitting at the back of the stove. "Actually, I hardly slept a wink. I was too nervous about today."

Martha Rose pulled out a chair and motioned for Laura to take a seat. "I understand how you feel. I was a ball of nerves on my wedding day, too."

"Really? Except for that incident with the mouse the other night, I've never seen you act nervous or upset about anything."

"I wasn't really nervous about the mouse. Just wanted to get it out of my kitchen." Martha Rose got another chair and seated herself beside Laura. "I think all brides feel a bit anxious when they're about to get married."

Laura took a long, slow drink from her cup. "I hope I can make Eli happy."

"You love him, don't you?"

"Of course I do."

"Then just do your best to please him. Always trust God to help you, and your marriage will go fine; you'll see."

Laura nodded, but she wasn't sure it would be as easy as Martha Rose made it seem. Especially since she didn't have any idea how she was going to put her trust in God.

※

When Pauline heard a knock on her bedroom door, she pulled the pillow over her head. A few seconds later, the door opened, and her mother called, "What are you still doing in bed? We'll be late for Eli and Laura's wedding if we don't get a move on."

"I'm not going."

"Not going?"

Pauline pushed the pillow aside and groaned. "I'm not feeling so well."

Mom took a seat on the edge of the bed and placed her hand on Pauline's forehead. "You don't have a fever."

"Maybe not, but my head is sure pounding. It feels like it's going to split wide open."

"Maybe once you've had some breakfast you'll feel better."

"I'm feeling kind of *iwwel*, too. In fact, I'm so nauseated I doubt I could keep anything down."

"Are you sure you're not just looking for an excuse to stay home from the wedding because you don't want to see Eli marry someone else?"

Unbidden tears rolled down Pauline's cheeks, and she swiped at them with the back of her hand. "I can't go to that wedding, Mom. I just can't deal with it."

Mom offered Pauline a look of understanding as she patted her arm. "Jah, all right then. You stay here and rest in bed." She slipped quietly from the room.

Pauline rolled over so she was facing the wall and let the tears flow. She knew she had to find the strength to deal with this somehow, but if she stayed in Lancaster County, where she would see Eli and Laura so often, she didn't think her broken heart would ever mend. Maybe she would consider going to visit Aunt Irma in Ohio for a while. She might even stay there indefinitely.

The wedding began at eight thirty, with the bride and groom and their wedding party already sitting in the front row. The ministers then took their places, followed by the parents of the bride and groom, the groom's grandparents, other relatives, and friends. The men and women sat in separate sections, just as they did at regular church services.

When everyone was seated, Eli's brother-in-law, Amon, announced a hymn from the *Ausbund*. On the third line of the song, all the ministers in attendance rose to their feet and made their way up the stairs to the room that had been prepared for them on the second floor. Eli and Laura followed them to the council room.

Laura drew in a deep breath as she glanced down at her light blue wedding dress, which was covered with a white organdy apron. *Am I really doing the right thing? Will Eli and I always be as happy as we are right now? I've given up so many things to become Amish, but can I be content to do without worldly things for the rest of my life?*

She glanced over at her groom standing straight and tall and looking as happy as a child with a new toy. He was so handsome, dressed in a pair of black trousers, a matching vest, and a collarless, dark jacket. Accentuating Eli's white cotton shirt was a black bow tie, making him look every bit as distinguished as any of the lawyers who worked at her father's law firm.

Once they had entered the council room upstairs, Laura and Eli were instructed to be seated in two straight-backed chairs, where they received encouragement and words of advice from the ministers. Then Bishop Wagler asked if Eli and Laura had remained pure. With a solemn expression, Laura was glad she could answer affirmatively, along with Eli.

The bride and groom were then dismissed, while the ministers remained for council among themselves. This would be the time when they would decide who would take the different parts of the wedding ceremony.

Eli and Laura were met at the bottom of the stairs by their attendants. When they returned to the main room with the young men leading the women, the congregation sang the third verse of "Lob Lied," the second hymn sung at most Amish church services. The wedding party came to the six chairs reserved for them and sat in unison, the three women facing the three men.

As the congregation finished "Lob Lied," the ministers reentered the room and took their respective seats. Deacon Shemly delivered a sermon, alluding to several Bible verses related to marriage. When the sermon was over, they offered a silent prayer. All those present turned and knelt, facing the bench on which they had been sitting. Laura was relieved to see that her parents did the same.

When the prayer was over, the congregation stood, and the deacon read a passage of scripture from Matthew 19, verses 1–12. When he was done, everyone returned to their seats.

Next, Bishop Wagler stepped forward and delivered the main sermon, which included several more biblical references to marriage. Then, looking at the congregation, he said, "If any here has objection to this marriage, he now has the opportunity to declare it."

There was a long pause, and Laura glanced around the room, half expecting Pauline to jump up and announce that she was in love with Eli and would make him a better wife than Laura ever could. However, there was no sign of Pauline, and for that, Laura felt hugely relieved. Maybe Pauline had stayed home today, unable to deal with seeing Eli marry someone other than herself. Laura couldn't blame the woman. She would feel the same way if she were in Pauline's place.

"You may now come forth in the name of the Lord," the bishop said, motioning for Eli and Laura to join him at the front of the room. Laura felt the touch of Eli's arm against hers, and it gave her added courage. This was it. This was the moment she had been waiting for all these months.

There was no exchange of rings, but when the bishop asked Eli if he would accept Laura as his wife and not leave her until death separated them, Laura felt as if the tie that bound them together was just as strong as if they had exchanged circular gold bands. As Laura answered a similar question from the bishop, she couldn't help but notice that her groom's eyes were brimming with tears, and the smile he wore stretched from ear to ear. She knew without question that he really did love her, and she hoped they would be this happy for years to come.

When the wedding ceremony was over, Eli and Laura moved outside to the front lawn, while the benches were moved aside and tables were set up for the meal. Even though there was a chill in the air, the sun shone brightly, and the sky looked as clear and blue as the small pond behind his parents' home. It was a perfect day for their wedding, and Eli was content in the knowledge that Laura was now his wife.

Many who had stepped outside came over to offer Eli and Laura their congratulations, including Laura's parents. When Wesley and Irene hugged their daughter, Eli noticed the tears in their eyes, and he felt a pang of guilt. He knew he was the cause of Laura leaving her fancy life and becoming one of the Plain People. Because of her love for him, she wouldn't see her own family so much, and he wondered if she had any regrets about giving up all the modern things her wealthy father could offer and Eli couldn't.

When Wesley shook Eli's hand, Eli smiled and said, "I'll take good care of your daughter. I hope you know that."

Wesley nodded. "I believe you're an honest man, and I can see how much you love Laura."

"Jah, I do."

"Please, let her keep Foosie," Irene put in. "Our daughter needs a touch from home."

Eli grinned. "I'll speak to Mom and Pop about the cat. I'm sure they won't mind having a pet inside as long as it's housebroke."

"Oh, she is." Laura reached for Eli's hand. "Foosie's never made a mess in the house. Not even when she was a kitten."

Eli's sister stepped up to them, along with Amon and little
Ben. Martha Rose hugged Eli and Laura, then excused herself
to go help in the kitchen. Laura bent down and scooped Ben
into her arms, and he kissed her on the cheek. It was obvious
that the child was enamored with her, and she seemed to like
him equally well.

She'll make a good mudder, Eli mused. *Lord willing, maybe
we'll have a whole house full of kinner.*

Ω

The wedding meal was a veritable feast. Wesley had never
seen so much food in one place. Long tables had been set up
in the living room and adjoining room, and the benches that
had been used during the ceremony were placed at the tables.
Eli's parents invited Wesley and Irene to sit at a table with
them, while Laura and Eli took their place at a corner table
Laura had referred to as the *eck.* They were served roasted
chicken, mashed potatoes, bread filling, creamed celery, coleslaw, applesauce, fruit salad, bread, butter, jelly, and coffee.
Then there were the cakes—three large ones in all.

"After eating so much food, I probably won't sleep
a wink tonight," Wesley said, nudging his wife with his
elbow.

She grimaced. "Can't you restrain yourself and practice
moderation?"

Johnny reached for another piece of chicken and snickered. "No man can practice moderation when there's food
involved."

"Our two children do look happy, don't they?" Irene
said, leaning close to Eli's mother, who sat on her left.

Mary Ellen nodded. "For a while, I wasn't sure things

would work out between the two of them, but now that Laura's joined the church and has proven herself, I've come to believe things will turn out okay."

Johnny thumped Wesley on the back. "I'll bet in another year or so, you two will be makin' a trip back here to see your first grandchild."

As Laura and Eli sat at their corner table, eating and visiting with their guests, Eli eyed Laura's plate and noticed that she hadn't eaten much at all.

"Eat hearty, *fraa*." Eli needled her in the ribs with his elbow. "Today's our wedding day, and this is no time to diet."

She turned to face him. "If I eat too much today, I might have to go without food for the rest of the week."

He snickered. "Jah, right."

Laura glanced across the room and nodded at her parents, sitting at a table with Eli's folks. "Mom and Dad seem to be having a good time, despite the fact they hardly know anyone."

Eli nodded. "Want to sneak away with me for a bit?"

"Sneak away? As in leave this place?"

"Jah. I think it's time for us to get a little fresh air."

They pushed away from the table and slipped out the back door.

"I'll race you to the creek," Eli said, once they were on the porch.

"You're on!"

Laura was panting for air by the time they reached the water, and so was Eli. She collapsed on the grass, ignoring the chill, and Eli dropped down beside her, laughing and tickling Laura until she finally called a truce.

"So, it's peace you're wanting, huh?" Eli teased. "All right, but you'll have to pay a price for it."

Laura squirmed beneath his hands. "Oh, yeah? What kind of payment must I offer the likes of you, Eli Yoder?"

"This," he murmured against her ear. "And this." He nuzzled her neck with his cold nose. "Also this." His lips trailed a brigade of soft kisses along her chin, up her cheek, and finally came to rest on her lips. As the kiss deepened, Laura snuggled closer to Eli.

When he finally pulled away, she gazed deeply into his dazzling blue eyes. "I love you, Eli, and I always will."

"And I love you, my *seelich*, blessed gift."

Laura and Eli spent their first night as husband and wife at Martha Rose and Amon's house so they could help with the cleanup the following morning. Then they would live with Eli's parents until their own place was finished, hopefully by spring. The thought of living with her in-laws caused Laura some concern. Would Mary Ellen scrutinize her every move? Would Laura be expected to do even more work than she had while living with the Zooks?

Forcing her anxiety aside, Laura stepped into Martha Rose's kitchen. Eli had kissed her good-bye some time ago and left with his brothers to take the benches that had been used yesterday back over to the Hiltys' place, where church would be held next week. Laura knew her folks would be here soon to say their good-byes, and she hoped Eli would be here in time.

Martha Rose was busy baking bread, but she looked up and smiled when Laura entered the room. "Did you sleep well?"

Laura shuffled across the kitchen, still feeling the effects of sleep. She nodded and yawned. "I'm sorry I overslept. After Eli left to take the benches back, I must have dozed off again."

"Guess you needed the rest. Yesterday was a pretty big day."

"Yes, it was." Laura reached for the pot of coffee on the stove.

"There are still some scrambled eggs left." Martha Rose gestured with her head toward the frying pan at the back of the stove. "Help yourself."

Laura moaned. "After all I ate yesterday, I don't think I need any breakfast."

"Breakfast is the most important meal of the day, and now that you're a married woman, you'll need to keep up your strength."

Laura dropped into a chair at the table. "What's that supposed to mean?"

"Just that you'll soon be busy setting up your own house."

"Not really. Eli and I will be living with your folks, remember?"

Martha Rose nodded. "Jah, but not for long. If I know my brother, he'll be working long hours on your future home." She winked at Laura. "He's a man in love, and I think he'd like to have you all to himself."

Laura felt the heat of a blush stain her face. "I—I'd like that, too."

"So, dish up plenty of eggs now."

Laura opened her mouth to offer a rebuttal, but the sound of a car pulling into the yard drew her to the window. "It's my parents. They've come to say good-bye." She jerked open the door and ran down the stairs. If she was going to get all teary-eyed, she'd rather not do it in front of Eli's sister.

As soon as Mom and Dad stepped from the car, the three of them shared a group hug.

"I'll miss you," Laura said tearfully.

"Be happy," her mother whispered.

"If you ever need anything—anything at all—please don't hesitate to call." Dad grinned at her. "I know you Amish don't have phones in your houses, but you can always call from a payphone or from one of your English neighbors' like you did before."

Laura nodded as a lump formed in her throat. She didn't know why saying good-bye to her folks was so hard; she'd been away from them for some time already. Maybe it was the reality that she was a married woman now—an Amish woman, to be exact. There could be no quick plane trips home whenever she felt the need, and it wasn't likely that Mom and Dad would come here to visit that often, either.

"We should really go inside and say good-bye to your new sister-in-law," Mom said as she started for the house.

"Where's Eli?" Dad asked. "We do get to tell our son-in-law good-bye, I hope."

"Eli went with his brothers to return the benches we used at the wedding," Laura explained. "He's not back yet."

Mom's mouth dropped open. "The day after your wedding?"

Laura nodded.

Dad glanced at his watch. "We should leave soon if we're going to make our plane."

"I'm sure Eli will be here shortly, but if you can't wait, I'll tell him—" Laura's words were halted by a piercing scream. At least she thought it was a scream. She turned toward the sound coming from the front porch and saw Foosie clinging to one of the support beams, hissing and screeching, with Amon's two dogs yapping and jumping after her.

"Foosie must have slipped out the doorway behind me." Laura turned back to face her parents. "I'd better go rescue her, and you two had better get to the airport. You don't want to miss your flight."

Mom gave Laura a quick peck on the cheek, then climbed into their rental car. Dad embraced Laura one final time, and just before he took his seat on the driver's side, he said, "Don't forget to call if you need us."

Laura nodded and blinked back tears. She offered one final wave, then raced toward the house.

CHAPTER 21

Laura had visited Eli's parents' home several times, but she'd never had occasion to use the rest room. It wasn't until she and Eli moved her things to his house and were settled into their room that Laura was hit with a sickening reality. Despite the fact that most Amish homes in the area had indoor bathrooms, the Yoders still used an outhouse.

"I'll never be able to use that smelly facility," she complained to Eli as they prepared for bed that night.

He flopped onto the bed with a groan. "I can't do anything about it tonight, but I promise as soon as our own home is done, it will have a bathroom."

"That will be fine for when the time comes that we get to move, but what about now? I'll need a *real* bathroom here, too, Eli."

"I'll see about turning one of the upstairs closets into a bathroom when I can find the time."

"Why can't your father or brothers build the bathroom?"

"They're busy with other things, too, and to tell you the truth, I don't think having an inside bathroom is all that important to any of 'em."

Laura paced back and forth in front of their bedroom

window. "So while I'm waiting for you to find the time, how am I supposed to bathe?"

"We have a large galvanized tub in the washroom for that. You'll heat water on the stove, and—"

"What?" Laura whirled around to face him. "I can hardly believe you would expect me to live under such primitive conditions!"

Eli looked at her as if she'd taken leave of her senses. "Calm down. You'll wake up the whole house, shouting that way." He left the bed and joined her at the window. "You've gotten used to living without other modern things, so I would think you could manage this little inconvenience. After all, it's really not such a *baremlich* thing."

She squinted. "It's a terrible thing to me. And this is not a 'little' inconvenience. It's a catastrophe!"

"Such resentment I see on your face." He brushed her cheek with the back of his thumb. "You've done well adjusting to being Amish, and I'm proud of you."

How could she stay mad with him looking at her that way? His enchanting blue eyes shone like the moonlight, and his chin dimple looked even more pronounced with his charming smile.

Laura leaned against Eli's chest and sighed. "Promise me you'll build us a decent bathroom as soon as you can."

"I promise."

The next few weeks flew by as Laura settled into her in-laws' home. There wasn't as much privacy as Laura would have liked, but she knew the situation would only be temporary.

One evening as she and Eli were in their room looking

at some of the wedding gifts they had received, Laura commented that her favorite gift was the oval braided rug in rich autumn hues that Martha Rose had made. With a smile of satisfaction, she placed it on the wooden floor at the foot of their bed. "Look how well it goes with the quilt I purchased at the farmers' market that first day we met." She motioned toward the lovely covering on their bed. "These two items can be the focal points in our room."

Eli raised his eyebrows. "I don't know anything about focal points, but the rug does looks good." He pulled Laura to his chest and rubbed his face against her cheek. "Almost as good as my beautiful wife."

"Eli, you're hurting me. Your face is so scratchy!"

He stepped back, holding her at arm's length. "It'll be better once my beard grows in fully."

She stared up at him. "I know Amish men are expected to grow a beard once they're married, but I'm going to miss that little chin dimple of yours."

Eli grinned. "It'll still be there; you'll just have to hunt for it."

Laura giggled. "You're such a tease."

He tickled her under the chin. "And that's why you love me so much, jah?"

She nodded and gave him another hug. "I surely do."

❧

Eli knew Laura wasn't happy living with his folks, and the absence of an indoor bathroom was only part of the problem. Almost every day when he came home from work, she greeted him with some complaint about his mother. He wasn't sure if the problem was Mom's fault or Laura's, but he hoped it would work itself out.

One Saturday, Eli decided to take Laura out for lunch at the Bird-in-Hand Family Restaurant, which had always been one of his favorite places to eat.

"This is such a nice surprise," Laura said, as the two of them were seated at a table inside the restaurant. "It's been so long since we did anything fun, I'd forgotten what it was like."

Eli snickered. "I think you're exaggerating some, but I'm glad you're enjoying yourself."

Laura glanced at the buffet counter behind them. "I might not be enjoying myself so much after I count up the calories I'll be consuming here today."

Eli's forehead wrinkled. "You worry way too much about your weight, Laura. What are you gonna do when you're in a family way?"

Laura opened her mouth as if to respond, but Selma and Elmer Hostetler stepped up to their table just then.

"Did I hear that someone's expecting a boppli?" Selma asked with a curious expression.

Laura's face turned red, and Eli shook his head. "Not us, but my sister is."

"So I heard." Selma smiled. "How many kinner are you two hoping to have?"

"Oh, as many as the good Lord allows," Eli replied.

Laura's mouth dropped open like a broken window hinge. "Huh?"

Elmer nudged his wife on the arm. "What kind of question is that for you to be askin' these newlyweds? You're worse than our outspoken daughter, and now you've embarrassed Laura."

Selma's face had reddened, too, and Eli felt the need to change the subject. "Speaking of Pauline. . .is she here with you today?"

"Nope. She moved to Kidron, Ohio, last week."

"Kidron? What's she doing there?"

"Went to be with her aunt."

Selma shifted her weight from one foot to the other as she cleared her throat. "I. . .uh. . .think she needed a change of scenery in order to get over her breakup with you. I'm sure she'll be back when she feels ready."

Eli couldn't help but feel a little guilty for being the cause of Pauline leaving her family, but what should he have done—married the girl just to make her happy?

"We ought to get ourselves some food and get back to our seats, don't ya think?" Elmer nudged Selma again.

"Jah, sure. Enjoy your meal," she said, nodding at Eli and then Laura.

When the Hostetlers moved away, Eli stood. "Guess we'd better get some food now, too."

Laura made no reply; just pushed away from the table and moved over to the buffet counter with a disgruntled expression. When they returned to the table a short time later, Eli felt a sense of concern seeing how little food she had put on her plate.

"Aren't you hungry?"

"I was until Pauline's folks showed up."

"Why would them stopping by our table make you lose your appetite?"

Laura took a drink from her glass of iced tea before she spoke. "Well, let me see now. . . First, Selma embarrassed me by asking if I was pregnant; then she asked how many children we planned to have. As if that wasn't enough, she made sure you knew why Pauline has moved to Ohio." She grimaced. "Didn't that make you feel uncomfortable, Eli?"

"Jah, a bit, but Selma's right about Pauline needing a change of scenery, and I'm sure it is my fault that she decided to go."

"How can it be your fault? You told me there was nothing but friendship between you and Pauline. I never understood why she thought there was more."

Eli shrugged. "I guess she wanted there to be, and when I started seeing her again after you and I decided it would be best if we went our separate ways—"

Laura held up her hand. "Just a minute. It was you who decided that, not me."

He nodded. "You're right, but that was before you'd made the decision to become Amish."

She leaned forward, staring hard at him. "So if I hadn't made that decision, would you have married Pauline?"

Eli took a sip of his water, hoping it would help cool him down. What he'd wanted to be a pleasant afternoon for the two of them was turning into a most uncomfortable situation, and if he didn't do something soon, they might end up in an argument.

"Well, Eli. . .are you going to answer my question or not?"

He set his glass on the table. "I can't rightly say, but I don't think I would have married her."

"You don't *think* so? If you never loved her, then marrying her shouldn't have been an option." Laura's voice had risen so high, Eli feared those sitting nearby would hear. "I'll bet you would have married her if I hadn't agreed to become Amish, wouldn't you?"

He put a finger to his lips. "Let's talk about something else, okay?"

"Let's just eat our food and forget about conversation."

"That suits me fine." Eli bowed his head for silent prayer, and when he lifted it, he noticed that Laura had already begun to eat. He didn't know if she had joined him in prayer or not, but he decided it was best not to ask. They could finish this discussion later.

On the buggy ride home, Laura kept her eyes shut, hoping Eli would think she was asleep and wouldn't try to make conversation. The last thing she wanted was another argument, and she was pretty sure they would quarrel if she told him all the things that were going on in her mind.

When Laura felt the buggy turn sharply and heard the wheels crunch through some gravel, she figured they had pulled into the Yoders' driveway, so she opened her eyes.

Before they got to the yard, Eli pulled back on the reins and guided the horse and buggy to the edge of the driveway.

"What are you doing? Why are we stopping?"

"So we can talk."

"There's nothing to talk about."

"I think there is."

She drew in a deep breath and released it with a weary sigh. "What do you think we need to talk about?"

"This business with you thinking I would have married Pauline, for one thing. If I've told you once, I've told you a hundred times, Pauline and I were never more than friends."

"She wanted it to be more." Laura balled her hands into fists. "I think your mother did, too."

"Mom? What's Mom got to do with this?"

Laura pursed her lips as she squinted. "Oh, Eli, don't look so wide-eyed and innocent. We've been living with your folks several weeks now. Surely you can feel the tension between me and your mother."

He merely shrugged in response.

"She's mentioned Pauline a few times, too. I think she believes Pauline would have made you a better wife."

A vein on the side of Eli's neck began to bulge, and Laura wondered if she had hit a nerve.

"Your mom is always criticizing me," she continued. "I can never do anything right where she's concerned."

"I don't believe that."

"Are you calling me a liar?"

"No, but I think I know Mom pretty well."

"You don't know her as well as you think. She scrutinizes my work, and she—"

"Enough! I don't want to hear another word against my mamm!"

As the days moved on, Laura became more frustrated. Nothing seemed to be going right. Their house still wasn't done; Eli wasn't nearly so cheerful and fun-loving anymore; Foosie was an irritant to Eli's mother; Laura dreaded the extra chores she was expected to do; and worst of all, she couldn't stand that smelly outhouse! She was on her way there now and none too happy about it.

On previous trips to the privy, she'd encountered several disgusting spiders, a yellow jackets' nest, and a couple of field mice. She was a city girl and hated bugs. She shouldn't have to be subjected to this kind of torture.

Laura opened the wooden door and held it with one hand as she lifted her kerosene lantern and peered cautiously inside. Nothing lurking on the floor. She held the lamp higher and was about to step inside when the shaft of light fell on something dark and furry. It was sitting over the hole.

Laura let out a piercing scream and slammed the door. She sprinted toward the house and ran straight into Eli, coming from the barn.

"Laura, what's wrong? I heard you hollering and thought one of Pop's pigs had gotten loose again."

Laura clung to Eli's jacket. "It's the outhouse. . .there's some kind of monstrous animal in there!"

Eli grinned at her. "*Kumme*—come now. It was probably just a little old maus."

"It was not a mouse. It was dark and furry. . .and huge!"

Eli slipped his hand in the crook of her arm. "Let's go have a look-see."

"I'm not going in there."

He chuckled. "You don't have to. I'll do the checking."

Laura held her breath as Eli entered the outhouse. "Be careful."

She heard a thud, followed by a loud *whoop*. Suddenly, the door flew open and Eli bolted out of the privy, chased by the hairy creature Laura had seen a few moments ago. It was a comical sight, but she was almost too frightened to see the full humor in it.

"What was that?" she asked Eli, as the two of them stood watching the critter dash into the field.

"I think it was a hedgehog," Eli said breathlessly. "The

crazy thing tried to attack me, but I kicked him with the toe of my boot, right before I walked out of the outhouse."

Laura giggled as her fear dissipated. "Don't you mean, 'ran out of the outhouse'?"

Eli's face turned pink, and he chuckled. "Guess I was movin' pretty fast."

The two of them stood for a few seconds, gazing into each other's eyes. Then they both started laughing. They laughed so hard, tears streamed down their faces, and Laura had to set the lantern on the ground for fear it would fall out of her hand. It felt good to laugh. It was something neither of them did much anymore.

When they finally got control of their emotions, Eli reached for her hand. "I'll see about indoor plumbing as soon as spring comes; I promise."

CHAPTER 22

Wesley sat on the couch, staring at the Christmas tree. The little white lights blinked off and on, and the red bows hung from the evergreen branches in perfect order—but this Christmas would be anything but perfect.

He glanced at the unlit fireplace. A garland of fake holly had been strung across the mantel, but there was no Foosie lying on the rug by the hearth.

The Christmas cards they had received were stacked neatly in a red basket on the coffee table, but the only card that mattered to him was the one they'd gotten from Laura and Eli. It had included an invitation to come there for Christmas, and Laura had even suggested they stay there with them. Wesley had wanted to go, and he'd even been willing to adjust his work schedule so they could, but Irene wouldn't hear of it. She had insisted that she couldn't leave town during the holidays because she had too many commitments.

"Yeah, right," he mumbled. "She just doesn't want to give up all the modern conveniences she's convinced she can't do without."

"Who are you talking to, Wesley?"

He glanced at the doorway and was surprised to see Irene

standing there holding a large poinsettia plant in her hands.

"I didn't hear you come in. Did you just get home?"

She nodded and placed the plant on the end table near the couch. "I've been out shopping."

"That figures."

"What was that?"

"Nothing."

Irene slipped off her coat and laid it neatly on one end of the couch. Then she took a seat in her recliner and picked up the remote. "How come you're not watching television? Isn't it about time for your favorite show?"

"I get tired of watching TV."

"Since when?"

"Since I came to the conclusion that there are better things I can do with my time."

"You mean like sitting here staring at the tree?"

"Christmas is just a few days away. It seemed like the thing to do."

She wrinkled her nose. "Are you being sarcastic?"

"I wouldn't dream of it."

"Wesley, are you still pouting because we can't go to Pennsylvania for Christmas?"

"What do you mean, 'We can't go to Pennsylvania'?" He stood and began to pace. "We could have gone if you weren't so busy with *things*."

"Those *things* are important, and I—"

He stopped pacing and whirled around to face her. "Don't you miss our daughter? Wouldn't you rather spend Christmas with her than go to some silly ball?"

"Of course I'd like to be with Laura, but I've been planning this gala affair for several months." She released a sigh.

"How would it look if the person in charge of the Christmas ball wasn't there to see that everything went according to plan?"

He grunted and started across the room.

"Where are you going?"

"Upstairs to bed. I'll need to get my beauty rest if I'm going to escort Princess Irene to the ball on Christmas Eve."

Laura stood in front of the living-room window, staring out at the blanket of pristine snow covering the ground and every tree in the Yoders' yard. It looked like a picture post-card, and despite the fact that Laura missed her parents, she felt happier today than she had in weeks.

She moved away from the window and took a seat in the wooden rocker by the fireplace. Even though there was no Christmas tree inside the house or colored lights decorating the outside of the house, a few candles were spaced around the room, along with several Christmas cards from family and friends. *Guess I did end up with an Early-American look after all. It's just a little plainer than I had expected it to be.*

Laura spotted the Christmas card they had received from her parents, along with a substantial check, and her heart clenched. *I do miss Mom and Dad, and I wish Eli and I could have gone there for Christmas or that they would have come here. But Mom was involved with a Christmas ball she'd planned at the country club, and even though Dad sounded like he wanted to come, he never seems to get his way where Mom's concerned. Maybe he should take lessons from Eli and his father. They don't have much trouble making a decision, even if it goes against what their wives might want.*

Eli had been looking forward to Christmas. He'd made Laura a special gift, and this afternoon, his sister and her family would be joining them for Mom's traditional holiday feast.

"Life couldn't be any better," he said to the horse he was grooming. "Maybe later we'll hitch you up to the sleigh, and I'll take my beautiful wife for a ride."

The horse whinnied as if in response, and Eli chuckled. "You kind of like that idea, don't you, old boy?"

Eli entered the house a short time later, holding Laura's gift under his jacket. "Where's my fraa?" he asked Mom, who was scurrying around the kitchen.

She nodded toward the living room. "Your wife's in there. I guess she thinks I don't need any help getting dinner on."

Eli merely shrugged and left the kitchen. No point getting Mom more riled than she already seemed to be. He found Laura sitting in the rocking chair, gazing at the fireplace. *"En hallicher Grischtdaag!"*

She looked up and smiled. "A merry Christmas to you, too."

Eli bent down and kissed the top of her head. "I have something for you."

"You do? What is it?"

Eli held his jacket shut. "Guess."

She wrinkled her nose. "I have no idea. Tell me. . . please."

He chuckled and withdrew an ornate birdhouse, painted blue with white trim.

"Oh, Eli, it's just like the one you showed me at the farmers' market the day we first met."

He smiled. "And now you will have a place for it, come spring."

She accepted the gift, and tears welled in her eyes. "Thank you so much. It's beautiful."

"Does my pretty fraa have anything for her hardworking husband?" Eli asked in a teasing tone.

"I do, but I'm afraid it's not finished."

"You made me something?"

She nodded. "I've been sewing you a new shirt, but your mom's kept me so busy, I haven't had time to get it hemmed and wrapped."

Eli took the birdhouse from Laura and placed it on the small table by her chair. He pulled her toward him in a tender embrace. "It's okay. You'll get the shirt finished soon, and I'll appreciate it every bit as much then as I would if you'd given it to me now."

Laura rested her head against his shoulder. "I love you, Eli. Thanks for being so understanding."

Silent prayer had been said, and everyone sat around the table with expectant, hungry looks on their faces. Mary Ellen had outdone herself. Huge platters were laden with succulent roast beef and mouthwatering ham. Bowls were filled with buttery mashed potatoes, candied yams, canned green beans, and coleslaw. Sweet cucumber pickles, black olives, dilled green beans, and red-beet eggs were also included in the feast, as well as buttermilk biscuits and cornmeal muffins.

Everyone ate heartily. Everyone except for Laura and little Ben. Their plates were still half full when Mary Ellen brought out three pies—two pumpkin and one mincemeat—along with a tray of chocolate doughnuts.

Ben squealed with delight. "*Fettkuche!*"

"No doughnuts until you eat everything on your plate," Martha Rose scolded.

Ben's lower lip began to quiver, and his eyes filled with tears.

"Being a crybaby won't help you get your way," Amon admonished.

"He's only a child." Laura pulled one of the pumpkin pies close and helped herself to a piece. "Surely he can have one little doughnut."

All eyes seemed to be focused on Laura, and Ben, who had moments ago been fighting tears, let loose with a howl that sent Laura's cat flying into the air.

"Now look what you've done." Amon shook his finger at Ben. "You've scared that poor bussli half to death."

Foosie ran around the table, meowing and swishing her tail. Laura bent down and scooped her up, but the pinched expression on Mary Ellen's face was enough to let her know that in this house, cats didn't belong at the table. Laura mumbled an apology and deposited Foosie back on the floor.

"You're not settin' a very good example for the boy, Laura." This reprimand came from Eli's father. "If you're not gonna eat all your food, then I don't think you should take any pie." Johnny looked pointedly at Eli. "What do you think, son? Should your fraa be allowed to pick like a bird, then eat pie in front of Ben, who's just been told he can't have any fettkuche 'til he cleans his plate?"

Laura squirmed uneasily as she waited to see how Eli would respond. She felt his hand under the table, and her fingers squeezed his in response.

"Don't you think maybe you should eat everything else first, then have some pie?" Eli's voice was tight, and the muscle in his jaw quivered. Was he upset with her or only trying to please his father?

"I'm watching my weight, and the only way I can keep within my calorie count is to leave some food on my plate."

"You could pass up the pie," Mary Ellen suggested.

Laura grimaced. Why was everything she did always under scrutiny? Why did she have to make excuses for her behavior all the time? She pushed away from the table. "I'm not really hungry enough for pie, anyway." She gave Eli a quick glance, then rushed out of the room.

CHAPTER 23

S pring came early, and the building of Eli and Laura's home resumed as soon as the snow had melted. It couldn't be finished soon enough as far as Mary Ellen was concerned. Ever since Eli had married Laura, she had tried to be a good mother-in-law, but it wasn't easy when Laura seemed so distant and often touchy. Here of late, she'd been acting moodier than ever, and Mary Ellen wondered if *she* might be the cause of Laura's discontent.

"Why don't the two of us do some baking today?" she suggested to Laura one morning after breakfast. "We can make a couple of brown sugar sponge rolls. How's that sound?"

Laura groaned. "Do we have to? I'm really tired this morning, and I thought it would be nice to sit out on the back porch and watch the men work on my house."

Mary Ellen's forehead wrinkled. "Are you feeling poorly?"

"I'm fine. Just tired."

"Maybe a good spring tonic is what you need." She opened the cupboard near Laura and plucked out a box of cream of tartar, some sulfur, and a container of Epsom salts. "All you have to do is mix a little of each of these in a jar of water. Then take two or three swallows each morning for a few days, and you'll feel like your old self in no time at all."

Laura's face paled, and she coughed like she was about to gag. "I'm fine, really. Just didn't sleep well last night. A few cups of coffee, and I'll be good to go."

Mary Ellen shrugged and stepped aside. "Suit yourself, but remember the spring tonic in case you're still not up to par come morning."

"Danki. I'll keep it in mind."

As they rode home from church one Sunday afternoon, Eli worried. Laura had seemed so pensive lately. Had someone said or done something to upset her? He offered her a smile. "Sure was a good day, wasn't it?"

"Uh-huh."

"Is there something troubling you? You seem kind of down in the dumps today."

She shrugged. "I'm just getting tired of going to other people's houses and seeing that they have indoor plumbing, while we still have none."

"I said I'd build one in our new home, and I'm still planning to put one in Mom and Pop's house as soon as I find the time."

"You've been saying that for months, Eli, and it's taking a lot longer than I thought it would." She grunted. "I can't stand that smelly outhouse!"

Eli glanced over at her and squinted. "I'm working every free moment I have, and so are Pop and my brothers. Can't you learn to be patient?"

Laura sat staring straight ahead with her lips pursed and said nothing.

"The Bible says, 'The trying of your faith worketh patience.' It's in the book of James."

"My faith in things getting better has definitely been tried, and so has my patience," she mumbled.

Eli blinked. Was there no pleasing this woman? He'd said he would install indoor plumbing in their new home. That ought to be good enough.

"Eli, could I ask you a question?"

He blew out his breath. "Not if it's about indoor plumbing."

"It's not."

"Okay, ask the question then."

She reached across the seat and touched his arm. "Do you think Pauline Hostetler would have made you a better wife?"

Eli lifted one eyebrow and glanced over at Laura. "Pauline? What's she got to do with anything?"

"I just want to know if you think—"

"I can't believe you would bring that up again, Laura. You should know by now how much I love you."

Her eyes filled with tears and she sniffed.

"What's wrong? Why are you crying?"

"Your mother and I were doing some baking the other day, and she brought up the subject of Pauline."

"Oh? What'd she say?"

"Just that Pauline is a good cook and likes to bake." Laura's voice rose a notch. "I'm sure she thinks Pauline would have made you a better wife than me."

Eli pulled sharply on the reins, steered the buggy to the side of the road, and gathered her into his arms. "I love you, Laura. Only you."

"I'm glad to hear that." Laura snuggled against his jacket. "But that doesn't take care of things with your mother. Do you have any idea what I can say or do to make her realize that I'm a better wife for you than Pauline could ever have been?"

Eli touched her chin lightly with his thumb. "You'd best leave that up to me."

When Eli and Laura entered the house a short time later, Laura went up to their room, saying she was tired and needed a nap.

Eli found his mother sitting in the living room on the sofa, reading a book. Apparently his folks had gotten home from church quite a bit ahead of them. He decided this might be a good time to speak with her about the conversation she'd had with Laura the other day. "Mom, can I talk to you for a minute?"

She looked up and smiled. "Jah, sure. What's on your mind?"

He took a seat in the rocking chair across from her. "It's about Laura."

"Is she feeling all right? The other day she mentioned that she was really tired, and I suggested she take a spring tonic."

Eli winced at the remembrance of drinking his mother's sour-tasting tonics when he was a boy. "I don't think a spring tonic will take care of what ails my fraa."

"Is she still fretting over your house not being done? She's mentioned several times that she can't wait until it's finished." Mom's forehead wrinkled. "I think she's anxious to have her own place to run, and to tell you the truth, I'm looking forward to having my space, too."

"Jah, it will be good for both of you when the house is done." Eli sat there a few minutes, trying to formulate the right words to say what was on his mind.

"You're looking kind of pensive, son. Is there something more you wanted to say?"

He nodded. "Laura thinks you would have been happier if I'd married Pauline instead of her. When you mentioned how well Pauline can cook the other day, it really hurt Laura's feelings."

"I think Laura's too sensitive for her own good." Mom clicked her tongue. "I meant nothing by what I said."

"Are you sure about that?"

Mom stared at the book she held in her hands. "I—I suppose I was kind of hoping you would choose Pauline, but once your decision was made, I accepted it."

"Then why did you bring Pauline up to Laura, and why does Laura feel as if you don't approve of her?"

"As I said before. . .she tends to be rather sensitive."

Eli nodded. Laura was touchy about some of the things he said, too—especially in recent weeks.

"I'll apologize to her and try to be more careful with what I say," Mom promised.

"Danki. I appreciate that."

🎋

"I'm not feeling well. I think I'll stay home from church today," Laura mumbled when Eli tried to coax her out of bed two Sundays later.

"You were feeling all right last night."

"That was then. This is now."

"You should get up and help Mom with breakfast," Eli murmured against her ear.

She groaned. "I don't feel like helping today."

Eli touched her forehead. "You're not running a fever."

"I'm not sick. . .just terribly tired."

"Maybe you should consider taking Mom's spring tonic. It does put a spring in your step; I promise."

"I'm not taking any tonic. I would feel fine if I could get a little more rest."

Eli pulled back the covers, hopped out of bed, and stepped into his trousers. He walked across the room to where the water pitcher and bowl sat on top of the dresser. After splashing a handful of water on his face and drying it with a towel, he grabbed his shirt off the wall peg and started for the door. "See you downstairs in five minutes."

When the door clicked shut, Laura grabbed her pillow and threw it across the room. "Maybe I should go home to my parents for a while. I wonder how you'd like that, Eli Yoder!"

*

Laura was quiet on the buggy ride to preaching, and during the service she didn't sing. Not only was she still tired, but she felt irritation with Eli for not having any understanding and insisting that she get up and help his mother with breakfast this morning. He should have had a little sympathy and agreed that she could stay home and rest.

Laura's attention was drawn to the front of the room as Bishop Wagler began his sermon, using Mark 11:25 as his text. "In Jesus' own words, we are told: 'And when ye stand praying, forgive, if ye have ought against any: that your Father also which is in heaven may forgive you your trespasses.' "

Laura frowned. *That verse doesn't make any sense to me. How can I forgive Mary Ellen for her comments about Pauline the other day when she didn't even say she was sorry? And Eli never said he was sorry for the way he talked to me this morning, either.*

She glanced over at Martha Rose, who sat on the bench beside her. She wore a smile on her face and looked almost angelic. But then, Eli's sister always seemed to be happy, even when she had a bout of morning sickness or things weren't going so well. *Maybe it's because she doesn't have to share her home with her mother-in-law!*

"I thought Bishop Wagler's sermon was good, didn't you?" Eli asked as he glanced over at Laura on their trip home from church later that day.

She merely shrugged in response.

"If we don't forgive others, we can't expect God to forgive us."

Still no reply.

"I forgive you for throwing that pillow at me this morning."

Her mouth dropped open. "You knew?"

He nodded. "Heard it hit the door."

"I wasn't really throwing it at you," she said, as a smile tugged at the corners of her mouth. "Just venting was all."

"Because I asked you to get out of bed and help my mamm?"

"Jah."

Holding the reins with one hand, he reached his free hand over and took hold of Laura's hand. "Didn't mean to sound so bossy. Will you forgive me?"

She nodded and slid closer to him. "Of course I forgive you."

His eyebrows raised. "Is that all you've got to say?"

She sat silently for several seconds; then a light seemed to dawn. "I'm sorry, too."

He grinned and gave her fingers a gentle squeeze. "You're forgiven."

Laura leaned her head on his shoulder and sighed. "I'm glad we got that cleared up. Now if I could just get your mother to apologize for what she said to me about Pauline."

Eli's eyebrows raised. "She hasn't apologized yet? She said she was going to."

Laura shook her head.

"She probably got busy and forgot. Want me to have another talk with her?"

"No, just forget it. We'll move into our house soon; then things should be better."

CHAPTER

24

Eli and Laura's house was finally ready, and Eli had included a small bathroom, just as he'd promised. He and his father had also put one in their house, so Laura knew she would have that convenience handy whenever they visited his folks. Eli and Laura's new home had five bedrooms, a roomy kitchen, a nice-sized living room, and of course, the small bathroom.

Mary Ellen had given Eli and Laura some furniture, and Laura was glad to finally have a home she could call her own. It would be a welcome relief not to have Eli's mother analyzing everything she said and did. As far as Laura was concerned, the completion of her house was the best thing that had happened since she'd moved onto the Yoders' farm.

On the first morning in her new home, Laura got up late. When she entered the kitchen, she realized Eli was already outside doing his chores. She hurried to start breakfast and was just setting the table when he came inside.

"Your cereal is almost ready," she said with a smile.

He nodded. "Is my lunch packed? I have to leave for work in five minutes."

"Oh, I forgot. I'm running late this morning. Usually

your mother gets breakfast going while I make your lunch."

"It's okay. I'll just take a few pieces of fruit and some cookies." Eli opened his lunch pail and placed two apples, an orange, a handful of peanut butter cookies, and a thermos of milk inside. He took a seat at the table, bowed his head for silent prayer, and dug into the hot oatmeal Laura handed him.

"Can you stop by the store and pick up a loaf of bread on your way home tonight?" Laura asked, taking the seat beside him.

Eli gave her a questioning look.

"I won't have time to do any baking today. I have clothes to wash, and I want to spend most of the day organizing the house and setting out some of our wedding gifts."

Eli gulped down the last of his milk and stood. "Jah, okay. I know it's important for you to set things up the way you want them." He leaned over and kissed her cheek.

"Ouch! You're prickly!"

"Sorry." Eli grabbed his lunch pail and headed for the door.

"Wait! Can't you visit with me awhile this morning? You've been working such long hours lately, and it seems like we never get to talk anymore."

"We'll talk later. I've got to go now, or I'll be late for work."

Laura waved at his retreating form. When she shut the door, she sighed deeply and surveyed her kitchen. "This house is so big. Where should I begin?"

❦

As Laura stood at the kitchen sink doing the breakfast

dishes, she began to fret. Eli had changed since their marriage. He not only looked different, what with his scratchy beard, but he never seemed to have time for her anymore.

"Work, work, work, that's all he ever thinks about," she muttered. "If Eli cared about me the way he does his job, I'd be a lot happier. Whatever happened to romance and long buggy rides to the lake?"

A single tear rolled down her cheek, and she wiped it away with a soapy hand. "Life is so unfair. I gave up a lot to become Eli's wife, and now he won't even listen to me." Laura glanced down at Foosie, who lay curled at her feet. "Too bad Mom and Dad can't come for a visit." She sniffed deeply. "No. . .they're too busy, just like Eli. Dad has his law practice, and Mom runs around like a chicken hunting bugs, trying to meet all of her social obligations."

The cat purred contentedly, seemingly unaware of her frustrations.

"You've got life made, you know that?"

A knock at the back door drew Laura's attention away from Foosie. *Oh, no. I hope that's not Mary Ellen.*

She dried her hands on her apron and dabbed the corners of her eyes with a handkerchief, then went to answer the door.

To her surprise, Martha Rose and little Ben stood on the porch, each holding a basket. Martha Rose's basket held freshly baked apple muffins, and Ben's was full of ginger cookies.

Laura smiled. She was always glad to see her sister-in-law and that adorable little boy. "Come in. Would you like a cup of tea?"

Martha Rose, her stomach now bulging, lowered herself into a chair. "That sounds good. We can have some of the muffins I brought, too."

Ben spotted Foosie, and he darted over to play with her.

"What brings you by so early?" Laura asked as she pulled out a chair for herself.

"We're on our way to town to do some shopping, but we wanted to stop and see you first," Martha Rose answered. "We have an invitation for you and Eli."

Laura's interest was piqued. "What kind of invitation?"

"Since tomorrow's Saturday and the weather's so nice, Amon and I have decided to take Ben to the lake for a picnic supper. We were wondering if you and Eli would like to come along."

Laura dropped a couple of tea bags into the pot she'd taken from the stove before she sat down. "Would we ever! At least, I would. If Eli can tear himself away from work long enough, I'm sure he'd have a good time, too."

Martha Rose nodded. "We'll meet you there around four o'clock. That'll give everyone time enough to do all their chores." She waved her hand. "Speaking of chores—you look awfully tired. Are you working too hard?"

Laura pushed a stray hair under her head covering and sighed. "I have been feeling a little drained lately. I'll be fine once I get this house organized."

Martha Rose opened her mouth to say something, but Laura cut her off. "What should I bring to the picnic?"

"I thought I'd fix fried chicken, two different salads, and maybe some pickled-beet eggs. Why don't you bring the dessert and some kind of beverage?"

"That sounds fine," Laura answered, feeling suddenly lighthearted. They were going on a picnic, and she could hardly wait.

"How was your day?" Eli asked, as he stepped into the kitchen that evening and found Laura sitting at the table, tearing lettuce leaves into a bowl.

"It was okay. How about yours?"

"Busy. We got several new orders at the store today, and my boss said we might have to put in more overtime in order to get them done."

She groaned. "I hope not. You work too much as it is."

He placed his lunch pail on the counter and joined her at the table. He was too tired to argue, and it seemed like he never won an argument with Laura anyway, so what was the use?

"Your sister and little Ben came by today." Laura looked over at him and smiled. "She invited us to join their family on a picnic at the lake tomorrow."

"What time?"

"She said for supper, and that they'd be there by four."

"That might be okay. I'll need to work in my shop awhile, and I promised Pop I'd help him do a couple of chores, too."

"What time will you be done?"

"Probably by four, I would imagine."

"Then we can go on the picnic?" Laura's expression was so hopeful, there was no way Eli could say no.

He leaned over and kissed her cheek. "Jah, tomorrow we'll join my sister and her family for a picnic."

The lake was beautiful, and Laura drank in the peacefulness until she felt as if her heart would burst.

Martha Rose was busy setting out her picnic foods, and the men were playing ball with little Ben. Laura brought out the brownies and iced mint tea she had made, and soon the plywood table they'd brought from home was brimming with food.

Everyone gathered for silent prayer, and then the men heaped their plates full. Laura was the last to dish up, but she only took small helpings of everything. When she came to the tray of pickled-beet eggs, a surge of nausea rolled through her stomach like angry ocean waves. Pickled eggs were sickening—little purple land mines, waiting to destroy her insides.

Laura dropped her plate of food and dashed for the woods. Eli ran after her, but he waited until she had emptied her stomach before saying anything.

"You okay?" he asked with obvious concern.

Laura stood on wobbly legs. "I'm fine. It was the sight of those pickled eggs. They're disgusting! How can anyone eat those awful things?"

Eli slipped his arm around her waist. "Maybe you've got the flu."

She shook her head. "It was just the eggs. Let's go back to the picnic. I'm fine now, honest."

The rest of the day went well enough, and Laura felt a bit better after drinking some of her cold mint tea. She even joined a friendly game of tag, but she did notice the looks of concern Eli and his sister exchanged. At least nobody had said anything about her getting sick, and for that, she was glad.

A few days later while Laura was outside gathering eggs from the henhouse, she had another attack of nausea. She hadn't eaten any breakfast, so she figured that was the reason. Besides, the acrid odor of chicken manure was enough to make anyone sick.

On her way back to the house, she spotted Eli's mother hanging laundry on the line. Mary Ellen waved and called to Laura, but Laura only nodded in return and hurried on. She was in no mood for a confrontation with her mother-in-law this morning, and she certainly didn't want to get sick in front of her.

"I'm almost finished here," Mary Ellen called. "Come have a cup of coffee."

Laura's stomach lurched at the mention of coffee, and she wondered how she could graciously get out of the invitation.

Mary Ellen called to her again. "I know you're busy, but surely you can take a few minutes for a little chat."

Laura inhaled deeply and released a sigh. "All right. I'll set this basket of eggs inside, then be right over." *May as well give in, or Mary Ellen will probably report to Eli that his wife is unsociable.*

Laura entered the house and deposited the eggs in the refrigerator. Then she took a glass from the cupboard and went to the sink for a cool drink of water. She drank it slowly and took several deep breaths, which seemed to help settle her stomach some.

She opened the back door. "Well, here goes nothing."

When she stepped into the Yoders' kitchen a few minutes later, she found Mary Ellen seated at the table. Two cups were sitting there, and the strong aroma of coffee permeated the air.

Laura's stomach did a little flip-flop as she took a seat. "Uh, would you mind if I had mint tea instead of coffee?"

Mary Ellen pushed her chair aside and stood. "If that's what you prefer." She went to the cupboard and retrieved a box of tea bags, then poured boiling water from the teapot on the stove into a clean mug and added one bag. "You're looking kind of peaked this morning." she said, handing Laura the tea.

"I think I might have a touch of the flu."

"You could be in a family way. Have you thought about that?"

Laura shook her head. "It's the flu. Nothing to worry about."

"Would you like some shoofly pie or a buttermilk biscuit?"

"I might try a biscuit."

Mary Ellen passed Laura a basket of warm biscuits. "So, tell me, how long has this flu thing been going on?"

"Just a few days."

"If it continues, maybe you'd better see the doctor."

There she goes again, telling me what to do. Laura reached for the small pitcher on the table and poured some milk into the tea, stirring it vigorously. With a splash, some of the hot liquid splattered onto her hand, and she grimaced. "I'll see the doctor if I don't feel better soon."

Mary Ellen moved her chair a little closer to Laura's. "I. . . uh. . .have been meaning to apologize for bringing Pauline up to you a few weeks ago. I shouldn't have said anything about the woman's cooking skills."

"Apology accepted." Laura took a sip of tea. "Have you

heard anything about Pauline since she moved to Ohio?"

"Just that she got there safely and seems to like it well enough."

"Any idea how long she'll be staying?"

Mary Ellen shrugged. "Guess it all depends."

Laura drummed her fingernails along the edge of the tablecloth. "On how soon she gets over Eli? Is that what you mean?"

"Jah."

"Eli has told me several times that he and Pauline were never more than friends, but I guess she was hoping for more."

Mary Ellen wasn't sure how to respond, because the truth was she'd been hoping for more, too. She had always liked Pauline and had thought she would have made Eli a good wife. *Maybe if Eli hadn't played around during his rump-schpringe years so long and had settled down and joined the church sooner, he would have married Pauline. Probably wouldn't have met Laura, either.*

"Are you about finished with your tea? Would you like another cup?" she asked, hoping the change of subject might clear the air between them.

"I am almost done, but I'm feeling kind of tired all of a sudden, so I think I'll head home and rest awhile."

Mary Ellen studied Laura. Dark circles showed under her eyes, and her face looked pale and drawn. Either she'd been working too hard setting up her new household, or there was something physically wrong. She figured it would be best not to make an issue of it, though. No point in setting herself up to say something wrong and then need to apologize again. So she merely smiled and said, "Guess I'd better get busy making some pickled-beet eggs I promised Johnny he could have. Have a good rest of the day, Laura."

Laura nodded, pushed her chair aside, and dashed from the room.

Mary Ellen shook her head. "Something tells me there's a lot more going on with Eli's wife than she's willing to admit."

CHAPTER
25

Laura's nausea and fatigue continued all that week, but she did her best to hide it from Eli. She didn't want him pressuring her to see the doctor, or worse yet, asking a bunch of questions the way his mother had.

One morning, Laura decided to go into town for some supplies. She asked Eli to hitch the horse to the buggy before he left for work, as she still didn't feel comfortable doing that on her own. As soon as her morning chores were done, she set her dark bonnet in place over her white *kapp* and climbed into the waiting buggy.

When Laura arrived in town, her first stop was the pharmacy. She scanned the shelves until she found exactly what she was looking for. She brought the item to the checkout counter and waited for the middle-aged clerk to ring it up. He gave her a strange look as he placed the small box inside a paper sack. Laura wondered if she was the first Amish woman who had ever purchased a home pregnancy kit.

The test couldn't be taken until early the next morning, so when she got home later in the day, Laura found a safe place to hide it. The last thing she needed was for Eli to discover it and jump to the wrong conclusions. He would surely think she was pregnant, and she was equally sure she wasn't. She couldn't be. Of course, she had missed her monthly, but that wasn't too uncommon for her. Then what about the fatigue and nausea? Those were definite signs of pregnancy; even she knew that much.

Laura waited until Eli left for work the following morning before going to her sewing basket, retrieving the test kit, and rushing to the bathroom.

Moments later, Laura's hands trembled as she held the strip up for examination. It was bright pink. The blood drained from her face, and she sank to the floor, steadying herself against the unyielding wall. "Oh, no! This just can't be!"

She studied it longer, just to be sure she hadn't read it wrong. It was still pink. "I can't be pregnant. What will it do to my figure?"

Some time later when Laura emerged from the bathroom, her eyes felt sore and swollen from crying. She went straight to the kitchen sink and splashed cold water on her face.

I can't tell Eli or even my folks about this yet. I need time to adjust to the idea first.

"How long can I keep a secret like this?" she moaned. After some quick calculations, she figured she must be about eight weeks along. In another four to six weeks, she might be starting to show. Besides, if she kept getting sick every day, Eli would either suspect she was pregnant or decide she was definitely sick and take her to the doctor.

"What am I going to do?" she wailed, looking down at Foosie, asleep at her feet.

No response. Just some gentle purring from the contented-looking cat.

Laura glanced out the window and saw the mail truck pull up to the box by the road. "Guess I'll walk out and get the mail while I think about this situation some more."

Laura found a stack of letters in the box and was surprised to see one from Darla. She hadn't heard anything from her friend from school in several months, and she'd figured Darla had probably forgotten her by now.

Back in the kitchen, Laura took a seat at the table and opened Darla's letter. It didn't say much except that she had a few days off from her job in Philadelphia and wondered if Laura would like to meet her for lunch at a restaurant near Strasburg on Friday of next week.

Laura figured there was plenty of time to get a letter sent back to Darla before Friday, so she moved over to the desk on the other side of the room and took out a piece of paper and a pen. Having lunch with Darla wouldn't solve her immediate problem, but at least it would be a nice outing and was something to look forward to.

Before Laura left the house the following Friday, she wrote Eli a note telling him where she was going and that she would try to be back in time to get supper going before he got home. Then she hitched one of their most docile mares to the buggy and headed out.

When Laura pulled into the restaurant parking lot some time later, she was pleased to see Darla's little sports car parked there. She climbed down from the buggy, secured the horse to the hitching rail, and headed into the restaurant.

She spotted Darla sitting at a table near the window and hurried over to her. "Hey, it's good to see you," she said, taking a seat on the other side of the table. "Thanks for inviting me to join you."

Darla smiled at first, but then her forehead wrinkled as she frowned. "I barely recognized you in those Amish clothes. You sure have changed."

Laura nodded and held out her hands. "Just look at my nails."

Darla shook her head and grunted. "Every one of them is broken." She stared at Laura, making her feel suddenly uncomfortable. "You look tired. What do you do, work all day and never sleep?"

Laura reached for the glass of water the young waitress had just brought and took a sip. "I do work hard, but my fatigue doesn't come from just that."

"What then? Did you jog all the way here or something?"

Laura would have laughed if she hadn't felt so crummy. She wished there were some soda crackers on the table, because she needed something to help calm her nausea.

"You're looking kind of pasty there, kiddo. Are you feeling sick?"

Laura nodded, and tears welled in her eyes. "I—I'm pregnant."

Darla's eyebrows lifted high on her forehead. "I knew marrying that Amish guy would bring you nothing but trouble."

"I don't need any lectures," Laura snapped. "Besides, I could have gotten pregnant no matter who I'd married."

"So what are you going to do about it?"

"Do?"

"Yeah. It's obvious to me by the look on your face that you're anything but happy about being pregnant."

Laura sighed. "I enjoy being around Eli's nephew, and I would like to have a baby of my own sometime. I just hadn't expected it would be this soon or that I would feel so rotten." She looked down at her still-flat stomach. "I wonder how long it will be before I lose my shape."

"Probably won't take too long at all. How far along are you?"

"A little over eight weeks, according to my calculations."

"Good. Then it's not too late to have an abortion."

"A what?" Laura nearly choked on the water she'd put in her mouth.

"You don't want to be pregnant; am I right?"

"Well, no, but—"

"There's a clinic in Philly, and I can make the appointment for you if you'd like." Darla leaned across the table. "No one but you and me would ever have to know, and I'm sure you would feel better once this was all behind you."

Laura shook her head. "Oh, no, I couldn't. . . ."

"If money's a problem, I could float you a loan."

"This is not about money." Laura's voice rose to a high pitch, and her hands trembled so badly, she had to set her glass down to keep from spilling the water.

"If you've got enough money, then what's the problem?"

"The problem's with the abortion, Darla. I could never do anything like that."

"Why not?"

"It—it's against the Amish beliefs to take the life of an unborn baby." The tears Laura had been fighting to keep at bay spilled over and dripped onto her cheeks. "And I would never dream of doing such a thing." She placed her hand against her stomach. "This baby is part of me and Eli, and even though I'm not looking forward to being fat and unattractive, I want to make him happy. I want to do what's right."

Darla's gaze went to the ceiling. "Not only have you changed in appearance, but I can see that you've gotten all self-righteous and sappy now, too."

Laura gripped the handles of her black purse and pushed away from the table. "This was a mistake," she said through clenched teeth. "I should never have agreed to meet you for lunch."

"Where are you going?"

"Home. To tell Eli I'm going to have his baby."

Laura lifted the teakettle from the back of the stove and poured herself a cup of raspberry tea. This afternoon she felt better than she had in many days, and the reason was because she had put Darla in her place and decided to come home and wait for Eli so she could give him the news of her pregnancy.

She thought about little Ben—always playful and curious, so full of love, all cute and cuddly. Laura had never cared much for children until she met Ben. She loved that little boy and was sure she would love her own child even more.

If Laura had listened to Darla, it not only would have ended her baby's life but it would also have ruined things between her and Eli. She was sure she would have been excommunicated from the Amish church, too.

Did Darla really think Laura could take the life of her unborn child and go on as though nothing had ever happened? While Laura might not understand all the biblical implications of the Amish beliefs, she did want to be a good wife to her husband, and she was sure that having Eli's child would only strengthen their marriage. She would just have to work twice as hard at counting calories once the baby came so she could get her figure back as quickly as possible.

The screen door creaked open, pulling Laura out of her musings. Eli hung his straw hat on a wall peg and went to wash up at the sink. "I hope supper's about ready, because I'm hungry as a mule!"

"There's a chicken in the oven, and it should be done soon." Laura turned to him and smiled. "I was wondering if we could talk before we eat, though."

He shrugged. "Sure, what's up?"

She motioned him to sit down, then poured him a cup of tea. "How do you really feel about children, Eli?" she asked, keeping her eyes focused on the cup.

"I've told you before, someday I hope to fill our house with kinner."

"Would November be soon enough to start?"

His forehead wrinkled.

"I'm pregnant, Eli. You're going to be a father soon."

Eli stared at her with a look of disbelief. "A boppli?"

She nodded.

He jumped up, circled the table, pulled Laura to her feet, and kissed her so soundly, it took her breath away. "The Lord has answered my prayers!" He grinned and pulled away, then started for the back door.

"Where are you going?"

"Over to my folks'. I've got to share this good news with them. Have you told your parents yet?"

She shook her head. "I wanted to tell you first."

"Guess you should go over to the neighbors' after supper

and use their phone. I'm sure your folks will be as happy about this news as I know mine will be."

Laura swallowed around the lump in her throat. She hoped they would all be happy.

Laura hung the last towel on the line and wiped her damp forehead with her apron. It was a hot, humid June morning, and she was four months pregnant. She placed one hand on her slightly swollen belly and smiled. A tiny flutter caused her to tremble. "There really is a boppli in there," she murmured.

She bent down to pick up her empty basket, but an approaching buggy caught her attention. It was coming up the driveway at an unusually fast speed. When it stopped in front of the house, Amon jumped out, his face all red and sweaty, his eyes huge as saucers. "Where's Eli's mamm?" he panted.

Laura pointed to Mary Ellen's house. "Is something wrong?"

"It's Martha Rose. Her labor's begun, and she wants her mamm to deliver this baby, just like she did Ben."

Laura followed as Amon ran toward the Yoders'. They found Mary Ellen in the kitchen, kneading bread dough. She looked up and smiled. "Ah, so the smell of bread in the making drew the two of you inside."

Amon shook his head. "Martha Rose's time has come, and she sent me to get you."

Mary Ellen calmly set the dough aside and wiped her hands on a towel. "Laura, would you please finish this bread?"

"I thought I'd go along. Martha Rose is my friend, and—"

"There's no point wasting good bread dough," Mary

Ellen said, as though the matter was settled.

Amon stood by the back door, shifting his weight from one foot to the other. Laura could see he was anxious to get home. "Oh, all right," she finally agreed. "I'll do the bread, but I'm coming over as soon as it's out of the oven."

When Laura arrived at the Zooks' some time later, she found Amon pacing back and forth in the kitchen. Ben was at the table, coloring a picture. "Boppli," he said, grinning up at her.

Laura nodded. "Jah, soon it will come." She glanced over at Amon. "It's not born yet, is it?"

He shook his head. "Don't know what's takin' so long. She was real fast with Ben."

"How come you're not up there with her?"

Amon shrugged. "Mary Ellen said it would be best if I waited down here with the boy."

"Want me to go check?"

"I'd be obliged."

Laura hurried up the stairs. The door to Martha Rose and Amon's room was open a crack, so she walked right in.

Mary Ellen looked up from her position near the foot of the bed. "It's getting close. I can see the head now. Push, Martha Rose. . .push!"

Laura's heart began to pound, and her legs felt like two sticks of rubber. She leaned against the dresser to steady herself.

A few minutes later, the lusty cry of a newborn babe filled the room. Tears stung the backs of Laura's eyes. This was the miracle of birth. She had never imagined it could be so beautiful.

"Daughter, you've got yourself a mighty fine girl," Mary

Ellen announced. "Let me clean her up a bit; then I'll hand her right over."

Martha Rose started to cry, but Laura knew they were tears of joy. She slipped quietly from the room, leaving mother, daughter, and grandmother alone to share the moment of pleasure.

Laura had seen Dr. Wilson several times, and other than a bit of anemia, she was pronounced to be in good condition. The doctor prescribed iron tablets to take with her prenatal vitamins, but she still tired easily, and Eli felt concern.

"I'm gonna ask Mom to come over and help out today," he said as he prepared to leave for work one morning.

Laura shuffled across the kitchen floor toward him. "Please don't. Your mom's got her hands full helping Martha Rose with the new baby. She doesn't need one more thing to worry about."

Eli shrugged. "Suit yourself, but if you need anything, don't think twice about calling on her, you hear?"

She nodded and lifted her face for his good-bye kiss. "Have a good day."

Eli left the house and headed straight for his folks' house. Laura might think she didn't need Mom's help, but he could see how tired she was. Dark circles under her eyes and swollen feet at the end of the day were telltale signs that she needed more rest.

He found Mom in the kitchen, doing the breakfast dishes. "Shouldn't you be heading for work?" she asked.

He nodded. "I wanted to talk with you first."

"Anything wrong?"

He shrugged and ran his fingers through the back of his hair. "Laura's been working too hard, and I think she could use some help."

"Want me to see to it, or are you thinking of hiring a *maad*?"

"I'd rather it be you, instead of a maid, if you can find the time."

She smiled. "I think I can manage."

"Danki." Eli grasped the doorknob, but when another thought popped into his head, he pivoted back around. "Do you think Laura's happy, Mom?"

She lifted an eyebrow in question. "Why wouldn't she be? She's married to you, after all."

He shrugged. "I ain't no prize." His eyebrows drew together. "Do you think she's really content being Amish?"

Mom dried her hands on a towel and moved toward him. "Laura chose to become Amish. You didn't force her, remember?"

"I know, but sometimes she looks so sad."

"Ah, it's just being in a family way. Many women get kind of melancholy during that time. She'll be fine once the boppli comes."

Eli gave her a hug. "You're probably right. I'm most likely worried for nothing."

CHAPTER

26

A few days before Eli and Laura's first anniversary, Eli arrived home from work one afternoon and found Laura lying on the sofa, holding her stomach and writhing in pain.

Alarm rose in his chest as he rushed to her side. "What is it, Laura?"

"I—I think the baby's coming."

He knelt in front of the sofa and grasped her hand. "When did the pains start?"

"Around noon."

"What does my mamm have to say?"

"She doesn't know."

"What?" Eli couldn't believe Laura hadn't called his mother. She'd delivered many babies and would know if it was time.

"I wasn't sure it was labor at first," Laura said tearfully. "But then my water broke, and—"

Eli jumped up and dashed across the room.

"Wh-where are you going?"

"To get Mom!"

❦

Laura leaned her head against the sofa pillow and stiffened

when another contraction came. "Oh, God, please help me!" It was the first real prayer Laura had ever uttered, and now she wasn't even sure God was listening. Why would He care about her when she'd never really cared about Him? She had only been pretending to be a Christian. Was this her punishment for lying to Eli, his family, and even herself?

Moments later, Eli bounded into the room, followed by his mother.

"How far apart are the pains?" Mary Ellen asked as she approached the couch.

"I—I don't know for sure. About two or three minutes, I think," Laura answered tearfully. "Oh, it hurts so much! I think Eli should take me to the hospital."

Mary Ellen did a quick examination, and when she was done, she shook her head. "You waited too long for that. The boppli's coming now."

Eli started for the kitchen. "I'll get some towels and warm water."

"Don't leave me, Eli!"

"Calm down," Mary Ellen chided. "He'll be right back. In the meantime, I want you to do exactly as I say."

Laura's first reaction was to fight the pain, but Mary Ellen was a good coach, and soon Laura began to cooperate. Eli stood nearby, holding her hand and offering soothing words.

"One final push and the boppli should be here," Mary Ellen finally said.

Laura did as she was instructed, and moments later, the babe's first cry filled the room.

"It's a boy! You have a son," Mary Ellen announced.

Laura lifted her head from the pillow. "Let me see him.

I want to make sure he has ten fingers and ten toes."

"In a minute. Let Eli clean him up a bit," Mary Ellen instructed. "I need to finish up with you."

"Mom, could you come over here?" Eli called from across the room. His voice sounded strained, and a wave of fear washed over Laura like a drenching rain.

"What is it? Is something wrong with our son?"

"Just a minute, Laura. I want Mom to take a look at him first."

Laura rolled onto her side, trying to see what was happening. Eli and Mary Ellen were bent over the small bundle wrapped in a towel, lying on top of an end table. She heard whispering but couldn't make out their words.

"What's going on? Tell me now, or I'll come see for myself."

Eli rushed to her side. "Stay put. You might start bleeding real heavy if you get up too soon."

Laura drew in a deep breath and grabbed hold of Eli's shirtsleeve. "What's wrong?"

"The child's breathing seems a bit irregular," Mary Ellen said. "I think we should take him to the hospital."

"I'd like Laura to be seen, too," Eli said with a nod.

※

Laura had only gotten a glimpse of her son before they rushed him into the hospital nursery, but what she'd seen concerned her greatly. The baby wasn't breathing right. He looked kind of funny, too. He had a good crop of auburn hair, just like Laura's, but there was something else. . .something she couldn't put her finger on.

"Relax and try to rest," Eli said as he took a seat in the

chair next to Laura's hospital bed. "The doctor's looking at little David right now, and—"

"David?" Laura repeated. "You named our son without asking me?"

Eli's face flamed. "I. . .uh. . .thought we'd talked about naming the baby David if it was a boy."

She nodded slowly. "I guess we did. I just thought—"

Laura's words were interrupted when Dr. Wilson and another man entered the room. The second man's expression told her all she needed to know. Something was wrong.

"This is Dr. Hayes," Dr. Wilson said. "He's a pediatrician and has just finished examining your son."

Eli jumped to his feet. "Tell us. . .is there something wrong with David?"

Dr. Hayes put a hand on Eli's shoulder. "Please sit down."

Eli complied, but Laura could see the strain on his face. She felt equally uncomfortable.

"We still need to run a few more tests," the doctor said, "but we're fairly sure your boy has Down syndrome."

"Are you saying he–he's going to be handicapped?" Eli's voice squeaked, and his face blanched.

"Quite possibly. The baby has an accumulation of fluid in his lungs. It's fairly common with Down syndrome. We can clear it out, but he will no doubt be prone to bronchial infections— especially while he's young."

Laura was too stunned to say anything at first. This had to be a dream—a terrible nightmare. This couldn't be happening to her and Eli.

"Once we get the lungs cleared and he's breathing well on his own, you should be able to take the baby home," Dr. Hayes continued.

"Take him home?" Laura pulled herself to a sitting position. "Did you say, 'Take him home'?"

The doctor nodded, and Eli reached for her hand. "Laura, we can get through this. We—"

She jerked her hand away. "We've just been told that our son probably has Down syndrome, and you're saying, 'We can get through this'?" She shook her head slowly. "The baby isn't normal, Eli. He doesn't belong with us."

Eli studied Laura a few seconds. "Who does he belong with?"

"If he's handicapped, he belongs in a home for handicapped children."

Eli looked at her as if she had lost her mind. "That's not our way, Laura. We take care of our own—even the handicapped children."

"But I don't know how."

"You'll learn, same as other parents with handicapped children have done."

Laura turned her head toward the wall. "Leave me alone, Eli. I need to sleep."

He bent to kiss her forehead. "I'll be back tomorrow, and we can talk about this then."

As soon as Eli left the room, Laura reached for the phone by the side of her bed. It was time to call Mom and Dad.

❧

"Meade Residence, this is Wesley speaking."

"Dad, it's me."

"Laura, it's good to hear your voice. Your mother and I were just talking about you. We were wondering how you're doing and—"

"Is Mom there?"

"Yes, she's out in the kitchen."

"You'd better put her on the phone. I have something important to tell both of you." Laura's voice trembled, and he felt immediate concern.

"Irene, pick up the phone in there," Wesley hollered. "Laura's on the line."

A few seconds later, his wife came on the phone. "Hello, Laura. How are you, dear?"

Laura sniffed and sucked in her breath, like she was choking on a sob. "N-not so good, Mom. The baby's here, and—"

"You've had the baby? Oh, that's wonderful. What did you have?"

Wesley shifted the phone to his other ear while he waited for Laura's response. If she was only calling to tell them that the baby had been born, would she sound so upset?

"The doctors have some more tests to run, but they think David—our son—might have Down syndrome."

Wesley winced as he heard his wife's sharp intake of breath. "Laura, could you repeat that?"

"The baby was born this evening, and his breathing is irregular. He's got auburn hair like mine, but he doesn't look right, Dad." There was a pause. "The doctors told us awhile ago that they suspect Down syndrome, and Eli expects—" Laura's voice broke on a sob.

"Eli expects what, Laura?" Wesley prompted.

"He expects me to take care of the baby, even if he is handicapped."

"What? He's got to be kidding!" Irene's voice came through the line so shrill that Wesley had to hold the phone away from his ear. "Laura, if the baby is handicapped, he should be put in a home."

"That's what I said, too, but Eli said it's not the thing to do, and—" Laura coughed and sniffed. "I know nothing about caring for a disabled child, Mom. I'm not even sure I can take care of a *normal* baby."

Wesley's forehead beaded with sweat, and he reached up to wipe it away. "Do you want us to come there, Laura? I can see about getting some plane tickets right away."

"Oh, but Wesley, I have a hectic schedule with that benefit dinner I'm planning for the hospital guild this week. It would be hard for me to find someone to fill in for me at this late date."

He gritted his teeth. How could Irene think of a benefit dinner at a time like this? Didn't she realize how much Laura needed them right now? "If your mother's too busy, I'll fly out there myself."

Laura drew in a shuddering sigh. "Could you wait a few days—until we get the test results back on David, and Eli and I have had time to figure out what we're going to do?"

"Sure, I can do that. Maybe by then your mother will be free to come with me."

No comment from Irene. What was that woman thinking, anyhow?

"I'd better go," Laura said. "A nurse just came into the room to check my vitals."

"Okay, honey. Call us as soon as you have some news."

"I will. Bye."

As soon as Wesley hung up the phone, he headed straight for the kitchen. If nothing else got resolved tonight, he was going to give his wife a piece of his mind!

Chapter 27

The baby was brought to Laura the following day, and she could barely look at him. The nurse held David up and showed her that he had ten fingers and ten toes.

Fingers that are short and stubby, Laura thought bitterly. She noticed the infant's forehead. It sloped slightly, and his skull looked broad and short. The distinguishing marks of Down syndrome were definitely there. The doctor had been in earlier and explained that David might also be likely to have heart problems, hearing loss, or poor vision. He'd said that Down syndrome was a genetic disorder, resulting from extra chromosomes.

How could this have happened? Laura screamed inwardly as tears rolled down her cheeks. She looked away and told the nurse to take the baby back to the nursery.

Laura was still crying when Eli entered the room, carrying a potted plant. "I got you an African violet from the Beachys' greenhouse, and—" He dropped it onto the nightstand and moved quickly to the bed. "What's wrong? Is it something about David?"

She hiccupped loudly and pulled herself to a sitting position. "I just saw the baby and was told earlier that he does have Down syndrome."

Eli sank to the chair beside her bed and groaned. "I was afraid of that."

"I called my parents last night."

"What'd they say?"

"Mom said David should be put in a home."

"No."

"I think she's right, Eli. A disabled child would take a lot of work."

He nodded. "Jah, I know, but David has just as much right to live a normal life as any other child."

"But he's not normal, and I—I don't know how to care for him."

"Mom will be there to help whenever you need her."

Laura shook her head as another set of tears streamed down her cheeks. "I can't do this, Eli. Please don't ask it of me."

Eli rubbed his thumb gently back and forth across her knuckles. "God gave us David so He must have had a reason for choosing us as his parents. Now we'll love him. . .cherish him. . .protect him. . ."

Laura's eyes widened. "God was cruel to allow such a thing!"

"God knows what's best for each of us. The book of Romans tells us that all things work together for good to them that love God," Eli said softly. He pointed to the African violet. "Just like this plant needs to be nourished, so does our son. God will give us the strength and love we need to raise him."

Laura closed her eyes and turned her head away from Eli. Was she somehow responsible for this horrible nightmare?

Laura went home from the hospital the following morning, but the baby would have to stay a few more days. The doctors said he might be ready to take home next week, so this gave Laura a short reprieve. She needed some time to decide what to do about the problem.

Eli had taken time off from work to hire a driver and pick her up at the hospital, but soon after the driver dropped them off at home and Eli had seen that Laura was settled in, he left for work. It was better that way. She wanted to be alone, and if he'd stayed home with her, they would have argued about Eli expecting her to care for David.

Laura poured herself a cup of chamomile tea and curled up on the living-room couch. Reliving her dialogue with Eli at the hospital, her heart sank to the pit of her stomach.

She closed her eyes and tried to shut out the voice in her head. *God is punishing me for pretending to be religious. I tricked Eli into marrying me by making him think I had accepted his beliefs and his way of life.*

Laura's eyes snapped open when she heard a distant clap of thunder. She stared out the window. Dark clouds hung in the sky like a shroud encircling the entire house.

"The sky looks like I feel," she moaned. "My life is such a mess. I wish I had never met Eli Yoder. We should never have gotten married. I should not have gotten pregnant."

The realization of what she'd said hit Laura with such intensity, she thought she had been struck with a lightning bolt. "Oh, no! Dear Lord, no!" she sobbed. "You're punishing me for not wanting to be pregnant, not just for lying to Eli about my religious convictions." She clenched her fists so tightly that her nails bit into her skin as she grappled with the reality of the moment. "That's why David was born with Down syndrome—because God is punishing me." Laura fell back on the sofa pillows and sobbed until no more tears would come.

When the wave of grief finally subsided, she sat up, dried her eyes, and stood. She knew what she had to do. She scrawled a quick note to Eli, placed it on the kitchen table, and went upstairs.

❦

"Laura, I'm home!" Eli set his lunch pail on the cupboard. No sign of Laura in the kitchen. He moved through the rest of the downstairs, calling her name. She wasn't in any of the rooms.

She must be upstairs resting. She's been through a lot this week, so I'd better let her sleep awhile.

Eli went back to the kitchen. He would fix himself a little snack, then go outside and get started on the evening chores.

There was an apple-crumb pie in the refrigerator, which Mom had brought over last night. He grabbed a piece, along with a jug of milk, and placed them on the table. Not until he took a seat did Eli see the note lying on the table. He picked it up and read it:

Dear Eli,

> *It pains me to write this letter, even more than the physical pain I endured in childbirth. I know you don't understand this, but I can't take care of David. I just don't have what it takes to raise a handicapped child.*

*I have a confession to make. I'm not who you think
I am—I'm not really a believer. I only pretended to be one
so you would marry me. I tried to be a good wife, but I
could never seem to measure up.*

*Pauline was right when she said she would be better
for you. It would have saved us all a lot of heartache if
you had married her instead of me.*

*I hope you'll forgive me for leaving you in the lurch,
but I've decided to go home to my parents. I know I'm
not deserving of your forgiveness, but please know that
I do love you. I've always loved you.*

Always,
Laura

The words on the paper blurred. Eli couldn't react.
Couldn't think. Could hardly breathe. He let the note slip
from his fingers as a deep sense of loss gnawed at his insides.
*Laura wouldn't pack up and leave without speaking with me first,
without trying to work things out.*

When the reality of the situation fully registered, he
propped his elbows on the table and cradled his head in his
hands. "Oh, Laura. . .I just didn't know."

During her first few days at home, Laura slept late, picked
at her food, and tried to get used to all the modern conveniences she had previously taken for granted. Nothing
seemed to satisfy her. She was exhausted, crabby, and more
depressed than she'd ever been in her life. Things had
changed at home. Maybe it was she who had changed, for
she now felt like a misfit.

Today was her and Eli's first anniversary, and she was miserable. As she sat at the kitchen table, toying with the scrambled eggs on her plate, Laura thought about their wedding day. She could still hear Bishop Wagler quoting scriptures about marriage. She could almost feel the warmth of Eli's hand as they repeated their vows. She had promised to be loyal to Eli, to care for him and live with him until death separated them, but she'd failed miserably. A painful lump lodged in her throat. She deserved whatever punishment God handed down.

Mom entered the kitchen just then, interrupting Laura's thoughts. "This came in the mail," she said, handing Laura a letter. "It's postmarked 'Lancaster, Pennsylvania.' "

Laura's fingers shook as she tore open the envelope, then began to read:

> *Dear Laura,*
>
> *I knew you were upset about the baby, and I'm trying to understand. What I don't get is how you could up and leave like that without even talking to me first. Don't you realize how much David and I need you? Don't you know how much I miss you?*
>
> *David's breathing better now, and the doctors let him come home. Mom watches him when I'm at work, but it's you he's needing. Won't you please come home?*
>
> *Love,*
> *Eli*

Tears welled in Laura's eyes and spilled onto the front of her blouse. Eli didn't seem angry. In fact, he wanted her to come home. He hadn't even mentioned her lies. Had he forgiven her? Did Eli really love her in spite of all she'd done?

Maybe he doesn't believe me. He might think I made every-thing up because I couldn't deal with our baby being born handi-capped. He might want me back just so I can care for his child.

Laura swallowed hard and nearly choked on a sob. No matter how much she loved Eli and wanted to be with him, she knew she couldn't go back. She was a disgrace to the Amish faith, and she had ruined Eli's life.

The days dragged by, and Laura thought she would die of boredom. The weather was dreary and cold, and even though Mom tried to encourage her to get out and social-ize, Laura stayed to herself most of the time. She thought modern conveniences would bring happiness, but they hadn't. Instead of watching TV or playing computer games, she preferred to sit in front of the fire and knit or read a book. There was something about the Amish way of life she couldn't quite explain. At times when she'd been living with Eli, she had felt a sense of peace and tranquillity that had calmed her soul like nothing else she'd ever known.

It was strange, but Laura missed the familiar farm smells—fresh-mown hay stacked neatly in the barn, the horses' warm breath on a cold winter day, and even the wig-gly, grunting piglets always squealing for more food. Laura was reminded of something Eli had once said, for much to her surprise, she even missed the predictable wake-up call of the rooster each morning. She missed her plain clothes, too, and felt out of place wearing blue jeans again.

By the middle of December, Laura felt stronger physi-cally, but emotionally she was still a mess. Would she ever be able to pick up the pieces of her life and go on without

Eli? Could she forgive herself for bringing such misery into their lives?

If God was punishing her, why did Eli have to suffer, as well? He was a kind, Christian man who deserved a normal, healthy baby. He had done nothing to warrant this kind of pain. How could the Amish refer to God as "a God of love"?

Laura sat on the sofa in the living room, staring at the Christmas tree, yet not really seeing it. *What's Eli doing right now? Does he miss me, like he said in his letter? No doubt he and the baby will be spending the holidays with his parents. If I could turn back the hands of time and make everything right between me and Eli again, I'd even learn how to fix the pickled beets he likes so well.*

Laura glanced at her parents. They sat in their respective recliners: Dad reading the newspaper, Mom working on Christmas cards. They didn't seem to have a care in the world. Didn't they know how much she was hurting? Did they think this was just another typical Christmas?

A sudden knock at the front door drew Laura out of her musings. She looked over at the mantel clock. Who would be coming by at nine o'clock at night, and who would knock rather than use the doorbell?

Dad stood. "I'll get it."

Laura strained to hear the voices coming from the hall. She couldn't be sure who Dad was talking to, but it sounded like a woman. *Probably one of Mom's lady friends or someone from Dad's office.* She leaned against the sofa pillows and tried not to eavesdrop.

"Laura, someone is here to see you," Dad said as he entered the living room with a woman.

Laura's mouth dropped open, and she leaped from the

couch. "Martha Rose! What are you doing here? Is Eli with you?" She stared at the doorway, half expecting, half hoping Eli might step into the room.

Martha Rose shook her head. "I've come alone. Only Amon knows I'm here. I left him plenty of my breast milk, and he agreed to care for baby Amanda and little Ben so I could make the trip to see you." She smiled. "The bus ride took a little over twenty-seven hours, and Amon knows I won't be gone long. Besides, if he runs into any kind of problem with the kinner, he can always call on Mom."

Laura's heart began to pound as she tried to digest all that Martha Rose had said. "What's wrong? Has someone been hurt? Is it Eli?"

Martha Rose held up her hand. "Eli's fine. . .at least physically." She glanced at Laura's folks, then back at Laura. "Could we talk in private?"

Laura looked at Mom and Dad. They both shrugged and turned to go. "We'll be upstairs if you need us," Dad said.

"Thanks," Laura mumbled. Her brain felt like it was in a fog. Why had Martha Rose traveled all the way from Pennsylvania to Minnesota if there was nothing wrong at home? Home—was that how she thought of the house she and Eli had shared? Wasn't this her home—here with Mom and Dad? She studied her surroundings. Everything looked the same, yet it felt so different. It was like trying to fit into a pair of shoes that were too small.

When Wesley and Irene entered their room, Irene took a seat on the end of their bed and released a sigh. "I wonder what Martha Rose wants. I hope she's not here to try and talk Laura into going back to Pennsylvania with her."

"If she is, it's none of our business." Wesley leaned on the dresser and stared at her.

"You don't have to sound so snippy. I only want what's best for our daughter."

His defenses rose, and he marched across the room. "And you think I don't?"

"Calm down, Wesley. It's not like you to shout like that."

"I'm not shouting. I'm speaking my mind, which is something I should have done a long time ago."

Irene's chin trembled, and tears shimmered in her green eyes. The old Wesley would have succumbed to that pathetic look, but not anymore. He was tired of saying things just because they were what she wanted to hear. It was high time he stood up to her and said what was on his mind.

He took a seat on the bed beside her. "I love you, Irene, and I have ever since we met in college."

"I–I love you, too."

"But just because I love you doesn't mean I always agree with you or will do things your way."

"What are you trying to say?"

He tucked his thumb under her chin and tipped her head back so she was looking into his eyes. "I'm saying that I don't agree with you where Laura's concerned."

"What do you mean?"

"I think Laura's place is with her husband and baby."

Her eyes widened. "You can't mean that, Wesley. Laura's baby is handicapped, and he will need special care."

He nodded. "I think Laura is capable of giving David whatever help he needs."

"But she doesn't want to care for him; she's said so many times."

"That's because she thinks she can't, but I believe she can."

"What makes you so sure?"

He smiled and reached for her hand. "She's her mother's daughter—full of courage, determination, and strength she doesn't even know she has."

"You–you think that about me?"

"Sure do."

She leaned her head against his shoulder. "That's the nicest thing you've ever said to me, dear."

He kissed the top of her head. "Laura's place is with Eli, just as much as your place is with me."

※

"Laura, are you okay?" Martha Rose asked, placing a hand on Laura's trembling shoulder.

"I. . .uh. . .sure didn't expect to see you tonight." Laura motioned to the sofa. "Please, have a seat. Let me take your coat. Would you like some tea or hot chocolate?" She was rambling but couldn't seem to help herself.

Martha Rose took off her coat and draped it over the back of the couch. Then she sat down. "Maybe something to drink, but after we talk."

Laura sat beside her. "What's so important that you would come all this way by bus?"

"My brother has been so upset since you left. He told me he wrote a letter asking you to come home."

"Did he also tell you that I've been lying to him all these months?"

"About being a believer?"

Laura nodded.

"Jah, he mentioned that, too."

Laura swallowed hard. "Then you understand why I can't go back."

Martha Rose reached inside her coat pocket and pulled out a small Bible. She opened it and began reading. " 'If any brother hath a wife that believeth not, and she be pleased to dwell with him, let him not put her away.' " She smiled. "That's found in the book of 1 Corinthians."

Laura's eyes widened. "Are you saying Eli could choose to stay with me even though I'm not a believer?"

Martha Rose nodded. "It doesn't have to be that way, though."

"What do you mean?"

"You could give your heart to Jesus, Laura. He wants you to accept His death as forgiveness for your sins. 1 John 3:23 says, 'And this is his commandment, that we should believe on the name of his Son Jesus Christ, and love one another, as he gave us commandment.' "

As Martha Rose continued to read from the Bible, Laura was finally convinced of the truth in God's Word, and soon tears began streaming down her face. "Oh, Martha Rose, you have no idea how much I've sinned. I did a terrible thing, and now God is punishing me. How can I ever believe He would forgive me?"

"Romans 3:23 says, 'For all have sinned, and come short of the glory of God.' If we ask, God will forgive any sin." Martha Rose clasped Laura's hand.

"When I first found out I was pregnant, I—I didn't even want our baby."

"Why, Laura?"

"I was afraid of having a child. I know it's a vain thing to say, but I wanted to keep my trim figure." She gulped. "Even more than that, I wanted Eli all to myself." Laura closed her eyes and drew in a shuddering breath. "God's punishment for my selfish thoughts was David. I believe that's why He gave us a disabled child."

Martha Rose shook her head. "God doesn't work that way. He loves you, just as He loves the special child He gave you and Eli. God wants you to ask His forgiveness and surrender your life to Him."

"I—I want to change, but I don't know if I have enough faith to believe."

"All you need to do is take that first little step by accepting Jesus as your Savior. Then, through studying His Word and praying, your faith will be strengthened. Would you like to pray right now and ask Jesus into your heart?"

Laura nodded and bowed her head. After surrendering her will to God and asking His forgiveness for her sins, the peace she so desperately sought flooded her soul. When she went to bed that night, a strange warmth crept through her body. She felt God's presence for the very first time and knew without reservation that she was a new person because of His Son, Jesus. Martha Rose slept in the guest room across the hall, and Laura thanked God that her special friend had come.

Laura clung tightly to Martha Rose's hand as they stepped down from the bus. She was almost home, and even though she still had some doubts about her ability to care for a disabled child, it was comforting to know she would have God to help her. She scanned the faces of those waiting to pick up passengers. There was no sign of Eli or Amon.

"Are you sure they knew we were coming?" Laura asked Martha Rose, feeling a sense of panic rise in her throat.

"I talked to Eli at the furniture shop where he works, so I'm certain they'll be here." Martha Rose led Laura toward the bus station. "Let's get out of the cold and wait for them inside."

The women had no more than taken seats when Amon walked up. He was alone.

Laura felt like someone had punched her in the stomach. "Where's Eli? Didn't he come with you?" *Maybe he's changed his mind about wanting me back.*

"Eli's at the hospital," Amon said, placing a hand on Laura's shoulder.

Her stomach churned like whipping cream about to become butter. "The hospital? Is it the baby? Is David worse?"

Amon shook his head. "There was an accident today."

"An accident? What happened?" Martha Rose's face registered the concern Laura felt.

"Eli cut his hand at work, on one of those fancy electric saws."

Laura covered her mouth with her hand. "How bad?"

"He lost part of one finger, but the doctor said he should still be able to use the hand once everything heals."

"Oh, my dear, sweet Eli," Laura cried. "Hasn't he already been through enough? If only I hadn't run away. If only—"

Martha Rose held up her hand. "No, Laura. You can't go blaming yourself. Just as David's birth defect is no one's fault, this was an accident, plain and simple. In time, Eli will heal and be back at work."

Laura looked down at her clasped hands, feeling like a small child learning to walk. "Guess my faith is still pretty weak. I'd better pray about it, huh?"

Martha Rose nodded. "Prayer is always the best way."

Eli lay in his hospital bed, fighting the weight of heavy eyelids. Against his wishes, the nurse had given him a shot for pain, and now he felt so sleepy he could hardly stay awake. Amon had left for the bus station over an hour ago. What was taking so long? Maybe Laura had changed her mind and stayed in Minneapolis. Maybe. . .

"Eli? Eli?" A gentle voice filled his senses. Was he dreaming, or was it just wishful thinking?

He felt someone touch his arm, and his eyes snapped open. "Laura?"

She nodded, her eyes full of tears. "Oh, Eli, I'm so sorry!"

She rested her head on his chest and sobbed. "Can you ever forgive me for running away. . .for lying about my relationship with God. . .for wanting you to change when it was really me who needed changing?"

Eli stroked the top of her head, noting with joy that she was wearing her covering. "I've already forgiven you, but I must ask your forgiveness, too."

She raised her head and stared into his eyes. "For what? You've done nothing."

He swallowed against the lump in his throat. "For not being understanding enough." He touched her chin with his uninjured hand. "I think I expected too much, and sometimes I spoke harshly instead of trying to see things from your point of view. If I'd been a better husband, maybe you would have found your way to God sooner."

Laura shook her head. "It wasn't your fault. I was stubborn and selfish. That's what kept me from turning to God. I believed I could do everything in my own strength. I thought I could have whatever I wanted, and it didn't matter who I hurt in the process." She sniffed deeply. "When I finally found forgiveness for my sins, I became a new creature." She leaned closer, so their lips were almost touching. "I love you, Eli."

He smiled. "And I love you. Christmas is only a few days away, and I'm convinced that it's going to be our best Christmas ever." He sealed his promise with a tender kiss.

EPILOGUE

Laura stood at the kitchen counter, about to open the jar of pickled beets she would serve with the stew they'd be having for supper. She gazed out the window at Eli and their two-year-old son as they romped in the snow. David was doing so well, and she thanked God for him every day. He was such an agreeable, loving child. How could she have ever not wanted him? Eli had been right all along. David was special—a wonderful gift from God.

A soft *meow* drew Laura's attention from the window. She turned toward the sound, and her lips formed a smile. Foosie ran across the kitchen floor, and their nine-month-old daughter, Barbara, followed in fast pursuit.

Laura chuckled at the sight of her perfect little girl, up on her knees, chasing that poor cat and pulling on its tail. No wonder Foosie preferred to be outdoors these days.

"Life couldn't be any better," Laura whispered. Not only had she made peace with God, but her parents had also moved to Lancaster County, where her father practiced law at a small firm during the week and tinkered in his garden every weekend. Laura had finally come to realize that Eli's folks really did care about her, and she'd even made things right with Pauline, who had written her a letter not long ago, apologizing for her bad behavior.

As Laura poured the beets from the glass canning jar into a bowl, she looked up. "Lord, I thank You for the two wunderbaar children and the husband You gave to me, and I especially thank You for turning a fancy, spoiled English woman like me into a plain Amish wife who loves You so much. You have truly blessed me, and I ask for Your blessings on each one in our extended families."

Recipe for Laura's Pickled Beets

Ingredients:
- 3 quarts small beets
- 3 cups cider vinegar
- 2 tablespoons salt
- 4 cups sugar
- 1½ cups water
- 2 cinnamon sticks

Cook the beets in a large pan until tender and put into clean, hot canning jars. Combine the rest of the ingredients in a separate pan and boil until it becomes a syrup. Pour the boiling syrup over the beets, then seal. Cold pack them for 10 to 15 minutes.

THE HOPE CHEST

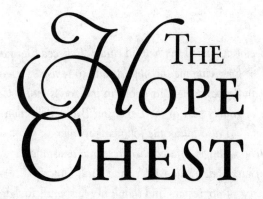

Brides of Lancaster County

4

To my daughter, Lorine, the recipient of my special hope chest.

With special thanks to my helpful editor, Rebecca Germany,
for giving me the opportunity to revise
and expand the four books in this series that
were originally part of the Lancaster Brides collection.
I also thank the following women
who willingly offered their research assistance:
Betty Yoder, Sue Miller, and Ruth Stoltzfus.
As always, I appreciate and thank my husband, Richard,
for his continued help and encouragement.
Most of all, I thank my heavenly Father,
who gives me the inspiration, strength, wisdom, and desire to write.

For thou art my hope, O Lord God:
thou art my trust from my youth.
Psalm 71:5

CHAPTER 1

Rat-a-tat-tat! Rat-a-tat-tat! Rachel Beachy halted under a giant birch tree. She would have recognized that distinctive sound anywhere. Shielding her eyes from the glare of the late afternoon sun, she tipped her head back and gazed at the branches overhead. Sure enough, there it was—a downy woodpecker. Its tiny claws were anchored firmly to the trunk of the tree, while its petite little head bobbed rhythmically back and forth as it pecked away at the old birch tree.

Hoping for a better look, Rachel decided to climb the tree. As she threw her leg over the first branch, she was glad she was alone and that no one could see how ridiculous she must look. She'd never really minded wearing long dresses. After all, that was what Amish girls and women were expected to wear. At times like this, however, Rachel wished she could wear a pair of men's trousers. It certainly would make climbing trees a mite easier.

Rachel winced as a piece of bark scratched her knee, leaving a stain of blood that quickly seeped through her dress. It was worth the pain if it would allow her to get a better look at that cute little wood-tapper, though.

Pik-pik-pik! The woodpecker's unusual call resonated against the trunk. *Rat-a-tat-tat!* The bird returned to the pecking process.

"Such a busy little bird," Rachel said quietly as it came into view, two branches above where she straddled the good-sized limb. She and her older sister, Anna, had gone to the river to get cooled off that afternoon, and Rachel had been the first one to head for home. Now she wished she had left the water sooner so she could spend more time studying this beautiful creature God had created and knew everything about. She was reminded of Psalm 50:11: *"I know all the fowls of the mountains: and the wild beasts of the field are mine."*

Rachel lifted one leg in preparation to move up another limb, but a deep male voice drew her attention to the ground. She halted.

"Hey, Anna, slow down once, would you, please?"

Rachel dropped down so her stomach lay flat against the branch. When she lifted her head a bit and peeked through the leaves, she saw her older sister sprinting across the open field. Silas Swartley was following her, his long strides making Rachel think of a jackrabbit running at full speed.

With his hands cupped around his mouth, Silas yelled, "Anna! Wait up!"

Rachel knew she'd be in trouble if Anna caught her spying, so she held as still as possible and prayed that the couple would move quickly on past.

Anna stopped near the foot of the tree, and Silas joined her there. "I—I really need to talk to you, Anna," he panted.

Rachel's heart slammed into her chest. Why couldn't it

be her Silas wanted to talk to? If only he could see that she would be better for him than Anna. *If Silas knew how much I care for him, would it make a difference?*

Rachel was keenly aware that Silas only had eyes for her big sister, but that didn't make her love him any less. As far as she could tell, Silas had been in love with Anna ever since they were children, and Rachel had loved Silas nearly that long, as well. He was all she wanted in a man—good-looking, kindhearted, interested in birds—and he enjoyed fishing.

She was sure he had many other attributes that made him appealing, but with Silas standing right below the tree where she lay hidden, she could barely breathe, much less think of all the reasons she loved him so much.

Rachel looked down at her sister, arms folded across her chest, body held rigid as she stood like a statue facing Silas. It was as if Anna couldn't be bothered with talking to him, which made no sense since she and Silas had been friends a long time. Silas had been coming over to their place to visit ever since Rachel could remember.

Silas reached for Anna's hand, but she pulled it away. "Just who do you think you are, Silas Swartley?"

"I'm your boyfriend, that's who. Have been since we were *kinner*, and you know it."

"I don't know any such thing, so don't try to put words in my mouth."

Rachel stifled a giggle. *That sister of mine. . .she's sure got herself a temper.*

Silas tipped his head to one side. "I don't get it. One minute you're sweet as cherry pie, and the next minute you act as if you don't care for me at all."

Rachel knew full well that Silas spoke the truth. She'd seen with her own eyes the way her sister led that poor fellow on. Why, just a few weeks ago, Anna had let Silas bring her home from a singing. She had to feel some kind of interest in him if she was willing to accept a ride in his courting buggy.

Rachel held her breath as Silas reached out to touch the ties on Anna's stiff, white *kapp*. Anna jerked her head quickly, causing one of the ribbons to tear loose. "Now look what you've done." She pulled on the edge of her covering, but in so doing, the pins holding her hair in a bun must have been knocked loose, for a cascade of tawny yellow curls fell loosely down her back.

Rachel wished she could see the look on Silas's face. She could only imagine what he must be thinking as he reached up to scratch the back of his head and groaned. "Why, you're prettier than a field full of fireflies at sunset, Anna."

Rachel gulped. What she wouldn't give to hear Silas talk to her that way. Maybe if she kept hoping. Maybe if. . .

Rachel thought about a verse in Psalm 71 that she had read that morning: *"But I will hope continually, and will yet praise thee more and more."*

She would gladly offer praises to God if she could win Silas's heart. Truth be told, the verse of scripture she should call her own might best be found in the book of Job, chapter 7: *"My days are swifter than a weaver's shuttle, and are spent without hope."*

Rachel figured she would most likely end up an old maid, while Anna would have a loving husband and a whole house full of children.

"Sometimes I wish I could wear my hair down all the

time," Anna said, pulling Rachel out of her musings. "Or maybe get it cut really short."

"Why would you want to do that?"

"Because I might look prettier if I. . .oh, never mind."

"Are you questioning the Amish ways? Now, what would your *mamm* and *daed* have to say about that?" Before Anna could answer, Silas added, "You've always been a bit of a rebel, haven't you?"

Anna leaned against the trunk of the tree, and Rachel dug her fingernails into the bark of the branch she was lying on. *What will my sister say to that comment?*

"My mom and dad would be upset if they knew I had mentioned cutting my hair short." Anna sighed. "Many things about the Amish ways are good, but sometimes I wonder if I might not be happier if I were English."

"You can't be serious."

"*Jah,* I am."

Rat-a-tat-tat! Rat-a-tat-tat! Pik! Pik!

"Say, that sounds like a woodpecker to me." Silas leaned his head back and looked into the tree where Rachel lay partially hidden.

She froze in place. If Silas should spot her instead of the bird, she'd be caught like a pig trying to get into Mom's flower garden. Anna would sure as anything think she had climbed the tree just to spy on her and Silas.

"Forget about the dumb old woodpecker," Anna said in an impatient tone.

Silas continued to peer into the branches. "Hmm. . .I know I heard him, but I don't see that old rascal anywhere."

"You and your dopey bird-watching. One would think

you'd never seen a woodpecker before." Anna grunted. "Rachel's fascinated with birds, too. I believe she'd rather watch them eat from one of the feeders in our yard than eat a meal herself."

Silas looked away from the tree and turned to face Anna again. "Birds are interesting little creatures, but you're right. . . I can do my bird-watching some other time." He touched her shoulder. "Now what was it you were saying about wanting to be English?"

"I didn't exactly say I *wanted* to be English; just that I sometimes wonder if I might not be happier being English." Anna pointed to the skirt of her long, blue dress. "Take these clothes, for example. It might be nice to enjoy the freedom of not having to wear a dress all the time."

Rachel sucked in her breath. Where was this conversation headed? If Anna wasn't careful, she might say something stupid and maybe get in trouble for shooting off her big mouth. Especially if the bishop or one of their deacons got wind of it. Truth was, Anna had been acting a bit strange of late—disappearing for hours at a time and saying some mighty peculiar things. Her conversation with Silas only confirmed what Rachel suspected. Anna felt some dissatisfaction with the Amish way of life. It wasn't like Anna climbed trees and saw her dress as a hazard. No, Rachel's prim and proper sister would never climb a tree.

Rachel knew that a lot more than wearing long dresses bothered Anna about being Amish. Not long ago, Anna had mentioned to Rachel that she wished she hadn't been so hasty to join the church and was worried that she might have made a mistake. When Rachel questioned her sister about it, Anna had quickly changed the subject. It made no sense, because Anna had never suggested such a thing before or immediately after joining the church. Something had happened between last fall and this summer to get Anna thinking this way.

"What would you suggest women wear, then—trousers?" Silas asked, jerking Rachel's attention back to the conversation below.

"Maybe."

"Are you saying that you'd wear men's trousers if you could?"

"I—I might. I could do some of my chores a bit easier if I didn't have a long skirt getting in the way." Anna paused. "If I weren't Amish, I could do many things that I can't now."

Oh, great! Now you've gone and done it. Why can't you just be nice to Silas instead of trying to goad him into an argument? Rachel shifted her legs, trying to get a bit more comfortable. *Can't you see how much the fellow cares for you, Anna? If anyone should be wanting to wear men's trousers, it's me—Rachel, the tomboy. At least I've got the good sense to not announce such a thing. And suggesting that you might want to try out the English world is just plain stupid, especially since you already had that opportunity during your* rumschpringe.

"I, for one, am mighty glad you're not English," Silas said, his voice rising an octave. "And you shouldn't even be thinking such thoughts now that you've joined the church, much less speaking them. Why, if your daed or any of our church leaders heard you say anything like that, you'd have some explaining to do, that's for certain sure."

Anna moved away from the tree. "Let's not talk about

this anymore. I need to get home. Rachel was way ahead of me when I left the river, so she's probably already there and has done half my chores by now. Mom let me have the afternoon off from working in the greenhouse, so I don't want her getting after me for shirking my household duties."

"Jah, well, I guess I need to be heading home, too." Silas made no move to leave, however, and Rachel had to wonder what was up.

Anna rolled and pinned her hair into place; then she put her head covering back on. Just as she started to walk away, Silas stepped in front of her. "I still haven't said everything I wanted to say."

"What'd you want to say?"

He shuffled his feet a few times, gave his suspenders a good yank, then cleared his throat loudly. "I. . .uh. . .was wondering if I might come see you one evening next week."

Rachel's heart missed a beat. At least it felt as if it had. Silas had been sweet on Anna a good many years, so she should have known the day would come when he would ask to start courting her. Only trouble was if Silas started courting Anna, then Rachel's chances would be nil, and she couldn't bear to think about that.

"You want to call on *me?*" Anna's voice came out as a squeak.

"Of course, silly. Who'd you think I meant—your little sister Rachel?"

That's what I wish you had meant. Rachel's pulse quickened at the thought of her being Silas's girlfriend and riding home from singings in his courting buggy. She drew in a deep breath and pressed against the tree limb as though she were hugging it. No sense hoping and dreaming the impossible. Silas didn't care about her in the least. Not in the way he did Anna, that was for sure. To him, Rachel was still a girl, five years younger than he was, at that. She knew he felt that way, because he'd just referred to her as Anna's "little sister." Besides, whenever Silas had come over to their house, he'd always spoken to Rachel as though she were a child.

"We've known each other for many years, and you did take a ride in my courting buggy after the last singing," Silas continued. "I think it's high time—"

"Hold on to your horses," Anna cut in. "You're a nice man, Silas Swartley, and a good friend, but I can't allow you to court me."

"Why not?"

"Because we're not right for each other."

"Ouch. That hurt my feelings, Anna. I always thought you cared for me."

Rachel could only imagine how Silas must feel. Her heart went out to him. How could Anna be so blind? Couldn't she see what a wonderful man he was? Didn't she realize what a good husband and father he would make?

"I'm sorry if I've hurt your feelings." Anna spoke so softly that Rachel had to strain to hear the words. "It's just that I have other plans for my life, and—"

"Other plans? What kind of plans?"

"I–I'd rather not say just now."

"You may think I'm just a big, dumb Amish fellow, but I'm not as stupid as I might look, Anna Beachy."

"I never meant you were stupid. I just want you to

understand that it won't work for the two of us." After a long pause, she added, "Maybe my little sister *would* be better for you, Silas."

I would! I would! Rachel's heart pounded with sudden hope. She held her breath, waiting to hear what Silas would say next, but disappointment flooded her soul when he turned on his heels and started walking away.

"I'll leave you alone for now, Anna, but when you're ready, I'll be waiting," Silas called over his shoulder. He broke into a run and was soon out of sight.

Rachel released her breath and flexed her body against the unyielding limb. Hot tears pushed against her eyelids, and she blinked several times to force them back. At least Silas and Anna hadn't known she was up here eavesdropping on their private conversation. That would have ruined any chance she might ever have of catching Silas's attention. Not that she had any, really. Besides their age difference, Rachel was sure she wasn't pretty enough for Silas. She had pale blue eyes and straw-colored hair. Nothing beautiful about that. Anna, on the other hand, had been blessed with sparkling green eyes and hair the color of ripe peaches. Rachel was certain Anna would always be Silas's first choice because she was so pretty. *Too bad I'm not schee like her. I wish I hadn't been born looking so plain.*

꧁꧂

When Rachel arrived home several minutes behind her sister, she found her brother Joseph replacing the bolts on an old plow that sat out in the yard. A lock of sandy brown hair lay across his sweaty forehead, and his straw hat rested on a nearby stump.

As she approached, he looked up and frowned. "You're late! Anna's already inside, no doubt helping Mom with supper. You'd better get in there quick, or they'll both be plenty miffed."

"I'm going. And don't be thinking you can boss me around." She scrunched up her nose. "You may be twenty-one and three years older than me, but you're not my keeper, Joseph Beachy."

"Don't go gettin' your feathers all ruffled. You're crankier than the old red rooster when his hens are fighting for the best pieces of corn." Joseph's forehead wrinkled as he squinted his blue eyes and stared at her dress. "Say, isn't that blood I see there?"

She nodded.

"What happened? Did you fall in the river and skin your knee on a rock?"

Rachel shook her head. "I skinned my knee, but it wasn't on a rock."

Joseph gave her a knowing look. "Don't tell me it was another one of your tree-climbing escapades."

She waved a hand and turned away. "Okay, I won't tell you that."

"Let Mom know I'll be in for supper as soon as I finish with the plow," he called to her.

As Rachel stepped onto the back porch, she thought about all the chores she had to do. It was probably a good thing. At least when her hands were kept busy, it didn't give her so much time to think about things—especially about Silas Swartley.

Silas kicked a clump of grass with the toe of his boot. What had come over Anna all of a sudden? How could she be so friendly one minute and almost rude the next? Worse than that, when had she developed such dissatisfaction with being Amish? Had it been there all along, and he'd just been too blind to notice? Was Anna going through some kind of a phase, like some folks did during their rumschpringe? But that made no sense, since Anna had already been baptized and joined the Amish church.

Silas clenched his fists and kept trudging toward home. *I love Anna, but if she's really the woman for me, then why is she acting so disinterested all of a sudden?* He still couldn't believe she'd suggested he start courting her little sister.

"Is that woman simpleminded?" he grumbled. "Rachel's still just a kinner. Besides, it's Anna I love, not her little sister."

As Silas rounded the bend, his farm came into view. A closed-in buggy sat out front in the driveway, and he recognized the horse. It belonged to Deacon Noah Shemly.

"Hmm. . .wonder what's up." He shrugged. "Maybe Mom invited Deacon Noah and his family to join us for supper tonight."

When Silas entered the kitchen a few minutes later, he found his folks and Deacon Noah sitting at the kitchen table, drinking tall glasses of lemonade. It didn't appear as if any of the deacon's family had come with him.

"Is supper about ready?" Silas asked, smiling at his mother. "I'm sure hungry."

Mom gave him a stern look over the top of her metal-framed glasses, which were perched in the middle of her nose. "Where are your manners, son? Can't you say hello to our guest before you start fretting over food?"

Silas was none too happy about his mother embarrassing him that way, but he knew better than to sass her back. Mom might be only half his size, but she could still pack a good wallop to any of her boys' backsides, and she didn't care how old they were, either.

"Sorry," Silas apologized as he nodded at the man who had come to pay them a visit. "When I saw your buggy, I thought maybe you'd brought the whole family along."

Deacon Shemly shook his head. "Nope. Just me."

"Noah came by to have a little talk with you," Pap said, running his fingers through his slightly graying hair, then motioning Silas to take a seat.

"What about?"

"Your friend Reuben Yutzy," the deacon answered with a quick nod.

Silas took off his straw hat and hung it on a wall peg near the back door. Then he took a seat at the table. "What about Reuben?"

The deacon leaned forward and leveled Silas with a piercing gaze. "As you already know, Reuben works for an English paint contractor in Lancaster."

Silas merely nodded in response.

"I hear tell Reuben's been seen with some worldly folks lately."

"As you just said, he works for the English."

"I'm talking about Reuben's off-hours." Noah gave his

full brown beard a few good yanks. "Word has it that he's been going to some picture shows and hanging around with a group of English who like to party some."

Silas frowned deeply. "I see."

"You know anything about this, son?" Pap spoke up.

"No. Why would I?"

"Reuben and you have been friends since you were kinner," Mom reminded.

Silas shrugged. "That's true, but he doesn't tell me everything he does."

"So, you're saying you don't know anything about Reuben being involved in the things of the world?" Deacon Noah questioned.

"Not a thing, and it's probably just a rumor." Silas scooted his chair back and stood. "Now, if you'll excuse me, I'd best see to my chores before supper."

"Reuben's folks are mighty concerned that if he's involved with the things of the world, he'll never decide to join the church. So, you will let me or one of the other ministers know if you hear anything, won't you?" the deacon called as Silas headed for the back door.

"Jah, sure."

Outside, on the porch, Silas drew in a deep, cleansing breath. What in the world was going on here? First Anna acting off in the head, and now all these questions about Reuben. It was enough to make him a nervous wreck!

CHAPTER 2

Rebekah sat in her wheelchair at the table, tearing lettuce into a bowl, while her oldest daughter stood at the stove, stirring a pot of savory stew. They'd been working on supper for the last half hour and still saw no sign of Rachel.

"Are you sure your sister left the river before you did, Anna?"

"Jah, Mom. Several minutes, in fact."

"Did she say she was coming straight home?"

"Not really; I just assumed she was planning on it."

"Hmm. . ."

Just then the back door opened, and Rachel stepped into the room—her face all red and sweaty, her eyes brighter than a shiny penny.

"Sorry I'm late." She hurried over to the sink to wash her hands and face.

Rebekah wiped her hands on a paper towel and reached for a tomato. "Anna said you left the river quite a bit before she did. What kept you, daughter?"

"I. . .uh. . .did a little bird-watching on the way home,

and Anna must have missed me somehow." Rachel picked up an empty pitcher and filled it with water from the sink. "Want me to set the table and fill the glasses?"

Rebekah nodded. "It seems as if you and Anna have been living in a dream world lately. Is this what summer does to my girls?"

Rachel shrugged. "I can't help it if I enjoy studying God's feathered creatures."

Anna turned from her job at the stove and frowned. "Sure is funny I never saw you on the way home. If you were looking at birds, then where were you—up in a tree?"

"What difference does it make?" Rachel's face flamed, making Rebekah wonder if up a tree was precisely where her daughter had been. Rachel had been climbing trees ever since she was old enough to run and play outdoors, always chasing after some critter, watching a special bird, or hiding from her siblings.

I wonder if I would have been a tree climber if I'd had the chance. Rebekah's thoughts pulled her unwillingly back to the past—back to when she'd been a little girl and a tree branch had fallen on her during a bad storm. The accident had damaged her spinal cord, and ever since then, Rebekah had either been confined to her wheelchair or strapped in braces that allowed her to walk stiff-legged with the help of crutches.

"What kind of stupid bird were you looking at, Rachel?" Anna asked, halting Rebekah's thoughts.

"It was a downy woodpecker, and it's sure as anything not stupid."

"Silas is such a *kischblich* man. He likes watching birds,

too, but I think it's a waste of time."

"Just because Silas appreciates birds doesn't make him a silly man." Rachel moved over to the table with a handful of silverware she'd taken from the drawer.

"And speaking of Silas, I know he brought you home from a singing awhile back. Seems to me he might want to start courting you pretty soon," Rebekah stated.

Anna silently kept stirring the stew.

"Might could be that you'll soon be making a wedding quilt for your hope chest." Rebekah smiled. "Or would you prefer that I make one for you?"

Anna pursed her lips. "It was just one ride in his buggy, Mom. Nothing to get excited about. So there's no need for either one of us to begin an Amish wedding quilt."

"Why not be excited?" Rebekah set the salad bowl aside and turned her wheelchair so she was facing Anna. "Silas has been hanging around our place for years now, and your daed and I both think he's a nice enough fellow. Besides, you're twenty-three years old already and joined the church last fall. Don't you think it's past time you considered getting married?"

Anna moved away from the stove and opened the refrigerator door. She withdrew a bunch of celery and took it over to the sink. "I'm thinking the stew needs a bit more of this; that's what I'm thinking."

Rachel headed back across the room, removed a stack of plates from the cupboard, and brought them over to the table. She looked a bit disgruntled, and Rebekah wondered if the girl might be jealous because Anna had a boyfriend and she didn't. She shifted her wheelchair to one side, making it easier for Rachel to reach around her, then glanced over at Anna again. "I think a lovely quilt would make a fine addition to someone's hope chest, and if Silas is so sweet on you, then maybe you should—"

"I'm sorry if Silas thinks he's sweet on me," Anna said. "I just can't commit to someone I don't love."

Rebekah clicked her tongue against the roof of her mouth. "*Ach.* I didn't mean to interfere. Guess I jumped to the wrong conclusion, but seeing as how you and Silas have been friends for so long, and since you let him bring you home from a singing, I thought things must be getting serious."

"Anna has other things she wants to do with her life. I heard her say so." Rachel covered her mouth with the palm of her hand, and her face turned red as a cherry tomato. "Oops."

"When did you hear me say such things?" Anna turned to face her sister, leveling her with a most peculiar look.

Rachel shrugged and reached for the basket of napkins in the center of the table. "I'm sure you said it sometime."

"What other things are you wanting to do with your life, Anna?" Rebekah asked.

Anna merely shrugged in response.

"If I had someone as *wunderbaar* as Silas after me, I'd marry him in an instant." Rachel's cheeks turned even redder, and she scurried across the room.

"My, my," Anna said with a small laugh. "If I didn't know better, I'd think my little sister was in love with Silas herself."

"Rachel's only eighteen—too young for such thoughts,"

Rebekah said with a shake of her head. "Besides, I'm sure she wouldn't be after your boyfriend, Anna."

"How old were you when you fell in love with Dad?" Anna asked.

"Guess I wasn't much more than nineteen. Even so—"

The back door flew open, interrupting Rebekah's sentence, and her twelve-year-old daughter, Elizabeth, burst into the kitchen. Her long brown braids, which had been pinned at the back of her head when she'd gone outside awhile ago, now hung down her back. "Perry won't let me have a turn on the swing. He's been mean to me all day, Mom."

Rebekah shook her head. "You know your twin brother likes to tease. The little *galgedieb*. I wish you would try to ignore that scoundrel's antics."

"But, Mom, Perry—"

Rebekah held up one hand to silence Elizabeth. "It's almost time for supper, so please run outside and call your daed and your *bruders* inside."

"Oh, all right, but if Perry starts picking on me again—"

"You'll just ignore him."

"I'll try."

Rebekah shook her head as Elizabeth went out the back door. "That youngest daughter of mine has a lot to learn about ignoring a tease." She clicked her tongue. "Why, I can't tell you how many times I had to endure teasing when I was a girl."

"Did your brothers and sisters tease you?" Rachel asked as she placed a napkin beside the plate nearest her.

Rebekah nodded. "Sometimes, but most of my teasing came from kinner outside my family—those who thought my handicap was something to joke about, I guess."

"Anyone cruel enough to make fun of someone who's disabled ought to be horsewhipped," Rachel muttered.

"I agree," Anna put in.

Rebekah smiled. She was glad her daughters felt that way.

Rebekah's husband, Daniel, and their oldest son, Joseph, entered the room just then, and Elizabeth and her twin brother, Perry, followed. Soon the family gathered around the huge wooden table, and all heads bowed for silent prayer. When it was over, Daniel glanced at Joseph. "Did you get that old plow put back together today?" he asked, as he filled his plate with a generous helping of stew.

Joseph nodded. "Jah, I did. Should be able to use it again tomorrow morning."

Daniel pulled his fingers through the ends of his full brown beard, now lightly peppered with gray. "No matter what those English neighbors of mine may think, I say you can't replace a reliable horse and plow with any kind of fancy equipment."

"Horses aren't always so reliable," Anna put in. "I've known 'em to be downright stubborn at times."

Daniel cast a curious look in her direction but made no comment.

"I've been wondering, don't you think we need to modernize a bit?" Anna continued. "I mean, working the greenhouse would go much better if we had a telephone. . .even one outdoors on a pole."

Daniel frowned. "We've gotten along all these years without a phone, so why would we need one now?"

Everyone fell silent, but as Rebekah watched her eldest

daughter fiddle with her food, she sensed the frustration Anna felt and wondered if she should say something on her behalf. Before Rebekah could say a word, Anna pushed her chair aside and stood. "I'd like to be excused."

Daniel nodded, but Rebekah felt the need to protest. "You've hardly eaten a thing, Anna."

"I'm not so hungry." Anna lowered her head, causing her long lashes to form crescents against her pale cheeks.

"Let her go," Daniel said. "Just might could be that going without supper is what she needs to help clear her head for better thinking."

Rebekah had never been one to usurp her husband's authority, even if she didn't agree with everything he said. So with a quick nod, she replied, "Jah, all right then."

Anna rushed out of the room without another word, and Rebekah released a sigh. Her oldest child had been acting a mite strange of late, and it had her more than a bit worried.

Rachel leaned against the back of her chair, her shoulder blades making contact with the hard wood. *Such a silly one, that sister of mine. She seems so dissatisfied with her life these days. Guess maybe she doesn't know how good she's got it.*

As soon as the rest of them had finished supper, Rachel cleared the table and helped her mother and Elizabeth do up the dishes and clean the kitchen.

"Many hands make light work," Mom said, as Rachel handed her a platter to dry.

Rachel nodded and glanced toward the hallway door

leading to the stairs. Too bad Anna was in her room sulking. If she'd been down here in the kitchen helping, like she should have been, they would probably be done already.

When the last dish was finally dried and put away, Rachel turned to her mother and said, "I think I'll go upstairs and see how Anna's doing. Unless you've got something more for me here, that is."

Mom shook her head. "Nothing right now. I was thinking about going outside to check on my herb garden." She glanced at Elizabeth, who was drying her hands on a terry cloth towel. "How'd you like to join your old mamm outside?"

Elizabeth wrinkled her freckled nose. "You ain't old."

Rachel noticed the smile that crossed her mother's face—that sweet, dimpled expression that made her so special. Even with Mom's disability, she rarely complained. From all Rachel had been told, their mother had been confined to a wheelchair most of her life. But Mom didn't allow her disability to hold her back much. It was Rachel's understanding that her mother had been quite independent when she was a young woman and had decided to open the greenhouse she'd named Grandma's Place.

Rachel smiled to herself as she thought of the stories Dad and Mom often told about their courting days and how they almost didn't marry because of some silly misunderstanding. Mom had convinced herself that Dad only wanted her because he loved flowers so much and hoped to get his hands on her business. It took some doing, but Dad finally made her believe he loved her most, not the plants and flowers. At last, they got married. They ran the greenhouse together, and a year later, baby Anna was born.

Mom had said she thought it was a true miracle, the way God had allowed her to give birth despite her partial paralysis. Rachel could only imagine how her mother must have felt when she kept having one miracle after another. Two years after Anna was born, Joseph arrived. Another three years went by, and Rachel came onto the scene. Mom must have thought she was done having *bopplin*, because it was another six years before the twins made their surprise appearance.

Five miracles in all, Rachel mused. *I would surely feel blessed if God ever gave me five children.* She drew in a deep breath and released it with such force that Mom gave her a strange look.

"You okay, Rachel?"

"Jah, I'm fine; just thinking is all."

"Were you daydreaming again?"

Rachel nodded. Daydreaming was nothing new for her. As far back as she could remember, she had enjoyed fantasizing about things.

"Say, how did you get that blood on your dress?" Mom asked suddenly, as she stared at the spot on Rachel's skirt where she'd injured her knee.

"Oh, just scraped my leg a bit," Rachel replied with a shrug. No point in explaining how it had happened. Mom would probably lecture her about it being unladylike and dangerous to go climbing around in trees.

"Want me to take a look-see?"

"No, it's nothing. I'm ready to go up and see Anna now."

"Go on ahead. Maybe you can talk some sense into her about courting Silas."

Rachel winced, feeling like she'd had a glass of cold water thrown in her face. Surely Mom didn't mean for her to actually try and convince Anna to let Silas court her. If she did that and was successful in getting Anna to agree to do what Silas wanted, then Rachel knew the chance of him ever deciding to court *her* would be slim to none.

Anna lay on her bed, staring at the plaster ceiling and tumbling things over in her mind. She thought about her encounter with Silas and wondered if somehow Rachel could have been nearby and overheard what they'd said. She wondered, too, why Silas kept pressuring her to let him court her and couldn't seem to take no for an answer.

Her mind went over the conversation that had gone on at the table during supper, and she realized that her folks would have a conniption if they knew the thoughts that had been going through her head of late.

A soft knock at the door roused Anna from her musings, and she rolled onto her side. "Come in."

Rachel poked her head into the room. "Mind if I join you for a while?"

Anna motioned her sister into the room. "Why's Dad have to be so stubborn?" she asked after Rachel had taken a seat on the bed beside her. "Can't he see there's a place for some modern things? He's the reason I got so upset at supper, you know." A stream of tears trickled down her cheeks, and she swiped at them with the back of her hand.

"People often blame things on the previous generation because there's only one other choice," Rachel said in a near whisper.

Anna sat up, swinging her legs over the side of the bed.

"What's that supposed to mean?"

"The other choice would be to put the blame on yourself."

Anna sucked in her protruding lip and blinked several times. "How dare you speak to me that way!"

"It's true."

Anna jerked off her head covering and pulled out the pins that held her hair in place; then she began to pace the room with quick, nervous steps.

"Are you unhappy being Amish? Is that the reason you've been acting so strange lately?"

Anna released a sigh. "Not unhappy, really, but if I weren't Amish—"

"But you are Amish, and you should be happy being such."

"Shouldn't I have the right to choose how I want to live and with whom?"

Rachel nodded. "Of course you should, but you're already baptized into the church, and if you were to go against the *Ordnung* now, you'd be shunned, and that's a fact."

Anna sniffed. "Don't you think I know that, Rachel?" She moved over to the window and stood looking out at the darkening sky. "What'd you come in here for, anyway—to pummel me with a bunch of questions?"

"Of course not. I just wanted to see how you were doing."

"I'm fine."

"Okay. I'll leave you alone then."

"*Danki.*" Anna released a sigh of relief when she heard the bedroom door click shut. She wasn't ready to tell anyone her secret yet—not even Rachel, whom she knew she could trust.

Silas shielded his eyes from the glare of the morning sun as he strolled through the small village of Bird-in-Hand. He'd come in early today with the intent of speaking to his friend Reuben, who was supposed to be painting a new grocery store in town.

He found Reuben around the back of the supermarket, holding a paintbrush in one hand and a giant oatmeal cookie in the other.

"I see you're hard at work," Silas said with a grin.

Reuben chuckled and popped the cookie into his mouth. "I do need to keep up my strength, you know."

"Jah, I'm sure."

"What brings you to town so early?" Reuben asked, as he applied a glob of paint to the side of the wooden building.

"I came to see you."

"So now that you see me, what do you think?"

Silas shook his head. "Always kidding around, aren't you?"

Reuben's blue eyes fairly sparkled, and he pulled his fingers through the back of his thick, blond hair, which was growing much too long for any self-respecting Amish man. Silas had to wonder how come his friend wasn't wearing his straw hat, especially on a day when the sun was already hot as fire. He was about to voice that question when Reuben asked a question of his own.

"You heard any good jokes lately?"

Silas shook his head. "Nope. Have you?"

Reuben nodded but kept right on painting. "My boss

told me a real funny one the other day, but I can't remember it now."

"How come you don't give up this painting job and go back to helping your daed on the farm? I'm sure he could use the extra pair of hands."

"I don't like farming so much anymore. In fact, I'm thinking about starting a whole new life for myself."

Silas rocked back and forth on his heels, trying to think of the right thing to say. He had been helping his dad work the land ever since he'd finished his eighth-grade education. That was nine years ago and he was still happy staying at home on the farm. It was hard for him to understand why an Amish man, born and raised on a farm, preferred painting to working the land. But then he guessed everyone had different likes and dislikes.

"So, what's new with you?"

"Not so much." Silas shifted from one foot to the other. "Deacon Shemly was at our place yesterday. Said he'd heard some things, and he seemed to be kind of concerned."

Reuben stopped painting and turned to face Silas. "Things about me?"

Silas nodded. "Are they true?"

"Are what true?"

"Have you been running around with some English fellows?"

Reuben's brows furrowed. "You planning on telling anyone what I say to you?"

Silas shook his head. "Thought I'd ask, that's all."

Reuben grunted. "I haven't done anything wrong—just going through rumschpringe, same as you did before joining the church. I'm smart enough to know what I'm doing."

Silas shook his head. "One thing I've learned is never to mistake knowledge for wisdom. One might help you make a living, but the other helps you make a life."

Reuben flicked a fly off the end of his paintbrush. "Let's just say I've learned that we only live once, and until I'm ready to settle down, I aim to have me some fun. I plan on keeping my truck for as long as I can, too."

Hearing the way his friend was talking put an ache in Silas's heart, the same way it had when he'd spoken with Anna yesterday. He didn't understand why some of the young people he knew seemed dissatisfied with the old ways. Well, he might not be able to do much about Reuben, but Anna was another matter. If he could figure out a way to get her thinking straight again, he was determined to do it.

CHAPTER 3

The following morning, Rachel awoke to the soothing sound of roosters crowing in the barnyard. She loved that noise—loved everything about their farm, in fact. She yawned, stretched, and squinted at the ray of sun peeking through a hole in her window shade. Today the family planned to go to the outdoor farmers' market, where they would sell some of their garden produce as well as a bunch of plants and flowers from Mom and Dad's greenhouse.

Before Rachel headed down the stairs to help with breakfast, she looked out her bedroom window and saw Dad, Joseph, and Perry out by the buggy shed, getting their larger market buggy ready to go.

The sweet smell of maple syrup greeted Rachel as she entered the kitchen a few minutes later, and she noticed right away that Mom sat in her wheelchair in front of one of the lower counters, mixing pancake batter. Anna stood in front of the stove, frying sausages and eggs, while Elizabeth was busy setting the table, which held a huge pitcher of fresh maple syrup.

"*Guder mariye*," Rachel said cheerfully. "What can I do to help?"

"Good morning to you." Mom glanced up at Rachel, then back to the pancake batter. "You can go outside and tell the men we'll be ready with breakfast in about ten minutes."

Rachel nodded, then made a hasty exit out the kitchen door. Dad and Perry were still busy loading the back of the buggy, while Joseph hitched the brawny horse that would pull it.

"Mom says breakfast will be ready in ten minutes," Rachel announced.

"You can go get washed up," Dad said with a nod at Perry.

Rachel's freckle-faced brother pointed to the boxes of green beans sitting on the grass. "What about those?"

"You stay," Dad said, nodding toward Rachel, "and you go," he instructed Perry. "I'll see to the boxes."

Perry straightened his twisted suspenders and took off in a run. Looking at his long legs from the back side, Rachel thought he appeared much older than a boy of twelve. From the front, however, Perry's impish grin and sparkling blue eyes made him look like a child full of life, laughter, and mischief.

Rachel stood quietly beside her father, waiting for him to speak. His shirtsleeves were rolled up to the elbows, and she marveled at how quickly his strong arms loaded the remaining boxes of beans. When the last box was put in place, Dad straightened and faced her. "Do you think you could do me a favor?"

Rachel twisted one corner of her apron and stared at the ground. Her father's favors usually meant some kind of hard work. "I—I suppose so. What did you have in mind?"

Dad bent down so he was eye level with Rachel. "Well now, I know how close you and Anna have always been. I was hoping you might let your mamm and me know what's going on with her these days."

Rachel opened her mouth to respond, but he cut her off. "Fact of the matter is Anna's been acting mighty strange lately, and we need your help finding out what's up."

Rachel wrinkled her nose. Was Dad saying what she thought he was saying? Did he actually want her to spy on her sister? If Dad thought she and Anna were still close, he was sorely mistaken. Here of late, Rachel and Anna didn't see eye-to-eye on much of anything. Rachel knew if Anna's talk about learning more of the English ways ever reached Mom and Dad, they would be very concerned. That was obvious by the way Dad had reacted last night when Anna suggested they should modernize some. Rachel didn't want to be the one to tell them what was going on inside Anna's stubborn head. Not that she knew all that much. Fact was she wouldn't have known anything at all if she hadn't overheard Anna and Silas's conversation while she was hiding in the tree.

"So what do you say?" Dad asked, scattering Rachel's thoughts.

She flicked her tongue across her lower lip. "What exactly am I expected to do?"

"To begin with, your mamm's told me that Anna has a suitor, yet she's not the least bit interested in being courted by that nice fellow."

"You must mean Silas Swartley. He's sweet as molasses on Anna, but she won't give him the time of day."

Dad glanced toward the front of the market buggy, where Joseph stood fiddling with the horse's harness. "Kind of reminds me of your mamm when I was tryin' to show her how much I cared."

Rachel listened politely as her father continued. "Sometimes a man shows his feelings in a strange sort of way." He nodded toward Joseph and chuckled softly. "Now take that big brother of yours—we all know that he's sweet on Pauline Hostetler, but do you think he'll do a thing about it? No way! Ever since Pauline returned from Ohio, Joseph's been making eyes at her, but he won't make a move to ask her out. That boy's gonna fool around, and soon some other fellow's bound to come along and win Pauline's heart. Then it'll be too late for my *bleed* son."

Rachel knew all about Joseph's crush on Pauline, as well as his bashful ways. He had been carrying a torch for Pauline ever since Eli Yoder had dropped her flat to marry Laura, the fancy English woman from Minnesota. The fact that Pauline was three years older than Joseph didn't help things, either. Rachel had to wonder if the age difference bothered Pauline the way it did her brother. It seemed rather strange that the twenty-four-year-old woman still wasn't married. Either she'd never gotten over Eli, or Pauline simply wasn't interested in Joseph. He sure wasn't going to take the initiative; Rachel was sure of that.

"Well, I'm thinkin' that if anyone can talk to Anna about giving Silas a chance, it would be you," Dad said, cutting into Rachel's contemplations one more time. "She needs to know that she's being foolish for snubbing someone as nice as Silas."

She swallowed hard. If her father only knew what he was asking of her. It was hard enough to see Silas hanging around Anna all the time. How in the world could Rachel be expected to talk Anna into something she really didn't want to do? Truth be told, Rachel would just as soon slop the hogs every day for the rest of her life as to tell Anna how stupid she was for snubbing Silas. But she knew her father probably wouldn't let up until she had agreed to his request.

Rachel let her gaze travel over their orderly farmyard for a few seconds as she thought things through. "Jah, okay. I'll have a little talk with Anna about Silas," she finally agreed.

"And you'll tell us if anything strange is going on with your sister?"

Rachel nodded, feeling worse than the thick scum that would no doubt be covering much of their pond by late August. "Okay, Dad. I'll tell you what's going on."

Joseph cringed as Rachel walked away. He hadn't eavesdropped on purpose, but he couldn't help hearing part of Dad's conversation with Rachel. Should he say anything about it—maybe give his thoughts on the whole thing?

He approached his father cautiously, his mind searching for just the right words. "Say, Dad, I caught some of what you were saying to Rachel, and I was wondering if it's such a good idea for her to be meddling in Anna's life."

Dad whirled around. "If I want your opinion, I'll ask for it."

"Sorry, I just thought—"

"How much of our conversation did you hear, anyway?"

"Just that you were hoping she could talk to Anna about giving Silas the chance to court her."

Dad nodded. "I said that all right."

Was that a look of relief he saw on his father's face? Had he said some things to Rachel that he didn't want Joseph to hear? If so, what had he said? Could it have been about him?

"I like Silas. He's a hard worker, and I think he would make Anna a fine husband, don't you?"

Joseph shrugged. "I suppose. I just don't think—"

Dad gave his stomach a couple of pats. "I don't know about you, but my belly's sure starting to rumble. Let's go eat, shall we?"

"Jah, okay." As Joseph followed his father to the house, he wished it had been he who'd been asked to speak with Anna. Rachel and Anna had always been close, and if Rachel started butting into Anna's business, she might not take so kindly to it. Besides, Joseph and Anna were closer in age, so she might be more apt to listen to him.

The farmers' market where Rachel and her family were heading was eight miles from their farm. Today the trip seemed even longer than usual, and the cramped quarters in the buggy combined with the hot, sticky weather didn't help much, either. Rachel had felt a bit cross all morning, and now she was even more agitated.

Dad and Mom rode in the front of the buggy, with Elizabeth sitting between them. Two benches in back provided seating for Rachel, Anna, Joseph, and Perry. Behind them, they'd stashed the boxes filled with produce, plants, and fresh-cut flowers. Mom's wheelchair was scrunched in back, as well.

The temperature was in the nineties, with humidity so high Rachel felt her dress and underclothes sticking to her body like flypaper. When they finally pulled into the parking lot, she was the first one to jump down from the buggy.

Perry tended to the horse, while Joseph and Dad unloaded the boxes and carried them to the spot where they set up their tables. Elizabeth and Rachel followed, with Anna a few feet behind, pushing Mom's wheelchair over the bumpy terrain.

Everyone scurried around to help set up their tables, and soon the Beachys were open for business. People started buying right away, and whenever they were between customers, Rachel and her siblings were allowed to take turns wandering around the market.

Rachel took a break around noontime and headed for a stand advertising cold cherry cider. A tall, gangly Amish fellow waited on her. Freckles covered his nose, and he looked to be about nineteen or twenty. Rachel didn't recognize him and figured he must be from another district.

"It's a mighty hot day, isn't it?" he asked, giving her a wide grin.

"Jah, it surely is warm." She handed him some money. "I'd like a glass of cherry cider, please."

He bent down and removed a jug from the ice chest underneath the table, then poured some of the cider into a paper cup and handed it to Rachel. "Here you go."

"Danki."

Rachel drank the cool beverage quickly, then moved on to another table where Nancy Frey, the Amish schoolteacher in their district, sold a variety of pies.

Nancy smiled up at Rachel. "Are you here with your family?"

"Jah. We're selling produce and lots of flowers and plants from my folks' greenhouse." Rachel pointed across the way. "Our tables are over there."

"I sure hope business is better for you than it has been here. Pies aren't doing so well today."

Rachel licked her lips as she studied the pies on Nancy's table. "Apple-crumb, shoofly, and lemon sponge are all my favorite."

"Would you like to try a slice?" Nancy asked. "I already have an apple-crumb cut."

"It's real tempting, but I'd better not spoil my appetite, or I won't be able to eat any of the lunch I brought along."

Nancy smiled. "How's your mamm doing these days? The last few times I've seen her, she was in her wheelchair. Doesn't she use her crutches anymore?"

"She does some, though I think it's difficult for her to walk like a stiff-legged doll. Mom says the older she gets, the harder it is, so she uses her wheelchair more often than the braces these days." Rachel fanned her face with her hand. "Well, guess I'll be moving on. It's awful hot and muggy today, so I think I'll see if I can find a bit of shade somewhere."

Nancy nodded. "I know what you mean. If I weren't here alone, I'd be doing the same thing."

"I'd be happy to watch your table awhile," Rachel offered.

"Danki, but my sister Emma will be along soon. I'm sure

she'll be willing to let me take a little break."

"All right then. See you later, Nancy." Rachel moved away from the table and found the solace she was looking for under an enormous maple tree growing in the field behind the market. She was about to take a seat on the ground, when she caught sight of Silas Swartley. Her heart slammed into her chest as she realized he was heading her way.

Silas gritted his teeth as he made his way to the backside of the farmers' market. He had just come from the Yutzys' table, and the few minutes he'd spent talking to Reuben's folks had made him feel sick at heart. They'd told Silas that they had a pretty good inkling of what their son was up to. . .or at least they knew some of it. Silas was sure Reuben hadn't told his folks everything he'd been thinking of late, but then, he hadn't really told Silas all that much the last time they'd spoken, either.

Reuben had always had a mind of his own, even when they were children attending the one-room schoolhouse together. Silas remembered one time when Reuben had skipped school and gone to the lake for a day of fishing. When he'd come back to school the following day, Reuben had expressed no repentance. The ornery fellow had bragged about the three fish he'd caught and how he'd gotten out of taking the spelling test they were supposed to have that day. Even though Reuben had to stay after school every day for a week and do double chores at home, he hadn't been tamed in the least.

Silas drew in a deep breath. He figured he'd best forget

about Reuben, because it wasn't likely that his stubborn friend would listen to anything he had to say. Might be best for him to concentrate on Anna, since she suddenly seemed discontent with her life. He hoped to change all that, though. If Anna would agree to court him, maybe soon they could talk about marriage and settling down to starting a family of their own.

Silas had decided to head out to the field behind the market to think things through, when he noticed Anna's little sister Rachel sitting under a giant maple tree. *Hmm. . .she might be the one I need to talk to.*

He hurried across the grassy area and plunked down beside her. "Hey, Rachel. What's new with you?"

Rachel couldn't believe Silas had taken a seat beside her, but it tickled her pink that he had. "Not much new with me," she said. "How about you?"

"Same old thing, I guess." Silas removed his straw hat and fanned his face with the brim. "So, what are you doing out here by yourself?"

"Trying to get cooled off." For one crazy moment, Rachel had an impulse to lean her head on Silas's shoulder and confess her undying love for him. She didn't, of course, for that would have been far too bold. And it would have only proved to him that she really was quite immature.

"Sure is a warm day we're having. Whew! Even under the shade of this big old tree, it's hot."

She nodded and looked upward.

"What are you lookin' at?"

"Oh, I thought I heard a bluebird whistling."

Silas tipped his head way back. "Really? Where is it?"

"I'm not sure. Maybe I'm just hearing things—hoping a bluebird might show itself."

Silas chuckled. "I thought I was the only one who liked to listen for the bird sounds."

"You're not alone; that's one of my favorite pastimes."

He glanced over at the people crowding around all the market tables. "Say, Rachel, I was wondering if we could talk."

"I thought we *were* talking."

He grinned and dropped his hat to his knees. "I guess we were, at that. What I really meant to say was, can we talk about your sister?"

Rachel frowned. She might have known Silas hadn't planned to talk about her. She shrugged, trying not to let her disappointment show. "What about Anna? She's the sister you were referring to, right?"

Silas lifted his gaze toward the sky. "Of course, I meant Anna. It couldn't be Elizabeth I want to talk about. I'm no cradle robber, you know."

Rachel felt as though Silas had slapped her across the face. Even though he was speaking about her twelve-year-old sister, she still got his meaning. She knew Silas wouldn't dream of looking at her because she was five years younger than he. Besides, what chance did she have against the beauty of her older sister?

In a surprise gesture, Silas touched Rachel's chin and turned her head so she was looking directly at him. Her chest fluttered with the sensation of his touch, and it was all she could do to keep from falling over. "Did you hear what I said, Rachel?"

"I–I believe so, but what was it you wanted to say about Anna?"

"You and your sister are pretty close, isn't that right?"

She gulped and tried to regain her composure. "I used to think so."

"Anna probably talks more to you than anyone else, correct?"

Rachel shook her head. "I think she tells her friend Martha Rose more than she does me these days."

Several seconds went by before Silas spoke again. "I suppose I could talk to Martha Rose, but I don't know her all that well. I'd feel more comfortable talking to you about Anna than I would to her best friend."

Rachel supposed she should feel flattered that Silas wanted to speak with her, yet the thought of him using her only to learn more about Anna irked her to no end.

"Okay," she said with a sigh. "What is it you want to know about my sister?"

"Can you tell me how to make her pay me some mind? I've tried everything but stand on my head and wiggle my ears, yet she still treats me like yesterday's dirty laundry. I tell you, Rachel, it's got me plumb worn out trying to get sweet Anna to agree to courting."

Sweet Anna? Rachel thought ruefully. *Silas, you might not think my sister's so sweet if you knew that she has no plans to let you court her.*

Rachel felt sorry for poor Silas, sitting there all woebegone, pining for her sister's attention. If she wasn't so crazy about the fellow herself, she might pitch in and try to set things right between him and Anna. "I think only God can get my sister thinking straight again." She looked away, studying a row of trees on the other side of the field.

"You're kind of pensive today," Silas remarked. "Is it this oppressive heat, or are you just not wanting to help me with Anna?"

Rachel turned to face him again. "I think a man who claims to care for a woman should speak on his own behalf. Even though my sister and I don't talk much anymore, I know her fairly well, and I don't think Anna would like it if she knew you were plotting like this."

Silas's forehead wrinkled. "I'm not plotting. I'm just trying to figure out some way to make Anna commit to courting. I thought maybe you could help, but if you're gonna get all peevish on me, then forget I even brought up the subject."

Now I've gone and done it. Silas will never come to care for me if I keep making him mad. Rachel placed her trembling hand on Silas's bare arm, and the sudden contact with his skin made her hand feel like it was on fire. "I—I suppose it wouldn't hurt if I had a little talk with Anna," she mumbled.

A huge grin spread across Silas's summer-tanned face. "You mean it, Rachel? You'll really go to bat for me?"

She nodded slowly, feeling like she was one of her father's old sows being led away to slaughter. First she'd promised Dad to help Anna and Silas get together, and now she'd agreed to speak to Anna on Silas's behalf. It made no sense, since she didn't really want them to be together. But a promise was a promise, and she would do her best to keep it.

CHAPTER 4

That Sunday, church was to be held at Eli and Laura Yoders' place. They only lived a few farms from the Beachys, so the buggy ride didn't take long at all.

Many Amish carriages were already lined up near the side of the Yoders' house, but Dad managed to find an empty spot near Eli's folks' home. Joseph helped Mom into her wheelchair, while Dad unhitched the horse and put him in the corral; then everyone climbed out of the buggy and scattered in search of friends and relatives to visit before church got started.

Rachel noticed Silas standing on one end of the Yoders' front porch, and she berated herself for loving him so much. She was almost certain he would never love her in return. She wasn't sure he even liked her. She either needed to put him out of her mind or figure out some way to make him take notice of her.

Silas seemed to be focused on Anna, who was talking with Martha Rose Zook and Laura Yoder at the other end of the porch. *Guess I'd better speak to Anna soon, before Silas comes asking if I did.* Rachel joined her sister and the other two

women, but she made sure she was standing close enough to
Anna so she could whisper in her ear. "Look, there's Silas.
He seems to be watching you."

"So?"

"Don't you think he's good-looking?"

Anna nudged Rachel in the ribs. "Since you seem so
interested, why not go over and talk to him?"

Rachel shook her head. "It's you he's interested in,
not me."

"I think we'd better hurry and get inside. Church is about
to begin," Anna said, conveniently changing the subject.

Rachel followed her sister into the Yoders' living room,
where several rows of backless, wooden benches had been
set up. She would have to speak to Anna about Silas later
on, even though she knew it would pain her to do it.

The men and boys took their seats on one side of the
room, while the women and girls gathered on the other.
Rachel sat between her two sisters, and Mom parked her
wheelchair alongside a bench where some of the other
women sat.

All whispering ceased as one of the deacons passed out
the hymnals. In their usual chantlike voices, the congregation
recited several traditional German hymns. Next, one of the
ministers delivered the opening sermon. This was followed by
a time of silent prayer, where everyone knelt. Then Deacon
Shemly read some scripture, and Bishop Wagler gave the
main sermon.

During the longer message, Rachel glanced over at
Anna, who sat twiddling her thumbs as she stared out the
window.

What's that sister of mine thinking about? Rachel had a terrible feeling that Anna's interest in worldly things might lead to trouble. What if Anna were to up and leave the faith?

Rachel clenched her teeth. *No, that can't happen. It would break Mom and Dad's hearts, not to mention upsetting the whole family. Why, we'd have to shun our own flesh and blood!* She shuddered just thinking about the seriousness of it. Right then, she vowed to pray more, asking the Lord to change her sister's mind about things. She would even make herself be happy about Anna and Silas courting if it meant Anna would alter her attitude.

Rachel felt a sense of relief when the benediction was given, followed by a few announcements and the closing hymn. It wasn't that she didn't enjoy church, but all those troubling thoughts rolling around in her head made her feel fidgety and anxious to be outside.

Once the benches had been moved and tables set up, the women served a soup-and-sandwich lunch. Rachel and Anna joined several other young women as they brought out the food to the men. After the men finished eating, the women and children took their places at separate tables.

When the meal was over and everything had been cleared away, men and women of all ages gathered in small groups to visit. The younger children were put down to nap, while the older ones played games on the lawn. Some of the young adults joined in the games, while others were content to just sit and talk.

Rachel didn't feel much like playing games or engaging in idle chitchat, so she decided to take a walk. Walking always seemed to help her relax and think more clearly. She left Anna talking with a group of women and headed in the direction of the small pond near the end of the Yoders' alfalfa field.

The pool of clear water was surrounded by low-hanging willow trees, offering shade and solitude on another hot, sticky day in late July. Feeling the heat bearing down on her, Rachel slipped off her shoes and socks, then waded along the water's edge, relishing the way the cool water tickled her toes. When she felt somewhat cooler, she plunked down on the grass. Closing her eyes, Rachel found herself thinking about the meeting she'd had with Silas the day before. She'd only made one feeble attempt to talk to Anna about him and knew she really should try again. It was the least she could do since she had made a promise.

A snapping twig caused Rachel to jump. She jerked her head in the direction of the sound and was surprised to see Silas standing under one of the willow trees. He smiled and lifted his hand in a wave. It made her heart beat faster and was just enough to rekindle her hope that he might actually forget about Anna and come to love her instead.

"I didn't know anyone else was here," Rachel murmured, as Silas moved over to where she sat.

"I didn't know anyone was here, either." Silas removed his straw hat and plopped down on the grass beside her. They sat in silence for a time, listening to the rhythmic birdsong filtering through the trees and an occasional *ribbet* from a noisy bullfrog.

Rachel thought about all the times Silas had visited their farm over the years. She remembered one day in particular when a baby robin had fallen from its nest in the giant maple. Silas had climbed that old tree like it was nothing, then put the tiny creature back in its home. That day, Rachel gave her heart to Silas Swartley. Too bad he didn't know it.

"I just talked to Reuben Yutzy," Silas said, breaking into Rachel's thoughts. "He's been working for a paint contractor in Lancaster for some time now."

She nodded but made no comment.

"Reuben informed me that he's leaving the Amish faith." Silas slowly shook his head. "Can you believe it, Rachel? Reuben's been my friend since we were kinner, and I never expected he would want to leave." The lines in Silas's forehead deepened. "Since he started working for that English man, Reuben's been doing a lot more worldly things. I tried talking to him the other day, but I guess nothing I said got through. Reuben's made up his mind about leaving, and he seems bent on following that path."

"Many of our men work in town for paint contractors, carpenters, and other tradesmen," Rachel reminded. "Most of them remain in the faith in spite of their jobs."

"I know that's true, but I guess Reuben's not one of 'em." Silas gave his earlobe a quick tug. "Reuben told me that he bought a fancy truck awhile back, but he's been keeping it parked outside his boss's place of business so none of his family would know."

Rachel fidgeted with her hands. She wanted to reach out and touch Silas's disheartened face. It would feel so right to smooth the wrinkles out of his forehead. She released a deep sigh instead. "Things are sure getting *verhuddelt* here of late."

Silas nodded. "You're right about things being mixed-up. I think something else is going on with Reuben, too."

"Like what?"

"I'm not sure. He dropped a few hints, but when I pressed him about it, he closed up like a snail crawling into its shell. Said he didn't want to talk about it right now." Silas grimaced. "I'm thinking maybe a woman is involved."

"An Englisher?"

"Might could be. It wouldn't be the first time an Amish man fell for an English woman." Silas shrugged. "That's what happened to Eli Yoder a few years back, you know."

"But Laura joined the Amish faith."

"That's true, but it's an unusual situation and doesn't happen very often."

Rachel slipped her socks and shoes back on before she stood. "I should be getting back to the house, I expect. If Mom misses me, she'll probably send Joseph out looking, and I'm not in any mood to deal with my cranky brother today."

"Joseph's not happy?"

"Nope. He's got a big crush on Pau—" Rachel covered her mouth with the palm of her hand when she realized she had almost let something slip. "As I was saying, I need to head back."

"Wait!" Silas jumped to his feet. "I was wondering if you've had a chance to speak with Anna yet."

Rachel's face heated up as she turned to face him. "I—I haven't said much to her on the subject, but I still believe it would be best if you spoke with her yourself, and you'd better do it soon, before it's too late."

"How's things at your place?" Rebekah asked her friend Mary Ellen as the two of them sat on the front porch visiting and watching the children play on the lawn.

Mary Ellen smiled. "Never a dull moment with Eli and Laura's two living right next door. Those little ones keep Laura hopping all the time."

Rebekah sighed and maneuvered her wheelchair closer to the swing where Mary Ellen sat holding Martha Rose's little girl, Amanda. "Sure wish I had a couple of *kinskinner* like this one to love on."

"You'll have grandchildren sooner than you think." Mary Ellen gave her granddaughter's chubby legs a little squeeze. "I heard that Silas Swartley's been courting your Anna, so I wouldn't be surprised if a wedding wasn't in the near future for them."

Rebekah shook her head. "Silas did take Anna home from a singing awhile back, but from what I've been told, there's nothing more to it. Of course, that's not to say that Silas wouldn't like for there to be more. Me either, for that matter."

"Silas seems like a nice enough fellow. I would think Anna would be anxious for him to come calling."

"My eldest daughter's not acting like herself these days." Rebekah lowered her voice some. "Fact is, I'm kind of worried about all three of my oldest kinner."

Mary Ellen's eyebrows lifted high on her forehead. "How come you're worried?"

"Well, Anna's been saying things to rile her daed, like

how come he doesn't want to put in a phone at the green-house and maybe he should modernize some."

"Maybe she thinks you'd have more customers if you had a phone."

"That could be, but the fact that she won't let Silas court her when they've been friends since they were little makes me wonder if she's got her eye on someone else, or maybe she's just feeling discontent with things."

"Why would she be discontent? She joined the church last fall, so I would think she'd be all settled in by now."

"I can't really say what's going on with her." Rebekah shrugged. "Maybe it's just my imagination, or maybe it's some kind of phase she's going through. I'm hoping it will pass real soon."

"You said all three of your oldest have you worried. What's going on with Joseph and Rachel?"

Rebekah's voice lowered another notch. "Joseph is carrying a torch for Pauline Hostetler, and he hasn't got the courage to tell her that he cares. That's made him kind of moody lately."

"I see. And Rachel? What's her problem?"

"I'm not sure about Rachel. She's been acting strange for some time, kind of like a young woman in love, only she doesn't have a boyfriend, so I know that's not the case."

Mary Ellen bent her head and kissed the top of Amanda's head. "If they could only stay sweet and innocent like this little girl, we grandmothers wouldn't have so much to worry about."

Rebekah chuckled. "Jah, but knowing us, we'd find something else to fret over."

Rachel and her family had begun packing up to leave the Yoders' place, when she noticed Silas had Anna cornered next to his courting buggy. Her sister didn't look any too happy, and Rachel couldn't help but wonder what was being said. She inched a bit closer, hoping to catch a word or two. Eavesdropping had become a habit, it seemed, but she couldn't seem to help herself. Besides, it wasn't like she was doing it on purpose. People just seemed to be in the wrong place at the wrong time.

"I think it would be best if you'd forget about me," she heard Anna say. "You really should find someone better suited to you."

Silas shuffled his feet a few times, turning his hat over and over in his hands. "Don't rightly think there's anyone better suited to me, Anna."

"If you think about it, you'll realize that we don't have much in common. Never have, really." Anna shrugged. "On the other hand, I know who would be just right for you."

Me. . .me. . . Rachel squeezed her eyes shut, waiting to hear Silas's next words.

"Who might that be?"

"Rachel."

"Don't start with that again, Anna."

Rachel's eyes snapped open. She had to give up this silly game of bouncing back and forth from hope to despair. It only proved her immaturity, which was exactly why Silas saw her as a mere child.

"She likes a lot of the same things you like, Silas. Besides,

I think she's crazy about you." Anna nodded toward her family's buggy, where Rachel stood, dumbfounded and unable to move. She would probably never be able to look Silas in the face again.

Silas didn't seem to notice Rachel, for he was looking right at Anna. "As I've said before, Rachel's not much more than a kinner. I need someone who's mature enough for marriage and ready to settle down."

"Rachel is *eighteen*, soon to be *nineteen*," Anna said. "Give her a few more months, and she'll be about the right age for marrying."

"But it's you I love, Anna." Silas's tone was pleading, and if Rachel hadn't been so angry at her sister for embarrassing her that way, she might have felt pity for the man she loved.

"Rachel, are you getting in or not?" Dad's deep voice jerked Rachel around to face him.

"What about Anna? She's still talking to Silas over by his buggy." Rachel pointed in that direction, but Dad merely grabbed up the reins.

"I'm sure Silas will see that Anna gets home," Mom put in. "After all, you did mention that he's sweet on her."

Rachel's throat ached from holding back tears, and she reached up to massage her throbbing temples. Silas thought she was just a child, and he was in love with Anna. At the rate things were going, she might never get to use the things she'd put in her hope chest. She glanced Silas's way one last time, then hopped into the buggy and took her seat at the rear.

Joseph glanced over at her. "Why are you lookin' so down in the mouth?"

"It's none of your business."

"I'll bet she'll tell me. I'm a girl, and girls only share their deepest secrets with another girl. Isn't that right, sister?"

Before Rachel could answer Elizabeth's question, Perry put in his two cents' worth. "Aw, Rachel's probably got a bee in her kapp 'cause she don't have a steady boyfriend yet. She's most likely jealous of Anna gettin' to ride home with Silas." He gave Rachel an impish smile. "That's it, huh? You're green with envy, right?"

"Leave Rachel alone," Mom called from her seat at the front of the buggy. "If she wants to talk about whatever's bothering her, she will. Now, let's see how quiet we can make the rest of this ride home."

As Anna pressed her body against Silas's buggy, she felt like a mouse cornered in the barn by a hungry cat. Couldn't Silas just accept the fact that she didn't love him? Why did he keep going after her like this? If only she felt free to tell him what was on her mind. If she could just reveal her secret. . .

"So, what do you have to say, Anna? Can I give you a ride home so we can talk some things through?"

Silas's pleading voice pulled Anna's thoughts aside, and she gritted her teeth. "Danki for the offer, but I think I'll just walk home today."

His eyes widened. "On a hot day like this, you want to walk all the way home when I'm offering you a ride in my open buggy?"

She nodded. "There's really nothing more for us to say, so I'd appreciate it if you'd leave me alone."

Silas pulled back as if he'd been slapped, and his face turned bright red.

Anna hated being rude, but Silas obviously didn't want to take no for answer, and speaking so bluntly seemed to be the only way she could get through to him. "I don't mean to hurt your feelings, Silas, but it wouldn't be right for me to lead you along when I know we can't have a future together."

"We could have if you'd give it half a chance."

"Sorry, but I can't do that."

"Why'd you accept a ride home in my buggy after the last singing then?"

Anna swallowed hard. How could she offer an answer to that without revealing her secret? "I probably shouldn't have accepted that ride, and I'm sorry if you got the impression that it meant anything more than just a friendly ride home." Anna stepped away from Silas's buggy and darted off before he had a chance to respond. She had to get away now before she ended up telling him the truth.

Chapter 5

The following day, Rachel felt more fretful than ever. She'd hardly said more than two words to anyone all morning and was sorely tempted to tell Anna that she had overheard some of her conversation with Silas yesterday. In fact, she was working up her courage and praying for the right words as she hung a batch of laundry on the line.

When Anna came out of the greenhouse and headed in Rachel's direction, she decided this was as good a time as any. Rachel waved and called for her sister to come on over. Anna merely gave a little nod and kept walking toward the barn. A short time later, she emerged with one of the driving horses, then began to hitch the mare to the buggy parked nearby.

Rachel dropped one of Perry's shirts into the wicker basket, but before she could move to intercept Anna, their mother called, "Where are you going?"

"I've got to run some errands in town," Anna explained. "Then I may stop by and see Martha Rose for a bit."

"You be careful now," Mom called. She sat on the front porch in her wheelchair, shelling peas into a large ceramic bowl sitting in her lap.

"I will," Anna hollered, as she stepped into the buggy.

"And don't be out too late, neither. There was a bad accident last week along the main highway. It was getting dark, and the driver of the car didn't see the Amish carriage in time."

"I'll be careful, Mom." Anna flicked the reins, and the horse and buggy were soon out of sight.

Rachel walked back to the wicker basket, bent down, and snatched a pair of Dad's trousers. "Guess I'll have to catch Anna later on," she mumbled.

"Rachel!"

"Jah, Mom?"

"When you're done with the laundry, I'd like you to go over to the greenhouse and help your daed awhile. I've got several things here at the house needing to be done, so it doesn't look like I'll be able to work out there today."

"What about Anna? She's the one who likes working with flowers."

"She's running some errands in Paradise."

Rachel already knew that. What she didn't know was why. Couldn't *she* have gone to town so Anna could have kept working in the greenhouse? Life wasn't always fair, but she knew there was no point in arguing, so she cupped her hands around her mouth and hollered, "Okay, Mom! I'll go over to the greenhouse as soon as I'm finished here."

※

Silas's morning chores were done, but he had a few errands to run for his dad. He decided this would be a good time to stop by the Beachys' greenhouse and have a little talk with Anna. Maybe he'd even buy Mom a new indoor plant or something she could plant in her flower garden. That would give him a good excuse for stopping at Grandma's Place, and it might keep Anna from suspecting the real reason for his visit.

Half an hour later, Silas stepped inside the greenhouse and was surprised to see Rachel sitting behind the counter, writing something on a tablet. "Guder mariye," he said, offering her a smile. "Is Anna about?"

"Nope. Just me and my daed are here today." She motioned toward the back room. "He's repotting some African violets that have outgrown their containers."

Silas's smile turned upside down. "I thought Anna usually worked in the greenhouse. She isn't sick, I hope."

Rachel tapped her pencil along the edge of the counter. "She went to Paradise. Had some errands to run."

Silas scratched the back of his head. "Hmm. . .guess maybe I can try to catch up with her there. I have some errands to run today, too." He turned toward the door, all thoughts of buying a plant forgotten. If he hurried, he might make it to Paradise in time to find Anna. The town wasn't so big, so if she was still running errands, he was bound to spot her. "Have a nice day. See you later, Rachel."

Anna. . .Anna. . .Anna. . . Rachel gripped her pencil so hard, her knuckles turned white. Was getting Anna to agree to court him all Silas ever thought about? He hadn't bothered to ask how Rachel was doing or even make any small talk about the weather.

"I heard the bell ring above the door," Dad said as he entered the room. "Did we have a customer?"

Rachel was about to answer when she felt a sneeze coming on. She grabbed a tissue from the box under the counter, leaned her head back, and let out a big *ker-choo!*

"*Got segen eich*—God bless you."

"*Danki.*"

"You're not coming down with a summer cold, I hope." Dad's forehead wrinkled, and he looked at Rachel with obvious concern.

She shook her head. "I think I'm allergic to all these flowers. I do okay with the ones growing outside, but being cooped up with 'em in here is a whole different matter."

"Guess working in the greenhouse isn't exactly your idea of fun, huh?"

She turned her head away as she felt another sneeze coming on. "*Ker-choo!*" She held her finger under her nose. "Truth is, I would rather be outside."

"How come the doorbell jingled and we have no customers?" Dad asked, making no mention of her preference.

"It was Silas Swartley. He was looking for Anna, and when I told him she was running errands in Paradise, he hightailed it right out of here."

Dad chuckled. "Love is in the air. There's no doubt about it."

Rachel nibbled on the end of her pencil, remembering the way Silas always looked whenever he spoke of her sister. It made her sick to her stomach, knowing he was so sweet on Anna when she didn't love him in return.

Dad grinned like an old hound dog that had just been

given a bone. "Someday your time will come, Rachel. Just be patient and have the hope that God will send the right man your way."

"I'm hoping," she mumbled. "Hoping and praying for a miracle."

By the time Silas had reached the town of Paradise, his horse was breathing heavy, and the poor animal's sides were lathered up pretty good. Silas knew he shouldn't have made the gelding trot all the way there, but he'd been in such a hurry to see if he could find Anna that he hadn't thought about what he was doing to his horse.

He pulled up to the back of the variety store and secured the horse to the hitching rail that had been put there for Amish buggies. "Sorry about making you run so much," he said, as he rubbed the horse's flanks with a rag he'd taken from the back of the buggy. "I'll get you a bucket of water, and then you can rest while I go inside and see if there's any sign of Anna."

Silas took care of his horse first thing. Then he hurried into the store. After checking every aisle and asking both of the women who worked in the store if they'd seen Anna Beachy, he realized that Anna wasn't in the store, nor had she been there any time today.

"Guess I'll have to check somewhere else," he mumbled as he climbed back in his buggy. "She couldn't have left town already."

For the next hour, Silas drove around Paradise, checking inside every store and asking all the clerks if they had seen

Anna. Not one person remembered seeing her, and Silas thought it was more than a bit strange. If she had really come to town to run some errands, then surely he would have spotted her by now, or at least someone would have remembered seeing her come into their store. Maybe Anna had changed her mind about going to Paradise and had gone to one of the other small towns in the area to do her shopping.

Silas knew it would take too long for him to travel from town to town looking for Anna, and he'd probably miss her anyway. Finally, with an exasperated groan, he took his seat in the buggy again and gathered up the reins. "There's no hurry getting home," he mumbled. "So I may as well let my horse walk all the way."

It was after nine o'clock, and the sun had nearly set, yet Anna still hadn't returned home. Dad and Mom sat on the front porch, talking about their workday, while Rachel kept Elizabeth entertained with a game of checkers she'd set on the little table at one end of the porch. Joseph and Perry were out in the barn, grooming the horses and cleaning Joseph's courting buggy.

Rachel had just crowned her last king and was about to ask her little sister if she wanted to give up the game and have another piece of funny-cake pie their Mennonite neighbor had given them earlier that day, when a horse and buggy came up the graveled drive. It was Anna, and before she even got the horse reined in, Dad was on his feet.

"Why are you so late, daughter?" He ran toward the

buggy, shaking his finger all the way. "You sure couldn't have been running errands all this time."

The porch was bathed in light from several kerosene lamps that had been set out, but the night sky was almost dark. Rachel knew Anna wasn't supposed to be out alone after the sun went down because of the risk of an accident, even with the battery-operated lights on their buggy.

Rachel peered across the yard and strained to hear what Anna and their father were saying. *Sure hope that sister of mine hasn't done anything foolish.* An unsettled feeling slid through Rachel as she watched Anna step down from the buggy.

"Your mamm and I were gettin' worried," Dad's deep voice announced.

Mom coasted down the wheelchair ramp. "Oh, thank the Lord! I'm so glad to see you're safe."

"Sorry. I didn't realize it was getting so late," Anna apologized.

"Well, you're home now, and that's what counts. We can talk about where you've been all this time after I get the horse and buggy put away." Dad quickly unhitched the mare and led her off toward the barn.

"Anna, where's your apron and head covering?" Mom asked, as Anna stepped in front of the wheelchair.

Rachel studied her sister closely. Sure enough, Anna wasn't wearing anything on her head, and the black cape and apron she'd been wearing over her dark blue cotton dress when she'd left home were off, too. No cape. No apron. No head covering. What in the world was that girl thinking?

Anna reached up to touch the top of her head. "I. . .uh. . . guess I must have left my kapp someplace."

Elizabeth stepped off the porch. "That makes no sense, sister. How could you have left your kapp anywhere when it's supposed to be on your head?"

Anna shot Elizabeth a look that could have stopped the old key-wound clock in the parlor, but she pushed past her little sister and stepped onto the porch without any comeback at all.

"Wait a minute, Anna." Mom propelled herself back up the ramp. "We need to talk about this, don't you think?"

"Can't it wait until tomorrow? I'm kind of tired."

Rachel gulped. If Anna were a few years younger, she would have had a switch taken to her backside for talking to their mother that way. What in the world had come over her?

"It may be getting late, and you might be tired, but this is a serious matter, and it won't wait until tomorrow," Mom said with a shake of her head.

Anna pointed at Rachel, then Elizabeth. "Can't we talk someplace else? No use bringing the whole family into this."

Mom folded her arms and set her lips in a straight line, indicating her intent to hold firm. "Maybe your sisters can learn something from this discussion. I think it would be a good idea if they stay—at least until your daed returns. Then we'll let him decide."

Rachel sucked in a deep breath and held it while she waited to see what Anna's next words would be.

"Guess I don't have much say in this." Anna folded her arms and dropped to the porch swing with a groan.

Elizabeth moved back to the checkerboard. "Are you

gonna make your next move, Rachel? I just took one of your kings while you were starin' off into space."

Rachel jerked her thoughts back to the game they'd been playing. "I don't see how you managed that. . .unless you were cheating. I *was* winning this game, you know."

Elizabeth thrust out her chin. "I wasn't cheating!"

Rachel was about to argue the point further, but the sound of her father's heavy footsteps on the stairs drew her attention away from the game again.

"Joseph's tending the horse." Dad looked down at Anna, who was pumping the swing back and forth like there was no tomorrow. "Now, are you ready to tell us where you've been all day?" A muscle in his cheek began to twitch, and Rachel knew it wasn't a good sign. "Why aren't you wearing your apron and kapp, Anna?"

Rachel flinched, right along with her older sister. Their father didn't often get angry, but when he was mad enough to holler like that, everyone knew they had better listen.

"I. . .uh. . ." Anna stared at the floor. "Can't we talk about this later?"

Dad slapped his hands together, and everyone, including Mom, jumped like a bullfrog. "We'll talk about it now!"

Anna's chin began to quiver. "Couldn't I speak to you and Mom in private?"

He glanced down at Mom, who had wheeled her chair right next to the swing. "What do you think, Rebekah?"

"I guess it might be best." She turned her chair around so she was facing Rachel and Elizabeth. "You two had better clear away the game. It's about time for you to get washed up and ready for bed anyway."

"But, Mom," Elizabeth argued. "I'm almost ready to skunk Rachel and—"

Rachel shook her head. "You'd better do as Mom says. You can skunk me some other time." She grabbed up the checkerboard, let the pieces fall into her apron, folded up the board, then turned toward the front door. As curious as she was about where Anna had been and why she'd come home without her kapp or apron, Rachel knew it was best to obey her parents. She would have a heart-to-heart talk with her rebellious sister tomorrow morning. Until then, she'd be doing a whole lot of praying.

❧

As Anna sat on the porch swing, waiting for her sisters to go inside the house, her mind swirled with confusion. If she told her folks the truth about where she had been all day, it wouldn't just get her in trouble. She would be breaking a promise she'd made not to say anything yet about her plans.

She closed her eyes and clenched her fingers until they dug into the palms of her hands. *If I make up a story to tell Mom and Dad, and they find out later that I lied to them, they'll be crushed, and I'll be in big trouble; that's for certain sure.*

Someone touched Anna's knee, and she opened her eyes. Her mother had pushed her wheelchair even closer to the swing, and her father stood directly behind the chair. "Anna, are you ready to tell us where you've been all day?" Mom asked in a near whisper.

Anna swallowed around the lump in her throat as tears blinded her vision.

"You'd best be tellin' us now." Dad's wrinkled forehead and squinted eyes let Anna know that he was nearly out of patience.

"I. . .uh. . .was with Silas Swartley all day," Anna said in a shaky voice. She sniffed a couple of times and blinked in an attempt to clear away her tears.

Mom's lips turned into a smile. "Why didn't you just say so in the first place? We have nothing against Silas; you know that."

"What about your apron, cape, and kapp?" Dad motioned to the front of Anna's dress, devoid of its cape and apron. "You had all three on when you left home earlier. How come you're not wearing any of 'em now?"

Anna drew in a deep breath and blew it out quickly. "Well, I. . .uh. . .the thing is—"

"Quit thumpin' around the shrubs and tell us the truth!"

"I'm not wearing my apron and cape because I spilled ice cream all over myself."

"And the head covering?"

Anna's face heated up. She was getting in deeper with each lie she told, but she felt like a fly trapped in a spider's web and didn't know what to do.

"Answer your daed's question, Anna," Mom prompted. "Where's your kapp, and why aren't you wearing it now?"

"Silas. . .well, he wanted to see how I would look with my hair down, so I took the head covering off and removed the pins from my hair for a short time."

Mom gasped, and Dad stomped his foot.

"I know it was wrong, but it felt right at the time, and after I pinned up my hair again, I forgot to put the kapp back in place." Anna glanced toward the buggy shed. "Guess I left the kapp, along with the apron and cape, inside the buggy."

"We're glad you and Silas are courting, but we can't have you running off like that without telling us where you're going," Mom said, reaching out to pat Anna's knee again.

Dad shook his finger in Anna's face. "And I won't stand for you taking off your kapp and letting your hair down in front of Silas. Is that understood?"

"Jah."

"You're a baptized member of the Amish church now, not some *eegesinnisch*—willful—teenager going through her rumschpringe days."

Anna stared down at her hands, folded in her lap. "I know, Dad, and I'm sorry. Don't know what came over me, really."

Mom smiled. "You're in *lieb*, that's what. Young people do all kinds of things they'd not do otherwise when they're in love with someone."

"That doesn't give her the right to be doin' things she knows are wrong and could get her in trouble with the church," Dad put in.

Mom lifted her hand from Anna's knee and clasped her hand. "She knows what she did was wrong, and I'm sure she won't do it again. Right, daughter?"

Anna nodded as tears rolled down her cheeks. She knew what she had really done today wouldn't set well with her folks when they learned the truth, and the lies she'd just told them had only made it worse. But she didn't feel she could undo any of it now. Later, once everything had been said and done, she would tell them both the truth. In the meantime, she had to keep the promise she'd made for a little while longer.

CHAPTER
6

When Rachel came downstairs the following morning, she found Mom and Anna busy fixing breakfast.

"You're late." Anna stirred the oatmeal so hard Rachel feared it would fly right out of the pot. "How do you think you're going to run a house of your own if you can't be more reliable?"

"Anna Beachy, just because you got up on the wrong side of the bed doesn't give you the right to be *schlecht* with your sister this morning." Mom sat at the kitchen table, buttering a stack of toast, and the look on her face let Rachel know she wouldn't tolerate anyone being crabby this morning.

Rachel hurried to set the table, deciding it was best to keep quiet.

Anna brought the kettle of oatmeal to the table and plopped it on a pot holder, nearly spilling the contents. "Like as not, you'll be getting married someday, Rachel, and I was wondering if you'd care to have my hope chest."

Rachel glanced at her mother, but Mom merely shrugged and continued buttering the toast. Anna was sure acting funny. Of course, she'd been acting strange for several weeks now, but today she seemed even more unsettled. Rachel could hardly wait until breakfast was over and she had a chance to corner Anna for a good talk. She was dying to know where her sister had been last night and what had happened during her discussion with their folks.

"I've already got a start on my own hope chest, but thanks anyway." Rachel gave Anna a brief smile.

"I'd sure like to go to Emma Troyer's today," Mom said, changing the subject. "She's feeling kind of poorly and could probably use some help with laundry and whatnot. Trouble is, I've got too much of my own things needing to be done here and out at the greenhouse, as well."

Anna's eyes brightened some. "I'll go," she said almost too quickly as she went to the refrigerator and took out a pitcher of milk.

Mom nodded. "If you don't dally and come straight home, then I suppose it would be all right. You'll have to wait until this afternoon, though. I need help baking pies this morning."

"This afternoon will be just fine."

Rachel could hardly believe her ears. Wasn't Anna in any kind of trouble for coming home late last night and not wearing her apron, cape, and kapp? What sort of story had she fed the folks so that Mom was allowing her to take the buggy out again today? Worse yet, if Anna went gallivanting off, Rachel would probably be asked to help in the greenhouse for the second day in a row. She'd planned to do some bird-watching this afternoon and maybe, if there was enough time, go fishing at the river. From the way things looked, she'd most likely be working the whole day, so there would be no chance of her having any kind of fun.

"Did I hear someone mention pies?" Elizabeth asked as she skipped into the room. "I sure hope you're plannin' to make a raspberry cream pie, 'cause you know it's my favorite."

Mom reached out and gave the child a little pat on the backside when she sidled up to the table. "If you're willing to help Perry pick raspberries, maybe we could do up a few of your favorite pies." Her forehead wrinkled slightly. "Our raspberry bushes are loaded this summer, and if they're not picked soon, the berries are liable to fall clean off. Now that would surely be a waste, don't you think?"

Elizabeth's lower lip jutted out. "I don't like to pick with Perry. He always throws the green berries at me."

"I'll have a little talk with your brother about that. Now, run outside and call the menfolk in for breakfast."

"Okay, Mom."

Elizabeth scurried out of the room, and Mom clicked her tongue. "That girl has more energy than she knows what to do with."

Rachel smiled, but Anna just took a seat at the table and sat staring across the room as though she were in a daze.

A few minutes later, Dad and the brothers came in along with Elizabeth, whose exuberance continued to show as she rushed over to the table.

"Slow down," Dad admonished. "The food's not going anywhere."

"I know, but I'm hungry," the child said as she pulled out a chair beside Mom's wheelchair.

Dad merely grunted in response, and everyone else took

their seats, as well. As soon as the silent prayers had been said, Elizabeth began eating.

"Guess you really were hungry," Mom said with a chuckle.

Rachel glanced over at Anna, who seemed more intent on pushing the spoon around in her bowl than in eating any of the oatmeal she had prepared. If only she could get into Anna's head and figure out what she was thinking.

Conversation at the table was kept to a minimum. Everyone seemed anxious to finish the meal and get on with their day. When breakfast was over and the dishes had been washed, dried, and put away, Anna excused herself to go feed the hogs, and Rachel headed to the henhouse to gather eggs. After she was done, she hoped she might be able to have a little chat with her big sister.

With basket in hand, Rachel started across the yard, wishing she could go for a long walk. The scent of green grass kissed by early morning dew and the soft call of a dove caused a stirring in her heart. There was no time for a walk or even for lingering in the yard, because she had chores to do and knew she had best get them done quickly if she wanted to catch Anna before she left.

A short time later, Rachel reached under one of their fattest hens and retrieved a plump, brown egg. A few more like that, and she'd soon have the whole basket filled. By the time she had finished the job, ten chunky eggs rested in the basket, and several cranky hens pecked and fussed at Rachel for disturbing their nests.

"You critters, hush now. We need these eggs a heap more than you, so shoo!" She waved her hands, and the hens all scattered.

When an orange and white barn cat brushed against Rachel's leg and began to purr, she placed the basket on a bale of straw and plopped down next to it. She enjoyed all the barnyard critters. They seemed so content with their lot in life. Not like one person she knew, who suddenly seemed so dissatisfied and couldn't give Silas the time of day.

"What am I going to do, Whiskers?" Rachel whispered. "I'm in love with someone, and he don't even know I'm alive. All he thinks about is my older sister." Her eyes drifted shut as an image of Silas flooded her mind. She saw him standing in the meadow, holding his straw hat in one hand and running his long fingers through his dark chestnut hair. She imagined herself in the scene, walking slowly toward Silas with her arms outstretched. Closer and closer she came to him, until. . .

"Sleepin' on the job, are you?"

Rachel's eyes popped open, and she snapped her head in the direction of the deep voice that had pulled her out of her pleasant reverie. "Joseph, you about scared me to death, sneaking up that way."

He chuckled. "I wasn't really sneaking, but I sure thought you'd gone off to sleep there in your chair of straw." He sat down beside her. "What were you thinking about that put such a satisfied smile on your face?"

Rachel gave Joseph's hat a little yank so it drooped down over his eyes. "I'll never tell."

Joseph righted his hat and jabbed her in the ribs with his elbow. "Like as not, it's probably some fellow you've got on your mind. My guess is maybe you and Anna have been bit by the summer love bug."

Rachel jabbed him right back. "I wouldn't talk if I was you. Anyone with halfway decent eyesight can see how much you care for Pauline."

"Pauline doesn't see me as anything more than a friend. When she came back to Pennsylvania after her time of living in Ohio, I'd thought maybe I might have a chance, but she doesn't seem to know I'm alive." He gave his right earlobe a quick tug. "I wonder if it's our age difference that bothers her, or maybe she just doesn't find me appealing."

Rachel touched his shoulder and gave it a gentle squeeze. "I wouldn't take it personal if I was you. I've got a hunch that Pauline's thinking about the age difference, same as Silas."

Joseph's eyebrows lifted. "That makes no sense, Rachel. Silas and Anna are the same age."

Rachel could have bit her tongue. If she wasn't careful, she would end up telling her big brother that she was crazy in love with Silas and wished like everything that he loved her, too.

"Speaking of Anna, has she ever told you that she's in love with Silas?"

Joseph leaned over to stroke the cat's head, for Whiskers was now rubbing against his leg. "She hasn't said anything to me personally, but she's been acting mighty strange here of late. I hear tell she got in pretty late last night; and some other times, Anna's whereabouts haven't been accounted for, either. What other reason could she have for acting so sneaky, unless she's been seeing Silas in secret?"

Rachel remembered Silas saying he was going to Paradise yesterday and that he hoped to find Anna there. Could she possibly have spent the day with him? She really wanted to know.

Rachel grabbed the basket of eggs and jumped up. "I've got to get these back to the house. See you later, Joseph!" She tore out of the barn and dashed toward the hog pen, where she hoped to find Anna still feeding the sow and her brood of piglets. In her hurry, she tripped over a rock and nearly fell flat on her face. "Ach! The last thing I need this morning is to break all the eggs I've gathered."

She walked a little slower, but disappointment flooded her soul when she saw that Anna wasn't at the pigpen.

Back at the house, Rachel found Mom, Anna, and Elizabeth rolling out pie dough at the kitchen table. Each held a wooden rolling pin, and Rachel noticed that Elizabeth had more flour on her clothes than she did on the heavy piece of muslin they used as a rolling mat.

"You're just in time," Mom said with a nod of her head. "Why don't you add some sugar to the bowl of raspberries on the cupboard over there?"

Rachel put the eggs in the refrigerator, then went to the sink to wash her hands. "Elizabeth, it sure didn't take you and Perry long to pick those berries. How'd you get done so fast?"

"Mom helped." Elizabeth gave Rachel a wide grin. "Her wheelchair fits fine between the rows, and she can pick faster'n anybody I know."

Mom chuckled. "When you've had as many years' practice as me, you'll be plenty fast, too."

Rachel glanced at Anna. She was rolling her piecrust real hard—like she was taking her frustrations out on that clump of sticky dough. Every once in a while, she glanced at the clock on the far wall and grimaced. Rachel figured this probably wasn't a good time to be asking her sister any questions. Besides the fact that Anna seemed a might testy, Mom and Elizabeth were sitting right there. It didn't take a genius to know Anna wasn't about to bare her soul in front of them.

Rachel reached for a bag of sugar on the top shelf of the cupboard. She'd have to wait awhile yet. . .until she had Anna all to herself.

The pie baking was finished a little before noon, and Anna, who seemed quite anxious to be on her way, asked if she could forgo lunch and head on over to Emma's.

"I suppose that would be okay," Mom said. "I could fix you a sandwich to eat on the way."

Anna waved her hand. "Don't trouble yourself. I'm sure Emma will have something for me to eat."

Mom nodded but sent Anna off with a basket of fresh fruit and a jug of freshly made iced tea. "For Emma," she stated.

Rachel finished wiping down the table, then excused herself to go outside, hoping her sister hadn't left yet. She saw Anna hitching the horse to the buggy, but just when she was about to call out to her, Dad came running across the yard. "Not so late tonight, Anna!"

Anna climbed into the buggy. "I'll do my best to be back before dark."

Dad stepped aside, and the horse moved forward.

Rachel's heart sank. *Not again! Am I ever going to get the chance to speak with that sister of mine?* With a sigh of resignation, she turned and headed back to the house. Today was not going one bit as she'd planned.

CHAPTER 7

Rachel gripped the front porch railing, watching as Anna climbed out of the buggy and began to unhitch the horse. It was almost dark. She could hardly believe her sister would be so brazen as to disobey their parents two nights in a row. *What kind of shenanigan is Anna pulling now? Why is she acting so defiant all of a sudden?*

Before Rachel had a chance to say anything to her sister, Dad was at Anna's side, taking the reins from her. "Late again," he grumbled. "You know right well we don't like you out this late. You'd better have a good excuse for this. Something better than what you told us last night."

Rachel wanted to holler, "What did you tell them last night?" Instead, she just stood like a statue, waiting to hear Anna's reply.

Anna hung her head. "I. . .uh. . .need to have a little heart-to-heart talk with you and Mom."

"Fine. I'll do up the horse, then meet you inside." Dad walked away, and Anna stepped onto the porch. She drew Rachel into her arms.

"What was that for?" A feeling of bewilderment mixed

with mounting fear crept into Rachel's soul.

Anna's eyes glistened with tears. "No matter what happens, always remember that I love you."

Rachel's forehead wrinkled. "What's going on, Anna? Are you in some kind of trouble?"

Anna's only response was a deep sigh.

"I've been wanting to talk to you all day—to see why you've been acting so strange and to find out how come you were late getting home last night."

Anna drew in a shuddering breath. "Guess you'll learn it soon enough, because I'm about to tell Dad and Mom the truth about where I was then and why I'm late again tonight."

"Weren't you running errands in Paradise yesterday?"

Anna shook her head.

"And today—didn't you spend the day at Emma Troyer's?"

"I went to Lancaster both times," Anna admitted as she sank into one of the wicker chairs sitting on the front porch. "I know you probably won't understand this, but I'm going to have to leave the Amish faith."

Rachel's mouth dropped open. "What? Oh, no. . .that just can't be!"

"It's true."

"But how can you even think of doing such a thing now that you've been baptized and joined the church? Don't you know what it will mean if you leave now?"

A pathetic groan escaped Anna's lips, and she began to cry.

Rachel knelt in front of the chair and grasped her sister's trembling hand. "I'm guessing the folks don't know," she said, hoping this was some kind of a crazy mistake and that as soon as Anna was thinking straight again, she would say it was only a joke and that everything would be all right.

"I made up some story about why I was late last night."

"What story was that?"

"I said I was with Silas all day, and the reason I wasn't wearing my cape and apron was because I spilled ice cream all over me."

"And the kapp? How come you weren't wearing that last night?"

Anna winced as though she'd been slapped. "I lied about that, too. Said Silas wanted to see me with my hair down, so I took the kapp off and forgot to put it back on before I headed home."

Rachel's mind whirled like Mom's gas-powered washing machine running at full speed. First Anna had said she wasn't interested in Silas; then she'd lied and said she was. It made no sense. And why would her sister do something so bold as to let her hair down in front of Silas—or anyone else, for that matter?

The words Rachel wanted to speak stuck in her throat like a wad of chewing gum.

"You. . .you. . .really lied to the folks about all that?" she finally squeaked.

Anna nodded.

"And they believed you? I mean, you said the other day that you had no interest in Silas."

"I know, but I wanted to throw them off track." Anna swallowed so hard her Adam's apple jiggled up and down. "I've got to tell them the truth now; there's no other way."

Rachel made little circles with her fingers across the bridge of her nose. This wasn't good. Not good at all. Anna had been lying to Mom and Dad and saying things about leaving the Amish faith. How could she be so mixed-up? What in the world was happening to their family?

Rachel had every intention of questioning her sister further, but Dad stepped onto the porch just then. "Let's go into the kitchen, Anna." He pointed at Rachel. "You'd better go on up to bed."

Obediently but regretfully, Rachel stood, offering Anna a feeble smile. At this rate, she would never find out the whole story.

When Rachel entered the kitchen, she discovered her mother working on a quilt. A variety of lush greens lay beside vivid red patches spread out on the table, making it look like a colorful jigsaw puzzle.

"Isn't it nice?" Mom asked as she glanced up at Rachel. "This is going to be for Anna's hope chest, seeing as to how she's got herself an interested suitor and all. Why, did you know that she snuck off yesterday just to be with Silas Swartley? The little scamp told us she wasn't interested in him, but it seems she's changed her mind."

Before Rachel could comment, Dad and Anna entered the room. "*Gut nacht*, Rachel," Dad said, nodding toward the hallway door.

"Good night," Rachel mumbled as she exited the room, only closing the door partway. She stopped on the stairwell, out of sight from those in the kitchen. She knew it was wrong to eavesdrop, but she simply couldn't go to bed until she found out what was going on with her sister.

"Anna, you said you had something to say," Dad's voice boomed from the kitchen. "Seems as though you ought to start by explaining why you're so late."

"She was probably with Silas again," Mom interjected. "Anna, we don't have a problem with him courting you, but we just can't have you out near dark by yourself. It's much too dangerous."

Rachel knew Anna was taking the time to think before she spoke, because there was a long pause and a shuffling of feet. Suddenly, her sister blurted out, "I lied about me and Silas. He's not courting me, and I–I'm sorry to be telling you this, but I'll be leaving the faith."

Goose bumps erupted on Rachel's arms as she peered through the crack in the doorway and saw Mom's face blanch.

"You're what?" Dad hollered.

"I–I'm leaving because I got married today."

"You were supposed to be at Emma's," Mom said as though the word *married* had never been mentioned.

"What are you talkin' about, girl?" Dad sputtered. "How can you possibly be married?"

"Reuben Yutzy and I got married today by a justice of the peace in Lancaster." Anna's voice sounded stronger by the minute. "We've been seeing each other secretly for some time now, and yesterday we went to get our marriage license."

Rachel clasped her hand over her mouth as she stifled a gasp. This was worse than she had imagined, and it simply couldn't be true.

"What caused you to do such a thing?" Dad's back was

to Rachel, and she could only imagine how red his face must be.

"If it's Reuben you love and wanted to marry, why did you hide it?" Mom's voice quavered like she was close to tears. "Why didn't Reuben speak with one of the deacons about the two of you getting married? We could have had the wedding this fall, and—"

"I'm sure you must know that Reuben hasn't been baptized or joined the church yet, and he doesn't plan to, either." There was a pause, and Anna cleared her throat a couple of times. "So that means I'll have to leave the Amish faith in order to be with him."

"You can't be serious about this!"

"Daniel, you'll wake the whole house." Mom's voice lowered to a near whisper, and Rachel had to strain to hear what was being said.

"I don't care if I do wake everyone! This is most serious business our daughter has brought to us tonight."

"Can't we at least discuss this in a quiet manner?" Mom asked in a pleading tone.

Dad shuffled his feet a few times, the way he always did whenever he was trying to get himself calmed down. A chair scraped across the kitchen floor. "Sit down, daughter, and explain this rebellious act of yours."

Rachel stood twisting the corners of her apron, too afraid to breathe. Nothing like this had ever happened in the Beachy home, and she couldn't imagine how it would all turn out.

"Reuben and I have been in love for some time, and I was hoping he would decide to join the church, but he wants to go English, so if I'm to be with him, then—"

"You could have told him no—that you wouldn't marry him unless he joined our church."

"Dad, please try to understand. I love Reuben so much, and I feel that my place is with him no matter which world we must live in."

"So you just snuck off and got married without consulting any of us first? Is that the way we do things in this family, Anna?" When Mom stopped speaking, she released a muffled sob.

Dad leaned over so he was looking Anna right in the face. "Why'd you wait so long to tell us this? Why weren't you honest from the beginning?"

"I was afraid if I was up front with you about this that you wouldn't understand and would try to talk me out of marrying Reuben."

He nodded. "That's right. We would have. Any decent parent would try to make their kinner understand the consequences of a choice such as this."

Mom let loose with another sob, and it nearly chilled Rachel to the bone. She leaned against the wall, feeling as if her whole world was caving in around her. How could she have been so blind? Anna had been telling her that she didn't love Silas, yet she'd been leading the poor fellow on. She'd been acting secretive and kind of pensive lately, too. Rachel should have asked her sister what was going on much sooner. If Anna had been straight with her about things, maybe she could have talked some sense into her stubborn head.

"As you probably know, Reuben's got himself a job working for a paint contractor in Lancaster," Anna continued.

"That's where we plan to live—in an apartment Reuben found for us. I just came home tonight to explain things and gather up my belongings. Reuben's home telling his folks now, too, and he's coming to get me in the morning."

"I won't hear this kind of talk in my house!" There was a *thud*, and Rachel was pretty sure her father's hand had connected with the kitchen table.

"Oh, Daniel, now look what you've gone and done," Mom said tearfully. "All my squares are verhuddelt."

"Our daughter's just announced that she's gotten married today and plans to leave the faith, and all you can think about is your mixed-up quilting squares? What's wrong with you, *fraa*?"

"But. . .but. . .Anna was raised in the Amish faith," Mom blubbered. "She's been baptized and has already joined the church, so we'll have to shun her now."

"Don't you think I know that already?"

Rachel chanced another peek to see how things were looking. Dad paced back and forth across the faded linoleum. Mom had gathered up the quilting pieces that had been scattered all over the table. Anna just sat with her arms folded.

"I know you don't understand my decision to go English with Reuben, but I love him ever so much."

Dad slapped his hands together, and Rachel jumped back behind the door. "You're our firstborn child, Anna, and it's gonna break our hearts if you run off and leave your faith behind."

"I'm not giving up my faith in God," Anna defended. "We'll find another church where we can worship God."

"Are you sure you can't talk Reuben into staying Amish?"

"No, Mom. Reuben's set on leaving. He likes having a truck to drive, and he enjoys many other modern things."

"Maybe I should have a little talk with that young fellow. Might could be that he'll come to his senses once I set him straight on a few things."

"Please, Dad, don't do that. I'm sure it will only make things worse."

"You'd have to give up your way of dress if you left," Mom said.

"I know."

"Since Reuben's not joined the church, he won't be shunned, but you will be, Anna. Surely you must realize the seriousness of this."

"I know it won't be easy." Anna sighed. "For Reuben's sake, I'll just have to deal with it."

Dad's fist pounded the table again. "You can't do this, Anna. I forbid it!"

Rachel shuddered. Whenever their father forbade anyone in the family to do anything, that was the end of it, plain and simple. No arguments. No discussion. But if Anna was already married to Reuben, then she had to consider what he wanted now, didn't she?

Anna sucked in a huge sob. "I'm sorry, Mom and Dad, but my place is with Reuben, and the two of us will be moving to Lancaster in the morning no matter what anyone says."

Rachel had heard all she could stand, and a raw ache settled in the pit of her stomach. She turned and tiptoed up the stairs as quickly as she could. Her oldest sister was about to be shunned, and there wasn't a thing she could do about it.

Morning came much too quickly as far as Rachel was concerned. To make matters worse, she had awakened feeling as though she hadn't slept at all. Part of her heart went out to her sister, for she seemed so sincere in her proclamation about loving Reuben and needing to leave the Amish faith because of his desire to go English. Another part of her heart felt sorry for poor, lovesick Silas. What was he going to say when he got wind of this terrible news? He'd been friends with Anna a long time and had brought her home from a singing not long ago. He must believe he had a chance with her.

And what about the greenhouse? Who would help Mom and Dad with that? Anna had been working there for several years, and the folks weren't getting any younger. Eventually they would need someone to take the business over completely.

Rachel slipped out of her nightgown and into a dress, feeling like the weight of the world rested on her shoulders. She was sure that she would be asked to fill in for Anna at the greenhouse. Joseph liked flowers well enough, but he was busy working the fields, and Dad often helped in the fields, especially during harvest season. If Rachel were forced into the confines of the stuffy, humid greenhouse, she would hardly have any time for watching birds, hiking, or fishing. She knew it was selfish, but she was more than a little miffed at Anna for sticking her with this added responsibility.

A sudden ray of hope ignited in Rachel's heart. With

Anna leaving, Silas might begin to take notice of her.

She poured some water from the pitcher on her dresser into the washing bowl. *Guess I could even tolerate working with flowers all day if I had a chance at love with Silas.*

The idea stuck in Rachel's mind like unbuttered taffy, and she splashed some water on her face, hoping the stinging cold might get her thinking straight. As the cool liquid made contact, she allowed her anxiety to fully surface. Silas wasn't going to turn to her just because Anna was no longer available. Besides, even if by some miracle he did, Rachel would be his second choice. She'd be like yesterday's warmed-over stew.

Her shoulders drooped with anguish and a feeling of hopelessness. She wasn't sure she wanted Silas's love if it had to be that way. But then, she *was* a beggar, and beggars couldn't be choosy.

Rachel hung her nightgown on a wall peg and put her head covering in place. She might look ready to face the day, but in her heart she sure wasn't ready. She hated the thought of going downstairs. After everything that had gone on between Anna and the folks last night, Rachel had a pretty good notion what things would be like with the start of this new day. As much as she might like a chance with Silas, she didn't want it this way. Anna's leaving would affect them all.

A sudden knock on the door startled her. "Who is it?"

"Rachel, it's me. Are you up?" Anna called through the closed door.

"Just getting dressed. Tell Mom I'll be right down to help with breakfast."

"Could I come in? I need to talk to you."

"Jah, sure."

When Anna opened the door, Rachel saw immediately that she had been crying. Probably most of the night, truth be told. She also noticed that her sister's hope chest was at her feet.

Anna bent down and pushed the cumbersome trunk into Rachel's room. "I can't stay long," she said in a quavering voice. "I'll be leaving soon, but I wanted you to have this before I go."

Rachel's heart slammed into her chest. Should she tell Anna she had been listening in on her private conversation with the folks last night or play dumb? Probably wouldn't be a good idea to let her know she had been eavesdropping.

"You're leaving?" she mumbled.

Anna nodded.

"Where are you going?" Rachel asked, making no mention of what she knew about Reuben or saying anything concerning the hope chest Anna had slid to the end of her bed.

"Last night after you went upstairs, I told Mom and Dad that I've been secretly seeing Reuben Yutzy."

"Really?"

"Jah."

"But Reuben's not a member of the church yet, and from what I hear, he's kind of wild."

Anna frowned. "Reuben's got a hankering for some modern things, but he's really a nice fellow." She took a seat on the edge of Rachel's bed. "The thing is. . .well, Reuben and I got married yesterday."

"You. . .you did?" Rachel hated playing dumb like this, but if Anna had any idea that Rachel already knew about her plans, she'd probably be too miffed to share anything else that was on her mind.

"We went to Lancaster and got married by a justice of the peace. Then a few hours later, Reuben went home to tell his folks, and I came here to tell ours. Last night was the final time for me to sleep in my old room, because this morning, Reuben's coming for me. We'll be leaving."

Rachel sucked in her breath and flopped down beside her sister. "But. . .but where will you go?"

"We'll be living in an apartment in Lancaster." Anna sighed. "Of course, the folks are pretty upset, but they need to realize that I love Reuben, and my place is with him now."

"What about your hope chest?" Rachel's voice dropped to a near whisper. "Won't you be needing all your things now that you're married and about to set up housekeeping?"

Anna shook her head. "The apartment Reuben rented is fully furnished. Besides, the things in that chest would only be painful reminders of my past." She nodded at Rachel. "Better that you have 'em."

Rachel was sorely tempted to tell her sister that there wasn't much point in her having one hope chest, much less two, since she would probably never marry. She thought better of it, though, because she could see from the dismal look on Anna's face that saying good-bye was hurting her badly.

"If you renounce your faith, you'll be shunned. You've been baptized into membership, Anna. Have you forgotten that?"

Anna blew out her breath. "Of course I haven't forgotten. Leaving my home and family is the sacrifice I have to make. There isn't any other way that I can see."

Rachel jumped up. "Yes, there is! You can talk Reuben into forgetting all this nonsense about going English. You can stay right here and marry Reuben again in the Amish church." Strangely enough, Rachel found herself wishing Anna had accepted Silas's offer to court her. With him, at least, she knew Anna would be staying in the faith.

What am I thinking? Here I am, so in love with Silas that my heart could burst, and I'm wishing my sister could be making plans to marry him.

Rachel's vision clouded with tears as she thought about how this news would affect the man she loved. "What about Silas? You rode home with him in his courting buggy from a singing not long ago. Didn't that mean anything?"

Anna dropped her gaze to the floor. "I—I didn't mean to lead Silas on, but even if I weren't planning to leave, I wouldn't have married Silas. I don't love him. I never have."

Rachel planted her hands on her hips as she stared hard at her sister. Anna seemed almost a stranger to her now. What had happened to her pleasant childhood playmate? Where had the closeness she'd once felt with Anna gone?

"Silas is a wonderful man, and he loves you. Doesn't that count at all?"

Anna lifted her head to look at Rachel. "I'm sorry for Silas, but I have to go with my heart." She drew in a deep breath. "What do *you* want out of life, Rachel?"

Rachel swallowed hard. "That's easy. I want love. . . marriage. . .and lots of kinner."

"Since you're so worried about Silas, why don't you try to make him happy? Maybe the two of you will marry someday, and he'll give you a whole houseful of children."

Rachel shook her head. "I wish I could make Silas happy, but I can't, because he doesn't love me."

CHAPTER 8

Not one word was said during breakfast about Anna's plans to leave. It was almost as if nothing had gone on last night. Rachel figured her folks either were hoping they could talk Anna and Reuben out of leaving and into getting married again within the church or had already begun the shunning.

When breakfast was over, Dad went outside. Rachel was at the sink doing dishes, and when she glanced out the window, she saw him hitch up the buggy and head on down the road. She thought it was odd that he hadn't said where he was going.

A short time later, Dad returned with Deacon Byler following in his own closed-in rig. Rachel was out in the garden with Elizabeth when she saw the two men climb down from their buggies.

Rachel straightened and pressed a hand against her lower back to ease out some of the kinks. The deacon stepped close to the garden and nodded at her. "Where's your sister Anna? I'm here to speak with her."

Before Rachel could reply, Anna came out of the house,

lugging an old suitcase down the steps. She wasn't wearing her kapp, cape, or apron. At least she wore a dress, and her hair was pinned up in a bun.

Deacon Byler marched right on over to her. "I understand you and Reuben Yutzy are planning to leave the Amish faith."

Anna nodded. "That's right. My husband will be here soon to pick me up."

"Your husband, huh?"

Anna nodded again.

Rachel dropped the beet she had just dug up and held her breath, for she feared the worst was coming. Even though she couldn't do anything about Anna leaving, she knew she must do something to offer a little bit of support. "Keep working," she told Elizabeth. "I'll be right back." She hurried across the yard to stand beside Anna.

Anna gave Rachel a sad smile. Then she turned to face the deacon again. "I don't like disappointing my family, and I feel awful about the lies I told them, but I'm a married woman now, and I've got to be with my husband."

The deacon crossed his arms as his forehead wrinkled. "Deacon Shemly is speaking with Reuben right now, so maybe he can convince him to stay and become a member of our church."

Anna shook her head. "I doubt he'll change his mind."

Deacon Byler turned toward Dad. "I guess we need to wait and see how things go between Deacon Shemly and Reuben."

Dad nodded.

The deacon headed back to his buggy, and Anna looked up at her father with tears shimmering in her eyes. "Sorry, but I don't think Reuben will change his mind, which means I won't, either."

Dad said nothing in return. He stared at Anna for a few seconds as if he were looking right through her. Then he stalked off toward the barn.

Rachel didn't know what she could say, either. She felt sick at heart over the way things were going, and reality settled over her like a dreary fog. If Anna left the faith, nothing would ever be the same at home.

"No one understands the way I feel," Anna moaned. She took a seat on the top porch step and rested her chin in the palms of her hands.

Rachel seated herself beside Anna and reached over to take her hand. "Being in love can make us do things we never expected we'd do."

Anna nodded and sniffed deeply. "I hate the thought of leaving home or being shunned by my family, and I did try to talk Reuben into joining the church, but he's determined to leave."

Rachel squeezed Anna's fingers, though she didn't think the gesture offered much comfort. "Guess I'd probably do the same thing if the man I loved was determined to leave home and had asked me to marry him and leave my family and friends."

Anna glanced over at her and squinted. "Are you in love with someone?"

Rachel chewed on her lower lip a few seconds. Finally, she nodded.

"Mind if I ask who?"

"I–I'm in love with Silas Swartley."

A smile lifted the corners of Anna's lips. "I thought so."

"You thought so?"

"Jah. I've had a feeling for some time that you had an interest in him."

"Has it been that obvious?"

"To me, at least. I've seen the way you look at Silas with such longing, and the things you've said about him being so good-looking and nice made me realize you must care for him."

Rachel released a sigh. "Silas has been in love with you for a long time, Anna. He doesn't see me as anything more than a child, so it makes no difference how I feel about him."

Anna opened her mouth as if to reply, but Reuben pulled up in his fancy red truck, interrupting their conversation. She stood and glanced back toward the house, then looked at Rachel again. "I spoke with Mom right after breakfast and told her I'd be leaving as soon as Reuben showed up, but she didn't want to come outside, so we said our good-byes in there."

Rachel stood, too, smoothing the wrinkles in her long, green dress and swallowing against the lump in her throat. "I guess she thought it would be too painful to see you drive away." She grabbed Anna in a hug. "I'm sure gonna miss you. Write soon and let me know how you're doing, okay?"

Anna nodded fiercely as tears welled in her eyes. "I know the brothers are already out in the fields, so would you tell them good-bye for me?"

"Jah, sure."

"And Dad, too."

"Why don't you tell him yourself? I haven't seen him come out of the barn, so I'm guessing he's still in there."

Anna shook her head. "You saw the way Dad looked at me when Deacon Byler was here. He's awful angry about this decision I've made, and I doubt he'd even want to say good-bye."

Reuben tooted the truck's horn, and Anna picked up her suitcase and hurried down the steps. She stopped off at the garden to give Elizabeth a hug, then opened the passenger's door of Reuben's shiny red truck and climbed right in.

Rachel sank onto the porch step with a groan.

⁊

Reuben had just started to back the truck up when Anna's father came running out of the barn, waving his arms.

Hoped welled in Anna's soul. Maybe Dad wanted to tell her good-bye after all. Maybe he didn't want her to leave with this awful dissension between them. "Better wait and see what he wants," she said, looking over at her husband.

"Jah, okay." Reuben put his foot on the brake, and Anna pushed the button to let her window roll down. But Dad went around to Reuben's side of the truck, not hers.

"Guess you'd best roll down your window then," she said to Reuben.

He grunted but did as she asked.

As soon as the window was down, Dad stepped close to the truck and leaned over until his head was nearly inside. "Did Deacon Shemly come by your place this morning?"

Reuben's only reply was a quick nod.

"I guess he didn't talk any sense into you, or you wouldn't be taking my daughter away."

"I'm not trying to cause any trouble for your family, but I've gotten used to so many modern things since I started working for Vern Hanson, and I've become used to having a truck that I don't think I could do without."

Dad's eyebrows drew together as a deep frown crushed his strong features. "Oh, but you think it's okay for me to do without my daughter?"

Reuben reached across the seat and took hold of Anna's hand, which gave her added courage and made her feel just a bit better. "I love Anna, and she's my wife now, so she belongs with me."

"If you love her so much, then you ought to be willing to join the Amish church and keep her from being shunned."

"This isn't just Reuben's decision," Anna said, leaning across the seat so she could look her father in the eye. "I've been feeling kind of discontent here of late, and—"

"And nothing!" Dad clapped his hands together. "You're only doin' this to please this young man, and apparently neither of you cares about who you're hurting in the process of having what you think you want." He stepped away from the truck and slowly shook his head. "Well, go on then. Go on out into the English world and forget you ever had an Amish family who cared about you!"

Tears clogged the back of Anna's throat and her vision blurred. "I love you, Dad. I love all my family, but my place is with my husband." She looked over at Reuben and managed a weak smile. "Let's go now, shall we?"

Reuben took his foot off the brake and turned the truck around. As they headed down the driveway, Anna turned and saw Rachel standing on the porch, waving at them. Anna waved back as tears coursed down her cheeks. When Reuben pulled onto the main road, she lifted her hand in one final wave, and then they were gone.

As Rebekah sat in front of the window overlooking the back porch, watching her firstborn child drive away, it was all she could do to keep from breaking down. All the expectations she'd had for her daughter had been dashed away in one fell swoop. She wanted to swaddle Anna in a blanket—keep her warm and safe. But it was too late for that now; her baby was gone.

She drew in a deep breath and closed her eyes as her mind took her back to that wonderful day when Anna had been born. . . .

"It's a girl," Rebekah whispered, as Daniel entered the birthing room, wearing an anxious expression. "God has given us a miracle baby."

Daniel bent his head to kiss Rebekah's cheek. Then he reached out his finger and stroked the side of the baby's tiny head. "She's a miracle, all right." He glanced back at Rebekah and smiled. "She's a beautiful child, and she looks just like her mamm."

Tears welled in Rebekah's eyes. "All those months I spent asking God for a miracle, I never expected Him to answer in such a wunderbaar way." She kissed the top *of the baby's downy head.* "Let's *call her* Anna *after my dear grandma; is that okay?"*

"That's fine by me." Daniel's smile widened. "If the next one's a boy, then I get to name him, though. Agreed?"

She smiled and nodded. "Jah, *sure. If God chooses to give us another miracle, you can name the* boppli *whatever you choose."*

As Rebekah's thoughts drifted slowly back to the present, the pain in her heart lessened a bit. If God could perform so many miracles, allowing her to give birth to five babies after the doctors had said she might never conceive, then He could do anything.

"Dear Lord," she whispered in prayer, "You blessed Daniel and me with our special kinner to raise, so now I'm committing my oldest child into Your hands and asking that You give her a life full of love, joy, and miracles beyond measure." She paused as tears clogged her throat and clouded her vision. "Please let Anna know that we love her despite the shunning she's brought on herself by choosing to marry Reuben and go English."

CHAPTER 9

Rachel tossed and turned in her bed for most of the night. Knowing Anna wasn't in her room across the hall left a huge empty spot in her heart. Until recently, she and Anna had shared secrets and hopes for their future. For some time, Rachel had known something was going on with Anna, but she'd thought her sister was only going through a phase that would pass. Never in a hundred years would she have suspected that Anna was interested in Reuben or that the two of them had been secretly courting. And the fact that they'd run off and gotten married by an English justice of the peace was the biggest shock of all.

Rachel closed her eyes and tried to picture Anna married to Reuben, making their home in Lancaster, wearing English clothes, and living the fancy, modern life.

"Does Silas know about this yet?" she whispered into the night. Surely Silas's heart would be broken when he heard the news, for he'd lost Anna not only to the modern world, but to one of his childhood friends, no less. Thinking about Silas helped Rachel feel a little less sorry for herself, and it was a reminder for her to pray for him.

Ping! Ping! Rachel rolled over in bed. What was that strange noise? *Ping! Ping!* There it was again. She sat up and swung her legs over the side of the bed. It sounded like something was hitting her bedroom window, but she couldn't imagine what it might be.

She hurried across the room and lifted the window's dark shade. In the glow of the moonlight, she could see someone standing on the ground below. It was a man, and he appeared to be tossing pebbles at her window, of all things.

"Who's wanting to get my attention at this time of night?" Rachel muttered as she grabbed her robe off the end of the bed.

Quietly, so she wouldn't wake any of the family, she tiptoed in her bare feet down the stairs, being careful not to step on the ones that creaked. When she reached the back door, she opened it cautiously and peered out. She could see now that it was Silas Swartley standing on the grass, bathed in the moonlight.

Rachel slipped out the door, closing it quietly behind her, and dashed across the lawn. "Silas, what are you doing out here in the dark, throwing pebbles at my window?"

He whirled around to face her. "Rachel?"

She nodded. "What's up, anyhow?"

Looking more than a bit befuddled, Silas shifted his long legs and gave his suspenders a quick *snap*. "I. . .uh. . . thought it was Anna's window I was throwing stones at. I've been wanting to speak with her for several days but never seem to get the chance."

Rachel's heartbeat quickened. So Silas didn't know. He

couldn't have heard the news yet, or else he would have realized Anna wasn't here. She took a few steps closer and reached out to touch his arm. "Anna's not in her room, Silas."

"She's not? Where is she, then?"

Rachel's lower lip quivered, and she pressed her lips tightly together, trying to compose herself. This was going to be a lot harder than she'd thought. "I hate to be the one telling you this, but Anna ran off and got married last night. She left home this morning."

Silas's mouth dropped open like a window with a broken hinge. "Married? Left home?" He stared off into space as though he were in a daze, and Rachel's heart went out to him. She had to tell him the rest. He had the right to know. Besides, if he didn't hear it from her, he was bound to find out sooner or later. News like this traveled fast, especially when an Amish church member left the faith to become English.

"Anna married Reuben. They're leaving the church, and—"

"Reuben Yutzy and my Anna?"

Rachel nodded. The motion was all she could manage given the circumstances. Even in the darkness, she could see the pained expression on Silas's face.

"This can't be. It just can't be," he muttered.

They stood staring at each other as crickets creaked and the cornstalks in the field beside her house rustled in the night air. Rachel's shoulders rose and fell, as she struggled not to cry. If only she had the power to turn back the hands of time and make everything right. If she could just think of a way to make her sister come home. But what good would that do? Anna was already married to Reuben, and nothing Rachel could say or do would change that fact.

Silas began to pace. "I knew Reuben was dissatisfied with our way of life. I also knew he was hanging around some English fellows who seemed intent on leading him astray." He stopped, turned, and slowly shook his head. "But I had no idea Anna was in on it, too. I thought I knew her better than that."

Rachel trembled. She didn't know if her shivering was from the cool grass tickling her bare feet or if it stemmed from the anger she felt rising in her soul. There was only one thing she was certain of—Silas was trying to lay the blame on her sister's shoulders.

"Anna wasn't *in* on this. She became *part* of it because she loves Reuben and wanted to be with him."

"Did she tell you that?"

"Not in so many words, but she did say she and Reuben have been secretly seeing each other and that they're in love. She made it clear that her place is with him."

Silas grunted. "She probably influenced him to make the break. Anna always has been a bit of a rebel."

Rachel's heart thumped so hard she feared it might burst wide open. How dare Silas speak of her sister that way! She gasped for breath, grateful for the cool night air to help clear her head. "Anna might have a mind of her own, but she's not the kind of person who would try to sway someone else to leave the church. I know for a fact that it was Reuben who wanted to go English, and I believe Anna loves him so much that she couldn't say no."

Silas drew in a deep breath, trying to get control of his emotions. It seemed his whole world was falling apart, but he knew he had no right to blame Anna for it. He'd just talked to Reuben a few days ago, and his friend had made it clear that he wanted many of the things the world had to offer. He was working for an English man, had bought a fancy red truck, and had even told Silas that he wasn't happy being Amish anymore. Truth be told, Silas had halfway expected Reuben to leave the faith. What he hadn't expected was that Anna would be leaving, too—especially not as Reuben's wife.

"If I had it in my power to make things turn out differently, I surely would," Rachel said, breaking into Silas's troubling thoughts.

When he looked down at her, he noticed that her chin quivered like a leaf caught in a breeze. For one brief moment, Silas was tempted to take Rachel into his arms and offer comforting words. Trouble was, he had no words of comfort. . .for Rachel or himself. All he felt was anger and betrayal. His friend had taken his girl away, and Anna had led him on all these years. How could he come to grips with that knowledge and not feel bitter?

Silas dipped his head in apology. "I'm sorry for snapping at you, Rachel. I know none of this is your fault. It's just such a shock to find out you've lost not one, but two special friends in the same day." He sniffed. "This had to be going on between Reuben and Anna for some time, and I was just too blind to see it. What a *dummkopp* I've been, thinking Anna and I had a future together. Why, I chased after her like a horse running toward a bucket of fresh oats, even though she kept pushing me away. She must have thought I was *ab im kopp*."

Rachel grabbed hold of his arm and gave it a shake. "Stop talking that way! You're not a dunce, and you're not off in the head for loving someone. Reuben had you fooled, and Anna had our whole family fooled." She shook her head. "No one's to blame but Anna and Reuben. They should have been honest with everyone involved. They shouldn't have waited so long to tell us their plans, and they should never have lied to cover up what they were doing."

Silas nodded. "You're right, Rachel. They deserve to be shunned."

"That's the part I dislike the most. It's hard enough to have Anna leave home, but to realize we're gonna have to shun our own kin is the worst part of all." Rachel grimaced. "Since Reuben hasn't joined the church, he won't be shunned at all, but my poor sister will be paying the price for his selfishness."

"That was her choice, so she ought to be prepared for the consequences." Silas blew out his breath and took a few steps back. "Guess I should be gettin' on home. My mission here is over. As much as it pains me to say it, Anna's out of my life for good."

Rachel rubbed her hands briskly over her arms like she might be getting cold, and for the second time, Silas was tempted to embrace her. He caught himself in time, though, remembering Anna's words the other day when she'd said she thought Rachel might be interested in him. If he hugged her, even in condolence, she might get the wrong idea. No, it would be better if he didn't say or do anything that might lead Rachel on. Things were messed up enough. No sense making one more mistake.

"See you at the next preaching service," Silas said before he turned and sprinted up the driveway where his horse and buggy stood waiting. Rachel would have to find comfort from her family, and he would find solace through his work on the farm.

Anna glanced over at her husband sleeping as soundly on his side of the bed as a newborn babe. A lump formed in her throat as tears gathered in her eyes. She loved Reuben so much and wanted to be with him at all costs, but it pained her to know how much she'd hurt her family by leaving the Amish faith to join Reuben in the modern, English world. During their secret courtship, she had tried several times to convince him to stay Amish, but he'd flatly refused. That meant she either had to break up with him or agree to go English, too.

It's so strange, she thought, as she slipped out of bed and padded across the room to stand in front of the window, *but there were times when we were courting that I actually thought I would be happier living the English way of life. Now I'm not so sure.*

She glanced around their small, sparsely furnished bedroom, devoid of many decorative items. It wasn't that Reuben didn't want fancy things; they just didn't have enough money to buy much yet, and since they hadn't had a traditional Amish wedding, they'd received no wedding gifts, either.

Anna pulled the curtain aside and stared at the moonlit

sky. *Guess I'll need to look for a job soon so we'll have enough money to pay the rent on this apartment, make Reuben's truck payment, and be able to buy a few fancy electronic gadgets Reuben's been wanting to have.*

Tears slipped from her eyes and rolled down her cheeks. *Dear Lord, help me to be content with the life Reuben wants us to have, and help my folks understand the decision I made to go English.*

Chapter 10

On the first day of August, an unreal stillness hung in the hot, sticky air. The inside of the house felt like an oven, so Rachel had wandered outside after lunch, hoping to find a cool breeze. She found, instead, her younger brother and sister engaged in an all-out water skirmish.

Squeals of laughter permeated the air as the twins ran back and forth to the freshly filled water trough, filling their buckets and flinging water on one another until they were both drenched from head to toe.

Rachel chuckled at their antics and stepped off the porch, thinking she might join them. The flash of a colorful wing caught her attention instead. Her gaze followed the goldfinch as it sailed from tree to tree, finally stopping at one of the feeders in the flower garden. When it had eaten its fill, it flew over to the birdbath on the other side of the yard. Dipping its tiny black head up and down, the finch drank of the fresh water Rachel had put there early that morning.

Rachel loved watching the birds that came into their yard. Loved hearing their melodic songs. Loved everything about nature.

"*Per-chick-o-ree*," the finch called.

"*Per-chick-o-ree*," Rachel echoed.

She watched until the bird flew out of sight; then she moved across the yard toward the clothesline. In this heat, the clothes she had washed and hung this morning were probably dry.

Rachel had only taken a few clothes off the line, when she heard a small voice nearby. Apparently Elizabeth had given up her water battle with Perry, for she was crouched next to the wicker basket, staring up at Rachel with an expectant look on her face. The child's hair, which was supposed to be secured at the back of her head in a bun, hung down the back of her wet dress like a limp rag.

"Elizabeth, did you say something to me?" Rachel asked.

The child nodded.

"What was it?"

"Dad says Anna and Reuben won't make it in the English world and that they'll come to their senses and return home again. I was wondering what you thought about that."

Rachel knelt next to her sister and wrapped her arms around the little girl's shoulders. "We're all hoping Anna and Reuben will return to our way of life, but we need to face the fact that it might not happen."

"How come?"

"Reuben has it in his mind that he wants to live as the English do, and the last letter I got from Anna said she's working as a waitress at some restaurant in Lancaster. She and Reuben are married now, and they've settled into an apartment there."

"Why can't they live here with us?" Elizabeth asked, her

blue eyes looking ever so serious.

Rachel drew in a deep breath and blew it out in a rush. How could she explain something to her little sister that she didn't fully understand herself? "Well, it's like this, Elizabeth—"

"That'll be enough, Rachel!" Dad's deep voice cut through the air like a knife. He grabbed hold of Elizabeth's arm and pulled her to her feet. "Get on up to the house and change out of those wet clothes. Your mamm's been looking for you, and I'm sure she's got something useful you can be doing."

"But Dad, Rachel was trying to tell me some things about Anna and Reuben."

"We've had enough talk about Anna and her wayward husband."

Elizabeth tipped her head as she stared up at their father with questioning eyes. "We hardly talk about my older sister anymore."

"And it's for the best." Dad gave Elizabeth a little push as he turned her toward the house. "I said your mamm could use your help with some things, so be off with you now."

With head down and shoulders slumped, Elizabeth trudged off. Dad watched until she disappeared into the house; then he turned to face Rachel. "You ought to discourage Elizabeth from talking about Anna. The child's still young and doesn't understand all the things of the world yet. She might think what Anna's done is perfectly okay with us."

"Elizabeth meant no harm in asking, and I didn't think it would hurt to try to explain things a bit." Rachel's eyes filled with tears, and she blinked a couple of times, hoping to keep them at bay. Things were bad enough around here; she didn't want any hard feelings between her and Dad.

"Jah, well, be careful what you say from now on." Dad's voice softened some. "We've lost one daughter to the world, and I don't want my other kinner getting any such thoughts." He turned toward the greenhouse, calling over his shoulder, "When you're done with the laundry, I could use your help. We're likely to have a lot more customers still today."

Rachel grabbed a towel from the line and gave it a good snap. "Always trouble somewhere," she mumbled.

When the back door opened and slammed shut, Rebekah looked up from where she sat at the table, rolling out the dough for an apple-crumb pie. Elizabeth rushed into the room, her clothes soaking wet, her long hair streaming down her back, and wearing such a scowl on her face.

"What's with the long face, daughter? Did Perry get the best of you again?"

Elizabeth nodded, and her chin trembled slightly.

"Was it so bad that he made you cry?"

"No, Mom. It's what Dad said to me, not anything Perry did this time."

Rebekah swiveled her wheelchair so she was facing Elizabeth. "What'd your daed say that has you so upset?"

"He says there's been enough talk about Anna, and he called Reuben *wayward*." Elizabeth wrinkled her forehead. "What's that mean, Mom?"

Rebekah motioned her daughter over to the table, then turned her wheelchair back around. "Have a seat, and I'll try to explain things a bit."

"Jah, okay." Elizabeth pulled out a chair and plunked down, letting her elbows rest on the table. "So what's *wayward* mean?"

"*Wayward* means that someone's kind of lost their way."

"Reuben's lost?"

"Sort of."

"Does that mean Anna's lost, too?"

Tears sprang to Rebekah's eyes as she thought about the choice her firstborn child had made when she'd agreed to marry Reuben and leave the faith. She drew in a deep breath and released it with a huff that lifted the ties of her kapp. "Anna's lost to us in many ways, because her decision to leave our church means we'll have to shun her now."

Elizabeth nodded soberly.

"But she's still part of our family, and it will always be so." Rebekah touched Elizabeth's shoulder and gave it a gentle squeeze. "No matter what happens in the days ahead, we'll love her and accept her decision to go English the best way we can."

"Dad, too?"

Rebekah swallowed around the burning lump pushing against the back of her throat. "Someday I hope he'll come to grips with all this, but in the meantime, I think it's best if we keep quiet about Anna whenever your daed's around."

"What's gonna happen when Anna comes for a visit? Can we still talk to her like she's our sister?"

"Jah, of course. She can't share a meal at the same table

with us, and we're not supposed to have any business dealings with her, but there's no rule that says we can't talk to her."

Elizabeth nodded. "Want me to help with the pie makin' now?"

"As soon as you've changed out of those wet clothes and we get your hair put back in place."

Elizabeth pushed away from the table and scurried out of the room. Rebekah resumed rolling out the mound of dough she'd left waiting on the cloth-covered table. Things would go better soon. At least she hoped they would.

❦

"Ah-ha! So this is where you've been all morning." Joseph squinted and shook his finger at his little brother, who stood in front of the horses' watering trough, drenched with water from head to toe. "When I sent you back to the barn with one tired horse and asked you to bring another, I didn't think you'd be gone for nearly an hour."

Perry hung his head as he dragged the toe of his boot through the mud. "Sorry. I was hot, and Elizabeth came along, soon after I put Tom away—"

"The two of you decided to have a water battle, right?"

Perry lifted his head and gave Joseph a sheepish-looking grin. "You should have seen her, Joseph. She was so wet she looked like a drowned little *hundel*."

Joseph bit back a smile. He could only imagine how much water must have been thrown at his little sister's expense. She probably did look like a drowned pup.

"I didn't just play in the water 'cause I was hot, neither."

"Oh? What other reason might you have had?"

"When I came back from the fields with Tom, I spotted Elizabeth sitting on the back porch looking kind of sad." Perry blinked a couple of times and lifted his chin. "She's been awful gloomy since Anna left home, so I thought it might be good if I came up with something that would take her mind off Anna and make her laugh."

"That's admirable of you, Perry, but I didn't send you out of the fields to get cooled off or to try to make Elizabeth feel better about missing Anna," Joseph scolded. "I expected you to bring back a fresh horse, and you cost me nearly an hour's worth of work waiting on you, so now we'll have to stay in the fields that much longer."

Perry frowned. "Ah, it's summertime, Joseph. I oughta be able to have some fun, don't ya think?"

"You can have all the fun you want when your work's done for the day."

"By that time, I'm too tired to do much of anything but sleep."

Joseph ruffled his little brother's hair. "Summer's nearly over, and you'll be back in school soon. Then you won't have to work half as hard."

"Jah, right. Besides all my chores to do at home, I have to work my tired brain takin' all the tests Teacher Nancy gives us scholars." Perry grunted. "It's enough to make my head explode."

Joseph chuckled. How his little brother liked to exaggerate. He pointed to the barn. "Time's a-wasting, so let's get that horse you came after and make our way back to the fields."

"Jah, okay."

As they headed for the barn, Perry glanced toward the greenhouse near the front of their property, and frowned. "Sure doesn't seem right with Anna not helpin' the folks in the greenhouse anymore, does it?"

Joseph gritted his teeth. Nothing seemed right at their place these days, and Dad seemed to be affected by Anna's decision to go English most of all. Maybe it was because he was supposed to be the head of the family, and he felt as if he'd failed to live up to the job. Could be that Dad was more angry at himself than Anna. It might even be that he thought if he'd been a better father, Anna wouldn't have been led astray by Reuben.

"Did ya hear what I said about Anna?" Perry gave Joseph's shirtsleeve a tug.

"I heard. Just thought it best not to comment."

Perry raised his eyebrows but said nothing.

As they stepped into the barn, Joseph sent up a silent prayer on Anna's behalf and another for them all to feel less tension.

CHAPTER 11

It was another warm day, and Rachel, accompanied by Elizabeth, had gone to the town of Intercourse to buy some things their mother needed. Since Dad paid Rachel for working in the greenhouse, she bought a few new things for her hope chest—just in case.

"How about some lunch?" Rachel asked her little sister when they'd finished their shopping. "Are you hungry?"

Elizabeth giggled and scrambled into the buggy. "You know me, Rachel; I'm always hungry."

"Where would you like to go?" Rachel asked, tucking her packages behind the seat, then taking up the reins.

"I don't care. Why don't you choose?"

Rachel nodded and steered the horse in the direction of the Good 'n Plenty restaurant. The girls soon discovered that the place was crowded with summer tourists and that the wait would be about half an hour.

Elizabeth said she needed to use the rest room, so Rachel stood in the hallway outside the door, waiting for her. She grimaced when a man walked by wearing a base-ball cap with an inscription on the front that read BORN

TO FISH. FORCED TO WORK.

That's just like me. I'd love to go fishing every day and never have to work in the greenhouse again, but that's not likely to happen, I guess.

As the fisherman disappeared, Rachel caught a glimpse of a young Amish man coming from the door that led to the restaurant's kitchen. She thought nothing of it until she got a good look at him. It was Silas Swartley, and he was heading her way.

"It's nice to see you, Rachel. How are things?"

Rachel slid her tongue across her lips and swallowed hard. Why did Silas have to be so cute? Why had she allowed herself to fall in love with him? Except for biweekly preaching services, she hadn't seen much of Silas since that night he'd come to the house, looking for Anna. The fact that Rachel had been the one to give him the shocking news about her sister running off with his friend still stuck in her craw. It should have been Reuben or Anna doing the telling, not her. But no, they left without thinking of anyone but themselves. Seeing Silas standing here now, looking so handsome yet unapproachable, left Rachel speechless.

Silas held a wooden crate in his hands, and he shifted it slightly as he took a step closer to her. "Has the cat got your tongue, or are you gonna answer my question?"

"W–what question was that?"

"I asked how things are."

She swallowed again. "Oh, about the same as usual. How's it at your place?"

"Everything's about the same with us, too. I brought in a crate of fresh potatoes from our farm. This restaurant buys a lot of produce from us." Silas nodded his head toward Rachel. "How come you're here?"

"Elizabeth and I came to town for a few things. We're here for lunch." She suppressed a giggle. "Why else would we be at the Good 'n Plenty?"

Silas's summer-tanned face turned red like a cherry, and he stared down at his boots. "I. . .uh. . .don't suppose you've heard anything from Anna."

Rachel swallowed once more, only this time it was in an attempt to dislodge the nodule that had formed in her throat. It wasn't so surprising that Silas would ask about Anna. He was obviously still pining for her. Truth be told, Silas was probably hoping Anna would change her mind about being English and come home again. But even if she did, what good would that do him? Anna was a married woman now—out-of-bounds for Silas Swartley.

"Anna wrote me a letter the other day," Rachel said. "She's written to her friend Martha Rose a couple of times, too—and of course, to our mamm."

"What'd she say in her letter to you? Or would you rather not share that information?"

"It was nothing special." Rachel shrugged. "Just that she and Reuben are pretty well settled in now. She got herself a job as a waitress, and Reuben's still painting houses and all."

A lady wearing some strong-smelling perfume walked out of the women's rest room, and Rachel's nose twitched as she fought the urge to sneeze. "Guess they've got to have lots of money, since they're living in the modern world and will probably be buying all sorts of fancy gadgets."

Silas's dark eyebrows furrowed. "Sure wish Anna would've

waited awhile to marry Reuben and not run off like that. Maybe if she'd thought it through and given me more time to win her heart, things might have turned out differently for all of us."

From the things her sister had said about Silas, Rachel doubted he could have ever won Anna completely over, but she wasn't about to tell him that. No point hurting his feelings more than they'd already been. "Anna's gone now, and I'm pretty sure she's never coming back," she mumbled.

"How can you be so sure?"

"I just know, that's all. My sister and her husband are walking a different path now, and Anna made it clear in her letter that it was her choice to join Reuben in the English world, and she hopes we'll accept her decision."

Silas shook his head. "I've known Anna since we were kinner, and I always thought we were good friends. It's hard to accept the idea that there's no future for me and her now."

Rachel's heart ached for Silas, but more than that, it ached for herself. She was sure he would always love Anna, even if they couldn't be together. So much for hoping he might ever be interested in plain little Rachel. Hopeless, useless daydreams would get her nowhere, yet no matter how hard she tried to push it aside, the dream remained. "The future rests in God's hands," she mumbled as Elizabeth came out of the rest room.

"Jah." Silas turned and headed out the door.

🙢

Silas left the Good 'n Plenty feeling like someone had punched him in the stomach. Anna and Reuben weren't coming home. Old memories tugged at his heart. He had trusted Anna, and she'd betrayed that trust by sneaking off with his friend, the whole time letting Silas think she cared for him. Could he ever trust another woman not to hurt him that way? Even if Anna changed her mind and came back, he knew she would never be his. She was a married woman now. . .married to his friend Reuben.

Deep in his heart, Silas knew he had to accept things as they were and get on with his life, but no matter how hard he tried, he couldn't imagine any kind of life without Anna Beachy.

Poor Rachel. She had looked so sad. He figured Anna's leaving must have hurt Rachel as much as it had him, only in a different sort of way. He would have to remember to pray for her often. . .and all the Beachys, for that matter. No Amish family ever really got over one of their own running off to become English, and from the look he'd seen on Rachel's face today, he figured she had a long ways to go in overcoming her grief.

Silas climbed into his buggy and gathered up the reins. "Giddap there, boy," he said to his horse. "I've got some work waiting for me to do at home, so let's get going."

※

"Was that Silas Swartley you were talkin' to?" Elizabeth asked when she stepped up to Rachel.

"It was him all right."

Elizabeth stared up at Rachel. "Well, what'd he have to say?"

Rachel wrinkled her nose. "If you must know, little

naasich one, he was asking about Anna."

"I'm not nosey. I just wondered what he had to say, that's all."

"Jah, okay." Rachel knew that just because she felt frustrated over the conversation she'd had with Silas, it wasn't right to be snippy with Elizabeth.

"I think he used to be real sweet on our big sister. I heard Mom say somethin' about it to Dad once."

Rachel grimaced. "Jah, he was. I'm afraid he's still pretty broken up over her and Reuben leaving."

Elizabeth grabbed Rachel's hand and squeezed her fingers. "Anna's never comin' back, is she?"

"Probably not, unless it's just for a visit."

"Can we hire a driver and go to Lancaster sometime? I'd surely like to see my big sister again."

"That probably isn't such a good idea," Rachel said, pulling her sister along as they made their way down the hall. "At least, not right now."

"How come?" the child persisted.

"Because Dad won't like it. Maybe later, down the road, he'll be willing to let us go there."

"I miss Anna a lot."

"Me, too." Rachel felt sick at heart because she couldn't visit her sister. How could she explain all this to Elizabeth when she couldn't make sense of it herself? She knew if they went to Lancaster to see Anna without telling Dad and he found out about it, he'd be furious. Besides, that would be a sneaky thing to do, and there'd already been enough sneaking going on in their family lately, which she knew wasn't right. And what if Elizabeth took a liking to the modern way

Anna was living and decided to seek after worldly things herself? It might be better for everyone if they visited with Anna at their own place, not hers. Of course, Dad might have some things to say about Anna coming to visit them right now, too.

In all of Rachel's eighteen years, she couldn't remember ever seeing her father so angry and determined to make one of his children pay for a decision that went against his will. *Of course,* she reasoned, *Dad might be acting so perturbed because he's upset that Anna's leaving has put us all in a position where we have to shun our own flesh and blood.*

"Your table is ready now," a young Mennonite waitress said as they returned to the restaurant's waiting area.

Rachel smiled, glad for the diversion. Maybe after they were seated, Elizabeth's mind would be on filling her empty stomach and not on Anna. Might could be that the discussion would be dropped altogether, and they could eat a quiet, peaceful lunch.

Much to Rachel's chagrin, no sooner had they taken a seat at the table and placed their orders, than the questions began again.

"Are Mom and Dad really mad at Anna?" Elizabeth blinked several times. "They never talk about her anymore."

Rachel drew in a deep breath and offered up a silent prayer. She needed God's wisdom just now, for sure as anything she didn't want to make things worse by telling her sensitive, young sister something that might upset her even more.

"It's like this," she began, carefully choosing her words. "I'm sure the folks still love Anna very much, but they also love being Amish. They believe in the Ordnung and want to abide by the rules of our church."

Elizabeth nodded soberly. "I've tried talking about Anna several times, but Dad always says it would be best if I'd forget I ever had her as an older sister. How can I do that, Rachel? Anna's still my big sister, ain't it so?"

Rachel was tempted to correct the girl's English but decided it would be best not to make an issue of it right now. She reached across the table and gently touched Elizabeth's hand. "Of course she's still your sister, and nothing will ever change that. As I've told you before, Anna's moved away now, and she wants to live like the English."

Elizabeth's lower lip trembled. "She really don't want to be Amish no more?"

"I'm afraid not. But we can surely pray that someday she and Reuben will change their minds and be willing to reconcile with the church." Hot tears stung the backs of Rachel's eyes. Today had started off well enough, but after seeing Silas, talking about Anna with him, and now trying to make Elizabeth understand how things were, she felt all done in. She had no answers. Not for Silas, not for Elizabeth, and not for herself. As far as Rachel was concerned, her life would never be the same.

She lifted her water glass and took a sip. If only she could get Silas to take notice of her now that Anna was out of his life. She was here; Anna wasn't. If only God would make Silas love her and not her older sister, who was now out of his reach.

As she set the glass back down, a little voice in Rachel's head reminded her that God never forced a person to love anyone—not even Him. If Silas was ever going to get over losing Anna, it would have to be because *he* chose to do so, not because of anything Rachel might say or do.

I can still hope, though. Rachel was reminded of what the Bible said in Psalm 71:14: *"But I will hope continually, and will yet praise thee more and more."* She would definitely continue to hope.

CHAPTER
12

One evening, Rachel's family went out the front porch to sit awhile because it was still too hot inside the house to go to bed. Mom was in her wheelchair, mending one of Joseph's shirts. Dad sat beside her in the rocker, reading the Amish newspaper, *The Budget*. Joseph and Perry sat on the steps, playing a game, and Rachel shared the porch swing with Elizabeth. It was a quiet, peaceful night, in spite of the sweltering August heat.

Rachel mechanically pumped her legs as she gazed out at the fireflies rising from the grass like a host of twinkling lights. An owl hooted from a nearby tree, the gas lantern hanging nearby purred, and the sun dipped slowly below the horizon, transforming the sky into a hazy pink. If not for the fact that Rachel still missed Anna so much and had been forced to take her place in the greenhouse several hours a day, she would have felt a sense of contentment as she soaked up God's handiwork.

Of course, I've lost Silas, too, she reminded herself. Ever since Anna and Reuben had left, Rachel sensed that Silas was mourning his loss. She'd seen him at preaching services several times, and no matter how hard she tried to be friendly, he remained aloof. Maybe she should give up the hope of him ever seeing her as a woman he could love. "It's just a silly dream," she murmured.

"What'd you say?" Elizabeth nudged Rachel with her elbow.

Rachel's face heated up. "Nothing. I was only thinking out loud."

"Daydreaming is probably more like it," Joseph said with a chuckle. "I've never known anyone who could stare off into space the way you do and see nothing at all. A day-dreaming little tomboy, that's what you are."

Rachel grimaced. Was Joseph looking for an argument tonight? Maybe he'd had a rough day out in the fields. Could be that Perry had been goofing around and hadn't helped enough. Or the hot weather might be all that was making her big brother a bit cross.

"If you ever plan on any man marrying you, then you'd better turn in your fishing pole for a broom." Joseph shook his head. "A grown woman isn't supposed to climb trees, splash around in the river like a fish, and stand around for hours gawking at dumb birds."

Rachel folded her arms and squinted at Joseph. "I refuse to let you ruffle my feathers."

He snickered. "Aw, I wasn't trying to upset you. I was just funnin' with you, that's all. We need some fun around here, wouldn't you say?"

Rachel shrugged. "I thought maybe you were *gridlich* because you'd had a rough day."

"I think we're all a bit cranky," Dad spoke up. "A few

more sweltering days like this, and everything in the garden will dry up, like as not."

Mom nodded. "I've had to water things in the greenhouse a lot more than usual, too."

"Everyone has their share of troubles," Perry put in. "Did ya hear about Herman's Katie breakin' her arm?"

Rachel's ears perked right up. "Silas's mamm?"

Perry nodded. "Jah. Heard it from her son Sam this morning when we went fishin' at the pond near Swartleys' place."

"When did this happen?" Mom questioned. "And how?"

"Sometime yesterday. Sam said she fell down the cellar stairs."

Mom clicked her tongue. "Ach, poor Katie. How's she going to manage all her chores with only one good arm?"

"Guess her boys will have to chip in and help out more," Dad commented. "It's a downright shame she doesn't have any girls."

"I could give her a hand," Rachel volunteered, trying to keep the excitement she felt over the idea out of her voice. She did feel bad about Katie's arm, and she really did want to help, but the main reason she'd suggested it was because she thought if she went over there every day, it would give her a chance to see Silas.

"You helping Katie out is a nice thought," Dad said, "but you're needed here, especially in the greenhouse. August is a busy time, what with so many tourists coming by and all. I'm helping Joseph and Perry in the fields part of each day now, and we sure can't expect your mamm to handle things in the greenhouse all by herself."

"I used to manage pretty well when I was a young woman," Mom said with a wistful sigh. "Guess those days are well behind me now, because I get all done in if I try to do too much on my own anymore."

"How 'bout me?" Elizabeth chimed in. "I like flowers. Can't I help in the greenhouse?"

Mom looked over at Elizabeth and smiled. "I appreciate the offer, but I need someone at the house to keep things running and get the noon meal fixed for the menfolk."

Joseph turned to face his mother. "Say, I've got an idea."

"What might that be?"

"Why don't you ask Pauline Hostetler to help out with the greenhouse? I know for a fact that she loves flowers."

"And how would you be knowin' that?" Dad gave Joseph a quick wink.

His face turned beet red, and he started squirming a bit but gave no reply.

"Joseph's sweet on Pauline." Perry chuckled. "I saw him talkin' to her at the last preaching service."

Rachel couldn't believe her bashful brother had finally taken the initiative with Pauline. She thought this bit of news might be beneficial to her, as well. She jumped off the swing and raced over to her mother's wheelchair. "I really would like to help out at the Swartleys'. If Pauline agrees to work at the greenhouse, I'd even be willing to pay her with some of the money I've made this summer."

Mom's eyebrows drew together. "Now why would you do something like that? It's your daed and I who should pay any hired help, not you, Rachel."

Rachel shifted from one foot to the other. If she weren't

careful, she would end up giving away her plans to win Silas. "I—I just thought, since you'd have to pay someone to take my place, I'd be obliged to help with their wages."

Mom smiled. "That's very generous of you, Rachel, but it won't be necessary."

"I can help Katie Swartley then?"

"If it's okay with your daed, then it's fine by me," Mom said with a nod.

"Won't bother me none, as long as Pauline agrees to the terms." Dad looked over at Joseph, who seemed to be studying the checkerboard hard. "Son, since this was your idea, I think you should drive over to the Hostetlers' place tomorrow morning and ask Pauline if she'd like to work in the greenhouse for a few weeks."

Joseph's face turned a deep shade of red, but he nodded, and his lips turned up slightly. "Sure, I guess I can do that."

Rachel smiled, too. If things went well, by tomorrow afternoon she might be on her way to winning Silas's heart.

※

Anna released a sigh as she flipped off the air-conditioning unit in their apartment and took a seat on the sofa. It was too hot without it but too cold whenever it was left on for more than an hour. Oh, how she wished they had a big porch to sit on during the warm, humid days of summer, or even a few shade trees would help. But no, they were stuck in this dinky apartment with only a couple of windows, and nothing but the sidewalk and the street next to it to look at.

She longed for a view of the river, like the one not far from her folks' house. She missed the cows grazing in their pasture, the beautiful flowers growing in her mother's garden, the fresh produce she could pick at will, and she missed her family most of all.

The sharp ringing of the telephone caused Anna to jump. She hurried across the room to the small table where it sat and picked up the receiver. "Hello."

"Hi, Anna, it's me. Just wanted you to know that I'll be working later than I thought."

She glanced at the small clock sitting beside the phone. It was already seven, and Reuben should have been home an hour ago. "How come you have to work longer?"

"My boss got the job of painting a couple of rooms at his dentist's office. Dr. Carmen would like to have it done right away, but the only time we can work on the place is when he doesn't have patients. So we'll be starting it this evening and will work through the night if need be."

Anna grimaced, and a trickle of sweat rolled down her forehead. How was she going to endure this long, hot night without Reuben? How could she tell him that it was okay if he worked late again without letting the disappointment in her voice show?

"You still there, Anna?"

She shifted the phone to her other ear. "I'm here."

"Well, don't wait up for me, because like I said before, I could be pretty late."

"Okay. See you in the morning, then."

Anna hung up the phone and shuffled over to the window, feeling as if she bore the weight of the world on her shoulders. During the time she and Reuben had been secretly courting, she'd felt such a sense of excitement and looked forward to the future with him. Now, every day seemed monotonous and dreary—especially those days when Reuben worked late or didn't feel like visiting with her. All he seemed to care about when he came home from work was watching the television he'd recently purchased or sleeping in his lounge chair.

Oh, how she wished they could return to their old way of life, but whenever she mentioned the idea, Reuben got angry. She knew it would only drive a wedge between them if she continued to pressure him to go back home and join the Amish church. The best thing to do was quit pining for her old life and try to focus on her new life with Reuben in the English world.

CHAPTER 13

As Joseph guided his horse and buggy up the Hostetlers' driveway the following morning, his stomach did a little flip-flop. He'd talked to Pauline a couple of times since she had returned to Pennsylvania, but every time he got close to her, he felt like his tongue was tied in knots.

"Maybe I'll do better this morning," he said as he pulled on the reins to get his horse slowed down. "I sure hope Pauline's willing to work at the greenhouse."

Joseph halted the horse in front of the hitching rail near the barn and climbed down from the buggy. After he'd secured the horse, he sprinted around the back of the house and took the porch steps two at a time. He rapped on the door and was surprised when Pauline answered on the second knock.

"Guder mariye, Joseph," she said, offering him a pleasant smile and pushing back a tendril of pale blond hair that had escaped her kapp. "What brings you by our place so early this morning?"

He shifted from one foot to the other as he stared into her pretty blue eyes. "Well, I. . .that is—"

"Is something wrong? You're acting kind of nervous."

He took a deep breath and forced himself to stand still. "Guess I'd better start over."

She waited patiently for him to continue.

"The thing is, Silas Swartley's mamm broke her arm, so Rachel's offered to go over there and help out for a while during the daytime hours."

"That's too bad about Katie."

He nodded. "So if Rachel's over at the Swartleys' and Dad's helping me and Perry out in the fields, that means Mom will have to be alone in the greenhouse."

Pauline's eyebrows drew together. "Your mamm's not as young as she used to be, and I'm sure it must be hard for her to handle things in the greenhouse by herself."

"You're right, and that's why I'm here."

She tipped her head and looked at him in a strange kind of way. Then a light seemed to dawn. "Are you wanting me to come work in the greenhouse until Rachel's done helping the Swartleys?"

"Jah, if you're free to do so."

Pauline nodded enthusiastically. "I'd be happy to help, and I think I'd rather enjoy working around flowers every day."

Joseph released a sigh of relief. "That's good to hear. Jah, real good." He turned to go but pivoted back around. "I'll let the folks know you'll be over soon then, okay?"

She nodded. "I'll be there as quick as I can."

As Joseph climbed back into his buggy, a sense of hope welled in his soul. If Pauline came over to help in the greenhouse for a few days, he might get the opportunity to see her more. If he could work up the nerve, he might even be so bold as to ask if he could come calling on Pauline sometime.

Silas and his younger brothers, Jake and Sam, had just returned from the fields. Silas spotted a horse and buggy parked in the driveway, but before he could say anything, Jake hollered out, "Looks like we've got ourselves some company!"

Silas shrugged. "Probably one of Mom's friends come to see if she needs any help."

"I hope they brought something good to eat," Sam put in. "Now that Mom's arm is busted, she won't be doing much baking."

Silas flicked his twelve-year-old brother's straw hat off his head. "It's the same old story with you. Always hungry, aren't ya?"

Sam flashed him a freckle-faced grin and bounded up the porch steps. "Last one to the table is a *fett kuh!*"

"You'll be the fat cow." Silas raced his brothers into the kitchen, each of them laughing and grabbing at one another's shirts as they turned this way and that.

Jake and Sam made it to the sink first, because Silas had stopped short inside the door, his gaze fixed on Rachel Beachy, who seemed to be busy setting the table. She glanced over at him and smiled, and his heart felt as though it had stopped beating for a few seconds. He'd never noticed it before, but Rachel had two little dimples—one in each cheek. Had she never smiled at him before, or had he just been too blind to notice? Today Rachel almost looked like a mature woman. Could she have changed that much since he'd last seen her?

"Guess that's your buggy outside," Silas said, feeling as if his tongue had been glued to the roof of his mouth.

"It's mine, all right," she answered. "I'm here to help your mamm until her arm gets better."

Silas's mouth dropped open. "You're going to stay with us?"

"No, silly. Rachel will be coming over every morning and staying until after supper," Mom said.

Silas really felt stupid now. Here his mother stood at the stove, stirring a pot of soup with her one good arm, and he hadn't even noticed her until she'd spoken.

He removed his hat and hung it on a wall peg. "That's real nice of you, Rachel. Nice of your folks to let you come, too."

Rachel placed a loaf of bread on the table. "If Pauline Hostetler hadn't been willing to take my place at the greenhouse, I probably couldn't have come."

"Did ya bring anything good to eat?" This question came from Sam, who had already taken his place at the table.

"Samuel Swartley, where are your manners? Sometimes I don't know what gets into my boys." Mom shook her head and clucked her tongue. "Rachel came to help, not furnish the likes of you with all kinds of fattening goodies."

"Actually, I did bring some chocolate chip cookies." Rachel motioned toward a basket in the cupboard.

Sam started to get up, but Silas placed a restraining hand on his shoulder. "You'd better eat your lunch first, don't you think?"

"What's for lunch, and where's Pap?" Jake asked as he joined his brothers at the table.

"Vegetable soup and ham sandwiches, and your daed's not back from town yet," Mom answered.

Silas and his brothers waited until Rachel and Mom took their seats, and then all heads bowed in silent prayer.

Later, after everyone had eaten their fill, Rachel offered the cookies as dessert.

Silas smacked his lips after the first bite. "Umm. . . these are real tasty. You didn't bake 'em yourself, did you, Rachel?"

"Of course," she replied a bit stiffly. "I may be just a little tomboy in some folks' eyes, but I can cook, bake, sew, clean, and do most everything else around the house."

Silas didn't have a clue what he'd said to make Rachel go all peevish on him, but she seemed kind of miffed. He shrugged and reached for another cookie.

❦

As Rachel cleared away the lunchtime dishes, her mind focused on Silas, who had gone back out to the fields with his brothers. She wished she could figure him out. One minute he smiled and said how nice it was for her to help out, and the next minute he made fun of her, the way Joseph often did.

Was Silas really making fun of me? a little voice niggled at the back of her mind. *He did say my cookies were good, and he only asked if I had baked them.* Maybe she was being overly sensitive where Silas was concerned. Maybe she'd tried too hard to make him take notice of her by smiling sweetly and bringing those cookies. Maybe she should play hard to get, like some other young women often did when they were trying to get a man's attention.

"That wouldn't be right," Rachel mumbled, as she placed the dirty dishes in the sink. Besides, she wasn't Anna, so if Silas was ever going to take notice of her, it wouldn't be because she was playing hard to get.

"Did you say something?" Katie asked, stepping up to Rachel.

Rachel's face heated up. "Guess I was talking to myself."

Katie grinned. Her chubby cheeks always seemed to be wearing a smile.

"If you ever need someone to talk to, I've got a good pair of ears for listening."

"Danki. I'll keep that in mind." Rachel moved over to the stove to retrieve the pot of water she'd heated to wash the dishes. "I can finish up in here. I'm sure you're probably feeling tired by now. Why don't you go and rest awhile?"

Katie handed Rachel the dishrag. "I think I'll take you up on that offer. My arm's hurting a bit, so some aspirin and a good nap might do me some good."

"What else are you needing to have done today?"

"Let's see now. . . . It's too hot to do any baking, but if you feel like it, maybe you could mix up a ribbon salad. That's Silas's favorite kind." Katie nodded toward the pantry. "I think there are a few packages of Jell-O and some other ingredients you'll need in there. Last time I checked the refrigerator, we had plenty of whipping cream, milk, and cream cheese, so you should be able to put it together in time for supper."

A short time later, Rachel had prepared the ribbon salad and was just placing it inside the refrigerator when the back door swung open. Thinking it was probably Herman Swartley returning from town, Rachel turned toward the door and smiled. Her smile was quickly replaced with a frown when she saw Silas standing there, holding his hand and grimacing in obvious pain.

She hurried to his side, feeling as if her breath had been snatched away. "What is it? Are you hurt?"

"I got a big old splinter in my thumb, and it's all your fault."

Rachel's hands went straight to her hips. "My fault? How can you getting a splinter be my fault?"

Silas lowered his head sheepishly. "I took a handful of your cookies out to the fields, and after I ate a few, I forgot to put my gloves back on. Next thing I knew, I was grabbin' hold of the wagon, and here's what I've got to show for it." He held up his thumb for her inspection.

Rachel bit back a smile, even though her stomach did a little flip-flop as she thought about how much the sliver must hurt. "So, it's my fault you weren't wearing your gloves, huh?"

He nodded and looked her right in the eye, which made her stomach take another big nosedive. "If you weren't so good at making cookies, I wouldn't have grabbed a handful. And if I'd had my gloves on, I sure wouldn't have all this pain right now."

Silas's voice had a soft quality about it, yet he spoke with assurance. Rachel thought she could sit and listen to him talk for hours. "Take a seat at the table, and I'll have a look-see," she instructed. "Do you know where your mamm keeps her needles and such?"

Silas's eyes were wide, and his mouth hung slightly open. "You're not planning to go pokin' around on my thumb, are you?"

She tipped her head to one side. "How else did you expect me to remove that old splinter?"

Silas swallowed so hard she saw his Adam's apple bob up and down. "Guess you've got a point." He nodded toward the treadle sewing machine positioned along the wall nearest the fireplace. "I think you'll find all your doctoring tools over there."

Rachel went to the sewing machine and opened the top drawer of the wooden cabinet. She found plenty of needles, a pair of tweezers, and even a magnifying glass. She figured Silas's mother must have had some experience taking out slivers, since she had three boys and a husband.

"It might be best if you close your eyes," Rachel said, as she leaned close to Silas and took his hand in hers. This was the closest she'd ever been to him, and it took all her concentration to focus on that nasty sliver and not his masculine scent or the feel of his warm breath blowing softly against her face.

"I ain't no boppli." Silas clamped his teeth together. "So I'll keep my eyes open, thank you very much."

"As you like." Rachel jabbed the needle underneath the sliver and pushed upward.

"Yow! That hurts like crazy!" Silas's face turned white as a sheet of paper, and Rachel feared he might be about to pass out.

She clenched her own teeth in order to keep from laughing out loud. So Silas didn't think he was a baby, huh? "Maybe you'd better hang your head between your knees and take some deep breaths."

Once Silas had his head down, Rachel grabbed his hand again and set right to work. It was hard to ignore his groans and yowls, but in short order she had the splinter dug out. "Let me pour some peroxide over it and give you a bandage. Do you know where those are kept?"

Silas sat up straight and took several deep breaths before he answered. "In the cupboard. Just above the sink."

Soon she'd cleansed the wound and put a bandage in place. When Silas smiled at Rachel, she thought her heart had quit beating. *How could Anna have turned this special man away in exchange for Reuben Yutzy? I don't understand what she thought was so special about her want-to-be-English husband.*

"Danki, Rachel. That splinter was a nasty one, and I don't think I could have taken it out myself."

"Gern gschehne—you're welcome."

Silas stood and started for the door but pivoted back around. "Say, I was wondering. . .that is. . ."

"What were you wondering?"

For several seconds, he stood with a faraway look in his eyes. Finally, with a shake of his head, he turned toward the door. "Never mind. It was nothing important."

The door clicked shut behind him, and Rachel sank into a chair. Was there any hope for her and Silas, or had she just imagined that he had looked at her with some interest?

With every step Silas took as he headed back out to the fields, he thought about Rachel and how motherly she had looked while she'd worked to remove the splinter from his thumb. Her pale blue eyes, framed by lush, dark lashes, and those cute little dimples made her look irresistible. Her voice, sweeter than a bluebird calling to its mate, had almost mesmerized him.

I'll bet she'll make some lucky fellow a good wife someday. She'll probably be a great mother, too, since she can bake such tasty cookies. He smiled. *And she's even an expert at removing slivers.*

He kicked at a stone with the toe of his boot. *What am I doin' letting myself think such thoughts? If I'm not careful, I'll end up thinkin' I've got feelings for that girl.*

"Girl," Silas mumbled as he bounced another rock across the dry ground. "That's all Rachel is. . .just a girl."

Silas didn't know why, but here lately, he'd begun to feel strangely attracted to little Rachel, and that bothered him more than he cared to admit. Maybe the best way for him to handle these strange feelings was to keep a safe distance from Rachel.

Jah, that's just what I'll have to do.

As Joseph headed home in his horse and buggy after running some errands in town, he was surprised to see Pauline walking along the edge of the road. He pulled on the reins and guided the horse over to the shoulder. "Where you heading?" he called to her.

"One of my buggy wheels broke, so I'm walking home to get some help."

"Climb in, and I'll give you a lift."

"Danki." Pauline stepped into the buggy. "Whew! Sure is a hot day. I didn't relish the idea of walking the next couple of miles to my place, so this ride is much appreciated."

"I'm more than happy to do it." Joseph smiled. "I'd offer to fix your wheel, but like a dummkopp, I forgot to put the toolbox in the buggy when I left home this morning."

"That's okay. My daed can do it." She tipped her head and smiled. "And you're not a dunce, Joseph Beachy."

His face heated up, and he gathered up the reins in order to get the horse moving again. He wished he could think of something else to say, but being this close to Pauline made him feel so nervous it was all he could do to keep his mind focused on his driving. If only he could think of some way to make her take notice of him. If he just weren't three years younger than her. Now that Eli Yoder was married and out of the picture, Joseph thought he might have a chance with Pauline, and if she could get to know him better, she might decide their age difference didn't matter so much.

"Have you been real busy this summer working in the fields?" Pauline asked, breaking the silence.

He nodded. "Mom says things have been busy at the greenhouse, too."

"Jah. We've had plenty of customers, all right." She sighed. "I've enjoyed working around the flowers and wouldn't mind doing it all the time."

He grunted. "My sister Rachel would argue with you on that."

"She doesn't like flowers?"

"Not the indoor kind. Says they make her sneeze."

"Maybe she's allergic to some of them."

"That's what she says, but I think it's just her excuse to get out of working in the greenhouse."

"Why doesn't she like working there?"

"She'd rather be outside climbing trees so she can get a better look at some dumb bird she wants to watch." Joseph glanced over at Pauline, and when she smiled, he found himself beginning to relax. He loosened his grip on the reins a bit and smiled in return.

"I guess Rachel's kind of a tomboy, huh?"

"Jah."

"I've never tried climbing a tree, and I think if I did, I'd probably fall out and break something."

"Rachel's taken a tumble or two over the years, but so far she's never broken any bones." He wrinkled his forehead. "If you want my opinion, she's way too old to be climbing up in trees."

"Next to working in my mamm's flower garden, my favorite thing to do is bake."

"What kinds of things do you like to bake?"

"Cookies. . .pies. . .cakes. . ."

The mention of food made Joseph's stomach rumble, and he hoped Pauline couldn't hear it. He coughed a couple of times, trying to cover up his embarrassment, and kept his eyes looking straight ahead.

They pulled into the Hostetlers' driveway a few minutes later, and he felt a keen sense of disappointment.

"Danki for the ride," she said, offering him another

pleasant smile that set his heart to racing.

"Gern gschehne."

Pauline stepped down from the buggy, and just before Joseph got the horse and buggy moving again, she looked up and asked him a question. "What kind of pie do you like, Joseph?"

"I like 'em all, but I guess shoofly's really my favorite."

"I'll bake you one soon as a thank-you gift for giving me a ride home."

"There's no need for that. I was glad to do it."

"You're a nice man, Joseph Beachy." Before Joseph could think of anything sensible to say, Pauline hurried off toward the barn.

Joseph clucked to the horse and headed back down the driveway, whistling a silly tune and smiling so hard his cheeks began to ache. Pauline had said he was a nice man, not a boy. Maybe there was some hope that she might take an interest in him—at least as a friend.

CHAPTER 14

Over the next few weeks, Rachel helped Katie every day she could. She got up an hour early in order to get her own chores done at home; then right after breakfast, she headed over to the Swartleys' place. Katie's arm seemed to be hurting less, but she would have to wear the cast for another three weeks, which meant she still had the use of only one arm.

Things weren't going as well with Silas as Rachel had hoped. Ever since the day she'd removed his splinter, he had seemed kind of distant. She had to wonder if he was trying to avoid her, although she couldn't think why, since she'd made every effort to be pleasant. It might be that Silas's aloofness was because he was so busy in the fields. On most days, she saw him only during lunch and supper, and even then, he appeared tired and withdrawn.

Today was Saturday, and Katie had enlisted the help of another Amish woman so Rachel could work in the greenhouse with Pauline. Dad had taken Mom, Elizabeth, and Perry to Bird-in-Hand, where they would be selling some of their plants and fresh-cut flowers at the indoor farmers' market.

Since Saturday was always a big day at the greenhouse, they didn't want to leave Pauline alone, and that meant Rachel was expected to stay and help out. Joseph also stayed behind, saying he had some chores to do.

As Rachel began watering plants, the musty scent of wet soil assaulted her senses, causing her to sneeze and making her wish she could be outside instead of cooped up in a much-too-warm greenhouse. She glanced over at Pauline, who was busy waiting on some English customers. The tall, blond-haired woman certainly had changed since she'd returned from Ohio. Instead of being distant and sometimes cross, Pauline had become outgoing and cheerful. Rachel could remember a few years ago when Pauline had been jilted by Eli Yoder. She hadn't tried to hide her bitter feelings.

Rachel couldn't be sure what had brought about such a dramatic change in Pauline, but she suspected it had something to do with the time Pauline had spent in Ohio. She was certain of one thing—Joseph was glad Pauline had returned to Pennsylvania. He seemed to have set his reservations aside about his and Pauline's age difference, because Rachel had noticed that for the last couple of weeks he'd been hanging around Pauline every chance he got. It made her wonder if she could do something to help Pauline and her big brother get together.

When the customers left the greenhouse, Rachel moved over to the counter where Pauline stood. "You can take your lunch break now if you want. I'll wait on anyone who might come in during the next hour."

Pauline nodded and grabbed the small cooler she used

as a lunch bucket from underneath the counter. "I think I'll eat outside. Might as well enjoy the good weather while it lasts. Fall's almost upon us. Can you tell?"

"Jah. Mornings and evenings seem much cooler now. Won't be any time at all until the leaves start to change."

Pauline was about to open the door, when Rachel called out to her. "I think Joseph's still in the barn. Would you mind going there and letting him know that the sandwich I made for him is in the refrigerator?"

Pauline smiled. "I think I can do better than that. I'll go on up to the house, fetch the sandwich and something cold to drink, then take it out to Joe myself, along with the pie I brought him."

Ah, so it's Joe *now, is it?* Rachel hid her smile behind the writing tablet she'd just picked up. Maybe she wouldn't have to play matchmaker after all. "What's this about a pie?"

"He gave me a ride home a few weeks ago after my buggy lost a wheel." Pauline's cheeks turned a light shade of pink. "When he mentioned that he liked shoofly pie really well, I said I would bake him one."

"That big brother of mine does like his pies. It's a good thing he works so hard in the fields, or he might be packing on some extra weight due to his hearty eating habits."

"There's not a speck of fat on Joe from what I can see. Lots of muscle, but no fat." The color in Pauline's cheeks deepened, and she dropped her gaze to the floor. "Well, guess I'd best be getting up to your house to get his lunch."

"See you later, Pauline. Oh, and tell *Joe* I said hello and that I hope he enjoys his lunch."

Joseph had just set out another bale of straw for the horse's stall he was cleaning when he heard the barn door open and click shut. He turned and saw Pauline heading toward him, and his stomach did its usual flip-flop. He hoped he would be able to speak to her without his tongue getting tied in knots again.

"I brought you some lunch, Joe," Pauline said, lifting the small cooler she held in her hands as she stepped up to him.

Joe? Since when had she started calling him *Joe?* Not that he minded the nickname. Truth be told, Joseph saw the familiarity as a good sign. Maybe Pauline was starting to have feelings for him—or at least see him as a good friend, which he hoped could be the beginning of something more.

He reached under his straw hat and wiped the sweat from his brow. "What did you make for me?"

"Actually, it was Rachel who made your sandwich and filled a jug with milk. I just offered to go up to the house and get it from the refrigerator and then bring it out to you." Her face turned kind of pink, and she dropped her gaze to the floor.

"Even so, it was nice of you." He studied her further, trying to get a feel for what she might be thinking.

The color in her cheeks deepened, and she giggled, kind of nervous-like.

"I. . .uh. . .also brought you that shoofly pie I promised to make for you a few weeks ago."

Joseph took the cooler and flipped open the lid. "There's

a whole pie in here, Pauline."

She nodded. "You said it was your favorite kind, and I didn't think a slice or two would do."

"Danki. That was sure nice of you." He licked his lips, and his stomach rumbled despite his best efforts to keep it quiet. "Would you care to join me? We could pull up a bale of straw and have ourselves a little picnic."

Pauline glanced over her shoulder, like she was worried someone might come through the door. Then in a voice barely above a whisper, she said, "I need to be honest with you about something, Joe."

He tipped his head in question.

"The cooler you're holding has my sandwich in it, too."

"It does?"

"Jah. When I volunteered to bring your sandwich out to you, I kind of had it in mind that we could eat our lunches together."

Joseph's lips curved into a smile as a sense of joy spread over him like a warm bath on a cold day. "I'd like that, Pauline. Jah, I'd like that a lot."

Silas wasn't sure it was such a good idea to be going to the Beachys' greenhouse today, but his buggy was already pulling into the graveled parking lot, so he figured he may as well carry out his plan.

When he entered the greenhouse, Rachel greeted him from behind the front counter, where she sat reading a book.

"I thought you'd be swamped with customers," he said,

removing his straw hat and offering her a smile.

Rachel jumped off her stool and moved swiftly to the other side of the counter. "We were busy earlier, but since it's almost noon, I think everyone must be eating their lunch about now." She took a few steps toward him. "I'm surprised to see you here today."

He shuffled his feet a few times and glanced around the room. "Uh, where's Pauline? I thought she was working here now."

Rachel nodded, and her eyebrows drew together. *Have I said something wrong?*

"Pauline does work here, but she's on her lunch break right now. Want me to see if I can find her?" As Rachel moved toward the door, her shoulders slumped.

Silas stopped her by placing his hand on her arm. "I didn't come by to see Pauline."

"You didn't?"

He shook his head.

"What did you come for?"

He rocked back and forth on his heels, with one hand balled into a fist and the other hanging onto his hat tightly. "I'm wondering. . .that is. . ."

"Are you needing a plant or some cut flowers? Mom and Dad took quite a few to the market this morning, but I think we still have a good supply in the back room."

Silas cleared his throat a few times, trying to decide the best way to broach the subject that had brought him here. He fanned his face with his hat, hoping the action might give him something to do with his hands, as well as get him cooled down some.

"You okay, Silas? You're looking kind of poorly. Want to sit awhile?"

"Maybe that would be a good idea." He pulled up an empty crate and plunked down with a groan. "Whew! Don't know what came over me, but I was feelin' a little woozy for a minute there."

"Maybe you're coming down with the flu or something." Rachel placed her hand against his forehead. Her fingers felt cool and soft, making it even more difficult for Silas to think straight.

"I'm not sick," he asserted. "It's just warm in here, that's all."

Rachel nodded and took a few steps back. "It's always a bit stuffy in the greenhouse, which is one of the reasons I don't like working here."

"What would you rather be doing?"

She gave him another one of her dimpled smiles. "Fishing. . .bird-watching. . .almost anything outdoors."

Their gazes met, and the moment seemed awkward. Silas swallowed hard. If he was ever going to ask her, he'd better do it quick, because right now he felt like racing for the door and heading straight home.

"The reason I stopped by was to see if you might want to go to the lake with me tomorrow. Your brother Joseph and me were talking the other day, and he mentioned that you like to fish. So I thought maybe we could do a bit of fishing, and if we're lucky, get in some bird-watching, too."

Rachel stood staring at him like she was in some kind of a daze. For a minute, he wondered if he would need to repeat himself.

"Since tomorrow is an off Sunday and there won't be any preaching service, I guess it would be a good time for some outdoor fun." Her voice came out in a squeak, and she blinked a couple of times.

He jumped up. "You mean you'll meet me there?"

She nodded. "How about I fix us a picnic lunch to take along? Fishing always makes me hungry, and later tonight I was planning to bake some more of those chocolate chip cookies you like so well."

"Sounds good. How about making some of that wunderbaar ribbon salad you fixed for our supper awhile back? That was awful tasty, too," he said with a wink.

Rachel smiled as her face turned a deep shade of red. "I think that can be arranged."

Silas licked his lips in anticipation of what was to come. He was glad he'd finally gotten up the nerve to ask Rachel to go fishing. "Let's meet at the lake around nine o'clock. How's that sound?"

"Sounds good to me," she said, walking him to the door.

⁂

"Say, Anna, wait up a minute, would you?"

Anna halted before she stepped out the back door of the restaurant where she worked. She was tired after a long day, and her feet ached something awful. The last thing she wanted to do was chit-chat with her coworker Kathryn Clemmons. She drew in a deep breath and turned around. "What's up?"

"The last time we talked, you said you hadn't found a church since you'd moved to Lancaster, so I was wondering if you and your husband would like to go church this Sunday with me and Walt."

Anna's heartbeat picked up speed at the mention of church. She'd been wanting to go, but whenever she mentioned the idea to Reuben, he always said he was too tired from working so much overtime. It seemed that all he wanted to do on Sundays was sleep or watch TV.

She swallowed hard, then chose her words carefully. "I appreciate the offer, Kathryn, but my husband's been working a lot of overtime lately, and Sundays are the only days he has to sleep in."

"That's too bad." Kathryn's dark eyes held a note of sympathy. "Maybe you could come this Sunday without him—so you can see if you would enjoy our church."

Anna swallowed again, trying to dislodge the persistent lump crowding her throat. Did Kathryn know how miserable she felt these days? Her life was nothing like she had envisioned it when she'd agreed to marry Reuben and go English. Instead of taking long walks together or enjoying a ride in Reuben's truck the way they used to when they'd been secretly courting, now they barely saw each other. And when they were together, Reuben was tired and cross, which only made Anna more lonely and depressed. She needed something that might help pull her out of this slump.

"I guess maybe I could go alone. Maybe in time, Reuben will feel up to joining me."

"You won't have to go alone." Kathryn placed her hand on Anna's shoulder and gave it a gentle squeeze. "Walt and I will be happy to come by and get you on Sunday morning.

Can you be ready by ten thirty?"

Anna nodded. "I'm sure I can."

As soon as Silas returned home, he went straight to the barn to get out his fishing gear. Besides the fishing pole, several fat worms, extra tackle, and line, he'd decided to take along his binoculars and the new book he'd recently bought on bird-watching.

He grinned as he grabbed his pole off the wall. It amazed him that Rachel liked to fish and study birds, but he was glad they had that in common. Neither one of his brothers showed the least bit of interest in watching birds or fishing with him, and now that Reuben was gone, he'd been forced to fish alone.

Silas frowned. He hadn't thought about Reuben for several weeks, and he wished he wasn't thinking of him now. Reminders of Reuben always made him think about Anna, and he wasn't sure he was completely over her yet. He'd loved her a lot, and she'd hurt him badly. A fellow didn't get over being kicked in the gut like that overnight. Matters of the heart took time to heal, and until a moment ago, Silas had begun to think his heart might be on the way to mending.

"I'll feel better once I'm seated on the dock at the lake with my fishing pole in the water and the warm sun against my back," he muttered.

"Who ya talkin' to, Silas?"

Silas whirled around. His brother Sam stood looking up at him like he was some sort of a bug on the wall. "I wasn't talking to anyone but myself, and you shouldn't go around sneaking up on others."

Sam scrunched up his freckled nose. "I wasn't sneaking. Just came out to the barn to feed the cats, and I heard you talking about going fishing."

Silas nodded. "That's right. I'll be headed to the lake in the morning."

"Can I go along?"

"Naw, I'd rather go alone. Besides, you don't even like to fish."

"I know, but it might be better than hangin' around here all day. Ever since Mom got that cast on her arm, she's been askin' me to do more chores."

"Things will go better soon. Mom won't always be wearing her arm in a sling. Besides, there won't be a bunch of chores for you to do on Sunday."

"I guess you're right about that." Sam turned to go, calling over his shoulder, "If it's a girl you're meeting tomorrow, could ya save me a piece of cake from the picnic?"

Silas pulled his fingers through the back of his hair. That little brother of his was sure no dumb bunny. Only thing was, it wouldn't be cake he'd be bringing home tomorrow, because Rachel had said she was going to bake his favorite kind of cookie.

Chapter 15

As Anna combed her hair in front of her dresser mirror, her mind was plagued with doubts. Did she really want to go to church this morning? If Reuben were going along, then she might be more in the mood. But to go alone didn't seem right. Of course, she wouldn't really be alone. Kathryn and her husband, Walt, would be with her. Still, it might be difficult to be with Kathryn, whose husband eagerly attended church every week, and not feel sorry for herself because Reuben showed no interest in anything spiritual these days.

Had he ever? Anna wondered as she turned to look at him sleeping in the bed across the room. Oh, sure, Reuben had attended church with his family throughout his growing-up years, but he hadn't been baptized or joined the church, which was a good indication that he hadn't taken anything of a spiritual nature too seriously yet. If she could only get him to go to church with her, that would be a step in the right direction.

Anna turned from the dresser and moved over to the bed. "Reuben, are you awake?" She nudged him gently with her hand.

"Am now," he responded with a muffled grunt.

She leaned over and kissed his forehead. "I'll be leaving for church soon. Are you sure you won't come with me?"

He pulled the covers around his ears and groaned. "Too tired. Need to sleep."

She released a sigh. Would there ever be a time when Reuben wasn't too tired? Would he ever come to realize that spending time with God—and with her—was more important than working so much or lounging around on Sundays?

"I'll see you shortly after noon." Anna whispered a silent prayer on her husband's behalf, then tiptoed out of the room.

As Rachel stood in front of the kitchen sink, doing up the breakfast dishes, she felt like hugging herself. The thought of going on a fishing date with Silas was enough to take her breath away. She couldn't help but wonder and, yes, even hope that Silas's sudden invitation was a sign that he was beginning to care for her.

Maybe she should start filling her hope chest with a few more things. If Silas enjoyed her company today, he might even offer to take her home from the next singing or young people's function. *Now that would mean we were officially courting.* Rachel smiled to herself. She would have to remember to thank Joseph for letting Silas know how much she liked to fish.

As Rachel's thoughts continued to swirl, she wondered how she could get away without telling her family that she planned to meet Silas at the lake.

She was alone in the kitchen at the moment, so as soon as she finished the dishes, she began packing the picnic lunch she'd promised Silas she would bring, hoping no one would come inside and see how much she'd stashed inside the wicker basket and small cooler she planned to take along.

Rachel had no more than shut the lid on the cooler, when Elizabeth and Perry bounded into the room.

"What's with the picnic stuff?" Perry asked. "Are ya goin' someplace, Rachel?"

She nodded. "I'll be leaving for the lake soon. I plan to do a bit of fishing."

Elizabeth stepped up to the table, where Rachel had placed the cooler and wicker basket. "Can we go along?"

"I don't think that's such a good idea."

"How come?" Perry questioned.

"You two like to throw rocks into the water, holler, and run around." Rachel pursed her lips. "That scares away the fish."

Elizabeth's lower lip jutted out, and Perry squinted at her as he wrinkled his nose.

A sense of guilt came over Rachel. She hated to tell the children they couldn't go along, but if she and Silas were going to get better acquainted, the last thing she needed was her rowdy brother and nosy sister tagging along.

"You meetin' someone at the lake?" Perry asked as he started to open the lid on the cooler.

She held the lid down with one hand and drew in a quick breath. "You two can go to the lake with me some other time, but today I'm going by myself."

Perry grunted and stomped out of the room.

"Guess I'll go with Mom and Dad when they call on some of their friends," Elizabeth said with a shrug.

Rachel leaned down and gave her sister a hug; then, grabbing up the cooler and picnic basket, she hurried out the back door.

The morning sun slid from behind a cloud as Rachel hitched the horse to the buggy a short time later. It was a bit chilly out, but the day held the promise of sunshine and blue skies. She was glad her folks hadn't insisted she go calling with them and was even more relieved that neither of them had asked any questions when she'd told them a few minutes ago that she planned to go fishing at the lake.

Rachel was about to climb into the driver's seat when Dad called out to her. "I'm not so sure I like the idea of you going to the lake by yourself."

"I've been fishing there since I was a kinner, and I've never had a problem. Besides, plenty of people are usually around, so I probably won't be alone."

Dad left Mom sitting on the porch in her wheelchair and hurried over to Rachel. "That may be, but it isn't good for a young woman to be running around by herself. I think you should take your sister or one of your brothers along."

Rachel placed the picnic basket under the front seat and turned to face her father. "I'm meeting someone."

He gave his beard a couple of yanks. "Ah, so my daughter has a beau now, does she?"

Rachel's face heated up. "He's not a boyfriend, Dad."

He chuckled. "So it is a fellow you're meeting, then?"

She nodded.

"Mind if I ask who?"

"It's Silas Swartley."

He winked at Rachel. "Should I be askin' your mamm to start makin' a wedding quilt?"

Rachel grimaced. "I knew I shouldn't have said anything. Like I stated before, Silas and I are just friends."

"Then why the big secret about meeting him?"

"I—I didn't want anyone jumping to conclusions."

Dad gave her arm a gentle pat. "Your secret's safe with me. Now run along and catch plenty of fish. Some nice, tasty trout would look mighty good on the supper table."

Rachel grinned and climbed into the buggy. Maybe Dad thought there might be some hope for her and Silas, too.

As Silas sat on the dock with his fishing line dangling in the water, he noticed several small boats on the lake, but no one else was on the dock or shoreline. Maybe he and Rachel would be alone all day. Did he really want to be alone with her? He'd thought he did yesterday when he asked her to meet him here. Now that he'd had ample time to think about it, he worried that he might have been a bit hasty making the invitation. What if Rachel thought he was interested in her as more than a friend? What if she thought this was a real date?

Silas stared across the lake, his gaze settling on a crop of trees where several crows sat, making their distinctive call of *caw, caw, caw*. Truth be told, he really did enjoy Rachel's company. The fact that she liked birds and fishing was a benefit, but it was her sweet spirit and appreciation for the simple things in life that had really captured his attention.

She isn't too bad-looking, either. Silas closed his eyes, and Rachel's pleasant face flashed into his mind. Her pale blue eyes and soft, straw-colored hair made her appear almost angelic. Whenever she smiled, those cute little dimples made him want to reach right out and touch her cheeks.

What am I thinking? Rachel is Anna's little sister. She's five years younger than me and isn't much more than a kinner. He shook his head. *Of course, I do know of some married couples where one is older than the other. Guess five years isn't really so much.*

Silas was driven from his inner conflict when he heard a horse and buggy coming. He turned and waved as Rachel directed her horse onto the grassy spot near the dock.

🐟

Rachel smiled and waved at Silas, who sat on the edge of the dock, holding a fishing pole and wearing an eager expression. Was it possible that he was as happy to see her as she was to see him? She prayed it was so.

"Catch anything yet?" she asked, as she stepped down from the buggy.

He shook his head. "Not yet, but then I haven't been here very long."

Rachel grabbed her pole from the back of the buggy, along with the can of night crawlers she'd caught last evening. When she walked onto the dock, Silas slid over, making room for her to sit beside him. "Sure is a nice day. Should have our share of trout in no time." He winked at Rachel, and her heart skipped a beat.

Does he have some feelings for me? She would cling to this glimmer of hope.

The sun shone brightly, the sky was a clear aquamarine, and the lake looked smooth as glass. Rachel felt a sense of peace settle over her as she cast out her line. It felt so right being here with Silas. If only. . .

No, I mustn't allow myself to start daydreaming. Today, I'm just going to relax and enjoy the company of the man I could surely spend the rest of my life with, if he was willing.

By noon, Silas had caught six trout and four bass, and Rachel had five of each. They both cleaned their own catch, then put the fish inside the small coolers they had brought along.

Silas eyed the picnic basket Rachel had taken from the buggy and placed upon the quilt she'd spread on the ground. "I don't know about you, but I'm starving," he said, as a dark flicker came into his eyes.

"I made plenty, so I'm glad you're hungry."

He dropped to the quilt. "What'd you bring?"

Rachel knelt next to the cooler and opened the lid. "Let's see now. . .ham-and-cheese sandwiches, dill pickle slices, ribbon salad, pickled beet eggs, iced tea to drink, and for dessert. . .chocolate chip cookies."

Silas licked his lips. "Yum. Let's pray; then we'll eat ourselves full!"

As Rachel and Silas ate their lunch, they shared stories, told jokes, and got to know each other better. By the time they'd finished eating, Rachel felt as though she had known Silas all her life. Actually, she had, but not on such a personal level. Silas, being five years her senior, had always hung around her older sister, so she'd never had the chance to learn what many of his likes and dislikes were. Today he'd shared his aversion to liver and onions, a dish his mother seemed intent on fixing at least once a month. He'd also talked about his love for God and how he had been praying for the Lord to have His will in his life.

"I believe strongly in prayer," Silas said with obvious conviction. "It's the key to each new day and the lock for every night."

"You're right about that." Even as Rachel said the words, she wondered if she was being sincere. Oh, she believed in prayer, all right. The problem was, she didn't pray as often as she should anymore. Since she'd been keeping so busy helping Silas's mother and trying to keep up with her chores at home, Rachel had let her personal devotions and prayer time slip. It was something she needed to work on, and right then she promised herself that she would spend more time with God.

Silas chewed on a blade of grass as he talked about Reuben and how he had persuaded Anna to go English with him. "If I ever have any kinner, I'm gonna hold a tight rein on 'em so they don't decide to leave the faith."

Rachel leaned back on her elbows and let his words digest fully before she answered. "Holding a tight rein could turn someone's head in the opposite direction. Take a baby robin, for example. If its mamm never taught it to fly and always kept it protected inside the nest, do you think that bird would ever learn to soar in the air?"

Silas scratched the back of his head and squinted. "Guess you've got a point. You're pretty bright for someone so young."

Rachel felt as though Silas had slapped her on the face with a wet rag. Why did he have to bring up her age? And just when they were beginning to have such a good time. "For your information, I'll be nineteen next Saturday. My mamm was married by the time she was my age, and—"

Silas held up one hand. "Don't get your feathers all ruffled. I sure didn't mean to offend you."

Rachel grabbed their empty paper plates and the plastic containers the food had been in and began slinging them into the picnic basket. Her face felt hot, her hands shook, and tears stung the backs of her eyes. She had wanted this day to be perfect. Maybe it would be better if they ended it now.

She stood and proceeded to move toward her buggy. "Guess I'll head for home."

Silas jumped up and ran after her. "You can't go now, Rachel. We haven't spent any time looking at birds."

She shrugged. "Maybe some other time. I'm not much in the mood anymore."

Silas placed a restraining hand on Rachel's arm. "Please, don't go. I'm sorry if I made you mad."

She swallowed hard, struggling to keep her tears at bay. Silas stood looking at her with those big brown eyes, and he really did look sorry. "I'm not exactly mad. I just get tired of everyone thinking I'm still a kinner." Her arms made a wide arc as she motioned toward the lake. "Could a child catch as many fish as I did today? Could a child have fixed such a tasty picnic lunch or baked a batch of cookies you kept on eating?"

Silas continued to stare at her a few more seconds, then in an unexpected gesture, he pulled her to his chest. "No,

Rachel, only a feisty young woman could have done all those things."

Rachel held her breath as Silas moved his fingers in gentle, soothing circles across her back. Was he about to kiss her? She wrapped her arms around his neck and nestled her head against his shoulder.

Then as quickly as Silas had embraced her, he pulled away. "Now that we've got that all cleared up, how's about I get my binoculars and bird-identification book, and the two of us can spend the next hour or so lookin' for some unusual feathered creatures?"

Rachel nodded as a sense of embarrassment rattled through her. Silas's sudden shift in mood hit her like a blow to the stomach, and she wondered what he must have thought about her brazen actions. Even though it was Silas who initiated the hug, she had taken it one step further. Truth be told, Silas had never led her to believe he had any romantic feelings for her. The embrace was probably just a friendly gesture.

"You get your gear, and I'll put away the picnic stuff," she said, scooting away quickly before he could see how red her face must be.

A short time later, Silas and Rachel were seated on the grass, taking turns looking through his binoculars as though their physical encounter had never taken place. In no time at all, they had spotted several gray catbirds, a brown thrasher, a few mourning doves, and several species of ducks on the lake. Silas looked each one up in his bird-identification book, and they discussed the various traits and habitats of those they'd seen.

"Do you have a bird book or binoculars of your own?" he asked.

Rachel shook her head. "Whenever I save up enough money, some other need always comes along, so I just jot notes on a paper about all the interesting birds I see." She was tempted to tell Silas that here lately, she'd spent most of her money buying more things for her hope chest, but she thought better of bringing up that subject. He might think she was hinting at marriage, and she wasn't about to say or do anything that would spoil the rest of the day. Except for that one misunderstanding, their time together had been almost perfect. Even if she never got to be alone with Silas again, she would always cherish the memory of this day.

Rebekah sniffed as she sat at the table reading the letter she'd received from Anna the day before. She'd been so busy when the letter arrived that she'd set it aside and had forgotten about it until she'd spotted it a few minutes ago, lying on the desk under a stack of bills that had also been in the mail.

Anna was doing well and wanted to come home for a visit—maybe for Rachel's birthday. That thought put a smile on Rebekah's lips. Wouldn't it be nice to have the whole family together to help celebrate Rachel's special day? Rebekah would fix a special dinner and bake a cake. Maybe she could talk Daniel into making a batch of homemade ice cream. How wonderful it would be to see Anna again.

"I've got the horse and buggy hitched. You about ready

to head out to your brother's place?" Daniel asked, stepping into the room.

Tears gathered in Rebekah's eyes as she lifted the letter she'd been reading. "I heard from Anna again yesterday. She wants to come home for Rachel's birthday."

The corners of Daniel's mouth drew down, and he leaned against the counter with his arms folded. "I don't think so."

"Why not?"

"She's under the ban."

Rebekah released a frustrated sigh. "It's not as if we can't speak to her, for goodness' sake. I think it would be good for her to be here to help celebrate her sister's birthday. I think—"

"No. Absolutely not!" Daniel's lips were set in a thin line, and his eyebrows furrowed, nearly meeting each other at the top of his nose.

"Won't you at least consider this?"

He shook his head.

Rebekah nearly choked on a sob. "She's our daughter, Daniel. Can't you find it in your heart to forgive her for leaving us?"

No comment.

"She's married now, whether we like it or not, and her responsibility is to her husband."

"She can stay with her husband, then. We don't need her around here filling our other kinner's heads with fancy ideas about her new way of life."

"I'm sure she wouldn't do that."

"We were both sure she was being courted by Silas."

Daniel grunted. "Yet she lied so we wouldn't know what she was up to with Reuben. Does that sound like someone we can trust?"

Rebekah opened her mouth to respond, but Daniel turned on his heels and headed for the back door. "The kinner are waiting in the buggy, so whenever you're ready to go, we can be on our way." He stepped onto the porch and closed the door.

Rebekah released a shuddering sob. How could she write Anna back and tell her she couldn't come to Rachel's party? What would it take to get through to her stubborn husband?

CHAPTER

16

After their enjoyable day at the lake, Rachel had expected Silas to be friendlier the following week. He wasn't. In fact, she saw very little of him, and when he did come to the house for meals, he seemed aloof and kind of cranky whenever someone spoke to him. Something wasn't right. She felt it in every fiber of her being. She wanted to ask him what was wrong, but there never seemed to be a good time, what with his family always around.

By Saturday, Rachel was fit to be tied. She had been forced to stay home from the Swartleys' again because Mom and Dad went to town for more supplies. That meant she was needed at the greenhouse, and even worse, it appeared as though her family had forgotten about her birthday. Not one person had said, "Happy birthday" during breakfast, and there was no sign of any gifts. It was such a disappointment not to be remembered on her special day.

Elizabeth and Perry had been left home this time, and they were still up at the house when Rachel walked out to the greenhouse. She put the OPEN sign in the window, lit all the gas lamps, and made a small fire in the wood-burning stove to take the autumn chill out of the room.

Rachel studied her surroundings, letting her gaze travel from the plants hanging by the rafters on long chains to the small wooden pots and lawn figurines sitting on shelves. Dad had made most of those things, and his expertise with wood was quite evident. Rachel knew her folks loved this greenhouse, and she was also aware that it had been one of the things that had brought them together. Even so, she had no desire to spend so much time helping out here. Today, of all days, she would rather be outside in the fresh air.

"It's my birthday. I should at least be allowed the pleasure of taking a walk to the creek." She plunked down on the stool, placed her elbows on the counter, and rested her chin in the palms of her hands.

Pauline showed up a few minutes later, and Joseph was with her.

"I thought you were out in the barn," Rachel said, nodding at her brother.

He shrugged, and his face turned a deep shade of red. "I was until I saw Pauline's buggy come down the lane."

"Are you planning to help out here today?" Rachel asked, a sense of hope welling in her chest. "If so, maybe I won't be needed."

"I wish I could, but Perry and I have got to get back out to the fields soon." Joseph cast a quick glance in Pauline's direction, then looked back at Rachel with a silly grin on his face.

"What are you doing here then, if it's not to work?"

"Came to see Pauline. That is, if you have no objections."

Pauline chuckled and elbowed Joseph in the ribs. He laughed and jabbed her right back.

At least somebody's happy today, Rachel thought ruefully. "I think I'll go in the back room and see if any of the plants need watering."

"Okay, sure," Joseph said, never taking his eyes off Pauline.

"Sickening. Downright sickening," Rachel muttered under her breath, as she headed for the middle section of the greenhouse. This day couldn't be over soon enough to suit her.

As Anna put the last of the clean dishes away in the cupboard, she glanced at the calendar on the kitchen wall. A pang of regret shot through her, and she groaned. Today was Rachel's nineteenth birthday, and Anna wouldn't be there to help her sister celebrate. She had received a letter from Mom the other day, saying that it wasn't a good idea for her to come visit just yet. While Mom hadn't actually said it was because of Dad's refusal to forgive her, Anna knew the truth. Dad didn't want her there for Rachel's birthday. Truth be told, he was probably afraid she might influence the younger children to do as she'd done and leave the Amish faith when they were old enough to make that decision.

At least Anna had mailed Rachel a card, and she hoped her sister had gotten it by now. Even so, a card and note weren't the same as being there and sharing the joy of the day with someone she loved.

She knew from Rachel's last letter that she'd been helping out the Swartleys, and she'd even asked Reuben if he'd be willing to drive her over to see Rachel at their place. But no, he'd told her this morning during breakfast that he would be working overtime again tonight and probably wouldn't be home until well after dark. Truth was, Anna didn't think Reuben had any desire to go home for a visit at all.

"Maybe it's for the best that I don't go home so soon, either," she muttered as she closed the cupboard door. After the way her father had acted the morning she'd left home, she wondered if she would ever be welcomed there again. Maybe someday she could talk Reuben into paying a visit to his folks, and then, if she could find Rachel or Mom alone at the greenhouse, she might be able to drop by and say hello. But how would she know if they were alone or if Dad was helping there, too?

Anna released a weary sigh, grabbed her lunch box, and turned toward the door. It was time to catch the bus for work, and she didn't want to be late.

Silas paced back and forth in front of his open courting buggy. Should he or shouldn't he make this trip? Would his intentions be misrepresented? What exactly were his intentions, anyway? He'd spent the last week trying to sort out his feelings for Rachel, yet he felt more confused now than ever.

Guess what I should have been doing was praying about all this, not trying to think it through by myself. Silas knew he'd been negligent in reading the Bible lately, and his only prayers had been the silent ones said before each meal.

I won't allow myself to move away from You, Lord. He thought about Reuben and Anna and wondered if they went to church anywhere or if they had fallen away from God when they'd left home. He was reminded that up until six months ago, he and Reuben had been friends. He knew from what Reuben's folks had told him that it had been a real disappointment when they'd discovered that Reuben had gone "fancy."

Then there was Anna. Beautiful, spirited, stubborn Anna. Silas had been in love with her since the first grade, when they'd started attending school at the one-room schoolhouse down the road. In his mind's eye, he could still see the back of her cute little head. He'd sat at the desk behind her for all of the eight years they'd gone to school. Anna, with her dazzling green eyes and hair the color of ripe peaches. She'd stolen his heart when he was six years old, and she'd broken it in two soon after he'd turned twenty-three. Would he ever be free of the pain? Would the image of her lovely face be forever etched in his mind? Could he learn to trust another woman?

"It does no good to pine for what you can't have," a voice in his head seemed to say. *"Get on with your life and follow Me."*

Silas moved to the front of the buggy, where his faithful horse patiently waited. He leaned against the gelding's side and stroked his silky ears. "What do you say, old boy? Do we take a little ride, or do we stay home?"

The horse whinnied loudly, and Silas smiled. "All right then. Let's be on our way."

Rachel had just put the CLOSED sign in the window and was

about to turn down the lights, when she heard a horse and buggy pull up in front of the greenhouse. Pauline had gone home fifteen minutes ago, and Rachel was anxious to head home herself. She released a sigh. "Guess I can handle one more customer yet."

She opened the front door, and her mouth dropped open when she saw Silas standing on the porch, holding a paper bag in one hand and a bouquet of orange and yellow chrysanthemums in the other.

"Well, well," she said with a giggle. "It isn't every day that someone shows up at the greenhouse carrying a bunch of flowers."

Silas chuckled. "Guess that's true enough. Most folks leave here with flowers, but it isn't likely they'd be bringing 'em in."

Rachel stepped aside to allow Silas entrance. "So what brings you here at closing time?"

He cleared his throat loudly, then handed her the flowers and paper sack. "Just wanted to give you these. Happy birthday, Rachel."

Rachel felt as though all the breath had been squeezed clean out of her lungs. This was such a surprise. Never in a million years had she expected a gift from Silas, especially since he'd been so distant all week. "Danki," she murmured. "How did you know that today was my birthday?"

"You said something about it when we went fishing last Sunday."

Rachel placed the flowers on the counter and opened the paper sack. When she looked inside, she let out a little squeal. "Binoculars and a bird-watching book! Oh, Silas, this is my best birthday present!" The truth was, it was her only present, but she wasn't about to tell him that. It was bad enough that her whole family had forgotten her special day; she sure didn't want to talk about it.

"I was hoping you might like it." Silas took a few steps closer to Rachel. "Now, whenever you see some unusual bird, you can look it up in the book and find out all about its habits and whatnot."

Rachel withdrew the binoculars. "These will sure come in handy."

Silas nodded. "I often put my binoculars to good use."

Rachel swallowed hard. Why was Silas looking at her so funny? Did that gentle expression in his dark eyes and the agreeable smile on his clean-shaven face mean anything more than just friendship? She couldn't come right out and ask, but she needed to know if she dared to hope.

As if he sensed her dilemma, Silas reached out and took Rachel's hand. "I enjoyed our time of fishing and looking at birds the other day. If the weather holds out, maybe we can find the time to do it again."

Rachel flicked her tongue back and forth across her lower lip. The sensation of Silas's touch did funny things to her insides. "I–I'd like that. I had a good time last week, too."

Silas let go of her hand, then turned and moved back across the room. "Guess I should be getting on home. Mom's probably got supper ready."

Rachel followed him to the door. "I need to go up to the house and see about fixing our supper, as well. My folks went to town this morning, and they still aren't back yet, so

I'd better be sure there's something ready to eat when they do get home."

When Silas got to the door, he turned and said, "I hear tell there's gonna be a young people's get-together over at Harold Landis's place two weeks from tomorrow. Do you think you might go?"

"Maybe." Rachel shrugged. "If I can get Joseph to take me."

He grinned. "From what I hear, your big brother's got a pretty good reason to bring his courting buggy these days. My guess is he'll be there early."

Rachel nodded. "You're probably right."

Silas opened the door. "Well, see you at preaching tomorrow." He bounded off the porch and climbed into his buggy before Rachel could say anything more.

She smiled to herself. "Guess this wasn't such a bad birthday after all."

A short time later as Rachel stepped out the greenhouse door, holding the bouquet of flowers and paper sack with the birthday presents from Silas, she decided to walk up the driveway and check the mailbox before she headed to the house to start supper. Since the folks had left early this morning and obviously weren't back yet, she figured any mail they may have gotten would still be in the box.

Maybe I'll get a card or two. It would be nice to know that someone else had remembered today's my birthday.

When Rachel reached into the mailbox a few minutes later, she was pleased to discover a card from Anna, along with a note. She placed the flowers on top of the mailbox and set the sack on the ground as she hurriedly read the note, anxious for any word from her sister.

Dear Rachel,

I hope this card reaches you in time for your birthday, and I hope your day is a special one. Reuben and I are doing fine, and we both keep busy with our jobs. Last week Reuben bought a CD player, and we have a TV now, too. I've spent most of the money I'd saved while working at the greenhouse on new clothes, as I needed something other than my plain dresses to wear now that I'm not Amish anymore.

It still feels strange not to wear my head covering, but I do wear my hair pinned up at the back of my head when I'm waiting on tables at the restaurant where I work. Reuben wants me to get my hair cut short, but I'm not sure I'm ready for that. Guess that's kind of silly, seeing as to how I used to say I'd like to have short hair.

I had wanted to be there for your birthday, but Mom's last letter said it would be best if I didn't come for a visit just yet. Besides, Reuben's been working lots of overtime lately, and even some Saturdays, so we probably couldn't have made it there on time anyhow.

I've started attending church with my friend Kathryn from work, but some Sundays, Reuben's so tired all he does is sleep, so he hasn't gone to church with me yet.

Write back when you can, and give my love to all the family.

As always,
Anna

Tears flooded Rachel's eyes, obscuring her vision. She missed Anna so much that it hurt. If only she hadn't fallen in love with Reuben and run off and gotten married. But then, if Anna hadn't fallen for Reuben, she might have ended up marrying Silas, and Rachel would have never had a chance with him.

Rachel cringed as she realized how selfish she was being. Wouldn't it be better to have her sister still living at home and being courted by Silas, than to have her living in the English world and being shunned by her family and friends? If Rachel could bring Anna home and make everything right again at home, she surely would—even if it meant giving up whatever was happening between her and Silas.

Rachel thought about Anna's comment concerning Reuben working long hours and not going to church. She hoped that didn't mean he'd fallen away from God. At least Anna was attending church. She would have to remember to pray for Anna, Reuben, and their marriage.

Rachel bent down and picked up the paper sack, then grabbed hold of the flowers. It was time to head up to the house and get busy with supper. It was time to set her pain of losing Anna aside and get on with life.

She stepped into the darkened kitchen several minutes later and had barely closed the door, when a gas lamp ignited, and a chorus of voices yelled, "Happy birthday, Rachel!"

"What in all the world?" Rachel's mouth fell open as she studied her surroundings. Mom, Dad, Joseph, Perry, and Elizabeth sat at the table, which was fully set for supper.

On one end of the cupboard was a chocolate cake, and beside it sat several wrapped gifts. "Elizabeth, did you do all this?"

Elizabeth smiled. "I helped, but Mom did most of the work."

Rachel's eyebrows drew together. "How could that be? Mom and Dad have been gone all day."

Mom grinned like a cat that had chased down a fat little field mouse. "Came back early so we could surprise you."

"But I never heard your buggy come down the lane. I don't see how—"

Dad chuckled. "We used the old road coming into the back of our property."

Tears stung the backs of Rachel's eyes, and she blinked to keep them from spilling over. Her folks really did care. They hadn't forgotten it was her birthday after all.

"What's that you've got in your hands?" The question came from Perry.

"Oh, just the mail." She placed the envelopes on the counter—everything except for Anna's card, which she had stuck under the band of the backside of her apron, not wanting the folks to see it. Dad might be upset by what Anna had said about buying a TV and Reuben not going to church. Besides, since the card was Rachel's, she saw no need to share it with anyone.

"I'm not talkin' about the mail." Perry pointed to the flowers and then to the sack she held.

Rachel's face heated with embarrassment. "It's. . .uh. . . a birthday present."

"Who's it from?" Joseph questioned.

"Silas Swartley," she said, trying to keep her voice from quivering.

"Rachel's got a boyfriend! Rachel's got a boyfriend!" Elizabeth taunted.

"No, I don't. Silas is just a good friend. That ought to be clear as anything."

Joseph snickered. "Oh, sure—about as clear as mud. He's a good friend, all right. One who gives you a birthday present and takes you fishing."

Rachel turned to face her father, and her forehead wrinkled in accusation.

He shook his head. "He didn't hear it from me."

Mom shook her finger at Dad. "You knew our daughter had gone fishing with Silas and you never said a word?"

"Rachel asked me not to say anything."

Rachel looked back at Joseph. "If Dad didn't mention it, then how'd you know?"

He shrugged. "Some other folks were out at the lake, you know."

"We never talked to anyone else." Rachel shook her head. "In fact, we were the only ones on the dock."

"That may be true, but there were some boats out on the water," Joseph reminded.

"Spies, don't you mean? I think some folks need to keep their mouths shut where others are concerned."

"Now, don't go getting into a snit about this," Mom said in a soothing tone. "There was no harm done, so come sit yourself down and eat your favorite supper."

Rachel had to admit the fried chicken and mashed potatoes did look tasty. She was plenty hungry, too, so she may as well eat this special supper Mom and Elizabeth had worked so hard to prepare. She would have a serious talk with Joseph later on. Then she'd find out who the informer had been.

❧

Rachel sat on the edge of her bed, looking over the presents she'd received earlier that day. It had been a good birthday, even if Joseph had let the cat out of the bag about her and Silas going fishing together. Joseph had told her later that it was Amon Zook who'd spilled the beans. Apparently, he'd been fishing on the lake with his son, Ben.

She chuckled softly. "Guess you can't keep anything secret these days."

Focusing on her gifts again, Rachel studied the set of handmade pillowcases Mom had given her and insisted must go into Rachel's hope chest. Dad's gift was a new oil lamp—also a hope chest item, since she already had two perfectly good lamps in her bedroom. Joseph and Perry had gone together on a box of cream-filled chocolates, which Rachel had generously shared with the family after supper. Elizabeth had made several nice handkerchiefs, and Rachel had put those in one of her drawers.

Then there was Rachel's favorite gift of all—the binoculars and bird-identification book Silas had given her. The candy was almost gone. The handkerchiefs would be useful in the days to come. The oil lamp and pillowcases might never be used if Rachel didn't get married. Silas's gift, on the other hand, was something she would use whenever she studied birds in their yard and the surrounding area.

Rachel scooted off the bed and stepped around the cedar chest at the end of her bed, opened the lid, and slipped the pillowcases and lamp inside. She hadn't given her hope chest much thought until recently. Now that Silas was being so friendly, there might be a ray of hope for her future.

" 'But I will hope continually, and will yet praise thee more and more,' " she murmured. "Thank You, Lord, for such a wunderbaar day."

As Rachel closed the lid of the chest, she caught sight of Anna's hope chest sitting in one corner of her room. She was tempted to open it and look through its contents, but she thought better of it. It belonged to her sister, and she still didn't feel right about snooping through Anna's personal things.

She did give the hope chest to me, her inner voice reminded.

Someday if Rachel ever married, she could find a use for the things in both hers and Anna's hope chests. She would wait awhile to see what was inside. In the meantime, she planned to start adding more things to her own hope chest.

CHAPTER

17

Silas felt a keen sense of excitement as he prepared to go to the young people's gathering that was to be held in Harold Landis's barn. A big bonfire would be blazing, and enough eats would be set out to fill the hungriest man's stomach. Neither the singing, bonfire, nor even the food was the reason he was looking forward to going, however. Simply put, Silas had discovered that he enjoyed spending time with Rachel, and he had a hankering to see her again.

He climbed into his freshly cleaned courting buggy, and his heartbeat quickened as he picked up the reins. The more time he spent with Rachel, the more he was drawn to her. Was it merely because they had so much in common, or was something else going on? Could he possibly be falling for little Rachel Beachy, in spite of their age difference or the fact that she was the sister of his first love? Would she be willing to accept a ride home with him tonight if he asked?

He clucked to the horse to get him moving. "I'd better take my time with Rachel, hadn't I, old boy? Elsewise, there might be no exit for me."

Fifty young people milled about the Landis's barn, eating, playing games, and visiting.

Rachel and Joseph went their separate ways as soon as they arrived, she with some other woman her age, and Joseph with Pauline Hostetler. That really wasn't such a big surprise, since he'd been hanging around her so much lately.

Rachel had just finished eating a sandwich and had taken a seat on a bale of straw, planning to relax and watch the couples around her who had paired off. She was pretty sure her brother would be asking to take Pauline home tonight, and it had her kind of worried. What if he wanted to be alone with his date? What if he expected Rachel to find another way home? It would be rather embarrassing if she had to beg someone for a ride.

She scanned the many faces inside the barn, trying to decide who might be the best choice to ask, should it become necessary. Her gaze fell on Silas, talking with a group of young men near the food table. It would be too bold of her to ask him for a ride, even if they had become friends over the past few months. It was a fellow's place to invite a girl to ride home in his courting buggy, not the other way around. Besides, she hadn't seen much of Silas lately. Every day last week when she'd been at his place helping his mother, Silas had been busy with the fall harvest. They hadn't had a real conversation since a week ago Saturday, when Silas dropped by the greenhouse to give her a birthday present.

Rachel noticed Abe Landis sitting by himself, eating a huge piece of chocolate cake. Abe was the same age as

Rachel, and they'd known each other a long time. She could ask him for a lift home, but there was one problem. Abe lived right here. He wouldn't be driving his horse and buggy anywhere tonight.

"Seen any interesting birds lately?"

The question took Rachel by surprise. She'd been in such a dilemma over whom to ask for a ride, she hadn't noticed that Silas stood right beside her. She glanced up and smiled. "Jah, I have."

Silas pushed another bale of straw closer to her and sat down. "You like my birthday present?"

She nodded. "A whole lot."

"Mom's getting her cast off soon. Guess you won't be coming around so much anymore." He stared down at his hands, resting on his knees.

Rachel studied him a moment before she answered. Did she detect a note of sadness in his voice when he mentioned her not coming over anymore, or was it only wishful thinking? If Silas knew how much she loved him yet didn't have feelings for her in return, the humiliation would be too great to bear. "I–I'm glad I could help out," she murmured, "but things will soon be back to normal at your house, so—"

"Rachel, would you like some hot chocolate?" Abe asked as he plunked down on the same bale of straw where Rachel sat. "I'd be glad to get some for you."

Silas's jaw clenched, and he shot Abe a look that could have stopped a runaway horse in its tracks. "Rachel and I were having a little talk, Abe. If she wants anything, I'll be happy to fetch it for her."

Rachel stirred uneasily. What was going on here? If she

hadn't known better, she might have believed Silas was actually jealous of Abe. But that was ridiculous. Abe and Rachel were just friends, the same as she and Silas. Abe was only being nice by asking if she wanted some hot chocolate. Surely he wasn't interested in her in a romantic kind of way.

Abe touched Rachel's shoulder. "What do you say? Would you like me to get you something to drink or not?"

Silas jumped up quickly, nearly tripping over the bale of straw where Rachel sat. "Didn't you hear what I said? If Rachel wants anything, I'll get it for her!"

Rachel's heart thumped so hard she feared it might burst open. Why was Silas acting so upset? It made no sense at all. Unless. . .

Abe stood, too. "Don't you think that ought to be Rachel's decision?"

Silas pivoted toward Rachel. "Well? Who's gonna get the hot chocolate?"

Rachel gulped. Were they really going to force her to choose? She cleared her throat, then offered them both a smile. "Me. I'll get my own drink, danki very much." With that said, she hopped up and sprinted off toward the refreshment table.

❧

Silas looked over at Abe and shrugged. "Looks like we two have been outsmarted."

"I think you're right about that." Abe started to move away but stopped after he'd taken a few steps. "Look, Silas, if Rachel and you are courtin', I'll back off. If not, then she's fair game, and I plan on making my move."

Silas's eyes widened. "Your move?" Heat boiled up his spine as unexpected jealousy seared through him like hot coals on the fire.

Abe nodded. "I thought I might ask her to go fishing with me sometime."

"Fishing?"

"Jah. I hear tell that Rachel likes to fish."

"Where'd you hear that?"

"Someone saw her at the lake a few weeks ago. Said she was sittin' on the dock with her fishing pole."

Silas squinted as he leveled Abe with a look he hoped would end this conversation. "That was me she was fishing with there."

"So, you two *are* courting then."

Silas clenched his fists. It wasn't in his nature to want to hit someone, and everything about fighting went against the Amish way, but right now he struggled with the impulse to punch Abe right in the nose. What was the fellow trying to do—goad him into an argument? He'd always considered Abe to be nice enough, but up until a few moments ago, he hadn't realized Abe was interested in Rachel.

Silas was still trying to decide how best to deal with Abe when Rachel returned, carrying a mug of steaming hot chocolate and a piece of shoofly pie. She smiled sweetly at both of them, then seated herself on the bale of straw.

Silas leaned over so his face was just inches from Rachel's. Her pale blue eyes seemed to probe his innermost being, and his heart begin to hammer. With no further thought, he blurted out, "I'd like to take you home in my courting buggy tonight, Rachel. Would you be willing to go?"

She took a little sip of her drink, glanced over at Abe for a second, then back at Silas. "Jah, I'd be willing."

Now that Rachel had accepted his invitation, Silas wasn't sure how he felt about things. Had he asked merely to get under Abe's skin, or because he really wanted to escort Rachel home?

He looked over at her, sitting so sweet and innocent, and knew the answer to his troubling question. He really did want to take her home. He enjoyed her company, maybe a bit more than he cared to admit. But the truth was, Anna had hurt him badly, and part of him was afraid Rachel might do the same thing.

Silas's disconcerting thoughts were jolted away when Abe slapped him on the back. "All right, I'm satisfied then." With that, Abe walked away, leaving Silas and Rachel alone again.

"What time were you planning to head for home?" Rachel asked as Silas took a seat on the other bale of straw.

He shrugged. "Whenever you're done eating your pie and drinking your hot chocolate."

"Aren't you going to have some?"

He chuckled. "I've already had enough food tonight for three fellows my size."

Rachel finished the rest of her dessert and stood. "Guess I'd better go find Joseph and tell him I won't be riding home in his buggy."

Silas reached for her empty plate and mug. "I'll put this away while you look for him."

"Danki." She offered him a heart-melting smile. He sure hoped he hadn't made a mistake by asking to take her home. What if she jumped to the wrong conclusion and thought one buggy ride meant they were officially courting?

I didn't have to ask her, Silas's inner voice reminded. *I could have conceded to Abe.* He gritted his teeth. *Never!*

Rachel turned and walked away, but her presence stayed with him like the smell of new-mown hay. He really was looking forward to taking her home.

Joseph had been sitting on a log by the bonfire, talking with Pauline for several minutes, when Rachel showed up. He had planned to seek his sister out as soon as he'd asked Pauline if he could escort her home tonight, but she'd beat him to it. There was only one problem—he hadn't spoke to Pauline yet.

"Silas just asked if he could give me a ride home," Rachel said, bending close to Joseph's ear.

He smiled. That was a relief to hear. At least now if Pauline said yes to his invitation, he would be free to escort her home without his little sister sitting in the buggy, listening to everything they said. "No problem. No problem at all. Have a good time, and I'll see you at home."

"Are you taking anyone home tonight?" she whispered.

His face warmed, and he knew it wasn't from the heat of the fire. "Don't know yet. Maybe so."

She smiled and nudged his arm. "Okay. See you at home then."

As soon as Rachel walked away, Joseph turned to Pauline. "Say, I was wondering if. . ."

"What were you wondering, Joe?"

He moistened his lips and swallowed a couple of times.

"Would you be willing to let me escort you home tonight?"

Pauline smiled at Joseph so sweetly that he thought he might turn into butter. "Jah, Joe, I'd be glad to ride home in your courting buggy."

He grinned. "Great. That's just real great."

CHAPTER 18

A sense of exhilaration shot through Rachel as she sat in Silas's open buggy with the crisp wind whipping against her face. She chanced a peek at her escort, hoping that he, too, was enjoying the ride.

Silas grinned back at her. "I think I smell winter in the air. Won't be too awfully long and we can take out the sleigh."

We? Does he mean me and him going for a sleigh ride? Rachel closed her eyes and tried to picture herself snuggled beneath a warm quilt, snow falling in huge, white flakes, and the sound of sleigh bells jingling in the chilly air.

"What are you thinking about?" Silas asked, breaking into her musings.

Rachel's eyes snapped open. "Oh, winter. . .sleigh bells. . . snow."

He chuckled. "Don't forget hot apple cider and pumpkin bread. Nothin' tastes better after a sleigh ride than a big mug of cider and several thick hunks of my mamm's spicy pumpkin bread."

"My favorite winter snack is popcorn, apple slices, and

hot chocolate with plenty of marshmallows."

"I like those things, too. Guess there isn't much in the way of food I don't like." Reaching into his jacket pocket, Silas withdrew a chunk of black licorice. "Want some?"

"No thanks." Rachel studied him as he chewed the candy. In spite of Silas's hearty appetite, there wasn't an ounce of fat on him that she could see. He appeared to be all muscle—no doubt from doing so many farm chores. *I would love him no matter how he looked.* It wasn't hard to picture herself and Silas sitting on the front porch of their own home, looking through binoculars and talking about all the birds nesting in their backyard trees.

She shook her head, hoping to bring some sense of reason into her thinking. Silas was only a friend, and he'd offered her a ride home from the gathering. That didn't mean he had thoughts of romance or marriage on his mind. She couldn't allow herself to fantasize about it, even if she did want more than friendship. She loved Silas so much, and each moment they spent together only made her more sure of it. She didn't want to feel this way; it wasn't safe for her heart. But no matter how hard Rachel tried, she couldn't stop herself from hoping that Silas might someday declare his love for her.

As they pulled into Rachel's yard, she released a sigh, wishing the ride didn't have to end so soon. If only they could keep on going. If only Silas would ask if he could court her.

He stopped the horse near the barn and turned in his seat to face Rachel. "Danki for letting me bring you home tonight. I enjoyed the ride a whole lot more than if I'd been alone."

"Me, too," she freely admitted.

"You're a special girl, Rachel. I can see why Abe would be interested in you."

"Really?" Rachel's breath caught in her throat, and her cheeks burned with embarrassment. The admiration in Silas's voice had sounded so genuine.

"Jah, I mean it." His gaze dropped to her lips.

For one heart-stopping moment, Rachel had the crazy idea of throwing herself into his arms and begging him to love her. She knew better than to let her emotions run wild, and she had too much pride to throw herself at him.

"Sure you don't want some licorice?" Silas asked, giving her a crooked grin.

All she could do was shake her head, her thoughts were so lost in the darkness of his ebony eyes, where the moonlight reflected like a pool of water.

Rachel's heart pulsated when Silas slipped his arms around her waist and pulled her close to his chest. She tipped her head back and savored the sweet smell of licorice as his lips met hers in a kiss so pleasing it almost lifted her right off the buggy seat. This was her first real kiss, and she could only hope her inexperience wasn't evident as she kissed him back with all the emotion welling within her soul.

Suddenly, Silas pulled away, looking shaken and confused. "Rachel, I'm so sorry. Don't know what came over me. I sure didn't mean to—"

Rachel held up her hand, feeling as though a glass of cold water had been dashed in her face. "Please, don't say anything more." She hopped down from the buggy and sprinted toward the house as the ache of humiliation bore down on her like a heavy blanket of snow. She wasn't sure why Silas had kissed her, but one thing was certain—he was sorry he had.

All the way home Silas berated himself. Why had he kissed Rachel like that? She must think he was off in the head to be doing something so brazen on their first buggy ride.

As Silas thought more about it, he realized as much as he'd enjoyed the kiss, it hadn't been fair to lead Rachel on like that. She might think because he took her home, then went so far as to kiss her, it meant they were a couple and would be courting from now on.

Was that what it had meant? Did he want to court Rachel? Was he feeling more than friendship for her, or did he only want to be with her because she reminded him of Anna?

Silas slapped the side of his head. "What am I thinking? Rachel's nothing like her older sister. Nothing at all. Guess I'd better commit the whole thing to prayer, because I sure enough wasn't expecting this to happen tonight, and I definitely don't have any answers of my own."

"Sure is a nice night," Pauline said, as Joseph directed his horse and open buggy down the road toward her home.

He nodded. "Jah, sure is." *Especially since you're sitting here beside me—that makes it an extra-special night.*

She looked over at him and smiled, and his heart skipped a beat. "You have a nice buggy, Joe." Her hand slid over the leather seat. "It's obvious that you take real good care of it."

"Danki. I try to keep it up to snuff."

They rode in silence for a time, with the only sounds being the steady *clippity-clop* of the horse's hooves and an occasional nicker. But Joseph didn't mind the quiet. It felt nice to ride along with his *aldi* beside him. At least he hoped Pauline was his girlfriend now.

"What's your family hear from Anna these days?" she asked, breaking into his thoughts. "Is she getting along okay out there in the English world?"

Joseph jerked his head at the mention of Anna's name.

"Did you hear what I said, Joe?"

"Jah, I heard. Just thinkin' is all."

"About Anna?"

He gave a quick nod in reply. He didn't want to spoil the evening by talking about his willful sister. He just wanted to concentrate on having a good time with Pauline. Was that too much to ask?

"Is Anna doing all right?"

He shrugged. "Mom and Rachel have both had letters from her, and from what they said, I guess she's doing okay."

"Mind if I ask how you feel about her leaving?"

"Guess what I feel is a mixture of sadness and anger at her for bringing a shunning on herself, not to mention the hurt she's caused our folks." He grimaced. "Mom doesn't talk about it much, but you can see the look of sadness on her face whenever Anna's name is mentioned."

"That's understandable."

"And Dad—well, he's just plain angry with Anna for running off the way she did, and if he weren't Amish and not given to violence, I'll bet he'd seek Reuben out and punch him right in the *naas*." Joseph's grip tightened on the reins, and a muscle in his cheek quivered.

"Are you angry with Anna and Reuben, too?" Pauline spoke quietly, but her pointed question cut Joseph to the quick.

He nodded. "Jah."

Pauline touched his arm again, only this time her fingers moved up and down in a soothing gesture. "You might not agree with Anna's reasons for leaving the Amish faith, but it was her choice, and the Bible says we must learn to forgive."

"It's not always so easy to forgive when so many people have been hurt."

She nodded. "I know that better than anyone. I was terribly hurt when Eli jilted me and married Laura. I felt that she was an Englisher who didn't belong with our people."

Joseph made no comment, waiting to see if she would say anything more.

"While I was living with my aunt and uncle in Ohio, I came to realize I had to forgive both Laura and Eli. Carrying around all that anger and bitterness was keeping me separated from God." Pauline smiled. "When I released the anger and confessed to God that I'd sinned, I was finally able to forgive those I thought had trespassed against me."

"I know you're right about me needing to forgive Anna, but seeing how Mom, Rachel, and the rest of the family have been affected by all this makes it that much harder."

"Maybe you need to ask yourself how you'd feel if you were in Anna's place."

"What do you mean?"

"If you'd fallen in love with someone the way Anna did Reuben, and then that someone had decided to leave the faith, what would you have done?"

Joseph stared straight ahead as he kept the horse going steady and contemplated her question. If Pauline had proclaimed her love for him and then said she wanted to leave the Amish faith for the modern, English life, he guessed he probably would go with her. He loved her that much.

He released one hand from the reins and reached over to take hold of Pauline's hand. "Well—if it was someone I truly loved, then I guess I would have gone English, too."

She smiled and squeezed his fingers. Did she know what he was thinking? Did she know how much he cared?

CHAPTER 19

For the next two weeks, Rachel continued to help out at the Swartleys' as often as she could, and for the next two weeks, she did everything possible to avoid Silas. It made her sick to her stomach to think that he had actually kissed her and then felt sorry about it. She really must be a fool if she thought she had any chance of winning his heart. After that embarrassing episode, she was sure he would never ask her to go fishing again, and he certainly wouldn't invite her to take another ride in his courting buggy.

Silas had tried talking with Rachel on several occasions, but she kept putting him off, saying she was too busy helping his mother. Rachel knew her time of avoidance was almost over, for today's preaching service was being held at their home and was about to begin. She was sure Silas and his family would be here soon.

The three-hour service seemed to last longer than usual, and Rachel squirmed on her bench, trying to focus on the songs, sermons, and prayers. Maybe her discomfort was because she had a view of the bench where Silas sat across the room. Beyond the flicker of a smile, she had no idea what he was thinking. Was it the kiss they had shared two weeks ago? Was he waiting for church to be over so he could corner Rachel and tell her he didn't want to see her anymore? If she kept busy in the kitchen, maybe she could avoid him again today. That's what she planned to do. . .stay busy and away from Silas.

Things went well for a while, but tables had been set up out in the barn for eating, and shortly after the noon meal was served, Rachel went back to the house. She planned to get another pot of coffee for the menfolk and carry out one of the pies she and Mom had baked the day before.

Much to Rachel's surprise, she discovered Silas in the kitchen, leaning against the counter with his arms folded. "I was hoping you'd come in here," he said, taking a few steps in her direction.

She moved quickly toward the stove and grabbed the pot of coffee.

"How about going for a walk with me, so we can talk?" he asked, following her across the room.

Rachel averted his gaze and headed for the door, forgetting about the apple pie she had planned to take back to the barn. "As you can probably see, I'm kind of busy right now."

"You won't be helping serve all day. How about after you're done?"

"I don't think we have anything to talk about, Silas."

He stepped in front of her, blocking the door. "Please, Rachel. . .just for a few minutes. I've wanted to talk to you for the last two weeks, but there never seemed to be a good time." He smiled. "Besides, I had some stuff to pray about."

Rachel nodded slowly. "Jah, me, too."

"So can we meet out by the willow tree, say, in one hour?"

She shrugged. "Okay."

At the appointed time, Rachel donned a heavy sweater and stepped onto the front porch. The afternoon air had cooled considerably, and a chill shivered through her. She caught sight of Silas out in the yard, talking to his cousin Rudy. She started across the lawn but stopped just before she reached the weeping willow tree. Silas was saying something to Rudy, and her ears perked up. Rachel was sure he had mentioned her sister's name, but she wondered why Silas would be talking to his cousin about Anna.

A group of children ran past, laughing and hollering so loud she couldn't make out what either Silas or Rudy was saying.

David Yoder, a little boy with Down syndrome, waved to Rachel, and she waved back, hoping he wouldn't call out her name. The last thing she needed was for Silas to catch her listening in on his conversation.

The children finally wandered off, and Rachel breathed a sigh of relief. She leaned heavily against the trunk of a tree and turned her attention back to Silas and his cousin.

"So you're really in love with her, huh?" she heard Rudy ask.

"Afraid so," Silas answered. "Don't rightly think I'll ever find anyone else I could love as much, and it's tearing me apart."

Rachel's heart slammed into her chest. Even after all these months, Silas still wasn't over Anna. *That's probably why he said he was sorry for kissing me. Most likely, he was wishing it had been Anna and not me in his courting buggy.*

Tears burned the backs of Rachel's eyes. She should have known better than to allow her emotions to get carried away. Silas cared nothing about her, and apparently he never had. He still loved Anna and probably always would, even though she was married and had left the Amish faith. She knew many people carried a torch for lost loves, and because of their pain, they never found love again. Mom had told her once that it almost happened to Rachel's great-aunt Mim. She was jilted by her first love, and for many years she carried a torch for him. Finally, she set her feelings aside and learned to love again. But that was only because she had allowed the Lord to work on her bitter spirit. Rachel wasn't so sure Silas wanted to find love again—especially not with her.

Tired of trying to analyze things, Rachel spun around. She was about to head back to the house, when she felt someone's hand touch her shoulder. "Where are you heading? I thought we were going for a walk."

Rachel shrugged Silas's hand away. "I heard you talking to Rudy. If you're still pining for Anna, then why bother taking a walk with a little *kinner* like me?"

Rudy, who was walking next to Silas, raised his eyebrows and moved away, but Silas kept pace beside Rachel. When she didn't slow down, he grabbed hold of her hand and pulled her to his side. "We need to talk."

Like a tightly coiled spring, Rachel released her fury on him. "Let go of me!" Her eyes burned like fire, and she almost choked on the huge knot that had lodged in her throat.

"*Was is letz do?*"

"Nothing's wrong here. I guess everything's just as it should be—or at least the way I figured it was."

Silas opened his mouth as if to say something more, but Rachel darted away without a backward glance. She had been a fool to think she could make Silas forget about Anna and fall in love with her. She'd been stupid to get caught up in a dumb thing like this. . .letting herself hope for the impossible. The one thing she had enjoyed most about her friendship with Silas was how comfortable they seemed with each other. Not anymore, though. That had ended when she'd heard him tell Rudy that he was still in love with Anna. If Silas wanted to pine his life away for a love he would never have, then that was *his* problem. Rachel planned to get on with her life, one way or another.

Silas groaned as he watched Rachel race up the steps and disappear into her house. One of the Beachys' dogs howled, and the mournful sound echoed in his soul. Rachel had heard something he'd told Rudy, but she'd refused to let him explain. Now everything was ruined between them, and it was a bitter pill to swallow. He was sure there was no chance of a relationship with Rachel, because she obviously didn't trust him. Maybe with good reason, too.

Truth of the matter, Silas hadn't been so good at trusting lately, either. He'd said he never wanted to move away from God, but he felt himself slipping away and knew if he didn't do something soon, he might sink into despair.

He moved slowly toward his horse and buggy, kicking at

every stone in his path. No point in hanging around here anymore. Maybe he should accept things as they were and just get on with his life.

"Jah, that's what I'll do," he mumbled as he gave one more rock a hefty kick with the toe of his boot. "I'll forget I had ever considered courting Rachel Beachy!"

⁂

"Are you about ready for bed?"

Rebekah turned her wheelchair away from the fireplace and smiled at Daniel. "Soon. Just thought I'd stay up awhile longer and try to get some more mending done."

He moved across the room to stand by her chair. "Are you sure you're not looking for some excuse to wait up for our two oldest kinner?"

"Anna's the oldest," she reminded.

Daniel grunted. "I think it's better if we don't mention her name."

Tears gathered in Rebekah's eyes, and she was powerless to keep them from spilling over. "Why must you be so unforgiving?"

"I'm only thinking of what's best for everyone concerned."

"Everyone concerned?" Her voice rose a notch. "How can you say it's best that we don't talk about our own flesh-and-blood daughter—that we won't welcome her home for a visit?"

Daniel crouched on his haunches and extended his hands toward the fire. "It's gettin' awful chilly at night now. Won't be long until the snow flies."

Rebekah released an exasperated groan. "Changing the

subject won't alter the fact that I don't agree with you on something, husband."

He shrugged.

"Neither will giving me the silent treatment."

"I'm not doing that, Rebekah. I just don't want to talk about our wayward daughter tonight."

"When can we talk about her?"

He shrugged again.

"Anna may have gone English, and she may be under the ban, but she's still our daughter, Daniel."

"Don't ya think I know that?" He sat a moment longer, then stood and reached for her hand. "Sorry for snapping. It just upsets me to think that she would join the church and make us think she and Silas had been courting and then sneak off and get married to Reuben Yutzy by a justice of the peace. Reuben's the one with the hankering for modern things; I'm sure of it."

"That may be, but Anna did marry him and agree to go English."

"That's what troubles me so." He rose to his feet. "Guess I must have failed as her daed somehow."

Rebekah shook her head. "You didn't fail, Daniel, and neither did I. We've raised our kinner the best we can, so we mustn't cast any blame on ourselves for the decisions they choose to make." She paused a moment to gauge his reaction, but Daniel just stood shifting his weight from one foot to the other.

"It's not our place to judge," she added. "Only God has that right, you know."

He bent to kiss her forehead. "I'm heading to bed now.

Don't be too long, okay?"

She nodded and released a sigh. If Daniel didn't want to talk about this, there wasn't much she could do except pray. She had been doing a lot of that since Anna left home, and she would continue to do so until her prayers were answered.

CHAPTER 20

Rachel felt a sense of relief when Katie Swartley's cast finally came off and she was able to stay home, even if it did mean spending more time helping Pauline in the greenhouse. Anything would be better than facing Silas every day. Knowing he was still in love with Anna and unable to quit loving him herself, Rachel felt a sense of hopelessness like never before. Everything looked different—the trees weren't as green, the birdsong wasn't as bright. She had nothing to praise God for anymore, and her times of prayer and Bible study happened less often.

That night, the young people were gathering at the Hostetlers' place. Joseph had already made it clear that he was going, and it was obvious that he and Pauline were officially courting. Even though Rachel was happy for them, she couldn't help feeling sorry for herself.

"Are you going to the singing?" her brother asked, as they met in the barn that morning before church.

She shook her head. "I don't think so."

"Why not? It could be the last one for a while, what

with the weather turning colder."

She shrugged. "I'd planned to work on my hope chest tonight."

Joseph took hold of her arm as she started to walk away. "It's Silas Swartley, isn't it? You haven't been acting right for the last few weeks, and I have a hunch it's got something to do with your feelings for him."

Rachel felt a familiar burning at the backs of her eyes, and she blinked rapidly, hoping to keep the tears from falling. "I'd rather not talk about Silas, if you don't mind." She shrugged Joseph's hand away. "I need to feed the kittens, and if I'm not mistaken, you've got a few things to do before we leave for church."

Joseph moved into the horse's stall without another word, and Rachel released a sigh of relief. She and Joseph might not always see eye-to-eye, but at least he cared enough about her feelings to drop the subject of Silas.

As Rachel rounded the corner of the barn, she noticed Dad down on his knees beside the woodpile. His face was screwed up in obvious pain, and the deep moan he emitted confirmed that fact. Rachel rushed to his side and squatted beside him. "What's wrong? You look like you're hurting real bad."

"I strained my back trying to lift a hunk of wood for your mamm's cooking stove. Must have bent over wrong." He groaned. "Don't think I can get up on my own, Rachel. Can you go get Joseph?"

Rachel patted her father's shoulder. "Jah, sure. Just hang on a few more minutes and try to relax." She jumped up and bolted for the barn.

Joseph was busy getting one of their buggy horses ready, when Rachel rushed back into the barn with a worried expression. "You'd better come, Joseph. *Schnell*—quickly. Dad's in need of your help."

His eyebrows lifted in question. "I'm busy with the horse, Rachel. Can't Dad get Perry to do whatever needs to be done?"

Rachel clutched his arm as he was about to lead the horse out of its stall. "Dad's hurt his back and can't even stand up. Perry isn't strong enough to get him on his feet, much less help him into the house."

Realizing the seriousness of the situation, Joseph closed the stall door, leaving the horse inside. "Where is he?"

"Out by the woodpile."

Rachel raced from the barn, and Joseph was right behind her. They found Dad down on his knees, his forehead dripping with sweat.

Joseph grabbed Dad under one arm, and Rachel took hold of the other. "On the count of three," Joseph instructed. "One. . .two. . .three!"

Dad moaned loudly when they pulled him to his feet. Walking slightly bent over, he allowed them to support most of his weight as they made their way slowly to the house.

They found Mom sitting in her wheelchair at the kitchen table, drinking a cup of tea. Elizabeth and Perry sat across from her, finishing their bowls of oatmeal.

"Ach, my!" Mom cried. "What's wrong, Daniel? It appears you can barely walk."

Dad grunted and placed his hands on the edge of the counter for support. "My fool back went out on me, Rebekah. Happened when I was getting more wood." He swallowed hard, like he was having a difficult time talking. "Guess I'll have to make a trip to town tomorrow and see Doc Landers for some poppin' and crackin'. He'll have me back on my feet in no time."

Joseph glanced over at Rachel, and she gave him a knowing look. The last time Dad's back went out, it took more than a few days' rest or a couple of treatments with the chiropractor to get him back on his feet. There was no doubt about it: Dad wouldn't be going to church this morning, and more than likely, he'd be flat on his back in bed for the next couple of weeks. That meant more work for Joseph and probably less time for him to spend courting Pauline.

That evening when Silas arrived at the singing, he looked around, hoping to see Rachel. She'd seemed so distant lately—nothing like the fun-loving Rachel he'd gone fishing with a few weeks ago. Maybe he'd have a chance to clear things up with her. Even if he had no possible chance at a future with Rachel, he would still like to be her friend. He remembered how much fun they'd had fishing and studying birds, and his heart skipped a beat at the thought of their kiss.

Silas caught sight of Joseph sitting on one side of the Hostetlers' barn, sharing a bale of straw with Pauline. He hurried over and squatted down beside them. "Did Rachel come with you tonight? I haven't seen any sign of her."

Joseph shook his head. "She stayed home. Said something about working on her hope chest."

"Hmm. . ."

"Besides, our daed hurt his back this morning, and Rachel figured Mom would be needing her help to wait on him."

Silas's forehead wrinkled. "Sorry to hear that. No wonder I didn't see him at church today."

"Jah, and he had to go straight to bed after it happened."

"Will he be able to help you finish the harvest or do any chores at all?"

"I doubt it; he's in a lot of pain—could barely get into bed." Joseph frowned. "Guess that means Perry might have to miss a few days of school so he can give me a hand with some of the chores. I'll be busy helping our Amish neighbors who come to help with the harvesting, and I sure can't do that plus all the other jobs needing to be done."

"No, I guess not." Silas thought he should say more, but Joseph had turned his attention to Pauline, so Silas let his thoughts shift back to Rachel.

Wonder why she would be working on her hope chest? After the way she acted the other night, it was fairly obvious she was done with me. Sure as anything, Rachel isn't stocking her hope chest with the idea of marrying me.

Suddenly, a light seemed to dawn. Maybe Rachel and Abe Landis were more serious about each other than he'd realized. Silas released a groan as he stood. Maybe it was for the best. Rachel might be better off with Abe. They were closer in age, and Abe probably hadn't said or done anything to make Rachel mistrust him.

After Rachel had finished helping Mom and Elizabeth clear the table and wash the supper dishes, she excused herself to go to her room.

"You're not sleepy already, are you?" Mom rolled her wheelchair across the kitchen to where Rachel stood by the hallway door. "Since your daed's in bed and Perry's in his room reading to him, I thought maybe we three women could work on a puzzle or play a game."

Elizabeth jumped up and down. "That sounds like fun. Let's make a big batch of popcorn, too!"

Rachel felt bad about throwing cold water on their plans, but she had work to do upstairs. Besides, she wasn't fit company for anyone right now. "Maybe some other time. I'd planned to work on my hope chest tonight."

Mom's eyes seemed to brighten. "I'm glad to hear that, Rachel. I was beginning to wonder if you were ever going to take an interest in marriage or that hope chest your daed made for your sixteenth birthday."

I've got an interest, all right. Trouble is, the man I want is in love with my married sister. Rachel sure couldn't tell Mom what she was thinking. She knew that even though her mother rarely spoke of Anna anymore, she still missed her and was terribly hurt by Anna's decision to go "fancy." There was no point in bringing up a sore subject, so Rachel smiled and said, "See you two in the morning."

As soon as Rachel got to her room, she knelt on the floor in front of her hope chest. The last time she had opened it, she'd been filled with such high hopes. Back then, she and

Silas seemed to be getting closer, and she'd even allowed herself to believe he might be falling in love with her. For a brief time, she'd been praising God and remaining hopeful. But her hopeful dream had been dented when Silas said he was sorry for kissing her, and it had been smashed to smithereens when she'd overheard him telling his cousin that he still loved Anna. "What's the use in having a hope chest if you aren't planning to get married?" she mumbled. "I could never marry anyone but Silas, because he's the only man I'll ever love."

Rachel lifted the lid and studied the contents of her hope chest. There was the lamp Dad had given her, along with the pillowcases Mom had made. She had purchased a few new items, as well—a set of dishes, some towels, and a tablecloth. She'd also made a braided throw rug, some pot holders, and had even been thinking about starting a quilt with the double-ring pattern. There was no point in making one now. The best thing to do was either sell off or give away most of the things in her hope chest. She pulled out the set of pillowcases and the braided throw rug, knowing she could use them in her room. The other things she put in a cardboard box, planning to take them to the greenhouse the following day.

Since Christmas wasn't far off, she was fairly certain she could sell some things to their customers. Anything that didn't sell she would take to Thomas Benner, the owner of the variety store in Paradise, and see if he might put them out on consignment. Maybe she would use the money she made to buy a concrete birdbath for Mom's flower garden. If she got enough from the sales, she might also buy several bird feeders from Eli Yoder, which would bring even more birds into their yard. At least she could still take some pleasure in bird-watching—even though it would have to be without Silas.

Rachel's only concern was what her mother would think when she saw all the things for sale in the greenhouse. Mom had seemed so hopeful about Rachel adding items to her hope chest. If she knew what was really going on, she would probably get all nervous, thinking she'd have to wait until Elizabeth grew up before she could plan a wedding. Of course, if things kept on the way they were with Joseph and Pauline, Mom could be in on their wedding plans.

Rachel closed the empty chest, and in so doing, she spotted Anna's hope chest. All these months it had been sitting in the corner of her room, and never once had she opened it. It was all she had left of her sister. If she opened it now, memories of Anna and reminders of how much she missed her older sister would probably make her cry.

Rachel moved over to Anna's hope chest and knelt beside it. She ran her fingers along the top of the chest as tears slipped from her eyes and rolled down her cheeks. "Oh, Anna, wasn't it bad enough that you broke Silas's heart by marrying Reuben? Did you have to move away and go English on us?" Rachel nearly choked on a sob as she turned away from Anna's hope chest, feeling as if a heavy weight rested on her shoulders. Would she ever see Anna again?

As Anna prepared for bed, her thoughts went to home. Several weeks had passed since she'd received a letter from Mom or Rachel, and it made her wonder if something might be wrong. Could Dad have found out they'd been writing to her? Maybe they'd been too busy working in the greenhouse to write anything lately.

She sighed as she stared at her reflection in the mirror. She not only wore different clothes, but she'd cut her hair a few weeks ago, and that made her look so much different. "I wonder if anyone in my family would recognize me now," she murmured.

"I recognize you," Reuben said, as he stepped up behind her and wrapped his arms around her waist.

She leaned her head against his broad chest and smiled. "I would hope so."

He nuzzled her neck with his cold nose.

"Do you ever miss your folks?" Anna asked.

"Jah, sure, but now I've got you, and you're my family."

"How come you don't go home and visit them?"

"I will when I feel the time is right."

She turned to face him. "You're not being faced with a shunning the way I am, so you can go back anytime you want, and nothing much will have changed."

He shook his head. "That's not so."

"What do you mean?"

"I haven't said anything about this before because I didn't want to upset you, but I ran into my brother Mose the other day, and he said Mom and Dad are still pretty peeved at me for leavin' the way I did. They think it's a sin and a shame that I didn't join the church, and Mom told Mose that I deserve to be shunned, regardless of whether I'd joined the church or not."

"Maybe in time your folks will come to understand."

Anna swallowed past the lump in her throat. "I'd like to visit my folks soon, but I'm waiting to hear from Mom again so I know when's a good time to go and whether Dad will allow me to come or not."

Reuben frowned. "A shunning in our district doesn't mean your family can't speak to you. They just aren't supposed—"

She put her fingers against his lips. "Can we talk about something else? This conversation is making me feel depressed."

He leaned over and kissed the tip of her nose. "How about we don't talk at all and just go to sleep? I'm pretty tired, and tomorrow my boss has scheduled us to begin a paint job on a big grocery store, so I really should try to get a good night's sleep."

"You're right; I need to be up early for my job, too." Anna flicked the light switch on the wall and crawled into bed. Maybe in the morning before she left for work, she would write Rachel and Mom both a letter and see what was up.

CHAPTER

21

Silas tossed and turned most of the night, punching his pillow, thinking about Rachel, and asking God to pave the way for them to be together. He had to see Rachel again and try to explain things. Even if she never wanted him to court her, he needed to clear the air and make her understand the way he felt. If only they could spend more time together. As he finally drifted off to sleep, visions of Rachel's sweet face and her two little dimples filled his senses. If only they could be together. If only. . .

When Silas awoke the next morning, he'd come up with a plan. Rachel had been kind enough to help out at their place when his mother had broken her arm, so now he could return the favor. If he helped Joseph in the fields most of the day, mealtimes would be spent in the Beachys' kitchen. It would be a good opportunity to see Rachel and maybe get in a word with her. Since Rachel's dad was laid up right now, he was sure his help would be most welcome. He would speak to his dad about the idea, and if Pap had no objections, then Silas would head on over to the Beachys' place right after breakfast and volunteer his services.

Rachel had just finished washing and drying the breakfast dishes when she heard a horse and buggy pull into the yard. She peeked out the kitchen window and gulped when she saw who it was. Silas had climbed out of his buggy and was heading toward the house.

Joseph and Perry were in the fields, Elizabeth was at school, and Dad and Mom had gone into town to see Doc Landers. That left Rachel alone at the house. Silas had obviously seen her through the window, because he waved. Rachel sighed. She had no choice but to open the door.

"Guder mariye," Silas said when Rachel answered his knock. "I missed you at the singing last night."

"I had other things to do."

"So I heard." Silas's forehead wrinkled. "I also heard your daed hurt his back."

Rachel nodded. "It goes out on him now and then. He's at the chiropractor's right now." She had no plans to invite Silas inside, so she stepped through the doorway and joined him on the porch, hoping he would take the hint and be on his way.

"I came to help Joseph in the fields. He said your daed won't be up to it now, and since we're all done harvesting over at our place, I figured I'd offer my services here."

Rachel breathed deeply and noticed the stinging sensation of the freshly mown hay hovering over their farm. She flicked an imaginary piece of lint off the sleeve of her dress and tried to avoid his steady gaze. "It's nice of you to offer," she murmured. "Perry stayed home from school to help Joseph today, but it won't be good if he misses too many days."

"That's what I thought." Silas shifted from one foot to the other. "I. . .uh. . .was kind of hoping you and I could have a little talk before I head out to the fields."

"I've got to get to the greenhouse and open up."

"I thought Pauline worked there now. Or did she find herself some other job?"

"She still helps us some because Mom's not up to working full time anymore. But Pauline has chores at her house to do every morning, so she usually doesn't get here until ten or after."

Silas cleared his throat. "Okay, I'll let you get to it then." He pivoted and started down the steps, but when he got to the bottom, he halted and turned back around. "Maybe later we can talk?"

She raised her gaze to meet his and slowly nodded. "Jah, maybe."

❦

Silas noticed tears clinging like dewdrops to Rachel's long, pale lashes, and it was all he could do to keep from pulling her into his arms. Before their misunderstanding, he'd been drawing closer to Rachel, and some of his old fears had been sliding into a locked trunk of unwanted memories. Now he wondered why they had drifted apart and if he could do anything to bring them close again. Maybe the real issue was trust. Did she trust him? Did he trust her? Were either of them trusting God as they should?

A deep sense of longing inched its way into Silas's soul

as he continued to stare at Rachel. He had missed seeing her every day, and if the look on her sweet face was any indication of the way she felt, then he was fairly certain she had been missing him, too. Still, she seemed bent on keeping her distance, and he thought it best if he didn't push. At least not now.

"See you later, then." Silas offered Rachel what he hoped was a pleasant smile, then waved and headed off in the direction of the fields.

Rachel entered the greenhouse a short time later, carrying her box of hope-chest items as confusion swirled around in her brain like a windmill flapping against a strong breeze. It was kind of Silas to offer his help, but how would she handle him coming over every day? She had tried so hard to get Silas out of her mind, and him wanting to talk had her concerned. Was he planning to tell her again how sorry he was for that unexpected kiss he gave her a few weeks ago? Did he want to explain why he still loved Anna, even though they could never be together?

Rachel already knew that much, and she sure didn't need to hear it again. She'd made up her mind. She was not going to say anything more to Silas other than a polite word or two no matter how many days he came to help out. Somehow she must keep her feelings under control.

Rachel shivered as goose bumps erupted on her arms, and she knew it wasn't from the chill in the greenhouse. "Get busy," she scolded herself. "It's the only thing that will keep you sane."

As soon as she had the fire stoked up, she quickly set to work pricing her hope-chest items; then she placed them on an empty shelf near the front door. She had no more than put the OPEN sign in the window when the first customer of the day showed up. It was Laura Yoder, and Rachel breathed a sigh of relief when she saw that the pretty redhead was alone. The last time Laura had come to the greenhouse, she'd brought both of her children along. Barbara, who was two and a half, had pulled one of Mom's prized African violets off the shelf, and the little girl had quite a time playing in all that rich, black dirt. Laura's four-year-old son, David, had been so full of questions. The child's handicap didn't slow him down much, and like most children his age, David was curious about everything.

As much as Rachel loved children, it tried her patience when they came in with their folks and ran about the greenhouse like it was a play yard. If it was disturbing to her, she could only imagine how her other customers might feel. Most Amish parents were quite strict and didn't let their children get away with much, but Eli's Laura seemed to be more tolerant of her children's antics. However, Rachel was pretty sure Laura would step in and discipline should it become absolutely necessary.

"I see you're all alone today," Rachel said, as her customer looked around the store.

Laura nodded. "I left the little ones with Eli's mamm. I've got several errands to run, and I figured I could get them done quicker if I was by myself." She chuckled. "Besides, Mary Ellen seems to like her role as *grossmudder*."

Rachel smiled. "I guess she would enjoy being a grand-mother. Let's see. . .how many grandchildren does she have now?"

"Five in all. Martha Rose has three kinner, as I'm sure you know. And of course, there are my two busy little ones. Mary Ellen's son, Lewis, and his wife are expecting most any day, so soon there'll be six."

"So I've heard."

"Since I'm an only child, my kinner are the only grand-children my folks have, and they spoil those two something awful." Laura moved over to the shelf where Rachel had displayed her hope-chest items. "You've got some nice things here. If I didn't already have a set of sturdy dishes, I'd be tempted to buy these." She fingered the edge of a white stoneware cup.

"Guess the right buyer will come along sooner or later," Rachel remarked, making no reference to the fact that the dishes were from her hope chest. Mom hadn't been too happy when she'd learned that Rachel was bringing them here, but Rachel was relieved when she chose not to make an issue of it. Truth be told, Mom was probably praying that Rachel's things wouldn't sell and some nice fellow would come along and propose marriage soon.

"How's the flower business?" Laura asked.

"Oh, fair to middlin'." Rachel didn't feel the inclination to tell Laura that except for the need to help out, she really didn't care much about the flower business. Laura seemed like such a prim and proper sort of lady. She probably wouldn't understand Rachel's desire to be outdoors, enjoy-ing all the wildlife God had created.

Sometimes Rachel wished she had been born a boy, just so she could spend more time outside. Even baling and bucking hay would be preferable to being cooped up inside a stuffy old greenhouse all day.

"Have you got any yellow mums?" Laura asked, breaking into Rachel's thoughts.

"Mums? Oh, sure, I think we've got several colors. Come with me to the other room and we'll see what's available."

Rachel studied Laura as she checked over the variety of chrysanthemums. Even though her hair was red and her face was pretty, she looked plain, just like all the other Amish women in their community. Except for the proper way Laura spoke, it was hard to imagine that she'd ever been a part of the fancy, English world. Rachel had only been a girl when Eli Yoder had married Laura after she'd chosen to become Amish. She had no idea how Laura used to look dressed in modern clothes or even how the woman felt about her past life. She had met Laura's fancy English folks a few times, as they'd moved to Lancaster County to be closer to Laura some time ago.

Maybe I should ask her a few questions about being English. It might help me better understand why Anna left home and what her life is like now.

She took a step toward Laura. "Say, I was wondering about something."

Laura picked up a yellow mum and pivoted to face Rachel. "What is it?"

"I know you used to be English."

"That's true. Although it seems like a long time ago to me now."

"You've probably heard that my sister Anna married Reuben Yutzy awhile back, and the two of them left the faith and moved to Lancaster."

Laura's expression turned solemn. "Jah, I know about that."

"Except for the letters we've had from Anna, we've had no other contact with her. My daed's not one bit happy about Anna leaving home the way she did, and he doesn't want her to come here for a visit." Rachel's voice faltered, and she paused a moment to gain control of her swirling emotions. "It sure hurts knowing she's no longer part of our family."

"She's still part of your family, just not of the Amish faith anymore." Laura touched Rachel's shoulder. "I'm sure it's not easy for any of you, or for Anna, either."

Rachel's eyes filled with tears, and she sniffed. "You really think it pains her, too?"

"I'm almost certain of it." Laura released a quiet moan. "I know it hurt my folks when I left the English world to become Amish, but we stayed in touch, and pretty soon my daed surprised me by selling his law practice and moving out to a small farm nearby. He still practices law, but in a smaller office in Lancaster now." She smiled. "Even though my folks are English, they're living a much simpler life than they used to, and we get to see a lot more of them, which makes me happy."

"Do you think there's a chance that Anna and our daed will ever mend their fences—even if Anna and Reuben never reconcile with the church? Maybe even come to the point where we can start visiting each other from time to time?"

Laura clasped Rachel's hand. "I'll surely pray for that, as

I'm sure you're already doing."

"I'm praying for that and a whole lot of other things."

Laura followed Rachel back to the front of the greenhouse, where Rachel wrapped a strip of paper around the bottom of the plant and wrote up a bill. Laura paid her, picked up the mum, and was about to open the front door, when Pauline rushed in. Her cheeks were pink, and a few strands of tawny yellow hair peeked out from under her kapp. "Whew! It's a bit windy out there!"

Laura laughed. "I can tell. You look like you've been standing underneath a windmill."

Pauline giggled and reached up to readjust her covering, which was slightly askew. "Sure is a good day to be indoors. I'm glad I have this job working at Grandma's Place."

Wish I could say the same, Rachel thought ruefully. Philippians 4:11, which Mom often quoted, popped into Rachel's mind: *"For I have learned, in whatsoever state I am, therewith to be content." Okay, Lord, I'll try harder.*

Pauline asked about Laura's children, and Laura spent the next few minutes telling her how much they were growing. She even told how her cat, Foosie, had paired up with one of the barn cats. Now the children had a bunch of fluffy brown-and-white kittens to occupy their busy little hands.

It amazed Rachel the way the two women visited, as though they had always been friends. She knew from the talk she'd heard that it hadn't always been so. Truth be told, Pauline used to dislike Laura because she had stolen Eli's heart and he'd married her and not Pauline. Then Pauline had gone to live with her aunt and uncle in Ohio for a time, no doubt to get away from the reminders of what she'd lost.

Rachel could relate well to the pain of knowing the man she loved cared for someone else and didn't see her as anything more than a friend. She couldn't imagine how Pauline had gotten through those difficult years after Eli had jilted her and married a woman who used to be English. It amazed her to see that there was no animosity between the two women now.

Laura finally headed out, and Pauline got right to work watering plants and repotting some that had outgrown their containers. She seemed so happy doing her work that she was actually humming.

"I was wondering if you'd mind me asking a personal question," Rachel asked when Pauline took a break and sat on the stool behind the cash register.

"Sure, what is it?"

Rachel leaned on the other side of the counter and smiled. She hoped her question wasn't out of line and wouldn't be taken the wrong way. "I know you and Laura were at odds for a while because of Eli, and I was wondering what happened to make you so friendly with one another."

Pauline smiled. "I'll admit that I used to be jealous of Laura because I felt she stole Eli away from me. It hurt so bad that I finally went to Ohio to live with my aunt and uncle. I learned a lot while I was there, and I grew closer to the Lord. By the time I returned to Lancaster County, I realized that I had to give up my bitterness and forgive Laura and Eli for hurting me. So, I apologized in a letter; then I went to their house and had a little talk with them."

Rachel's interest was piqued. "Mind if I ask what was said?"

Pauline shrugged. "Nothing much except I told Laura

I was sorry for making her so miserable, and then she apologized, too. The thing was, I knew in my heart that Eli had never been in love with me. He and I were only good friends. I should have been Christian enough to turn loose of him and let him find happiness with Laura. Truth be told, Eli probably did me a favor by marrying her."

Rachel's eyebrows shot up. "Really? How's that?"

"If he'd married me, I never would have gotten to know Joe so well, and we. . ." Pauline blushed a deep crimson. "Guess you've probably figured out that I'm in love with your brother."

"Jah, and I'm sure he feels the same way about you." Rachel glanced across the room at her hope-chest items. "Say, do you think you might be interested in some things for your hope chest?"

Pauline grinned. "Maybe so. I'll have a look-see."

⁂

"I can't figure out why this stupid CD player isn't working," Reuben grumbled, as he punched a couple of buttons and turned some knobs.

Anna kept her focus on the road for fear that Reuben might hit something while he was busy looking at the CD player in his truck instead of watching out for traffic the way he should be doing.

"Everything costs a lot, but it seems like nothing ever works right," Reuben complained. "Maybe I need to trade this truck in and get a newer one."

Anna grimaced. With their tight finances, the last thing they needed was a larger truck payment. "When I went to church last week, the preacher made some good points about people putting too much emphasis on things and not enough on God."

Reuben merely grunted in reply.

"I wrote down one of the verses of scripture he quoted. Proverbs 15:16: 'Better is little with the fear of the Lord than great treasure and trouble therewith.' "

"This CD player is trouble, all right," he admitted. "Guess I'll have to learn to live without it until I have enough money to get it fixed. We've got bills to pay and groceries to buy, so having music to listen to as we drive to work every morning will have to wait."

Anna smiled. "I don't miss it, really. Having some quiet time so we can talk is kind of nice, don't you think?"

He nodded. "With the long hours I've been workin', we don't get to see each other much anymore."

"That's true. Even our Sundays aren't spent together when you sleep most of the day."

Reuben's forehead wrinkled, and he gripped the steering wheel a little tighter. "Are you tryin' to make an issue of me needing to get caught up on my rest?"

"No, no. I just meant—"

"We can talk about this later. There's no point in you being late for work." He pulled the truck into the parking lot on the backside of the restaurant where Anna worked and stopped. "Since I'm starting work two hours later than usual today, I'll probably be working late tonight, so you'd better plan on catching the bus home."

"What else is new?" Anna mumbled, as she opened the truck door.

"What was that?"

"Nothing. Have a good day, Reuben."

When Joseph entered the restaurant in Lancaster, where he'd decided to have some breakfast, his stomach rumbled. He'd had an early dental appointment and hadn't eaten anything before he'd left home. After he'd left the dentist's office, he'd run a few errands, and now that the numbness in his jaw had finally worn off, it was time to fill his belly with a bit of food.

An English woman escorted Joseph to a table near the window, telling him that his waitress would be there shortly. As he waited, he stared out the window and thought about Pauline. It still seemed too good to be true that she was willing to let him court her, but he wasn't complaining in the least. Every chance he got to be with her was like candy in his mouth. He wished she could keep working at the greenhouse indefinitely so they could see each other more. For that matter, he wished he could quit working in the fields and work at the greenhouse, too. Maybe someday when Mom and Dad retired from the business, he could take over. And maybe if Pauline was willing to marry him, the two of them could run the greenhouse together. Rachel wasn't likely to want it.

"Can I bring you something to drink before you order your meal?"

Joseph turned at the sound of a woman's voice. It was a voice he thought he recognized. When he looked up at the waitress who stood next to his table, his mouth dropped open. "Anna?"

Her cheeks turned pink, and her mouth hung slightly open, too. "Joseph. I didn't realize it was you until I saw your face."

"I thought I recognized your voice, but I barely recognize you at all." He frowned deeply. "What have you done to your hair?"

Anna reached up to touch the blond curls framing her slender face. "I. . .uh. . .decided to try it short for a change." The color in her cheeks deepened. "Reuben likes it this way."

Joseph folded his arms and glared up at his sister. "Reuben's the only reason you left the faith, isn't he?"

Her gaze dropped to the floor. "Neither Reuben nor I have anything against the Amish way of life, but Reuben didn't want to give up his truck, so—"

"You left just to please him then—so he could have his stupid old truck?"

She shrugged. "Sort of."

He gritted his teeth. "Either you did or you didn't, Anna. Which is it?"

She lifted her gaze to meet his again. "All right then; I did leave to please Reuben, but lots of things about the English way of life I enjoy, too."

"More than being with your family? Or have you already forgotten about us?"

"Of course I haven't forgotten, but Reuben's my family, too."

Joseph sat fuming as he stared at the menu lying before him.

"I need to wait on some other customers, so what would you like to order?"

"If I place an order with you, then it's the same as doing business with you, and we both know that's not allowed."

Tears pooled in Anna's eyes, and she blinked a couple of times. "Would you like me to see if another waitress is free to take your order?"

He shook his head and pushed away from the table. "My appetite's gone, so I'll just meet up with the driver I hired to bring me to town and be on my way home. Mom or one of the sisters can fix me something to eat."

Anna took a step toward Joseph, but he moved quickly away. Seeing his older sister dressed in English clothes and wearing her hair cut short was a painful reminder that she was no longer Amish and had chosen Reuben and his fancy English ideas over her own family. All he wanted to do was get as far away from Anna as he possibly could.

CHAPTER 22

Daniel's back took nearly two weeks to heal, and Silas went over to the Beachys' place most days in order to help with chores and the last of the harvesting. In all that time, he never had his heart-to-heart talk with Rachel. It wasn't because he hadn't tried. He'd made every effort to get her alone, but she always made up some excuse about being too busy to talk to him. Silas was getting discouraged and had about decided to give up, when suddenly an idea popped into his head. Last Friday had been his final day helping out. Daniel had assured him that he was feeling well enough to start doing some light chores, and with the help of their neighbors, all the hay had been baled and put away in the barn, which was a good thing, since they'd had some snow since then. Silas wouldn't be going back to the Beachy farm—at least not to help. However, that didn't mean he couldn't pay a visit to the greenhouse.

He stepped up to his mother, who stood at the sink, doing the breakfast dishes. "I'm going out for a while, Mom. Should be back in plenty of time for the noon meal, though."

Her forehead wrinkled as she turned to face him. "In this

weather? In case you haven't noticed, there's a foot of snow on the ground, with the promise of more coming from the looks of those dark clouds in the sky." She nodded to the window.

"I'm taking the sleigh, so I'm sure I'll be fine."

"Mind if I ask where you're going?"

"Over to the Beachys' greenhouse."

Mom gave Silas a knowing look, but he chose to ignore it. "Say, if you're heading to the greenhouse, would you mind seeing if they have any nice poinsettias? I'd like one to give my sister Susan when she comes here to celebrate her birthday next week."

"Jah, sure, I can do that." Silas leaned over, kissed his mother on the cheek, and started for the back door. "See you later, Mom."

Since none of Rachel's hope-chest items had sold yet and Pauline had decided not to buy any, Rachel thought it might be time to take them into town and see if Thomas Benner would sell them in his store. Storm clouds were brewing that morning, and Dad wouldn't let Rachel take the horse and buggy to town, saying he was worried she might get caught in a snowstorm. She had been hoping to get her things into the variety store in time for the busy Christmas shopping season, but now she would have to wait until the weather improved. Besides, Mom had come down with a nasty cold, and it wouldn't be fair to expect her to work with Pauline in the greenhouse while Rachel went to town.

Rachel donned her woolen jacket and headed for the

greenhouse. She had talked her mother into going back to bed and had left a warm pot of fenugreek tea by her bedside. Mom was resting, and Rachel would be all by herself until Pauline showed up. If the weather worsened, Pauline might not come today. For that matter, they might not have any customers. Who in their right mind would want to visit a greenhouse when the weather was cold and snowy?

Shortly after Rachel opened the greenhouse and stoked up the wood-burning stove, she heard a horse and buggy pull up. Figuring it was probably Pauline, she flung open the door. To her astonishment, Abe Landis stepped out of a closed-in buggy and offered her a friendly wave. She hadn't seen Abe since the last preaching service, and then she'd only spoken a few words to him while she was serving the men their noon meal.

"Those angry-looking clouds out there make me think we might be in for another snowstorm," Abe said when he entered the greenhouse. He wore a dark wool jacket, and his ears protruded out from under the black hat perched on his head.

Ears that are a mite too big, Rachel noticed. An image of Silas sifted through her mind. *Abe's not nearly as good-looking as Silas, but then—as Dad often says—looks aren't everything.*

"What can I help you with, Abe?" Rachel asked, as she slipped behind the counter and took a seat on her stool.

Abe removed his hat, and it was all Rachel could do to keep from laughing out loud. A thatch of Abe's hair stood straight up. It looked as though he hadn't bothered to comb it that morning.

"I really didn't come here to buy anything." Abe jammed

his free hand inside his coat pocket and offered her a lop-sided grin.

"What did you come for then?"

"I. . .uh. . .was wondering if you'd like to go with me to the taffy pull that's gonna be held at Herman Weaver's place this Saturday night."

Rachel wasn't sure what to say. She didn't want to go to the taffy pull with Abe. He was a nice enough fellow, and she'd known him and his family a good many years, but he wasn't Silas. If Rachel couldn't be courted by the man she loved, then she didn't want to be courted at all. Of course, she could go as Abe's friend. Still, that might lead the poor fellow on, and she didn't want him to think there was any chance for the two of them as a couple.

"So, what's your answer?" Abe prompted. "Can I come by your place on Saturday night and give you a lift to the Weavers'?"

Rachel nibbled on her lower lip as she searched for the right words. She didn't want to hurt Abe's feelings, but her answer had to be no. "I'm flattered that you'd want to escort me to the taffy pull, but I'm afraid I can't go."

Abe's dark eyebrows drew downward. "How come?"

She swallowed hard. "My mamm has a bad cold, and my daed just got on his feet after a painful bout with his back. I think it's best for me to stick close to home."

Abe nodded and slapped his hat back on his head. "Good enough. I'll see you around, then." With that, he marched out the door.

Rachel followed, hoping to call out a friendly good-bye, but Abe was already in his buggy and had taken up the reins. Maybe she'd made a mistake. Maybe she should have agreed to go with him. Wouldn't having Abe as a boyfriend be better than having no boyfriend at all?

She bowed her head and prayed. *Lord, if I'm not supposed to love Silas, please give me the grace to accept it. And if I'm supposed to be courted by Abe, then give me the desire for that.*

Rachel heard a horse whinny, and she glanced out the front window. A sleigh was parked in the driveway, and she recognized the driver. Rachel's heart hammered in her chest, and her hands felt like a couple of slippery trout as she watched Silas step down from his buggy and hurry toward the greenhouse. She couldn't imagine why he would be here. The harvest was done, and Dad's back was much better. Maybe he'd come to buy a plant for someone.

Silas rubbed his hands briskly together as he entered the greenhouse. His nose was red from the cold, and his black hat was covered with tiny snowflakes. Dad's prediction about the weather had come true, for the snow was certainly here.

Rachel moved toward the counter, her heart riding on waves of expectation. Silas followed. "It's mighty cold out, and I'm glad we got your daed's hay in when we did. Guess winter's decided to come a bit early." He nodded toward the door. "Say, wasn't that Abe Landis I saw getting into his buggy as I pulled in?"

"Jah, it was Abe."

"Did he buy out the store?"

She shook her head. "Nope, didn't buy a thing."

Silas raised his eyebrows. "How come?"

"Abe stopped by to ask me to the taffy pull this Saturday

night." Rachel stepped behind the counter. "Can I help you with something, Silas?"

He squinted his dark eyes, and Rachel wondered why he made no comment about Abe's invitation.

"I came by to see if you have any poinsettias. My mamm's sister lives in Ohio, and she's coming to visit next week. Mom thought since her birthday's soon, she would give her a plant."

Rachel stepped out from behind the counter. "I believe we still have one or two poinsettias in the other room. Shall we go take a look-see?"

Silas followed silently as they went to the room where a variety of plants were on display. Rachel showed him several red poinsettias, and he selected the largest one.

Back at the battery-operated cash register, Rachel's hands trembled as she counted out Silas's change. Just the nearness of him took her breath away, and it irked her to think he had the power to make her feel so weak in the knees.

"Seen any interesting birds lately?" Silas asked after she'd wrapped some paper around the pot of the plant and handed it to him.

Glad for the diversion, she smiled. "I saw a great horned owl the other night when I was looking up in the tree with my binoculars. The critter was sure hootin' like crazy."

Silas chuckled; then he started for the door. Just as he got to the shelf where Rachel's hope-chest items were placed, he stopped and bent down to examine them. "These look like some mighty fine dishes. Mind if I ask how much they cost?"

"The price sticker is on the bottom of the top plate."

Silas picked it up and whistled. "Kind of high, don't

you think?" His face turned redder than the plant he held. "Sorry. Guess it's not my place to decide how much your folks should be selling things for."

Rachel thought about telling Silas that it wasn't her mom or dad who had priced the dishes, but she didn't want him to know she was trying to sell off her hope-chest items. It was none of his business. "I hope your aunt enjoys the poinsettia," she said instead.

Silas gave a quick nod and opened the front door. "I hope Abe knows how lucky he is," he called over his shoulder.

Rachel slowly shook her head. "Now what in the world did he mean by that? Surely Silas doesn't think Abe and I are courting." Of course, she hadn't bothered to tell him that she'd turned down Abe's offer to escort her to the taffy pull. But then, he hadn't asked.

Rachel moved over to the window and watched with a heavy heart as Silas drove out of sight. She glanced at the dishes he'd said were too high-priced and wondered if he had considered buying them, maybe as a gift for his aunt's birthday.

"Guess I should lower the price some." Rachel felt moisture on her cheeks. She had been trying so hard to be hopeful and keep praising God, but after seeing Silas again, she realized that her hopes had been for nothing. He obviously had no interest in her. Rachel wondered if God even cared about her. Hadn't He been listening to her prayers and praises all these months? Didn't He realize how much her heart ached to be loved by Silas?

※

As Joseph finished up his chores in the barn, he kept going

to the door and checking to see if Pauline's buggy had shown up at the greenhouse yet. Ever since that day when he'd seen Anna at the restaurant, he'd been stewing over things, and he thought he might feel better if he talked to Pauline about it. She'd been understanding and willing to listen the last time he'd discussed Anna with her, and she had been full of good advice. Only trouble was he still hadn't found it in his heart to forgive his sister for leaving home and going English on them. It still pained him to think of Anna dressed in fancy clothes and wearing her hair cut short, and the idea of her and Reuben living in the fancy English world gave him a sick feeling in the pit of his stomach.

Joseph peered out the barn door one more time and was happy to see Pauline's buggy coming up the driveway. He slipped out the door and ran toward the greenhouse. Pauline was just getting out of her buggy when he arrived.

"Guder mariye, Joe." She offered him a friendly smile. "It's good to see you."

"It's good to see you, too." He motioned toward her buggy. "Could we sit in there awhile and talk, or do you have to get into the greenhouse right away?"

"I'm a little earlier than usual, so I have a few minutes to spare."

"Great." He opened the door on the side of the buggy closest to her and helped her inside. Then he went around and took a seat on the other side.

"Is something troubling you, Joe?" she asked. "You look upset."

He grunted. "I saw her the other day."

"Who?"

"Anna."

"Did she come to your place for a visit?"

"No. I ran into her at the restaurant in Lancaster where she works as a waitress."

"How's she doing?"

"Fine, as far as I could tell, but she doesn't look like Anna anymore."

"You mean because she's not wearing Plain clothes?"

"That, and she's cut her hair real short." Joseph gritted his teeth and gripped the buggy seat so tightly that his fingers ached.

"I'll bet she did look quite different."

Joseph sat staring straight ahead.

Pauline reached over and touched his arm. "Did seeing Anna that way make you feel sad?"

"Not sad, really. More mad, I'd have to say." He grimaced. "I could hardly stand to see my sister looking that way, and since I'm not supposed to do any business with a shunned member of the church, I walked out without letting her wait on me."

Pauline offered him a sympathetic smile. "I thought you were going to forgive Anna and move on with things."

"I can't go against the church and do business with her."

"I'm not suggesting that." She paused a moment and flicked her tongue across her lower lip. "I just think you need to forgive Anna for hurting your family and treat her kindly when you do see her."

Joseph shrugged. "Probably won't be for some time, 'cause I'm not likely to go back to that restaurant again."

"She might come here for a visit, though."

"Not if Dad has anything to say about it."

"He's still angry, too?"

He nodded. "I think it would take something big for him to let Anna come home to see any of us."

"Big, like what?"

"Like a death in the family or something."

Pauline shook her head. "Let's hope there's nothing like that on the horizon." She reached over and took hold of Joseph's hand. "I've been praying for you, Joe. Praying for all your family."

He smiled and squeezed her fingers. "Danki. I appreciate that."

For the next few days, snow poured from the sky like powdered sugar, but by Saturday morning, the weather had improved some. So Rachel convinced Joseph to hitch up the sleigh and drive her to the variety store in Paradise. It was the second week of December, but there was still a chance that people would be looking for things to give as Christmas presents. She'd finally sold some towels and a few pot holders from her hope chest to a couple of customers who'd come into the greenhouse, but she needed to get rid of the dishes, the kerosene lamp, and the tablecloth.

Thomas Benner was more than happy to take Rachel's things in on consignment, although he did mention that they would have had a better chance of selling if she'd brought them in a few weeks earlier. Rachel sure didn't need that reminder. She wished she'd never started filling her hope chest.

By the time Rachel left the store and found Joseph, who'd gone looking for something to give Pauline for Christmas, snow was beginning to fall again.

"We'd best be gettin' on home," Joseph said, looking

up at the sky. "If this keeps up, the roads could get mighty slippery. I wouldn't want some car to go sliding into our sleigh."

"You're right; we should leave now." Rachel climbed into the sleigh and reached under the seat to withdraw an old quilt, which she wrapped snugly around the lower half of her body. "Brr. . .it's turning cold again."

Joseph picked up the reins and got the horse moving. "Jah, it sure is."

Rachel glanced over at her brother. He seemed to be off in some other world.

"Are you okay?"

"Sure. Why do you ask?"

"You seem kind of pensive today."

"I was just thinking about something Pauline told me the other day."

"Oh? What was that?"

He shrugged. "She's been giving me some advice lately."

"What kind of advice? Or would you rather not say?"

"I don't mind saying. It might feel good to talk more about it."

"More about what?"

"The way I've been feeling about Anna going English."

Rachel noticed the wrinkles etched in her brother's forehead. "How have you been feeling about the whole thing?"

"Not so good. Not good at all."

"I don't think any of us feels good about it, but it's a fact we can't change, so as Mom said after her last letter from Anna came, 'We must accept Anna's decision and quit brooding over it.' "

Joseph nodded. "Pauline said pretty much the same thing, only she took it a step further by telling me I needed to forgive Anna."

"Pauline's right about that. We all need to forgive Anna for leaving home the way she did—including Dad."

"I'm workin' on it," Joseph mumbled.

"Glad to hear it." Rachel smiled. "So, why don't you tell me what you got Pauline for Christmas?"

He smiled, too, and his mood seemed to brighten. "I bought her a pair of gardening gloves and a book about flowers."

"She should like that since she enjoys working in the greenhouse so much."

Joseph nodded. "She's sure changed a lot here of late, don't you think?"

Rachel bit back the laughter bubbling in her throat. "I think you've been good for her."

His dark eyebrows lifted. "You really think so?"

"I do."

"Well, she's been good for me, too."

"She's not worried about your age difference anymore?"

He shook his head. "Doesn't seem to be."

"And you're okay with it?"

"Jah."

"I'm glad." At least things were going well for someone in Rachel's family.

"Come spring, I'm thinking about asking her to marry me." Joseph glanced over at Rachel. "Don't you go sayin' anything to anyone about it, though, you hear?"

"Oh, I won't. It's not my place to be doing the telling."

"I'm sorry things didn't work out for you and Silas."

Rachel grimaced. "It wasn't meant to be, that's all. I just have to learn to be content with my life as it is. There's no point in hoping for the impossible. Job in the Bible did, and look where it got him."

"Think about it, Rachel. Through all Job's trials, he never lost hope." Joseph glanced over at her again and smiled. "In the end, God blessed Job with more than he'd lost."

Rachel drew in a deep breath and released it quickly. "I guess you're right, but it's not always easy to have hope. Especially when things don't go as we'd planned."

"Life is full of twists and turns. It's how we choose to deal with things that makes the difference in our attitudes. Take Silas, for example. . .I saw him the other day and mentioned my encounter with Anna at the restaurant."

"What'd he say?"

"He didn't seem all that affected when I mentioned Anna's name."

"Well, what could he say, Joseph? Anna's a married woman now, and there's nothing Silas can do about it." She sighed. "I'd been hoping that he might take an interest in me, but it doesn't look like that will ever occur. Truth is, not much of anything I hope for ever seems to happen."

"Our hope should be in the Lord, not in man or in our circumstances."

Rachel stared straight ahead. She didn't want to talk about Job, hope, or even God right now. She was too worried about the weather. The snow was coming down harder, and the road was completely covered. She watched the passing scenery, noting as they approached the one-room schoolhouse that the yard was empty. No Amish buggies. No scooters. No sign of any children or their teacher. "School must have been dismissed early today. Teacher Nancy probably thought it would be best to let the kinner go before the weather got any worse," she commented.

"Jah, you're probably right."

They rode along in silence until a rescue vehicle sailed past, its red lights blinking off and on and the siren blaring like crazy.

"Must be an accident up ahead." Joseph pulled back on the reins to slow the horse.

Rachel's body tensed. She hated the thought of seeing an accident, and she prayed one of their Amish buggies wasn't involved. So often, horse-drawn carriages had been damaged by cars that either didn't see them or had been traveling too fast. Lots of Amish folks had been injured from collisions with those fast-moving English vehicles, too.

Their sleigh had just rounded the next bend when they saw the rescue truck stopped in the middle of the road. Flares threw light along the highway and on a dark blue, mid-sized car pulled off on the shoulder. Rescue workers bent over a small figure. Several Amish children clustered around, and the sheriff directed traffic.

"We'd better stop. It could be someone we know." Joseph pulled the sleigh off the road; then he and Rachel jumped out.

They had only taken a few steps when a familiar voice called out, "Joseph! Rachel! Over here!"

Rachel glanced to her right. Elizabeth dashed across

the slippery snow and nearly knocked Rachel off her feet when she grabbed her around the waist. "It's Perry!" she panted. "He was hit by a car!"

CHAPTER

24

Rebekah had just put a pan of chicken in the oven to bake when she heard a car pull into the yard. She rolled her wheelchair across the floor and peered out the low kitchen window. The car that sat in the driveway belonged to Sheriff Andrews. The family had met him a couple of times when buggy accidents had happened near their home. The sheriff got out of his car, glanced around the yard as though he was looking for someone, then started for the house.

Rebekah was about to head for the door to see what he wanted, when she noticed a horse and sleigh come up the driveway, with Rachel in the driver's seat and Elizabeth sitting in the seat beside her. Goose bumps erupted on Rebekah's arms. Where were Joseph and Perry, and what had happened that had brought the sheriff to their place?

Just as the officer reached the back porch, Daniel came rushing out of the barn. He stopped at the sleigh a few minutes, apparently to speak to the girls, then hurried toward the house.

Rebekah maneuvered her wheelchair over to the door

and opened it quickly. The sheriff stood on the porch with Daniel. Rachel and Elizabeth had gotten out of the sleigh and were running toward the house, as well.

"What is it?" Rebekah looked up at the sheriff, then over at Daniel. "What's happened?"

Sheriff Andrews took a step toward her and bent down so he was eye level with her. "I'm sorry to have to tell you this, Mrs. Beachy, but there's been an accident on the road near your place, and I'm afraid your son's been seriously injured."

"My son? Which son?" Rebekah felt as though she were in a daze.

"Your daughter said his name is Perry."

Rebekah covered her mouth with the palm of her hand and gasped. Daniel released a deep moan.

"How. . .how bad is he hurt?" she squeaked.

"What happened?" Daniel asked at the same time.

The sheriff opened his mouth as if to reply, but Elizabeth bounded onto the porch just then. "Perry's been hit by a car!" she shouted. "I'm sure he's dead!"

The next several hours were like a horrible nightmare for Rachel, and she was sure the rest of her family felt the same way. Perry had been taken by ambulance to the hospital in Lancaster, and Joseph had ridden up front with the driver while the paramedics tended to Perry in the back. Mom, Dad, Rachel, and Elizabeth rode with the sheriff.

When they arrived at the hospital and spoke with the emergency-room doctor, he told them that Perry was dead.

The sheriff had explained how the driver of the car that ran into Perry had hit a patch of ice and swerved off the road. All the other Amish children who'd been walking home from school with Perry and Elizabeth had witnessed the accident.

When they returned home later that night, Rachel offered to fix the family something to eat, but no one was hungry. Elizabeth, who appeared to be in shock, had to be carried to bed by Joseph. Dad was busy comforting Mom, who hadn't stopped crying since she'd been given the news that her youngest son was dead.

Rachel took a seat at the kitchen table and let her head fall forward into her hands. She still couldn't believe that young, impetuous Perry, who had been making jokes at breakfast that morning and talking about the things he wanted to do after school, was gone. She felt sure her little brother was up in heaven with relatives and friends who had gone on before him, but despite the knowledge that Perry was with Jesus, she would always miss his mischievous face. She knew the rest of the family felt the same way—especially Mom, who had lost her youngest child, born just fifteen minutes after Elizabeth had entered the world.

Rachel lifted her head and moaned as her thoughts went to Anna. She needed to be told about Perry as soon as possible. After all, Anna was still a part of their family, even if she had moved away.

⚜

Early the following morning, several women came to the

house with food and offers of help. One of them was Martha Rose Zook, Anna's friend.

The others joined Mom in the kitchen, but Rachel touched Martha Rose's arm and nodded toward the living room. "Can I speak with you a minute?"

"Jah, sure."

As soon as the two of them had taken seats on the sofa, Martha Rose turned to Rachel and said, "I'm so sorry about Perry, and I'd like to help in any way I can."

Rachel forced a smile. If she smiled, maybe it would be easier not to cry. "I spoke with Mom this morning after breakfast, and we want Anna here for the funeral."

"And well she should be."

"The thing is. . .we know your husband, Amon, has a phone in his place of business now, so we were wondering if you might be willing to call Anna and let her know what happened to Perry."

Martha Rose nodded. "Of course I will."

Rachel glanced toward the door leading to the kitchen. "It might be best if you didn't say anything to my daed about this. No point getting him any more worked up than he already is."

"I understand." Martha Rose gave Rachel a hug.

Rachel found the gesture to be comforting, but having someone's sympathy made it more difficult for her not to cry. Tears had been clogging her throat ever since she'd first seen Perry's lifeless body lying by the side of the road, but she'd refused to give in to them. She needed to be strong for the rest of the family, and she knew if she started crying, she might not be able to stop.

"If Anna comes for the funeral, then Dad will just have to deal with it," she murmured.

Martha Rose pursed her lips like she was thinking the matter over. She finally nodded and said, "I won't say a word."

❦

Joseph couldn't keep his mind on his chores. All he could think about was Perry and how much he would miss the little scamp. He could still picture the wild expression on Elizabeth's face when he and Rachel had pulled up to the accident and seen Perry lying by the side of the road. She, along with several others from their school, had witnessed the accident, and seeing Perry struck down by the out-of-control car must have been a real shock for them all. Elizabeth and her twin brother had always been close, despite their constant bickering. It would be difficult for Elizabeth to get through the funeral, which was to be held at their house in a few days.

He ambled over to the bales of hay stacked against the barn wall and lifted one bale into his arms. He needed to feed the livestock, and other jobs waited to be done. Life didn't stop because of a death in the family, even though he might wish it could.

Joseph tried not to think of anything but the job at hand as he forked hay into the horses' stalls and filled their troughs with fresh water. He'd just finished with the last horse and was preparing to move on to the mules, when he heard the barn door open and shut.

"Joe, are you in here?"

"I'm here, Pauline." He set his pitchfork down and hurried to the front of the building, anxious to see the woman he loved.

Pauline stood near the door with a grievous expression on her face. "I'm so sorry about Perry. Is there anything I can do? Anything at all?"

He nodded and moved quickly to her side. "You can give me a hug, that's what."

She opened her arms, and he went willingly into her embrace. Tears clogged the back of his throat as he struggled to remain in control of his raging emotions. "It's not fair, Pauline. Life's not fair. God shouldn't have taken my little brother."

She patted his back in a motherly fashion. "I've never lost anyone so close to me, and I don't truly know how you're feeling, but I do know that God understands your pain, and He wants to help you through this."

Joseph tried to speak, but his words came out garbled.

"Let the tears flow, Joe," she said, hugging him tighter. "I'll cry right along with you."

He knew he couldn't fight the ball of emotions that threatened to suffocate him, so he gave in and wept until the shoulder of Pauline's dress was saturated with his tears.

Finally, he lifted his head and stepped back. "Danki for being here for me."

She nodded, as a film of tears swam in her eyes. "That's what friends are for."

"I—I was kind of hoping we could be more than friends."

She tipped her head and blinked a couple of times. "Oh?"

"I'm in love with you, Pauline, and if you'll have me, I'd like us to get married next fall."

She smiled and wiped her eyes. "I love you, too, Joe, and I'd be honored to be your wife."

CHAPTER 25

Anna stared out the window of Reuben's truck, watching the passing scenery yet not really seeing it. She was finally going home to see her family, only this was not the homecoming she had wanted it to be. Instead of going to a family member's birthday supper or celebrating some special holiday with them, she was going home to view the body of her little brother who had gone to heaven to be with Jesus. Would she be accepted by her family today? Would Dad, who had been determined that she not come home for a visit these past months, speak to her?

"You okay, Anna?" Reuben asked, as he reached across the seat to touch her arm.

She turned to face him and blinked against the stinging tears obscuring her vision. "I'm feeling a little uneasy about things."

"Are you afraid you'll break down when you see your brother's body?"

"I'm concerned about that, but I'm also worried about how I'll be accepted today." She glanced down at the long, black skirt she'd chosen to wear for this somber occasion. It wasn't a Plain dress, but at least she hadn't worn slacks or a fancy dress that would draw attention to her clothes.

She reached up to touch the short curls framing her face and grimaced. "I wonder what my folks will have to say about my hair?"

Reuben grunted. "I think you're worried for nothing, Anna. I'm sure everyone will be so glad to see you that they won't even be thinking about your hair."

Anna released a sigh and pushed her full weight into the back of the seat. Truth was, even though she'd said a few times that she wished she could cut her hair, she'd only done it to please Reuben. He had wanted her to do it before they'd left the Amish faith. Of course, she would never have done anything so bold or defiant then, especially since she had already become a baptized member of the church. Even after leaving the church, she'd been hesitant to cut off her hair, but Reuben had kept insisting.

Reuben took hold of her hand and gave her fingers a gentle squeeze. "It'll be all right, Anna. Everything will work out just fine."

❦

The funeral for Perry was a solemn occasion. Friends, relatives, and neighbors quickly filled up the Beachys' house for the service. The wall partitions had been removed so the speaker could be seen from any part of the three rooms being used. Perry's plain pine coffin had been placed on a bench against one wall in Mom and Dad's bedroom. Rachel's immediate family sat facing the coffin, with their backs to the speaker, who stood at the doorway between the kitchen and living room.

It sent shivers up Rachel's spine to think of her little brother's body lying in that coffin. In this life, she would never again have the pleasure of seeing him run and play. Never again hear his contagious laugh or squeals of delight when a calf or kitten was born. Never hug him or ruffle his hair the way she'd often done whenever he'd been in a teasing mood. It wasn't fair. Rachel wondered why God had allowed such a horrible thing to happen. Wasn't it bad enough that they'd lost Anna to the English world? Did God have to take Perry, too? She had to keep reminding herself that even though her little brother's days on earth were done, he did have a new life in heaven and was probably happier now than he'd ever been in this life.

Before Rachel had entered her parents' bedroom, she'd seen Silas and his parents come into the house. Silas had offered her a sympathetic smile, but she'd only nodded in response and gulped back the sob rising in her throat.

Rachel was miserable without Silas as a friend, and she didn't have Anna as a friend anymore, either. Even though Martha Rose had called Anna on the phone and told her about the funeral, she wasn't here, which meant she must have decided it was best not to come.

Unbidden tears slipped out of Rachel's eyes and rolled down her cheeks in rivulets that stung like fire. *If only things could be different. If only. . .*

Rachel barely heard the words Bishop Wagler spoke during his funeral message. Her thoughts lingered on her sister and how much she had hurt the family by going

English. Anna had hurt Silas, too, and because of it, he had spurned Rachel's love.

The service was nearly over, and the assisting minister had just begun to read a hymn, when Rachel caught a glimpse of Anna and Reuben, who had slipped into the room. She had to look twice to be sure it really was Anna. Her modern sister was dressed in English clothes—a black skirt and matching jacket. The biggest surprise was Anna's hair. She'd cut it short, just like Joseph had said, and it made her look so "English," despite the little black scarf she wore on the back of her head.

When the service was finally over and everyone had vacated the rooms so the coffin could be moved to a convenient viewing place in the main entrance, Rachel and her family stood. As soon as the coffin had been set in place inside the living room, everyone present formed a line to view Perry's body.

Rachel knew the funeral procession to the cemetery would begin soon afterward, and she wanted a chance to speak with her sister now, just in case Anna and Reuben didn't plan on staying. So as soon as she had seen Perry's body, she sought out her sister, who had already made her way out of the house, with Reuben at her side.

Rachel had only taken a few steps when she was stopped by Silas. "I'm sure sorry about what happened to Perry." He paused, his gaze going to the casket, then back to her again. "It doesn't seem right, him being so young and all."

Rachel stood staring at him, feeling as if she were in a daze. When Silas said nothing more, she started to move away. To her surprise, he reached out and gave her a hug. She held her arms stiffly at her side and waited until he pulled back. She was sure his display of affection was nothing more than a brotherly gesture. Besides, it was too little, too late as far as she was concerned. Rachel knew she needed to weed out the yearning she felt for Silas. It would only cause her further pain to keep pining away and hoping for something that never could be.

She bit her bottom lip in order to keep from bursting into tears, then turned quickly away.

Anna and Reuben were about to step off the porch, when Rachel showed up. "Anna, hold up a minute. I want to talk to you."

As Anna turned to face her sister, her eyes flooded with tears. "Thanks for asking Martha Rose to get word to me about Perry. I—I just had to come." She glanced over at Reuben, and he took hold of her hand.

"Of course you did, and it's only right that you should be here." Rachel nodded toward the door. "I know it's kind of cold out here, but could we talk a few minutes?"

Anna looked to Reuben as though seeking his approval.

He nodded. "I'll go back inside and see if I can speak with my folks while you two talk." He gave Anna a quick hug, then returned to the house.

Rachel led Anna over to the porch swing, and they both took a seat.

"Do you think this is a good idea?" Anna asked. "If Dad sees you talking to me, he might be pretty miffed."

Rachel shrugged. "There's no rule that says I can't talk

to my own sister."

Anna nodded and swallowed hard. "Martha Rose said Perry was hit by a car, but she didn't know any of the details. Can you tell me how this horrible thing happened?"

Rachel drew in a shuddering breath. "Joseph and I were heading home from town in the sleigh. As we came around the bend not far from our house, we saw the accident. A rescue vehicle, the sheriff's car, and the car that hit Perry were parked along the side of the road." She paused and swiped at the tears rolling down her cheeks. "Our little brother never regained consciousness, and he died soon after he got to the hospital."

"The roads were pretty icy, I heard."

Rachel nodded. "I'm sure the driver of the car didn't mean to run off the road. It was an accident, but still. . ." She sniffed. "Perry was so young. It just doesn't seem right when a child is killed."

Anna blinked a couple of times to keep her own tears from spilling over. "Sometimes it's hard to figure out why God allows bad things to happen to innocent people."

Rachel reached up to wipe more tears from her eyes. "Mom would remind us that the Bible says God is no respecter of persons and that the rain falls on the just, same as it does the unjust."

"That's true, but it's still hard to accept such a tragedy." Rachel nodded.

"How are Mom and Dad dealing with Perry's death?" Anna asked. "I only saw them from a distance, and I wasn't sure if I should try to talk to them right now." She glanced away. "From Mom's letters, I'd have to say that she's forgiven me, but I think Dad must still hate me for leaving the faith and all."

Rachel shook her head. "He doesn't hate you, Anna. He and Mom are disappointed, of course, but you're still their flesh and blood, and if you were to come back, they would welcome you with open arms."

Anna flexed her fingers, then formed them into tight balls in her lap. "I won't be coming back, Rachel. Reuben's happy living the modern life. He likes his painting job, and I–I'm content to work as a waitress."

"You could have done those things and still remained Amish."

"I know, but Reuben really needed a truck to get him back and forth to work, not to mention traveling from job to job."

Rachel merely shrugged in response. She probably didn't understand how important Reuben's vehicle was to him, Anna figured. Maybe he did put too much emphasis on worldly things, but Anna didn't think it would be right to discuss that with Rachel. At least not right now.

"How are things with you and Silas these days?" Anna asked, feeling the need for a change of subject.

Rachel gave no reply other than a brief shrug.

"Are you going to tell me about him or not?" Anna pried. "I can see by the look on your face that you're in love with him."

Rachel shook her head. "There's not much to say. Silas and I are friends, nothing more."

"Has he taken you anywhere or come calling on you at the house?"

"We did a few things together for a while there, but it didn't mean anything to him, I'm sure."

"That's too bad. I was kind of hoping that, after I left home, Silas's eyes would be opened and he'd see how good you are for him."

Rachel stared at the porch, and Anna's heart went out to her. If there was something she could do to make Silas see how good Rachel was for him, she surely would.

"You never really said—how's the rest of the family taking Perry's death?"

A fresh set of tears pooled in Rachel's eyes. "It's been mighty hard—especially for Mom and Elizabeth. Perry was still Mom's little boy, and even though Elizabeth and her twin argued sometimes, I know she still loved him."

Anna was about to reply, but Joseph stepped out the door and headed their way. She hoped he wouldn't make an issue of her being here. Maybe he wouldn't speak to her at all.

※

Joseph tromped across the porch and stopped when he got to the swing. "Hello, Anna," he mumbled.

"Hello, Joseph."

"I came out to tell you two that everyone went out the back door and they're climbing into their buggies already. We need to head for the cemetery now."

Rachel stood, but when Anna didn't join her, she turned back toward the swing. "Aren't you coming? You can ride with me and Joseph."

Anna stared down at her clasped hands, struggling with

her decision. "I'm not sure I should. Some folks might see it as an intrusion."

Rachel shook her head. "How could they? You're part of our family. You have every right to be at Perry's burial."

Anna looked up at Joseph, obviously waiting to see what he would say.

He nodded and reached out to touch her arm. "You and Reuben are welcome to ride in the buggy with me and Rachel."

Anna's chin trembled as she smiled up at him. "Thank you, brother Joseph."

"You're welcome." A feeling of relief flooded Joseph's soul, as he and Rachel stepped off the porch, and Anna went back into the house in search of her husband. Joseph really had found forgiveness in his heart toward his sister, and for the first time in many weeks, he felt a sense of peace.

❧

A horse-drawn hearse led the procession slowly down the narrow country road, with the two Beachy buggies following. Behind them, a long line of Amish carriages kept pace, and Silas Swartley's was the last. He felt sick to the pit of his stomach, thinking how it would feel to lose one of his brothers. Even if they didn't always see eye-to-eye, they were kin, and blood was thicker than water.

At the cemetery, everyone climbed out of their buggies and tied their horses to the hitching posts. Perry's coffin, supported by two hickory poles, was carried to the open grave and placed over it. Relatives and friends gathered near.

Silas stood near his own family, directly across from

the Beachy family. He was surprised to see Anna standing between Rachel and Joseph, and Reuben nearby with his parents and younger sister. Silas's heart stirred with strange feelings when he saw Anna wearing modern clothes. Her hair was cut short, and it looked like she might be wearing a bit of makeup. Such a contrast from the Anna Beachy he'd known as a child. She no longer resembled the young girl he'd fallen in love with so many years ago.

Silas glanced over at Rachel. Her shoulders drooped, and tears rimmed her eyes. She looked exhausted. His heart twisted with the pain he saw on her face. If only she hadn't shut him out, he might be of some comfort to her now.

Maybe it was best this way. She didn't trust him anymore, and he wasn't sure she should. What had he ever done to make Rachel believe he cared for her and not her sister? The truth was, until this very moment, he'd never truly seen Anna for what she was—a modern woman who seemed more comfortable dressed in English clothes than she did the Plain garb she'd grown up wearing.

Silas forced his attention back to the graveside service. Long straps were placed around each end of the coffin, and the pallbearers lifted it with the straps, while another man removed the supporting crosspieces. The coffin was then slowly lowered into the ground, and the long straps were removed. The pallbearers grabbed their shovels and began to fill the grave. Despite the snow they'd had a few days ago, at least the ground wasn't frozen; that made the men's job a little easier. Soil, mixed with snow and gravel, hit the casket with loud thumps, and with each thump, Silas noticed Rachel's shoulders lift and fall back.

When the grave was half filled, the men stopped shoveling. The bishop read a hymn, and the grave was then filled the rest of the way. The service was closed after everyone had silently said the Lord's Prayer.

Silas's heart went out to Rebekah Beachy, who sat in her wheelchair, audibly weeping. She clutched her husband's hand on one side, and her youngest daughter stood on her other side next to Joseph. Elizabeth sobbed hysterically, and when family members turned from the scene and moved toward their buggies, Joseph lifted the little girl into his arms. It was time to return to the Beachys' for a shared meal.

CHAPTER

26

Since so many people attended Perry's funeral, they needed to eat in shifts, so some went outside to the barn while they awaited their turn for the meal.

Rachel knew Anna would not be welcome to eat at any of the tables with her Amish friends and relatives, so she set a place for her and Reuben in the kitchen at a small table near the fireplace.

"That's okay," Anna said with a shake of her head. "I'm not really all that hungry."

"You've got to eat something," Rachel argued. "You're already skinny enough, and we can't have you losing any more weight."

"We'll both eat something," Reuben said as though the matter was entirely settled.

Anna finally nodded and took a seat at the table. It was obvious to Rachel that her sister was ill at ease, but even so, she was glad Anna and Reuben had come. She just wished Dad would say something to Anna instead of looking the other way whenever Anna came near. It pained her nearly as much as losing Perry to see her flesh-and-blood sister being treated that way. And for no good reason; Dad didn't have to give Anna the silent treatment. Shunning didn't require silence, so Dad was just being stubborn and spiteful, as far as Rachel was concerned.

When the meal was over, Rachel returned to the kitchen, hoping to speak to her sister before Anna and Reuben returned home. Reuben was nowhere in sight, but she spotted Anna and their mother sitting at the small table where Anna and her husband had eaten their meal. Clearly Mom had been crying, for her eyes were red, and the skin around them looked kind of swollen.

Rachel slipped quietly away, knowing that Anna and Mom needed this time alone.

She scurried up the steps and went straight to her room, realizing that she, too, needed a few minutes by herself. She'd been so busy helping with the funeral dinner and trying to put on a brave front in order to help others in the family who were grieving that she hadn't really taken the time to mourn.

As Rachel stood in front of the window, staring at the spiraling snowflakes that had just begun to fall, her thoughts kept time with the snow—swirling, whirling, falling all around, then melting before she had the chance to sort things out.

Oh, God, why did You have to take my little brother? Why did Anna have to hurt our family by leaving the faith? Rachel trembled. *And how come Silas has to pine away for Anna and can't see me as someone he could love?*

Deep in her heart, Rachel knew that none of these things were God's fault. He had allowed them all right, but certainly

He hadn't caused the bad things to happen. God loved Perry and had taken him home to heaven. Anna hadn't left home to be mean. She'd only done it because of her love for Reuben. Love did strange things to people; Rachel knew that better than anyone. Look how she had wasted so many months hoping Silas would fall in love with her and trying to gain his favor. It wasn't Silas's fault that he couldn't seem to get over his feelings for her sister. Anna had hurt Silas badly by running off with Reuben, and he might always hunger for the love he'd lost.

Rachel had to get on with her life. Maybe God wanted her to remain single. Maybe her job was to run the greenhouse and take care of Mom and Dad. It was a bitter pill to swallow, but if it was God's will, she must learn to accept it as such.

Rachel walked to the corner of her room. Maybe Anna would like to take something from her hope chest. Surely she could put a few of the things to good use in her new English home.

Rachel opened the lid and removed some hand towels, several quilted pot holders, and a few tablecloths—all things she was sure Anna could use. Next, she lifted out the beginnings of a double-ring wedding quilt. Its colors of depth and warmth, in shades of blue and dark purple, seemed to frolic side by side.

Rachel's eyes filled with tears as she thought about her own hope chest, now empty and useless. She had never started a wedding quilt, and the few items she'd stored in the chest had either been sold or were on display at Thomas Benner's store. Rachel had no reason to own a hope chest anymore, for she would probably never set up housekeeping with a husband or have any kinner of her own. Maybe her destiny was to be an old maid.

Shoving her pain aside and reaching farther into the chest, Rachel discovered an old Bible and an embroidered sampler near the bottom. Attached to the sampler was a note, and a lump lodged in her throat as she silently read the words.

> *Made by Miriam Stoltzfus Hilty.*
> *Given to my mamm, Anna Stoltzfus,*
> *To let her know how much*
> *God has changed my heart.*

Rachel knew that Miriam Stoltzfus was her great-aunt Mim and that Anna Stoltzfus was her great-grandmother. She noticed a verse embroidered on the sampler:

> *A merry heart*
> *doeth good*
> *like a medicine.*
> *—Proverbs 17:22*

A sob tore at Rachel's throat as she read the words out loud. She clung to the sampler as if it were some sort of lifeline. The yellowed piece of cloth gave her a strange yet comforting connection to the past.

Rachel's gaze came to rest on the old Bible then. She laid the sampler aside and picked up the Bible, pulling open the inside cover. Small, perfectly penned letters stated: *"This*

Biwel *belonged to Anna Stoltzfus. May all who read it find as much comfort, hope, and healing as I have found."*

Rachel noticed several crocheted bookmarks placed in various sections of the Bible. She turned the pages to some of the marked spots and read the underlined verses. Psalm 71:14 in particular seemed to jump right out at her: *"But I will hope continually, and will yet praise thee more and more."* Rachel had been reciting this same verse for several months. Was God trying to tell her something?

Rachel was about to turn the page when another underlined verse from Psalm 71 caught her attention: *"For thou art my hope, O Lord GOD: thou art my trust from my youth."*

Hot tears rolled down Rachel's cheeks as the words of verse 5 burned into her mind. All this time she'd been hoping to win Silas's heart. She had praised God for something she hoped He would do. Never once had it occurred to her that the heavenly Father wanted her to put all her hopes in Him. She was to trust Him and only Him, and she should have been doing it since her youth. Instead, she had been trying to do everything in her own strength, because it was what she wanted. When Silas didn't respond as she'd hoped he would, her faith had been dashed away like sunshine on a rainy day.

Rachel broke down, burying her face in her hands. "Dear Lord, please forgive me. Help me to learn to trust You more. Let my hope always be in You. May Your will be done in my life. Amen."

Rachel picked up the precious items she'd found in Anna's hope chest and turned toward her bedroom door. The Bible belonged to Anna's namesake, and she should have it. The sampler belonged to Great-Grandma Anna's daughter, Miriam, and Anna should have that, as well.

❧

"It's so good to see you again, Anna."

Tears welled in Anna's eyes as she sat at the table beside her mother. "It's good to see you, too."

"We've missed you, daughter."

"I've missed you, as well."

"You can still come home, you know." Mom reached for Anna's hand.

"I can't, Mom. My place is with Reuben now."

Mom's eyes swam with tears. "I'm not asking you to leave your husband, but I'm hoping Reuben will want to return to our way of life, too."

Anna shook her head. "I don't think he'd ever be willing to give up his truck or the TV programs he enjoys watching."

Mom stared at the table. She obviously didn't know how to respond.

Anna moistened her lips with the tip of her tongue, wishing she knew how to express everything that was on her mind. "I must admit I've come to enjoy some things about the modern way of life, too."

"Like wearing short hair?" Her mother's wounded expression and mournful tone of voice let Anna know that Mom disapproved of her new look.

Anna reached up to touch a wayward curl. "It was Reuben's idea that I cut my hair. He thinks I look prettier this way."

Mom clicked her tongue, which Anna knew meant she was very displeased. She was about to explain things further, when her father stepped into the room.

"Some of our guests are leaving now, Rebekah," he said, nodding at Mom. "Might be good if you went into the other room and said good-bye."

Mom sat for a few seconds as though she was contemplating his suggestion. Then she motioned to Anna and said, "Aren't you going to say hello to our daughter, Daniel?"

He grunted and gave his beard a quick pull. "Not much to be said, is there?"

Anna's heart felt as if it would break in two. Why couldn't Dad find it in his heart to forgive her? Why couldn't he at least try to talk things through?

Mom maneuvered her wheelchair away from the table. "I'll tell you what, Daniel. I'll go say good-bye to our guests, and you can visit with Anna awhile."

Dad blinked a couple of times as if he couldn't quite believe what Mom had just said, but to Anna's surprise, he pulled out the chair across from her and sat down.

Mom gave Anna a quick wink and promptly wheeled out of the room.

Anna drew in a quick breath and prayed for the right words to say to her father. "Dad, I—"

"Anna, I want you to know—"

They'd spoken at the same time. "Go ahead, Dad," Anna said.

He shook his head. "No, you started speaking first."

She swallowed hard as she stared at his face. Was his pained expression from losing his youngest son, or was her being here today what had caused Dad's obvious agony? "I—I just wanted to say how sorry I am for hurting you and the rest of the family. I know it was wrong to hide the fact that I'd been seeing Reuben secretly, and I know it was wrong for us to sneak off and get married the way we did."

Dad sat stoically, apparently waiting for her to continue.

Anna swallowed once more, hoping to push down the lump that had lodged in her throat. "Reuben and I won't be returning to the Amish faith, but we do want to keep in contact with our families—come here for visits and all."

Still nothing from her father. He remained silently in his chair, wearing a stony expression.

"I know you don't understand, but I love Reuben so much, and even though I probably wouldn't have decided to leave the Amish faith on my own, it's what he wanted. If I was going to be with him, I knew I had to make a choice."

He nodded slowly, and tears gathered in the corners of his eyes. "Love does that to people. Fact is, it can cause 'em to make all kinds of sacrifices." He glanced toward the door leading to the living room. "Your mamm and I had a few problems when we were young and some misunderstandings that nearly kept us apart."

Anna gave a quick nod. She'd heard from Mom about some of her courtship with Dad and knew they'd almost not gotten married.

"For a time, your mamm thought I only wanted to marry her so I could get my hands on the greenhouse. But I finally convinced the silly woman that it was her I loved and not her business." Dad shifted in his chair. "I even offered not to work there if she'd take me back. Said I'd spend the rest of my days workin' at my daed's dairy, though it wasn't my first choice." He stared right at Anna and offered her a smile. "So you see, I do understand in some ways what caused you to move away. You wanted to be with Reuben so much that you were willing to give up the only way of life you'd ever known."

Anna nodded, and tears rolled down her cheeks.

"I'm still not happy about you and Reuben goin' English, mind you, but I am trying to understand." He extended his hand toward her. "And I do still love you, Anna."

She clasped his fingers, feeling the warmth and strength and reveling in the joy of knowing she was still loved. "I love you, too, Dad."

Anna wasn't in the kitchen when Rachel returned, but Mom sat at the table with her head bowed. Not wishing to disturb her mother's prayer, Rachel slipped quietly out the back door. She found Joseph and Pauline sitting side-by-side on the porch. They looked so good together. Rachel was happy Joseph had found someone to love.

Joseph turned when Rachel closed the screen door. "Oh, it's you, little sister. Nearly everyone's gone home, and we didn't know where you were. Anna was looking for you."

A sense of panic surged through Rachel. "Did Anna and Reuben leave already?"

Joseph shook his head. "Naw. She said she wouldn't go without talking to you first."

"Reuben's still inside talking with his folks, but Anna said something about taking a walk down by the river."

Pauline removed her shawl and handed it to Rachel. "If you're going after her, you'd better put this on. The snow's let up now, but it's still pretty cold."

Gratefully, Rachel took the offered shawl. "I think I will head down to the water and see if Anna's still there. I've got something I want to give her."

Rachel started out walking and soon broke into a run. The wind stung her face, but she didn't mind. Her only thought was of finding Anna.

The rest of Silas's family had already gone home, but he wasn't ready to leave just yet. He wanted to hang around and see if he could offer comfort to Rachel. She hadn't looked right when he'd seen her earlier, and after lunch he'd gone looking for her, but she seemed to have disappeared. He figured she must be taking Perry's death pretty hard, and it had pained him when she hadn't even responded to his hug. She'd felt small and fragile in his arms—like a broken toy he was unable to fix. It was as if Rachel were off in another world today—in a daze or some kind of a dream state.

He remembered hearing his mother talk about her oldest sister and how she'd gone crazy when her little girl drowned in the lake. He didn't think Rachel would actually go batty, but she was acting mighty strange. He couldn't go home until he knew she was going to be okay.

Silas decided to walk down to the river, knowing Rachel often went there to look for birds. Just as he reached the edge of the cornfield, mottled with snow, he spotted someone standing along the edge of the river. His heart gave a lurch when he saw the figure leaning over the water. Surely, she wasn't thinking of—

Silas took off in a run. When he neared the clearing, he skidded to a halt. The figure he'd seen was a woman all right, but it wasn't Rachel. It was her sister Anna. He approached slowly, not wanting to spook her.

She turned to face him just as he stepped to the water's edge. "Silas, you about scared me to death. I thought I was all alone out here."

"Sorry. I didn't mean to frighten you. I was looking for—"

"I used to love coming down here. It was a good place to think. . .and to pray." Anna dropped her gaze to the ground. "Sorry to say that since I left home I haven't done as much praying as I should. I have started going to church with a friend, though, and I've come to realize that the only way to deal with life's problems is to walk close to the Lord."

Silas nodded. "Praying is good. I think it goes hand in hand with thinking."

Anna smiled and pointed to the water. "Look, there's a big old trout."

"Rachel likes to fish." Silas couldn't believe that even a silly trout made him think of Rachel.

Anna grinned. "I think you and my sister have a lot in common. She likes to spend hours feeding and watching the birds that come into the yard."

"I know. I bought Rachel a bird book and a pair of binoculars for her birthday."

"I'm sure she liked that."

"I thought so at the time, but now I'm not sure."

Anna touched the sleeve of Silas's jacket. "How come?"

He stared out across the water. "She thinks I don't like her. She thinks I'm still in love with you."

❧

Rachel stood behind the trunk of a white birch tree, holding her breath and listening to the conversation going on just a few feet away. She'd almost shown herself, but when she'd heard her own name mentioned, fear of what Anna and Silas were saying kept her feet firmly in place. Was Silas declaring his love for her sister? Was he begging her to leave Reuben and return to the Amish faith? Surely Silas must know the stand their church took against divorce.

"But you're not in love with me now, are you, Silas?" Anna asked.

Rachel pressed against the tree and waited for his response. She was doing it again—eavesdropping. It wasn't right, but she could hardly show herself now, with Silas about to declare his love for Anna. Her thoughts went back to that day many months ago when she'd heard Silas say to Anna, *"When you're ready, I'll be waiting."* Was he still waiting for her? Did he really think they had a chance to be together?

"I used to love you, Anna," Silas said. "At least I thought I did." There was a long pause, and Rachel held her breath. "Guess maybe we'd been friends so long I never thought I'd fall in love with anyone but you."

"Have you fallen in love with someone, Silas?" Anna asked.

Rachel chanced a peek around the tree. Silas stood so close to Anna he could have leaned down and kissed her.

He didn't, though. Instead, he stood tall, shoulders back and head erect. "You were right when you told me once that Rachel is good for me. I love her more than anything, but I doubt we'll ever be together, because I don't know what I can do to prove my love to her."

Feeling as if her heart would burst wide open, Rachel jumped out from behind the tree. "You don't have to do anything to prove your love. What you said to Anna is proof enough for me!"

Silas jumped back. His foot slipped on a patch of snow, and he nearly landed in the water. Rachel raced forward and caught hold of his hand. "Be careful now. You'll get what I have for Anna all wet," she said, as he pulled her close to his side.

Anna stepped forward. "What have you got for me, Rachel?"

She lifted the sampler and their great-grandmother's Bible. "I found these at the bottom of your hope chest, and I thought maybe you'd like to have them."

Anna's eyes flooded with tears. "Great-Aunt Mim's sampler and Great-Grandma's Bible. Mom gave them to me for my hope chest several years ago, but I'd forgotten all about them."

Rachel handed the items to her sister. "I read some passages I found in this old Bible and was reminded that I need to put my hope in the Lord and keep trusting Him, not hope for the things I've wanted or try to do everything in my own strength." She looked over at Silas. "I thought I'd have to learn to live without your love, but now—"

Silas placed two cold fingers against her lips. "Now you'll

have to learn to live as my wife. If you'll have me, that is."

She nodded. "Jah, I'll have you, Silas."

He leaned down to kiss her, and Rachel felt as if she were a bird—floating, soaring high above the clouds—reveling in God's glory and hoping continuously in Him.

EPILOGUE

One year later

Rachel stood on the lawn, her groom on one side, her brother and new sister-in-law on the other. Two weeks ago, Joseph had married Pauline, and today the young couple were offering their congratulations to Rachel and Silas. Both couples had received double-ring wedding quilts from their mothers, and today Rachel's heart held a double portion of happiness. The only thing that could have made her day more complete would have been to share it with her older sister. But apparently Anna and Reuben hadn't been able to come, for Rachel hadn't seen any sign of them during the wedding ceremony.

On an impulse, Rachel glanced across the yard and was surprised to see Anna and Reuben walking toward her.

"Excuse me a minute," she whispered to Silas. "I need to speak with my sister."

Silas nodded and squeezed her hand. "Hurry back, fraa."

Rachel smiled and slipped quickly away. She drew Anna off to one side, and they exchanged a hug. "It's so good to see you. I was hoping you had received my invitation to the wedding and that you would be able to be here today."

"I'm sorry Reuben and I didn't get here in time for the ceremony. He had a little trouble with his truck this morning, so we were late getting started. I did want to wish you well and give you this, though." Anna handed Rachel a brown paper sack.

"What is it?"

"Take a look."

Rachel opened the bag, reached inside, and withdrew a sampler. At first she thought it was the same one she'd given to Anna a year ago, but when she read the embroidered words, she knew it wasn't:

> *"For thou art my hope, O Lord GOD:*
> *thou art my trust from my youth."*
>
> *—Psalm 71:5*

"I thought it would be something you could hand down to your children and grandchildren." Anna placed her hand against her stomach. "That's what I plan to do with the Merry Heart sampler Great-Aunt Mim made all those years ago."

Rachel's eyes widened. "You're in a family way?"

Anna nodded. "The baby will come in the spring."

"Do Mom and Dad know that they are going to be grandparents?"

"I told them a few minutes before you came outside." Anna smiled, and her eyes filled with tears. "Dad and Mom want me and Reuben to come visit more often after the baby is born." She glanced around the yard as though someone might be listening. "I'm sure a few in our community still might exclude us from some things, but as long as we feel welcome within our own families, that's what counts."

Rachel hugged her sister. "I'm glad things are better between you and Dad."

Anna nodded. "Reuben and I had a long talk awhile back. We decided that we both want to stay English, but we're attending church together now, and we're reading our Bibles and praying every day."

"I'm happy to hear that, and I thank you for coming today." Rachel held the sampler close to her heart. "I'll always cherish this, and every time I look at it, I'll not only be reminded to put my hope in Jesus but I'll think of my English sister, who is also trusting in God."

Anna pulled her fingers through the ends of her hair, which she had let grow long again. "That's so true."

"Well, I'd best be getting back to my groom, or he's likely to come looking for me," Rachel said with a giggle.

Anna nodded. "Tell him I said to be happy and that he'd better treat my little sister right, or I'll come looking for him."

Rachel hugged Anna one last time; then she hurried toward Silas. She was glad she had opened her sister's hope chest last year, for if she hadn't, she might never have found Great-Aunt Mim's special sampler and Great-Grandma's Bible, so full of hope found only in God's Word.

When Rachel reached her groom, he pulled her to his side. "I love you, Rachel, and I pray we'll always be this happy together."

Rachel leaned her head against his shoulder. "If we keep

God at the center of our lives and put our hope and trust in Him, the love and happiness we feel today will only grow stronger." She smiled and looked up. "The Lord is truly my hope, and I pray that all of our future children and grand-children will put their hope and trust in Him, too."

Rachel's Ribbon Salad

Ingredients:
- 3-ounce box of lime gelatin
- 3 cups boiling water, divided
- 3 cups cold water, divided
- 1 small can crushed pineapple
- ½ cup chopped walnuts
- 3-ounce box of lemon gelatin
- 8-ounce package cream cheese
- ¾ cup whipped cream
- 3-ounce box of raspberry gelatin

Dissolve lime gelatin in 1 cup boiling water. Add 1 cup cold water, crushed pineapple, and nuts to the gelatin, then pour into an 8x8 pan to make the first layer. Chill in the refrigerator until set. Dissolve lemon gelatin in 1 cup boiling water, then add 1 cup cold water. When the mixture becomes cool, add the cream cheese and whipped cream. Pour this mixture over the first layer of gelatin that has already set. Return to refrigerator and let set again. Dissolve raspberry gelatin in 1 cup boiling water. Add 1 cup cold water and mix well. Pour over the top of the first two layers, return to the refrigerator, and chill until set.

About the Author

New York Times bestselling and award-winning author **Wanda E. Brunstetter** is one of the founders of the Amish fiction genre. She has written more than 100 books translated in four languages. With over 11 million copies sold, Wanda's stories consistently earn spots on the nation's most prestigious bestseller lists and have received numerous awards.

Wanda's ancestors were part of the Anabaptist faith, and her novels are based on personal research intended to accurately portray the Amish way of life. Her books are well-read and trusted by many Amish, who credit her for giving readers a deeper understanding of the people and their customs.

When Wanda visits her Amish friends, she finds herself drawn to their peaceful lifestyle, sincerity, and close family ties. Wanda enjoys photography, ventriloquism, gardening, bird-watching, beachcombing, and spending time with her family. She and her husband, Richard, have been blessed with two grown children, six grandchildren, and two great-grandchildren.

To learn more about Wanda, visit her website at www.wandabrunstetter.com.

Other Books by Wanda E. Brunstetter:

Prairie State Friends Series
The Decision
The Gift
The Restoration

Sisters of Holmes County Series
A Sister's Secret
A Sister's Test
A Sister's Hope

Kentucky Brothers Series
The Journey
The Healing
The Struggle

Indiana Cousins Series
A Cousin's Promise
A Cousin's Prayer
A Cousin's Challenge

Brides of Webster County Series
Going Home
On Her Own
Dear to Me
Allison's Journey

Brides of Lehigh Canal Series
Kelly's Chance
Betsy's Return
Sarah's Choice

The Discovery–A Lancaster County Saga
Goodbye to Yesterday
The Silence of Winter
The Hope of Spring
The Pieces of Summer
A Revelation in Autumn
A Vow for Always

Other Books
Amish Front Porch Stories
The Brides of the Big Valley
The Beloved Christmas Quilt
Lydia's Charm
Amish White Christmas Pie
Woman of Courage
The Amish Millionaire
The Christmas Secret
The Lopsided Christmas Cake
The Farmers' Market Mishap
Twice as Nice Amish Romance Collection
The Hawaiian Quilt
The Hawaiian Discovery
The Blended Quilt